WHAAM!

John Gardiner

Dedication

Betsy, Nada and Troy

1968

(STREET FIGHTING MAN)

CONTENTS

I
SATORI IN SAIGON

Calligraphy Of A Summer Happening. '68 rose like a fiercely burning Phoenix from the ashes of '67: a blinded Regulus, Christopher Featherstone gazed unblinkingly into the dazzling depth of space beyond his car's windshield, stalled in the congested arterial highway adjacent to the University by the calligraphy of a Summer Happening. The student Free Speech Movement obstructing traffic with their presence was bleached of definition by the light's intensity. Spilling shapelessly across the highway these existential anarchists anchored his state of mind as he attempted to cast his reverie adrift into summer's satori. **WE ARE THE INFANTRY OF MAO'S CULTURAL REVOLUTION** soaked a massive banner in blood-red type: the infamous red book released in a shower from the chanting students landed on the bonnet of his car. As if besieged by summer's overheated ennui the vacationing students had roused themselves to surge through the urban terrain in their unpatriotic Mao-masks. Featherstone's car radio caught the timpani of this new wave of revolution in the wavelengths of Jimi Hendrix's *Purple Haze* as the boiling traffic slowly crawled westward again into the afternoon sun. The eye of the windshield burned on in a Turnerian explosion of light. One by one the red books fluttered open briefly before falling away from the bonnet onto the roadway.

Séance On A Summer Afternoon. Psychedelic *Purple Haze* and summer heat as abrasive as pumice brushed Fabian Roxburgh as he reflectively finger-flicked the page of a bizarre letter-collage held in his other hand. Various seemingly random images and newspaper editorials had abstractly arranged themselves on the floor as they fell, forming in his mind the cartography of a political failure-of-nerve mapping the future defeat of the US in 'Nam. The letter-collage fell too: having sliced open the anonymous envelope he discovered it to be his obituary ... **FABIAN ROXBURGH (1940-1968).** Smooth as olive oil, the scarlet blood clot of Mao's red book held in one hand against her breast, the young girl he had literally carried off from the anarchist rally the previous evening, (to the cries of *rapist!*), serenely minimalist in her youth's eighteen years, twirled her Mao-beret on a forefinger and waited in the shadow of her little-rich-girl persona as if the world was about to stop and she could get off. Among the unwashed anarchists she immediately commandeered his sensibility with her pungent softness, her sympathetic sweetness veiling intransigent rebelliousness, made him her instant spectator when his journalistic mission was to create a red book bonfire of Chairman Mao's infiltration of the minds of Western youth and sympathetic intellectuals. She had woken him just as dawn crimsoned the sky saying he was talking in his sleep. He had been dreaming, of being swallowed by the boa constrictor of the lazy Mekong as its smooth belly slithered through 'Nam. The obituary-as-collage had been discovered in her red book, but he was certain she was not the creator. When he had asked her for her name she had responded in a private school voice: "Just think of me as a virgin-on-the-precipice, ready to free fall into the year's adventures." Leaving her on her hands-and-knees vacantly studying the editorial cut-outs on the floor he showered, but on stepping back into the room she had vanished, leaving only the warm-flavored essence of her absence. Better to erase any hopes of her ever being his *Now* girl. 'Nam's séance of images silently flickered on the television screen.

The Wild One. Temporarily routed by roving motorcycle police the Gang of Five student agitators withdrew their cadres back to the University grounds where they created a Ho Chi Minh Trail amid the Spanish sandstone arcades. Wielding a megaphone aimed more at the ebb-and-flow of arriving news teams eager for sensationalist images to broadcast on the evening bulletins, supplementing the visual footage from 'Nam, the fiery Che Guevara understudy leading the Gang of Five kept up a stream of commentary. "Look out Capitalist running dogs, we're the Children of the Cultural Revolution!" The news cameras dutifully recorded this verbal expressionism flung at the bourgeois canvas of monogamous domestic felicity. "Bring on America's sons to the dinner table of 'Nam. Chow down as they are massacred and eaten by the Revolution! Only anarchy brings security!" National Guardsmen strained the sinews of their immaculately groomed uniforms and gripped their precision machine-tooled rifles at the correct Pythagorean angle of address.

Amazons Fighting Maoists. Solemn, funereal, dressed in designer battle fatigues, truncheons belted at their hips and led by a statuesque barn-stormer of a woman, a female cortege bore a Pop Art assemblage through the University arcades and set it down on an expanse of pavement in full view of the news cameras shielded by the National Guardsmen. Identifiable as a plaster cast model of David's famous revolutionary painting, *Death of Marat*, this piece of street theater would elude today's television audience of the news bulletins, but deliver its purpose to inflame and outrage them. The statuesque stunner laid a bloodied knife beside the bath in which slumped, not a representation of Marat stabbed by a female martyr of the Revolution, but the Pop Art figurehead himself, Andy Warhol! Cameras now ignored the anarchists, here was something more controversial, for the statuesque warrior began a declamation, contemptuous of the Maoists. "You think *you* are the Revolution? *This* is the Revolution!" She energetically advanced on Che Guevara and threw Mao's red book in his face. "Bourgeois trash!" Immediately, the whirlpool of angry young women unleashed their truncheons and assaulted the strung out cadre of anarchists. Amazons fighting Maoists! Existential nuclei smashed together releasing a spray of debris. As wailing police sirens blue-shifted and the National Guardsmen uniformly advanced the Amazon Queen shouted across them at the news cameras: "W-O-M-I-N is the next evolutionary model!" The canvas of three-dimensional space began bending with the cartography of bleeding and bruised protagonists until the gravity exerted by the National Guardsmen pulled them into their crushing orbit.

A Crucifixion. Anchored at leisure in the placid ocean's suburbia of wide-open spaces lay the Westwood's schooner seemingly minted from Croesus himself. Christopher Featherstone's astrologer had said 1968's Rubicon would be a cusp he crossed over into uncharted waters divided by Scylla and Charybdis and asked if he was a strong swimmer. A motorboat powered him toward the schooner's exoskeleton and he pondered whether his clients would require him to climb up onto the center mast's crucifix if he failed to bring home their daughter. Welcomed aboard by Calvin Westwood he dipped his head under a shade awning and was introduced to a supine Mrs. Westwood ... Samantha Westwood! Fortunately he was immediately offered a martini of his choice and could compose himself as his glance was held by the fabulous Bathsheba, remembering the same Medusa-look freezing his heart that lost weekend back in 1964. She betrayed no signs of recognizing him. Calvin Westwood handed him a martini and gestured to a deckchair. "Well, a conservative-looking Private Investigator, Sam. But are you after-all just another anti-hero?" Featherstone's long-frozen heart began to thaw and melt, or was it perspiration from the oppressive heat? "You could say I am rather allegorical-looking."

Their Lost Weekend In 1964. Molded by her chic forties, Samantha Westwood's gradually fading, Titian-haired beauty preserved by wealth, reclined as if on a canvas in acrylic oils. Her hand barely had strength enough to raise her martini glass. Christopher Featherstone's repressed bourgeois instincts were paralyzed by his erotic memory of their lost weekend back in 1964. The ocean's gravity-waves imperceptibly undulated the schooner just as he was lamenting how his loins lacked animation these days. "Featherstone, now there's a name in conflict with itself! Relax. Unbend. You look like you're studying for the role of Private Investigator in a movie. Too stiff!" Calvin Westwood exampled the listless ennui of a new-made sixties millionaire already settling now for the *status quo*. "It's my lazy Anglo-Saxon charm ... The language of my subconscious." Featherstone desperately tried to burn his nude studies of Samantha Westwood in his mind's bonfire.

A Hard Day's Night. *Miranda Westwood is missing!* Entering his office's urban décor as a cell where he might attain satori, Christopher Featherstone shuttered the windows against the full impact of the afternoon sun. He gathered up some random mail and catalogues from the floor and tapped a wall barometer: stormy weather was imminent. Sunk in reverie contemplating Samantha Westwood's unexpected apparition aboard the schooner he drifted across the box-like office like the cut-out silhouette of an urban monk. The fabric of his shirt was still impregnated with the salty tang of the ocean breeze. Flowing by his office the arteries of roadway outside were choked with traffic. What was The Beatles' song all over the radio that weekend in 1964?

The Beat Generation's Time Was Over. Beat! Music had the *beat* now not prose or poetry or the rhythm of living. "Am I virtuous? Then I will certainly perish under its shroud!" Calvin Westwood explained how Miranda's untamed minx had run away before, offering him his diary recording the Odyssean adventure of his search for her: she had chased after the fantasy of The Beatles during their tour in '64. Now her petulance to embrace freedom was not so easily controlled, she was turning eighteen. So it was during Miranda's escapade that weekend in '64 Samantha Westwood (using a *nom de plume*, Jane Greer) had booked into the Hotel Plaza and begun a weekend's erotic reverie with him before vanishing from his life as mysteriously. He had imagined at the time she was emotionally responding to the breakdown of his marriage and his seeing himself as *The Forgotten Man*. He tabled photographs of Miranda, two-dimensional fragments from which he would have to locate her co-ordinates in three-dimensional space. Gathering shadows heightened the office's psychological austerity. Somewhere the cartography of Miranda's three-dimensional presence was displacing, bending the space of the city, her movements creating a distortion he would need to identify, preventing her ongoing escape through four-dimensional time. The Beat Generation's Time was over. The phone rang, its resonance the very antithesis of his satori's *beat-time*.

Obituary-As-Collage. A three-dimensional collage of movements within the four corners of the room's cube, hearing a singing viola line's emanation drift through the partitioning wall, Fabian Roxburgh looked through his reflection-as-painting on the glass window, across the cubist illogic of the city. But of more immediacy was the mysterious collage of his obituary composed of the following: (i) **PAINTING** – *Death of Chatterton* by Henry Wallis. Here perhaps was Journalism's poetry of death configured *à la Boheme*, a corpse as pale as paper. (ii) **BOOK** – *The Spy Who Came In From The Cold* by John Le Carré. Tropically overheated 'Nam being the new Berlin Wall in the global game of geopolitical dominos. (iii) **SONG LYRIC** – *Look To Your Soul* sung by Johnny Rivers. The Vibe is the Groove! (iv) **FLOWER** – An orchid soaked in Special Services camouflage, the tender grail's colour having ebbed to a nadir of darkness under the spell of political voodoo cast by Saigon. (v) **COCKTAIL** – *Bloody Mary*. Juice thickened, congealed in the glacial coffin of glass on which was cut the hammer-and-sickle: Lenin embalmed after spilling his blood for the Revolution.

Judy In Disguise (With Glasses). Barricaded within the University grounds, *papier-mâché* effigies of US and South Vietnamese leaders, President Johnson and Ky being the centerpiece, preaching the Gospel of American Righteousness, burned through the night to the sounds of commercial radio. A girl-next-door from Millionaire's Row eluded the police presence by avoiding the University entrances and joined the throng of student agitators on campus. She identified a pentacle of leaders, a Gang of Five, and transformed it into a Star of David by assertively interrogating the ring leader's non-intellectual demeanor and then drawing his gaze with the silkiness of her solo dancing to the song on the radio. Fresh flames licked and smoked the President's effigy wrapped in the Stars and Stripes as Stephen Maxwell shouted to her above the song's instrumental break: "Are you with us, girl-next-door, or are you just the cartoon of a revolutionary for the capitalist newspapers?" Exuding appropriate impudence, seamlessly dancing on, full of teasing provocation, she answered: "And do I look like I'm studying to sing and square-dance in some swank nightclub for boys-next-door, like you?"

Silhouettes. Evening's luscious purple wash of color quickly imploded to indigo-black and the wave-lapped beach scene assumed the quality of a photographic negative held up to moonlight. Elegiac glimmers of onboard light cast by the offshore schooner vibrated the ocean surface into a mineralized glitter. An isolated silhouette was faintly visible moving around the schooner. Was it Samantha Westwood's languorous socialite-in-crisis, drained by ennui with a world no one understood anymore, rising from the afternoon-long martini-hour to confront the horizon's unsurpassable barrier drawn against Eternity's proscenium? The mysterious symbol of the schooner's crucifix-mast held by the binoculars completed the scene's negative image outlined in space. "Who then has Miranda been seen with?"

Treasure Troves. Mornings: Christopher Featherstone thoughtfully considered Calvin Westwood's cryptic diary record strung together during Miranda's disappearance in 1964. Traces of feminine perfume and discursive handwriting soaked a few pages, producing a rare *frisson*: he made out the words *Hotel Plaza* and the date of the entry! Perhaps too many dry martinis had faded her memory of that lost weekend casually inked in the diary. He established different search criteria for his own investigation. Black vinyl pressed as albums was now the currency of youth. Trawling through newspaper personals, backtracking several weeks, snatching bill posters advertising gigs by local and touring rock groups, he formulated his initial profile of Miranda's likely social interactions. Visits to recording studios, even a very obscure underground label, **LESBOS**, allowed him to engage with their personnel in meditations on the face of the eighteen year old heiress. Driving by the University he quickly pulled over and investigated the burnt-out effigies charred on crucifixes and the blackened tatters of American flags: acrid smells hung in the summer-heated air. He stepped over student agitators exhausted and sleeping on the lawn searching for Miranda. Looking over the chaotic scene one thing was clear, youth were composing their own psycho-political diagrams of dissent against an unforgiving world, and the lines made up one word: **REVOLT!** No tired old men here like the years of the French and Russian Revolutions!

The new *Internationale* was the pop song of the moment. Everyone he asked knew the girl-next-door in the photograph, even under her Mao-beret!

What Urban Apocalypse Awaits Saigon? Coronal, white-hot fragments of Charlie's grenade casually tossed into the street-side bar splintered the flimsy wooden internal support frames and tore through Fabian Roxburgh's Hawaiian shirt as he stood at the urinal. He remembered a ticking clock later, the moments soluble to one another, each absorbing its predecessor with advancing stealth. Even the Buddhists, supposed conquerors of the fear of death, had abandoned Saigon, surprising him, for they were reported to have seen through the illusion of war into Nirvana. No satori in Saigon for them! Let the Wheel of Rebirth spin on for unenlightened humanity! Summoning together the collage of his splintered psyche he rearranged the sequence of cut-outs from the Personals ... **SEEKING MAO-BERET MISSING FROM COLLAGE** ... obscure, cryptic, but *she* would know. His unsympathetic editor had spiked his latest *tour de force* as no more than a dose of Saigon Fever he had contracted: *What Urban Apocalypse Awaits Saigon?* A sharp knock at the door of his rented apartment and there she was, Mao-beret in hand, from which she removed and passed to him the Personals clipping. No explanations. No questions. A silent movie. What was her name? He considered frisking her but for the apprehension of what he might discover. When would the fog of war lift for at least one generation's respite?

Going To A Go-Go. *(The Lights Went Out In) Massachusetts* overlaid the clouded mood of the pinup posters, towering somber black-and-white images of Che Guevara, Jean-Paul Belmondo, Humphrey Bogart and Marlon Brando adorning the walls of the bedroom where she closeted herself, sitting cross-legged, chin-in-hand, elbow resting on a knee memorizing menus from magazines. Ignoring the shadowy specters gazing down from the walls she poutingly indulged his quirky fascination for posing her innocence against the façades, and photographing collages with a Pentax. She only moved energetically in the kitchen preparing their Spaghetti with Lamb Regù, sauce and pasta deliciously balanced: Virtue's fine spaghetti was dressed for the sauce of temptation. "Where shall we go after dinner?" Dancing-A-Go-Go she summoned passion enough to overwhelm her precocious self-awareness. Flashes of annoyance tortured her expression, not even softened by elaborately painted lotus petals opening out from the limpid pools of her eyes, and he realized his dancing was burdened with out-of-date clichés, more Roxy-A-Go-Go than Whisky-A-Go-Go. Tight-structured and disciplined pop songs sharpened her dancer's instincts to the delicate precision and swing of a Swiss time-piece, but when they moved on to the larger, psychedelic ballrooms where doodling, interminably drawn-out if hypnotic guitar solos deconstructed Time, she too spaced-out her dancing into sensual longeurs. Returning drained to the rented apartment before dawn crimsoned the skyline felt like an astronaut's splashdown after circling the Earth in the euphoria of zero-gravity!

Man Is Dead! Dragging the razor down his cheek in the converted living space immediately above his office Christopher Featherstone paused to catch details of a bizarre news item on the radio. Rinsing off shaving cream he heard how in the early hours of the morning unknown vandals had desecrated the altarpiece of a suburban drive-in movie screen. The violation took the form of a decoration in red paint *à la Jackson Pollock*. Interestingly enough, checking out the movie guide in the newspaper he discovered the movie scheduled for screening was a re-run of Brigitte Bardot's international *cause célèbre, And God Created Woman*. The kittenish screen goddess from the fifties was already passé, she was no Julie Christie, and a sub Art Nouveau Twiggy easily out-muscled her from the covers of the glossy magazines. Late the previous afternoon he had witnessed a piece of street theater dominated by the Amazonian stature of an explosive young woman of indeterminate age in a red-dyed T-shirt inciting her companions to create a bonfire of brassieres. Ironically, as Featherstone noted, the b of brassiere, round-sounding, evoked the outward curvature of the bra-less woman-in-red's breasts pressing through the T-shirt. Squeezing through the tight-packed crowd of onlookers he flung aside a brassiere warmed by feminine breasts which had caught him in the face. He made straight for the news crews jostling for advantage. "Does anyone recognize this Atalanta?" Placards framed challenging statements: **MAN IS DEAD!** and **THE CENTER OF THE WORLD IS NOT GOD, BUT WOMIN!** Featherstone recognized here was a heroine for a Beat novelist, a companion worthy of a Be-Bop saxophone solo! Then he slyly suggested to a journalist the statuesque stunner was none other than the grand-daughter of Simone de Beauvoir and Jean-Paul Sartre: she screamed *Sorbonne*!

Ignition Of Metaphysical Thought. Questioning his metaphysical identity on a glorious *South Pacific* evening spangled with glittering stars, Fabian Roxburgh wheeled his modified Chevrolet by the refreshment kiosk and pulled in alongside a convertible on the ascending wave-slope of bitumen. Imposing, a touchstone for the ignition of metaphysical thought, the flattened lantern of the drive-in movie screen seemingly concentrated the illumination of trillions of stars into the implosion of its two-dimensional space: surely a representation which would have drawn from Socrates a dialogue on the philosophy of Man's spatial relationship with God. "Please take me to the *drives*." Cruising alone earlier he had accelerated along the beachfront boulevards reflecting on the kinesthesia of the golden sunset deepening to a warmer orange halo effect. He recalled a poignant experience in 'Nam coming upon a blood-soaked young GI waiting to be evacuated, relishing his moment of satori in silence, tightly gripping a smoking Stars-and-Stripes on its pole, the charred black serration of remaining fabric gently fluttering in the fetid circulation of air. Could he risk an emotional charring by this inflammatory ingénue beside him in the Chevrolet? All the anguish of Socrates staring forlornly at the shadow-shapes silhouetted on the wall of the Cave of Existence descended upon him.

Daydream Believer. Death's prone and disheveled mannequins randomly spaced in the oozing, putrefying earth of 'Nam were mocked by the stylizations of living youth crowding the refreshment kiosk: pushing herself forward on tip-toes, lifting herself up on the counter with tensed, straightened arms, a lotus and a Peace symbol beautifully embroidered on the derriere pockets of her Levis, she deeply inhaled the invigorating aroma of hamburgers sizzling on an open grill and placed her order. The lights went down on a Brando double-feature: *The Fugitive Kind* and *The Chase*. Sensing the supple pressure of her lips fondling the sculpted glass mouth of a Coca-Cola bottle quickened his anima's sensibility, flushed the calcifications of 'Nam from his consciousness, but she was quite coy peering through the driver side window into the convertible. "The drive-in is for *necking*." Emptying the Coke bottle and unable to stifle a gaseous burp she slid aside her leather pouch on its shoulder strap, leaned forward, reached between her shoulderblades and unhooked her brassiere, slipping it free from under her unbleached muslin blouse. "You can kiss me if you like, the way you would your favourite actresses. But don't get any ideas about us." Sexually then this was her minimalist phase, where a few well-sequenced caresses thoughtfully exploring the landscapes of her torso, perhaps an arrangement of delicate sweeps like a Fantin-Latour still-life, would release the dove of romantic peace between them. Kisses hummed off her lips, and under his hand's palm and fingers her breast's simmering purée of flesh awakened echoes of sensations from the late-fifties at the drive-in with girls who had anything but the Cold War on their minds. Across the drive-in tonight hundreds of breasts were being caressed, mouthes were being sucked with kisses, delving for the mystery of sexual contentedness in a celluloid world where to be a *Star* incarnated insatiable pleasure.

Satori In Saigon I. *"The flames of (Saigon) were the aurora of the Liberty of the World."* (Benjamin Constant). Tet's anniversary eruption of fireworks set Saigon's suburbs ablaze. Incense and Peppermints, the leis of Flower Power wilting around the necks of youth from the Summer of Love, the fatuous lyric of *All You Need Is Love*, levitated with 'Nam's Buddhist monks to the Lotus Land, and any hoped-for satori was shattered forever. Millions of television screens aureoled the heads of families contemplating the dramatic events on the evening news bulletins: the All-Seeing-Eye was focused on Saigon!

Satori In Saigon II. *"War is delightful to those who have had no experience of it."* (Erasmus). Credibility gaps opened with the War's intensifying Inferno, this breaching of the sanctity of Saigon and the American Embassy compound itself. Infiltrating cadres of Viet Cong subversively appeared from the faceless masses, embodiments of Satan's disaffected advance guard, stunning America with the horror there is a *secret* casketed within fear within all of us threatening to burst open.

Satori In Saigon III. *"War is not sparing of the brave, but of cowards."* (Anacreon). Limp, crumpled rag doll torsos sprawled on the grass compound, totally relaxed, marionettes whose strings had been severed, unable to float away to Lotus Land. US Marines on guard duty too had been squeezed in death-by-suffocation by Saigon's geometry of space-time, the fabric of the city's continuum now their winding-sheet. Einstein's famed four-dimensional co-ordinates of Relativity have brought these Soldiers of Fortune together on Saigon's space-time grid: *Le Déjeuner sur l'herbe*! January 30, 1968! Only American families and loved ones are publicly permitted to weep and grieve for their fallen sons.

Fall Of The GI. Themed on collective salvation through the omnipotence, omniscience and omnipresence of perpetual Revolution, vigorously exampled by the disenfranchised Viet Cong, the Gang of Five existential anarchists orchestrated a wave of street theater presentations celebrating the explosion of Tet across 'Nam. The profound fall of the GI was hammered into the malleable substance of the mass consciousness as the Image of the Future. Prominent among the theatrical protagonists was a young heroine in a Mao-beret, celebrant of the certain liberation of Saigon from the American-backed South Vietnamese puppet regime, with the glamor Princes Ky and Thieu in their silk cravats, braided and decorative uniforms mercilessly parodied as a Hollywood Stage Show. Fabian Roxburgh's hermetic withdrawal inside the space of his own mind, with television running 24 hours a day in the background, symbolized an entombment relieved only by an occasional walk along deserted streets after midnight to ease his mental anguish. He too could have been marooned in 'Nam in '68! Before she disappeared, his young companion had prepared dinner, he watched her watching him watching her fan out delicate trout slices arranged on a plate, the flesh evocatively pink: Tet's onomatopoeia instantly reverberated deep in the American psyche. What he now knew to be her goodbye kiss had the revolutionary fire of chili sauce haloed on her lips.

Street Execution. Archangelic Air Cavalry swept in low like a sequence of power-chords from the rising generation of guitar-gods, the helicopter gunships shredding the youth brigades, scything through the cadres below as if reaping grass: a gentle flock of geese suddenly ascended and flew away in a V-formation. Falling with screams unheard above the fire power, the youth brigades were flattened along with the slender grasses beneath the blades of the helicopters. Gunfire swept with the ferocity of a breathing dragon, consuming the refuge of a bamboo thicket, splintering millions of fragments from the poles which tore away soft flesh from bone, stripping the Viet Cong for their crossing the River Styx. Shuddering remembrances ignited Fabian Roxburgh's brain-waves into patterns of newsprint as his *Dispatches From 'Nam* appeared in various Underground papers. Readers now waded upstream with the GIs in the muddy water-ways of 'Nam, each pressured footfall waiting to sense the trip-wire and activate an explosive device. He described nights in Saigon, how the facets of his skull's dodecahedron jewel were veined with imagery insoluble even to the forgetfulness of sleep. The keening urgency of the geese mimicked a flight of screaming souls fleeing the rhythm of death violently rocking the earth. Fabian Roxburgh's soul peered into the weightless crystal ball of his skull tarnished, fogged, clouded with smoky imagery the soft jelly of his eyes had witnessed. Now 'Nam's map signage could be understood: All roads in 'Nam led to Saigon! Swerving through outbound military traffic on the periphery of a murderous fire-fight, an incoming shell's explosion lifted raw earth and heaved it over the vehicle he was passenger in. TIME magazine fixed the perspective of his impressions on the grid of best-selling newsprint. All the arteries into the heart of Saigon calcified now with war's agonizing angina. Among the traffic of bustling actors strutting the Saigon stage-set was a battle-hardened Police Chief and on-cue, from the chaotic, smoke-laden labyrinth of streets emerged a Viet Cong insurgent fresh from acts of arson, rape and murder, ambushed by death: the handgun's hard-rock candy shattered the Viet Cong's crystal ball of a skull in a flash memorialized on film. Dutifully, TIME too indulged the science of Numerology, where body-counts became Revelation, as if the mathematical accumulation would rescue the awkward political equation of the War's ideological imbalances.

And The Winner Is ... Camera flashes welcomed the black-tie invitees up the red-carpeted staircase into the glittering space of the hotel's ballroom. Tables were arranged for dinner beneath dazzling chandeliers, metaphors for electric ideas traveling the brain-wave circuitry inside a human skull. Fabian Roxburgh's strange semi-delirious nausea intensified as he was walked through the open doors into the vast space-time of the ballroom whose walls pictorially imploded with sequences of prestigious photographs from 'Nam. These Press Awards for excellence in Journalism and Photojournalism adopted a self-congratulatory thirties movie-style ambience, were an exercise in socio-political morphology justifying Darwin's famous evolutionary dictum on the hierarchy of species. Sleep-walking by the mounted photographic murals Roxburgh experienced an unsettling vertigo beneath a kaleidoscopic chandelier, remembering his near-death scramble from the taxi on the road back into Saigon, half-choking on the loose earth covering the vehicle. Disorientated, as the dust-cloud settled, he saw exposed at his feet the blood-splattered corpse of a young woman, other faceless Saigonese scurrying to-and-fro as if late for an appointment with Death. Fragments from an earlier radio program drifted through the white noise of the assembled guests: he recalled to mind the John Lennon interview, in particular the announcement of the obligatory new Beatles single, wittily dubbed, *Hello* (Elvis) *Goodbye* (Elvis), inspired as he intimated by such classic Elvis films as *Spinout* and *Clambake*. Roxburgh steadied himself against a chair thinking of the clownish *Sgt. Pepper* uniforms so praised by the critical bandwagon, but in reality a snide UK smirk at the Grunts stripped down in the swelter of 'Nam's Summer of Love. *Sgt. Pepper* was the childish entertainment extravaganza of counter-culture, already reputed its finest hour, but 'Nam was the real War ... *A Whiter Shade of Pale*! Stepping across the feminine corpse that day Roxburgh had felt her entering death's spacetime with utter tranquility. When dinner began to be served the noxious odors overwhelmed and sickened his sensibility, evoking the stench of flesh barbecued by napalm, steaming intestines ripe with a belly full of bronze candy: he stumbled humiliatingly over chairs and patrons in his rush to vomit across the men's room floor. Such were the post-war sorrows of the survivor!

Homage À Ingres. Sunlight dwindled through the shutters in elongated ellipses of shadow and space's winding-sheet shrouded Christopher Featherstone, caved in his office's existential loneliness, Miranda Westwood's still-thin dossier lying under his hand. Walking to his favorite diner he paused at a store window where a television news item showed graphic footage of an anarchist assault on the previous evening's Press Awards. Stampeded, the *beautiful people* indecorously tripped over full-length evening gowns and were splattered with paint and invective. Youth's penchant for convenience-store Maoism struck him as absurd, although the generational drift-effect certainly loosened the tectonic plates holding society together. After scanning the familiar menu his thoughts revisited scenes from that tumultuous weekend in '64 with Samantha Westwood, and her anonymous *Homage à Ingres*. "Tell me, if I am a painting, whose? What subject?" Unquestionably, sublimely nude, *La Grande Odalisque*!

Aesthetic Of The Martini. Reviewing the nouveau *nouveau roman* narrative of his existence, Christopher Featherstone stood squarely on the deck of the schooner disappointed with Samantha Westwood's absence: had she simply strode across the ocean to the shore? Calvin Westwood frowningly handed him an itemized charge account to scrutinize. "Listen, Featherstone, if you are too exhausted to complete this race with Time ..." True, he did feel like a Blakean watercolour of a Man hopelessly pressing outward against the frame's containment, and thought of his own youth's electricity of oil paint illumining the promise of the future. "Prepare well for the return of your Prodigal Daughter, honor her with ... a masked ball!" Featherstone resembled Samantha's eyes liquefying to a translucence of otherworldly reverie: the colorless martinis they shared at the bar that lost weekend burning her cheeks to burgundy. All seductive delicacy the martini proved to be the drink *par excellence* of adulterers. Leaving the schooner in the motor boat Westwood provided, Featherstone varnished these emotions of remembrance as the frieze of the sky distilled from space's immense silence sunset's cloth of Turnerian brushstrokes, against which was raised the crucifix of the mast.

Freud's Surrealist Pop Songs. Comatose, physically inert, Fabian Roxburgh's period of hospitalization brought him a psychic chemistry of dreamscapes under medication, the metaphysical flying buttresses of imagery stretching Time to irrelevance. Dipped in aquamarine liquids of semi-consciousness his brain-waves became soluble to washes of far-off music audible on another plane from a close-by patient's radio. His white pillow during his wanderings through the labyrinth of dreamscapes pursued by pencil drawings of Picasso's Minotaur had the texture of a flattened and bleached skull. Later, convalescing, with pen-and-paper he expressed a dream-sequence as follows: (1) **SUMMER RAIN** by Johnny Rivers. Vietnam's monotonous wet season. A whiskey-sodden Jack Kerouac, *Desolation Angel*, wingless, collar turned up, was glimpsed riding the Mekong Delta freight trains trying to get himself close again to the heart of darkness of his once-celebrated prose. The *Lonesome Traveler* haltingly vanished into downpours shed by the Angels, a beaten Atlas no longer able to raise the three-dimensional world upon his shoulders. (2) **LOVE IS BLUE** by Paul Mauriat. Miranda Westwood's painted lotus eyes gazed at him from above, melting with the liquidity, the transparency of Vermeer's oils, the corona of her Mao-beret so much dark space against light's aureole holding her face suspended in space. Then Bunuel's long-bladed razor sliced the soft globe of her eye and jelly oozed, but the blindness was his, for she vanished from sight. (3) **GREEN TAMBOURINE** by The Lemon Pipers. The moon's double-cream camembert rose over the green twilight of the Mekong delta silhouetting a stream of incoming helicopters. Was the brief moon's Miranda's face, and darkness the anti-establishment halo of her Mao-beret? (4) **GOIN' OUT OF MY HEAD** by The Lettermen. Dream's Time displacement interchanged epochs, where Elvis' '58 crew cut and *GI Blues* regalia, saw him stationed in Saigon in '68, the Fort Lauderdale of 'Nam. Thousands of Hondas sped through the streets while on the beach at Da Nang The Beatles in *Sgt. Pepper* uniforms performed *Do The Clam*! (5) **BABY, NOW THAT I'VE FOUND YOU** by The Foundations. Half-awakening from 'Nam's surrealistic space, whose foreground was dominated by a feminine corpse whose flowing blood quickly congealed across the dusty roadway in a sweeping scarf of black satin, he sensed a visitation hovering by his bedside. A square-shouldered Aegean Goddess with the morphology of a perfuming rose-as-woman, leaned over him whispering. Aureoled by overhead lighting her fall of hair's liquefying *frottage* muffled her voice in its veil of oil paint. Withdrawing, she melted back against the lighting as red-into-white *sfumato* before vanishing. He could not recall through the haze of semi-consciousness her spoken words.

Jewel-In-The-Heart-Of-The-Lotus. The stench of urine lingered, sharpening his sensibilities during this early phase of his convalescence, hopefully not his own. Gorgeously layered lotus petals blossomed from her nirvanic-spaced eyes. Twin Jewels-in-the-Heart-of-the-Lotus regarded his prone torso and limbs with oblique detachment, the seeming effortlessness with which a space capsule is magnetized yet eludes the Earth's gravity. "Did you visit me in a red T-shirt? Read me my obituary? Will you tell me your name?" Turbaned in a perennial Mao-beret, her skin breathing close by and brush-coated in caramel-and-banana, she astrally levitated him through the fog of his 'Nam sickness with her voice: "Miranda Westwood."

SO ENDS THE BLOODY BUSINESS OF THE DAY.
(Homer)

II
ZONES OF SHADOW

Tango à la Che. Che Guevara, would-be tango dancer leading the world's young revolutionaries into The Promise Land, forehead imperiously crowned with his infamous beret, loomed large from a popular counter-culture banner, strictly black-on-white, silk-screening a cartouche in Spanish sandstone as Christopher Featherstone followed the reverberant echoes beyond an archway deeper into the heart of the University. Che's stylized tango of Revolution and Mao's messianism now duetted as strophe-and-antistrophe in the dramatic consciousness of youth gathering in the grounds of the world's universities. Featherstone reflected on whether the corridors of the University would ever again be tombs lined with the sarcophagi of holy virgins sainted in classical learning. The scene assumed a three-dimensional presence: the silhouetted Hydra of existential revolutionaries swayed to anthemic pop songs and animated conversation, the fabric of modern existence being singed by war and youth's tango of militancy with the authorities à la Che, the evening seemed parched ready to explode in flame. Featherstone brooded over a sign stenciled on a head-high block of Spanish sandstone: **HO CHI MINH WAY**. Sparks scattering severed the Hydra, and uniform cheers took up a chant as the ring leader climbed onto a make-shift dais and with an eruptive branch on fire wrote up a burning slogan against the kohl-lined evening: **U.S. OUT! U.S. OUT! U.S. OUT!** The *Good Vibrations* wavelength of '67's Summer of Love now segued in '68 to the *I'm-Fixing-To-Die-Rag*! Suddenly absorbed in the coils of collective madness as the activists showered the approaching frontage of National Guardsmen with rocks and smoldering branches pulled from the bonfires, Featherstone ran for safety coolly pondering a famous question posed by Socrates two-and-a-half millennia previously: *What is it that makes the young good?* Answer: *The Laws*!

Siege. Police searchlights swept the University's façade. Visible across the bitumenized moat of the highway from a second floor window in the Ivy League dormitory named after St. George, a massive banner unfurled against the Spanish Palace lit up with the face of Che Guevara, questioning the logic of a University's existence in a world committed to perpetual revolution. Minutes earlier, nursing bruises and abrasions from their scuffles with police, a quintet of activists accompanied by Christopher Featherstone made the sanctuary of St. George's college and busted inside a dormitory room. Stumbling over bean bags someone found a light switch. Vacated for the summer vacation, existential detritus from previous occupants littered the space's psyche. Two wilting, soiled jasmines collapsed side-by-side into a bean bag, their heads coronaed by the square album covers of Jimi Hendrix's *Are You Experienced?* and Cream's *Disraeli Gears* stapled to a wall. Where though was Miranda Westwood? Stephen Maxwell kneeled on the floor and switched on a small-screen television set relaying newsreel footage of the siege of the Citadel of Hue. Can openers worked on jumbo cans of cold baked beans. Smarting from a truncheon blow across his lower back Featherstone moved away from the window.

Citadel Of Hue. The *Desolation Row* jasmines, bare-footed now, ripped calico skirts sweeping the floor, smelling of cold baked beans, suspiciously questioned Featherstone: "So what's your angle then on Miranda-the-invisible?" Illusions had hardened to stone, as resistant as the compacted blocks being pounded by artillery walling up the Citadel of Hue. Zooming in close a camera caught the archaeological recovery of a torso's dust-coated shoulder-and-arm being lifted from out of collapsed rubble, the measured stature of a shiny plastic body-bag nearby: the Grunts lifted the lifeless body with a tenderness comparable with the Raising of Jesus from the Cross. Delivering his eulogy of symbolized disillusionment, Stephen Maxwell squatted between the bruised jasmines, his arms about their slumped shoulders; "It's just a plastic world out there, man, running on plastic Time, shit through a plastic hourglass turned by *The Man.* Time is made of cellophane, man, you understand? Flowers, man, not cellophane. Flowers breathe, cellophane suffocates." Each stone executioner's block in the Citadel of Hue created in the minds of the Grunts a three-dimensional zone of death splashed with blood!

Zones Of Shadow I. *"War loves to seek its victims in the young."* (Sophocles). Fabian Roxburgh pondered the serendipity of the draft card as he looked up from turning the pages of a newspaper: 300,000 Draftees in 1968! *Lady Madonna* previewed on the radio saw the mysterious Miranda Westwood emerge from the bathroom's chiaroscuro where she had been hand-washing her brassiere. Where were the *free love* friendship kisses promised by her generation for him? On the television newsreels American youth were gate crashing the garden party at Hue. Carnival firepower accompanied street theater in full swing. Compared to these actors in Hue-as-Performance-Art Miranda congealed a Vermeeresque domesticity, even if her breast's sepia outline was too strongly sexual for the flimsy muslin fabric of her blouse. Fingertips tingled with the anticipated sensation of measuring their parabolae: on the black-and-white television screen, in extreme close-up, a GI's finger erotically squeezed the curve of a trigger and the rifle jumped.

Zones Of Shadow II. *"Better pointed bullets than pointed speeches."* (Bismarck). Fabian Roxburgh's scrapbook accumulated pages of newspaper cuttings, **TIME** and **NEWSWEEK** editorials, column inches overflowing with analysis of the Tet Offensive and now the Siege of Hue. *Open City! Cinema verité* reported everyday from the Citadel at Hue. Zing went the strings of the heart of patriotism vibrated by Hue's evocation of Stalingrad. The Grunts hunkered behind stone blocks splashed with blood weren't swallowing the political rhetoric Stateside, just Charlie's cheap but deadly bronze candy (Made in China). For amusement Roxburgh had Miranda listen to a comedian on the radio doing impressions of President Johnson in comically emotional denial: "There will be no atomic bomb used for the relief of Khe Sanh. Thank you, and *Amen*, General Gordon!"

Zones Of Shadow III. *"Military glory – that attractive rainbow that rises in showers of blood, that serpent's eye that charms destiny."* (Abraham Lincoln). Fabian Roxburgh commissioned noted illustrator, Celeste Hawthorne, to compose sequences of cartoon frames describing the drama unfolding of Grunts gate crashing the party at Hue, juxtaposing the Citadel's stone blocks with Warhol's grocery carton Pop Art sculptures. Above the fog of creeping tear gas Huey Cobras struck with force. Pen-and-ink bled the red spectrum plateau of earth at Khe Sanh into cartoon frames. Celeste magically evoked Khe Sanh's Elysian field swept by the swish of Maharishi robes and Sgt. Pepper's hangers-on, her pen's artistry as fluent as flutes drifting from Hippie communes Stateside. And the subtitle tie-in? ... *be-in* ... *love-in* ... *die-in* ...

Deliquescence. Two crucifixes, yin-and-yang, geometrizing sexual abstinence languidly stretched in the hypercubic space of the apartment. Reflectively lowering a T-shirt over the freshly showered raisins of her taut nipples the gourmet-child addressed herself to the fresh collages papering the living room. A Delphic veil descended upon her expression as she hand-washed her clothes in the bathroom, his words to her echoed like a Voice in the Wilderness. How could the affluence of suburbia induce such sadness? When he spoke to her of his despair at not being on the correspondence quest hunting down the Minotaur entrenched in Hue's Imperial Palace, she continued focusing on the news item sketching details of Jimi Hendrix's arrest and jailing in Sweden for trashing his hotel room. Everyone was in the front-line fighting except him! She shrugged: *That's the point!* When he said revolutions became uncontrollable. And when he journalized the futility of freedom ever rising now from its imprisonment deep in the existential dungeon of 'Nam's three-dimensional space she simply ambled over to the blazing window and gazed up into the surreal azure sky. Superimposed collages of Mao's pulpy sponge face, infamous antithesis of handsomeness, more a perverse waxwork eunuch, juxtaposed with Lyndon Baines Johnson's and Richard M. Nixon's, themselves sculpted after Roman coin portraits, without laurel crowns of victory, formed a mural to her movements during the midday heat, her pubis damp with honey as were his loins. Languorous with heat exhaustion, her torso's sculptural *oeuvre* lay a brushstroke of impastoed oil on the bed's canvas. Eyes following his sharper sexual keenness, she burned up the remnants of the bullet-ridden-Stars-and-Stripes-in-tatters already exposing his wounded Ego. Still, she created in the convalescing space of his apartment an emotional lily pad effect, brightening the pool of inertia into which his sensibilities had deliquesced.

When Is An Ugly Duckling A Swan? Shadowing the mirror's spatial zone with the innocence of a Disney cartoon, Miranda Westwood's oil painting chemistry hardened in glass, her visceral ice reflection sexually unreachable, so Fabian Roxburgh returned to the television screen where the crumbling Acropolis of Hue resisted US encroachment. Khe Sanh's *lonesome cowboys*, worthy stars auditioning for a Warhol movie, suddenly danced to the rhythm of exploding mortars shuffling across the red earth ballroom: fragments of shrapnel pinned medallion shapes to the purple heart of a brave young Lieutenant, psychologically tore open empathy wounds in Roxburgh's sensibility. Suddenly the imagery of his collages swirled across the floor as a gust of warm ghosted breeze billowed through the veil of curtains. An audible crash startled his psyche: Miranda stooped over the jagged asymmetry of a fractured mirror, reflected in fragmentation by the sizable splinters of glass. Glancing up at him, trapped, looking-out from the fragments, no longer whole, her dying swan posture welcomed his Nureyev effect of lamentation. Later, he contemplated with her, illustrated the significance of the shattered mirror of the Milky Way, its portrait of the fallen Archangel hopelessly fragmented and unrecognizable.

A Sweet Little Rock'n'Roller. Solo dancing, spaced-out waifs of the Sgt. Pepper's generation, dripping in eastern fragrant oils, crowded the stoops of inner city apartment blocks, the architectural squalor redolent with music-conversation-fashion to Christopher Featherstone pausing before a building under a lighted street lamp, unable to disrobe the velvet fur electricity of the overheated summer evening. Somewhere inside a Zen-organ droned on, and octopi guitar lines undulated a seemingly endless psychedelic melody inhaled from the marijuana fumes. Then a heavily chromed street-rod in midnight-blue, wide-wheeled and crêpe-soled, definitively not a vehicle for hippie tripping, rolled menacingly by Featherstone, its car radio blazing out the chorus of *Devil With The Blue Dress On*: a visually sartorial moment evocative of the Democratic Age. Up at a second floor window Miranda Westwood moved into the frame for air and stood there suspended with arms upraised, posing him a question: "Y?" Later he trailed the *sweet little rock'n'roller* back to the University dormitory college where the Gang of Five were waiting and they all squeezed into her car. Featherstone searched for them in the open air rock festival, *Battle of the Bands*, losing them in the languid smoke-haze of the crowd, but thankful for the invaluable details of her charge account all the same. He caught the logo of **LESBOS** records and eased himself closer to the stage. A familiar, statuesque Amazon with broad Ursula Andress shoulders fronted a rocking four-piece and launched herself at the microphone, her voice's Simone de Beauvoir seriousness addressing the lyric:

I am woman and I talk
So don't ever command me to silence.
I am woman and I walk
So don't ever read me evolutionary science.

Hells Angels' *old ladies* were hoisted on-stage and began assaulting the Amazon and her band. Swinging the microphone the shapely Hippolyte fought back fiercely. A riot ensued: water cannon, police on horseback, running skirmishes, newspaper column inches.

Tuesday Weld, Art Nouveau And Newton's Laws Of Motion. From the ocean's solar-etched mass of softened aquamarine glass waves smoothly lifted. Statues molded from Greek *thought* beachcombers-with-Malibus contemplated the Venetian masterpieces golden with light reclining in the cool ebb-and-flow of the foreshore. His dramatic fall from lucidity to opacity memorialized by the dark-lensed aviator sunglasses he slipped on, solitary Fabian Roxburgh juxtaposed this ideal white beach with the Paradise Lost of Khe Sanh's bleak red clay plateau, trenched and sand-bagged by semi-naked Grunts surfing the waves of VC assaults. A car's tocsin jolted him. Long-time high school friends in a dazzling midnight-blue street-rod, all gleaming chrome like their personae, pulled over to the sidewalk to buzz him. "Hey, Roxburgh, how long have you been back from 'Nam this time?" Paddling a Malibu into the cartography of glassy waves with them stretched space with elastic silences. Surfing embellished the wave's pristine symmetry with sculptural attitude. Exuberant Art Nouveau creations of the sixties, young women immersed themselves in the slippery wave plasma, shining angels contrasting the earthly corpses floating in the putrid rice paddies of 'Nam as if parallel universes co-existed in spacetime. Sunset's elegiac wistfulness cast zones of shadow across the foreshore of the glorious beach. "Tuesday Weld has vanished from our fantasies. So who's the hippie nymphet we saw you with the other evening?" Towelling dry, Roxburgh visualized himself shedding the arabesque of a metamorphosis as the fog of 'Nam momentarily dissipated, naked in the sea, naked in the setting sun. "She's like ... Newton's Laws of Motion!" Untouched by the disorienting dream of 'Nam his friends laughed at the mystery. "Well, those hippie clothes hang off her like the mood of her emotions!" Crossing the shadow-swept boulevard, Roxburgh took a glancing caress from a touring convertible, and lunging for his dislodged aviator sunglasses as he described an acrobatic ballet in his fall to the roadway, glimpsed the striking upper physique of a statuesque woman in a red T-shirt behind the wheel. Night descended early, fading on a strangely familiar face whispering to him.

Rabelais, Boccaccio And Dante. Savoring his martini while watching lines of evening commuters disperse from the inner city's citadels of finance, Christopher Featherstone transcribed a name, *Jane Greer*, vertically down the page of his notebook, drawing solace from the deliberate substitution. The diner's tried-and-true menu could not tempt his thoughts from his relationship with the triangular *ménage à trios*: he conceived Calvin Westwood's imaginative choice as follows:

Foie Gras
Crocodile Ragoût
Char-grilled Lamb Cutlets
Patridge Roasted in Pepper
Caramelised Pumpkin and Fig Fritter

Rabelais' figural gluttony, Boccaccio's adulterous appetite, contrasted his pure Beatrice being let loose on the wild streets of a latter-day Florence, where she has denied her politically inept Dante her salutation. Featherstone determined to read *him* more carefully.

Out Of The Past. A neon psychedelic light-show illuminated the upper living space over his office. Lying fully clothed along the crystal catafalque of the bed listening to an elegiac late Beethoven String Quartet (op. 130) he summoned up remembrance of Samantha Westwood's sexual cartography of his personae, beginning with her choices for dinner.

Sole Soufflé Flavoured with Cognac
White Asparagus Purée

With flesh as thin as apple shavings through which drizzled perfume saturated in Chanel No. 5 she engaged his capitalized I with the haunting echo of her O forming a nude union of mathematics ... **Phi.** Her squid-ink eyes that afternoon of recognition on the schooner suffused him in a fog of ecstasy despite her Monica Vitti-like existential ennui. Beethoven's monumental fugue explored her displacement in his existence's spacetime continuum.

Mao Is Very Now! Perfecting his investigative voyeurism, Christopher Featherstone identified Miranda Westwood's numerous excursions during the early phase of her disappearance: (i) Hanging off the driver side window of a very stylish if old-fashioned midnight-blue street-rod, flirting with the occupants. (ii) Baiting the formations of National Guardsmen by inserting flowers in the barrels of their precisely-angled rifles, then indulging in the desperate pyromania of her existential anarchists of the Cultural Revolution – *Mao is the moment!* (iii) Visiting recording studios listening to playback tapes of this year's omnipotent album, helping rivet the lyric of the year to melody. (iv) Holding conversations with a 'Nam correspondent via the newspaper Personals.

Chartreuse of Candied Oranges
Chocolate Sorbet
Melting Lemon Tart with Rich Cream

More worrying was Miranda's pursuit by a tall statuesque woman braless under a red T-shirt, endowed with Ursula Andress' shoulder-width; the ice-slurried breasts of these radical virgins evoked reminiscences of Artemis and her Actaeon-slaying handmaidens.

A Butterfly Pinned To Ixion's Wheel. Heavy raindrops tattooed the glass panes of the studio attic's skylight windows. Mountains of black cloud unleashed a summer thunderstorm deluging the city. The sextet of anarchists moved among poster displays arranged in Celeste Hawthorne's studio space. Stephen Maxwell immediately recognized the Amazon Queen's portrait affixed to the **LESBOS** record logo. Celeste glanced up from her work table. "Would you like to hear the 45? She's Clytemnestra in a Greek tragedy, revenge is on that woman's mind. Still, the arrangement is lush with hippie wildflowers. Her voice though has a Spartan timbre ...

> In case you haven't heard I have the freedom of a bird.
> I move like mist across a hill without your ego's sudden chill.
> Invisible bird inside a cage, love's imprisoned by your rage.
> Tell me you're leaving
> Leave me to my grieving ...

"See what I mean, her voice is a butterfly pinioned to Ixion's Wheel. What about some Hendrix then? *Red House*? I can do a variation on Salvador Dali for you: *The Discovery of 'Nam by Lyndon Baines Johnson*." Fiery fingers of sunlight plunged through the taffeta brocade of cloud shredding its tissue.

The Sixties Epicenter Will Be Here, On Campus, In '68! While the Star of David geometrically formed by the motion of the anarchists on the floor space of the studio as they surveyed the collection, Celeste returned to her inking a massive poster commissioned by a consortium of left-wing (or Humanist) academics: Grunts waded into the murky Acheron of the Mekong obviously unaware they were now noir-shades, each unwrapping Uncle Ho's bronze candy with their names on, a pole-driven ferry approaching out of the gloom. Miranda Westwood stood transfixed, sorting through a folio of posters featuring the likeness of Fabian Roxburgh as (i) James Dean seated in his racing Porsche hours before his fatal accident, and his empyrean passage East of Eden into immortality. (ii) Humbert camouflaged leering after Lolita (quotations identified the protagonists) in her bathing suit, pre-teen pinup, worthy prize for a Renaissance Man adrift in the twentieth-century. (iii) Socrates of neo-classical provenance imbibing the truth serum, hemlock. Miranda swung around to face the silent television screen flickering with a news correspondent reporting on the block-by-block urban fighting in Hue. Celeste's illustrator eyes followed her Iphigenia movements back to Stephen Maxwell's elbow where she peered at a poster he exulted over. "Look, **THE SIXTIES EPICENTER IS HERE, ON CAMPUS, IN '68!** Mao's educational de-construction will at last realize God's Plan on Earth!" Compared with the vividness of the *dramatis* *personae* in the studio how drained and grainy the newsreel footage flickering on the television screen appeared, almost Hollywood thirties make-believe, with a supply plane lumbering onto Khe Sanh's dangerous plateau, mortar rounds dancing after the beast: *Thunk! Thunk! Thunk!* "My posters make politicized violence palatable, for usually the blow is to the conscience, unlike a police truncheon to the kneecaps!"

Morality Is Personal Choice. Loins faded to a feeble ember glow, an ink line drawing, Christopher Featherstone handled the **LESBOS** 45 catching at the singer's name on the label, **HELENA STEELE**, suddenly feeling himself the sculpture of a *lost man* frozen by time in a glacier of conservatism. Too monochrome to paint a masterpiece, too politically uncool for these swinging sixties, just a drifting lone wolf doomed to wander further from the Adonis of his youth, he listened as Celeste asked: "Who is this young Eurydice you're searching for?" *(Sittin' On The) Dock Of The Bay* underlined his hopelessness while she prepared him tea in bone china and sliced through a dripping double-layer chocolate cake. "Beardsley's draughtsmanship inspires us all. Yes, sexually." These water-torture moments of sexual lucidity as he fell into this Penelope's web and sunset's skyline resembling the burning manuscript of a New Testament had him roused enough to confess: "I'm a Zen rock these days soaking in a stream of waved sand." From a woven basket of freshly baked bread her ink-stained fingertips picked at the heart of a sliced loaf. "So, are you hard-crusted with a fluffy centre like this loaf, or pumpernickel?" She played him a stack of 45s, her sublime ebony eyes, her modelled lips after those of the French chanteuse, Mireille Mathieu, stretching time until he discovered his physical entombment and thoughts content enough to gaze up at the stars through the skylight. With zones of shadow descending she melted any crystallization of awkwardness: "If you have any electricity how about lighting up my evening for me? Shall we *Do The Clam*?"

Quantum-A-Go-Go. Uninhibitedly taking off her clothes, peeling away layers of illusion, Celeste allowed him to astrally sense the almond in its delicate shell vibrate with auto-suggestive pleasure-to-come, through her body's flesh-tinted bone china, while her fingers' artistry felt after his tanned, if weathered antiquity. Contrasting sexual skin tones with him, she asked: "How does a man in his forties kiss?" Thinking of the Westwoods drinking martinis through '68, of Miranda circulating the scene, Featherstone camouflaged a Pre-Raphaelite kiss on the French chanteuse's mouth, while his thought's voice-over rationalized how purity's spillage was unavoidable in a world undergoing revolution. Celeste's *ombre*, abstract expressionism as biology, transliterated the simpler cartoon of missionary sex to a complex novella of postures and caresses and immediately she was lit, fully alight and radiating. Subsidence relaxed her to a pleasurable composure before her ink-stained fingers helpfully sheathed a condom and they initiated a jive of subatomic particles interchanging sexual music ... Quantum-A-Go-Go! Later, her Sleeping Beauty glassed over by the studio attic through which the tranquilized evening had him pondering how his own epiphany subsided quickly enough. Awaking, he stilled himself, for her heavy black pencil analyzed their intimacy for her collection, but he was not discomforted by her sketching his naked torso knowing she would rarely open the folio to reflect on him in the future. "You said last night you've been *around*. Was that a pun?" Celeste put a fresh record on the turntable, Velvet Underground's *White Light/White Heat*, before answering: "Well, yes, numerous men have been around my studio."

Lost In Action. Flowers overflowing vases aerated the clinically tranquil hospital ward. Visible through a window was some geometry of electric-blue sky. Fabian Roxburgh had fallen to the roadway and the surreality of his mind's mirror had splintered. He could feel the dense oil paint bruising of his flesh. Sleeping through the night he had felt angel fingers dressing his abrasions but swimming back through to consciousness the tenderness of pressing his memory's bruises proved too painful. Miranda sat at his bedside, slightly hunched, probably bored, chewing her lower lip, her eyes vaguely scanning a radical newspaper lying beside his arm on the bed. "Look, I brought you a poster, shall I unroll it for you?" How was it youth's consciousness had become shadowed in the penumbra cast by Chairman Mao? The chameleon colors of hippiedom fiercely contrasted the Grunts in 'Nam dust-coated in red clay earth. Where was the Wooden Horse to bust 'Nam wide open? After Miranda left he noticed the newspaper and began reading. There it was, under *Dispatches From 'Nam*, his obituary: *Celebrated Vietnam War Correspondent, Fabian Roxburgh, lost in action: (1940–1968)*. A photograph fell from the newspaper, showing Miranda engaged in sexual cartography with a student agitator!

In A Monastery Garden. Butterflies-in-flight embroidered on her well-worn Levis, Miranda twirled with excitement, no longer Mao-sodden with his cultural anaesthesia, after Fabian Roxburgh announced their embarkation upon a quest for purification. "Are we truly cutting-out of this scene? Of the pattern? Cool! Where is this monastery?" Cruising in the borrowed midnight-blue street-rod they traveled north pulling off the highway towards the monastery's citadel with the sun's antique eye overhead. Miranda's holiday-mood, tipping successive bottles of Coca-Cola to her thirsty lips, throwing the flourish of her Jimi Hendrix scarf to the onrushing summer breeze, holding her musketeer's plumed hat in place with a hand, erased her alter ego of teenage political temptress for a time at least. Roxburgh allowed his amnesia of the years '60-'63 to revivify with memories under this incendiary immersion in her emotional napalm. Would the glorious sunshine years of the early sixties ever return? Her psychedelic blouse working loose, the colorful plumage of her broad-brimmed hat a striking montage, she burst free of the street-rod and ran over the Zen-like shadows laid on the earth by the stone-blocks of the monastery.

Sand Traps. Vintner monks busily tended trellises of grapevine. Musical brethren deep within the monastery's citadel vocalized a famous Requiem. Fabian Roxburgh pressed against the stone edifice sensing the rocket and mortar barrages reducing Hue's Imperial Palace to rubble. But who would honor the martyred blood of the

Grunts spilling over the stones at Hue? Before him were symmetrically equidistant traps laid by a mysterious assailant. Sunset bloodied the surfaces of the monastery. While Miranda entertained the monks he stood in the dusty courtyard recalling a patrol he had joined in 'Nam headed by a dog handler. The monastery loomed over him. Obsequious zones of shadow embedded him in a kind of psychic imprisonment. How many Grunts at Hue had discovered their *treasure* buried beneath the floor of the Imperial Palace? The dog had faithfully and fatefully discovered to Roxburgh and his handler an excrement-smeared barb of arrow booby trapped for a footfall to trigger, release and impale the abdomen. Miranda re-emerged with a smothering leap into his arms, her caress like sweet syrup poured over warm cake. Hours passed exploring the spiritual zones of the monastery. Her feet laid aromatic trails across the *crème brulée* sand dunes following the contraction of the sun westward. A bronze seascape freshened by an onshore breeze cooled the *flambé* summer day. Moonrise came, unfolding a golden rose from a skyline dyed in rich purple. Hurling herself level against the sloping flank of a dune she asked: "Can you kiss me like Robert Redford does Jane Fonda on screen?" Renoir-on-the-beach, so much caviar-in-blue-jeans, she lay on the creamy toffee flow of sand dune feeling his kiss smoke her head's space like the monastery's censer!

Mythological Encounter. Boarding the Westwood's schooner from the powerboat, Christopher Featherstone glimpsed Samantha sunbathing, tanning her years of decadence, the smoothly rounded arc of her derriere dipping in the bright colors of her one-piece bathing suit. Beneath her marbled face, slightly bronzed, creamed against too much weathering by Time, emotions were veiled or non-existent, her smile's vague woodcut was sharpish. "Who are you, Mr. Featherstone?" Her manner of address delivered him the *recoil*. A silverware coffee service awaited them under an awning. "A lapsed Platonist." He handed her the 45 he carried, with its **LESBOS** record logo visible, a sliced-through pomegranate: "Miranda's voice is audible in the back-up vocal." Looking across the ocean's volatile phosphorescence, away from her still very agreeable-looking physique soaked in martinis, he felt Celeste's heavy black pencil clinging to his loins, her sexual caricature annealing to flesh and muscle. "What were Miranda's last words to you?" Now he understood, only with Iphigenia's sacrifice would the sails fill with Aeolus' breath and the schooner cleave for the shores of Troy! "Well, inside a blank sheet of white paper she wrote: **HOLD THE SQUARE.**" The physique of her voice's image agitated a still-felt resonance between their torsos' two-pronged tuning fork. "Miranda's carousel ride through Hippieland ... I'm so out-of-touch, you understand. And you ... your wife and children ... are you still abandoned?" Thrilling to her remembrance he experienced all sunbeams suddenly become stationary. "There are no water nymphs in Hylas' reflective pool." Samantha murmured a curious phrase he heard as, *amour fou*, but she asked aloud: "No *echoes*?"

Fixing A Linear Narrative. Posing her arabesque *à la Danaë* painted by Rembrandt, Samantha held up the **LESBOS** 45, pondering the pomegranate logo, while Christopher Featherstone remembered the barely visible scar along her calf's curvature. Had the martinis starved her of an appetite for sex? Suddenly she plunged over the side of the schooner into the marine-blue coolness of the ocean. Surfacing, her transformed head-sculpture above the water-plane, her body entombed below, she possessed the freshness and clarity of a Warhol portrait on silk screen. A tuning fork of harmony was struck.

The Philosopher's Stone. Walking an aisle of typists and clerks, entering the vaulted, oak-paneled office, introduced to the new partner in Williamson & Lovegrove, chartered accountants, Christopher Featherstone orchestrated his observations, feeling an inert nakedness at being financially sketched. Bridget Lovegrove calmly offered him her hand and effortlessly seated herself behind the Rembrandt bible of his accounts ledger, already open on her massive jarrah desk. Ink's unguent anointed the stereoscopic space of the sacred leaves, the precision of penmanship a subtle contrast in red-and-black. Over pleasantries, Featherstone spoke of perhaps beginning a New Testament, his accountant stylized in a rather austere dress-line worthy of placement in stained glass, her polished up purity aureoled by framed certificates adorning the wall behind her. She spoke of Time as being his truest friend, financially speaking, her eyebrows lifting at his proposal of investing in an obscure record label, the pomegranate logo of **LESBOS** drawing from her allusions to *The Ancient Mariner*, the small-label music business being an albatross. "Profitability is sustained long-term with a mining portfolio. Consider how the recent nickel boom has increased your financial stability. Iron ore, Mr. Featherstone, iron ore." Sunlight filtering through a window into the office created a chrysanthemum effect of her hair's halo. "Iron ore? But is it The Philosopher's Stone?" Her phone rang. He respectfully ran his eye down a column of alimony payments visible on the ledger. Then he was electrified to hear her mode of address, for she was a chameleon, in naming the caller on the line: Calvin!

One-Hit Wonder. Turning over the pages of the evening edition headlined by North Korea's boarding and seizure of the American spy-ship, *Pueblo*, Christopher Featherstone listened to more of the vinyl groove of the **LESBOS** record, thinking of Demeter and Persephone and their shopping patterns revealed by their charge accounts. Lyric and music sank deep into the substratum of his thoughts as he left the office, strolled downtown to the Hotel Plaza, entered the bar and ordered a martini.

> Her eyes are like a lotus blooming with love
> My heart is a tambourine swept by the wings of a dove.
> Something's happening to make my rhythm skip a beat
> Revolution's coming and we're turning up the heat.

Drenched in the atmosphere of his lost weekend he drove down to the beach where zones of shadow flickered between the glazes of sunset and moonrise. Sinking between the curvaceous folds of sand dunes he fixed upon the Whistlerian silhouette of the schooner poised on the ocean's tranquil canvas. Wings on fire, a seagull sketched a calligraphy of aerial bliss, described in motion the cartography of gravity-waves, rendered space rubbery with displacement. Smeared in sunset the moon's butterfly metaphored the lyric in Featherstone's thoughts. Washes of silken dye were blocked for life's cartoon-effects: soon the ocean's quicksilver mirror cradled the full face of the glowing moon.

S.P.Q.R. Banners strident with slogans presented the human face of socialism to the formations of news media gathered to witness the gladiatorial spectacles being shaped by the events of 1968. Familiar existential anarchists and a tribe of Amazons with a new-look feminine etiquette accelerated the momentum of anti-authoritarianism, their meta-political dance ebbing-and-flowing from the University into the heart of the inner city. Images flashed around the Globe shattered the mirror of surreality clouding with sprays of Democracy's debris. (i) **LET ADAM STAY IN PARADISE, W-O-M-I-N DON'T NEED HIM!** Led by a statuesque Amazon, beardless women in a tight-knit sit-in spilling from the corridors of a female college dormitory, sang the lyric of a pop song they were hoping to chart and become their anthem of social deconstruction (sexual freedom on their terms). (ii) **TEAR UP THE YELLOW BRICK ROAD!** Student agitators flushed with brusque attitude carried a bed through the inner city streets in which effigies of President Johnson and the South Vietnamese *fly-boy*, Ky, lay together in coitus, a sculpted bomb suggestive of a penis. Stilt-walkers smoothly strode by, boxes of the gnomic red book were distributed to pedestrians, megaphones were thrust into the faces of the police cordons and Karl Marx beards were everywhere. Jeering and jostling began in earnest with the unauthorized burning of the bed, canisters of tear gas exploded, a youth was felled in mid-stride by a police truncheon, and a young girl in a Mao-beret was photographed for the news bulletins in a pieta's lamentation over him. (iii) **BUY-IN: SELL-OUT!** Huddled at an impromptu press conference before banks of microphones, a Gang of Five in shirts sewn from the flags of the U.S., Australia, China, Russia and the Viet Cong, harangued the imperialistic forces, their message loud and clear: No more would youth be sold to war like newspapers ... the axis of the dialogue between youth-as-the-future, and the urban bourgeoisie-as-the-past, had shifted forever. (iv) **CREDIBILITY GAPS!** Panning images of the orchestral desks of the UN Assembly being conducted by left-wing *prima donnas* in an anti-American Symphony were juxtaposed with a television documentary on youth's transformation through the sixties. A voice-over to visual imagery conjured halcyon moments ... teenagers blowing bubblegum, teenagers rotating hula hoops, teenagers dancing the *Twist* ... reflective of years untarnished by today's turmoil. (v) **OUR HAIR IS GETTING LONGER SO GET USED TO IT!** Mortar boards replaced by dunce caps, this year's University graduates paraded before the newsreel cameras, while a young girl with a softened vanilla face and wearing a Mao-beret grinned down the barrel of a National Guardsman's rifle as if it were a long-stemmed flower before arranging her hat over it. All the talk these days was of forging a Tao to Freedom.

The Cartography Of Khe Sanh. Cooking explosives limned the faces of the Grunts on the hill in 'Nam's most dreaded zone of shadow, Khe Sanh, in shades of fear, for raindrops of red clay earth fell from the sky. Among the Grunts who had financial portfolios in the munitions industry Stateside? In *Dispatches From 'Nam* Fabian Roxburgh composed valedictory orations from the University of Khe Sanh. Awaiting the forlorn salvation of meta-politics to bring them home, the Grunts exhibited phenomenal stoicism in the face of the fallen Archangel's legions and their mindless, self-sacrificing tenacity to uphold Ho Chi Minh's venerable wisdom, willingly releasing their lost souls from three-dimensional space. Plumes of black smoke fired with brimstone ascended over the architecture of the School of Life. Taxiing C130s dragging tailgates swept along the plateau's airfield observed by prostrate Grunts buried in sandbag-covered bunkers. Radios blasted out the pop song, *Words*, the Grunts hugged their flak jackets and called along the line: Everybody Uptight – Get Outa Sight!

III
A FEATHERSTONE ON THE BREATH OF GOD

Sea Cruise. Fulsome curvatures of two-dimensional sailcloth billowed as the schooner cleaved a linear Newtonian motion across the shimmering soft-glass of the ocean's dimensionless plane. Christopher Featherstone emerged from the sumptuously furnished interior, a psychological space wherein he had been musing over Memory's dilution by Time, immediately glimpsing Samantha Westwood sunbathing in quasi-nudity to soak up a late-burst of autumnal warmth. Rising, arching her suppliant back in the style of Mary Magdalene from Renaissance canvases, she revivified a repertory of psycho-sexual hieroglyphs remembered by Featherstone as he observed her retreat from the bow of the schooner beneath some rigging. In the Pentecostal late-afternoon sky the translucent fabric of the breeze molded itself to the torso of a cloud. Samantha's faintly burnished enamel style, she was *Madame Récamier* reclining in an encroachment of deep-violet shadow, imbibing the chemistry of her favourite pre-dinner martini, contrasted sunset's lava seeping from the horizon. "Your boulevardier's manner surprised me. I expected a cynical Beat poet on Sam's recommendation of you." Calvin Westwood considered again the hypercubic fragment of the monastery's stone veneer angle visible beyond the sand dunes. Featherstone saluted the comment, lost though in the gossamer raiment of Samantha's self-thought, her luxuriant odalisque as subdued as the schooner now anchored offshore for the night. Had Westwood noticed the exultant silhouette dancing across the twilit crest of a sand dune and her companion defined against the idyllic skyline? "Featherstone – this *Free Speech Movement* – why will she never talk to me?"

Pieces In An Existential Mosaic. Dinner-table conversation beneath a forming architecture of cloud softly illumined by moonlight and starlight, those fragmentary remains of Paradise blown across spacetime, and with molecules of flavor bursting upon their palates from bowls of *Veal Scaloppine* soaked in *Marsala* intertwined with sinuous pasta, appeared like pieces in an existential mosaic. "Professionally I mean, your morality must now be made of stone, experience chipping away any resemblance to the *Image* that monastery symbolizes." Featherstone listened, his thoughts placing in spacetime the ineffable jewel of Hue until the inner flaws of the Viet Cong lined its structure and the U.S. had to crack and break open the facets one-by-one. Samantha twirled her sinuous pasta around her fork, momentarily raised the curtain and then let it fall: "Of what is our voice an echo? Listen to the monks chanting, entombed in the monastery." Fringed by surf the ocean's tapestry drew to itself threads of moist moonbeams. Lying in his bunk-bed Featherstone's thoughts evoked Samantha's sculpted breasts frozen beneath a sheet in the adjoining cabin, her pale-fleshed column insoluble to the autumnal glazes of his *lost weekend* caresses, her halo of memory now increasingly translucent.

The Expulsion! Strikingly sculptural shading her eyes on the bow of the schooner Samantha Westwood watched them wade ashore from the motor boat and ascend the sand dune. Footsteps in the soft sand trailed away towards the monastery. When questioned and offered a contemporary photograph, monks politely mentioned a couple, calling themselves *Adam and Eve*, who hurriedly vanished the previous evening, not in a chariot of fire but a midnight-blue street-rod. Featherstone pondered the leitmotifs of spiritual conquest inter-threaded about the precincts of the monastery, knowing the monks experienced the stone-structure as something muslin-thin whereas his shoulder found it immovable. "Our tragedy is, every beautiful woman's face soon fades to the ghost of a wife." Calvin Westwood kicked up puffs of fine dust as he strode off through the sand dunes.

A Seraph Ascending From Paradise Lost. A late Beethoven String Quartet op. 127 unraveled logical Time through the afternoon. Sitting in the Remington typewriter was a page of the feminine Westwood's retail temptations. The bedroom curtain swished, papers swirled, eddied like two-dimensional space brushed by the room's three-dimensionality. With the sun's autumnal relaxation and the sky's absorption of black Christopher Featherstone left his office's geometrical space and walked his mind through the labyrinthine streets of Hue, where President Johnson's re-election campaign lay in utter ruins, copious GI blood spilling across the rubble, all energy sapped. GIs mimed time-travelers fresh from World War II! Outside a discotheque he pressed himself into a deep-cut embrasure on glimpsing Miranda Westwood's ever-vanishing *objet d'art* disappear through the cavernous entrance. Who was actually leading this dance? Out on the crowded floor she danced cooler than a Seraph ascending from Paradise Lost. Towards midnight, on an impulse, he drove out to the barricaded University, following the luminous bayou of stars along which the moon drifted, identified the cut-out silhouettes of familiar anarchists and listened to Stephen Maxwell's Gang of Five listen to *The Ballad of Bonnie and Clyde*. After ascending the University clock tower following the challenge laid down by the popular song, removing the hands from its face, the existential anarchists triumphantly chimed: "No more Time! ... No more Work! ... No more Money!" Thinking of the mauve-dusted sand dunes from which the monastery's hyperbole levitated, Featherstone unobtrusively sat in the airport lounge behind the façade of a newspaper featuring Communism's Zen master, Chou En-Lai. How the moon's pearl cast into the surf that evening illumined Samantha Westwood on the bow of the schooner such that their memory of the *lost weekend's* causal circuitry flashed: but perhaps the burnt depletion of that hot candle had suffered too great a melt-down! Miranda waved off her journalist, handsome, fashioned after an early-sixties beachcomber, destination, Saigon. Curled in the Remington was an invoice typed up for the Westwoods. Featherstone listened to another late Beethoven String Quartet as Quetzalcoatl's ascension announced 1968 would be a very hot war!

Dispatches From 'Nam. Christopher Featherstone subscribed to the Underground journal searching for Fabian Roxburgh's signature pieces: with scissors he cut out the column inches and pasted them together on cardboard. (i) Operation Pegasus – Ostensibly the 1st Air Cav raised the Siege of Khe Sanh, these traveling salesmen with their catalogue of weaponry saturating its existential space, but Communists were not willing consumers and shied away from the purchase. Still, the Phoenix of another Kennedy rose from the ashes at this time as a portend ... of what? Someone was spreading a new word ... Vietnamization. (ii) VC Execution Sites – Sly and the Family Stone cut a big hit with *Dance To The Music* to ease America's pain over the *Mephisto Waltz* of the VC. For grace, morality and ethics attained their ultimate definition with the living burial of numerous French priests, whose torsos captured on film so loosely clung to the Earth they would save. Only the *Te Deum* of Hueys flying overhead, avenging angels, brought solace, for somewhere a boiling bath of napalm would anonymously strip the perpetrators for Hell. (iii) Stars-and-Stripes – A Sword was hammered on the anvil of Hue and a clean flag draped the coffin nobly borne by Marines. Grief collapsed across the coffin in the fabric of the flag, each sacred star in the mosaic symbolic of an extinguished pulsation of light from the Earth. A poster modelled *à la Vermeer* showed a *Woman in Blue Reading a Letter* (or telegram announcing the fall of her son), backdropped by a map of 'Nam and the site of his death marked with an algebraic X.

Memphis, Tennessee. Elvis' city burned. Another masterpiece was forever flawed. Christopher Featherstone looked from afar into the darkness now clouding the space of the mirror which is Memphis, Tennessee. Civil Rights oratory, typified by, *I have a dream that one day this nation will rise up and live out the true meaning of its creed: We hold these truths to be self-evident; that all men are created equal*, swept to fulfillment, but not in 1968! No, not 1968. Now the glorious shadow cast by a pillared Man from a motel balcony was locked away in a coffin dragged by humble mules. A Man attained his Damascene satori in Memphis, had transformed into a beautifully plumed Bird of Paradise. Featherstone mused long upon the soul's body being simply an object cast away like an abandoned fur coat: Sun Records too had set on Memphis, its famous songs lost to the *Sgt. Pepper* generation ... *Blue Moon of Kentucky*, *Mystery Train*, *Baby Let's Play House*, *I Forgot To Remember To Forget*. Looting and tear gas kissed goodbye to the thrill of Rockabilly days ... *I've looked over and seen the Promised Land.* Grim-faced leaders in close-up on black-and-white television deepened the mood of hopelessness.

A Surrealist's Marvel To Paint. Banded by shadow cast through the slatted louvers Christopher Featherstone listened to the rhythm of high heels click down the corridor and pause outside the door of his office. Swinging open the door a stunning Bride dressed in Russian red, her shoulder-to-waist wedge comparable to Ursula Andress' torso, filled the *sfumato* of the framed space, her presence sucking everything out of the office, the very air crystallizing to frost. She stepped across the threshold into the three-dimensional space of his office like Lucretia falling from Rembrandt's canvas, a white handkerchief in her hand pressed under her heart as if staunching a fatal wound. Swept to his feet in a tidal surge of emotion, Featherstone now recognized her anatomical paradigm from the street theater he had witnessed, and he stood as motionless as Medusa's lover as her walk's living sculpture approached his desk. Now he saw the immaculate white handkerchief was to daub the exquisitely carved marble tears freezing on her cheek. As she reached forth to politely shake his hand the bronzed compasses of her legs widened as if to measure in him those resistors to sexual currents, stoicism and cynicism. Featherstone released her hand sensing its capability to caress his heart into submission and the wallet from his jacket. Her stunning outfit was a crinoline waterfall from broad shoulders, over the no-longer naked breasts of her Republicanism, flowing with the contour of her hips, and as she precisely seated herself he experienced an infusion of ice able to freeze out even Faye Dunaway. "Mr. Featherstone ... my name is Helena Roxburgh."

How Old Is The Old Testament? "Falling in love is too easy, why is falling out of love so hard?" Pausing for effect, physically styled after a feminine torch burning for dramatic righteousness of her *cause*, Helena Roxburgh allowed her fingers to fondle a waist-high bust of Beethoven standing off in the corner of the office. "No *Maltese Falcon?*" Already the psychic dissonances established by her physicality clouding space eroded his ethical boundaries. "Adulterer!" The enunciated word formed a knot in the grain of her voice. "Seducer!" Reseated again like a carving of smooth-textured and colored ice she mimed a striptease of breathless despair and helplessness. "Some photographs are there, Mr. Featherstone ... her naked skin painted in veils of flowers is his idea of a joke: a mad Ophelia played with by a faithless Hamlet. But men are not men these days. If only someone would pass him a poisoned chalice, dip a sword-point in curare and plunge it through his heart!" Now her voice warped spacetime, its *découpage* suggestive of Shakespeare, Featherstone divining she might be setting him on a path to Infinitude where he would certainly lose his way. He was Dante here without Virgil's guidance: this was no Beatrice! Helena Roxburgh's eyes were solid panes of glass, the telling of her story emerging from space's *sfumato* into a richer Technicolor, in Cinemascope ... MGM! "Will you consider taking me on as a client over lunch then?"

Electrical Circuit Breaker. Boldly, provocatively themed in Russian red Helena Roxburgh strode into the restaurant leaving electric footprints for Christopher Featherstone to follow. Her subsequent perusal of the menu though was a smokescreen as she established a synthetic equilibrium between her personae. Featherstone purposefully softened his accessibility knowing she would get him to sleep-walk for her anyhow, that she was an actress sculpting a characterization, but at least she was calling him back from the exile of his divorce, and Samantha Westwood was unattainable. Every carefully chosen phrase she spoke offered moral compromises. Beyond the plate-glass windows of her eyes the specter of a question suffused her brain's circuitry in a *sfumato* filtering out the light of truth: "Does he need money or sex, or both?" Featherstone's lucid consideration of her face immediately opened up the consequential affair of King David and Bathsheba, and her husband Uriah the Hittite, on the pulpit of his mind where the lesson tolled the sequel of any involvement with *her*. But she did make of a man a passionate classicist of dead languages! He casually turned in three-quarter profile as their entrée was served and saw, eating *tête-a-tête*, Calvin Westwood and his own accountant, Bridget Lovegrove, a sight wildly spinning his emotional compass. Helena Roxburgh snapped her fingers in his face to refocus his attention: "I can see that you too have abandoned worthless Ideals, and have been orphaned by your wife." Suddenly raising her eyes Bridget guiltily entangled his, keeping Westwood occupied, while Helena collapsed space to a Black Hole: "Tell me, are you licensed to carry a firearm? Do you have a shoulder holster?"

The Ballad Of Bonnie And Clyde. Christopher Featherstone discharged the hand-gun at the far-off target, reeled in the human silhouette and counted off his *kills*. Cruising and thinking later he planned a nocturnal visit and search of Helena Roxburgh's (nee Steele) apartment, having identified an eclectic Underground feminist journal she contributed to and investigated more of her involvement with **LESBOS** Records. She was as menacing as lines by Catullus! Veiled in bars of instreaming, late-afternoon sunbeams, staring at the office door which had framed her statuesque Amazon, remembering her supple movements as lithe as a Jaguar, he considered stenciling on the frosted glass: **CHRISTOPHER FEATHERSTONE TELEOLOGICAL PRIVATE INVESTIGATOR.** Memphis rioted. Lying inert on the oak desk was the gleaming anatomy of a hand-gun. Superbly machine-tooled it was nevertheless a non-thinking torso. "Let the gun do its own thinking, its own talking." Had she said those words over lunch, or had he thought them? Television newsreel footage of coast-to-coast rioting backdropped him walking and describing the Zen of a Cartesian circle inside the cube of his office as he prepared the bureaucracy of his investigation. *"Mine eyes have seen the glory of the coming of the Lord."*

The Struggle Is The Thing. The State Office of *Births, Death & Marriages* had no official record of a *Roxburgh, Helena*. Christopher Featherstone slipped a skeleton key into the door of her apartment and swung it open. His surveillance took him to an obscure club affiliated with **LESBOS** Records where she sang away the nocturnal hours.

Surveying the mirage of her low-rise ranch-style apartment he considered what model of truth he could build from the physical reality of her possessions. (i) Furniture – Architecturally and spatially the style was honeymoon hacienda. In her bedroom he approached the sarcophagus noting the covers draped its form like a flag did a coffin. The motions of her thought while making love could be traced there, reminiscent perhaps of Duchamp's famous *Nude Descending A Staircase*. Ingres' ice in his sketch laid on the mirror threatened to thaw. (ii) Wardrobe – Sliding open the structure had him breathing carbon monoxide! Running a hand along the suspended corpses of her clothes he thought of an alchemical parallel, how the soul's fourth-dimensional angel of incidence when incarnating equaled the human persona's three-dimensional angle of reflection. Then he glimpsed the strawberry syrup of her magnificent evening gown and he knew she did not go to Church on Sundays! With a forefinger he loosened his shirt collar moistened with perspiration. These clothes were surgical bandages for her damaged psyche. (iii) Books – The geometry of thinking being the structure of existence, Featherstone stood at the table on which was spread cut-up journals, magazines and newspapers, the empty spaces in their pages perhaps the hidden realms of her feminine self removed from visible sight. She had aliases. Her book titles rejected God as Narrator. (iv) Photographs – From her immersion in photographic fluid emerged a heroine-as-orphan. Lightly dusted frames held a defiant and magisterial teenage Amazon maturing into her contemporary version. *Causes* aureoled her face-masks, she was soluble to existential responsibilities. Featherstone closed the door behind him and glanced up at the iced curve of the moon: he would have to be careful, she was obviously a skillful and ruthless shadow-boxer!

They Awoke From Their Underworld Sleep. News helicopters high over the inner city flashed images of a crucifix of streets filling with a mass of protesters. Space warped as one mass moved and surged before stabilizing. Into the loins of the inner city crossroad the anti-war demonstrators flowed, the skyscrapers creating rivers of people in a Valley of Death. Close by the open coffin symbolically honored in a central position where the arms of the street-crucifix met, Christopher Featherstone observed Miranda Westwood and her long-haired Ganymede harangue the crowd through megaphones: "The System? No, the cistern! They're selling The President, but we're not buying!" A pretty flautist tripped along the ranks of National Guardsmen taunting their fixed bayonets phallically angled, others with flower badges sewn on jeans and jackets offered peace symbols instead of bullets, but the impassive line held firm. "Awake, arise, or be forever fallen!" Stephen Maxwell raised an arm and smoking from his fingertips was a burning draft card. National Guardsmen advanced and the crowd stampeded: Featherstone stumbled and lost sight of Miranda.

An Archaeological Discovery. Crushed and scuffed by the rioters, breathless, Christopher Featherstone sought refuge in the lobby of a hotel ... the *Plaza*! The *maître d'hôtel* commiserated and offered him the washroom followed by refreshment at the bar. Time decelerated and began to flow backward as he emerged from the washroom and wandered through into the ambient intimacy of the classic bar. Echoes awoke for Samantha Westwood's cool and brittle marble presence stood stationary in an atmospheric glow of low-lighting having recognized his disheveled appearance. Some words of recognition hung suspended in her throat as he approached but he remembered her O!, its musical legato extended with the pulse of a bowed cello. Then her voice's subtle perfume was released: "Mr. Featherstone, you seem to have been buffeted by the riot going on outside. Please, let me order you a drink." Fate had exactly transcribed their presences from 1964 to 1968! Her perpendicularity, the supple Doric swelling of her hips and abdomen swathed in the corporate affluence of her clothes, full with the richness of Pre-Raphaelite chalks in the spatial chiaroscuro of the bar, melted him like a candle cup holding a lit flame. She signaled the barman they were choosing a table for lunch. "Tell me about Miranda." Featherstone prayed their faces would rhyme with truth. Her voice's minimalism was as strikingly harmonious as a Mondrian canvas. He allowed the waiter to deliver their pre-lunch drinks before speaking: "Miranda's passport is valid, she has been browsing travel agents for brochures on India, Paris and Chicago, gathering flight information." Submerged in wealth, Samantha closed her hands around her Manhattan and she inwardly reflected on his words, then she looked straight at him as if he were a burning monk seated opposite her. "Calvin is hopeful these fads will pass with time. You know, Mr. Featherstone, one day she asked us to *tune in, turn on*, then she dropped out of our lives." Featherstone realized just how valuable a third eye would be right there and then to establish just how far the broadening vista of time-past had receded for her since their *lost weekend* in 1964. "Innocence is a prehistoric skeleton in the museum of life." Space's existential shroud enveloped them with this aphorism and slivers of frost formed around the arabesque of her ageless beauty, but he remembered her depths within the hotel's luxurious bedclothes, how her breath blew him as effortlessly as a feather. When their orders were taken she spoke again: "Featherstone is a name full of ambiguity, is it not? Both light-and-heavy, ticklish-and-monumental, air-and-earth in polarity. You are not happy either, being divorced?" He translucently colored as this masquerade became more deeply etched in forgetfulness. "I borrowed a Sargent for the weekend once and have carried the image with me ever since. Yes, I am unhappy divorced, but I pay the alimony." Her eyes said: *"Yes, you made a Titian Venus of me!"*, but all he received was the silence of her mouth's perfect lipstick impression left on her martini glass. Lunch followed, and she had Chicken with Rocket & Almond Pesto, with Prosciutto Rosemary Mushrooms, cuisine-as-aphrodisiac while his conversational arrows continued to be deflected in flight. He asked after her memories of the hotel and she answered by suggesting a visit to The Factory, a new warehouse gallery she supported by purchasing contemporary works of art. Featherstone had already plunged to an Archangelic death and become lost in spacetime having fallen in love with another man's property, so he accepted the invitation.

The Factory. Silk screen portraits eased the ennui of the modern *installationist* into the commercial art market and announced the malaise induced by three-dimensional space (the Renaissance) had been well and truly conquered. Samantha Westwood strolled among the elegant phantasms erased of emotion, silk screens of pop singers and well-known fashion models alongside political anti-heroes, allowing the flat, monochrome shadow of conversation fade, while Christopher Featherstone clung to her 24-carat aureole knowing that if he stopped thinking about her he would cease to exist. Suddenly she touched his arm, laid her voice on her spoken words as if it were a hand restraining him: "Mr. Featherstone, is that sexual tenderness, or ennui you are experiencing?" He stood before a selection of Celeste Hawthorne's worked-up drawings, including a sprawling full-length study of himself, nakedly realized, post-coital, an archaeological discovery he panicked Samantha would purchase. Hadn't she seen him naked at forty? "How *perfunctory* the artist has been with you. But has she extracted your *essence?*" After thanking him for a thought-provoking afternoon she took her own inner-city street map for traveling from life-to-life and disappeared into the river of pedestrians. Featherstone returned to his office, played another late Beethoven String Quartet, and visualized how the oil portrait of her presence anchored light in the three-dimensional space of his existence.

Inertia Of A Feather And A Stone. In a vacuum a-feather-and-a-stone fell with the same acceleration, conjuring the Physics of the fall of souls into incarnation, from fourth-dimensional space into three-dimensional space. Unraveling the diagrammatic design of Helena Roxburgh's consciousness resembled understanding a serpent's calligraphy within a square of sand. Had they been in pursuit of each other across incarnations and were now locked together in the vice of three-dimensional space for refining and final polishing? Life's manuscript was already blackened by flame, meanings erased by the burnt serrations: so was he a *Feather on the Breath of God*, or plummeting *brimstone*? Escaping his office and the cerebral mathematics of the Beethoven Quartets he made the journey by car back to the monastery among the sand dunes.

Wine And Bread. Monks roamed free among the alleys of vineyards and fruit trees, changeless in their rejuvenation, offering him wine and bread, the sublime metaphysical axis of Christ's cartouche ablaze in an embrasure of stained glass. Christopher Featherstone's once-youthful Titan had diminished in stature, the bow of Time was drawn and curving, the linear shaft of his arrow readying to fly free ... according to Relativity! The ocean's amniotic fluid washed the foreshore below the sky's fading azure wallpaper festooned with rose-and-orange clouds. Driving non-stop to the monastery he had been conscious of dragging a magnetic field of existentialism but more telling were the footprints criss-crossing the sand dunes like strands of incarnational computer code. Silica's textural linings of dune and stone shaped into the geometry of the monastery enchanted him as the opaque autumnal sun disappeared from the pale grey flanks of sand and drew forth a cloth of plum-violet sky over the scene. Starlight curved around the sun!

I Think, Therefore I Am. Acid soaking the fabric of Christopher Featherstone's lifestyle smoked as he rang off and replaced the receiver. Sexually she could only be the hammer-and-sickle, the proclamation of woman-in-revolt, yet he locked his office and strolled the corridor, passed out of the building thinking impure thoughts of her: Helena Roxburgh. How could she lose him this way in the mist of her voice's Fauve slash, mold him as easily as a glassblower working molten glass, glove his feelings the way a puppeteer does? Her hyperbolic monologue on *The Ballad of Bonnie and Clyde* generated an expressionist spatiality around her visible presence in his office where she postured herself with the innocent-soothing balm of her statuesque passivity. A colorful convertible with the hood's carapace up, suggestive of her red-dyed blouse stiffened to burnished armor, braked by the curb, the passenger-side door swung open and he belatedly climbed inside. Helena Roxburgh's immaculately tailored and coiffured model-for-an-anarchist sat behind the wheel where he visualized her preparing herself for a trial-by-jury. "Mr. Featherstone – may I call you Christopher? – I too am abandoned. So please don't just give me illusions. Are you a Cartesian detective?" Featherstone knew instinctively now she suspected him, of something, of *everything*!

Scenic Drive. Accelerating, the convertible clearly delineated vectors of betrayal, negotiating the interchanges leading to the coastal sunbelt, Helena Roxburgh's hair bound by a scarf, her eyes camouflaged by dark sunglasses, her posture behind the wheel vividly, breezily sculptural. The imagery of her copious legs working the clutch, accelerator and brake pedal was evocative of a sculpted Amazon fighting off a rapist ... Theseus? The surrealism of the early morning mist perfumed the boulevard of palm trees. "Have you ever had occasion to transgress the Law?" A lone strand of her hair's fishing line floated free of the scarf. "Do you have a cool trigger finger?" The folded wad of paper money passed into his hand was loaded with her fingerprints. "Will you teach me how to fire your hand-gun?" She had caught him summer-dry and set him ablaze with her raw fire. Stopping the car they ambled down to the beach, varying psychological terrain, where the Aegean contour of her clothed pubis was brushed by the freshening sea breeze and she manoeuvred an opportunity to slip her hand inside his jacket. "No shoulder holster?" Was this how the modern woman emulated falling for a middle-aged man? "Christopher – someone disturbed my apartment. Am I a palette from which you could paint a masterpiece? Following my divorce?" Walking around the convertible's dust-glazed windshield she climbed behind the steering wheel. Parking at the airport they checked arrival times and browsed the duty free stores. Below them under the mezzanine level Miranda Westwood emerged from the crowd and scanned the arrivals board.

A Falcon In Flight. Focused like a falcon in flight, Helena Roxburgh pursued the couple through the crowded airport lounge, her right hand empty of the hand-gun Featherstone already visualized molded to her grip, and rising to a ninety-degree arc at shoulder level. Helena's kissing at the beach was strictly Hollywood, adherence to the script, pure dissimulation of course, but as an exile he welcomed any haven of affection these days. Miranda Westwood and her anti-hero, Fabian Roxburgh, lured them through the crowd outside where they hailed a taxi, her unheard conversation very mannered compared to his speeded-up animation. Driving distilled an even purer existentialism from Helena's persona as she finally identified their taxi on the highway leading into the city and settled in behind at an observable distance. Featherstone still felt like smudged red chalk lifted from the paper on which this polymath Amazon was sketched. Perhaps he had better study the Art of Falconry!

Residual Radio Waves From The Big Bang. Abruptly raising his head from the oak table, the question exploding at the speed of light in Christopher Featherstone's mind was, not who pulled the trigger cutting down Kennedy, rather, who fired the Cosmic Gun shattering the crystalline Ptolemaic spheres, sending a bullet through the *Planck moment* tearing into the soft, quiescent torso of three-dimensional space. Proliferating imagery occupied the cloud chamber of his mind in contemplation, how the cosmic bullet softened in flight, passing like a daub of oil paint from its singularity, splattering space with itself, hemorrhaging into clotted galaxies: the Assassination of God perhaps? *Beginnings* troubled him during this time, the spinning *stones* of the galaxies skimming across the ocean of space, or were they *feathers* expiring with the breath of God-in-death? Various pieces of music self-explored his psyche, but for what purpose?

> Beethoven: String Quartet op. 127
> Bruckner: Symphony No. 8 (adagio)
> Wagner: Götterdämmerung (Siegfried's Death and Funeral March)
> Scriabin: Vers la flamme op. 72

Keeping Miranda Westwood under surveillance he utilised the mirrors in a clothing store to observe her buying modish jeans, himself unseen. Question: why two legs flowing into a torso? Jeans stood inert on a display, then Miranda stepped into them and they were animated, they swivelled, were stretched by her limbs-in-motion. Man's spatial diminution in being-and-existence puzzled him, and the question of two legs flowing into the unity of a torso and then sweeping free again into two arms. That afternoon seated in his office he held in one hand his polished gun and in the other an invitation to a *Happening* that evening.

A Middle-aged Pan Caught In Aspic. The night sky lay bloodied in pools of *white* warping its fabric as Christopher Featherstone determined to alchemise any acid of criticism from his thoughts. He idly turned the pages of the program booklet and circulated among the *avant garde* society crowd swimming to-and-fro in affectation across the lower floor of the multi-level gallery. He paused before vacant wall-space specially prepared for the hanging of fresh canvases. Professional society page photographers queued for the most marketable pictorial images to sell. "Christopher – the mood is positively gelatinous, and you look like a philosophic detective in aspic. What are you doing here, since when is a *Happening* your scene?" So, the perfumed invitation did not originate from Celeste Hawthorne! Unexpectedly, her *objet de luxe* manoeuvred at his elbow, champagne in hand, *hors d'œuvre* raised from a passing waiter's tray, herself a decorative ornament amidst the swarm of feminist mænads on the prowl for some hapless Orpheus to desecrate. "And when are you going to employ a secretary to take your calls?" She exhibited her etiquette as if it were a poster she had designed on the inequality of the sexes. "Celeste, I saw your full-length nude study of me, a middle-aged Pan caught in aspic. Can it be wise for me to publicly flaunt so low a *décolletage*?" Gathering applause focused their attention on a spiralling cavalcade of elegant mannequins, albeit with facial expressions of Burne-Jones beauty, descending a staircase, led by the provocative Amazon, Helena Roxburgh. Celeste leaned close to Featherstone's ear: "You were touchingly autumnal, I thought." She observed the Amazonian svengali orchestrate in space two tableaux, bizarrely modelled after Delacroix's *Liberty Leading The People* and *Greece Expiring On The Ruins Of Missolonghi*.

Aphrodite Rising. Fabrics fell away and the quantum foam smoothing out the symmetry of the young Burne-Jones beauties memorialized the torso of every Aphrodite rising from marble and canvas throughout the centuries. Horizontal canvases lay across the floor like Japanese tatami mats. Nude, splashes of radiance, exhibitionist thrill-seekers, the tableau of women had the audience catch its breath wondering whether sexual acts were to be performed on the canvases as an expression of feminist emancipation. Their silvery haze of arabesques began to be coated, layered, swathed in rainbow colors of oil paint, the foliage of pubises soaked up brilliant textures, and then the canvases were caressed by their torsos and limbs creating a spontaneous free-form art, an irrevocable severance from the tradition of Titian-Velasquez-Rubens-Delacroix. When the Zen calligraphy of these canvases stood silent on the walls, to which price tags were being attached, the devotees of satori masked in kaleidoscopes of color reascended the spiral staircase to the upper levels of the gallery.

Still-life. *Scarborough Fair* softly played, and Christopher Featherstone noticed the radio dial permanently taped to the pop music station. Celeste rose from the white porcelain sculpture of the toilet and moved through the studio loft with toothpaste lusciously foaming about her French chanteuse mouth, the bubbles a magnification of quanta. In these long-wavelength moments of Zen calm before the contours of a mutual eroticism would collide in sex's horizontal ballet his eyes fell on her as on a textbook. Outside the studio neon signage refracting through the windows repetitively cast her face in washes of varying silk-screen colors. Languid incense smoked space. Chiaroscuro lighting evoked a brocade of shadowy flesh as their motion in the space of the studio mutually warped them closer together. Celeste's *ombre*, precisely coiffured, was brushed by his penis as her breasts touched the canvas of his chest, itself a soft meadow, in a ritualistic enfoldment. "Anatomically, are men improving as lovers?"

The lifeless inertia of his suit suspended from nearby hangers suggested a troubling metaphor in his thoughts. "No, but women are!" Her noir-eyes were sliding fingertips, a sweep of pen-and-ink over paper, then her porphyry lips absorbed the torso of his mouth within hers. Her totemic earthing herself astride him in an exquisite intimacy, molding him to her preferred sexual cartography embossed on the stretched canvas sheet on the bed, had him contemplating whether her chalk rendering of his nude torso would hang on some gallery wall for centuries measuring the passage of Time. Sexually resuscitated by her as a Florentine masterpiece, impressed how she bridled his libido, he lifted himself from the full horizontal, thinking how his marathon of Eros had exhausted itself following the break-up of his marriage, and peered beyond the arabesque line of Celeste's anatomy. He glimpsed emerging from the chiaroscuro a canvas propped on an easel, mirroring back to him a preparatory oil study of Helena Roxburgh! Collapsing back onto the bed he knew Celeste sensed him sexually falter, for she hurried him toward his *Planck moment* and he soon relaxingly floated like Pan in aspic. Later, standing by the window he welcomed the pink sash of cloud girdling the horizon, and the golden sunbeams beginning to groove the city streets. A lovely white dove fluttered down and paused on the window ledge.

Scarborough Fair. A Molotov cocktail smashed the window, bounced across the oak desk over Christopher Featherstone's shoulder and rolled into the middle of his office. The inflammable device exploded in a spray of debris, a mosaic of glass burst asunder as he instinctively fell behind the table, preparing to embrace mutability, become another casualty of the sixties. Shock-waves of combustible chaos covered him in splintered fragments and papers settled back like a swirl of fallen autumnal leaves catching alight. Mortality's flavor filled his nose, seared his tongue, a turbulence of vibration suffused the lattice of his body's chemistry. But no harmonic disturbance violated the silence of his incendiary immersion and as death's momentous emptiness filled his quantum model he pondered whether three-dimensional space wasn't actually *the other side. Scarborough Fair's* ghosted flow presaged his tranquil discernment of spacetime's intersecting planes. Mechanistic principles reasserted themselves as he lay self-embedded in the spacetime of hospital. A barely identifiable voice whispered how he survived death's absolute zero. How had he shuffled free of that autumnal quilt of burnished leaves? "Elizabeth – have you come from the shades of Pemberley for me?" His ex-wife smiled: the lineaments of her vanishing Fragonard beauty did not wear well in 1968. "The children visited you yesterday, but were traumatized by your delirium. And a Bridget Lovegrove left her business card. Christopher, last week I received a surprise envelope in the mail, a reproduction of some nude chalk study of you. Can you explain that?" Featherstone was consubstantial though with other *membranes*, surveying the coastline of his persona in spacetime swept by the tidal currents of cosmic oceans, existing in thought, thinking confirming existence!

IV
ASSASSINATION OF AN UNARMED PROPHET

Flower Power. Music's halo-effect lingered on but poetically as a dying fall. The Maharishi's fantasy, bearded smile, nectar voice, danced in the thoughts of the new Messiahs following his footsteps to his ashram in India. Faces decorated with the tears of compassion, England's new princes imbued with the mysticism of *Sgt. Peppers*, The Beatles levitated across an oriental carpet of flowers, ornamented in coronas of incense, for dialogue with the gathered Press corps. Fresh buds at the fingertips of the Maharishi they now commanded the world's youth with a weaponry of flowers. Squeezing into the entourage while a musical divertimento of sitar and tabla established a suitably reverent mood, Miranda Westwood, bathed herself in flowers, her motif of spiritual chastity, thought of appearing on television across the world. Fabian Roxburgh, necklaced in leis of sweet-smelling blossoms, hitching up his full length kaftan, listened to the platitudes, the buzzing of bees clinging close to the blossoms of these new Messiahs. But where were Dylan, Kerouac and Elvis? "Our soul and human persona are wrestling for supremacy on Earth." Time's elixir made India drowsy for the compassionate serenity of the Buddha's face but where did one stand in relation to God suffering from acute dysentery? Coming from 'Nam Roxburgh sought solace for the crack widening in the egg shell of his mind. Miranda asked: "Fabian, are we invisible yet? Free of illusion?"

Tomb Of The Unknown Scholar. Threatening southern autumnal skies lowered over the picturesque University. Banners sloganized with rhetoric hung from cloisters raised in Spanish sandstone. Sit-ins sand-bagged inside lecture theaters awaited the arrival of busloads of police in riot gear. The landmark clock tower measured Time. A press contingent set up microphones and a transistor radio could be heard previewing Elvis' *U.S. Male* single, but as one journalist was overheard joking, conscious of the tensions unsettling the current stalemate between students and the police, his 1960 offering, *It's Now Or Never*, might have been more appropriate. Everyone sensed a psychological *frisson* prepared to tear apart the paradigm of the sixties modelled by Kennedy's illusory Camelot. Marshalling before the University precincts the police squads were hardly preparing an exhibition of Performance Art, neither were the student activists rehearsing a Broadway musical's feel-good show tunes. Media press conferences were now a popular Theater of the Absurd, stages from which to deliver soliloquies exalting Revolution. Stephen Maxwell's provocative posture, close-pressed around the bank of microphones with the Gang of Four, conveyed the urgency of his message: "Revolution is mushrooming all over the planet, hanging in the air like fallout. Let me tell you, we will fight *now*, before you draft us to 'Nam. We'll die here, in these corridors, out there in the streets, rather than in 'Nam, so keep the body-bags at home. The Summer of Love was your last chance, now comes the Summer of Revolution! Historic May! Get ready the bonfires of draft cards. Let's not stand here face-to-face with the police and think we're going to dance *The Twist*. No! You geriatrics out there had better start moving and make the leap across the Generation Gap. We see the end of your Time, we see the Apocalypse ... *now*!" Shields interlocked, truncheons beating a rhythm, the Roman legion of police advanced onto the campus grounds and moved along the corridors. Cascades of water-cannon drenched and dispersed the front-line cadres of students linked arm-in-arm. Dragged off, immobilised by truncheon blows, unceremoniously bullied into police vans, fingers and faces clung to the bars in shock and desolation: the poetry of innocence lay bruised and bleeding under autumnal skies and beamed into the nation's living rooms on the evening news bulletins.

Amazons And Beauty Queens. Looping footage of historic beauty contests culminating in Miss Worlds and Miss Universes drew rapturous applause from the party-goers standing watching the oversize screen. Dancing on the ballroom to *Do You Know The Way To San Jose?* the textbook beauty queens were partnered by waxwork men in black tuxedos while up on the screen women were so many glamorous still-points of swim-suited radiance, their smoothly sheered pubic fleeces marble-like for the inner thigh hemlines. A liquidity of rainbowing perfumes intermingled with clouds of cigarette smoke, a chemistry through which passed the chandelier effects of dazzling evening gowns and aureoled hairstyles. Suddenly the music paused, conversation faded and near-perfect expressions on the faces of the impossibly beautiful women masked surprise and then shock. Simultaneous with Helena Steele's imposing entrance and her Amazon cortege accompanying her like figurines from classical amphorae new music began, her latest single on the **LESBOS** label:

> Act your age, act your sex,
> Sex is all the rage, but worst with your ex.
> Be a feather, be a stone,
> Sex is all the rage, but better when you're alone.

The swaggering Amazons brought in their arms assembly-kits, brassieres, girdles, high-heeled shoes and numerous cosmetic products which they irreverently dumped in the middle of the ballroom. Helena gestured toward the screen where the sanitized contortionists were postured in erotic tableaux for the audience. "What is my name? Who am I? An artefact from some Victorian painting? What are my expectations?" Commercialised feminine space closed into a delicious architecture of physical honeycomb as the tuxedoed men kneeled to fondle the visually sculpted icons, the protrudent tubes of lipstick being especially provocative. Brawling Amazons struggled, kicked, scratched and squirmed while being forcibly carried off in the arms of the security gendarmes, there was a dramatic spillage of drinks and slippage of *hors d'oeuvres* among the colliding guests. Photographs later appeared in Underground magazines with poignant captions parodying Beauty Pageants.

Sexual Milkshakes. "Mrs. Featherstone – your ex-husband's expression reminded me of an ice-floe networked with cracks: this act of violence has widened the fissures in his psyche. Shouldn't he convalesce longer in hospital?" Elizabeth Featherstone thoughtfully surveyed the office's burnt-out casket inlaid with charcoal, laying a hand to her throat as she contemplated the drama of the moment of explosion, of fragments penetrating soft flesh. Arson squad detectives patiently sifted the scene for further evidence. Insurance valuers assayed the financial cost as Bridget Lovegrove worried her copper-haired chrysanthemum might absorb any lingering smoke, for she had another lunchtime rendezvous with Calvin Westwood and any acrid odor tarnishing her purity could deaden arousal of their erogenous zones. For the choreography of adultery modelled specific sculptures as fragile in a sense as still-photographs, formalised set-pieces camouflaging glacial interstices of absence from each other, in which thought devised a algebra of sexual intensities calculated for resolution. What if Samantha Westwood engaged Christopher Featherstone to gather adulterous evidence about Calvin and herself for divorce proceedings? The ideology of surveillance disintegrated the coherence of her thinking's horizontal chain of cause-and-effect, the simplistic mechanics of coitus she had laid out with the precision of a page of double-entry book-keeping in her accountant's journal, everything finely balanced and underlined for auditing. Elizabeth Featherstone frowned curiously: "Yes, Miss Lovegrove, the ambiguity in the name, Featherstone, became symptomatic of the malaise in our marriage with the passage of Time. Initially though, I confess, he was once my milkshake, my thirst quencher."

I Love Paris In The Springtime. Sartre, the Rodin of Existentialism, settled his stylistic sculpture at a café table joining Fabian Roxburgh and Miranda Westwood on the evening of the 10-11 May. Dusk's burning topaz atmosphere brooded, contrasting Miranda's sparkling absurdist sketch, her anti-establishment manners, as the famous philosopher, a veritable Napoleon of existential thinking, observed streams of youth running by the café bearing aloft the fluttering *tricolor*. Camus' ghost ironically remained alive to companion Sartre on another campaign of defeat, and together they could walk back down the hill, death being no asylum at all. Roxburgh had brought Miranda with him to the desert of Paris but already the halo of the Maharishi stood shattered like the store windows they passed, following the road maps of Eric Clapton

Cream solos pouring from transistor radios. Miranda's existential Eurydice moving through these suburbs of Hell led to the barricade on the *rue d'Ulm* and blended with the swirling dynamism of the students preparing their own DMZ. Roxburgh nervously watched her wholeheartedly engrossed in the gathering of material from road works and building sites, awash in a sudden religious beautification unnoticed before, and thought of the bloodied wine lingering on the lips of Sartre's evening wine glass. Earlier he had glimpsed the whipping dragon of the North Vietnamese delegation's flag in the breeze, surely an ominous sign. Cafés had organised a telephone relay system to support the student activities: war had been declared. Police assumed the offensive at 2.15am with a barrage of grenade guns, phalanxes moving on the barricades: paving stones lay in David's sling-shot aimed at the Goliath, General de Gaulle. Beneath the running feet Paris' tectonic plates quaked, the Earth's axis tilted, students were given refuge in adjoining flats by sympathizers, canisters of tear gas smashed through windows, Miranda was lost to Roxburgh in the chaos of smoke and noise. Trampled, choking with tear gas, eyes stinging, he was arrested, emerging from the inchoate textures behind the police lines. Somehow he produced his journalist's credentials and convinced the police he was there for the Paris talks and was allowed to recover inside a Black Maria. Whenever the smoke cleared the street resembled a collapsing Cubist scene, form fragmented, colorless and abstracted, then a semi-nude young woman emerged vigorously manhandled by police. Miranda, ash-coated, her skin reminiscent of the white mold of cheese, thankfully gazed into his eyes, a shuddering evocation of the old woman's expression they had stood before earlier in Delacroix's *The Massacre of Chios*. Gone was her vividness, her mobility and prodigious zest, pleasure had chilled to cold marble in her veins, and from the transistor radio on the floor of the van could be heard Cream's *Strange Brew*.

Physician, Heal Thyself! "Whom do I resemble, Miss Lovegrove, Bogart as Marlowe? *Was this the face that launched a thousand ships?* Should I preside, like Lear, over the division of my assets? Will you be my Fool?" Visible from the hospital verandah clouds held an immense tonnage of water suspended in space. So, Calvin Westwood was authoring chapters in the romantic narrative of her existence. Thinking herself unobserved, Bridget lifted her salamander tresses and flung them back, and profiled the fractal curvature of her nearside breast, perhaps tiring of his ponderous gallantries for she peeled him an orange and squeezed some of the scented juice over her fingers. If all beauty was symmetrical those clouds suggested so many Apollonian blondes. Fruit's three-dimensional form ripened inside its two-dimensional skin before peeling away of its own accord. Bridget's moist lips resembled a wet autumnal red leaf the breeze plastered against the glass frontage of the verandah. Aroused by the aroma of her feminine clothing absorbing the odor of decaying flowers, Christopher Featherstone imagined her fingers languidly fondling her nipples, puzzled how the geometry of sleep segued into three-dimensional space, how the sculpture of dreams really formed. Brought to the sharp edge of absurdity by his rambling conversation, Bridget became prosaic: "How do you feel, in yourself?" Calvin Westwood had obviously conquered the latitude and longitude of this maturely pretty woman, but not her quanta. "Post-coital, Miss Lovegrove. Meltingly aglow. Horizontally polarised, flattened by spacetime, thinking of crossing the event-horizon of death, I formed a question in my thoughts: Who are the spiritual accountants balancing the physics of Newton's Laws? Such questions physician the diseased mind, you see. Now I find the four-dimensional man in spacetime I planned to meet in '68." Bridget held the sculpted tautness of a red lioness in reaching out a hand and touching his forehead. "While the nurses were changing your dressings the other day I glimpsed the lacerations, and thought your torso a current image of society ... a bloodied mess." Decalcomania! Consciousness was just gouache sliding between the planes of three-and-four dimensional space from which the visible imprints of human personae coalesced as images. His wounds miraculously healed over but his contemporary self-portrait in the mirror seemed unrecognizable.

Art For Art's Sake. Discharged from hospital where he was collected by his ex-wife he suggested a movie, his restlessness and revisionism surprising her considering the sexual anaesthesia of their final months together. Perhaps the coal-black space of the movie theater, showing *Planet of the Apes*, gave him an opportunity to deconstruct his psyche, restore the Statue of Liberty in his life, for he was concealing something beneath the spatial surface of his existence. Later she drove him to the cryptic symbol of what remained of his office space. Christopher Featherstone listened to his ex-wife's confessions overlaying the mosaic of pop songs on the car radio. "Have I become as fat as a buttered potato?" Their asymmetrical framing within the black-grained wall-space of his office had him using his third eye to reassemble her portrait's sepia silhouette motionless beside the charred oak desk. (i) Charcoal — the gentle curvature of her flattened shadow lay like a two-dimensional fingerprint whose sexual maze receded from him with the inflationary speed of the Universe. (ii) Chalk — marriage's Freemasonry of intimacy, rituals, ceremonies, initiations, was disturbed by the spectroscopy of adulterous behaviors, by absorptions and emissions. (iii) Pen-and-ink — Celeste Hawthorne's black-and-white Beardsley parody of himself as Philip Marlowe bemused Elizabeth, who said: "Your pretty accountant ... finds you *magnetic*. What shall I tell the children?" Unable to read her the poetry of Quantum Physics he answered: "We are strands of incarnations criss-crossed on the web of being, centrifuged by Einsteinian physics." (iv) Watercolor — Existence flowed around and through the quantum foam of their beings, boundaries melting into wave-particle dualities. Unconscious in hospital, dreams in washes of color mimetized Seurat's pointillism as recollected moments separated in frames of reference, became visible imprints like the geometry of miniature puncture wounds on his torso from the explosion. Elizabeth was afraid to touch him there in the fossilized remains of his office thinking his petrification might crumble.

Studio Time. "Here comes the sheriff in some western!" Nursing severe bruising from recent battles with police, Stephen Maxwell welcomed him to sleep over in his

University dormitory, and invited him along to EOS Records' recording studio where his brother's rock group, *The Pléiades*, had assembled to lay down some tracks. Carrying an Elizabethan miniature of Samantha in his thoughts, Christopher Featherstone experienced himself as increasingly unrhymable with the unfolding rhythm of 1968 as he listened to these youth mourn in music, giving the melody endless run-throughs but struggling for a lyric. Featherstone filtered out the crushed diamond percussion and focused on the statuesque guitar chords dissolving into arpeggios, from which some frothy fermentation of organ cascaded, then hurriedly scribbled some lyrics on music manuscript.

> Who is going to make my coffee,
> Who is going to iron my jeans?
> Can I tempt you to be free,
> And ride away in my cream-coloured limousine?
> We could measure mystic mountains,
> Go and catch a falling star.
> We could dance together in Trevi fountain,
> Make love while playing my guitar.
> Burn, baby, burn like a Phoenix on fire.
> Moan, baby, moan more sweeter than a lyre.

"What are these lyrics, man, a soul-map for your suffering psyche?" Jerome Maxwell sang them through a fog of sound, a bursting supernova, but all Featherstone could think of was Orpheus given studio time lamenting his sexual *Te Deum* for Eurydice. Featherstone prophesized: "Listen, even among revolutionary youth, Capitalism must make a comeback."

La Reforme, oui! Palms dirtied with revolution, pressed into closed eyes, Fabian Roxburgh hunched over his hooded portable typewriter: somewhere a French chanteuse could be heard on a radio. Croissant pastries, coffee and fresh baked bread aromatized the senses reeling still from the previous evening's existential adventure on the streets of Paris. Now a light-grey sky rendered the metaphysical formalism of the city, its geopolitical contours, opaque with Sartre's revolutionary existentialism – *no exit*! Gazing from the attic garret window to which they had retreated after being rescued by the landlady from the battle-scarred boulevard, Miranda Westwood sculpted space with her virgin olive oil incandescence, her torso's generous non-concealment showing him her bruises and abrasions. Brushing his itchy, close-scythed face stubble, Roxburgh recalled their evening with Sartre amid the barricades of Paris, organising the revolutionary cadres into grids, introducing himself as a southern Arcadian existentialist searching Paris for a story with a happy ending. Miranda interrogated the philosopher on his knowledge of popular song and offered him her Coca-Cola yo-yo to play with. Roxburgh gave the philosopher the *lie direct* ... existence is a man leaping from a plane, his parachute opening, trying to return again to the plane.

Existence is eternally unfinished. Existence itself is *bad faith*! "Where is my exit? Tomorrow I exercise my freedom and board a plane for Los Angeles. See, I reboard the aircraft!" Before Miranda and he left the café for the cobblestone front-line, and kissing at the barricade, before succumbing to spasms and vomiting as the tear gas grenades burst, Roxburgh handed Sartre a collage made up from *Les Temps Modernes*, featuring leading luminaries in *Sgt. Peppers* costumes: the headline read: **What Will Fire Up The Revolution? Hell Is Sartre!** Miranda chased a butterfly fluttering in the open window: she conjured up a heroine for Truffaut or Godard. And himself? *Don't Shoot The Journalist!*

Commedia Dell'Arte. Habitué of modern art galleries, Fabian Roxburgh considered the exhibition of *Warholisms* in the context of 1968, silk screens stretched across spacetime, the psycho-physical fabrics a patchwork of society masks questioning Marilyn, Jackie and Elvis as valid icons of the American psyche increasingly traumatized by the sixties. Pop comedy personified by Valerie Solanas delivered a June 3rd Manifesto to America. She daubed artistic space's silk screen in living vermilion, set acrylic flowing intensifying Warhol's already funereal pallor, for he floundered with the gracelessness of a *commedia dell'arte* buffoon. Collapsing, Warhol's iceberg hair came adrift with Time's mysterious coloration of death, his torso yielded to a kind of silk screen surrealism, was so much wax softening beneath the full pressure of the bullet's seal. The would-be assassin had trimmed her hair for this perfect, instantaneous Pop Art gesture of assertion, the shot though was a mere bagatelle of artistic criticism from a ventriloquist for the World's oppressed women. Warhol, celebrated as one who sculpted non-existence from existence now struggled to extricate his mortality from the web of silk screen imagery woven by him with such panache, his pale moon began to decline to a thinness of being beyond waxing. Later though, upon recovery, he resumed a public wall-portrait in his hospital bed *à la Madame Récamier* relaxing upon a divan. Miranda Westwood, orphaned on Los Angeles' silk screen illusion, Hollywood hopes dazzling her travel weary eyes, failed to register the news bulletins updating the world on Warhol's recovery, she possessed the innocence of another Iphigenia in the House of Atreus. Warhol, armed only with his silk screen genius, paintbrush blond hair and cortege of sycophants, survived assassination.

Worshipping The Golden Calf. Black-grained Hells Angels' sepia silhouettes revved their custom-built motorcycles to the music of *The Good, The Bad And The Ugly* and cruised the electrically charged streets of Los Angeles and the city bristled with their masculine-driven hauteur. Ionized in neon, Fabian Roxburgh and Miranda Westwood left a Chinese restaurant and idled away the early evening hours in pinball arcades and bowling alleys, double-strawed the quantum foam of milkshakes, browsed gleaming automobile showrooms and returning to their motel sat together on the balcony gazing at the cryptic ideogram of the shimmering swimming pool. *Postcards from LA* developed in Roxburgh's mind for transference to print. Orbiting the city in a hire car they gravitated to Malibu and Huntington Beach where Miranda's salty flesh of creamed macadamia deepened from sunburn pink to a pale bronze pallor. *Mrs Robinson* was all over the radio in this urban sunbelt taking the world beyond glamor. Roxburgh's mind looped *If I Were A Carpenter* and the euphoria of California's primary, its radiating *joie de vivre* of political stereotypes had him feeling like a redundant anti-hero strolling through a Godard film, justified when a shot rang out in the Ambassador Hotel heard across the Nation.

Is There A Doctor In The House? Assassins' bullets threaded by the Furies through the tapestry of spacetime consumed the imagery of Fabian Roxburgh's meditation on the rhythm of a celebrity's journey toward death. Under a star-studded Los Angeles night sky high above the city, framed by the famous **HOLLYWOOD** sign, remembering Sarajevo as much as Bobby Kennedy ebbing from life on the floor of the Ambassador Hotel kitchen, his eyes plotted the trajectory of an assassin's cosmic bullet evoked by a comet plunging through the soft plasma tissue of the Solar System. Cruising the immense curvatures of the freeway cloverleaves filled with the sculptural moldings of American cars he remembered Miranda Westwood's collection of empty mollusc shells laid on the table in the motel room. Later, towelling her hair dry after climbing from the swimming pool, she leaned herself forward over the detailed maps and photographs of Dealey Plaza, the architectural blueprints of the Ambassador Hotel spread across the floor of the motel and held in place by cans of Campbell soup. She remained puzzled with his dissertations on the significance of JFK's tragic motorcade and now his brother Bobby's descent and suffocation in the kitchens of Hell. For days in the motel room he studied the political coiffures of the Kennedy Dioscuri, poured over photographs of the black marble statues of the widowed sisters-in-law, especially fixated on their gazes balanced between life and death. Miranda consoled and coaxed his introversion with her elliptical virginity: "Fabian, you are my favourite kisser." From the balcony he watched her surface on the plasma of the swimming pool with the unfolding poise of a starfish and float upon the water's soft jewel. Kennedy's political speeches though were as thin as Warhol's pop art silk screen imagery. Ethel Kennedy's face modelled a cartography of grief shaped by Destiny, her dream of being First Lady like her sister-in-law being too soluble in the drainage of Time for the chemistry of these late-sixties. Roxburgh's revelation came as he kissed the image of Jackie's lonely enigma of a mouth and their catechism of silence brought into focus the erotic nature of the *ménage à trois* between the Kennedy brothers and herself. Soon they would all be casualties of Camelot's early-sixties optimism and lie in the Nation's morgue undisturbed by the breathtaking poetry of the Milky Way in which billions of suns were dying and being reborn.

Pentagram. (i) Samantha Westwood – From the purée of Christopher Featherstone's emotions she raised a *soufflé*. Her memory lay in his thoughts with the restfulness of a summer novel whose pages had the softness of curling flower petals … *Hypatia*. Divination of her sexual thoughts outside the liturgical rhythm of marriage melted the iced-over river of desire solidifying since their *lost weekend* and currents flowed again. Watching her mouth's sugar cube dissolve with colorless martinis as afternoon declined into evening he remembered convulsive lava flowing through her abdomen and loins that weekend. (ii) Elizabeth Featherstone – Even though their ice age of nostalgia melted years ago, even though autumnal leaves were crunched underfoot, an atomic clock ticked off memories and her voice haunted like droplets of oil paint merging on a canvas with painful imagery … Dali's *Paranoiac Astral Image*. In today's asymmetries of choice, was a wife's soul still a mirror reflection of her husband's. Portraits of absence hung in the space of their eyes looking at each other. He launched *The Pléiades* with a song in remembrance of her presence's sliced half-a-fig:

> With her sombre eyes of surreal rhyme
> She moves me like the curvature of spacetime
> Betrayed – my faith is blind
> Betrayed – pain slowly unwinds

(iii) Bridget Lovegrove – Could she be shaken Coca-Cola, an erotic zero's symmetry spinning off a balance sheet? Were her timekeeper suburban emotions earthed in sex as her gilt-copper hair's soaking space suggested? Certainly, her exteriorized beauty magnetized a male glance to focus on her in the manner she wished to be viewed, she caught at the intimate geometry of his meditation even as his ex-wife's fragile aureole began thinning now to invisibility. (iv) Celeste Hawthorne – In charcoal, chalk or pen-and-ink she described their straight-lined arabesque deep into the Tao of sex. Modelling as she carved their pieta in the marble of her sketchbook he listened to her talk: "So, are your thoughts full of laughing women then, or women saying their prayers? You strike me as being unfashionably stoic for a man coming off a failed marriage." (v) Helena Steele/Roxburgh – Her glance falling on the wasted inertia of his hand gun blocked his heart in ice. She was a textbook burner dancing to a dervish melody despite the leaflets of her pasted up on city windows highlighting her Amazonian metamorphosis in a red T-shirt. Listening to her record on the radio, her voice was a feathered quill dipped in vinyl ink, a stylus scratching the lyrics into audibility in stream-of-consciousness.

Grey Clouds Aureoled The Sun Like A Monk's Cowl. Teasingly austere the monastery's chrysalis filtered through the distance as the car windshield framed the rain-sodden dunes and held the enamelled arc of a spectacular rainbow. Elizabeth Featherstone slowed the heavy sedan as the dusk-silhouetted monastery stood bathed in whispers of rainfall. Clouds tiered on the pavilion of the horizon obscured her understanding why her ex-husband had freed himself from the cityscape and navigated to this remote monastery. Christopher Featherstone, the *faux* monk, laid his feet in the soil as doves burst from latticed windows and indulged in the sky's freedom and Elizabeth wheeled the sedan away down the roadway opening infinitely into darkness. Already he sensed his soul taking up his body's lyre to play as the monks' unison voices drifted like streams from an unsealed fountain. Geographically placed beneath the monumental cloud-sculptures the monastery defined architectural choices of symbolism, even as his footsteps illustrated his metamorphosis from Hippocentaur to his soul's palimpsest and the frontispiece of his persona radiated emblems of mystery. Walking beneath angles of stone as music emotionalised the structures of his mind release was accorded unknown legions of souls. The following evening strolling with the moon amid the barren vineyard he wound a pathway down to the beach where the disappearing sun painted the dunes and some moody wintery clouds which impastoed the skyline. Moonbeams though burned up the velvet stained glass sky and he yearned like the Lunar Goddess for the Sun God to fill his wholeness. Soon bells twinkled from the moon's tambourine and lacquer flakes of light across the gracefully sloped sand dunes evoked the scales of a serpent. His hours of meditation alone in the cell were veiled in myriad temptations, using his mind as a canvas across which he painted Samantha Westwood's portrait!

Who Struggles In The Dying Throes Of Assassination? Following the chalk-crested Tao of a sequence of dunes structured after a gigantic Zen garden, moving away from the incised entablature of the monastery's façade beyond which burned the Phoenix of a Great Fire, Christopher Featherstone contemplated light's seizure of shadow in an effortless wrestle and how it diminished its strength. Wounds to the psyche were overlaid by the very emptiness of the subterranean circle of sky, the scene proved medicinal for no poison flowed here, death's quietude pervaded the stillness. Only the calligraphy of dunes on the parchment of the landscape swirled an inscription about the tomb of the monastery. Later, lying within the monastic physique of his cubed cell, adrift amid the debris of martyrdoms, Featherstone experienced a glow of exquisite sensation, for the stained glass window opposite his bed evoked a spiritual cameo drenched in colour as lonely moonbeams touched the image of Jesus' unarmed prophet crucified in death. Sand particles had clung to his footfalls, yet the sweeping dunes receded as long-breathed wavelengths, proof of the curvature of space-time. When the rays of the lowering Phoenix had shivered deeper into the ocean he returned to the monastery's eurhythmy, hesitating at the door's threshold through which seeped potent aromas. How many doors had he opened, how many doors had he closed?

Biblical Alter-Egos. "Mr Featherstone – to whom were you referring in your letter? You mentioned an assassin guilty of a crime who stretches truth like soft rubber to elude prosecution and punishment, who rigorously denies any guilt, but do they have a name?" Bridget Lovegrove's numinous radiance cooled in the early morning sea-mist, very *soigné* there on the exposed beach, the illusion of her proximity, her orderliness and dreaminess contrasting the sculpted assemblage of the heavily armoured helicopter in which she had arrived. Christopher Featherstone lamented the erosion of his psyche as he pondered how her biblical motif came to be threaded into the tapestry of his existence. "Miss Lovegrove, we run like grain in timber, become tightly knotted impeding the flow, receive the stigmata of Original Sin. Last evening the splendor of the full moon rested on the monastery there like a sponge cake filled with creamy light. I banqueted alone." He stood haunted in confusion, like Ahasuerus maddened by Vashti's disobedience, entranced by Esther's queenly perfections, pausing to test the oiled hinges of his destiny swinging on the moment. Visibly curious, Bridget deliberated, her porously sketched-in presence finally flashing him her lightning thought: "Fly back with me, now! I'm not only thinking of your hip-pocket, as your accountant. Let me help you bring this would-be assassin to justice."

Diary Entries – June '68. (i) Seated amid the flower-runes of the Maharishi's Zen garden The Beach Boys memorialize super-human embryos inside the world-egg of Paradise. (ii) 'Nam's sink-hole gravity submerges the fallen and the moonscape of Khe Sanh welcomes the new American Forces Astronaut, General Abrams, with a rise-and-fall of earth-jarring curtains of loosened soil. (iii) Stephen Maxwell models himself on Daniel Cohn-Bendit addressing the world from resistance HQ on campus as the Latin Quarter is barricaded readying for Time's vertiginous spin on the axis of revolt. (iv) The superbly sculpted Amazon, Helena Steele, is located recording for **LESBOS** records where her lips are photographed embracing a harmonica with the fervor of an erotic kiss. (v) All feathered brilliance, dazzling green-and-gold, parrots in aereal flight leave a tall, white-fleshed eucalyptus tree as Bridget Lovegrove and Calvin Westwood embrace with searching eyes before lunch at a beachside restaurant. Pleasure cools within the geometry of a monastery's stone spaces and even the red roses in bloom cannot revive it. Dr Spock's generation says: "Our shoulder-length hair is here to stay, and you don't do our thinking for us anymore!"

Blue Hawaii – scene (i). Elvis, visceral as a fifties jukebox, hair sculpted in a symbolism of black jade, adorned with more leis than The Beach Boys sojourning with the Maharishi in Lotus Land, emerged from Honolulu's airport lounge into the paradisal brilliance of Hawaii as his circling limousine slowly approached. Shaded by aviator sunglasses, Fabian Roxburgh's eyes immediately identified the famous traveller from Memphis-to-Honolulu, his inexhaustibly handsome presence, and distracted Miranda from the freshening trade winds which had blown away the luscious hibiscus from her hair. "In lifting the Veil of Elvis, God has given us the electricity of His Own Portrait."

Blue Hawaii – scene (ii). Awash in Hawaiian ukuleles and steel guitars the hotel foyer allowed Elvis a royal entrance and he was immediately guided to the elevators for ascension to his penthouse suite. Miranda threw open the doors onto their hotel room balcony overlooking Waikiki Beach stripping clothes down to the glazed sheath of her flesh. Roxburgh leaned into the space of a mirror still feeling the sensation of her love bite dissolving with the touch of Eros' arrow into his neck. All Hawaii bloomed in a slow arousal of floral orgasms. Miranda stepped inside from the frieze of dreams and prepared herself as if a virgin bride by laying her golden caramel arabesque along the rectangular space of the bed. Sparkling diamond-dust glistened on the ocean and across the offshore reefs surf dissolved in softened vanilla ice-cream folds. "Miranda, did Elvis ever ask what metamorphosis Time would bring him? Music was simply invented for him, yet he barely troubles Billboard these days."

Blue Hawaii – scene (iii). Sexually iced in the sarcophagus of the bed, Miranda's sculpture melted his keening eagerness like a form of perfume treasured in a flower, how it holds and holds ecstatic shape. She briefly dipped herself in the tropically heated ocean before laying her oxidized bronze arabesque along a beach towel where slender calves were already roasting. Roxburgh paddled his surfboard for the outer reef of silver and the sparkling jewels of sunlight cresting the perfect waves. Suddenly a familiar presence emerged from the bowl with Byronic ease, like Nureyev on a wave-dance, poised, feeling the weight of the ocean's destined curve. Roxburgh too drew perfectly placed lines on the wave-tableaux, glimpsing Elvis paddle back out, the elasticity of flowing water caressing his backswept ducktails.

Blue Hawaii – scene (iv). Having dressed for dinner in the supper club, Roxburgh and Miranda strolled the foreshore where they fused with the tropical sunset's topaz incrustation. Mighty obelisks collapsed across the omnipotent flow of waves. Aglow with burning purple shadows the sun magnificently set about Miranda's shoulders. An after-dinner surprise in the supper club was Elvis' introduction and coaxing to sing, polishing the Philosopher's Stone of his voice with a revival of *Return To Sender*, an Orphean moment proving his artistry was furnished to outlast Time itself. When Hawaii's famous drums of the islands routine altered the rhythm, Roxburgh mused to Miranda: "Sartre in Paris. Elvis in Honolulu. His voice still romanticizes our emotions even if he has become imprisoned as *The Outsider*, his singing stifled by the existentialism of his movie career. He knows he is guilty of *bad faith* and steps into the icon of its characterization. His true heroism in these days of *Sgt. Pepper* is that he will not commit *suicide*."

Disobedience. Paris' Latin Quarter featured in the news bulletins resembled a post-Dickensian Inferno, the soluble imagery of youth no longer so many pretty flamingos in kaftans like last year's Summer of Love. Christopher Featherstone introduced Bridget Lovegrove to the dormitory's war-room where Stephen Maxwell donned a death's head mask as evening advanced across the University's Spanish sandstone matrices. Others too were war-painted up as the television screen unloaded images of jungle in 'Nam smeared in napalm. On the transistor radios the musical soundtrack was a bizarre collage of *Mony, Mony* and *Yummy, Yummy, Yummy* with Hendrix's searing revolutionary guitar and voice-print. Soon bonfires of textbooks illumined the University's caravanserai and inertia galvanized to combustion as the students' moving *bas relief* advanced across the Somme of the campus. Featherstone gripped Bridget's elbow and pointed to a striding Amazon and her followers spiral in a centripetal whirlpool upon the costumed revolutionaries taunting the cohorts of police. In his pocket was a photograph from the streets of Paris of a bloodied young woman, smudged beyond immediate recognition, being carried from the impact zone by a familiar journalist – was it Miranda Westwood though? Blown winter leaves swirled and scraped across the pavement as this Cecil B. de Mille spectacle intensified, scene from the definitive Movie of the Sixties, grandiose and tragic. "One day the Police will use live ammunition!"

V

THE WORLD-EGG CRACKS

Zeno's Paradox. Circumambulating the city's diagrammatic respiratory system with newsreels from 'Nam and the year's assassinations screening in his dreams, Fabian Roxburgh allowed the late-model sedan drift in orbit about the metropolis like the space capsule in *2001: A Space Odyssey*. Finally exhausted with these travelogues of dressing and undressing in motel rooms, of seeking sexual transubstantiation in the bread and wine of Miranda's Eucharistic presence but having to be satisfied with kissing the softened amber of her mouth, he drove on gazing at the immense billboard panels, Southern California's surreal art exhibition amid the chaos of freeways. Endless emblematic Arks massed from horizon-to-horizon as if queuing to embark for *Alpha Centauri*. Miranda turned a donut, each sugar grain on the skin reminding him of the sand clinging to her torso at the beach, its form a metaphor of the spacetime continuum in which he was trapped. In a burst of sound-waves gunshots disturbed the drone of traffic as he stood at the gas pump inserting the nozzle. With meaningless illogic two Negro youths wielding firearms crashed through the door of the gas station and ran over to an idling Lincoln Continental. Burning rubber the Lincoln slipped on the asphalt in screeching for the exit. Roxburgh tossed some notes at the gas pump and revved his sedan out into the Los Angelean maze after the accelerating Lincoln. "Fabian, what are you doing?" Miranda, licking a gelato, prettily petulant in her Hawaiian tan beside him, spun the car radio dial until *Jumpin' Jack Flash* gave the impetuous moment its mechanistic definition. The elegance of the sweeping cloverleaves curving space around the globe of the Earth, intersecting with the motion of millions of automobiles, assisted the Lincoln to vanish, become absorbed in the respiratory breathing of the city. "Fabian, we may be in Hollywood, but can you see any cameras?" Slowing into the nearest exit he brooded over this romantic still-birth with Miranda and the sedan descended into the empty Tao of Los Angeles.

Tutelage. "Celeste, the Earth hangs like a dew drop from Penelope's web strung across space, and this Apollo program aiming to put Man on the Moon will simply be an excursion to a wasted Zen garden." Christopher Featherstone escorted her to yet another student conference where the revolutionary cut-outs of Stephen Maxwell's Gang of Four sat cross-legged in the campus quadrangle of the University's monastery. Celeste's poster montages walled them in like Japanese silk screens on which were Pop Art portraits of the Faces of '68: (i) The Kennedy generations veiled in lace at funerals – erasures from the page of Time longing for amnesia's incubus. (ii) President Johnson and Richard M. Nixon – *The Dharma Bums* gorged on their own political rhetoric, their textural faces burdened with the Apocalypse of 'Nam. (iii) Mao and Che – High Priests of the counter-culture, illustrations from *Howl*. Helena Steele's substantially statuesque presence spear-headed an Amazonian charge through the crowd of students upsetting the marquee and cracking the eggshell of Transcendental Meditation, the OM of Revolution. Driving Celeste home afterwards Featherstone glanced across at her thoughtful presence feverishly filling her sketchpad with penciled remembrances of the riot.

Heartbreak Hotel. The earthquake of Paris' cobblestones and their rising in revolt agitated the lonely streets of this Southern Arcadian city half-way across the globe. No *Arc de Triomphe* liberated the skyline as Christopher Featherstone awakened from his dream of sub-atomic wave-particles traveling the freeway of his torso's circulatory system, the bursting wave-pulse of each breath expanding and collapsing his lungs. Beyond the window of the hotel room ebony clouds thinned and the moon's horse's hoof impressed its emblem in the fabric of space. Lately his intelligence had become a pilgrim obsessed with burial and resurrection, since his recovery from the shadowy tomb of his bombed-out office and surveillance of Helena Roxburgh. Seismic generational and gender drifts were occurring and turbulent paradigms were reshaping the cartography of the city. Featherstone knew he was crossing a perilous lake of fire shadow-boxing with Helena, enmeshing himself in the heavy web of rebellion these Sabine women with attitude were weaving from the loss of Paradise. Space bubbled now with the supernova of convulsive social change. A light came on in her upstairs apartment as Helios' amber blood congealed in the under-flesh of clouds modeling an immense torso reclining along the horizon. Had she been dreaming of being a virgin again for a night? He remembered Blake's aphorism: *The nakedness of woman is the work of God*. Helena though was a sexually disillusioned rose thrust forth from a lethal branch of very sharp thorns! She burnished the ballroom of the world with a new feminist imperialism, moved with a rhythm Featherstone realized was a dance-to-the-death, and was re-arranging the mosaic of music to eliminate men from the frieze. Trailing her through the city streets along which she summoned in imagination the ghosts of the aristocracy guillotined in the French Revolution he recalled another of Blake's poignant aphorisms: *A dead body revenges not injuries*.

Do You Have A Phone Number Where I Can Reach You? Standing on the sidewalk, his bruised Beat features half-reflected in a store window, Christopher Featherstone heard the voice, Samantha Westwood's voice, but his memory was deconstructing his inner photographs of their *lost weekend*, particularly the dissipation of its pessimism. "Samantha, Miranda is launching her embryonic self into the world. She is traveling overseas, Paris I believe." Her air-kiss and momentary pressure of her fingers on his arm were tissues dissolving as his thoughts wrestled with the concept of being's *non-locality* unless directly observed. Voices merged around them on the sidewalk like overlapping wave-interference patterns. Suddenly the buildings on the grid of city streets resembled curved slicings of space-time and falling through the space of his delirium bombs serenely emptied from the undercarriages of B-52s and exploded in a delicate *frottage* across the jungle landscape of 'Nam. Samantha's silver screen beauty surveyed the emotional blitzkrieg of his psycho-sexual fragmentation before her puzzled gaze as a thunderstorm flashed across the cityscape.

Comic Book Hippies. *Los Angelenos* screen-tested themselves everyday waitressing in restaurants, on the tennis courts of country clubs, body-building at the beach, cruising the interlacing freeway complexes, all brought together by the myth of a common journey. Aimlessly wandering the boulevards, listening to the car radio, their romantic broth cooled despite the scalding summer heat, they glimpsed the NBC sign and Fabian Roxburgh pulled over into a parking lot. Miranda's tamarind-glazed torso blended with the fabulous smears of oil paint characterizing the Miss California clones queued on the boulevard for entrance to the studios. "Fabian, it's bubblegum!" Miranda's Lolita protests smoldered as they seated themselves with the audience around the square stage, no doubt her thoughts singing with Hendrix's *Faberge* creations on guitar or a musical hall medley from *Sgt. Pepper*. Romanticized comic book faces, radiant with optimism, oblivious to the Sorbonne or Berkeley, focused on the illuminated square where four non-youthful personnel hunched on chairs awaiting their demi-god's *deus ex machina*.

The Light Of The World - (Elvis[2]). Suddenly God's microcosmic incarnation emerged from a darkened aisle and placed a footstep onto the illuminated square of the stage, Pythagorean solid, perfected pentagram of embodied Man. Lithe with eurhythmy, smiling with the effortless grace of a Buddhic lotus afloat on the surface of applause, colored in a Grecian patina, his noble lineage a fulfillment of Orpheus' triumphant return, Elvis paused glorying in all his illustrative power. Beside him, Roxburgh sensed Miranda's presence touched by an aura of divinity enveloping the studio, and she immediately shuffled her way closer to the stage, oblivious of the cameras filming this resurrection. Elvis[2]! Discipled, Roxburgh witnessed Orpheus-in-black-leather astrally ascend from Hades, his totality of being submerged in the idealism of Greek sculpture, the very definition of *miracle*, a flawless masterpiece, a new New Testament! His demi-god's sculpture squared on stage stood as a revivification of Antiquity dreaming of lost Golden Ages. Singing, Elvis' voice sonorously soothed with the power of a Pythagorean lyre the dissonance beginning to dismantle the symmetry of the Free World, thawed the Ice Age promise of the Cold War raging across the globe. His voice's foliage was more burnished, more autumnal, more Aeschlyan and self-transfiguring, but an assertion of triumph, that it would illumine what is dark within humanity and be eternally omnipresent. Hyperbole energized Roxburgh, emotion energized the structures of thought and Elvis' beauty, black-marbled poetry embodied independent of mortality in Time, existed forever in the mind which contemplated him. Elvis and the continuum of America were *One*!

Leaves From The Garden Of Elvis. The Biblical Elvis unveiled more of his parable over successive days and Miranda Westwood's captivation with the Colossus from Memphis assumed a religious fervour easing Fabian Roxburgh from the intricacy of her existence. Unlike the Maharishi, Elvis scattered, not literal lotus petals across the neophyte's Path, but the very musical emanation of God, attuning consciousness to the *Way* – through The Meditation Garden of Elvis! Sartre in the cafés of Paris, existentializing from the barricades, modelled how far incarnation's physical sculpture had abandoned the Divine Ideal, when compared with Elvis' metaphysical aura radiated from the sound-stage of the NBC studios. Long would the redemptive symmetry of Elvis in black Orphean leather resonate across the dream of Roxburgh's own aspiration to recover his Eurydice. Miranda positioned him before a mirror in their motel room attempting to style a kiss curl rakishly across his imperfect forehead, *à la Elvis*. "Does Elvis *really* exist? Does he still live in Pelugia Way? My egg shell has cracked!" De Gaulle's very exoteric head on the news bulletins reasserted its authority in France.

Pathos. "Climbing the mountain to understand the man proved too arduous." Elizabeth Featherstone spoke of severing the rope and letting herself fall away from her ex-husband's ascent of a stairway to the distant stars. "How do you find his aloof *othermanliness* then?" The wind howled outside and the winter storm unleashed frosted hailstones across the darkening city street frontage. Sharing cocktails at the Plaza, Samantha Westwood maneuvered the conversation back to the truancy and teenage rebellion of her daughter, martini-in-hand, hoping to smother this worldly-wise Emilia's suspicions with Othello's pillow. Two actresses confronted reality, evaluating themselves in the curved porcelain jug each presented to the other, the relative social spaces they occupied, both rather beautifully marbled and aged but no longer fresh with innocence. "So, Christopher collapsed, and you have temporarily allowed him to live aboard your husband's schooner? And he is engaged to locate your daughter? Why would you be a lifebuoy and throw yourself at him this way?" Memories of a chimerical intimacy intruded and coloured their surface sociability with a lashing sting even the dry martinis could not assuage. "Mrs. Westwood, some years ago Christopher mentioned a chance encounter, with a mysterious woman, in this very hotel I believe, does it hold any memories for you?" Memory's bouquet of sweet-fragranced roses evaporated with forgetfulness from the masked countenances of both women as they sheared the rope of their meeting.

Indiscretion. Thinking she recognized Elizabeth Featherstone framed by the driver side window, parked on the street outside an inner city apartment block, Bridget

Lovegrove reversed her car back parallel in the opposing lane and signaled to her. Elizabeth wound down her window out of politeness. "Mrs. Featherstone, have you seen your ex-husband? I have documents for him to sign." Cloud coverage and finely misted rain were suddenly lit up by sunlight piercing through and bringing a dazzle to the wet surfaces. A youngish middle-aged man exited the apartment block and climbed in the passenger side of Elizabeth's car. "Hello, Miss Lovegrove. I believe Christopher is recovering aboard the Westwood's schooner. Try the marina." Winding up her window so her words to her companion were lost Elizabeth pulled away from the curb.

The Outsider. Unshaven, too grizzled for comfort, Christopher Featherstone stood on the deck of the schooner at its winter mooring, feeling a barely perceptible rock through his feet. "You can stay here for the weekend if you like. Just remember, Calvin does not know you are here." Anchored in Time he dreamed of swimming for the horizons of past-and-future simultaneously with Byronic ease of expression, a *Don Juan* for the existential sixties. Samantha's icy Ravelian waters froze etiquette and all discussion of the connectivity of chance bringing them together again. She would not acknowledge she was *the she* at The Plaza. During the hours of his delirium they were veiled not in thoughts of the Savior, but of Samantha, her unraveling thread clinging to the tapestry of his self-image mirrored in the world. Roofed over with clouds of rich embroidery the sky brought to the ocean a texture of opaque porcelain. Completion of Time by Man was an impossibility, the question to be asked was: Could Man ever abandon Time altogether? Soon Nature dramatized Debussy's *La mer* so he descended to the spacious living quarters. Haunted by *The Fall*, of becoming an *Outsider* without the grace of redemption, he allowed reflections of Samantha poetically rise to the space of his mind and stand mirrored there. Perhaps he could attempt an escape act, re-twist his thoughts into strands of the Fates' rope, long frayed from over-use, and climb the precipice out of this world. Inaccessible women had often lured men this way, Dante being the very model and author of his longed-for salvation.

Two Pieces Of Mosaic. "What do they call Miranda's generation? The Discothèque Age? Featherstone talks to me in *the vocabulary of '68* as he phrases it, but strikes me as someone pursuing his own obsessions. Just listen to this, Sam." Calvin Westwood nodded to his private secretary arranging a vase of roses on a cabinet within the office and she moved to a portable record player. Samantha maintained her posture of anonymous sculpture, her academic realism, while the secretary had moved about the office with the solemnity of an attendee on a potentate, serving them coffee, but observed her now like tufted waves bursting free of the concentrated bud. "Apparently Featherstone has become a lyricist for some obscure pop group whose singer goes by the *nom de plume*, Vera Jane Palmer." Samantha glanced at the photographs on the desk, of Miranda and herself, then at the silhouetted ellipsis of the secretary curved over the portable record player in the rigid corsetry of her tailored clothes, erotically squeezed between the interstices of life, art and business.

I caught you walking with the actor in blue suede shoes,
He was reading to you from *A Streetcar Named Desire*.
Yeah, he was lighting you up like a burning fuse,
And I could tell your magnesium loins were on fire.

They tell me you're hearing the Music of the Spheres,
Then they tell me it's destined to end in tears.
They tell me the crystal is bound to shatter,
But what the hell does it all matter.

I saw you through the window ripping off his white tee-shirt,
As if you were reading him *A Streetcar Named Desire*.
Yeah, saw you dazzling him and playing the flirt,
Better be careful though setting his loins on fire.

They tell me he sets you spinning like a galaxy,
They tell me it's destined to end in ecstasy.
They tell me your passion's like a supernova,
But what the hell if it's all over.

Is this how the sixties are going to wind down,
The sun setting all over town?
The year's clinging to Time's rolling stone,
And my love's as meaningless as a wave's veil of foam
And my love's as meaningless as a wave's veil of foam
And my love's as meaningless as a wave's veil of foam

With precocious verve the secretary raised the 45 from the turntable while the curvaceous stalk of the vase held the rose of marriage barbed with thorns. Infidelity's frost crusted the leaves of memories in Samantha's thoughts as she left Westwood Holdings Ltd and walked beneath an arcing pedestrian crossover draped in banners dripping with revolutionary political statements. She stepped over a discarded newspaper on the pavement, its rain-soaked ink leaching away and considered her purpose in requesting the tablet of the 45 from the secretary, who only released it to her following Calvin's nod.

Lyricist Of The Tao. Embedded in the *trompe l'œil* of solace and renewal, all the world seemingly in Newtonian motion, Christopher Featherstone stood on the deck of the Westwood's schooner measuring the duration of his *becoming* within the vibratory chiffon fabric of space. "Will I see you tonight?" His *Teen Romance* question simply exposed the head of a lamb to the knife. Driving through the streets, acknowledging how his mind was actually an icon immanent with every possibility, he nevertheless pondered what he should be doing as a grown man, before on a whim deciding to re-investigate Helena Steele's ranch-style apartment. Space's ventriloquism accompanied his passage through the rooms. (i) Furniture – the honeymoon hacienda was decorated with a bizarre exhibition of inflated balloons on whose stretched curvatures were stenciled familiar portraits ... Mao ... Che ... Castro ... Nixon ... Dubček ... a puzzling enigma, extravagant metaphor of masculine heads filled with emptiness, ready to explode. Sexually, laid in the sarcophagus of her bed, would this chilled salamander ripple into a lascivious odalisque, become flaming *jouissance*, consuming the pyre? (ii) Wardrobe – Her evening gown's strawberry syrup would melt around her winter ice cream thighs with the visceral adherence of flame to flesh. He ran his fingers across the curvilinear silhouettes of her incarnational array of clothing suspended from hangers. A sudden blow stunned consciousness and he stumbled to his knees grasping the flimsy veil of clothes in sinking. Temporarily blinded by darkness, his consciousness dimmed like the brightness of the disobedient Archangel's, Featherstone awoke from the eclipse to focus Helena Steele crouched in marblesque resolve over him, the barrel of his hand gun aimed between his eyes. Surrendering to the moment's metaphysical vertigo, he murmured with wry humour: "I was wondering whether I would see you tonight."

Shadow-Boxing. Still tightly coiled in her crouch, sculpturally clothed, fingers tightening around the hand gun, Helena's comic strip feminine image threatened to explode the frame so Featherstone abruptly hit the inside of her wrist with his forearm. The gun automatically discharged into the carpet, the bullet locked in spacetime, freeing his consciousness, freeing him from the dream, galvanizing their quick-frozen tableaux from shock. Featherstone quickly elbowed her jaw line while his fingers tightened around her wrist. He scooped up the fallen hand gun while Helena lifted herself onto her elbows, legs spread awry, senses disorientated by the blow, but still physically dangerous. Featherstone then silently demonstrated how she should have reacted after chopping him across the back of the neck and retrieving his hand gun. Distanced, both hands holding the gun leveled, statuesque but loose, he sensed the ice crusting her lips as she spoke: "Can you think for all of us, all the time? When I first entered your office that day I know now I mistook you. You're just another worthless Hamlet! Ghosts frighten you." Saturnine, hooded, Featherstone moved away through the balloons and closed the apartment door behind him, his metaphysical purism rather resembling a Jackson Pollock canvas.

Homesickness. Carved out of midnight-blue space as if with a chisel, Christopher Featherstone walked the suburban street and confronted the abstract equilibrium of the house's façade where his ex-wife resided in its sanctum of contentment. Fault lines of misogyny merged his memories; women sitting in the engine of masculine existence were spark plugs! Cruising another suburb he searched for the urban lettering of Bridget Lovegrove's address. Rarefied silk pajamas her soul's apparel, Bridget sleepily answered the door bell, so contrasting his monochromatic sobriety aureoled by the porch light, his subversive anti-hero ambience, but she invited him inside and listened to him describe his skirmish with Helena. The bullet's reverberation through the space-time continuum impacting the canvas of his torso would have soaked its fabric *à la Harmony in Red*, the image's emotional impasto visualized in Bridget's expression. After sleeping for an hour or two on her living room sofa he showered and ironed his shirt and trousers before driving out to the airport. Early morning rain formed liquid pools of glass by the roadside and furrowed expanses of cloud lay reamed with dawn's golden grain. Fabian Roxburgh and Miranda Westwood emerged with their luggage, the white Californian fabrics showing off to maximum effect her bronzed flesh, while her world-weariness betrayed in her body language identified a new vibe shaping her persona, that her story was still without an ending. More striking was Miranda's expensive Sassoon haircut, the ultimate sixties helmet for space age travelers, *Born Free*! Trailing their taxi, Featherstone was increasingly surprised as they headed for the marina, and soon realized Miranda intended she and Roxburgh would crash aboard the schooner until they found other accommodation.

Good Morning ... Darling! A champagne-vinegar oozing suffused Miranda's aura as she squeezed close joining him over breakfast she had prepared from the schooner's well-stocked kitchen. "What are you thinking?" Rodeo Drive's boutiques of miniskirts designed to show off the sleekly tanned legs of Hollywood's starlets were already fading, as was the paralysis of Paris, and surely England's swinging pendulum was slowing, Hawaiian surf had flattened to the smoothness of this marina, as Fabian Roxburgh savored his buttered toast and considered Miranda's almost instantaneous displacement from scene-to-scene over the past month. Was her sexuality filtered through her cooking? Noises on deck brought a pause, feminine legs descended into the schooner's state room, puzzlement and surprise made the *ménage à trois* falter, space's *tabula rasa* permutated many possibilities. "Good morning ... darling!" Here was a collision of soft geometries seeking resolution, for Roxburgh broke down the frames of Samantha Westwood's facial expressions into a realization she came aboard expecting someone else to be there. Making himself one-dimensional he exited the state room and wandered the walkways of the marina. 'Nam's Hollywood labyrinth of movie settings and the dueling Minotaur of Communism's presence at its narrative heart beckoned with its beautifully grained scenery lit with the liquid shudders of exploding napalm. Miranda leapt off the schooner and jogged off into the distance before vanishing. Samantha Westwood slowly surfaced from the state room, her motion about the deck a sequence of asymmetrical nuances, Demeter's nobility remembered from Antiquity, and then she moved away towards her car like a fan gently closing.

Where Is Your Revolution At Then? Harder-edged under her Sassoon haircut, Miranda respectfully listened to the Cream album then began her story-telling, earning her stripes with the Gang of Five, passing around a well-circulated photograph of her taken from the Parisian barricades. Sartre's existential selflessness described through the impressionism of Miranda's voice inspired Stephen Maxwell with an intenser

Marxist totalitarianism. Eyes conjured the ghosts of her cuts and abrasions traced on her anatomy with a fingertip which the sun of Hawaii had bronzed over. "Let's wrap up in the American flag and immolate ourselves outside their Embassy!" Footage on the evening news followed a collection of statuesque Amazons, one with a swollen jaw, demonstrating in the city and releasing hundreds of inflated balloons which carried familiar faces ... Mao ... Che ... Castro ... Nixon ... Dubček ... until scuffles erupted with a cadre of student radicals running the gauntlet of the police trailing burning American flags.

The Party. Fabian Roxburgh addressed the collapsing geometry of his psyche by renting in an apartment block decorated with the inelegance of a hippie salon. Fondling an envelope lacerated with the anguish of handwriting, his other hand pouring straight bourbon into a glass he listened to a neighboring actress memorizing her lines to an unfamiliar modern drama. Late-night parties vibrated the screen of the separating wall and one day he glimpsed the actress shopping among the local supermarket aisles. Arrayed in convolvulus flower child motifs and biting into the luminous flesh of a crisp apple she obviously recognized him and approached. "Hello, stranger, why don't you come to our parties?" She smelt *eastern ... far eastern*! Roxburgh emerged from the shell of his aloneness and crossed the threshold into the crowded apartment resonating with an extended guitar solo. Linear, monosyllabic conversations were being strung together by souls dressed for youthful tragedies, the stylistic dissonances with the sacrificial Grunts in 'Nam all the more striking. "Hey, stranger, the way one dances is politically *Now*, or *Then*. We do anything we want, understand?" Towards morning the atmosphere held the painted heaviness of lowering clouds with Simon & Garfunkel's *Sounds Of Silence* on endless repeat. Already the skies over 'Nam would be smeared with the rouge of dawn. "Hush, hush, stranger, only move *withinness*, or *withoutness*, release the tension of your narcissism." When she wandered next door into his apartment she decorated its gloomy space in psychedelic splendour, painting with her thighs in her actressy motion, standing over his collages on *The Death of the City*, images of 'Nam and its expressways channeling the Grunts towards the mountains lined up in *Desolation Row*. "What shall I call you?"

Fleur ... French For Flower. Sexually, Fabian Roxburgh squeezed himself from the sheath of existential panache in which he had numbed his desires, feeling his loins a delta silted deep with memories of Saigon and his fateful glimpse of Jack Kerouac *On The Road* of the Mekong looking absolutely *beat*. "Reader's Digest sex is okay, but I'm not a home-maker, all my education is in this Cream album." Her hooded chrysalis of tissue engorged like a rose bud loaded with a hundred petals visible when she swung astride him with the virtuosity of an acrobat, had him day dreaming as he wandered the shopping aisles of the supermarket, thinking of the housewives leaning forward over the shelves and into the deep freeze, everyone erotically poised to be an *"Outside Woman"*. Rising from moments of post-coital immobility the French flower began to cover the abstract expressionist surfaces of his apartment with newspaper and magazine cuttings while he gazed at the television screen's serialized assaults on the mountainous hills of 'Nam. Non-existential exposures, the black-and-white images as economical as a mathematical equation, stretched the tautology of "Peace With Honor", and then Fleur passed across the mirror of his existence, sinuous in her cashmere sweater.

Atonal Architecture's Mathematical Logic. Asymmetrical with hypotheses for Helena Steele's behavior, placing her perfect Amazonian form inside the sphere of her invisible soul, Christopher Featherstone circled through his atonal relationships, so many images in curved mirrors, conscious of the flaws in and reflected from the glass. Sunset's ignition of a bayou enriched Bridget Lovegrove's hair, her torso's curvilinear *parfum flaçon* gloried in the glittering treasury of her persona sweeping to another rendezvous with Calvin Westwood, and just looking at her lucid passage across the architectural façade of a building rendered space illogical. Checking over Samantha Westwood's charge account details he browsed her favourite boutiques pretending he was on a buying spree for his ex-wife. Serendipity eluded these elliptical adventures, especially his re-visiting the Westwood's schooner at leisure docked in the marina, where he measured what his emotional and physical expenditure of energy would be in going to war with Helena Steele. Bridget proved his *gold reserve* and offered her sofa's space for him to dream of their *Cause* as she phrased the Helena Steele Case. One evening she agreed to accompany him to an off-beat, *outré* discothèque where Helena Steele performed, her presence's atonal architecture while singing the lyrics full of menace reciprocated by the underground audience. Factually and precisely Helena Steele loaded the band's equipment in a van and accompanied by the drummer maneuvered through the mathematical logic of her route back to her honeymoon hacienda. Bridget discreetly followed the sequence of logical images unfolding from the exit of the discothèque to the disappearance of the couple inside the hacienda-style apartment framed within her car's windshield. Exploratory lacquer nails gripped the steering wheel. Featherstone glanced down at the **LESBOS** record she purchased at the discothèque and lying in her lap. What logical images were standing in Bridget's thoughts from the patterns shaped by the evening's excursion?

Isolation Brings Its Own Vengeance. Softening Fleur's dazzle, lessening his blindness, Fabian Roxburgh abandoned his collages and plans for an exhibition, slowed his thinking by half-carrying her from another party and taking her in his hire-car to a drive-in movie. Her cartoon-drawing of her *true* flower child of a younger sister tagged along wearing an Indian sari and fragranced with the mystic east. Half-way into the movie, *The Producers*, falling rain streaked across the screen, continuing through the *Springtime For Hitler* number, fogging up the windows, so Fleur acrobatically climbed astride his loins, the visceral milkiness of her skin dissolving against him with the tenderness of summer clouds in a blue sky. Visible in the rear vision mirror her eternally silent sister's eyes were closed. Wetness layered the inside pane of glass from which the speaker was suspended. Her sister's fondness for yogurt which she casually took from the supermarket freezers and ate while shopping became a trigger of arousal only assuaged in these obscure experiences of sexual reverie. Anti-war posters pasted up across the apartment block excited and hallucinated his imagination that 'Nam was the tourist destination he longed to visit. Fleur's sister's boyfriend was drafted and Roxburgh promised her he would accompany him on R&R in Saigon.

The Co-Existentialism of Spacetime. Christopher Featherstone sliced Time into a cone of experienced memories trying to extricate himself from its enmeshing fabric and inhabit the *no-space* between the layers of imagistic film impressed there. The cyclonic point of the *Now* sucked images from the planar slices of the cone as he transposed his physical presence across the three-dimensional model of the city. Commissioned billboards lining the approach routes into the city evoked slices individualized from the continuum of Time, an anthology of images, passport memories carried with us on a journey of existential consequences, an exhibition of the absurdity of the human consciousness. Over coming days and nights Featherstone maintained a covert surveillance of Helena Steele, observing her materializations and de-materializations on the impressionably thin-sliced film of space, layering the cone of his memories with a narrative to determine whether *existence* precedes *essence*. Had the world-egg fallen into three-dimensional spacetime, through its planar slices of moments and was experiencing a widening crack: could the fall be reversed and re-assembly occur? Helena Steele had opened spacetime's Planck-moment firing off his hand gun and shattering the crystalline slices through which the bullet journeyed.

Dispatches From 'Nam I. "Looking for your Girl-Next-Door?" Stephen Maxwell's sly impudence punched the air as they walked briskly across the campus lawn towards the library. "Miranda told me she begged you to take her to Haight & Ashbury, man. She wanted to be rocked in cradle of our generation's counter-culture movement. Berkeley is our Hanoi, our Kremlin." Revolution tightened the musculature of Maxwell's face as he straight-arm saluted with a closed fist. Fabian Roxburgh gazed across the manicured lawn where student radicals were erecting a platform from which to address those beginning to gather near the scaffolding. "Just drop the Ashbury, Maxwell. Haight! Haight! Haight! is the only vibe there these days. Tell her I'm returning to 'Nam and look out for my obituary. She'll understand." Sweeping out of Saigon, on a whim, intuitively following some radar of emotional orientation, Roxburgh and his principal photographer hitched a helicopter ride into the Central Highlands where they holed up in a hilltop citadel. From the void of a foxhole he composed another series in his *Dispatches From 'Nam*, joining the yoga of the Grunts on the Hill, waiting for the swish of machine gun fire to scythe from the forestation. Here were so many Hamlets on the battlements of their own Elsinore! Disembodied GI voices from radio broadcasts issuing on the air-waves out of the Hanoi Hilton demoralized the Grunts curled up in the Orphic eggs of their foxholes. Roxburgh illustrated comparisons between the heroic young faces of the *G-eyes* in 'Nam fast-draining of resolution and those Angels of Democracy captured on World War II footage pushing forward at break-neck pace toward Victory. A downed F111 plunged behind a hill while the drifting parachute from which swung the pilot became absorbed by the screaming foliage, surviving only to disappear into the Viet-Cong tunnel system, emerge along the Ho Chi Minh trail for booking into the Hanoi Hilton. Across the skyline burnished orange brightened to gold.

Dispatches From 'Nam II. Bellying across splintered timber under a fusillade of blistering crossfire, Fabian Roxburgh only saw a blur of ink strokes for trees etched against the horizon, and wrote his observations of each Grunt precisely aligned to the cartography of his destiny on this Hill. Human faces born of soul suffocated in the earth or serenely lay exposed perfectly geometrized to the vanishing perspectives of death, all for the liberation of these mythological hills in the Central Highlands. Gasping with revulsion the photographer elbowed his way across intestines manuring the soil and the tremor in his frightened eyes was marbled with a gaze poised between life and death. Roxburgh peered through the churning arabesques of smoke as the nearby hilltop fused Heaven and Hell with napalm. Screaming souls drowned in napalm, the suffocating Styx burned with human carcasses, a claustrophobic foxhole was territory enough from which to observe the world-egg crack, its contents leak, ooze away. Night fell.

Dispatches From 'Nam III. His flak jacket shredded by shrapnel, a Colonel eased himself into the harmonic disharmony ensphering the shell-shocked Grunts coming down from the fresco of Paradise Lost, telling them of a dream he had, of the fallen Sons of America being shining stars on the fourth-dimensional flag spread before the Throne of God, sanctified by Him for raising in Everlasting Glory. Every heart possessed at that moment a stained glass delicacy capable of enduring a Crucifixion. Half-buried in dark-grained soil displaced by mortar, Roxburgh searched in vain for the Colonel and the souls he memorialized for the Grunts now assaulting the palimpsest of the hillside again, passing in-and-out from visibility-to-invisibility. Remnants of smoking jungle briefly caught alight with the sinking of the sun. Medics crawled everywhere through the inchoate morass, squeezed through sieves of devastated tree stumps to tend the wounded and dying. Thinking of Fleur's flowing milk contours, her acrylic opalescence, erotically kneeling to collect the spillage of contents from her American Indian style pouch, Roxburgh witnessed the column of a tree, the column of a man, fall.

VI
FLAMBÉ

WHAAM! 'Nam's virus raging in Fabian Roxburgh's consciousness ripped through his sensibilities with the percussive effect of a string of exploding firecrackers. A ceiling fan rotated above the crumpled bed, its rotor-blades unable to lift the room's Huey out of the war-zone into the pure empyrean realm, away from Paradise Lost. He glimpsed the slenderness of a silhouette in a one-piece camisole drifting about the room and imagined Sigmund Freud sitting in the dreams of his existence with the power of Rodin's contemplative *Thinker*. Every assault on the Hill evoked a remembrance of the Original Fall. Space was deliriously unhinged from the doors of perception by a mortar shell slamming into the hillside. Fragmented applause and laughter, mustachioed GIs grinning mixed up with 'Nam's cortege of death, biers of body-bags, Bob Hope's circus and shrill waves of whistles welcoming Raquel Welch, morphed away the sultry summer hours of his delirium. "Why am I suffering like this?" While dressing for her shift at the military hospital the mid-western nurse who mirrored back to him his look of hopelessness rotated the dial away from Armed Forces Radio to a renegade station broadcasting The Doors' *The Unknown Soldier*.

A Military Psyche Leavened By Democracy's Relaxation Of Doctrinal Will. Pushing aside sketches for more column-inches, Fabian Roxburgh fingered the plaster over the cut above his eyebrow, legacy from the mortar strike on the Hill, impatient for the end of the nurse's shift, hungering in his psyche for more spectacular B-52 raids carpet bombing the terrain north of the DMZ. Disillusioned by 'Nam's betrayal of the classic war movie he drove the nurse through the peripheral suburbia of Saigon where the VC strongholds had been loosened. Pressed up against him in the taxi her mid-western feminine tenderness was almost too cruel for his wounded psyche. Everywhere radios carried the soundtrack to 'Nam's action movie in three-dimensional spacetime, Vietnamese scurrying along the roadways beneath conical hats while *Angel of the Morning* had her humming along, but this was no Yellow Brick Road in Kansas. Later she leaned over his shoulder as he composed his *Dispatches From 'Nam*, evoking GIs marching through rice paddies and jungle infested with VC cadres while students Stateside bravely marched as if suffering unbearable deprivations of liberty and freedom, and hippies wrestled with their spaced-out visions of the Commune-as-Paradise. When she had returned to the military hospital he became transfixed by a song on the radio, Elvis' obscure *Your Time Hasn't Come Yet, Baby* and spontaneously thought of Miranda's smoothness of ice, of Fleur's smoothness of oil, the sweet hippie verdure of her loins fragranced with its idealism of the east. Statistical data published in dispassionate print itemized how more US personnel had perished in the first six months of '68 than the whole Year of Love, '67 ... radio requests featured *Dream A Little Dream Of Me*!

Waiting For The Sun. Flying north with Macbeth's famous soliloquy in his thoughts ...

> Tomorrow, and tomorrow, and tomorrow,
> Creeps in this petty pace from day to day,
> To the last syllable of recorded time;
> And all our yesterdays have lighted fools
> The way to dusty death. Out, out, brief candle!
> Life's but a walking shadow, a poor player
> That struts and frets his hour upon the stage,
> And then is heard no more; it is a tale
> Told by an idiot, full of sound and fury,
> Signifying nothing.

... Fabian Roxburgh sat in the Huey rivetted by the unblinking, staring faces of the GIs in sustained close-up around him, and imagined an intellectual collision between Kerouac, Elvis and Warhol on the tarmac at Khe Sanh, devised dialogues on the theme of existential *being-and-nothingness* with which to engage the troops. How convincing was the proposition *existence preceded essence* stripped naked in 'Nam's universal Hell?

Compass And Set Square. Funereal rain drizzled from the yeast of burgeoning cloud forms. A limp newspaper drenched with rain lay half-folded in the car park outside the terrestrial castle of Police Headquarters, headlining some domestic Law and Order drama in the community. Christopher Featherstone climbed the steps of the stone precinct rising towards the sky's diaphanous space above with the confidence of Crusader armor and paused inside the entrance. He scanned the Freemasonic minuet of Police Officers, their uniforms a ceremonial cuirass, moving with the stilted pride of Knights Templars, custodians of the Holy Grail, until he identified the on-duty desk sergeant from previous casework and approached. "Featherstone, someone rearranged that aesthetic nose of yours yet?" Shown to a wood-panelled office with glass windows, Featherstone shook the hand of his surrogate self-portrait, a caricature of a senior detective, a cliché of existential textures balanced by gravitas, and took in immediately the Freemasonic ring. Catholic crosses were hidden under the shirts of other officers, ethically opposing the compass and set square, creating ideological tensions he intelligently used. "Well, Featherstone, I listened to the record you gave me, then passed it on to my daughter. Do you still think this Fabian Roxburgh is in some kind of danger? He's overseas right now, in Vietnam." Clouds of cigarette smoke seeped into the office space. "We visited the hacienda, interviewed the Steele woman, and what did we come up with? No sign of a discharged firearm. Are you sure you haven't dreamed this? You were concussed in the explosion." Featherstone allowed him to finish, close the file and lean back in his swivel chair, hands behind his head. "Yes, and Tiepolo went Rococo! Life is absurd, like the crushing together of those wall-planes there into a diminished corner." Silence tilted the geometry of the moment. Rotating the Freemasonic ring on his finger, the senior detective ignored these obtuse *non sequitirs* and seemed to levitate upright out of the chair. "Featherstone, why do you keep reminding me of an actor? Have you thought of auditioning at the Playhouse? Reports identify you at these student demonstrations. Have you become a weekend anarchist, want to tear down society? Her hacienda smelt sensational. What do you mean, Tiepolo went Rococo?"

Circle Every Beginning With An End. After purchasing another copy of Helena Steele's 45 from **LESBOS** Records, Christopher Featherstone drove down to the marina and stood on the quay observing the Westwood's symmetrical schooner among the rhyming curves of the other moored yachts, before climbing aboard and proceeding to the state room. His fleeting hours with Samantha Westwood seemed erased from her consciousness so he determined to tell her about Helena Steele and the three-way arrows of fatalism existing between Fabian Roxburgh, Miranda and himself, hoping to energize her from this relaxed etiquette she neutralized him with. Calvin Westwood featured as a magazine millionaire in **TIME**, one of the *nouveau riche*, his portrait struck on the cover's paper medallion, its presence in the state room indicating a recent visit. Samantha's surface sociability had the seriousness of an Apollo Mission taking flight as they consumed her rocket-fuel martinis aboard the schooner and over *dinner à deux* of crisply sautéed fish in garlic lemon sauce. Featherstone squeezed his irresistible nostalgia for her magical likeness that *lost weekend* in '64 and to arrest the sudden avoidance of her gaze at him, her potent signal they were not anonymous to each other. "Lately I've been fascinated by Marie Curie's romantic radioactivity for her fellow physicist, Paul Langevin, who undertook the ritual of a duel in defense of their honor. No shots were fired, the gesture being symbolic. I never expected to see you again ..." Samantha coquettishly uncrossed her legs, turning her face away from him into the emotionally bruising shadows as she asked: "Would you symbolically duel for the honor of the woman you loved?" Wide-eyed, she listened to his unraveling of the strands of the pulp paperback drama so far, staring, frightened when he placed his hand gun on the low table and promised to watch over Miranda.

Revolutionary Mannequins. "The Fascists charged us again, they wore riot gear, we wore our paisley shirts and blue jeans. I know you see us as revolutionary mannequins standing behind the plate-glass window of the world, man, but we want our bourgeois psyches cleansed of sentimentality." Footprints melted the crystalline winter frost carpeting the lawn. Stephen Maxwell and the Gang of Five, quotations in Beardsley pen-and-ink against the pale light, half-saluted off Christopher Featherstone and made their way into the University dormitory and into the upper floor room where they discovered Miranda lying sprawled face down along a sofa, its stuffing oozing through the seams. "Hey, girl-next-door, where were you last night?" Freshly showered, her clothes ironed, Miranda entered the kitchen and began unpacking two bags of shopping: someone turned on the record player and *Jumpin' Jack Flash* defiantly crescendoed. "Last night? Last night is already ancient history." A newsreel bulletin from 'Nam had Maxwell scribbling names and cross-referencing an Atlas ... *Dau Tieng/Thua Thien Province/Ashau Valley* ... while they huddled together around the small black-and-white television screen hungrily eating Miranda's cooking, her grilled figs with goat's cheese drizzled in a dressing, adorned with sugar and chives. Night and day they played *Born To Be Wild*, singing the chorus, their new battle song for the barricades, while during lulls when they slept, Miranda put on The Doors' *Hello, I Love You ... (Won't you tell me your name)*, mesmerized by the images of Huey gunships unloading bronze candy by the bucketful into the thick dark-green jungle between a trench line filled with barechested GIs. Everywhere across Paris the heroes and heroines of May would be basking in a summer evening's twilight.

Hot And Cool Generations. "Glass holds a metaphysical transparency which metaphors something profound." Christopher Featherstone realized she had glimpsed the reflection of his approach in the expanse of glass but had chosen to remain stationary. On display in the showroom was a muscular Triumph motorcycle, a piece of sculpture resonating with memories of a cooler decade, the fifties, whereas the choppers of the sixties, the Hueys, possessed more firepower, more mobility, took one to more dangerous places. "I saw you from the dormitory window, talking to Stephen. What do you talk about?" Miranda could effortlessly pre-fabricate movie scenes around his three-dimensional stencil there in spacetime. "He keeps asking me what decade I inhabit. And whether I'm renting the billboard space." Photographs of Miranda plastered across billboards hung from the sides of inner city buildings and were strategically placed along freeway routes to capture the audience of gridlocked commuters. "Listen to the radio, something is in the air this year. Listen to the music. You shrugged! It's not just me, we're all in danger." Amazingly perfumed, sweeter than sunset-glazed pomegranate juice, comparable with her mother, Miranda turned and glimpsed hands holding the curve of the Triumph's gas tank in an erotic embrace. "Hey, Johnny!" A curious Elvis look-a-like emerged from the showroom's depth-of-field towards the motorcycle's sculpture and fleetingly held Miranda's eyes through the glass.

Westwood Holdings Ltd. Legs abandoned to swaying motion, her skirt and blouse an arabesque of gratuitous symmetry from shoulder-to-calf, Calvin Westwood's secretary fluidly opened the door and gestured him inside. Westwood stood hunched over a putter and played his stroke. Now a more tightly strung bow, the secretary efficiently gathered up an intray from the desk and closed the door behind her, infinitely magnetic, shaping the sexual filings of Everyman's thoughts in beautiful patterns about her person. "Infidelity is inbuilt with its own logic of discovery, right, Featherstone? The romantic duets of the nineteenth-century read well off the pages of a novel, but the carnal sting, the lash of desire, induces hysteria in puritans, and as a successful businessman, well, the written word is too abstract. Ever thought of emptying the mirror of yourself for once and getting a real job?" *Who* then was blackmailing Westwood? Featherstone surveyed the *luxuria* motifs, visualizing the secretary's academic Ingres nude, her sleek columnar silhouette in the semi-darkness, hair swept-up by her hands, perhaps more tempted by the aroma of the coffee-and-cake on its tray on the desk than the taste of Westwood ululating with pleasure. "Perhaps, when I recover from the illness of this existential life."

Helena Steele. Clothed in the crimson flame of a vermilion blouse she might have been dipped in the tear-drop of Matisse's paintbrush loaded with the heart of a red rose but a worm quickened there with the pride of a Biblical serpent. Known to him as *la bande à Steele* at **LESBOS** Records her companions modelled a roundel's portraiture inset with her impersonation of Eve.

Bridget Lovegrove. Top of her Class, Business School Graduate, how could she unzip her DNA to Calvin Westwood's modern gunslinger of high finance, become a devotee of flagellation, or fellation? The aquamarine clarity of her eyes, fresh with the healthy glow of tropical lagoons, became increasingly veiled with the ambiguity of Baudelaire's verse filtered through Gustav Moreau's watercolors.

Samantha Westwood. She re-invented Woman's face emerging from the World-Egg, moved free with ever-deepening organ music rhymed to the Milky Way's iceberg floating in the Sea of the Cosmos, her sudden supernova so remote it could only now ignite the sky of his mind. Living in a cashed-up marriage, impossibly wealthy, she had Featherstone dreaming of existing inside a work of art hanging from a wall in her home where they could gaze at each other. And still, that *lost weekend* in '64, with the image of her abandoned dress draped across the bed left him breathless with desire.

"I Will Bring An Honorable End To The War In Vietnam". The moon's Persian slipper rested on a nocturnal eiderdown of cloud low in the sky above the battered shield of Saigon. Death's mask hid the lineaments of youth and bone china flesh brittle with fear of amputation. Visceral with the blood of GIs on her hands the exhausted nurse extended the radii of her fingers in which he placed a straight Scotch and listened to her thoughts. "The tank took a direct hit and he tried to scramble free, half-escaping, bloodied, fabric buried in his wounds, the medics worked on him for hours, then he was gone." Fabian Roxburgh stood by the window watching the cartoon presence of the Vietnamese flow by in perpetual motion bound by the frames of their existence beyond which evening's diamante trim glowed. "Here we are, Fabian, me waiting for you to come along, your kisses full of the end-of-time sensations. Don't you feel it too, we have run out of time?" Roxburgh observed her sprawl across the crumpled bed in her silk stockings and roused himself to observe: "We'll always have 'Nam."

Saigon, Full Of Labyrinthine Movement. Soaked, porous to fatality, Saigon accelerated in corruption and extravagance and Fabian Roxburgh realized the strategically unthinkable, the city was doomed and the screaming souls of the fallen were gathering at its precincts for a final assault. Electioneering Stateside was building in intensity and Richard M. Nixon, hardly a worthy opponent for Ho Chi Minh and General Giap any more than President Johnson, became the Republican candidate as *friendly fire* took its toll in the Ashau Valley, a true reading of the war's barometer. Sweeping through Saigon on a Honda with the nurse holding tight on the pillion, Roxburgh sidetracked logic, just keeping up that forward-moving momentum until the tropical sun iced over her hair with richer auburn mists. Chiselled prose distilling the imminent collapse of South Vietnam in his *Dispatches From 'Nam* was immediately spiked by his editor precipitating his angry recall from the Minoan maze of Saigon. Tear drops varnished the nurse's tanned cheeks as she stood beside him in the airport lounge. A nearby transistor radio blasted out The Rolling Stones' *Street Fighting Man* and both knew the boulevards of Saigon were preparing the banners to welcome a victorious North. President Thieu killed Roxburgh with his cornered acceptance of the Vietnamization program. "You know I'll never see you again." Only fools fall in love against a backdrop of war!

Running Scared. LESBOS Records folded under mysterious circumstances. Christopher Featherstone stepped across the threshold after breaking the lock and wandered through the empty spaces. From among the debris he picked up a photograph and dusted off the publicity shot of Helena Steele. What paramilitary thoughts were scaffolded in the cupola of her Amazonian head? Under the octopi of galaxies on a cold winter night he chanced to observe her commanding presence on the sidewalk outside Her Majesty's Theater for a performance of *Tannhauser*. The intoxicating *Venusberg* music, erotically centripetal, asserted its supremacy over the *Pilgrim's Chorus*, but Featherstone's opera glasses searched the audience for Helena, remembering his trial in her nightingale bedroom and her bacchanale of clothes seducing him from himself. Swept up by the crowd in the crush of the exit they brushed against each other. "Too bad about **LESBOS** Records." Which ratios of the Zodiacal Egg held the dimensions of her embodiment in spacetime? She slowly detached her torso from the crowd, a dissociation as vivid as one of Gustav Moreau's feminine encrustations among a collection of Sargent socialites. After spending some time in a bar ruminating over this chance operatic encounter he approached the car park, fumbling for his keys in his tuxedo, stumbling to his knee on an uneven paving slab, then was luckily thrown hard but safely against the fender of an adjacent vehicle by the explosion.

Astral Shells. Flashing ambulance lights pulsed across the surface of the pavement where Christopher Featherstone's crumpled photograph of Helena Steele had fallen. Haulage chained the wreckage of his car to a trailer for forensic investigation. Half upright on a trolley he was slid inside the ambulance. Ears deafened by the blast he nevertheless heard the *Pilgrim's Chorus*, its caressing musicality, as the ambulance accelerated for the hospital, and thought of the divinity of the soul, how the astral shells of humanity were foreign incrustations deforming its Primal Beauty. Wheeled through Casualty nurses and doctors quickly examined the crust of his sensorial physique, that already tainted fragment, perverse with uncleanliness, abandoned to every discordant impulse, and were satisfied the *shell* was sound. Elizabeth, his Socratic iconography of a disappointed wife, arrived breathing shallowly and he realized the doctors had examined his wallet, calling her in to his side, but the Police pressed to interview him. The hospital's whitewashed inner façade and its homage to geometry, all clarity and stringent proofs, conjured an astral vision overlaid with outlined angels wandering the precincts of a physical reality, nursing a sick humanity. Elizabeth's décolletage, endlessly explored curvatures modelled after the movie goddesses of the fifties, held no currency now in the grittier sixties and the back-to-nature squalor of communal love-ins, where statuesque-on-a-pedestal classicism out of Ingres deferred to an earthier pose. Her voice faded across a horizon of *goodbyes* as Featherstone's thoughts succumbed to the swelling waves of *Tannhauser's* lushly orchestrated *Venusberg* music.

Parallels. Embodying purity, the light of a full moon, nurses busied themselves in the ward with a rhetoric of hand gestures and moving tableaux consistent with theater, were precise sundials, had the motion of timepieces, all of which entertained Christopher Featherstone. Squared in the geometric frame of the entrance he recognized the broad country-girl shoulders of Bridget Lovegrove and the operatic splash of her Titian-hair, a volcanic spillage contrasting the nurses clothed like angels in crosses of pure white flame. "Christopher – no blemishes! Elizabeth phoned me this morning." An indelible watermark of a welcoming kiss, invisible perhaps but felt, surfaced as prose on the page of his face, giving her pause. "You are well?" Featherstone mentioned the Police confirming earlier that Helena's alibi seemed watertight and they were pursuing their forensic investigation. Bridget's wide-ranging research, bringing half-the-story up to date, concerned a parallel she had discovered with a Baader-Meinhof group in Europe, and thought the themes of their activities might be intertwined, for Helena had spent periods with clandestine gangs in Ireland and Germany until recently. When a doctor visited and cast the eye of his surgical mind over him, Featherstone answered his questions with a wry humour: "Well, doctor, crowned with blindness I see only light." He spoke too of the surgeon's Masonic tools rebuilding the Temple of Man. When asked about the explosion he offhandedly shrugged that Helena Steele was most likely attempting to illuminate an Idea for him, bring to his understanding existence was modelled on an ethical relativity. Discharged from the hospital he carefully orchestrated the taxi ride back through the city and on a convoluted route finishing at the marina to ensure Helena was not following. Standing on the quay he observed Samantha Westwood emerge from the state room of the schooner.

Postcards From Prague I. Cream's double-album, *Wheels of Fire*, opened up the soundscape of the campus dormitory, Rock music's amplification rolling across the globe from the windows of the consciousness of youth. Leader of the paramilitary students, Stephen Maxwell strapped a headband around his shoulder-length hair and welcomed his Gang of Five inside as *Spoonful's* Faberge guitar creations decorated space, dissolving into the aromas of Miranda's cooking. All over the news bulletins were images of the Soviet conquerors riding triumphantly into Prague underscored by the pulsing arabesques of Clapton's feminine-toned and conversational guitar and Bruce's improvisatory bass exuding a self-contained sensuality. Prague's Summer of Love suddenly chilled as the citizens awoke to find columns of Soviet tanks crowding the city streets. Miranda's Mod Squad sensibility burned on in *Wheels of Fire* as she turned away from the television and stared through the dormitory window at the gentle flow of traffic by the University. Maxwell's voice zealously focused the Gang of Five on the Cold War tableau framed within the television screen. "Look, Dubček, your August moon ideas of socialism in the sixties are one thing, what happens to Czechoslovakia is something else altogether. Your blasé intelligentsia has been asleep to political reality in the swinging sixties. It would be hypocrisy to celebrate the invasion of South Vietnam by the North and now condemn the invasion of Czechoslovakia by Russia."

Postcards From Prague II. "The shell of socialism cracks wide open and we have re-birth of revolutionary fervor, the euphoria of anarchy. There are no stop lights in Prague for Soviet traffic!" Brezhnev barely yawned through his summer holidays, thoroughly enjoying this contemporary twist on the October Revolution, especially as Western radicals everywhere were scrawling **YES, TO SOVIETS ... NO, TO CZECHS** across campuses, and Underground newspapers were giving the kiss-off to *The Czech Road To Socialism*, and describing Czechoslovakia as a dead word in any language. "The Western Democracies are disintegrating so this is no time for capitalist sentimentality." Bonfires of conservative publications were held on campuses and banners raised high with Brezhnev's pompous epiphany in the face of Western condemnation of the invasion.

Postcards From Prague III. Teased for her ingratiating millionairess prettiness, Miranda slipped a wide belt through the loops of her jeans and adjusted the brass buckle and watched the caricatured faces of socialism mourn their blood-stained Czech flag, while the Gang of Five enjoyed the images of Dubček's party gate-crashed by 500,000 Warsaw Pact troops. Someone produced a scent bottle labeled **PRAGUE** to intimate Dubček's appalling revisionism, the stench of his imperialism offending

Brezhnev's inanimate bust suited up for the cameras. Miranda subsumed herself in the extraordinary innovation of *Wheels of Fire* as the shadows advanced with apocalyptic irresistibility across Prague, where there was no kissing of flowers in the barrels of Soviet tanks and the air-waves closed down. She read an article somewhere headed: **GLOBAL VILLAGE CANNABILIZED!** and thought she recognized in the anti-Marxist tone Fabian Roxburgh's handwriting.

A Soul More Ancient Than The Acropolis. Late-winter almond petals frosted over a pool of rainwater dammed against the curb of the street frontage outside Bridget Lovegrove's suburban home. A lion's mane of cloud, more coppery-red like Bridget's, flowed out of the rising sun as she reversed the car down the driveway and splashed through the pool of rainwater. "Christopher – this woman is dangerous." Yesterday he had glimpsed her in the city meeting Calvin Westwood, her white umbrella lustered after the membrane of a full moon. Rented billboard space carried Helena Steele's portrait: **HAVE YOU SEEN THIS WOMAN?** As they cruised by them on the route into the city they observed some prankster had pasted over massive posters of Elvis' face morphed into Mao's, eerie images fusing the initiators of populist Cultural Revolutions in their Time. "Yes, she's determined to fade me out." Together with the Senior Police Detective they examined the wreckage of his impounded car and the forensic report, so much detritus moraine now in the space of his glacial existence. Thumbing through one of her travel magazines in her car, where the calligraphy of her handwriting embellished the glossy page, he paused at the profound draughtsmanship of the Parthenon, a holiday destination perhaps memorialized by her soul. "Why did that Police Officer refer to you as James Bond?"

Ulysses Leaves Once More Calypso For His Native Shore. Lazily grinning through their beards the sit-around hippie companions welcomed Fabian Roxburgh as low-slung sunlight ebbed from the apartment. Steeped in the symbolism of the high-sixties they trailed Cream's *Sunshine Of Your Love* from apartment to apartment in the complex seemingly oblivious to the withering of Prague's *Spring of Socialist Enchantment*. Miranda's fingertips breathing pungent basil were absent from the cooking of dinner, improvised cauliflower-and-cheese, while the eating mimetized a kind of socialist cannibalism backdropped with the burning intensity of Cream's *Wheels of Fire* album. Roxburgh crashed on a sofa and dreamed of the Grunts dying in 'Nam. Friends collected him in the midnight-blue street-rod before dawn's expressionist skyscape defined the surf breaking offshore at the beach, only the waves were audible as they waxed down the Malibus. Chilled by the undulating crest of a wave's lip disintegrating and flowing across his torso, Roxburgh shivered his way out to the lineup of shadowy silhouettes. Wave spray flew from an immense coiffure of whitewater and crystallized across his torso as ice. Fleur's purificatory oils of myrrh and her sweeter odors had him sinking into a perfumed silk cloudiness of thought. After sunrise, with the sky touched by a Mont Blanc of cloud, while arcing his Malibu through a broad calligraphic sweep he recognized again the familiar figure from the airport, curious why his attractive companion was photographing him with a telephoto lens. His thoughts' fluid congealed as the quicksilver wave collapsed, beaching him on the foreshore.

Album Cover. "The soul walks a labyrinth of mirrors, surrounded by the reflections of myriad incarnations, all of which make up a composite portrait hung in the gallery of spacetime." Christopher Featherstone stood with Bridget on the foreshore as she photographed Roxburgh's twisting draughtsmanship across the entablature of waves. Soothed by the front-facing tranquility of Roxburgh modelled against the planar colors of wave-and-whitewater Featherstone followed the axis of his reflection while remembering album covers from '64: Time's distance had swept such sunburst scenes from them. "If we reflect on this whitewater here, all space is essentially explosive, from supernovæ to the sub-atomic world." Bridget cupped the camera's telephoto lens in the palm of her hand, her hair's elusive curves momentarily clouding space. "Christopher – you still haven't told me why he called you James Bond." Why was Time's distribution linear, why couldn't he leap back in years, or Bridget leap forward, what exultation of freedom that would bring! "Seeing your movie star beauty contrasted with my film noir shadow inspired him to hyperbole. The compliment was for you, Bridget." Flooded with an impenetrable indigo of thinking he allowed her silence to illuminate his emotional space and observed the ever-replenishing waves sculpted with arabesques modelled from the Parthenon surge forth.

Chicago! Caged on campus, derailed by a lull in student activism, television screens everywhere ignited with tensions surrounding the upcoming Democratic Convention, Stephen Maxwell considered the falling away of commentary between Miranda Westwood and himself. Cream's *Crossroads* perhaps indicated an emblematic *way* to Chicago if her journalist friend could be persuaded to buy plane tickets. With her retrogressive, geometric hair-bob, no longer fashionable, her blood-red mouth of late, Miranda imaged ambiguous moods, her glances straws of ice piercing his monologues before she melted away into the night. "Che walked for us the way, Ho Chi Minh shows us where to begin, our Time is *Now*!" The rococo sermonizing of Hubert Humphrey overlaid youth's frustration with authority while the iconic Mayor of Chicago inspired explosive anger, alarm and anxiety. Increasing friction rubbed the generations and their hatred of each other while fathers who had fought in World War II grieved over society's disintegration. Chicago unloosed a Medusa of politicians across the frieze of a city resembling more and more the twilight of Hades. The gaiety and otherworldliness, the ephemeral butterfly of '67's Summer of Love flickered in Grant Park, faded to the grey of their television screen as they sat watching the evening bulletins eating Miranda's pasta dressed in her homemade sauce. "Speeches are just museum pieces, man, dinosaurs of political expediency." On the mirror scrawled over in Miranda's blood-red lipstick was the phrase: *Meadows of the Mekong Delta mown by Death (Fabian Roxburgh).*

Are We Made Of The Right Stuff? Fabian Roxburgh leaned against the midnight-blue street-rod looking at the stranger's companion with her ever-ready camera. Were they responsible for his obituary? Photographs of a tall Amazonian woman, her torso's verticality favoring red T-shirts, genii of flame, her gaze and bearing touched by the world's sharp-edged absurdity, lay spread on the bonnet for him to study. "You say this exiled Amazon is scripting symbolic deaths for us? We live in a new age of martyrs, if the photographic frame of the world's magazines holds any truth. My own obituary has already been published, so are we made of *The Right Stuff*, that is the question to ask ourselves? See the dye washing through those clouds there, we have a tumultuous night ahead. Shoulder-to-shoulder with the Grunts in 'Nam I know life is proportionate to death's depth." Roxburgh drifted among the moustaches, headbands and badges asking after Fleur and her sister but their vague presences had assumed the substantiality now of mere ghosts, so he settled in to watch the evening news bulletins as images of the Chicago Democratic Convention became the lead item. Bearded, long-haired casualties from anti-Vietnam demonstrations, naked children frolicking in the Park, the relentless intensity of MC5 dismantling America's creaking patriotism, these were the Chicagoans descending into the twilight of Hades.

Pandemonium. Out of a fog of tear gas emerged a swirling vortex of youthful shades on the shoal of the Styx. From the axis of the hotel a vast equator of youth was assaulted by the Roman Legions of the Chicago Police Department, shields, guns, water cannon, tear gas and dogs being the arsenal arrayed against the music of MC5, long-hair and beards. Television relayed the images across the globe, of survivors stumbling hopelessly from the spray of water cannon, sustaining the blows of truncheons from leather-booted and capped Police officers, the sons and daughters of America's World War II heroes being crushed by Law and Order corseted in riot gear. "Man, will anyone get of there alive?" Where was Vice-President Humphrey, pro-peace advocate Eugene McCarthy, aspirants to the leadership of America? The television scenes proved to be an electrifying generational cataclysm from which the Yippies manoeuvred to be the moment's defining martyrs. Stephen Maxwell's Gang of Five stormed across the University campus: "We will never submit, we will never yield, we will deliver the blow!" Hubert Humphrey rose from the ashes of Chicago to oppose Richard M. Nixon but for youth Che had stamped himself in their minds as well as on their T-shirts. Summer ended with the aura of 'Nam suffocating the Spirit of America and now paralleled by the brutal Police assaults on the youth gathered in Chicago.

War Must Be For The Sake Of Peace (Aristotle). Fleur cooking eggs in the tenement apartment, Cream's extended version of *Spoonful* playing loudly, the repose of her contours, her strange merging of space with the soundtrack of Time's successive moments, disarmed Christopher Featherstone as Fabian Roxburgh ushered him inside. A tender-faced flower child supinely dozed on a sofa, the crossover of her sari skirt adrift revealing her limbs arranged like the runes of a Zen garden. "Cruising the highways of 'Nam death becomes profoundly affecting, I become less numb to its mystery, if you can understand that. Death turns existence inside out, like shell fragments tearing through the body exposing our inner contents. You have the face of Delacroix visiting the inner sanctum of a harem!" Featherstone listened, sensing Roxburgh was cutting himself out of a pattern and placing himself against the collage of a new existence whose background might resemble a Segal tableau, although he noticed in the fractured wall mirror their heads resembled Dante and Virgil. "Miranda reads the Personals – I'll compose a message. She's been my day dream of late-winter almond blossom you see blowing everywhere, the fruit is yet to come."

Towards The Spring Equinox. From the arms of a thousand almond trees blossom floated away like petals issuing from the aura of the Buddha. Space clouded over with the grace of a spiritual striptease. Stephen Maxwell suspiciously eyed Fabian Roxburgh's aviator sunglasses and didn't appreciate the latter's banter: "Have you heard Brezhnev's Czech joke? ... *Dubček!*" Maxwell snapped back a response: he hadn't seen Miranda Westwood since the day the tanks rolled into Prague. Youth evaporated so quickly as the human incarnation descended ever more swiftly into the twisting center of an Inferno. Featherstone noticed how youth's sub-cultures were already shadow-boxing with each other and pondered their interbreeding – who would be the offspring of the Gang of Five and Fleur and her flower child sister for example? Clasped in space of the womb the pearl matures to adorn the world. Seeking solace aboard the schooner Featherstone confronted the dragons undulating with the violin and cello lines in Beethoven's late String Quartets.

VII
CONTRAPPOSTO

As I Went Out One Morning. Haunted, haunting, the wispy flower child lay curled up asleep in the crèche of the midnight-blue street-rod, to Fabian Roxburgh's mind dreaming herself through these latter-days of the sixties. Turning to Christopher Featherstone climbing in the front seat beside him, he said: "Who's your friend then in the horn-rimmed glasses?" Under a watercolor early morning sky threatening a spring thunderstorm, Bridget Lovegrove's bourgeois bodhisattva waved them off with a lyrical reverie in her expression, the plasticene flower child unseen by her. "My accountant." Crawling along the street toward Helena Steele's hacienda apartment the street-rod was absorbed in the metaphysical fresco of a curtain of rain through which sunlight softly filtered and paused within an observable distance of the exit to the property. Featherstone noticed a buckled vinyl album, *John Wesley Harding*, melted by the sun lying on the rear seat under the flower child's knees. "Dylan's new music is too watery, a little frigid, like your accountant?" Soon the linear emergence of the Venetian-red delinquent from the hacienda, Helena Steele, a little opaque and distanced but the geometry of her stride clearly inebriated on discontent, focused their attention. "Featherstone ... look at her number plate!" A triple-six evoked a stimulus of biblical allusions as her car reversed into the roadway and accelerated away.

Drifter's Escape. Jolted awake as the street-rod swerved through traffic on the freeway in pursuit of Helena Steele vanishing inside a heavy shower of rain, the flower child unrolled the poster of her presence in a wash of Indian body oils and sat gazing through the windshield. Speeding up, Roxburgh allowed the street-rod to flow with abandon through the sprays of rainwater, searching for her profile recessed under the frieze of car hoods, while the flower child sprawled forward to turn on the radio and *I've Gotta Get A Message To You* burst from the speakers. "So, Featherstone, your accountant then, is she qualified in double-entry bookkeeping ... Heaven-and-Hell? Which side of the ledger do you occupy?" Passing the grisaille curves of cars spraying water from the roadway they climbed into a stave of music for a rollercoaster duet with

Helena Steele's vehicle as its silhouette emerged through the rain's impressionism. Featherstone breathed in the body oils oozing through the cheesecloth molded to the flower child's Art Nouveau sinuosity leaning across the front seat. "What do you say, Featherstone, this linear motion, friction ... or fiction? I'm having the same dream every night since returning from 'Nam. A Luciferan helicopter throbbing low, casting ideograms of ominous shadow across the quietude of suburbia, shattering the profound stillness." Quickly glancing at the flower child, noticing Featherstone's flared nostrils, he added: "Her sister is a full blush of magnolia blossom. From what you tell me, this Helena Steele woman is poison ivy." Side-by-side in vibrant horizontality as sunlight melted through cloud both cars maintained a sizzling velocity. Featherstone finally spoke, but in *non sequitir*: "Can you see her with a pair of knitting needles?" Sensing the allusion's seriousness, Roxburgh cocked a thumb-and-forefinger in a juvenile gesture at Helena Steele's profile and expressively blew across his smoking fingertip. "You mean, watching us mount the guillotine?" Misty red lights flashed ahead on the freeway's stave lines in an atonal wash. Tyres skidded and cars moon-danced across slippery roadway like particles colliding in a linear accelerator; a quantum moment of twentieth-century concrete poetry.

Compositional Stasis. "Whaam!" Bleeding, vomiting, Helena Steele stumbled from the smoking wreckage of her car crumpled against the pillar of a pedestrian walkover, her encrypted silhouette describing an abstract ballet before collapsing on the asphalt. Fabian Roxburgh's Tennessee Williams' anti-hero gunned the motor of the midnight-blue street-rod but eased off the accelerator as the flower child swung open the car door and glided over to Helena Steele's motionless sculpture half-sprawled across the verge. "I'll order a dozen red roses for her funeral in the rain." Contingency and fatality had metaphysically criss-crossed on the grid of three-dimensional spacetime, the insertion of the massive pylon through the plane of the freeway, its compositional stasis, proving a magnetic axis spinning Helena Steele from the orbit of their lives. Christopher Featherstone postulated his own compositional stasis within the melodrama played out that morning, thoughts of his estranged wife, Elizabeth, his *lost weekend* with Samantha Westwood, his existential séance with the psychic, Helena Steele, filling the intervals of time as they traveled in the street-rod. "Can honor or dishonor be weighed or measured, Featherstone, to determine which is the greater and which the lesser?"

A Folio Of Memories. "Are you still a Zen stone, or light as a feather?" Spring sunlight illumined Celeste Hawthorne's studio attic as Christopher Featherstone wandered among her folio of memories. "Still looking for Eurydice?" While a black-and-white television screen carried images of 'Nam via the news bulletin she shuffled through her stack of 45s and chose *Harper Valley PTA*, then served tea in her favored bone china cups, the illustrator's intensity behind her eyes undressing him for translation onto paper. Featherstone paused before an oil study of Helena Steele, nude, recumbent, broad-shouldered, her pubis rendered with the finesse of quasi-bonsai. "Eurydice? Elizabeth and I sexually centrifuged like cream from milk." Celeste stirred a whirlpool of chalk on paper, her lips physiologically precious, existentially French as she sketched his arousal: chalk clung to his naked loins as he realized she had provocatively framed herself before the Helena Steele portrait to sketch him.

Chalk's Quantum Foam Agitation. Beside Celeste's box of colored chalks Fabian Roxburgh noticed a cut-out of his obituary stapled to the cover of Mao's little red book. "Are you the world's most beautiful illustrator then?" He remembered Featherstone explaining she was employed on occasion by the Police to provide sketches as he encountered her nude portraits of Helena Steele and the Private Eye placed in a diptych, surely a calculus of failed sexuality despite the yin and yang eroticism of their respective arousals. "You've brought something of her fractured psyche into expression here. This morning she became a stretchered casualty when her car collided with a pylon on the freeway. She wants the world emptied of us – has she seen this portrait?" Leaving the studio Roxburgh ambled into a bookstore and scanned the shelves, browsing a selection of titles from John Clellon Holmes, Nelson Algren and Norman Mailer, thinking over Celeste's comment about Featherstone: "His odyssey takes him far from this lonely island." Voices roused him from this reverie and from the raised mask of the book he was holding he recognized Miranda accompanied by her student radical friend enter the bookstore. Carefully avoiding them by transposing aisles he observed their choices, Miranda selected *Franny and Zooey*, her friend flipped through *The Naked Lunch*. Roxburgh lamented in this scene how the frieze of reconciliation was crumbling, how the chalk outlines of their naked torsos had never agitated the white sheet of a bed's canvas together.

Contrapposto I. *In Search Of The Lost Chord*: Fabian Roxburgh visited the car wreckage impounded by Police forensics and was directed to a cardboard box in which was a stack of 45s with their fiery pink **LESBOS** label carrying a name in bold black: **HELENA STEELE**. Sifting through he selected a number of copies and carried them with him, the camber of his journey shaping a passage to the city hospital where he stood in a sterile corridor framed by the swinging doors' window leading into her ward. A gleaming wheelchair stood parked beside her bed, on which she lay as if entombed with the clinical silence of a mannequin, white plaster stretched above an eyebrow, her hair bound in a turban of bandages. For a moment he stood gazing through the slatted window banded by sunlight and shadow, then was roused by a familiar voice: "Fabian, who was it said: We are where we only imagine we are?" Christopher Featherstone noticed the 45s held in Roxburgh's hand. "Her voice's poison ivy is lipsticked into every groove of those 45s. Beware, she's an odalisque of Lilith." Featherstone raised a corner of the bedsheet so her foot extended free, each toenail ablaze in pillar-box red. "Yes, I agree, lying here she radiates an illusion of sugar frosting coating innocence. This woman is as two-dimensional as a sheet of paper – no sides, just back-and-front." Roxburgh controlled an impulse to touch her flesh colored like creamy mayonnaise but instead turned to move from the metaphysical space of the hospital rendered opaque with its existentialism.

Contrapposto II. *Do It Again*: The *papillon* wings of the flower child's sari and cheesecloth blouse dissolved in the sunlight sweeping the beach. Monet's impressionism of white-crested waves dancing on the walls of the Louvre paled before the sensual bolero of the surf's petticoats of whitewater undulating offshore. Nostalgia crystallized and melted with the warmth of the sun as Fabian Roxburgh paddled into a wave's soft tumescence and languidly played his surfboard through sweeping arcs as if he were a sculptor commissioned to render a Faun in marble. Standing on the beach the flower child fingered a mollusk, perhaps sensing her own soul's soft presence inside the encrustation of her physique's exterior, a tender echo barely audible above the world's crashing waves. Pressing his own feet into the sand, Roxburgh considered an analogy, how his own thoughts and feelings formed a smooth crust over a very soiled existence, the surface easily disturbed and broken so the world's imprint showed through. Then the lip of a wave spread for a respiratory kiss and the flower child's illusion vanished in thin air.

Contrapposto III. *Magic Bus*: Evening's kohl-blackened skyline lit up with the Technicolor drive-in movie screen on which was condensed some of Hollywood's more handsomely grained flesh. Fabian Roxburgh's hand cupped the underside of Fleur's bellied-out breast while her own fingers unzipped his trousers: she was sexually organic, he more a constructionist. The moon tenderly beamed through some off-screen foliage: the movie was *The Thomas Crown Affair*. Fleur defied being corseted in whalebone, her inner loins under his fingers more like the fluffed up petals of a wild rose, her orgasm a feathered dove flying across fluvial, stippled grass, but afterwards kissing her deeply he could not help but consider the metaphysics of sex all thinking and imagining. Spread like a languid nymph among spring flowers she contrasted Helena Steele blindingly luminous limned under a marble bedsheet as if awaiting rebirth from the cocoon. When they returned to the apartment block a party was still in full decline, the air heavier with aromatic intoxicants which subdued rather than excited, *The Who – Sellout* on the turntable, the flower child listlessly turning a prayer wheel, acquiescing to Astrology's soul-map.

Contrapposto IV. *I Am A Lonesome Hobo*: Miranda in her plumed, broad-brimmed Musketeer's hat-with-scarf, short-skirted in knee-high boots, flirted outside a motorcycle outlet with an Elvis look-a-like in a psychedelic-patterned shirt: a name, *Johnny*, carried to Fabian Roxburgh's ear. Miranda's aura of absence during this time when spring was healing the earth with luscious meadows of wild flowers kept turning him inside out like a glove. Elvis' iconoclastic decline, his vanishing like Orpheus, like Apollo, space's emptying of his singing presence, co-incided with the escalation of the conflict in 'Nam, as if the fallen Archangel seized the moment to destabilize humanity's recovery from World War II. Miranda's Marxist hanger-on, now growing a beard, appeared on the scene and words strident with jealousy were exchanged. Together they drifted into their favorite bookstore and Roxburgh experienced the sensation of his heart being slowly brushed along a cheese grater. Following them to the University dormitory he took out a drawing pin and fixed a copy of his obituary to the door, curiously observed by milling students, to whom he shrugged: *"Live A Little, Love A Little."*

Contrapposto V. *Down Along The Cove*: Bridget Lovegrove's fleet-footed choreography on the tennis court, her motion's aphrodisiac, sculpted in Grecian whites, the scent of her perspiring skin fragranced like an abstract painting, emblemized an angel suspended in space. All cool jade, lovely sounds vibrated space when ball-and-racquet were struck, as she pivoted a swishing backhand, stretched and balanced a forehand volley. Christopher Featherstone said to her one evening as she sat bare-shouldered contemplating volumes of accounting journals: "You should take off your glasses and be seen, everywhere." She returned him a glance evanescing with the purity of blowing almond blossom.

Catherine Deneuve: Chalked As Pure As Leonardo's St. Anne Cartoon. A cloud of pink-and-grey galahs swept across the surreal blue sky rendering its tissues of spatiality and rupturing the linear motion of the car traveling the straight arrow of roadway. Wildflowers and foliage loaded with spring carpeted the earth as the baroque fluidity of the car reached deeper into the Arcadian desert. "Who is in your fantasies these days?" Christopher Featherstone listened to the question but his sightline remained fixed on the vanishing point of the roadway and the horizon towards which they were traveling. The intelligence silhouetted in his ex-wife's profile behind the wheel held for him now a sparse interior comparable with the mindscape of this Australian geography, ruthlessly self-fixated, terraced with *nowhere's* insularity, a juxtaposition of illusions held by the frame of the windshield. On the car radio *The Pléiades* performed another of his power-driven compositions featuring electric organ:

> This trail of infidelity and the pain of its memory
> Leads me on into the night when once my days were so bright.
> We went to the Opera and saw *La Traviata*
> And I wondered how we once rocked each other in the cradle of our heart.

Illumined archaeology took shape and runes of etched glass dazzled from the façade of the Monastery. "Christopher – why were you murmuring the name, *Catherine*? Whenever your mind wanders into the escort agency of Imagination I feel alone, abandoned." With musical bees harmonizing about the trumpet bell of flowers Featherstone heard Christian harps vibrating with faith, the breeze wafting in from the ocean carrying the resonance of a Crucifixion to a burnt-out Hades of a land seemingly universes away from the original drama.

Delphine Seyrig: In Her Heart's Abandoned Garden A Pale Rose Blows. The soft vertebra of sand dunes flowed away from the ecclesiastical splendor of the Monastery. Benedictine monks faintly choired Berlioz's *Agnus Dei* as Christopher

Featherstone stood on the crest of a dune observing the opaque sun layered on the aquamarine chemistry of the ocean and the perfume of spring wildflowers diffused on the offshore breeze. The majesty of the Sun God's distance, esoterically, had him yearning to transcend his own physique as he wandered this deserted garden of a world unable to grieve for the beautiful roses dying everyday. Walking the terraces of dunes, their illusory archipelago of islands colored ice-blue shading to grey, he contemplated the sexual and emotional impastos of his own presence, his own aesthetic immersion in the weave of canvas which was three-dimensional incarnation, and lamented how his conversations with Elizabeth were no more than stains on a linen of silence, like perspiration. The roses blowing in the Monastery garden would endlessly prolong these memories.

Jean Seberg: Her Martyr's Hairstyle Encoded A Remembrance Of Joan Of Arc. The sky's vault of black crystal inset with the Milky Way's studded loin belt, slung low, and luminous with the rotund moon, muted the luster of the sculpted sand dunes as Christopher Featherstone pondered the esoteric significance of the proposed moon landing. Galaxies pulsed, electromagnetic thoughts in the cranium of God, strangely unsensed by the Benedictine monks, signals arrayed across the sky to be read and interpreted: the spectacular reach of Einstein palpitated his heart just as moments watching the actress Jean Seberg left him *breathless*. Later, by traditional candlelight, he perused the crumpled pages of a Bible and composed a song with an opening line ... *Though I walk in the shadow of the valley of death*.

Virna Lisi: Her Face Evoked The Cool, Ethereal Dew of Moonbeams. Against the monochrome stone geometry of the Monastery's façade a flight of birds juxtaposed pink with emerald and chrome-yellow, and from the bakery drifted aromas of wood-fired nut-cake. Moving through the metaphysical quietude, the empty intervals between the luminously uniform sand dunes, Christopher Featherstone considered the celestial architecture of the sky, how thought is but smoke to the fire within Cosmic Mind, a discoloration. This monumental mindscape had him conjuring up Virna Lisi's allegorical arabesques from the dunes' supple lines of recumbent energy, eroticism's fever chalked over the canvas with her ever-cool presence until the mystery of infidelity's faithlessness collapsed these reflections. Somewhere far-off the throb of a helicopter emerged from the profound silence enveloping the dunes. Walking back through the Monastery garden he paused before the skull of a deep red rose and pondered what thoughts dwelled inside its elemental presence. Lucid illusions filled the sight-line of geometric space, none more alluring than the conjuration of the actress Virna Lisi washing his soul in the mystery of infidelity, pure as watercolor dripping from the brush of his thoughts. A helicopter hovered against the tangible softness of some ornamental clouds.

Monica Vitti: A Lonesome Visionary Enclosed In The World's Shuttered Chamber. Perhaps the ever-present helicopter descending and ascending across the sand dunes modelled the space capsule designed to accomplish the future moon landing. Christopher Featherstone sliced up the spatial unity of the three-dimensional frame with a purpose to edit and reassemble these *mise-en-scènes* lensed by God. One morning a distant dancer-of-the-dunes appeared in quicksilver illusion, illumined by instreaming sunlight, a strange portent from the helicopter whose damascene blades fanned undulating whirlpools of sand about her presence. More troubling though was the hornèd shadow of the helicopter materializing from the azure flank of the sky's silken flank. Featherstone waited for the spiritual light passing through the sky's delicate crystal to transform into twilit shadow before returning to the Monastery. In his dreams Monica Vitti's attractively enameled face offered him the solace of her acting's sigh of compassion, always reflection-in-solitude, existential withdrawal, filtered through an intense radiation of immobility.

Mireille Mathieu: In Her Eyes Dwelled The Luminous Haze Of A Million Candles. Strolling the arcades of the Monastery, Christopher Featherstone imagined he wore the sacred hem of Rameses' fabulous purple robe swishing desert stone, bathed in the softened splendor of white décor of moon and lily while around him odorous incense ascended in offering from Earth to God. Of late the French chanteuse's glorious mouth vibrated his soundscape as often as the Beethoven String Quartets.

Visitation. Anchored offshore one morning, glimpsed with an elegiac thrill by Christopher Featherstone as he emerged from the planar modulation of sand dunes, the Westwood's yacht floated on a calm aquamarine sea, while prints of the belovèd's feet retreated along the shoreline. "Have you been waiting for me to come sailing by?" Samantha Westwood's amorous pulp of mouth, lyrical with these words, suddenly softening into intimacy with the question, established a sexual tremolo reaching far back into Time when Beauty was first molded from sin. Space's diaphanous textile, a gauzy fabric, linen flecked with pure golden thread, held her sublimely mature caryatid in erotic folds of cloth on the crest of a monochromatic sand dune. "With a kind of spiritual vertigo – I can't look up to Heaven, or down to Hell." Listening to his reply her hair's ambrosial plume swayed in the aqueous radiant warmth, her person metamorphosed from the corridors of the Plaza that *lost weekend*, as if she had conquered forgetfulness, then she said: "We should be two of the smart people, Christopher. We have reached and passed the *noir* moment for us – ageing." Dining on sautéed fillets of fish that evening together in the yacht's stateroom with sunset's amber luminescence burnishing the windows, Samantha all classical distinction, martini-in-hand, Featherstone pondered afresh their pose's passivity, twin sculptures corroded by Time.

A Glowing Alchemy Of Imagery. "Is this your inner desert?" Samantha's question, delivered amid the jellied glow of sand dunes, with moonrise dramatizing the absurdity of Creation, blended with the olfactory pleasures of her presence. A perfume aureoled her still-memorable beauty, illuminated her presence's decorative effect beneath the imperfect sphere of the moon forming the yolk of the Milky Way galaxy. Upon the thread of a necklace encircling her throat lay a succession of pearls: he illustrated for her a concept of Time running through a sequence of moments, all experience absorbed by the precious jewels, how past, present and future were then interchangeable. With the tension of his nostrils, the shape of his nose reveling in the long-held echo of her fragrance from that *lost weekend*, he told her: "Think of our strands of embodiments from which our souls weave the mesh of a tapestry, forming an adornment comparable with your pearl necklace." Samantha's contralto languor rarefied her accessibility so Featherstone inwardly washed his thoughts with memories, how on that *lost weekend* her abandoned dress draped across the hotel bed rendered him breathless with desire for her, how in the psychoanalysis of that time he was unrepentantly Freudian: sexual piety shaped his faith. During their sexual embraces astral feelings surged with the power of galaxies deep in the space of the star-sown sky. "Samantha, both of us have died a million times and still the tangled tresses of the Milky Way's hair have not been unfolded by the cosmic breezes."

Moonbeams Burned Up The Stained Glass. "This is my stone façade, my antiquated conception of myself." Ushered by Christopher Featherstone into the depth of the Monastery's sarcophagus, Samantha beheld the altarpiece, a *Coronation of the Virgin*, about which aromatic smoke from censers thickened. Standing back a little, his palate spiced with the aftertaste of existence, allowing Samantha's synthesis with the ambience, Featherstone witnessed how her torso's presence formed a seal in space: open the envelope and the fragrance of the soul would be released. "Christopher, only fools fall in love."

Party Time. A converted waterfront warehouse mounted the Underground Exhibition presided over by the local High Priests of Hippiedom. Someone had booked a print of Warhol's *Chelsea Girls* and it was screening in the basement. Décor *extras*, commune hippies and student radicals, ambled with bohemian insolence through the maze-like gallery space in search of catharsis. Hendrix's massive *Electric Ladyland* canvas musically sprawled through all spatial volumes, the student radicals' defoliant flushing out reactionary critics and curious bourgeois visitors to the exhibition. Television's universal presence bracketed to the four corners of the main display room relayed cyclic transmissions from 'Nam, shadowy images intersecting with the acrylic white walls festooned with rainbowing colors, against which moved silhouettes in kaftans and leis of lotus blossoms, and the more abrasive denim fabric of revolutionary thought. Whispers that the figure of Kerouac, declaiming poetry over the rim of his whisky glass, and bearing his abstract expressionist gaze towards *satori*, was circulating lost in the maze of exhibits, galvanized the High Priests from their hippie throne adorned with the era's paraphernalia to search for him. Others smoked and stared blankly at the mounted exhibits as if desirous of translating themselves into the interstice between the *possible* and the *impossible*. Crowds sluiced through the maze and then began thinning towards evening. Word-of-mouth spread the password: Happening! Accompanied by a divertimento of sitar-and-tabla a *sex-in* was initiated in the basement during re-runs of *Chelsea Girls*.

Who Is Vera Jane Palmer? Fabian Roxburgh preferred the stylization of his aviator sunglasses while viewing the new Goyas, *Naked Majas*, confronting the audience with their communal sex-in, a vivid dissonance of shifting generational identities guaranteed to generate publicity for the exhibition. His own collages stood submerged in a turbulence of slashing colour, and only Celeste Hawthorne deigned to give them more than a cursory glance. "Perhaps I should have exhibited a massive blow up poster photograph of **ME**. An artist's own body is the *Work* these days." Jolted, he glimpsed Miranda Westwood, carrying an armful of Astrology books, trailing behind a neo-Elvis incarnation carrying his torso like a crucifixion. Celeste's cosmopolitan veneer, her mouth a crimson conflagration, contrasted the fertility sculptures of the hippies and Miranda's *Electric Ladyland*, broad-brimmed Musketeer's hat-with-feather, this jaunty virtuoso-with-chalk as Featherstone described her. "Is she your *Girl From Ipanema* then? Do you know Johnny Esquire, who lives in balloons of bubblegum music? He couldn't find a quatrain in *The Rubaiyat*, he's so stupid! Relax, one day she'll grow away from these hippies and marry the millionaire." Sensing in Celeste the potency of *chartreuse*, Roxburgh focused on a large silk screen of a car crash, the sixties certainly being the decade of the automobile-as-vehicle-of-collective-catharsis entitled: **WHO IS VERA JANE PALMER?** Celeste noticed the gaze rivetted to his face like a pensive Hamletian mask. "Fate's rancor can be so lethal. Even blondes-with-brains won't get out of the sixties alive. And there's Johnny Esquire, chiseling away the dross of his persona hoping to find the Philosopher's Stone for a heart. As our mutual friend, Christopher Featherstone, told me while sketching him, "We're the soul's child chalked in flesh upon a three-dimensional canvas. Study the signs, sure we have a generation gap, but age will soon close it." Roxburgh had seen the nude keepsake she referred to, the masculine mandala's *plastique*, its classical linearity more a nineteenth-century narration *à la Ingres*, and looking into her eyes imagined his own image soaked to the skin in her chalks.

Stagflation. Miranda Westwood stood ironing a silk screen's stenciled slogan to the paper dress she chose to wear to the press conference: **LAW ≠ MORALITY**. Engravings of palmistry lay beside her Astrology books. Walking from the dormitories with the Gang of Four across the campus inside the paper dress she remembered Sartre in Paris in May and the café revolutionaries of the French Left, the students barricading the boulevards and the frenzied violence. Approaching the barrage of microphones assembled in the library for the press conference, someone asked her: "Are you a *Party* girl?" Stephen Maxwell elbowed aside competitors for the microphones, bearded now, wearing John Lennon glasses, his Peace symbol-on-a-chain prominently suspended from his neck. "Money is Law! Money is Morality! Let's ice Capitalism and zip up the body bag for good!" Miranda had asked him while holding the ironed paper dress against her camisole: "Stephen, would you duel for me?" She sensed a biblical anarchy pervading his sensibilities, of a dimension she headlined as follows: The World In Stephen Maxwell's Day! Even his catch-cry of *Freedom From Exploitation* inferred a wresting of his proletariat self-image from her feminine oppression. "Let us demand to see the hands of these Capitalist running dogs as they shuffle their deck of cards of philosophers, the deck is stacked. Western society is undergoing a nervous breakdown, time then to commit it to the asylum, its reality is intolerable." Shuffling uncomfortably in her paper dress, photographed by the press contingent, Miranda realized there was only the material Stephen Maxwell, nothing ethereal, and he regarded himself as Lucifer to Fabian Roxburgh's Archangel Michael. Either way she had no ownership of either *means* or *ends*!

I Thought I'd Catch Your Falling Star. Fabian Roxburgh turned the newspaper pages to the Personals and browsed the columns while Fleur wreathed herself in the perfumed veil of her cheesecloth fabrics. Her gamin baby doll of a sister had the rhythm of a moving shadow from the pages of the *Upanishads* while waiting on a *Postcard From 'Nam* from her conscripted boyfriend. Fleur's visibility skewed the perspectives, tilted the horizon of his attention as he scanned the columns, hopeful for some phrase, and there it was: *I Thought Existentialism Might Be My Thing*! Miranda's candy jar of a girl unwrapped the phrase he anticipated: *Peace Between Us Is The Best Thing That Can Happen*. So Peace was the hoped-for sign-off, Peace-and-Goodwill! Roxburgh gestured by crumpling the folds of appeasement in the napkin of Peace Talks. Cruising through the city later he saw how its corpse was bloating on the anti-war movement as student radicals rioted with the Establishment. On a whim he talked his way into the Tennis Club and sat drinking as brief showers swept across the grass courts. The sun's burn-off brought the players back and he noticed Bridget Lovegrove and Calvin Westwood partnering each other in a game of mixed doubles. Surprisingly, she possessed the elasticity of oil paint squeezed from the tube, a Van Gogh sunflower perhaps, in the gyre of her poses, compared with his still ballet's torpor. While men were hopelessly mesmerized a tearful melodrama was sure to be staged from this romantic dramaturgy. Escaping the claustrophobia of the apartment that evening Roxburgh drove Fleur to the drive-in where he could meditate on the shapes of various perimeters and the use of emptiness in the space of his world: the tennis court's flat screen from which Bridget hyperbolically twisted, the theater's flat screen where ageing adolescents varnished existence with the glamor of stylized romances. Why was his heart blocked-in-ice towards Fleur, and why did she accept the symmetry of their respective masks, the hopelessness of a shared champagne life together? Why had he ever imagined he could catch the falling star of Miranda Westwood's innocence?

Guess Who's Coming To Dinner? "Listen, Featherstone, be that philosopher who wouldn't charge a fee for his wisdom and you'll be singing that spiritual, *All My Trials, Lord, Will Soon Be Over*. Surveillance has moved on with the time, so shouldn't you be using James Bond's flair here?" Calvin Westwood, all urbane nonchalance Steve McQueen style, molded to the commercial *bric-à-brac* featured in his expansive office, drew back his putter and touched the golf ball across the carpet while his secretary abandoned herself to motion, intensely thinking about nothing. Christopher Featherstone pondered who could be blackmailing him: could it be his secretary of the lascivious comportment, for she exhibited a luxurious enough accessory for such a platinum-coated melodrama. "As I explained, Miranda is orphaned by this Revolution, and would benefit from a minder. And I think it would be useful if you could financially investigate **LESBOS** Records, under the guise of diversifying your investments." Westwood's contempt flashed, then the phone rang and his secretary answered it, a carnelian flush powdering her face: Featherstone intuited the caller to be Bridget Lovegrove. Territorial, parading the arrogance of his knotted tie, Westwood became elegantly superficial as the telephone conversation proceeded, culminating in complicity's insolence as he hung up and turned to Featherstone. "Be-in ... be-out ... sit-in ... sit-out ... What is this gibberish? They want to call it the *Now* Generation's coming-of-age. I'm diversifying into coastal real estate, Featherstone, and you should do the same. Instead of indulging in pornography. Someone mailed me this representation of you in chalk, and don't tell me it is Art!" Featherstone winced at the secretary's gratuitously attentive arabesques, another Arachne enmeshed on the web of the Time, the paragon of a mere ornament, and certainly jealous of Bridget Lovegrove. Suddenly a circuitry of understanding sparked, flashed, lit up between the triad and the conversation swung elliptical. "Viet Cong body-counts, how do they translate into dollars, and how long will this war's boom years last?" Featherstone listened patiently to the aesthetic of the new millionaires, then offered his own oblique *non sequitir*: "Our dream women of the fifties have suddenly aged."

Mekong's River Styx. Leaves of *Dispatches From 'Nam* fell from Fabian Roxburgh's typewriter. "We'll always have 'Nam." The song on the transistor radio was Eric Burdon's *Sky Pilot*. The mid-western nurse from Idaho or Wyoming, silhouetted in a slender one-piece camisole, traumatized and exhausted by the casualties lining up at the military hospital, spread the radii of her fingers across his perspiring shoulders waiting for him to give her the sleep of Reason. **CASUALTIES? HOW ABOUT TRUTH FOR STARTERS!** Roxburgh typed in bold print, then continued, *The scripted choreography of the Grunts and Charlie is so predictable now the Producers of 'Nam's live-action movie should be screaming:* **REWRITE! REWRITE!** Wrapped in a bathrobe the nurse lifted hair from the nape of her neck with a free hand and lay down on the bed speed reading her way through **TIME**. A surreal brightness, otherworldly and psychological hung over the Mekong's River Styx. With the nurse holding tight on the pillion of the Honda, her rich auburn mist of hair moist with the humidity, Roxburgh blended with the streaming motorcycles on the road-to-Nowhere, speeding through Saigon crossroads where emptiness and fullness were interchangeable. "'Nam verifies my view of myself, my authenticity, how I've become an everlasting exile." Coitus, although smothered in French, had the reticence of an étude amid Saigon's Mahlerian crescendos, and her orgasm with the creamiest voice imaginable haunted his days with the Grunts self-questioning their heroism in the Central Highlands.

I'll Be Your Baby Tonight. 'Nam's end-game played out by the White King puppetry of Ky and Thieu in a firmament of *showtime* delusions possessed a too-lateness for miracles, even though there was as undeniable musical poetry to the fiery arcs of tracer bullets streaming red across the night sky. What a photogenic war, with the cavalry of choppers tattooed with bullets arriving at Little Big Horn, *Homo Americanus* triumphant, cameras rolling, tape recorders switched on, the breadth of the canvas contracted to tens of millions of television screens every evening on the news bulletins! Fabian Roxburgh marveled at the Grunts' incredible disengagement, awash in after shave and the rhythms of transistor radios, wondering how they survived their jungle fire fights. Relaxing, they had the switched-off detachment of *extras* wandering about the movie set of 'Nam, waiting for the call to perform. Charlie had superior penetration of the jungle fastnesses, and the NVA carried with them the hostility of the world's élite intellectuals and *avant garde* academics towards America in their thoughts. Still, the US was militarily impervious to penetration on a scale capable of threatening their presence, so why were they losing? Roxburgh scrawled graffiti on walls everywhere he went, quoting Cicero: *An army is of little value in the field unless there are wise counsels at home.* Across the immeasurable emptiness of thick jungle decimated with defoliants two army divisions tried to frighten each other, then Roxburgh saw a careless correspondent take candy in the throat and slowly expire, any distillation of grief burned up in the criss-crossing fragments of fire as NVA silhouetted cut-outs stole frontline footage from the network contingents jostling for fame. "Suppose God exists, what then?" A Grunt permeated with the turgid odors of the jungle put this question to his companions. Johnson escalated the war but he wouldn't be around to de-escalate the conflict. From *GI Blues* to *Electric Ladyland*, how did such a trajectory eventuate in so few years? "Spooky ... spooky ..." Hueys bound on round-the-clock missions weighed the emerald scenery with their bronze candy, preceding the whirlwinds of napalm, frighteningly mobile, scorching the shoulders of the Grunts hunkered down in their foxholes. Existence was so capricious, a whole generation of NVA youth born to fry in napalm, their souls released screaming onto perpetual motion on Dante's terraced Inferno. Mesmerized, feeling the metaphysical claustrophobia suffocate him, Roxburgh sensed flakes of flesh peeling from napalm burns, torsos stumbling with the color of smoky charcoal before sinking to the earth never to rise again. Thus the scythe of Time leisurely ebbed and flowed through 'Nam. "Don't you feel it too, we've run out of time?"

VIII
BAGATELLE

The Girl Next Door Went A'Walking. "Democracy is asphyxiating, gasping for breath, and Authority stutters!" Stephen Maxwell's radical truculence shook the pages of the Sunday newspaper, tossing aside the glossy supplement carrying a photograph of Miranda in her paper dress at the press conference. Hendrix's version of *All Along The Watchtower* accompanied the drinking of coffee and eating of Miranda's voluptuous pastries while seated in the center of the dormitory room. Incensed, exasperated by her casting of horoscopes, her effortless making of the news, with the reporters more interested in the column inches of her paper dress than his declamation, Maxwell made a serious cut in the ice: "Where did you score those aviator sunglasses? From your sweetheart-next-door? Why do I still have to draw word-pictures for you? Study more Berkeley addresses instead of those horoscopes. She knows she's alive. She has a share portfolio from Daddy." Miranda's addiction to revolutionary etiquette proved transitory. "Nobody instructs me how to walk, talk or think." Moths swarmed around the street light visible from the dormitory. The Gang of revolutionary *fauves* feasted on her cooking unable to fathom her sculpted aloneness by the window, her symbolic exclusion precipitating Maxwell's angst: "Leaving? What direction are you taking? We all saw you as the girl-next-door in Hanoi, not Saigon! We could have been halves of a single revolutionary being, the density of the hammer-and-sickle. Instead, you courted those journalists in your paper dress like a beauty contestant in a lineup!" Miranda boxed-and-taped her collection of books and records while the revolutionary martyrs huddled watching the news bulletin, imaginary laurel wreaths encircling their brows, throwing clenched fists in the air when the politicized Olympic Games coverage came on. Having iced-over her political intelligence, become labeled a *Pepsi Yippie* in the Propaganda War, accepted the Establishment's key to her handcuffs, she abandoned the revolutionary love-in with wry humour: "Stephen, you see I'm just about head-high, almost a thinker, but not quite."

Tales Of Brave Ulysses. Vietnam's core issue swinging society abruptly Left, the inference of Fabian Roxburgh's letter to Christopher Featherstone from Saigon, in which he asked his friend to infiltrate *La Bohème* and retrieve his collages, its revolutionary catalyst, had western youth creating from these mid-sixties years an indelible scene of freedom-from-the-past. Featherstone approached Celeste and she welcomed the invitation to enhance her social visibility in Bohemia. Psychedelic flashing lights announced the premises identified in Roxburgh's letter, a freewheeling party spilling from the apartment block onto the street. "Christopher – just think of *La Bohème's* swelling **b** as a rounded nymph searching for her Faun." Lenin and Lennon posters, the obligatory Che and Mao, festooned the hallways, and from the loud music, *Tales of Brave Ulysses*, a champagne sea-foam of sound, semi-nude sirens emerged, as if all adolescence was now populated with fantasy figures. Featherstone leaned close to Celeste's ear: "In every innocent there is a portion of guilt awaiting expiation." Floral patterned girls, sinuous and straight from Modigliani metaphored fertility, for many semi-naked children danced to the music. Celeste commented: "This dance class is no Degas pastel, no *Swan Lake*, although I fancy there will be *Sleeping Beauties* early tomorrow morning." Featherstone visualized the poignant mirage of his own children in the radii of dancing gyrations. Hallucinating in the geometric angles of the hallways and apartments, nocturnal youth discussed their non-belonging, their anti-face in a world ruled by advertising jingles, the whole Madison Avenue *thing*, so Featherstone drifted through the smoke-haze dispensing his own hippie wisdom: "Consider, only *no-thing* can conceivably exist in *no-space*." Somehow leached of ambition, the young girls little more than impressions, the calligraphy of a stylus on a wax tablet, as Celeste imaged them, they talked in hushed voices of perpetually enduring sunflowers while listening to Clapton's soft self-portrait in guitar phrases. After the Police had finally subdued the raucous exhibitionism and the energy and volume dissipated in sleep, Featherstone and Celeste stepped over the slumbering torsos, so many portable tubes of oil paint squeezed onto furniture and across the floors, concluding the sixties aesthetic possessed the thinness of a cyclone in whose fabric they were all temporarily impressed: the eye of the hurricane offered a moment's surcease.

The October Movement. Balloons bursting with urine showered the Police line-up, its uniform rhythm stepping in time just prior to their imminent assault on the anti-war demonstrators. Guiding Elizabeth to an advantage point on the periphery of this war zone he glimpsed the Yippies in masks representing Ky, Thieu and Nixon singing *The Times They Are A'Changing* to their flag burning ritual, recognizing Stephen Maxwell at the heart of the centerpiece. He said to Elizabeth: "You could almost say the theme of the sixties is the vow youth have made never to cut their hair again. Almost a biblical remembrance, but then youth perfects the next generation's morality I suppose." Glass shards tore the flesh as a small group of demonstrators who were strong-armed through a store's plate-glass window by the mobilised Police. Blanketing tear gas soon enveloped the singing Yippies. Following the riot's pointless chaos and the Establishment had stabilized suppression and oppression on the student radicals, Featherstone and his ex-wife stepped across a banner reading **THE OCTOBER MOVEMENT** and lunched in a nearby restaurant. Elizabeth leaned her elbows on the table, her fingers interlaced as if ready to pray, the detritus of her fifties beauty recalling to him their fading wedding photographs. "Christopher – I intend to remarry." Reverberations from the incident of his fire-bombed car had unclamped his portrait of himself from the easel of his previous incarnations, so Elizabeth's statement rendered all nostalgia outmoded, the weight of her sexual presence, its historical *plastique* in his life, lessened and he heard himself saying: "Youth eternalizes Beauty, is Beauty's revelation. The despair of youth is to lose one's self-portrait in a mirror, its Narcissus effect." King David's fleece of *Psalms*, the fallacies of existence, souls sealed to death, eased the finality of her words. "Christopher – yours is a make-believe world with too many excesses. We have closed a succession of doors behind us now." Featherstone acknowledged her fears and uncertainties with his surveillance of clients undergoing divorce proceedings, his testifying in court on their patterns of intimacy, and frequent confrontations with aggrieved spouses, and glimpsed behind her façade a concern he might use his skills against her. A tidal wash of human pedestrians had already swept away signs of the demonstration, even the glass from the window frontage had been removed and the space boarded up. Acting was the ultimate absurdity, Man was useless, and the world was a tomb.

The Invisible Man. Sunset's avalanche of saffron and salmon leaves of cloud flaked and impastoed the horizon where the languor and lethargy of the schooner moored in the marina presented the skeleton of an enigma. Already feeling himself the *lost man* in the slippage of Time, Christopher Featherstone gazed at the massed fire leavened in the porthole glass of the schooner's state room, likening himself to a Shakespearian anti-hero sick with self-love, oblivious to the danger in which he is embroiled, and losing the power of soliloquy. Climbing aboard the schooner and entering the state room he identified Miranda Westwood swiveling on a stool at the bar, masked in aviator sunglasses, her posture insouciant with defiance, a barefoot statue on a pedestal, although she spoke first: "Well, we meet farce-to-farce: I've been listening to the sound of the sea. How often do my parents call on you here?" Her sculpted hostility with all the immediacy of Beat prose committed straight to the typewriter without reflection strangely relaxed him. "Why am I here? Why am I *anywhere*? Guess! Everywhere, it's an inquisition." Serrations edged her youthful persona as if she were casually torn from the pages of a glossy magazine editorializing survivors from Hippieland. "Samantha routinely drops by, for updates." The dappled sunset faded and twilit purple smothered the sky. Worldliness was hammering Virtue to the thinness of gold leaf and Featherstone imagined Miranda puzzled why the simple joys of girlhood were vanishing into the mists of amnesia. "Private Eye – *The Invisible Man*. I am the space where I am because this is the Westwood schooner, but why are you in the space where I am?" Featherstone deftly eluded her implication with humor: "I'm working on this year's Xmas single for *The Pléiades*. Of late I've been listening to the songs of '64 and asking myself did I ever know them. How strange they seem now." Miranda prepared dinner for them: *Whiting in Crème-Fraîche sauce with Pumpkin Mash*. Mother-daughter parallel twists of the DNA dismantled his thoughts like film footage at the editing desk, as Samantha's theosophic hues radiated through Miranda's consciousness.

"Stephen, he's bargain-basement, romantically, I know, and he didn't understand when I finally told him, only buildings take to the streets."

Juxtapositions. Meditating in a scallop shell of quietude Christopher Featherstone could faintly hear *Hey Jude* issuing from Miranda's cabin as he sketched the calligraphy of his thinking in sexual feminine imagery: (i) **MINIMALIST** – Elizabeth Featherstone – Her theological spacetime years brought him the solitude of the Sistine Chapel, sex became a plunge into ice cold water or an entwining of flaccid geometries, then the library of dreams was torched and they were left sifting through the ashes. Now she planned to remarry, resurrect herself as Canova's sculpture of Paolina Borghese as *Venus Vietrix*! (ii) **SURREALIST** – Samantha Westwood – Memory's delicate prism separated the colors of infinite longing for her divine reflection implanted in her person by her soul. Her hair's Créole fire sizzled the delicate wave of the silk sheets descending onto the horizon of the pale pillow. In a rush of spontaneous combustion she died into the gentle ripples of a shivering rose blowing from its stem. He remembered the sensation of his palm massaging cream into her softening heels, and her martinis of green olive, ice cubes, gin and dry vermouth, the patina of her flesh upon which jeweled coruscations of electricity scintillated. Why were they romantic Dioscuri fated never to banquet together beneath Renaissance altarpieces, a true Marriage at Cana? The miracle of water transformed to wine had been performed for them. (iii) **CLASSICIST** – Celeste Hawthorne – Unsheathing a tube of pillbox-red lipstick she rolled its Tuscan warmth around his naked outline on a sheet of paper, her fingers' adventurous traces of geometric touches a transmission of her own untrammeled sexual ecstasy. Then there was the erotic fold of cloth on her sublime caryatid modeling *Greece Expiring on the Ruins of Missolonghi*, décolleté and sweep of vulva sexually entrancing, a finished masterpiece for viewing through all Time. (iv) **VORTICIST** – Helena Steele – A Dadaist cut-up with a showgirl stride eager to regain Hippolyta's aristocracy, she bestrode space's tightly sheathed fresco like a prodigious genetic chimera, sexually ambivalent among her statuesquely adventurous companions. She imaged an explosive rose on the terraces of Dante's *Inferno*, her soul's black coal consumed in Venetian-red fire, besieged by apparitions singing the blank verse of Milton's *Paradise Lost (Books I and II)*. (v) **CUBIST** – Bridget Lovegrove – His inner eye thoughtfully unfolded along her athletic tennis legs as she stretched to serve, from ankle to trim derriere, the racy saltiness of her perspiration burning his lips. He imagined himself a sun-soaked Faun gazing as she floated like her tennis tunic caught up in the greening arms of an almond tree, the scene aureoled in flights of doves. Trouble was, she nestled like a pearl maturing in the clasp of Calvin Westwood's sexual space!

The Monotony Of Existence. "Miranda is to be the trustee of my fortune. The vineyard of Westwood Holdings will be hers someday. These apes she frolics with, she can only learn their guttural grunts, become a helpless forager. I always visualized her as young, beautiful of course, immortal." Raising his burgundy, Calvin Westwood reflected for a moment, affection overflowing, while Christopher Featherstone pondered the widening credibility gap between the generations. Samantha stabilized this thoughtful *ménage à trois*, seated like an Egyptian pharaoh, her torso a sacred shrine, her head a radiant cupola, her expression smooth as glass as she listened. Featherstone spaced a response by first tasting the food on his plate: "The world egg is full of surprises when the shell cracks. Youth is a *tabula rasa* from which impressions are easily washed, they ebb and flow with the tide of the Age." Calvin Westwood frowned at this display of manners adorned with knowledge and judgment, as if an unwholesome flow of human imagery floated to the surface of three-dimensional space before him: *The Winter's Tale?* "Featherstone – it strikes me the tidal flow of *every* Age is captive following captor." Westwood reached inside his jacket and took out his chequebook. "Let's leave wisdom for tomorrow, I have a meeting now where I'll be tapping the shell of a Faberge egg!"

A Subliminal Transmission Of Ecstasy. "Well, Christopher, you were rather amusing over lunch." Samantha half-swayed beside him, slow twisting he thought, establishing a comfortable rhythm as they moved along the sidewalk together. "The brevity of my wit is as a sunbeam soon buried in the world's dark cloud." Through the connectivity of chance Hotel Plaza approached bringing a subliminal transmission of ecstasy. "You believe this vogue for the beret is passing? ..." Featherstone understood signals so they walked on by shrouded in an inexpressible *déjà vu*. "What is important though, is whether Miranda's the kind of girl able to make an anarchist laugh. As she said to me the other evening, her latest passion is to pass through the Houses of the Zodiac." Acting was the ultimate absurdity in a make-believe world, so Featherstone stopped by **EOS** Records' studio, ushering Samantha inside the engineer's booth where *The Pléiades* listened to playbacks of their Christmas single.

> (Intro – sung)
> Christmas ... Christmas ... Christmas
> Poetry of our Eternal Day
> Christmas ... Christmas ... Christmas
> Prologue to a Divine Play
> (Verse)
> Bringing Christmas gifts from noble Kings
> Laying up treasures before the chimes of midnight.
> She's already asleep in her glow-worm dreams
> While Urania motions the stars to holy flight.
> (Chorus)
> Fading is the light in her window
> But her drowsing face is all aglow.
> Time glides over silver sands
> Tomorrow she'll hold my gifts in her hands.

Revolution Born Of A Daisy-Chain Of Flower Children. Drifting in a monsoon shower of flower petals across the nexus of Spanish sandstone, lovely surface moldings to the University façade, the devotees moved towards the sitar's evening raga shimmering from the inner quadrangle of lawn. Braless in muslin blouses, their feet sandaled, all their personal possessions in a loop of leather pouch, the Flower Children strolled across the floral tapestry of spring carpeting the pavement approaches to the quadrangle. Within this living and moving fresco of fragrance Christopher Featherstone and Samantha Westwood were a pair of more somber lithographs, although he delighted in the choreographic pleasure of walking with her beneath the silver monotone ring of the moon's bowl, his penetrative thoughts cloyed with her presence. "How certain are you Miranda is here this evening?" Discipled of the Maharishi, seated on a low platform, immersed in the reflective glow of candlelight which illuminated the gathered frieze of earthly deities, the guru modelled the expectation of sanctity while the sitar played. Featherstone recognized the Flower Children companions of Fabian Roxburgh, their jutting breasts in cheesecloth fabric soaked in heavily fragranced Indian oils, and briefly introduced them to Samantha as the successors to their own fabulous fifties generation. Fleur offered to enlace Samantha's hair with flowers, her presence having the elegance of timeless sculpture poised on a pedestal as she accepted the visual iconography and they joined the sit-in. "Is he God's surrogate self-portrait in the world?" Featherstone posed the question to Samantha as a tuft of feminine lotus petals gathered around the seated bud of the guru. A languor strangely intoxicated the gathering of devotees in their newly minted celestial armor. Aureoled with the soft flame of fragrantly anointed trimmings they dazzled. "Are we to witness a heavenly visitation, or a dissertation?"

The Evangelical I. Ripe for celluloid scripture the scene transformed as fugitives from *Paradise Lost's* abyss of spacetime muscled onto the low platform, a more analytic human plane compared with the levitating deities awash in incense and flower petals. A commanding figure with a swaggering, pervasive truculence wielded a megaphone, flanked by Stephen Maxwell and his Gang of Four, and his words embodied dissidence and dissonance, silencing the sitar. "Through God's eyes I witness His compassionate megalomania, and stand in *revolt*! I am here to turn your eyes from the window on the Garden of the World. History is but God's diary. He takes our life as being-and-existence, as His Original Idea in the first place. God is killing Himself in an act of suicide when he arranges our death. How do we commit suicide? By going to war! Man is sculpted by God, grotesquely aged, deformed by Him, and then uselessly cast aside into earth or fire. *Revolt*! Become metaphysical questioners ..." A wave of flower petals assaulted the Evangelist and his companions, someone yelled: "Hippies are the answer to the Age's great questions!" Fighting eventually quelled the impudent insurrection while the frieze of devotees surrounding the guru began a charismatic chant and the strings of the sitar took up the doctrinal affirmations.

The Coronation Of Jackie O. Christopher Featherstone surveyed the glittering impressionistic nuances of the ocean from the deck of the schooner moored in the marina. A shimmering martini glass masked Samantha's statuesque symmetry and alluded to the chilled silver bowl of the moon held by fingers of cloud with its lip sipping light from the Sun God. News of the widow-virgin's adultery in remarriage, Jackie O. a blushing bride again, seemed to evoke a symmetry, a parallel with Samantha and her regal presence that evening aboard the schooner promised a comparable surrender. Featherstone sensed the attainment of synthesis and equilibrium in the moment's breathtaking attentiveness and tension aroused by the news item and brief footage, although his conscience was molten with virtuous instincts too, especially as she so relaxingly glided aboard the schooner with him. Powdery wings oared a moth about the watery glow of a pier light, and Featherstone himself was buoyed with Samantha's listenable warmth, he rose on Icaran wings towards the under-curve of her martini glass bright with reflected sunlight from the moon above. Greek light and fire would deplume Jackie O. as she cruised the waves of the Mediterranean Sea in her fabulous trireme, dawn coating the ocean in legendary gold as she awoke tomorrow: what would marriage to Midas bring? "Please give me your ice cube, Christopher, I'm sizzling."

Mosaic. (i) Fingers of cloud curled around the martini glass of the moon and beneath the blur of subdued lighting the modeling of Samantha's face was radiantly idealized. Studiedly passive she too witnessed the wings of the moth sizzle and powder as the torso plummeted to the dark waters, barely troubling the Law of Displacement, perhaps an allusion to her own adventure that evening with Christopher Featherstone. (ii) Moist burials, Créole fire dowsed on the bayou of the marina-bound schooner, occupied Featherstone's immediate thoughts as the depth of the Icaran moth's echo reverberated on and Samantha's beauty filled his mind. (iii) *Luxe, calme et volupté*: As if caressing into being some thought-up mannerism *à la Baudelaire*, Samantha's fingers gently toyed with the erotic glove of her dress and rapture dilated Featherstone's loins. (iv) The out-curving petals of two roses searched for, felt after each other in the hyperbole of a kiss and two souls shaped the mold of two bodies to exquisite sensation. A stem burgeoned upward from the muddy darkness garlanded with a ravishing lotus, *trés pur*. (v) Her sheer pantyhose's sheath peeled away from her naked sculpture in a blaze of brightness. Sheets loaded with the spices of her reclining arabesque inspired Featherstone to reveal the Pompeiian fresco of his subterranean torso as faint moonlight again illuminated the circumference of the porthole. (vi) Curves of abdomen pressed together in the mosaic of a beehive, deliciously sticky in feeling, and someone breathed: *I Got Stung*! Kissing was as visceral as sculptors carving Aphrodites and Apollos for Greek temples and soon swollen lips were brimful of the juice from over-ripe pomegranates, with Samantha physically conscious of the melting of the glacier of her pubis' frost. (vii) *Jouissance!* A sliced pomegranate oozed delicious juice. Bed sheets exuded autumnally ripe fruit flavors during the lyrical synthesis of their torsos. A dense breathlessness undulated Samantha, she flooded and passion streamed forth from her expression like her hair caught by the sea breeze: the petals of a red rose blew and came away in the ecstasy of her *fall*. Later the rhapsody of her somnolence had Featherstone lamenting for yesterday when they were both younger.

Sign Of The Times. Gone was the scarlet effusion staining the skies over 'Nam. Quietude reigned in the commercial airliner as beautifully radiant raiment of cloud formed in the luminous empyrean. Fabian Roxburgh relaxed back in his seat focusing on postcard visions of Hippieland as the airliner's feather floated above some white calligraphy of cloud against the azure sky. Drinks were served arousing him from his peaceful reverie and a staccato imagery of war scenes intruded. Observing cloud-formations through the window he was reminded of the cyclonic turbulence and mobility of napalm rendering ignited candlesticks of branches and turning smoking trunks into pillars of fire. Safe in the air pressured cabin he recalled the cloud-like hissing of napalm and its horrendous engulfment of everything, his direct-to-camera commentary on a torching of a Vietnamese village and the rounding-up of suspects, epitomizing the whole blood-soaked aesthetic of the war. Why though did this scourge of Communism continue to exude an aura of indestructibility? Even the war-torn cities of America through the sixties promoted to the world export-rich Democracy was little more than hostile imperialism with Marxism a convenience store alternative. Carpets of napalm and carpets of flowers seemed bizarre contrasts of baroque political thinking as his generation gazed into future time instead of illuminating the reality of Now. Was Sartre on the streets of Saigon, smoking in cafes, talking up Existentialism, was everyone in 'Nam reading his books? Sickened with bile, Roxburgh closed his eyes to scenes swallowed in a furnace of napalm, to foliage instantaneously dissipating in ashes. Thrusting aside the dull journalism of newspapers he marveled at the ideological naivete of the Grunts fighting their way through the impenetrable political darkness of 'Nam, a generation sacrificed yet again to forestall the domino-effect of these Asian Goths and Vandals sweeping south. Soon the washed-out exterior of Australia's southern Arcadia appeared below, a coastline swept with surf, a leitmotif recalling the innocence of Hawaiians, then his eye fell on an editorial castigating an escalation of US bombing raids. But the equation was simple: US ground troops would have to physically take Hanoi, or NVA ground troops would have to physically take Saigon. Flying low over the body of the city the skyscrapers resembled curious stigmata hammered through the palms of each street block. As he descended to the tarmac a pretty flight attendant smiled with idyllic freshness and cleanliness, vivid with classical certainty that she was a sign of the times, that the flight into the future would be upbeat, for wasn't Aquarius dawning on the horizon?

When I Paint My Masterpiece. "Shall we awaken this canvas which was asleep and see what it was dreaming?" Celeste Hawthorne's sudden lightning flash of a laugh startled him as he emerged from her en suite bathroom into the gallery towel-drying his hair as she stripped a sheet from an easel painting. "Fabian, I've been studying your collages more closely, looking for signature-themes. Pop Art is really quick art, whereas you can see I'm deep-sunk in painting's day-dream." On a whim he re-directed the taxi from the airport to Celeste's studio where, although surprised, she welcomed him with the polished perfection of her artistic manners, and offered him refreshment and a shower. The gallery-studio's airiness, purity and vitality amid its stillness, her own mood's crisp buoyancy roused him a little from his mournful reverie. "Warmed by the sun there, your studio feels like the lovely breast of a dove compared with 'Nam's vulture. Coming home today I felt like I was falling through life like a stone the breeze can't support. From the repose offered by this chrysalis I might be able to rouse myself to flight again." Celeste embroidered her palette with myrtle-green, peacock-green, lacquer-green and maize-green while Roxburgh studied her proposed compositional entry for an esteemed National Art Prize, the finger of her paintbrush bringing a Delacroixan touch to the full-length portrait. Responding to the intimate authorship of painting, he remarked: "My own biography is about as rigorously researched as some tabloid piece." Suddenly haunted by the memory of Miranda Westwood's frigid existentialism staged for him in a theater of revolution, and Fleur's lush creaminess of personality he left the studio's chrysalis and hailed a taxi from the sidewalk.

Here I Am, Where Are You? Miranda had emerged from the chrysalis of her Hippie friends' Old Testament fashion statements, the aromatic oils of Kings, Proverbs and Psalms were no longer her fabric of the moment and her emerald leafage had returned. She referred to Christopher Featherstone amusedly as her *comic book detective*, square-jawed, moralistic, until she thought she recognized her mother's shade of lipstick on his shirt collar, inhaled her mother's perfume seeping from his clothes. Featherstone caught the chilled swathe of her glance paint him in the colors of a middle-aged roué and turned away to watch a sea bird launch its wingèd sails to the sky. Confused, Miranda returned to the schooner's galley and buried herself alive in the aromas of cooking, her culinary gifts, her unusual alliance with food rather quirkish for a modern girl. Over lunch Featherstone's conversation sapped her moodiness, knowing her role-playing existentialist to be a script defining her otherness from her father, and he talked of being shipwrecked on the golden reef of the family schooner, but now he must swim ashore and beach himself on the atoll of the world again. Savoring the vegetable stew of leeks, potato and tomato garnished with an olive gremolata, its savoury melt a more truthful gauge of her persona, he listened to her take up his metaphor and warn him to beware of hidden reefs over which the schooner was sailing. Saying *au revoir* later on the deck of the moored schooner with the aureole of the sun's horoscope spinning around her head tangled up in the aromas of her cooking, Featherstone genuinely praised her preference to stand apart from the chorus of revolutionaries in the intensifying Greek Tragedy of the Age. Both had raised their masks a little and peered from behind them. "Miranda, remember the sacrifice of Iphigenia, and the art of *mimēsis* as you educate your emotions." Still smothered in Samantha's lip-prints, enthralled by excess of her, he walked away from the marina to calyxes of birdsong igniting the spring skyline.

Symbolism. Beethoven's late String Quartets musically christened Christopher Featherstone's completely refurbished office chambers, carriers delivered furniture and appliances throughout the day while he hung a reproduction of G. F. Watts' thoughtful Victorian masterpiece, **HOPE**, and placed a companion marble bust of **CLYTIE** on a pedestal, her head averted away over one shoulder, her naked breasts strangely inviting, perhaps models for future clients. Should he have gone bohemian though, gone *Beat*, become a minimalist installation advertising himself as a sleuth, *à la Pop Art*? The Beethoven String Quartet elevated his thoughts to the defining essay of Life's transience, with its sonorities of hot yellows and autumnal oranges, while he waited for the telephone call to come. Miranda's teasing hide-and-seek interludes book-ending his more mundane surveillance work and court appearances both tore at and healed his tissues of guilt, his sexual offences and prudence as his own marriage collapsed to ground-zero, undoubtedly metaphored in the fire-bombing of his office earlier. All the richest prizes though eluded him: Elizabeth, Samantha, Celeste, Bridget. How could he keep the wounds from becoming gangrenous? Seated on the perimeter hugging sofa, convertible and functional as a bed, he relaxed amid graceful cushions listening to the String Quartet and conscious of the dynamism of moving sunlight shifting across the office space. With Zen calm a maple bonsai stood on a window sill. Fragments of memory dispersed when the telephone rang.

Adulterous Moments. "Miranda's duration of *becoming* will seem to her eternal." Christopher Featherstone looked into Samantha's limpid aspic eyes as she stood in his reincarnated office space with her head profiled against the famous painting of **HOPE**, her sexual mannerisms from their evening together on the schooner well camouflaged. Diamonds embedded in the clasp of her handbag glistened as vibrations of instreaming sunlight fell across her, torching her symbolic apparition from the library of his dreams. Her welcoming kiss' somnolence was further assuaged by his posture-perfect sensibility of her mood, nevertheless she unhurriedly unzipped her skirt letting it fall to a pedestal around her ankles. A thought's limp weight clung to her silken sensuality tautening the physical silence: sin's sap drunk by Eve from the Tree of Knowledge flowed through her veins, and Miranda's! Having undressed for Celeste's chalk-on-paper he stood naked in the gathering purple shadows of the office before Samantha had slipped her arms free of her brassiere. Years of sensory deprivation revived with the sweetness of Provençal honey, sex's soothing balm pleasant for jaded palates: she quietly spread her arms standing at his desk supporting her torso allowing him to explore her shoulder blades, from which Angel's wings had come away, and feel the erotic charge of her derriere pressed against his inner thighs. Reversals metaphored all their lives, as she explained later dining in her favourite restaurant, touched by his gallantry in ordering the *Beef Rossini* with *foie gras* and *truffles*, while she had the *slow-roasted rack of lamb*, a different kind of sensual immersion. She had allowed Featherstone to surfeit her own appetite, guiding him to isolate and follow through her personal sexual thread, using the functional sofa-bed to luxuriate in her feminine *jouissance*. "Now that we have crafted a sacrosanct moment we can isolate its memory, keep its bubble intact, and thereby not breach our sexual proprietary with our husbands and wives." Tangled up in her aromas, Featherstone found these words popped, fizzled and fumed in his mind, thrilling to the osmosis between her voice and her image while they shared desserts, an *Orange Drambuie Soufflé* and *blood plums in red wine with Mascarpone Tea Cakes*. She was being definitive in her avoidance of that burst bubble of a *lost weekend* in 1964, and an act of elopement was out of the question. Featherstone brooded upon these over-explicit sixties ringing with the emptiness of the Tao!

Be Sure To Wear Some Flowers In Your Hair. Christopher Featherstone thought of Lear descended into madness, of Ophelia naming flowers as he paused on the stoop of the apartment block peopled with flower children, and asked after Fabian Roxburgh, his room number. Quizzical looks translated to: *This is a commune, man, nobody owns or rents their own space here.* Everyone wore hair styled for Eternity and superficially the mood overflowed with the *joie de vivre* of a Golden Age. Vibrant strings from a sitar created a resonance and to walk the hallways and through rooms was to enter a Pop Art installation. Featherstone did not resist when two flower children crowned him with a hand-made bouquet of flowers and he glimpsed Roxburgh's flashing saber of a smile welcoming him with the brilliance of a latter-day hippie General Custer at Little Big Horn. "Who's this groovy hippie putting down the Word? Why, it's The Man! The flower children with interlocking arms are Fleur and her sister: how they gather into themselves all the affectations of these late-sixties. How have girls metamorphosed from Madison Avenue exponents of *The Twist* and the *Mashed Potato* to these psychedelic rag dolls dancing to *All Along The Watchtower* in so few years? Don't they look too fragile and languid compared with their older sisters?" Roxburgh ushered Featherstone into a space awash with saturated colors where they crashed and were joined by Fleur and her sister, to his eye still-forming symbols suspended in Time like milk-white Fauns over which the blades of Hindu deities were poised to render sacrifice. Struck by the intensity of their self-absorption, Featherstone began to suspect here was a generational bubble whose fabric was anything but tenuous, and therefore unlikely to burst and vanish.

The U.S. Flag Upon Display. The skyline's gold enamelling was succeeded by the churning sea of the Milky Way, elixir of the Hippie God when evening's split second lengthened to the duration of a lifetime. Christopher Featherstone recognized the Evangelist from the evening at the University, wisdom's lamp seemingly extinguished in his ascetic's mind as he motioned himself through the apartment block in a jacket cut from the pattern of the Stars-and Stripes. He was introduced to Featherstone as Eddie Phoenix, a rather bewildered and *seized* flower child on each arm, and offered them the following: "I cling to *nothingness*, though I tend the birth of these birds from the shell of the egg and they link me to the world." Fabian Roxburgh observed the flag's passage down a corridor, reviving momentarily from his mutual cannibalism kissing Fleur, to comment: "As these hippies disengage from the tapestry of society, he is re-weaving threads of attachment to bind them tighter. Watching him, I'm struck by the image of the discolored Mekong ferrying the Viet Cong, and how the company one keeps discolors one's own mind. Like Lucifer, his mentor, he has all the prowess of a lotus!" Haunted by the U.S. flag displayed as a jacket on the back of this bizarre Evangelist, Featherstone relaxed on the sofa in his office, his thoughts flashing with the mango flower flesh of Fleur and her untranslatable sister, their glancing eyes smooth as almonds but torrential with cravings, and of Roxburgh tossed on their thick pubic hair's circlet of illusion. Closing his eyes his thought's wax image melted into Samantha Westwood's breathless paradigm and the honey squeezed between her loins. To be collapsed upon a web of knowledge with full consciousness, powerless before the approach of the spider, Lucifer, while aeons of starry oceans ebbed and flowed across Time, brought a shudder to Featherstone's soul. The hiss of the abyss poisoned his senses as the elastic cosmos felt the powerful tread of Lucifer!

Bagatelle. Why was poetic space so gloriously animated with emotion? The Milky Way's shattered mirror evoked a burst heart, emotion lacerated with the sinister breezes flowing from the abyss, space ignited with the deliquescing jewels of the fabled Sun Gods. Christopher Featherstone felt himself fall into his mirror reflection as he ritually purified himself in the shower and shaved afterward. Beethoven's contrapuntal late String Quartets slid across existence's monochrome surface trying to establish a center of gravity. Open for business, the craftsmanship of surveillance, he saw Man metaphored torn asunder like the eternal discord of the Milky Way, teeming with a microcosm of impulsive thoughts mutating through Eternity's deformities of Beauty, a guttering of the fires of Incarnation, crusted with evil, an infection nothing could medicine. A fragile sensation burgeoned like the seed of a magnificent pomegranate sweetened by juice!

IX
GOWNED IN RUSSIAN RED

A Sixties Pageant. Boutique surfing with Fleur, tempting her to swivel free of her hippie sari and shimmy into the latest summer mini skirts, Fabian Roxburgh stood gazing into the pool of the full length mirror wondering who the Luciferan figure advancing towards him was. Fleur weaved among the racks of clothes, her voice obscured by Creedence Clearwater Revival's updating of the fifties classic, *Suzie Q*, rocking the boutique, but she was simply embroidery to the sixties' revolutionary fabric. The wizened cartography of Lyndon Johnson's face in the last days of his caretaker Presidency, black-and-white on the evening news bulletins, evoked the mask of an increasingly disordered society, or *global village*. Grizzled and ageing, Johnson's portrait contrasted the youth of the late-sixties as if not simply a generation separated them but centuries, millennia! Roxburgh drove Fleur and her flower child sister down to the beach where he surfed the waves' baroque silk screens with style and verve while they bared their jade-skinned torso and limbs to the November warmth. Of an evening, with *Suzie Q* pulsing through the apartment he addressed himself to his *Dispatches From 'Nam: Wingèd angels, Skyhawk spotter aircraft visibly survey the North Vietnamese manoeuvres across the DMZ, taking some ineffective ground fire, and lining up the approach routes for the incoming from the USS New Jersey. How smooth the faces of Ky and Thieu are, as if this cataclysmic confrontation were a phony-war or being enacted on a Hollywood film-set, while Johnson's face expresses in its cartography every US excursion into treacherous jungles and the taking of some forlorn hill. Freight trains of bronze candy crash into the NVA positions and more screaming souls are ferried into the Paradise Lost of their Hell.* Roxburgh looked up from the typewriter and Christopher Featherstone stood framed in the open doorway of the apartment.

Danger, Heartbreak Ahead. "So, our blood-splattered dove of peace is no longer hospitalized, and eager to renew acquaintance?" Drinking Fleur's odd-flavoured brew of tea, but declining the alfalfa sandwich, Christopher Featherstone had explained his tip-off from the Police and resumed surveillance of her activities. "That would explain the copy of Mao's red book left at the apartment, with my obituary stapled to the cover. Is she planning to resume her recording career?" Featherstone climbed into the midnight-blue street-rod, Fleur and her sister occupying the rear seat, and they arrived at the discothèque as Helena Steele launched her new combo into a version of *Danger, Heartbreak Ahead*, the lyric cajoling the female dancers and bristling with menace. Roxburgh danced with Fleur and her sister *à trois* when Featherstone declined to embarrass himself. Backstage, lost in the mists of the younger generation's self-awareness, drinking the poison of her voice enunciating the message in the song, he assumed an offensive posture and positioned himself to advantage. More a skeletal model than he remembered her, following her hospitalization, she recognized him immediately, soaked through with perspiration, her combo and back-up singers creating an embrasure-effect. "Miss Steele, your choric commentary on the song was no feckless imitation." Helena maintained her immobile centrality, then spoke slowly: "The nurses told me you visited me in hospital, but I doubt it was to lay healing hands on me. As you can see I have arisen without your intercession." Featherstone acknowledged his appreciation of her virtuosity with a tautening of his statuesque stance, and chose his metaphor carefully: "The foot soldiers in 'Nam have walked into a maze, but whatever path they travel, and there are many as the news bulletins show, they all lead to one center ... Death." Helena understood and swept by him supported by her back-up singers. Should he pray to the flower child's deity for a Third Eye to see deep into his destiny?

Afternoon Tea At The Tennis Club. Puzzled by the trigonometry of tennis, serve-and-volley across the court's two-dimensional plane of immaculate lawn, *jeu divin* beneath an azure late-spring sky, Christopher Featherstone hesitated before approaching Samantha Westwood seated alone under an umbrella. She was dressed for tennis, a sweater draped over her shoulders, legs crossed squeezing the seductive curve of her pubis, observing the mixed doubles with Calvin partnering Bridget Lovegrove. Featherstone longed to be molten and flowing together with her but their molds cast by the Gods were separated by spacetime, tombs held apart and buried for millennia in the pyramid of the world. Still, they had synthesized dream with realization, enjoyed if briefly the closure of a nimbus of egg, jellied yolk softly floating inside an unbroken shell, always a tantalizing thought. "Shall we read tea leaves together? Samantha, whenever I look at a tennis court, it strikes me as the model for a room without walls, in which intimate games are played with one's neighbor." Kneeling to tie up the laces of her tennis shoes, a sublime Olympiad Greek for a moment, Bridget was intimately whispered to by Calvin Westwood, watched over by Samantha's limpid portrait sheltered under an umbrella. "So, beneath the Ptolemaic spheres, what is happening?" Samantha gestured for him to join her under the umbrella, obviously conscious that even the royal descent of new millionaires was contaminated by infidelity and adultery, although the clean athleticism of tennis suggested a crystalline innocence pervaded existence. "To fall is natural, Christopher, witness gravity itself. Miranda spoke to me about Astrology, justifying her avoidance of Calvin and myself at this time because of a combustible conjunction of planets in the Houses: the aspects for reconciliation and understanding are unfavorable. Where can I find the anaesthesia I need? Every young Hymen is a poisoned chalice in her tunic there, every would-be Cupid a poisoned arrow." Featherstone savoured her presence's ripened fruit leaving the branch to be candied in syrup, then observed Calvin Westwood's vigorous tree-climbing on the tennis court, his finding the chalice in the bowl and his Phoenix inside, burning up in sex, certain to resurrect before his next visit. From the Persian-blue eyes of Bridget's incarnation of Artemis perspiration resembled the tears of a Phoenix as she stood talking to Samantha, drinking lemonade, citrus tang to mature palates. Careful in approaching his refurbished office since Helena Steele's release from hospital, Featherstone's surveillance identified her in the breastplate of the Red Archangel, Circe drugged on Revolution, circling the block.

Photographic/Epistolary Quotations. Christopher Featherstone cleverly devised a photographic/epistolary strategy involving Bridget Lovegrove: (i) **LETTERS** – Bridget composed a succession of letters addressed to Helena Steele using her Record Label's address, a ruse designed to ingratiate herself to gather information. Following suitable phrases of admiration Bridget became more daring; *"I want to be your stencil, please ink me into your life and work."* Shifting the emphasis she wrote of the Kremlin being her model, authoritarian and absolute, with just the right tone of submissiveness. (ii) **PHOTOGRAPHIC** – Using high-speed film and Fabian Roxburgh's 'Nam photographer they undertook intense surveillance of Helena Steele, capturing her at the discothèque, compiling a profile of acquaintances and of her residential mobility now she had abandoned the hacienda apartment. The Abstract Expressionist surfaces of her persona carried a rebellious aureole with high-visibility and she was always adorned with the statuesque idolatry of feminine admirers.

Stolen Kisses. "Sitting in the cramped dressing room, her back-up singers very languorous squashed among hanging garments, I suddenly felt her brushing my hair, with secretive strokes, camouflaged, while I explained my accountancy skills and what I could offer. I had occasion to observe her frigidity with the juvenile Casanovas knocking at her dressing room door. Her incandescence, as you warned me, is swift and lethal." Bridget Lovegrove turned away briefly as Helena Steele's combo took to the stage and a strobe light falling upon her highlighted how the crossover straps of her dress formed a crisp X, geometrically centred between her shoulder blades. Christopher Featherstone suggestively compared the women coupled together in the dressing room, Bridget's natural growth being of a genuine leaf spiraling about Helena's carved marble one, a juxtaposition tempting for a man approaching middle-age. "What did you say?" Bridget answered the question with grace: "What I feel about you, Christopher ... I like your face well enough, but would I want to smooch it? Like you she would sense my lying to her, and you know my stolen kisses belong to Calvin. Sex with other partners is impossible for a straight woman, my *jewel* is a brazier burning for him right now. Christopher, she's too frontal for me, and those tomato-red lips of hers ... *Psycho*!"

Malcontent Of The Year. Brooding on generational conspiracies surrounding 'Nam's contemporary political theatrics, and the five-year anniversary of JFK's assassination, the passage of a lifetime for today's youth, Stephen Maxwell strode across the campus grounds his existential self-definition a fading image. Could the anti-war movement be losing momentum? Emerging from below an arch of Spanish sandstone the Clytemnestra figure of Helena Steele imposed her presence on the quadrangle, her radical feminine devotees spreading into a semi-circle to gather Maxwell up in their wingèd formation. Most students avoided these public confrontations, disinterested in the Politics of Cruelty, the circularity of their existence contoured by Authority and smoothly polished, the dissonance of violence contracted to a television image on the evening bulletins. Maxwell stood puzzled before the proscenium arch of Spanish sandstone, on the stage perimeter of the quadrangle, unable to fathom this subversive subculture of young women, their tangential aspirations of liberation, surely a mere sideshow before the drama of the Vietnam War. "The man shall fall!" Maxwell threw his arms in the air *à la Richard Nixon* in his triumph, a stupefying non-verbal gesture conveying the hopelessness of the American Age. Helena Steele, dressed in her favoured Russian red soaking up the menstrual flow of the world's women, interpreted the mysterious joke within the words as a literal fact, but her glance clearly encompassed capitalized Man.

Invitations To A Masked Ball. Rehearsing in-studio another local garage band heavy on electric organ and fourth-dimensional guitar chords, signed for the **EOS** label, Christopher Featherstone worked through more contemporary lyrics with his favorite melodist. Front-runner for the name of the band was The Vibes, perfect caricatures for updating famous blues chords, *Get Smart* witticisms propelled by increasing amplification, and a general insolence captured in the rehearsal single, *Summer of Rage.*

> Let's all step out onto the streets this summer and die.
> Let's all step out onto the streets this summer and die.
> Walking through People's Park let's all get high.
> America is no Greece and 'Nam no goddam Troy.
> America is no Greece and 'Nam no goddam Troy.
> Walking through People's Park let's search and destroy.
> Revolution – Revolution's Summer of Rage
> Burning – Burning down society's cage.

Featherstone enthused the band members, inflamed their melt-down performances committed to tape with the suggestion they attack the lyric and blues melody with the vengeance of a Minotaur goring Agamemnon, until the amplifiers fused. "Where did a *square* like you find such true moments of expression?" Featherstone spoke of comparing portraits, say Richard Nixon's with Jimi Hendrix's, one throwing his arms in the air in victory, the other his Stratocaster, and asked what both images conveyed of the late-sixties. More and more he was visualizing spacetime as slices comparable with film-frames, seeing existence not as *flow*, but fragmentation, and therefore capable of re-editing. Transcendent resonances, subtle variations of thinking, spheres of sensation could be re-analyzed and re-integrated, primary among them the knock on his office door and entrance of Samantha Westwood earlier, her stepping across the space of the room a succession of framed moments curving pleasure's horizon. Kissing her cheek's velvet plum as she passed him the formal invitation to a Masked Ball devised by Calvin he inter-cut slices of memory into the scene from their *lost weekend* in '64, her nudity displayed with baroque flamboyance in the hotel suite bath, her head flung back with thoughts no more fathomable than those of Louis XV's mistresses erotically astride a divan in the paintings of Boucher. Quietude reigned in the late-evening as he fingered the ornate invitation and realized his statuesque soul chose the only form of stability in three-dimensional space, its human persona, but ultimately of what interest was this incarnation's passions and ambitions?

Dispatches From 'Nam. *"Like Roman Legions the ranks of National Guardsmen, clean-uniformed, helmeted, sterile in formal sameness, challenge the flute-playing Flower People of their own generation, a potent display of American yin-and-yang."* Fleur's reading voice solemnly banished endless replays of Cream's *White Room* from the turntables in the apartment block. Listening to this prose the gathered tenants-in-common were saying *No!* to the Somme of their generation, their stiff upper lips flowed with moustaches and beards, some wore the Stars-and-Stripes upon their backs, but in mockery. *"What is this ritualized camouflage? National Guardsmen, so prim and proper and precise, brutalized by Flower People, while the disheveled Grunts are brutalized by the jungles of 'Nam, and the fragile, conical-hatted peasants in pyjamas are blown along dusty roads by the blasts of war. What are we to make of Johnson and Nixon's hairstyle today, the cartography of their faces delivering policy on television, what are we to make of Jackie O. and Janis Joplin, and where is the metaphysical no-man's-land slickness and smoothness visible in Diana Ross, Smokey Robinson, James Brown and Marvin Gaye leading us? Sure, I've dipped in my oar, but it's dragging in a raging River Styx!"* Fleur's flower child sister dowsed Fabian Roxburgh in her heavily fragranced Indian oils as he spread his orgiastic carnival of collages across the apartment floor later, his prose tempting her to sexual abandonment among the autobiographical fragments. Sex exploded the domestic scene in a distillation of color where Matisse-meets-Pop-Art-installation, for the flower child wore a braless T-shirt dipped in an emulsion of tomato, recognized by Roxburgh as worn by Helena Steele! The late news bulletin carried images of a helicopter undercarriage stenciled in black pepper tracer fire plunging onto a smoke-rimmed LZ inter-cut with the pretentious puppet show ventriloquism of Paris peace talks.

The World Seen Through Horn-Rimmed Glasses. Smoothly anonymous in a tailored mid-sixties double-breasted business suit, idealized especially for accountants and given distinction by horn-rimmed glasses, Bridget Lovegrove focused Helena Steele approaching her glass-walled inner office and unconsciously teased her hair's bouffant.

"Miss Steele – welcome to my sanctum, for clientele privacy is paramount. Shall I arrange for coffee?" Masked behind her horn-rimmed glasses Bridget focused scarlet infused with jade, vibrant vermilion blushing milky opal flesh tones, and subdued a wave of *frisson* engendered by remembrance of moments in the discothèque when her hair was being brushed. "Am I to call you Miss Lovegrove, like your simpering clerks?" With economical omnipotence Helena imposed her Amazonian self-assurance inside the geometric envelope of space and Bridget felt the glassed-in office frost over although her horn-rims remained clear enough. She deftly teased from Helena obscure business and social connections knowing they would prove valuable to Christopher Featherstone, mapping them innocently enough, her questioning financially focused. Spreading the financial charts across Featherstone's office desk late that afternoon for them to examine Bridget perceived the encyclopedic density of thought crafted in his person, his Byronic *Don Juan* seriousness leavened with a modern sensibility, and he was clearly *on the rebound*. A subdued knock at the door suddenly echoed. While he answered, Bridget stood before **HOPE**, the painting's Wildean chloroform of color-texture quite smothering as if to render one semi-conscious of this world's pain. Miranda Westwood's rococo embellishment of youth undertook a barely audible conversation with Featherstone and he passed her an envelope. The fuse of a smile irresistibly burned during introductions. "Fabian appears to have lost interest in the Personals. I prefer to keep our relationship breathing with the occasional cryptic phrase but he seems to want a novel." Bridget thought she recognized the envelope being played with by Miranda as she spoke, the ornate scripting of its invitation. Here was precociousness diminished by the thought of sex's actual act of darkness. Now she half-blushed behind her horn-rimmed glasses, glimpsing her own luscious face in Featherstone's mind reflected as in a mirror, that luminosity in his eyes, gently veiled, the definition in his voice speaking to her, how his presence ruptured the normalcy of her existence. His adoration would remain sealed inside the envelope of his conscience, his character's wax hardened to the image of fortitude he purveyed, although the painting of **HOPE** held her eye. Miranda unconsciously curled up on the sofa mimicking the posture of **HOPE** in the painting, blindfolded by inner thoughts as she perused the calligraphy of the Masked Ball's invitation.

Masked Ball I. Shoulders swathed under Tyrian purple, brows crowned in laurel, face masked, Christopher Featherstone mimicked the carriage of the Imperial favorite at his zenith, moving among the hundred guests at the Westwood's Masked Ball, beneath dazzling chandeliers igniting the ballroom itself in a magnesium glow. Maintaining an implacable profile standing by the crystalline lotus of the punch bowl he observed numerous chamber-like encounters among the guests, then watched the constellation of dancing arabesques responding to Stan Getz's *bossa novas*, before identifying the Ball's hosts, King Solomon and the Queen of Sheba, Calvin and Samantha Westwood, mingling, talking, bringing light to the conversations. Intricately layered in eastern accoutrements, delicate golden chains adorning her cheeks, swinging from a headdress, jewels gracing her neck, Sheba inspired jealousy in a would-be lover that she was no more than Solomon's richly saddled mule, circulating his wealth among the guests to garner admiration. Featherstone promptly offered her a chalice of punch but she didn't immediately recognize the identity behind the mask of his presence's colonnade of rhetoric. "The Fame of Solomon is as renownèd as the commercialization of his wisdom. In his presence God Himself witnesses His Own magnificent flowering on Earth. And his Queen, *who is she that looketh forth as the morning, fair as the moon, clear as the sun, and terrible as an army of banners?* She is a golden desert rose unfolding harmony and peace poised before me amid this wasteland of wealth. So should royalty's necklace be bejeweled with infinitely expensive precious stones." Featherstone's conversational opening identified him and although she feigned ignorance, how her torso's mold dazzled in its ripening for the touch of adultery to bruise; words fell from her lips catching him by surprise, as she tasted the punch: "*Let him kiss me with the kisses of his mouth: for thy love is better than wine.* Shall we dance, Caesar, before you are assassinated in the Capitol, for I overheard some guests, personal friends I'll have you know, conspiring to seduce and abandon you." To the *bossa nova* rhythms she curved her motion with all the cloying baklava of Stan Getz's saxophone phrasing, burning and burning but never reduced to ashes. Caesar-and-Cyd-Charisse dancing they hoisted a sexual sail gathering every inch of breathy air flowing from the saxophone to fill its fabric, and she talked while saturated in motion: "*I sleep, but my heart waketh. By night on my bed I sought him, but I found him not. Saw ye him whom my soul loveth?*" Featherstone murmured something about his investiture in the purple and the scarlet thread of her mouth and of the sacrilegious moment of Caesar's assassination, how his name had become an ointment to salve the conscience of conspirators down the Ages. Remembering her pubis as a delicious pomegranate, his sexual insertions as a sword sliding into a scabbard of melting jewels, he said to her: "*Thy navel is like a round goblet which wanteth not liquor.*" With a falling countenance, serious as the faces on so many nineteenth-century English paintings of the School of Leighton, Waterhouse and High Victorians she gestured over his shoulder at Solomon and a brilliantly costumed woman conversing together beneath one of the indoor palm trees' explosion of frondage. "*My belovèd is gone into his garden, to the bed of spices.*"

Masked Ball II. "Solomon was surely explaining to you how he would go the way of all earth, I suppose. Decay is endemic, so a wealthy man, a Prince among men, should carve his own tomb in his lifetime." Christopher Featherstone brought his own aristocratic imagination to focus on the glorious seventeenth-century apparition who had concluded details with some assignation with Solomon beneath the palm frondage. Bridget Lovegrove's slippered feet peeped from below the hem of her fulsome veils of silk, her footfalls shaking the very foundations of the Westwood's House, but did she recognize *him* behind the mask, a chiseled Caesar: "Shall we dance? I observed you passing so poetically across the ballroom just now towards this palm tree with Maecenas, but he has abandoned you it would seem." Swivelling her airy equipage on the fulcrum of his hand she *bossa novaed* her stunning underneath arabesque swathed in tiers of glistening fabric, eroticizing herself on the sounds and rhythms of this music-softening marble, effortlessly, translucently absorbing herself in a subsequent samba, her torso and silks amorously kissing. A barely visible angler's strand of hair tickled his fancy in the pool of music, caught him up and played him like a fish, while she floated across the mirrors in the ballroom like perfume in glass compared to the other feminine militia. "You have rendered the man breathless: may he claim a lock of your hair?" Laughing, she released a kaleidoscope of tinctures onto the air: "What a timorous assault, for Caesar! You look like you've been gnawing on a bone all evening. Would you be my guardian sylph for an evening, or a middle-aged Faun?" Feather-bedded in her spacious gown she seemed poised for any amorous offense. Featherstone said: "May any Infidel nail himself to the Cross suspended from your virginal neck?"

Masked Ball III. Icarus splashed into a reflective pool set amid a symmetrical rectangle of lawn. Turning his upward gaze from a first floor balcony where he glimpsed Solomon and the dazzling cosmic fragrance of Bridget's silken incarnation, Christopher Featherstone surveyed the roasting carcasses of pig and lambs, stood a little adrift of the energetically talking guests, his own excellent *cedar of Lebanon* preoccupied with hostess duties. Presently, Hamlet dressed in *the trappings and suits of woe* approached, himself a consummate loner, a melancholic black-and-white etching at Solomon's feast, soon recognized as Fabian Roxburgh. How did he secure an invitation? Miranda Westwood! But where was she? *"Frailty, thy name is woman!* Let me then embrace my own emptiness. You see I carry the skull of my previous incarnation to soliloquize with, or on." Featherstone's laurel wreath of victory pressed into his skull like a crown of thorns thinking of Solomon effortlessly seducing the astonishingly vivid Bridget Lovegrove, feeding among her lilies while he languished for the honey and milk under Sheba's tongue, longed to be Icarus falling into her fountain, the well of her living waters. Rousing himself to respond to Hamlet, he said: "Where then is your celestial, and your soul's idol, the most beautiful ..." Hamlet's glance sharpened appreciably with this exchange and he raised a self-analyzing smile beneath his mask: "She too is suited in solemn black, wears an inky cloak, but sulks somewhere because a certain incomparable beauty is tonight *the observ'd of all observers*, and not herself, or the Queen of Sheba. I have transcribed quotations from Psalm 46 for these *beau monde* at play which I have been reciting to myself walking the *allée* of trees there, trying to fathom their mystery, for there certainly is one. Would you care to peruse the verses yourself?"

> God is our refuge and strength, a very present help in trouble.
> Therefore **WILL** not we fear, though the earth be removed, and though the mountains be carried into the midst of the sea;
> Though the waters thereof roar and be troubled, though the mountains **SHAKE** with the swelling thereof. Selah.
> He maketh wars to cease unto the end of the earth; he breaketh the bow, and cutteth the **SPEAR** in sunder; he burneth the chariot in the fire.

Featherstone observed Hamlet's *mould of form* move away down a path dissecting immaculately manicured lawn, indulging his taste for soliloquy, pausing to rest an arm on a large urn.

Masked Ball IV. *"I am black, but comely."* Mesmerized, Christopher Featherstone had discovered Miranda Westwood, unbelievably masquerading as the psychedelic icon of today's youth, Jimi Hendrix, wearing off-black face makeup, an Afro wig with bandana soaked in a dissonance of colour, a jeweled choker. Provocatively unashamed, she added: "I take whatever sex I please, and what pleases me." No wonder sweet bells were jangling in Fabian Roxburgh's mind! "He has worked so hard to melt my ice's purity, my *button* is small but very hard." The wispy add-on moustache was suitably lifelike. Featherstone wandered away from this violet in youth's primy nature fascinated with her pretense and success at eluding recognition by her mother and father while blushing right under their noses, perhaps conversing with them briefly. The first floor balcony was again illumined by those Olympian Gods while he floundered, earthbound, like Icarus, the wings of his laurel wreath could not raise him.

Late-Spring Scented With Its Death. Porphyro-without-Madeleine, Fabian Roxburgh ascended the apartment block, stepping over sprawled torsos now quiet as phantoms chained to ethereal space and glanced in on the flower child lying on the shore of the bed as if among sand dunes at the beach, her perfumed musk oozing onto the drugged air. He peeped closer at her remarkable eyelashes and the mouth licked in passion, pearls of perspiration absorbing the sandalwood fragrance in her pores, and pondered why the rock of his heart soaked in the sweet honey of these women had not lost its hardness. Even her Sivan dance astride him leaving him covered in telltale saffron paste stains and the cleanliness of her jasmine teeth aglow with a puzzled smile as he mastered this trial of strength and self-discipline, only drew from him the murmur: "I'll remember you on into my next life." Seated at the typewriter as Hamlet's photographic negative of his true presence he attempted more *Dispatches From 'Nam*, matching together the dissimilar *square* patches of the time: *No Thracian breeze has forestalled the US fleet, and considering the sacrifices made to the Gods, the Commander-in-Chief's tactic of pounding the DMZ and then ironically appeasing the North Vietnamese in Paris, Gay Paree, with Peace Talks smacks of a mind dislocated from the realities of Total War. What is Hanoi? What is Saigon? Surely the Commander-in-Chief now understands the North Vietnamese and Viet Cong are engaged in Total War! Burning on an LZ is the funeral pyre of a Huey. What penance the Grunts are enduring through the austere practices of a jungle existence, as someone mentioned to me, they are living through Hell-on-Earth to quicken the attainment of their next birth. Birds squawk, a Company's mascot parrot talks, but can they read Hamlet? Above the Grunts slogging waist-deep through a narrow stream a monkey freely swings from tree to tree, both knowing here is the terminus of Truth.* Drowsy as a rose, trailing a pungent scent compounded of many fragrances well slept in, Fleur drifted by and could be heard in the quietude flushing the toilet, and when she returned lazy fingertips dragged across his Hamlet costume during the retreat back to the bedroom.

When he joined her she muttered sleepily: "Shall I undress now?" Already though she was roaming the horizons of her dreamscapes, wherever they were.

Caesar's Crossing Of The Rubicon. Darkness' decomposition of light flattened space's imagery. Traversing the pre-dawn black void of the city's maze, feeling inside the skin of his own opaque shadow as Caesar, Christopher Featherstone made a precautionary circuit of streets in which his office block squatted three-dimensionally, as was now his custom. The bizarre malcontentedness of Helena Steele's nihilism, somehow triggered by associations he could not fathom, perhaps just a symptom of the Time, and her aspiration to martyr herself in some public manner had sharpened his instincts. Answers were not forthcoming and he did not especially seek them, with her. Over the course of numerous evenings he had followed her to a succession of random *safe houses* where friends and acquaintances would lodge her, so keeping her under reasonable surveillance was unrealistic, a neglect which made him as uneasy as Caesar should have been on the *Ides of March*. This rigorous surveillance rewarded him with the discovery that Helena Steele always deviated first by his office block where she noted every entrance and exit point. Investigations he undertook speaking with the other tenants and security people revealed she had become friendly with them, seeking information and establishing how to gain access late in an evening to throw a surprise party for him. Too late to park in the office block's undercover precincts because of the hour he chose a well-lit site nearby in the heart of the city and walked back. Occasional impastoed splashes from car headlights identified his shadow against a building. Coming to a starkly illuminated phone booth he dialed his office number and purposely allowed it to ring out. Passing through the security doors he quietly maneuvered his way along the corridor towards his darkened office looking for signs of disturbance and forced entry. Caesar crossed the Rubicon!

Dénouement With Style. Sculpted for extreme tension, Christopher Featherstone summoned up his memorization of the office layout, swinging open the door with a feigned casual nonchalance, glimpsing an upper torso carelessly backlit by a flash of neon bleeding through the window. A white-orange burst from a hand gun silhouetted by a subsequent eruption of flickering neon confirmed his wisdom in crouching low for the bullet tore into the frame of the door. Instinctively knowing she would be trigger-happy and precipitate he chanced himself on this method of approach, uncoiling to launch his shoulder into her hesitant and stationary sketch outlined against the window, throwing her off-balance as the hand gun again discharged. A sour aroma redolent of a discothèque's cramped dressing room enveloped his senses as she cushioned his fall against the edge of his desk and collapsed underneath him very bruised and winded. He snapped her wrist and the hand gun dropped away. Illumination momentarily blinded this salamander in a T-shirt, her living fire smothered, her flaming sulphur drawn from *Paradise Lost* neutralized of its menace by the cone of light from the desk lamp. Gone was the flare against the Russian red T-shirt and Helena Steele spearing space with a bullet destined for his heart.

Interrogation. "When all reasonableness is so recklessly abandoned one is clothed finally only in space with the bowl of cupped hands to eat out of. I am not going to ask you to take me to your mind's place of metaphor but I will tell you I have an antidote to this poison coagulated in the veins of Time. You and I are simply actors carefully arranged in a frame, contemporary motifs against which the bright scintillation of stars visible earlier as I approached the office highlighted the distance between Heaven and Hell. What is legible of the script you are working with may emerge later, perhaps in a palimpsest effect, but we cannot know everything about anyone, and precious jewels deep in the earth can only be perfected by extreme force." Christopher Featherstone had made other calls from the phone booth on the corner and now paused gazing down at the poisonous mandala of a woman still half-crushed against his desk. With a definitive touch the strand of her spider's web had trembled and come away isolating her from its tracery.

Confession. "Authority! Authority is not my oracle! These years of excess have been dominated by men eager for the fame of martyrdom, eager to soak up the clamour of media attention, to be angular in a smooth, round world. So my wrist is snapped, it will heal and my forefinger will again squeeze a trigger. The time has passed when a young woman will simply be lithe in a bikini climbing up and down the ladder of a swimming pool to induce a leer on the face of men. I am simply a summoning up of *no-thing* to fill a silence. Police sirens? Very precautionary of you! Why are you dressed in that ludicrous costume? The spillage of your red blood staining the purple fabric could have been so visceral an image, a theatrical moment for the prose of the newspapers to sensationalize. Beware, other silent scorpions will stalk you, the sting is but delayed." But her voice weakened with the crash of the Police stumbling down the corridor outside the office, its lambent candle flame shrinking before a rush of sudden breeze whistling across the terraces of Dante's *Inferno*.

Swamis At Leisure. Combing a hairstyle permanently out-of-fashion and smothering his face in shaving cream, Fabian Roxburgh longed for a bath of summer beach sand and Blue Hawaiian skies, a metaphysical canvas of sparkling waves to transfigure himself against, for perhaps they would assuage his ache for Miranda Westwood. Fleur's illusion surfaced on the sculptural flat plane of the bathroom mirror, her expression conveying the mathematics of morality as impenetrable as calculus in announcing Christopher Featherstone's arrival. Wheeling the midnight-blue street-rod from the curb, Roxburgh's meditative thought delved the kernel of Featherstone's news: "Could it be a theological problem? Like 'Nam is? You found this Cardinaless respectably *femme*, boringly *fatale*?" The ocean's rustling taffeta of space, with fluid, diaphanous, silken waves caressing the shoreline, disintegrated the box-like geometry of office and apartment block, evoked a serene Samadhi and redemptive grace following the year's dramas. "Well, Christopher, let's keep her strictly a limited-edition, a footnote to the sixties." Bridget Lovegrove's weekend had obviously passed in a post-coital daze, seated now in her glass-panelled office as if coming out of deep-freeze, half-rising to welcome Featherstone and Roxburgh before collapsing back. This Hypatia of chartered accountants, mistress of Heaven-and-Hell's double-entry book-keeping, converted devotees with her languorous Viennese mannerisms as much as her Californian grace on the tennis court, a veritable stunner in horn-rimmed glasses. Morbidly embarrassed to imagine himself her blackmailer, a victim he had fallen hopelessly in love with, Featherstone listened to Roxburgh caricature Helena Steele: "The *femme fatale* of these late-sixties has arisen, more dangerous because more political, and committed to wielding money, power and revenge on a wider stage. Christopher curled her scorpion's tail over her own torso and then struck, driving the sting deep." While he talked Featherstone sensed a thread of melody, atmospheric nuances of lyric gather inner audibility in his thoughts, anthem for a feminist martyrdom, music for a rock aria The Vibes could bring out in the New Year.

> Down at the discothèque
> Helena and all the girls
> Are dancing up a New Revolution.
> Boadicea and Joan of Arc
> Twiggy and Madame Mao
> Are dancing up a New Solution.

In The Furnace Of Revolution. The thin film of skin layering the festering boil of the city burst and the poison of revolt flowed, ironically just as South Vietnam relented and admitted the NLF to the Paris peace talks, with Stephen Maxwell's megaphone the voice of the protesters sweeping up the constricted artery of the Terrace into the conservative heart of the CBD. Humanity's global whimper down the centuries was said to reach the ear of God, even over the *howl* of the cosmic Big Bang, and the cartoon deaths of millions in interminable wars said to be sketches for eventual transfer to a canvas of *The Resurrection* beyond even the dreams of a Michelangelo. Revolution-and-Resurrection! Humanity was forged from the unthinkable furnace of the Big Bang whose sparks now filled the night-sky in a blaze of cold brilliance. Christopher Featherstone stepped aboard the schooner to usher in the martini season of summer with Samantha Westwood. Let the eternally vibrating galaxies form their spiraling blast patterns from the war between Heaven and Hell, humanity's residual imprint from the smashing of the diamond chalice scattering across the sky was similarly a sphere in turmoil, but this evening Samantha honoured him with her heart's rose on the lovely breast of her silken gown. Over the culinary symmetries of her cooking

Featherstone said: "In this storm of existence, ploughing through the heaving ocean, our soul has fixed us like the prow of a trireme, certain to sink ... Perhaps someday an archaeologist will discover remnants of our being drowned in the Sea of Time and ponder the significance of what he is gazing upon. Samantha, the prow of the trireme is guided by a pilot and we are turned into the storm by a hand on the wheel to out-face its passions." With remarkable prescience Samantha murmured: *"L'anné dernière à Marienbad*!"

X

BLUE CHRISTMAS

I. Literary - *À la recherché du temps perdu* (Proust). Christopher Featherstone took tea-and-madeleine with Celeste Hawthorne on the cusp of summer for she was sketching in chalks illustrations from the fabulous literary creation, his own bedside reading for the coming months. Impressions drew from him these conversational observations: (i) "Opening the first volume is to remove the dewdrop from a *parfum flaçon*, for a genie levitates and transforms the monochrome space of the page, a flattened plane, although luminously black-and-white, like a bud drawn from narcissus leaves." (ii). "A soul's silhouetted personae, gripped in a loosening coil of sentences, begin to unravel and flow against the fabric like brushwork, now Renoir's, now Monet's, now Moreau's." (iii). "The light of Genius manifests in a mosaic of characterizations, remodeling the perspectives of a lifetime's sweeping arc." (iv). "The rose matures reaching for Paradise, but Life is snared by thorns increasingly erect, tearing at the human sensibility, so can glory be attained through the Art of Substitution?"

II. Musical – Poème d'Extase (Scriabin). Sailing among the offshore islands on the Westwood's schooner, a weekend sea cruise along the Arcadian coastline, Christopher Westwood lounged on deck with Samantha, martinis in hand, enjoying sunset's display of profound repose. But the spray of raying ecstasy faded as the day's brilliant brass melody diminished to one harmonious chord in diminuendo. A sublime odalisque within the breathing space of open ocean, schooner-and-Samantha conjured sensations of delirious yearning as evening's organized silence descended, and the breeze which had earlier filled sailcloth to bursting fell away, leaving Featherstone with an unsustainable, imperfect illusion. Stinging a little with sunburn, her flesh the epiphany of a fully mature rose, Samantha visited him in his office, a statuesque Cyd Charisse in perpetual motion, listened with him at the tomb of Scriabin's soul, succumbed to the immutable orchestration of voluptuous longing, became imbued with a sonorous orgasm. Later they had pre-dinner drinks at a cocktail lounge designed for assignations and sipped their favourite martinis with Scriabin's *Poème d'Extase* still reverberating through their sexual afterglow.

III. Visual – The Fable of Arachne (Velàsquez). Bridget Lovegrove's calligraphy, a spidery handwriting covering her accountancy journals in a web of numbers, herself a transfigured Arachne weaving Christopher Featherstone and Calvin Westwood upon her loom, embroidered and interwove their financial and sensual lives, became an inexhaustible ribbon fusing them all. Lying in semi-darkness on his office's sofa, neon flushing the window-space, Featherstone considered incarnation's curious pattern, its embroidery of the fabric of space-time, of light threaded with coloured cloth interwoven through body-and-soul as a wave pulses through the ocean. The web of the window cascaded with a neon iridescence and in the visitation of mythological dreams as he slept Bridget came to him with a smile diaphanous through sensual lace. Molten in a cuirass of webbed drapery bejeweled with her haunting calligraphy she was equidistant yet simultaneous in space with Samantha Westwood, herself lucidly contoured, marblesque perhaps, but electric with unparalleled virtuosity on a sexual loom!

The Lion Lay Down With The Lamb. Cleanly sterile, uniformly inert, parade-ground perfect in formation the National Guardsmen formed an impenetrable barrier to the picturesque softness of the Flower Children bejeweled in dewdrops of colour, as if their interior illuminations were being made visible to the world. Doves erupted from the midst of the amorphous assembly of Flower Children, garlands of divinity for the manifestation of these delicate angels approaching the phalanx of National Guardsmen, imaged like the Lambs of God, and among them Fabian Roxburgh glimpsed Miranda Westwood's more commercial cliché. Were the rosettes of delicately sculpted paint Fleur and her sister had patiently adorned themselves with imaginary wounds to come should the National Guardsmen open fire? Roxburgh marveled how the Rose of Youth had now unfolded this generation's petals too far for them to ever recover the purity of a bud's innocence again. Over the rim of a calyx Fleur addressed an impassive National Guardsman: "Did you ever spend childhood summers among flower-cups drinking in their beauty? Or did you prefer to fondle your make-believe bullets instead of these gentle flower-buds?" Could such imagery from the canvas of '68 leave profound traces on the time-to-come? Numberless flowers-of-youth advanced on the National Guardsmen hoping the muscular forms of their exhausted and bruised blossoms would weigh down the rifle barrels!

Be-In Be-Out. "So, who is this Eddie Phoenix, and Johnny Esquire?" Fabian Roxburgh suffered from languor's arousal as camphor and sandalwood oozing from the sisters' smudged copies of each other was now synchronous with his breathing in the space of the apartment, where the air possessed the texture of curiously flavoured paste. "The Paganini of Existentialism perhaps?" Camelot was forever besmirched, student ideologues were arguing off-campus these days, were the protégées of icons such as

Che, Mao and Ho, and marginalized living was all the rage. Cheesecloth skimmed off the *love me* arabesques of the sisters swathed in a floral aroma of murmuring voices. Their sunflower faces loaded with pollen prepared to gaze eternally at Helios through the summer. Moving with soothing unreality a group of communal residents squeezed into the apartment to deliver a seasonal message. "Peace, man. Look, as you serve the military Stock Exchange in 'Nam, our *Be-In* here can't be your scene, so we request you find somewhere else to crash. This has been such a *heavy* year for us, man, and we're from different scenes, the jigsaw arrangement isn't a cool fit." Roxburgh graciously accepted his descriptor as a *square* and cut straight to formula, telling them: "Christmas in 'Nam is looking good for me, and I can see in the New Year on some Golgotha."

E-L-V-I-S. Television attained an exquisite apotheosis when Elvis illuminated the surface of the screen his face's translucent pastel radiantly idealized. Fabian Roxburgh now witnessed the edited version of the NBC Special filmed in June beamed across the world, the destiny of the name **E-L-V-I-S** emblazoned in defiance of the fallen Archangel's ascendancy through 1968, a year shaped for falls from Grace, beginning with the tragedy of the Tet offensive swinging humanity toward nihilism's futility. **E-L-V-I-S**, letters inscribed by God Himself miraculously effected a revelation, transcended the negativity of the year, for he was simply too handsome ever to copy, too breathtaking in trans-human beauty, the beginning of a new Antiquity future generations would marvel at amid the chaos of a world gone mad. Armoured like God's warrior in Renaissance black chalk, his smile's unprecedented illumination dazzling against the burnished glow of his face, Elvis commanded America's ceremonial reconciliation with its Spiritual Destiny, reaffirmed the National Identity at the nadir of a world-wide crisis. During a commercial break, Roxburgh touched a barely involved Fleur and explained how the spatial nuances from being among the audience and the edited film version transformed his understanding of this moment in Time: "Orpheus on Mount Olympus can only be enchanted by this illusion of Elvis, and the allusion to his own loss of Eurydice, for in marrying Priscilla surely he too will lose her. How like a golden death mask of some mighty Pharaoh Elvis' face is, timeless and eternal in its beauty; Fleur, we are all Elvis' shadows!" Elvis' daring membrane of black leather, the musicalisations of his posture, baroque affirmations of the Absolute, the renaissance of lyricism in his miraculous voice, a silken thread weaving their tapestry of songs, left Fleur untouched, her ears marble her expression a mask. A glass dome descended upon Roxburgh's mind for Elvis awakened having vanished for a time in a MGM sleep of dreams, but he knew, like Orpheus, the demi-god would have to vanish having *become* life already, divine breath. "Elvis absolutely believes in the personae of his songs, but does the listener? We have entered the voice and *become* as a generation. World War II devastated and pared back the Earth so Elvis might be revealed as a dazzling seam of gold in the reef of divine music."

Feathers Heavy As Stone. Practicing tennis serves on court with a club coach, Bridget Lovegrove dazzled in the whitest of tunic fabrics, its hemline ecstatically fluttering, the elastic grip of her briefs on her inner thighs, rhythmically stretching and relaxing, widening the fissures in Fabian Roxburgh's conscience. "Standing motionless at the net there, serene, inside the space-time of the court, even God would hold-in His breath." Christopher Featherstone had sauntered over and was welcomed by Roxburgh's spoken thought delivered with a passionate in-rush of breath. This visual slice of time integrated with the skin of space created impastoed splashes of romantic grace exuberant with intertwined harmonies unexpectedly scripted into these revolutionary days. Featherstone became tangential, seating himself at the table, trying on Roxburgh's aviator sunglasses and feeling circumscribed by a kaleidoscope of vanities: "Fabian, you mentioned on the phone leaving for 'Nam, but wouldn't you prefer to script a Christmas romance here? Bridget has the lips of a sibyl, and she told me of some new clients of hers, Eddie Phoenix and Johnny Esquire ..." Running off court with a curious skip and gathering up a towel from her tennis bag, Bridget joined them rubbing her liquefied hair, sipped her waiting orange juice and soaked up the perspiration glistening her flushed flesh. Casually, his eyes only aligned with Bridget's lineaments being toweled dry, Roxburgh asked: "Are you undertaking surveillance of these hustlers?" Handing off the sunglasses, Featherstone smiled with his sly allusion: "Hustlers? Yes, a couple of feathers fallen to Earth from the dark Archangel's wing!" Bridget's sibylline mouth came away from the chilled glass of orange juice.

Flight Of An Archangel. Burdened with the expectations of a Delacroixian lithograph, perhaps Hamlet in the graveyard of the world soliloquizing over Yorick's skull, Eddie Phoenix laid a caressing hand on the glass-bubble of the helicopter's cockpit and paused, before swinging himself aboard. Observing everything some distance from the helipad, Christopher Featherstone felt the rush of stifling summer air swirl his suit into undulations as a convertible *coupé* accelerated by onto the two-dimensional space of the tarmac, Johnny Esquire at the wheel and beside him a commandingly beautiful Nefertiti figure vaguely resembling the famous pop star's wife. Raising the towering black fleece of her hair with both palms as he kissed her, Johnny Esquire himself possessed a hairstyle worthy of the expressive dimensions of ink in a caricature cartoon *à la Rowlandson*. Following the *coupé* on its circuitous ambulation through the city and the suburban by-ways Featherstone remembered the helicopter's exploration of the Westwood's schooner and glimpsed the insect-eye of its glass-bubble, wings drooping, from the crest of a dune close by the Monastery precincts. While the talons of Helena Steele may have been withdrawn from the flesh of his existence a far more ominous and dangerous shadow began to cast its all-too-familiar outline across his dreams. Awakening he immediately transcribed this dream-sequence: (i) Helen of Troy *aka* Priscilla Presley astral traveled with Hermes *aka* Elvis Presley to Egypt, a pair of wandering exiles traversing the sand dunes sweeping up to the Sphinx. (ii) Hermes' smooth-skinned, burnished mask transmigrates into a Phoenix from whose eye a tear falls in which is imaged Christ's face. (iii) Featherstone crosses a courtyard with its chequerboard effect and falls into a sarcophagus modelled on a *coupé* whereupon he dies and floats on a papyrus funeral barge along the Nile. (iv) Aeons of incarnations of spiritual debauchees fuse into the feathers of the mighty fallen Archangel's wing-beat sweeping through three-dimensional space trying to lift Heavenward. Disturbed by these visionary portents Featherstone awaited the coming of dawn with moonlight-and-Beethoven puzzling through the power of dreams to slice up space-time and re-arrange the scenes from past, present and future so they were simultaneous with each other.

Romance Via A Telephoto Lens. Obscure advertisements published in idiosyncratic journals and magazines named after modern icons, **CHE ... MAO ... HO ... JACKIE**, and calling for a revamped Salvation Army under the wing of Lucifer, surfaced illustrating analogies between God's Disciples and the fallen Archangel's; the fringe benefits of prizes and holiday camps formed a glossy attraction, and a travel agency offered cut-price tours of sacrilegious sites. Christopher Featherstone undertook investigations into the sudden appearance of these journals but had to conclude their manifestation was inexplicable. Eating *chocolate torte* with Samantha Westwood aboard the schooner he spread first editions of the journals across a low table. "Look closely at the photographs ... you can see why I hurried over." Cleverly transposed shots of Calvin and Bridget *en flagrante delicto* amid a series of décors both indoors and outdoors, telephoto shots taken from a sweeping helicopter of Samantha and himself kissing on the prow of the schooner populated the pages along side the *Thoughts* of Che, Mao and Ho, and images of the sharp political fashion sense of Jackie O. "But ... these advertisements are for swinging couples ... *us*! Neither Calvin nor I will divorce, Christopher. Who is responsible for this?" A peeling scent of orange sprayed the room. The excitation engendered by her glance brushing him in the semi-darkness of the state room sizzled like perfume touching red hot coal. Scandal's dark side of a mirror now obscured the palimpsests of baroque lovemaking, the rococo aeration of their minds afterward, leaving so much dead-space for time simply to remember *L'année denière à Marienbad*!

Resurrection Of The Elvii. "Is death a life-event? The metaphysical cusp is blurred so who possesses the definitive answer?" The twang of Bridget Lovegrove's racquet serving, the aerial leap of her arabesque too translucent for mortality against the sky's azure tincture, the frothy milkshake of her laugh as she cried, *Ace!*, drew from Fabian Roxburgh these speculations. The tennis ball's missile flew deep into the circumference of the court but he was distracted by her fleet-footed approach to the net. A breath of breeze raised her tunic's hem in a *frottage* of undulations and he thought he glimpsed her *ombre* perspiring and soaking the fabric of her briefs. Between games they paused to drink tall glasses of lemonade under the shade of a courtside umbrella. While she fenced with silences on court, parry-and-thrust, rolling the frosted glass across her temples she challenged him: "So, you've offered me a two-edged sword, Fabian, talking of Vietnam and Elvis: how did you phrase it – *The Elvii have resurrected from the Summers of Love and Revolution*. And I have been leafing through your *Dispatches From 'Nam*, quite devastating. You say Christopher has persuaded you to go into battle with this metaphoric sword held before you like a Cross. Or are you planning to plunge it into your heart?" Bridget's racquet scythed the air in whipping strokes as she moved back to the baseline. Elvis' glorious abstraction had imbued December and the approaching celebration of the Saviour's Divine Incarnation with a psychic *frisson* crystallized in Roxburgh's quest to displace all competing idols for Bridget's devotion and adoration!

A Theological Problem. "Miranda, our dream is for our life to run parallel with our imagination," Christopher Featherstone mused lowering the volume of the Beethoven String Quartet, "but we are all children of very mortal parents." Exposure of adulterous secrets in the pages of **JACKIE**, a journal with beautifully crafted illustrations and graphic design, had brought Miranda Westwood to his office with her family skeletons disinterred for public viewing. Featherstone stood in the frame of a window from which he observed workmen installing cables of Christmas decorations and lights in preparation for the annual city pageant of floats. Speechless, Miranda exited, slamming the door behind her, but what purificatory rites could cleanse any of their houses? Leaving early, conscious the treasures of his liaison with Samantha, visualizations which haloed his thoughts about her, had been well and truly looted he rendezvoused with Elizabeth for coffee, noting her portraiture had been touched up by the divine Eros. "All in all, Elizabeth, humanity's probability of abandoning God runs high, if we remember Antiquity's pious duplicity." Was this cleansed Renaissance portrait just a *doppelgänger* though? "Honestly, Christopher, for how much longer are you going to be guided by blindness?" Had he said *Yes!* then to perpetual blindness?

Who Will Be The New Messiah? Resplendent stars brightened above the drive in movie screen as the lights went down. Perfumed colour flowed from the projector's brush beamed at the massive screen. Inside the cabin of the midnight blue street rod Fabian Roxburgh couldn't keep his persona flattened, two-dimensional, all surface, for to his lucky romantic throw of the dice Bridget Lovegrove agreed to an evening at the drive in before his departure for 'Nam. She said she easily buried the magazine libels in the sarcophagus of her heart, entombed them to remember them in her wizened old age, to brush them off occasionally and reflect on the transience of Time. Steve McQueen's incisive existentialist, *Bullitt*, compact as a Wittgenstein proposition, reminded her of Eddie Phoenix, especially the voice within his somber mask, but she was soon kissing him, neutralizing the screen's nihilism with an upsurge of eroticism. "Some men kiss me with the same coldness as when I pressed my lips to the mirror as a young girl, but the experience with you is a stepping *through* into the mirror itself!" The strength and turbulence of women in imagining sex far exceeded the physical performance of coitus itself, and conversation more potently peeled back the façade than a series of colour-by-number caresses of the torso, pleasurable though they might be. The glittering nocturnal firmament, penetrative yet impenetrable, stretched Time to immeasurable lengths and thereby exposed existence to incalculable evils. Steve

McQueen, not *Sgt. Pepper*, assumed the probability of being the *Now* Generation's Messiah, for the Carnival of Love was well and truly over!

Tragic Idyll. Like struck crystal, her heart shattering even as the timbre rang free, Samantha Westwood lay on the deck of the schooner fated with the heaviness of **JACKIE** magazine's revelations, weighed to earth with passion's momentum, her martini glass not deep enough to wash away the stain. Calvin Westwood half-slumped against a mast gazing seaward where smooth hemispheres of stone embedded in a breakwater were washed to glistening surfaces by the surf. Sail flapped in the breeze bound by rope, Samantha and Calvin each glancing speculatively toward differing horizons, the sky's emptiness crystalline with infinitesimal fragments of splintering sunlight, arrows unloosed by passion dividing to bury in the hearts of other lovers. A mutual erotic dynamism first consecrated at the altar had dissipated like shattering glass struck by a coloratura soprano and now four lovers were bloodied in the weakening cohesion!

Fairytale Ending. Celeste Hawthorne's fingertips fondled the bloodied carnation symbolically placed in the lapel of Christopher Featherstone's suit. Presented to Elizabeth following the civil ceremony, and identified as the artist who had captured her ex-husband in textured chalks for public viewing, she was all vibrant conviviality, a delightful companion: "Yes, Elizabeth, I am responsible for the transfiguration of this ecclesiastical sleuth, and he has come up reborn like a New Testament prophet. And you have cut a fresh block of marble from the mountain and can carve again." Featherstone guided Celeste onto the dance floor hoping the dance would still the resonant echo filling his heart's hollow gourd, and even attempted a witticism: "While your humour is unsparing of my fallibility, Celeste, just remember you too have locked the Princess, your soul, in a tower beyond reach, inaccessible."

Surfing Breaks All Sexual Taboos. Fabian Roxburgh's sculptural latticework all over the waves, his offering himself ritually to the summer swells, a sacred cleansing prior to his embarkation for 'Nam, contrasted his existential failures with Miranda and Fleur, although Bridget communicated how she divined unexplored dimensions in his psyche. The aroma of her clothes quickened his sensibility and the baroque variations in her postures beneath these fabrics formed silhouettes as memorable as those of his illustrations on the wave-frescoes. Could this encounter be his life's quintessential orientation? Entering the whitewater Bridget soaked herself through and slithered astride the Malibu, Roxburgh lying slightly behind her paddling through an oncoming wave, the hemline of her bathing suit clinging wetly to her derriere, her gasp as the curl dissolved across them choked with water. How the turbulence of physical activity saturated her eroticism with intensifying *frissons*!

EOS RECORDS. Engaging a publicist, Paulette Taylor, EOS Records, at the suggestion of Bridget Lovegrove, brought saturation promotion to The Vibes hoping to maximize Christmas sales of the single written by Christopher Featherstone. Paulette's portrait was enciphered with photogenic qualities conducive to the seduction of radio executives and programmers, and Featherstone sensed she decomposed sex to commission ratios and financial outcomes. Still, her deep-freeze public persona, ice-coloured but bloodied with the stain of her red lips, her mouth like a moving heart inside a block of frozen water, held Time firmly in an Ice Age during negotiations and the publicity campaign. Featherstone watched the record spinning on the turntable and listened to his lyrics while Paulette distractedly diarised her own interior thoughts, as if there was no correlation between the product, the single, and its actual promotion in the marketplace. "Mr Featherstone – Bridget tells me you are buying up back catalogues of songs for your investment portfolio. Isn't that being seriously uncool, considering everything today is geared for self-promotion, for being self-created and totally free?" Leafing through a Pop Magazine, Eve striving for knowledge and understanding, herself an ice-sculpture, Paulette considered the pre-Christmas chart placings as a presentation of evidence of his folly: *I Heard It Through The Grapevine ... Love Child ... Abraham, Martin and John ... Both Sides Now.*

A Day At The Races. "Elizabeth then is remarried?" Symbolic of *soul*, Primal Beauty's exemplar, Samantha Westwood outfitted in late-sixties high fashion, aureoled with a spectacular hat as was customary at the Summer Racing Carnival, modelled the truth that this inner presence could sculpt some glimpsed vision of itself in three-dimensional form. Meeting clandestinely at the barrier of the mounting yard where the horses paraded and circled before half-floating onto the track, surrounded by blooming roses, Christopher Featherstone welcomed her opening question hoping it would shatter the crystal sphere which had distanced them from each other. "Miranda ... Miranda is lost to me. Christopher, is that how you feel now about Elizabeth?" Power personified, yet delicate as wingèd Pegasuses, the horses thundered down the straight stretching for the finishing post, the vociferous crowd forestalling an answer. "Aren't we simply helpless spectators these days?" Featherstone thought of dead Eurydice and of the Roman Coliseum, our back catalogue of lyrical moments, of the chart placings of Imperial Poets and Gladiators and handed her a glass of consolatory champagne. "Will your children live with Elizabeth and her new husband?" Levelled emotionally by the question, a guilt-edged passion seething with forlorn resignation, noticed but not understood by Samantha, he pondered whether his Orestes and Electra felt exiled while Aegisthus paraded the honeymoon scene in Agamemnon's clothes.

Is Lucifer A Misogynist? Seen dramatically throwing her torn-up race tickets into the air like confetti, Paulette Taylor magically appeared in a broadening space, Christopher Featherstone's field-of-vision, before the tent serving flutes of champagne, then Eddie Phoenix was glimpsed approaching her from a Bookmaker's totem counting his winnings. "Christopher, do you know them?" Phoenix's minimalism, his insular profile of misogyny, contrasted Johnny Esquire's likeness to the archetypal Pop Star, emphasized by the Egyptian Goddess with high-piled hair addressing them with the silhouetted incisiveness of a classic stele. "Distantly. I begin to see the wisdom of the

Gods in disallowing humanity to integrate their day dreams with three-dimensional space!"

Freud and 'Nam. Sinking into sleep's aqueous solution crystals soon formed around the substance of Fabian Roxburgh's recurrent dream, super-saturating his psyche, imprisoning images like chemicals stimulating film which he could not edit from his slumber. *With enameled grace cascades of bronze candy strafed the Ho Chi Minh trail searching for human flesh to digest in. Film in the camera rolled, he shouted his commentary above the noise, buffeted by the wind whipping inside the helicopter. Gravity's falling sensation, hollow and uncontrollable, had him flailing like the stricken Huey descending in an erratic logarithmic spiral on its axis of impending death: his cameraman slumped over, bleeding profusely, himself tightly gripping a railing, the breeze suddenly chillier, sound suspended as the chopper fell.* Through the cloudy solution of semi-consciousness and disorientation Bridget Lovegrove knelt over him, faintly perfumed, re-establishing again the harmony of her bedroom walls and furnishings, a touchable geometric realism soothing his embarrassment in imagining she was an angel easing him from the fatal wreckage of the crashed Huey. Sleepily disheveled herself she gently seized upon his reawakening aliveness, helping raise himself back across the bed, where he puzzled why he was massaging his clenched fist. Minus her horn-rimmed glasses, still naked from their coitus earlier, geometrically supple against her bedroom's rococo wallpaper, her expression wide-eyed and visibly excited by the obvious trauma of his dream, she vividly realized for him *the faith that looks through death.* Eating toast and fig jam with her at breakfast in the morning, he said: "As a young boy I would have a recurring dream, of myself running, earthbound across a country scene, futilely chasing an eagle, its wings spread, effortlessly gliding on the air currents, free, eventually disappearing while I collapsed with exhaustion. Tomorrow I fly back to 'Nam ..."

Rebels Break Commandments. Exotically dressed, Calvin Westwood stepped up to the tee and purposefully addressed the ball, and how sweetly it swished and soared down the lush centre of the fairway, contrasting Christopher Featherstone's haphazard slice among the tall trees which columned the course. "Men *rebel*, Featherstone, for existence is simply hypocrisy. Sam is my Faberge egg, priceless, admirable, someone I can't live without, a museum treasure I know others have looked at and admired." Featherstone searched the undergrowth for his ball, located it and wedged it onto the fairway and made a further approach shot to the far-off green. Striding beside Westwood he commented which just the degree of levity of address: "Your golf ball too is a Faberge egg, you stroke it as if it were more than a plaything." Westwood registered the lash with a wry smile, always the tireless observer, hence a successful entrepreneur: "Bridget Lovegrove has taken herself out of my hands and stands in a glass case, looking at me with *that* look." Putting his bogey Westwood held the pin for Featherstone, who had the effrontery to talk as he stroked the ball: "And you want to engage me to discover who is taking her out of this glass case? The screen of life is so thin it perforates easily and we vanish, so we cling to some image of ourselves or someone else even as the film is burning up and we disappear. Our vision gradually darkens, Westwood, and we engage in games of substitution hoping to prolong some brightness." Westwood emasculated Featherstone in the game, and over drinks in the clubhouse pondered: "For God to chisel a Commandment against adultery in the tablet, one of the Ten, it must have been universal among men and women through the Ages. Well, Featherstone, nothing has really changed, has it?"

Where Have All The Flowers Gone? Brandishing a tee shirt stenciled **STREET FIGHTING MAN** inside the Stars-and-Stripes Stephen Maxwell galvanized student agitators now on summer vacation to initiate continuous discontent and dissent under a banner **SOLIDARITY = EXERTION OF POWER**. (i) **Political** – Right Wing Trade Unions were threatened with violence if they did not swing behind moves to legally abort Nixon's Republicanism and its feared flow-on effect across the Western World. Effigies of political figures as eunuchs were ritually incinerated with press coverage. (ii) **Social** – New territory of exposure presented itself for incisive ridicule and the flotsam and jetsam of Hippiedom was castigated in speeches and print by radicals as a softening of the Will of Marxism. It was observed with disgust how the counter-culture's rich harvest of grain was grinding down in flour towards 1970, its answer to Camelot simply *Blowin' In The Wind*! (iii) **Sexual** – Uneasy with the purism of the resurgent Feminists, the torture of high-heeled shoes, the dehumanization of marriage, and the male Ego-is-the-spy rhetoric, the student radicals found the enemies of husband, wife, boyfriend, girlfriend too ill-defined, the Gargantuan rape of 'Nam an outrage, a *cause* attracting larger and more violent demonstrations. Under the city Christmas lights one December evening Christopher Featherstone and Stephen Maxwell crossed paths and briefly talked, until the latter's rendezvous with Eddie Phoenix materialized. "Well, Stephen, what does 1969 hold, for we will soon be chained to another year in Time together?"

God The Mathematician. Under a night sky filling with shining crystal fragments Christopher Featherstone journeyed north and only slowed when the Monastery architecture loomed out of the desert space with the stillness of a Zen rock aesthetically placed by God in the garden of the World. Nearby, a white-flanked eucalypt pierced the darkness, aureoled by the sonorous polyphony of the chanting monks, enriching their safety deposit casket of prayers against Judgment Day. "Samantha, it is time for us to be ahead of parting as if it has already occurred, but you have been for me recently a finite impression of infinite expression. Can you hear already the peeling resonance of bells ringing out the old year? You will always be embroidered in my memory's tapestry, every recollection an enfoldment I can re-edit into my thinking, and your voice will be a fluctuation between three-and-four-dimensional space wherever I am physically located." In the mathematics of morality he had imperfectly resolved the test questions presented to him. Haunting Gregorian chants were disturbed by the rhythm of a low-throbbing helicopter banking across the intelligible geometry of the Monastery.

A Fall of Kings. The sand dune cast in bronze sunlight at dawn resembled the flexed bicep of an arising earth-deity. As if repulsed the helicopter lifted above the crested horizon. How did Lucifer's blasphemous stain soak across the pure linen of God's thinking? Reflection enfolding reflection, Christopher Featherstone watched the breeze scroll over the calligraphy of his imprints impressed in the fine-textured sand, conscious how stone shattered glass and thought unstitched the tapestry of *being-and-existence* until frayed threads blew in the wind and humanity was no more unified with God than the scattered stars in the night sky. When the helicopter quietened he wandered into a garden luxurious with blooming roses. Crossing the windswept dunes late in the afternoon he encountered Eddie Phoenix measuring some bizarre geometric space in the sand, his eyes glancing skyward seemingly over-burdened with the imagery of *Revelations*. Standing like Iago exhibiting Othello false proofs, Phoenix would only say: "God's postponement of the Second Coming, and His annual recycling of the First, now a laughable pastiche, signals the victory of the Fallen Archangel is certain, and soon a new Crown will descend on a nobler brow!"

Letter I. Fabian Roxburgh To Bridget Lovegrove. *Bob Hope's Christmas Show, his wit as old-fashioned as Bismarck's-on-'Nam, both wellsprings of nihilism overflowing with seasonal good cheer for the applauding Grunts, is about as effectual in lifting morale as Santa Claus and his sleigh-driven reindeer landing on the rooftops of Da Nang's airbase. The Vietnamese are stealing everything flowing in from the States and any attempt to discipline these infractions threatens to create a diplomatic incident. So I lie here beneath my stifling room's ceiling fan thinking of Elvis, how he endures his measureless beauty, paradigm of a demi-god, otherworldly, wondering about the dissociation of the phrase Elvis-and-'Nam ... Lennon-and-'Nam though is possible. And the Beat hipsters of the fifties are unrecognizable out here for all Ginsberg's posturing coast-to-coast in the States. Nor are there any Andy Warhol look-a-likes, although he was gunned down. Bridget, if only you could glimpse the faces of the Grunts from Idaho, so visually baffled by the jungles of 'Nam, as if they have suddenly fallen asleep in their towns and farms, astral traveled here and woken up dressed in battle fatigues ...*

Letter II. Fabian Roxburgh To Bridget Lovegrove. *Serenity, whatever happens, is miraculous, and the intimate space of a drive in movie theatre shared with you, or paddling out in the surf in tandem with you, were such moments, perhaps valedictory moments. If only I could condense the sky into my bath here and cleanse myself in its blueness! The Marx Brothers' vaudeville sketch of the Paris Peace Talks is hilarious, a farcical diplomatic uproar over seating plans and table shapes, but the Viet Cong aren't laughing, to them KIA's and WIA's are meaningless, considering the hits they've taken in this Operation south of Saigon through December alone. So, if you hold one those Peace-With-Honor tickets ... tear it up now. Tomorrow we're going to shoot a little historical footage ...*

Letter III. Fabian Roxburgh To Christopher Featherstone. *Christopher, already 30,000 KIA's, and 14,000+ in '68 alone, but as you poignantly put it to me ... Paradise Lost relishes a human tragedy. So I forward you Notes from a Theatre of the Absurd. Hopelessness* *enervates the Fire Zones, for there is no Pattonesque forward thrust to take Hanoi out here, no symbolic end-point, no terminus. Yesterday, to illustrate my point, I sped up-and-down the Mekong in a patrol boat, hardly comparable to crossing the Rhine, such a dissipation of energies. Now I'm scribbling these lines hunkered down with a patrol catching fire, although Hueys like a swarm of mosquitos power by sweeping the board clean, and here come trails of napalm billowing in pompous robes melting everyone's flesh. Crawling around I don't touch anything, ever, except my own person, nobody's weaponry, as we ebb-and-flow towards the precipice of death ... over there lithe ghosts are cut down in mid-stride. Death is such an effortless surrender! O for the flight of Daedalus! Let me brush the sand and debris from the page ... a mortar hit and vomited earth, sprayed the Grunts with human viscera ... God must be sickened by the sight of it all. Ahead of me shadows are pausing to listen huddled in the shell of a foxhole ... blood leaks everywhere like the ink staining this once-white page ... and still the Giacometti figures emerge in the distance, charred sculptures blackened by napalm ...*

Moonshot! Apollo 8 orbited the Moon on Christmas Eve, sheltered beneath a pale gold umbrella as a spectacular star-burst erupted, and wise voices were heard saying humanity's voyage through the sixties was approaching a terminus. America, not Vietnam, lowered an astronaut's reflective face shield against the brilliance of God and followed His footsteps laid across the sky like the Buddha's lotus petals, symbolically launched the National Soul and so many hopes with the Apollo 8 capsule. Against the eerie blandness of Infinity the Earth's incandescence blazed, contrasting the black acne of craters on the fallen Archangel's face, a veritable blossom floating on streams of cosmic breezes, testing the proposition there was no existence beyond human imagination. Where in the astrolabe's divine mirror could the eye find war? Clouds gowned the Earth's torso in nothing but ethereal light. For a moment an immense quietude soothed the beauty of the world and then the lonesome silver surfers caught the last wave home! *All things that rise will fall!*

1969
(ON THE THRESHOLD OF A DREAM)

CONTENTS

I
WHAAM!

Cracks In The Façade. Saffron tinctures brightened the eastern skyline. Beyond the surf's restful wave-curves a schooner's Spanish treasure lode gained visibility, sails magnificently ballooning with the offshore breeze. No longer leveled to two-dimensionality as a wave powered shoreward the ocean strongly silhouetted Simon Freeman angling the rail of his surfboard down-the-line, chasing the shadow of Infinity. Surfacing in shallower water he stood adorned in frothing foam, an Elizabethan ruff collar of whitewater, the whole beach scene dyed in the silk screen freshness of Pop Art, summer's tranquilizing flavours bringing him to ponder why Fabian Roxburgh would leave their pastel southern Arcadia for the emerald humidity of 'Nam's hellish terrain. Half-asleep on the golden *chaise longue* of a loin of sand dune, the keys of a midnight-blue street-rod clasped in his hand, the dazzling schooner bending for the horizon under spread canvas measuring the distances dividing their lives, he mused on the ashramic *Summer of Love* and the harvesting of the flower children. Spinning the radio dial by the latest casualty figures from 'Nam he tuned in BJ Thomas' *Hooked On A Feeling*, his surfboard racked, his hippie-length hair now conservatively styled and bleached by the sun, and accelerated the midnight-blue street-rod down the boulevard.

Presentiment Of A Classical Incarnation. Shadowed with inhibitions, but debonair, impeccably suited so as to be sculpted in angular lines yet very symmetrical, a late-sixties *bon viveur*, Cornell Bedford-Brown moved through the front entrance of The Playhouse. Presided over by a mammoth setting of Roy Lichtenstein's oil-and-magna *Temple of Apollo*, cast-and-crew onstage listened to the production's Director, so Bedford-Brown quietly lowered himself into an aisle seat in the semi-darkness. Half-immersed in chiaroscuro like himself, off to one side, he glimpsed a figure observing the ritual of rehearsal, a Mephistophelian silhouette seared as if by Hell's blow-torch, immovable until a revving Harley wheeled onstage, its twin-forks elongated like Ann-Margret's chromed legs, and astride the saddle sat *Elvis'* mirage, presentiment of a classical incarnation. Deafening rhythmic beats and psychedelic lighting engulfed the stage setting as the cast-and-crew dispersed. Hailed by the Producer, who hurried up the aisle on recognizing him, Bedford-Brown rose and in glancing across the empty theater realized Mephistopheles had vanished.

The Off-Broadway Theater Company. "WHAAM! is contemporary, ground-breaking, a test for censorship in the theater, the beginning of a new epoch." Bedford-Brown listened to the Producer, sensitive to the controversy and publicity surrounding the staging of this Rock Musical, but sensationalism could prove profitable. "Very well, Calvin Westwood himself has personally entrusted me with the financial management and responsibility for his investment. He made clear to me that his daughter, who I understand is among the cast, is not to know of her father's philanthropy, she is to rise or fall with the fortunes of the Company and its Productions." Introduced to the Scenarist, Celeste Hawthorne, an essay on French-styled beauty, a delectable illustration in colored chalks, he welcomed her handshake even as the vibrations of the pre-recorded orchestrations physically passed through them both, and he sensed himself somehow trapped in the angle of her sidelong glance, a stele sculpted from an entablature of classical marble, frozen in a long-time past. **WHAAM!**, indeed.

Chariot Races In Space-Time. *Speed*, abbreviating Time, provided condensed conversation between Christopher Featherstone and the young man endlessly cruising the quadrants of city streets in a dust-coated Chevrolet classic, their dialogue rapturous with evocations of Heaven's War with the fallen Archangel. "Get in!" Rescued when the Chevrolet's passenger door swung open, Featherstone nursed a glancing blow to his forehead from an anti-war placard, having been swept along by the demonstrators, and soon realized this bronzed knight was focused on trailing a custom-built Harley, Johnny Esquire in the saddle, weaving the long-limbed chrome forks through the crowd. Duelling with the Harley on the freeway, drawing level, the young man leaned from the Chevrolet's window, challenging Esquire: "Tell Phoenix from me, I've had a visitation from Hamlet's ghost, who said ... *Remember me ... Adieu ... Adieu ...*" Dropping by an oceanside apartment where the floors were papered over with collages, or *looms weaving a tapestry*, introducing himself as Jason Palmer, the young man described to Featherstone various *architectures of imprisonment* being prepared to capture and hold the fallen Archangel. Visible from the balcony the glassy ocean decrystallized and surfers exposed reefs of carved diamonds across the wave entablatures with their curving maneouvres.

WHAAM! (Eros And Psyche). Pre-recorded, anthem-chords announced a contemporary Daphnis and Chloe curtain-raiser, hippie *nymphs-a-go-go* vigorously pagan dancing before the *Temple of Apollo* backdrop, then segueing into a gentler back-beat rhythm with the entrance of Eros and Psyche from opposite wings of the stage. Each spatially unaware of the other they duetted:

(Eros)
Ribbons float from her hair on the summer breeze
Whenever she sings of her love for me
I circle her in love's orbit but freeze
Oh let me be ... your Streetcar Named Desire
(Psyche)
Oh let me be ... your Stranger in a Strange Land
(Eros)
Oh let me be ... your blazing Wheel of Fire
(Psyche)
Oh let me be ... the Burning Bow in your hand

Memorably melodic, impressing Cornell Bedford-Brown, who spoke now of a promotional album and radio air-play, a visual and aural spell was invoked by the performance to suspend space-time beyond the inner architecture of The Playhouse. What was the curious *frisson* experienced as the Chorus interblended with the duettists, feeling as powerful as the slipstream of an Archangel's wing beat struggling for freedom?

Money To Burn! Remembering his moments with Celeste Hawthorne as so many chalk sketches, Cornell Bedford-Brown sampled the pages of a brochure being designed by the Production's Publicist, Paulette Taylor, her dynamic presence's bondage to **ME**, radiating *what is forbidden intoxicates!* "A Pop Art Happening – and you're suggesting we suit ourselves up in dollar bills and ignite ourselves in the foyer?" Smooth-textured like a satin lining, lascivious as a swimming cobra breasting a stream, Paulette opened the office door and motioned a Mephistophelian figure inside, introducing Eddie Phoenix, the chameleon Bedford-Brown had recognized earlier. "Yes, Cornell, a symbolic bonfire, for we know our philanthropist benefactor has *Money To Burn*!" Jupiter's refrigerated ice configured in her physiognomy, especially the mobility of the famous *red spot* in the lineaments of her mouth, proved astronomically captivating viewed through the telescope of his bachelor's sensibility.

Paganism And Christianity Squared By Time. Exiting via the stage door *nymphs-and-satyrs* dispersed through the city. Swinging her shoulder-bag, Aquilina Kingsley shouldered herself alongside Alexander Chamberlain, *Psyche-and-Eros* in **WHAAM!**, gazing after Miranda Westwood impulsively sprinting after the long-limbed Harley down the Terrace. "All eyes are on Miranda, of course, but she's one stone that doesn't cling to flesh; she's no peach, Alexander." A classic Chevrolet accelerated after the Harley. "Have you noticed, her high-summer sorbet freshness never melts even under the most grueling of rehearsals?" Sleek, suggestive of menace, a midnight-blue street-rod curb-crawled up to them, Simon Freeman leaning from the window inviting an introduction. Lane-hopping, eyes straying to Aquilina holding on in the back seat,

Freeman squared time on the journey while she and Chamberlain amused themselves singing:

> (*Eros*)
> Oh let me be ... your Imperial Theme
> (*Psyche*)
> Oh let me be ... your Theme For A Dream
> (*Eros*)
> Oh let me be ... your Celestial Sign
> (*Psyche*)
> Oh let me be ... your portrait by Lichtenstein

"Hey, Aquilina, do you know Alexander's the *Son-Of-A-Preacher-Man*, has an ecclesiastical lineage?" Catching the treble clef of her exhausted perfume on an inhalation, feeling a burning quiver stretching his heart's bow-string, Freeman swiveled to follow her disembarkation on the pavement outside the University dormitory, thrilling to her words in Chamberlain's ear: "I can see why you haven't introduced your friend earlier, he's fetchingly handsome, just a little starchly suited up. Have you discussed our nude scenes in **WHAAM!** with him yet?"

Portrait Of The Archangel (I). WHAAM's lyricist, Christopher Featherstone, thoughtfully strolled through the displaced dimensions of the Oceanside apartment, where black-and-white television images from the Belfast sectarian riots erupted in populist Art's heretical *Popism*, a *Happening* of religious confrontation. Stepping like a Reformation seraphim from the poetry of Shelley, and poised on the balcony like an instrument of martyrdom anchored to the geometry of spacetime, the mysterious Jason Palmer loaded his psyche with this portrait of the fallen Archangel: (i) **PHYSICS** – a feather miraculously swayed in space from *a far Eden of the purple East* as the swelling organ of the Big Bang crescendoed like the helicopter sweeping the nearby sand dunes, exciting rebellion's electricity of danger. (ii) **CHEMISTRY** – sonorous, metallic elements from the Periodic Table became soluble to every evil manifest through the spiral of the DNA structures of humanity. (iii) **BIOLOGY** – broad-chested as the Cosmos itself, weighted with phalanxes of galaxies arrayed across the battleground of space-time, the fallen Archangel created labyrinths of incarnations for humanity to lose itself in, the fecund spillage of the Milky Way testament to his permanently emptying scrotum; the hidden constellation of the **SCORPION** paralyzing the soul of Man. (iv) **PSYCHOLOGY** – Emperor of mannerisms, delirious with desecrations, somehow an anguished resonance in God's Own Thought, a perverse brain-wave, the Archangel endlessly multiplied and recycled his personalities through the *white room* of space-time. (v) **ECOLOGY** – a dark-mantled shroud of infinite depth, lit with the lustre of ebony jewels mined from the Cave of space-time, the very model for the tedium of an existential Earth, Theater of the Absurd, presented a sterile promontory from which the Archangel brooded over the Act of Creation ... his own! Disturbed by the Vision, Featherstone joined the inconsolable Palmer on the balcony where the strangely ominous helicopter circled the sand dunes like a long-leashed falcon controlled by the Archangel.

Letter I. Fabian Roxburgh to Bridget Lovegrove. *How do we forestall the slippage of years and stay among the young in '69? You have rescued my address book ... and turn the leaves of fiction? The sky is forever weeping here on the road from Belfast-to-Londonderry where humanity is in dress rehearsal for the Apocalypse. Meteors of stones shower the civil rights marchers to raise up martyrs to a Christian cause. Time is the wave we all must surf and kinship is but a mechanical device easy to break down. How I miss the balm of your scented oils and evenings together at the drive in — sketch with me a tree in your mind, branches thinning as leaves fall, and you have a picture postcard of me placed in the space-time continuum of Northern Ireland.*

Letter II. Fabian Roxburgh to Christopher Featherstone. *Crimson-and-clover, a splash of blood caked on a leaf, a GIs? Curling petals of white hot metal peel from a tank's armour-plating while all along the watchtower of the skies F111's scream revenge and embroideries of napalm consume a village's farmyard simplicity. Do you get the picture? But not the exquisitely perverse and primal smell! Tensing tendrils twist thought into unconsciousness but I escape the enclosure of 'Nam to think again. Where am I? The Catholic virgins of Northern Ireland (where are these late-sixties in evidence here?) and the promiscuous, more militant Protestants are unleashing a ferocity of sectarian hatred unknown to me: the GIs in 'Nam are ambivalent even if their killing machine is infinitely more efficient. What bruises are being drawn forth here! And the passage through the thorns of each day tears my sensibility to shreds. The fallen Archangel has sprung the mechanism of revolution, he strolls the pearly floor of Belfast's metropolis, a city of his Archangelic design if ever I've seen one, bringing the Irish to a permanent Finnegan's Wake: how many corpses will decompose here?*

Who Are We Looking For? Two Pop Art flower children, Fleur and her sister squeezed into an installation of sleeping *objets d'art* arrangements, their slumber an illusion softening the outlines of hopelessness pervading the hippie-generation. Lt. John Kirby, on R&R from 'Nam, carried letters for the youngest flower child, and was accompanied through the apartment by Johnny Esquire and Eddie Phoenix, Dioscuri who met him at the airport with questions about a foreign correspondent by the name of Fabian Roxburgh. Sifting the psychometry of the bizarre collection of *objets d'art*, trying to fathom their significance, Lt. Kirby noted: (i) The stripped-down engine-block for a 357 Chevy, time capsule of his own younger days when he would frequent the cataclysmic combustion of *Drag City*. Who was renovating the antique sculpture? A manual opened for assemblage of the jigsaw arrangements of spare parts lay on the floor, dusted over as if untouched for weeks. Eddie Phoenix hissed: "Who plans to *drag* me out on the strip?" (ii) Album covers constelled the walls of the apartment in an oblique geometry of parallelograms, shifting as if under the influence of hallucinogenic mind-substances, the flower children sleeping through the singing voices. Lt. Kirby read the symbolism in *Cheap Thrills* by Big Brother & The Holding Company asleep beside *20/20* by the Beach Boys, where *Ball and Chain* melted into *Cabinessence* as if light-years had passed in duration between 1959 and 1969. (iii) Soup tins were stacked as if representing the thought-structure of some dangerous vortex which had gripped the hippie-generation. But perhaps this sculptural solemnity of a mass marketed product stood as a Franciscan *homage*, symbol to a new religious awakening, a vow to poverty among this generation's flower children. (iv) An ancient Remington typewriter modelled the sixties generation's neurosis to explain everything, *vis-à-vis, the medium is the message*, and from the alphabetic pattern, from the mosaic inlay of words on a page, Lt. Kirby isolated ... **ATOMKRIEG**. Dialogue scripted on rejected pages crumpled-and-balled might have been for a hippie Broadway musical. (v) Postcards from Paris, London, Saigon, LA and Belfast seeped with imagery evocative of the territorial war between Heaven and Hell, all with Fabian Roxburgh's signature, fragments written from the front-line by an evangelical missionary Lt. Kirby identified with. Turning them over he too caught at the thinness of the screen of life in three-dimensional space, understanding the bohemian rancor infecting the cities, randomly, non-geometrically arranged across the surface of the globe.

Sonnet Cast In Speed. Overalls stained in oil-and-grease, Simon Freeman half-sprawled across the sculpture of the dragster, longer-leggèd than Ann-Margret, signaling the mechanic to ignite the motor, then glimpsed a highly-polished Chevrolet fresh from the car wash wheel through the gates and approach the workshop. Peeling off sunglasses a vaguely familiar figure descended from the Chevrolet and wandered over to the dragster, eyeing off its torso's authority, carved from mineralized substance, sensing the *puissance* of its inertial horse-power in the resonance of its revving motor. He strode the length of the long-limbed dragster and returned to its thigh, a metallic womb ribbed in chrome, his presence clearly in bondage to speed. Freeman noticed a Harley cruise by the workshop gates, its cavalier's legs exposed, a captive Queen of the dark suites of a set of playing cards in the pillion seat. Following his gaze the young stranger moved a step closer to the gates as the Harley vanished: "Priscilla! Now there's a Shakesperian sonnet worthy of a recitation from the throat of Elvis!

> Against my love shall be, as I am now,
> With Time's injurious hand crush'd and o'er-worn;
> When hours have drain'd his blood and fill'd his brow
> With lines and wrinkles; when his youthful morn
> Hath travell'd on to age's sleepy night;
> And all those beauties whereof now he's king
> Are vanishing or vanish'd out of sight,
> Stealing away the treasure of his spring;
> For such a time do I now fortify
> Against confounding age's cruel knife,

That he shall never cut from memory
My sweet love's beauty, though my lover's life:
His beauty shall in these black lines be seen,
And they shall live, and he in them still green.

So, what's your scene?" Spellbound, puzzled, Freeman studied the hyperbole of the young imagist, balancing him against his Chevrolet's misogynist's extremity, before responding: "Eighteen months ago I fell under the spell of *Sgt. Pepper* and devotionally became a hippie, succumbed to the call of our generation. Now, I'm committed to selling-out, and I sell cars during the week in a city showroom. On weekends I am for heroic racing, I prefer the salesmanship of fluted motors, tuned for speed-runs on the stave of our Time." Shaking hands in a parting gesture, the young man said: "Do you know Eddie Phoenix, one of the Archangel's auxiliaries? I want to challenge him while strapped in this dragster's electric chair! Then the fabric of history will shake again with the imagery of this chariot circling Troy, another Achilles dragging Hector's torso."

Recognition As A Status Symbol. Remembering now Aquilina's dormitory Simon Freeman wheeled the midnight-blue street-rod down the highway and eased up in a queue of cars stalled at some traffic lights adjacent to the University entrance, an edifice of rising Spanish sandstone inset with a massive clock-face. A legion of revolutionary shadows streamed onto the roadway, a thousand placards and banners protesting the war in 'Nam, and emerging from the heart of this peopled chaos there appeared a Gang of Five leading flaming effigies of political figures, smoke from the flames turning the setting sun redder than Ann-Margret's aureole of hair. Curiously, the leader of the anti-war demonstrators seemed distracted, as if he recognized the street-rod, then was swept onward through the University grounds. Traffic began clearing, and Freeman thought he glimpsed Miranda Westwood addressing her swift steps towards the male dormitories, until she too seemed to recognize the car and hailed him from a respectful distance, but continued on inside the dormitories. Asking female students after Aquilina's dormitory, wondering if he smelled too much of motor oil and gasoline, Freeman stood outside the door listening to the musical phrasing of a violin, then knocked. Unblinking, radiating a finishing-school innocence, starched in classical music manuscript, still balancing a violin under her chin, a young woman with a blonde back-knot answered the door. "Does Aquilina have some social visibility apart from **WHAAM!**? I mean, is she seeing anyone, not being home?"

Anthem To Hippie Heaven. Bustling backstage, while the Chorus of nymphs and satyrs suitably dishabille, rehearsed under direction in the footlights, singing more of **WHAAM!**'s anthem to narcissism, perfecting the arrangement's inner canonic voicings and melodic rhythms, particularly the lyric

Life up your eyes and focus them
(On the face inside your mirror)
Be the eyes in your belovèd's face
(Deep inside your mirror)
And let him be your halo of immortality
Let him be your romantic history
(And lift you to Hippie Heaven)

Aquilina Kingsley obliquely questioned Alexander Chamberlain. "Tell me, your friend, the disillusioned hippie, now brash car salesman, what prompted this regression from deep-to-shallow?" *Déjà vu* exiting the stage door, Miranda glimpsed the eternally elusive Johnny Esquire astride his revving Harley, while Chamberlain stood on the sidewalk pursued by Aquilina dancing some flamboyant steps of sociability into his physical orbit. "Laura, my oldest friend, said Simon called by for me thinking *I* was resident at the dormitory." She eagerly dipped her head and followed him inside the midnight-blue street-rod, the car radio raucous with Janis Joplin's *Piece of My Heart.* "You both must stay to dinner, Laura is a virtuoso in the kitchen as well as with her violin!"

Conversation I. "Alexander here, Eros' icon in **WHAAM!**, endlessly disputes with the nymphs and satyrs on the pre-eminence of *existential cool* versus *hippie priesthood*, as the primary posture for a young man in the late-sixties."

Conversation II. "Aquilina dreamed last night your fetching handsomeness exploded her mind like one of Dali's disintegrating *Madonnas*: she was all light-headed, spacious as a hippie emptied of reality."

Conversation III. "How can you misrepresent the truth so boldly? That was *your* dream of Miss Miranda Westwood! No, Simon, the imposition of **WHAAM!**'s lyrics, and your style behind the wheel of this car, had me dreaming of a Lichtenstein cartoon which is a backdrop in the show ... awakening, I glanced at your framed photograph, thinking, *Good Morning, Darling!*"

Conversation IV. "Aquilina, these nude scenes with Alexander, is it just pantomime, because he won't 'fess up with me how real you intend to be, he just half-closes his eyes as if you're already naked in the mirror of his mind."

Conversation V. "Just have our bail money arranged for delivery to Court once you hear we've been arrested!"

Quartet At Dinner. Statuesque idolatry defined Alexander Chamberlain's alignment with Laura Devonshire over dinner as alcoholic refreshment constructed a pop art assemblage of cans on the floor of the dormitory apartment, and refills of tall ice cold lagers were emptied. Sveltely silhouetted in flower-sewn jean cut-offs, barefooted, Laura remembered Simon Freeman and her friend's interrogation of her, shrugging that the thread of Chance was easily severed. Fourth-point of a square deviating into a parallelogram, Alexander had been suitably obtuse, forced to observe Laura prepare a dinner and respond to her sparse banter: "Observing Aquilina, I think an actress has to learn to be flexible and yielding in many directions, but I'm not so sure about an actor. Our time is especially theatrical, do you feel that?" Alexander sampled some herb frittata as her voice's aubergine purée quipped to Aquilina how she thought he resembled a playing card image, being handsome enough in the line of modern actors, if a little poker-faced. Asparagus, fresh beans and sardines in a garlic vinaigrette covered Simon's reference to his ecclesiastical pedigree and Laura gave him a serenely gliding glacier of a glance stalling in a full-face enquiry for him to respond. "Certainly, it was the pulpit or the stage for me, but either way I get to moralize on the world. From the pulpit of course I could only harangue the fallen Eves among the congregation, on stage I get to seduce them, and in front of a live audience." Hiccupping after a draught of chilled lager, teased by Alexander's allusion, Aquilina assured Simon: "We croon together, but haven't *moaned*. Except on stage in our *undress* rehearsal, and soon before a live audience!"

Sculpted On A Poet's Page In Rhyme. "Would you play the scene for me, now?" Simon Freeman's alcohol-soaked question slept through dessert, a deliciously over-sauced chocolate cake in brandy custard, but revived when a leisurely Laura amused herself with Stephane Grappelli stylings on *Sweet Georgia Brown*. Her fingering and bowing the violin intensely eroticized Alexander Chamberlain as he moved with visceral awkwardness from the floor where they had collapsed to *dim, dim the lights*. "Aquilina, if Laura cues us in with her violin, yes, I'll sing for my supper." How her softened self-portrait electrified the violin, imaged through a mind soused like a peach saturated in liqueur while Aquilina hummed the melody to her, and he thought the embroidery of chiaroscuro would shadow his undressing. Simon began laughing uncontrollably: "Alexander embarrasses himself! Will your singing be as *sharp*? Eros' *dart* is to penetrate ... your heart?" Merely a hand's-breadth separating them, Aquilina (Psyche) sitting like an angel's sculpture over Alexander's (Eros) tomb, her naked pubis' vanishing curve interiorized for absorption, his exteriorized penis invulnerable to alcohol, shaped for sculpting, they duetted while Laura sight-read the melody and Simon listened.

A grey sea
And yellow moon
Low
Seaweed-scented
Beach and ocean's
Flow
The sky's fading tempera scene

Holds your silhouette on its delicate screen
Our future is forever dawning
Forever dawning, forever dawning, forever dawning
Below
...
Look at that storm threatening deep in the night
Aphrodite's playing out my heart strings like a kite
My feelings are taking the punches of soul horns
And already I'm lying on a bier for you to mourn

"Such swelling-to-bursting, Alexander, I mean your lungs!" Laura's summer sunshine brushed legs varnished the chiaroscuro with a powerful Leonardo-effect, Madonna-with-violin, and her voyeurism sweetly ethereal, as if he were a playing card held in her hand for a game of poker where the stakes were low. The aroma from smoke-charred effigies drifted across the University grounds where the head of the Revolution and his limbs had been separated from the torso of the mob and were being man-handled by counter-revolutionaries into Police vans. Brushing flakes of ash from his crumpled clothes Simon collapsed against the cool flesh of his midnight-blue street-rod, thinking of Aquilina's ambiguous kiss and her appraisal of his features as a taller Perry Como look-a-like filtered through Steve McQueen, giving him her actressy, audience-savvy gaze as Alexander and he stumbled away from the dormitory.

Poster Imagery. White-fleshed, dressed in Coca Cola being shaken as she walked onto the pedestrian crossing, Paulette Taylor's modern version of some classical masterpiece bringing an extension to the dimensions of Paradise Lost's pavement with every motioning step, eventually became conscious of the monosyllabic Chevrolet cruising the curbside, the young man behind the wheel of the chariot as heavily etched as an Old Testament prophet. Angling towards a glass-walled building where Eddie Phoenix and Johnny Esquire were examining a stylized poster for **WHAAM!** with a self-adoring performance art she sensed the handsome young man's thoughts in the Chevrolet were dancing a gentle foxtrot with her. Once inside her office Phoenix rolled up the rogue poster ripped from the building's glass-frontage: "His name is Jason Palmer and his fingerprints are all over this poster. Like us all he was hurled flaming from the ethereal sky but aspires to re-grow Archangelic wings and roll back Eternity." Made up in the combustible colors of a Pop Art cartoon-in-a-frame, Phoenix-and-Esquire her expansive wings but with varying skin dyes, Paulette gave the assembled guests Voluptua's mouth welcoming them to the Publicists' luncheon. Cameras flashed preserving her Jupiteran lineaments for posterity. Feasting from the trays of circulating *hors d'oeuvres* Palmer confronted the unholy trinity, caressing the perfect curve of her upper shoulder: "Does stone feel the sensations of rain, frost and sunburn?"

Scenes In Summer's Aquatint. Johnny Esquire's reflection of Elvis' time-tested hairstyle, his hoped-for leap from a Jack-to-a-King, momentarily distracted Cornell

Bedford-Brown from listening to Paulette Taylor: "The stage lends itself to the sartorial etiquette of Mythology. We'll sharpen the focus of our publicity on the show's nudity closer to opening night. Heighten the impact, abruptly increase the crescendo, rather than let Time diminish our intention to mere novelty." Celeste Hawthorne unveiled her scenarist's designs, incarnations for the flattened perspectives of Pop Art, her own person's re-interpretation of the late-fifties a characterization based on that decade's mass production principles and dutifully noted by Bedford-Brown. Guiding her with a Chevalier's courtesy from the building into the aquatint of an Arcadian summer afternoon he was caught off-guard when she asked him: "How motivated are you by heritage?" The sixties had increasingly traumatized the Goddesses of the fifties, widowed many, and the new generation abandoned trophies not considered worth salvaging, yet their sexual sophistry remained undiminished. "Can we ever finitely rule a heavy line under the past and let it sink away into the Ocean of Time, the Titanic-of-History?" Johnny Esquire vigorously kick-started and gave throttle to his Harley observed by Miranda Westwood, a collage straight from **WHAAM!**'s songbook on the twilight of the sixties.

Rock Arias. Commissioned to illustrate Eddie Phoenix's crusade to launch World War III, Celeste Hawthorne discussed sexual plagiary with Cornell Bedford-Brown immersed in post-coital oblivion: (i) Ingres – *La Grande Odalisque* – moving the discreet fan of her pubis she effortlessly disrobed the psychology of the fifties Man and honored him with the *high finish* of her orgasm. (ii) Guérin – *Henri de la Rochejaquelin* – his thighs and penis carved with the strength of marble, a visualization of Paulette Taylor's confidential *ideal* evoked at the Publicists' luncheon: "I chill a man with the perfection of my orgasm, and the stricture I am building a portfolio of the foremost sexual sculptors of our Age, with physiques who can accomplish the deed." (iii) Goya – *The Nude Maja* – Plagiarizing Art's preservation of the smile of eternal orgasm, Celeste arrayed her voluptuous post-coital arabesque in the marble creases of the bedsheet, nestling against Bedford-Brown's terrestrial crucifixion which lay there as if for placement in a tomb. (iv) Rembrandt – *Joseph Accused by Potiphar's Wife* – Excited by the vicarious thrill of seduction and denunciation, Celeste brought to the otherness of their sexual dream a calligraphy of sketches of Bedford-Brown singing a sequence of Old Testament lyrics as rock arias.

Mythology Meets Feminism. A modern nude version of Delacroix's *Greece On The Ruins of Missolonghi*, dripping oil paint beneath the stage light-shifts, while the horizontal **I** of Miranda Westwood's flute suffused the scene in turquoise, Psyche sang lyrics extolling the transition from the Age of Pisces to the Age of Aquarius. More nudes swathed in neon, masked evocations of Aquarius, began crowding the stage-in-rehearsal, the pre-recorded orchestration camouflaging the crashing sounds from the back stalls of the theater. Aeschylan stresses gathered in intensity as a battalion of placard-wielding women headed by a tall Amazon armored in red burst along the aisles towards the stage apron. Paralyzed amid blocking stage-moves the Director was brusquely man-handled and swept aside by the Amazon and tumbled into the front stalls. Alexander Chamberlain's dress rehearsal Eros eluded the pile-driver thrust of a pole bearing a placard screaming: **MAKE WAR ON MEN, NOT LOVE!** A Pop Art *Elvis à la Roustabout*, Johnny Esquire tore free a stage prop and felled two women assailants exacerbating the ugly mood, and in the escalating frenzy the Amazons began demolishing the set while the cast and crew scattered for *exits* and safety. Showers of paint rained upon the cast, Miranda and Aquilina wearing a decalcomania of rainbows veiling their nakedness!

Swing Down, Sweet Chariot. Revolving Police and Ambulance lights flashing across the sidewalk outside The Playhouse already awash with the neon-splashed tableaux of the cast and crew signaled a reactive, inert Authority, disinterested in a *Rock Musical à la Antique*, and therefore offering no *Orders of the Sacred Heart* to the battle-wounded. Cornell Bedford-Brown surged through the jostling crowd of onlookers, a puzzled Mark Antony to Paulette Taylor's queenly Cleopatra stepping free on the other end of the sidewalk's stage, working a news crew in her shoes with fashionably snipped-off toes, her flamboyant rectangular pillbox hat, always the headline-grabber. Luminously outlined, caressed in neon, Miranda Westwood recognized Christopher Featherstone's face emerge through a gauze of light like an exhausted visionary, and handed him her elbow-jointed flute. Woven into a tapestry of nymphs, all daubed in a kaleidoscope of paint colours, Aquilina climbed into an ambulance, a frost hardening her gracefulness towards Eros sidewalk-dancing for the onlookers. A creeping Chevrolet hovered in existential pursuit of Eddie Phoenix, the pure rebel, ideal-less, his coal-black eyes burnt-out, any smoulder extinguished, seemingly invisible to the Police, the vehicle like an Old Testament Prophet's fabulous chariot.

Theme For A Harold Robbins Novel. Fresh editions of Eddie Phoenix, now spotlessly uniformed as a hospital orderly, centrifuged kaleidoscopic impressions of the Archangel's fall into the architecture of three-dimensional spacetime, *Pandemonium's* terrestrial oracle of the aluminum trolleys wheeling emergency patients into operating theaters for surgery. Jason Palmer lounged against a Coca-Cola machine tipping the lip of a bottle to his lips, observing movement through the passenger terminal of emergency out-patients, conscious of the compression-and-stretching of Time as trolleys entered and emerged from swinging doors, the clinical procession of nurses and medics desperate to preserve in spacetime the jellied plasma of suffering human flesh in the which the soul was immersed. Well-dressed in a pin-stripe suit, Christopher Featherstone entered the main vestibule, as tough as Kerouac prose, gazing at Palmer as if upon some Byzantine frontispiece, and together they walked the hospital corridors, through an exit and located the over-parked Chevrolet. "Helena Steele and her puritanical Amazons, today's revolutionary adventuresses reborn straight from Paris, 1794, I should think, just might be Man's *Terror* in the future." Green neon silk-screened Miranda Westwood's quizzical portrait there in the space of the streetscape. The synaesthesia of Johnny Esquire's Harley Davidson peeled away from the curb,

Paulette Taylor's *créateur de mode* astride the pillion, one hand holding her pillbox hat, so Miranda bustled inside the Chevrolet and leaned forward over the front seat. "Don't let them melt away!"

Comic Book Universe. Pop Artists had emerged as the twentieth-century's highwaymen out on Highway 61, chasing down the lumbering coaches of historical artworks, silk screening off their imagery and giving back to all and sundry commercial comic book versions, a thought trailing through Alexander Chamberlain's consciousness while the ice-cold lagers cooled and soothed. The baroque music stylings of The Beach Boys drifted in from next door, accompanied by half-pleasurable cries in obbligato ... *All I Want To Do* ... chimeras of intimacy, arrows dipped in the blood of his heart aimed at Laura Devonshire's but repulsed by her purity's breastplate. His alter ego, Eros, was just a sight gag to her, a lifeless skeleton, compared to her virgin's draughtsmanship and devotional interweaving with her friend, Aquilina Kingsley. Anxiety dreamed her face as she listened to the evening's drama: "Going public, this Pop Art spectacle, with you both dancing undressed-to-kill, will only incite violence." Eros' taut bowstring resonated, but she was rubbing out his chalk outline from her affections, although Aquilina attempted to rescue him, reviving him with: "Come on, Eros, out with the songbook, we'll sing ourselves out of this one!" Quietly, feeling Laura's seraphic veil descend, Eros and Psyche sang away Time ...

> *(Eros)*
> Oh let me be ... your Age of Enlightenment
> *(Psyche)*
> Oh let me be ... your Marriage of Figaro
> *(Eros)*
> Oh let me be ... your apocalyptic moment
> *(Psyche)*
> Oh let me be ... your partner in a tango

II
THE AMUSEMENTS OF A YOUNG GIRL

Journey To The Crematorium. A hand's icicle at her throat, the flower child's drooping leaf hanging loose on the bough of Fleur's arm, drifting on the tide of people like so much existential wreckage, she stood on the baking airport tarmac as the plane taxied nearer. Tresses loosened, groovily-patterned hippie skirts fluttering in the scorching summer breeze, the sisters contrasted the military tightness of dynamic and volume forming up as a guard-of-honor to receive the casket, two post-bloom orchids ready for silk-screening on aluminum and hanging in a gallery as a representative image of the Age. Christopher Featherstone witnessed their radiance of youth dimming even in the overwhelming brilliance of the brightening summer sunshine. Pious Christian souls flying in formation, wingèd albatrosses passed low overhead as the soldier's torso floated by in its flag-draped casket, and silk screen repetitions of the faces of the dead accumulating in 'Nam seemed mirrored in the immaculate guard-of-honor addressing themselves to the ceremonial on the tarmac. Nearby, Jason Palmer's face emulated a Renaissance bronze, observing Lt. John Kirby's stylized reality intersect the plane occupied by the mourning sisters, and Featherstone was conscious how their briefly intercrossing lives sizzled with electric currents of the Age, always threatening to short-circuit. As the funeral cortege prepared for the journey to the crematorium, Palmer approached, always poised to say the unsayable, his glance weighing the fractal profile of Bridget Lovegrove's curvatures: "We chain our thoughts, emotions, life to a statue which is simply a copy of the soul, and when we fall from the frieze of existence miss the stage direction's true significance." Throbbing somewhere out-of-sight but brutally audible was the kick-start rumble of Johnny Esquire's Harley Davidson given maximum throttle.

The Fallen Soldier's Natal Horoscope. "How do we cremate our pasts?" Jason Palmer's question echoed close to the ear of Eddie Phoenix, scene-stealer, his role of usher at the crematorium giving him a semblance to the Prince of the fallen Archangel's, and was over-heard by Bridget Lovegrove's chilly salamander, a sculpted lioness of a grieving woman and therefore tamed. Leaving the immaculately trimmed emerald lawn the funeral train followed the draped casket, led by the aegis-bearer, Eddie Phoenix, and his psychic resemblance to the fallen Archangel, through the portals into the womb of the crematorium where the song of mourners raised its hymn. Lt. John Kirby handled and supported the grieving sisters, their faces bloodless masks and only partially visible beneath veils but clearly showing they were at the very expiration of all thought, as if he were caressing wavelets of white roses ready to expire and fall. Haunting as the frieze of mourners was, placed against the crematorium's marble entablature, and the resonance of the sung hymn, Palmer's thoughts filled with *Crimson and Clover*, song of the moment, and he suddenly glimpsed the eyes of the flower child mirroring him, double-tracking his thoughts. A monogrammed handkerchief displayed in his respectful dark suit, Christopher Featherstone escorted Bridget Lovegrove over to the wreaths of flowers, drawing her attention to a circular evocation illustrating the fallen soldier's natal horoscope, a gift from Miranda Westwood!

Footprints. Brilliant-in-sunshine, Simon Freeman's midnight-blue street-rod rolled alongside Aquilina Kingsley waiting in the driveway, a chain of burning sunbeams gold braceleted about her lyrical sketch dressed in a sari-with-bikini-brassiere. With laughing lips of rhyme she swung open the door: "Why, Simon, darling, this car is truly a masterpiece, a work of Art! And already both of you are double-parked in the space of my heart!" Alexander Chamberlain followed her tresses gathered up in a pretty ribbon undulant with perfume, through the spacious rooms of her parents' bungalow, beyond the glass-frontage to the swimming pool, where a glimpse of Laura Devonshire's luminous palpitation, a blinding cloud-white façade of loveliness, preparing to enter the aquamarine water in the milky fluid of a one-piece bathing suit, had his heart's inner wingspan flying on Eros' flame. With icèd perfection she moistened her curves in the jeweled water and melded seamlessly as she stroked the length of the pool. Aquilina's parents prepared the barbecue, sizzling garlic prawns and sunburned rumps of steak on the hot plate, while she tore Simon's sensibility to shreds with repartee: "Your magnificent car has lengthened your stride, its imprints: its footprints have carved a path to my door, so now you can throw away the map I gave you the other evening. What a handsome piece of flesh you are, even if your intellect needs ripening, freshening up!" Surfacing, water rilling from her hair, Laura rested both elbows on the edge of the pool, loosening her restraint to say: "Welcome, *Son-Of-A-Preacher-Man*."

Coconut, Frozen Ices And Nudity. Carved wooden bowls held portions of *chicken-in-a-cashew-salad-aromatic-with-coconut-dressing*, and lunch was backdropped by a fireworks display of glorious parrots suddenly ascending from suburban trees, their senses perhaps excited and aerated by the flavor of coffee being poured. Prepared by Aquilina, but mentally crossing themselves, her parents questioned *three Acts of nudity for nudity's sake*, nor were they connoisseurs of Pop Art, but were intrigued by Alexander Chamberlain's ecclesiastical background and pagan incarnation as Eros. The heady afternoon slowed, loaded with an opulence of explosive aromas, and they cooled the icons of their personae in the glistening swimming pool, feasted burning lips on frozen ices, and licked away the perfect summer imagery of Pop Art itself!

Purpose. Against a nocturnal copper skyline the speeding midnight-blue street-rod traveled parallel to a sunset forestalling the emergence of twilight, as if Arcadia aspired after an Arctic summer. When the street-rod smoothly slowed for a red traffic light a dazzling Chevrolet, dreamier than sculpted reverie carved in marble by Canova, eased alongside and Simon Freeman recognized the silhouette of the masculine visitation that day at the workshop, leaning toward the passenger side window. Aquilina half-climbed across Freeman's lap, both hands gripping the window ledge, ambiguously coquettish: "Hey, Stanley Kowalski, you have no sister beside you, so where are you headed?" Amused, alert in a spectating Camus kind of way, Jason Palmer gunned the Chevrolet: "To meet the *redeemed*, up the golden stairs there, just over the hilltop, in the Land of my Father's Mansion!"

The Wild Bunch. Sensually intermingled, twisted in a breathless kiss, evocatively intimate on the rear seat of the street-rod, Simon Freeman and Aquilina were oblivious to the detonation of imagery illuminating the drive-in theater screen. Moved to the front seat, Alexander Chamberlain and Laura sensed the vibration of kissing rippling outward, he still searching for the secret staircase into her persona's temple, yet to attempt the turning key of a kiss. During Intermission, Jason Palmer mysteriously appeared, bending under the low-ceilinged window frame of the midnight-blue street-rod: "Light effortlessly refracts through glass, but can I?" Tammy Wynette's syrupy, pomegranate voice belting out *Stand By Your Man* on the car radio, contrasted the virtuosity of Laura's marblesque pose profiled to his presence close to the car window, then her smooth-planed pinewood cheek reddening with fire felt his fingertips. Chamberlain precipitously reached across and clasped the *puissance* of Palmer's wrist, breaking the spell of his fingertips: Laura breathed: "Who *are* you?" A silver luminary over Palmer's shoulder, the moon's scimitar watermarked the sky in sizzling magnesium, as he answered: "*Nothing* is the word I would describe myself with, but I am *no-thing*. I'm amusing myself writing a screenplay, and looking for actors to give my apothegms a voice in the world." Sauntering back from the diner's kiosk, Aquilina and Simon Freeman were welcomed by Palmer: "Johnny Esquire is cruising around with a very wicked *Ann-Margret*, Priscilla's stiff Egyptian Nerfetiti on the pillion, just looking for trouble, but that dance team is no competition for my solo Chevy."

Whitman, Wordsworth And 'Nam. White-hot *iron-in-the-soul* characterized Lt. John Kirby's immersion in the atmosphere of the hippie commune network, the hive of the apartment block, redolent with smoking incense, melting as he escorted Fleur and her sister along the corridors, the younger flower child listlessly spinning a prayer wheel just inside the door of the overcrowded room where they crashed in exhaustion across a divan. Wound in Indian saris, hems sweeping the floor, more wraiths drifted into

the apartment rendering the flow of Time in slow-motion and a *peace-pipe* was offered
Lt. Kirby to smoke with them. Child-like, *out of the cradle endlessly rocking*, a Walt
Whitmanesque figure in a perspiring kaftan emerged through the haze, momentarily
spoke with Fleur and the flower child before cornering Lt. Kirby. "She's heavy as
marshmallow, man. The epidemic of 'Nam ... what might you be bringing us from
the ooze of the Mekong?" Lt. Kirby found his consciousness floating inside a empty
balloon of *thinking* unable to form a caption there, until after a seeming aeon gazing
upon the flower child who was now cooking eggs, he said to Walt Whitman: "A faith-
that-looks-through-death." Then the frames in the story were a blur, an evanescence of
I, disembodied dialogue sticking to his memory like footprints in molasses ... "Your
in-ness and out-ness, man, is the breath of Brahma ... We begin to scratch this leprous
scab on the flesh of society, called 'Nam ... *Goodbye Cream* is just threadbare cliché,
man, a sell-out, the tide is ebbing."

Déjeuner d'affaires Ballard. Poison sieved through honey, supervising workmen
rebuilding the stage-sets for publicity photographs, Paulette Taylor paused beside a
Temple column adorned with a climbing mass of tendrils erupting in floral chakras,
the air clouded with verbal paraphrases as some of the cast rehearsed their lines
and lyrics. Fleur auditioned as a replacement for one of the nymphs injured in the
disruptive fracas, strangely energized by the stage décor, Pop Art Reader's Digest
versions of classical masterpieces, and to Alexander Chamberlain all the nymphs were
as spring flowers banked around the icy torrent of Paulette Taylor's Mont Blanc. Proud
of her status as a *boutique* Publicist, Paulette Taylor strode into the restaurant and
glimpsed Cornell Bedford-Brown signal from a semi-circular leather-bound booth,
fresh iced water ready to cool her lips, her first words being: "So many late-edition
scenes being added to the script, and now *Déjeuner d'affaires Ballard*, if you will be
my *Illuminated Man*." Shopping after lunch, very *haute couture*, modeling herself in a
succession of ornate mirrors while Bedford-Brown followed too stiffly, a cold-blooded
Faun, she slipped on the skin of an exclusive pair of long-sleeved burnt-cream gloves,
erotically moving her arms in slow-motion Tai Chi. Her movements cut the air like a
smoothly severed fig, the calculated sorcery of her demeanor fluidly inflected to invite
promiscuous touches, and not simply from Bedford-Brown's eyes!

Countdown. (i) 15.00 hours – Tossing their conversational bouquet aside, letting
audible words fade, interiorizing thought as monologue, Paulette Taylor laid her fingers
on Cornell Bedford-Brown's arm as if avoiding sharp rose-thorns, feeling his loins
inside their trousers touch hers. (ii) 15.05 hours – Unzipped, unbuttoned, trousers fell
to a pedestal about his feet, the column of his torso being traced with creeper-lines
of moving touches by her fingertips, speech between them now complete elision. (iii)
15.10 hours – Tranquility hummed as afternoon shadows veiled his stylized head lifted
into chiaroscuro, then his mouth aroused her noir-silk *décolleté* and her remembrance of
his features became a flaky fresco, something sensed beyond her heartbeat and centered
thought. (iv) 15.15 hours – Her bed's immobility configured a spectrum of intimate

aromas loosening from the folded-back sheets across which she descended. Dense couplet on the bed's stele his tense bough clung to the red apple threatening to fall. She observed surprise re-mould his playing card expression when she took him halberd-in-hand and her own Ace of Hearts melted deeper into the bed. (v) 15.30 hours – Now riding the meteor with the stretch-contraction-stretch of a cheetah speeding after an impala she remembered from a television documentary she brought to the surface of her consciousness palimpsests already modelled from her cartography of previous sexual experiences. (vi) 15.35 hours – Pearls of perspiration lustered his flesh and his deep-sea diving breaths expanding his chest erotically softened the porphyry marble of her pubis all the way to her womb. Her infolding jewel dissolved, her orgasm splashes of waved color from a psychedelic poster. (vii) 15.40 hours – Sexually aroused as a red summer poppy impressed with a Maltese Cross, she remembered one of Celeste Hawthorne's observations, obviously applicable to Bedford-Brown: "Even though we dutifully scrape the canvas, stains remain embedded in the weave, summoning up a wraith of imagery coloring subsequent embracings."

The Live Adventures Of Mike Bloomfield And Al Kooper. Slipping free of the snakeskin of language Eddie Phoenix half-slithered across the stage towards Miranda Westwood who was studying the manner of Paulette Taylor offering herself as a free aperitif to Johnny Esquire. Seepage of decaying melody eased from her gelatinous-toned flute. The julienned sweep of her lips, softened and malleable from practice, offered Phoenix her piqued impressions of Paulette Taylor: "Notice how this flurry of sexual activity has fluffed open her hairstyle like chrysanthemum petals. Look at that touch: Johnny is being tenderized, already a beached octopus." Seeking a more agèd vocabulary Phoenix escorted her through the stage door and into his parked car, continuing non-talkative but observant for sight of a dazzling Chevrolet whose brilliance of reflective curves soon appeared in the rear vision mirror. Driving one-handed, half-leaning from the window of the Chevrolet, Jason Palmer's antique head swept by the on-rushing summer breeze, he studied the strata of anxiety exposed in Miranda profiled against Phoenix's half-visible shadow. *"Him there they found squat like a toad, close at the ear of Eve, assaying by his devilish art to reach the organs of her fancy, and with them forge illusions as he list, phantasms and dreams."*

The Eloquence Of A Puritan. The charcoal horizon lightened to tangerine, sunrise and the brightening sky laughed away the vault of darkness from the Arcadian beach, where offshore a sleek schooner lay anchored. Leaning over the parked Chevrolet, to Alexander Chamberlain's Chekhovian despair, Laura Devonshire's reflection filmed over the windshield glass, two unfathomably beautiful *objets de luxe* fusing as the sun span above the horizon bursting with golden showers. Aquilina Kingsley's high-note laughter as she splashed in the surging whitewater of the foreshore with Simon Freeman contrasted Laura's formal spreading of her towel on the sand and metamorphosing herself from the musical sketch in Chamberlain's mind to the heat-curled page of a paperback novel, read with seductive longing. All lightness and flexibility she herself read in his eyes more the eloquence of a Puritan and with a soft-wax gesture impressed with a virgin's thinking, said: "Alexander, I have seen you naked, an unfinished Eros, singing with Aquilina, rare bravery in a man, so what, or who, is your Achilles heel?" Glancing into the distance along the beach she noticed a sequence of monolithic Pop Art billboards rising above the sweeping crests of sand dunes.

Love Affairs. Leaning from the frieze of a wave's entablature Jason Palmer's meditation delved something Christopher Featherstone had said: "I am manacled to the oar of that schooner there, and dragged through the Ocean of Time." Linearly graphed he sucked the salted lip of the wave in a passionate kiss.

Auras. Poised in arabesques sketched in the colored chalks of flesh-tones and bikinis, contestants in the beach's beauty pageant lined up along a trestle raised in the sand before a judging marquee. Sizzling honeycomb scented the gentle sea breeze from Greek marble unbesmirched beneath sapphire skies. Having surfed the restorative waves, feeling enameled in the colour of the ocean, Jason Palmer isolated a beautiful source of illumination on the beach, *her* motion's ripple of harmonies as spiritual as a cherubim's spaceless sculpture in fourth-dimensional embodiment! Recognizing him immediately, Aquilina Kingsley stepped across the sand toweling herself dry, accompanied by Simon Freeman: "'Tis a manly leg you have, stranger. What a fanciful pantomime it would be, to parade you men up on the trestle there, for us to hand the palm to the most handsome, and *accomplished*. You might win a prize." Laura Devonshire stood pinioned to Hope, not by Eros' arrow, but the signature glance of the Seraphim masquerading in the fading handsomeness of Man before her, a rhapsodic recognition torturous to Alexander Chamberlain. "*L'aura*, sovereign, transcendent, may mighty Angels trace a perfect circle around you with the compass of their illustrious experiences in Paradise!" Unintelligible to the others they laughed, although the fire of Eros sparked on the anvil of his mind, which even the coolness of the ocean could not assuage. Palmer blushed in Laura's thoughts with the evocation of sunset while ice burned through the spheres of Eros' demesne. Leaning in at the window of the Chevrolet as Palmer turned the ignition key, Chamberlain said: "Laura is the dream I'm immersed in, you understand? Take your Miltonian tragedy, and play Adam with someone else!"

Letter III. Fabian Roxburgh to Christopher Featherstone. *Saigon is under artillery bombardment – Fire is here, Fire is there, Fire is all around! Fire crackles and growls, Fire roars and howls, even as we hit the ground! Gold candy passing from belts through an M60, splintering timber, shredding foliage, fed to Charlie out there in the boondocks, Made in USA, is not sweetening the war – an NLF suicide squad took out 36 personnel – traveling across a flooded meadow the other day we came across a sign: You die, GI. Where are the Audie Murphys in this war? Evasion is the bias here, it better serves VC and NLF infiltration, and the GI prefers to be a painted soldier on a Tour of Duty, touring the shanty towns, bars and massage parlors. 'Nam, this worthless crust of earth, this other-Eden, symbol of worldly discontent, can* *never conclude a peace-with-honor, honor being an abstraction, a cipher, and how can America scrawl its signature on an ignoble document blooded with Communist treachery?*

Letter IV. Fabian Roxburgh to Bridget Lovegrove. *Here in my Iliadic banishment I think of you standing inside the elbow-wall of your office, visible through the glass, waiting for Calvin Westwood's phone call – I know that paralysis. Humility in war is hypocrisy, yet is a grace when falling in love, and that is why it defines Heaven-and-Hell. Saigon is a suburb of Pandemonium, the very shape of 'Nam's curvature resembles the fallen Archangel's folded wing, as Christopher illustrated in his letter. Beaten copper skies burn with the smouldering afterglow of an Archangelic fall lining the walls of the Great Pit into which we too have ignobly descended. Even now I visualize you on the tennis court, vivacious and impeccably tailored in your tunic, the twang of your racket strings in my ear, wishing I could partner you in a game, see you leap across the net in victory. Instead, under fire out in the boondocks, I was running wild light as a feather in a hurricane – how can I not be sad when our thrones in Heaven have been abandoned?*

Portrait Of The Archangel (II). Singing fragments from the songbook of **WHAAM!** revolved in Christopher Featherstone's mind as sunset's hyperbole embraced the figure of Jason Palmer leaning upon the balcony of the Oceanside apartment. Hyperspace contracted to the dimensions of the black-and-white television screen relaying footage from 'Nam of the post-Tet offensive, contrasted the contours of Palmer's presence sharpened as if cut-out by a knife from the sphere of the sun, evoked a severing of the multi-dimensional planes of existence of his seraphic form incarnate to pursue the fallen Archangel. Featherstone's psyche overloaded with this portrait of the Archangel: (i) **PHYSICS** – Blackly cut-out from the golden sun, a helicopter's flighted engineering approached the Oceanside apartment, the opacity of the bubbled-eye of the cockpit focused on Palmer defiant on the balcony, measuring how he bestrode Eternity in pursuit of the Archangel. (ii) **CHEMISTRY** – DNA's genetic code, the language of the double helix, was determined to be self-directing, capable of speech summoning up from the Periodic Table the immortal words ... **I AM!** The fallen Archangel's double helix is coded with the famous words ... **I REBEL!** (iii) **BIOLOGY** – Evening falling, from the balcony Palmer indicated a galaxy's coconut, ovary spawning trillions of milky webs to which creation clung, a vine of vices to be pruned. On the battleground a scorpion would have to be pinioned inside a circle of sacred fire. (iv) **PSYCHOLOGY** – Lucifer's brain-waves agitated space and raining black stars (negative film-image of the Cosmos) fell out of luminous Heaven. The searing crescendo of the plummeting Archangel into three-dimensional space's geometric prison dragging humanity in his slipstream deafened Man for aeons. Entombed in silence and forgetfulness humanity's brain-waves barely oscillated with aspiration and could only mimic the Emperor of mannerisms cloaking the world in flat-line shadow. (v) **ECOLOGY** - The fallen Archangel brooded over his *gnomes* polishing up jewels of ebony thought and rotating them through the generations as evolutionary observations on being-and-existence. Featherstone realized the singing fragments revolving in his thoughts were a fourth-dimensional structure engineered by Palmer and leveraged across the credulous mind of humanity, a bridge to cross the Milky Way's immortal river raging through the deep ravine of the Cosmos.

How The World Was Metamorphosed. Led Zeppelin's breathtaking musical excursion through *Dazed and Confused* resuscitated the sleeping torsos of the hippie wraiths lethargic with a drugged humanity they despised, and arose in seeming immortality. Fleur's fingers allowed the songbook of **WHAAM!** to slip free, her sister paused over her container of yogurt, sucked fingers locked between her lips, the walls of the apartment resonated in a Dionysian dance, kaftans undulated with the *frisson* of Jimmy Page's guitar playing. Waves of aether announced a new *sound* flowing through the world! Psychedelia was solarized, and *Sgt. Pepper's* aural negative imagery was forever smudged out-of-focus, youth's engagement with the world metamorphosed like the stunning Zeppelin-on-fire image gracing the album cover.

Is There No Awakening From Insomnia? Imagist body-builder, running his hands adoringly along the arabesque of the dragster, the chromaticism of its musical motor rising and falling with the diastole-and-systole of his heartbeat, Simon Freeman first felt the enclosure of shadow before noticing Eddie Phoenix at his elbow. "Your friend, the Ptolemaic Palmer, assures me you can harness chaos with this vehicle and drag off the Archangel's gravitational grid, soar through the crystal spheres. Let me tell you, the grid of three-dimensional space is littered with the wreckage of sacrificial crashes, the Archangel is unbeatable on his turf." Headlights beaming, his midnight-blue street-rod edgy with insomnia, Freeman accelerated from the garage and exercised the car's muscles on the freeway, before calling by Aquilina's home awakening the household. Parking at the beach they wandered bare-footed down to the foreshore, observed a star fall from the sky's zenith, the metallurgy of the dragster clinging to Freeman's persona like protective armor, and he perceived, in gossamer fragility, the quasi-invisibility of a spider's web enmeshing them all. Aquilina's fingers snapped before his interior gaze: "Simon, give me the eloquence of your kiss that I might master the language of its tongue!"

I Can't Quit You Baby. Lt. John Kirby's *papier-mâché* dishabille, branded with Cain's self-image of imperfection contrasted the flower child's clichéd Baby Doll *naiveté* as they stylized a resemblance to dance on the floor of the Discothèque. Elusive despite her intense soporific languor, the flower child welcomed being burdened with the banality of her hippie lifestyle, toiled not like the lilies-of-the-field, literally, and curved languidly through her dancing as if entranced. Holding the double-echo of herself in the polished silver space of a mirror she re-adjusted a head-band, her expression looking as if she had sucked all the sweetness from the sugar-cube of existence, which Lt. Kirby attributed to the finality of the cremation, the dispersion of *his* being into nothingness comparable with the cool precision of disintegrating galaxies visible across the sky. Crazily reeling across the pavement outside the Discothèque a spaced-out youth shoved Lt. Kirby but fell away as if through sight of a ghost and collapsed against the building. Cooking breakfast while Fleur rehearsed, the flower child leaned her skin of stone against the memory of Lt. Kirby dancing, idly dipping her fingers in a tub of yogurt, remembering his rising phallus pressed against her loins as he kissed her goodbye.

Evening Raga. Chancing upon the recital advertised in the newspaper, Jason Palmer elbowed his way to the front of the University auditorium cradled within the wing of his guardian Archangel, applauding loudly as the sitarist, tabla player and Laura Devonshire devoutly moved onstage. Water spilling over hot coals and simmering quietly was the evocation of Laura lyrically sketched, raising the violin-and-bow to cascade a raga from fourth-dimensional into three-dimensional space, while the symmetry of her torsion as she rotated pleasure on her presence's spiritual axis, intertwined and meshed with the scintillating runs of the sitar. Agitated emotional *frottage* blew from the wavèd crests of flowing melody when it chanced Alexander Chamberlain and Jason Palmer crossed glances in the audience, the chargèd tension increasing when both glimpsed the *bas-relief* of Eddie Phoenix pressed into the stele of an exit side-door, Johnny Esquire's formula Elvis cut-out slouching there too with crossed arms. Back-stage following the recital's encore, introduced to the sitarist and tabla player by Laura, Chamberlain and Palmer held the syllables of two stones in admiration, both attaining serenity simply in her presence, duly noted by the visiting musicians, who bowed away over touching fingertips. "Laura, come with me and I'll show you where your playing has created the crayon sketch of the Milky Way across the canvas of the sky!"

Dramatis Personae From Paradise Lost. Losing the long-leggèd dynamism of Johnny Esquire's Harley when a traffic light flashed orange-to-red and his speeding Chevrolet made the intersection, Jason Palmer powered away from the Oceanside boulevard, sweeping north towards the two-dimensional architectural structure of billboards anchored among the sand dunes. Escorting Alexander Chamberlain and Laura from the car he guided them into the labyrinth of billboards illumined by moonlight, cartoon images *à la Lichtenstein* illustrating the Archangelic crash described in John Milton's *Paradise Lost*. "Very amusing. And are all your girlfriends representations of our Grandmother, Eve?" Chamberlain emotionally contracted, for Laura's expression suddenly flooded in moonlight, conveyed a metaphysical subtlety perhaps inspired by her year's Juilliard Music School training: "Alexander, poetry is like music, its rhythms keep the globe of the Earth spinning, keeps our contemplation of Heaven hopeful for redemption." Throbbing low, a punishing physical sound, vibrations annunciated the approach of a helicopter, its shadow inlaid on the moon and Laura half-gasped to see the concentration in Palmer's face, as if he were actually face-to-face with the infinite depth of the fallen Archangel. Re-seated behind Palmer in the Chevrolet, Chamberlain inhaled Laura's aroma as he touched her neck with his lips, but she held and held the ambiguously veiled eyes dominating the rear vision mirror when suddenly the car screeched backward in reverse. Johnny Esquire's Harley barely escaped the collision as the Chevrolet smoked rubber on the roadway and propelled forward.

Yin, Yang And Einstein. The twang of the tennis racquet's banjo-strings accompanying the elegant calligraphy of Bridget Lovegrove's arabesque patterned her presence on the grass court as a celestial Cherubim graced in matter, bottled up like a rare fragrance in a *parfum flaçon*. Propelled back-and-forth, *yin* in flight, *yang* curving the spatial web of tennis strings, the ball's Tao of emptiness illustrated the miracle of the erotic relationship between inertia and energy. Plucking the taut lip of the tennis net, Bridget said to Aquilina: "Sweet coz, does he have a mind though like an empty camera?" Aquilina laughed and swung her racquet through a practice serve: "My portrait is developing in the frame, but, sweet coz, I would just have to say to him, *roll over, Lassie*, and I could play with him to my heart's content." Marvellously toned by the athletic tension of tennis, electrifyingly supple too in the layered petals of their spotless tunics, they served-and-volleyed a set observed by Christopher Featherstone and Jason Palmer in an ellipse of shadow cast by an umbrella.

Romance Is All Mannered Sentiment. "Well, two Dharma Bums wandering in from *Paradise Lost*, as Fabian would introduce you, if he were here instead of fallen through the tears in the fabric of the world! Hello, Christopher, your friend gives the impression he is very tall." Burnished bronze, displaying the luster of Phaëton, Jason Palmer rose to take the hand of Bridget Lovegrove and Aquilina Kingsley, both women moist with salted perspiration, swabbing themselves with towels. Sparkling mineral water glistened in the jewels of her eyes when he said: "My soul stretched my DNA spiral to its own height." Bridget lamented that Featherstone had buried his words in a crypt of silence as she responded: "Ah, very tall, with your head in the clouds too!" Palmer observed the deepening shafts of thought into which Featherstone had descended, possessed of the internal equilibrium of a Zen stone dropped into the Ocean of Time, sinking never to rise again, and remembered his standing on the foreshore watching a schooner for hours, roused whenever a vague feminine figure emerged on deck. Under Featherstone's palm on the table lay a 45rpm record sleeve, the label **EOS** visible, and a name: **HELENA STEELE**, while Bridget bunched up a cluster of her hair's red grapes with a hand. A transistor radio played new up-to-the-minute sounds, *Born On The Bayou*, and the words of Featherstone gazing across the summer ocean at the schooner were smothered in resonance: "She's my romance-in-stained-glass, Abelard to Eloise!"

Tickle Me With The Archangel's Feather. An eye of azure sky pierced the showroom window. A film crew assembled by Jason Palmer, today his featureless face unstained like clear glass, set up elaborate shots of dazzling car models revolving slowly on turntables. From the wide doorway's rectangular volume of sunlight emerged Johnny Esquire's contrivance of arch poses *à la Elvis* circa *Tickle Me*, his life-exhaustion already evident, Priscilla hanging back off his presence silhouetted in the framed space. Eddie Phoenix materialized, the very mirror of the world's sorrow, stepping by Simon Freeman over to where Palmer's epigraph pressed against the carved armour of a late-model showpiece, the revolving turntable slowly spinning them apart. "I'll see you out in Drag City, and we'll see how you perform on the shifting tectonic plates of the world's chaos. Just remember what you told me, Palmer, about God being the Perfect Poet, and we'll compare a stanza or two of His with the Mighty Archangel's." Paulette Taylor's mechanistic mould dipped through the soluble streams of sunlight pouring through the door like a rubbing of ink, one of this year's automobile models sculpted in the space of the showroom, fresh from a lunchtime test drive with Phoenix aboard the fallen Archangel's wingspread.

Colouring-Book Images For Meditation. Stunningly choreographed, nymphs-and-satyrs, introduced by Miranda Westwood's dulcet flute, the stage's altar beneath a breathtaking Celeste Hawthorne backdrop, chorused with ethereal gravity a **WHAAM!** set-piece:

> *(Chorus: layering the vocal throughout)*
> Guess Who's Doing Transcendental Meditation?
> Guess Who's Doing Transcendental Meditation?
> *(Eros)*
> Clothes
> Camouflage
> You.
> Braless
> Prophet's
> Muse.
> Mandala
> Peace
> Choose.
> *(Chorus)*
> Guess Who's Doing Transcendental Meditation?
> Guess Who's Doing Transcendental Meditation?
> Passion's
> Tao
> Lose.
> Emotion's
> Sky
> Blues.
> Karma's
> Rebirth
> Cruise.
> *(Chorus)*
> Guess Who's Doing Transcendental Meditation?
> Guess Who's Doing Transcendental Meditation?

Cornell Bedford-Brown's coloring-book Muse for '69 puzzled him, for her every caress, every kiss seemed borrowed, but from where? Miranda Westwood's silk screen portrait-in-green, her thoughts heavy with the Zodiac from her Astrologer's latest reading, betrayed her obsession with Johnny Esquire, strange manifestation of the duality of existence's pattern, considering his choice of designer-and-design compared with Elvis'. In the dressing room later, Bedford-Brown glimpsed through the half-open door, Miranda trying on a wig modelled after *Ur-Priscilla's* fabulous ziggurat chignon hairstyle circa her 1967 wedding ceremony, and teasing out her eyes Cleopatra-style!

Drag City's Oeuvre Of Symbols. Awash in an iridescent fantasy of sweeping spotlights like a psychedelic floorshow in a Discothèque the fabulous *quarter-mile* channeled the adrenalin of the building crowd of onlookers. Eternity's crystallization of an Old Testament Prophet's day dream of a Chariot of God stood in the physiognomy of *Simon Freeman & Co.'s* millennium dragster. Aquilina Kingsley and her cousin, Bridget Lovegrove, strode by in sunflower dresses, *homage à Van Gogh*, while above the *quarter-mile* straight a helicopter hovered, its searchlight sweeping its length, while Freeman's dragster rolled up to the start line as phallic as the sword of Solomon. Jason Palmer's film crew zoomed in on his descent into the dragster where his pulsing groin was visibly glutted with horsepower. Arm raised from the driver's seat in the adjacent dragster, Eddie Phoenix defiantly released John Milton's forgotten book from his fingers where it was caught up in the helicopter's down-draught, the spine came apart and half-shredded fragments swirled away, molecules in the chemistry of the author's profound consciousness lost to Time awaiting rebirth. Light dropped from red-to-green and the twin arrows of prophecy plunged for the terminus of the *quarter-mile* straight. As explosively lyrical as the blank verse description of the fallen Archangel's *Planck-moment* in modern Physics Eddie Phoenix's dragster disintegrated, and when the ambulance arrived, when he was cut free of the harness, he resembled under the garish psychedelic light-show a fractured portrait by Picasso!

I Started A Joke. Romantically, a grain of hypocrisy twisted through the wood, knotted the texture of Lt. John Kirby's feelings for the flower child in her moments of mourning, the vanishing of the casket into the crematorium leaving them a living tableau practicing the Art of Waiting. Why had he so written his life's scenario on the pages of the Book of Fate, now unable of course to erase the entry, even if he placed the offending hand in fire, what possessed him to master the apotheosis of loneliness on the subterranean continent of 'Nam?

Einstein's Famous Equation: (The Argument). *On me let Death wreck all his rage; under his gloomy power I shall not long lie vanquished; thou hast giv'n me to possess life in myself for ever; by thee I live; though now to Death I yield ...* (John Milton)

III
AS I OPENED FIRE ...

Stonedhenge. Lightning-rod of revolt, megaphone-in-hand, Eddie Phoenix cajoled Stephen Maxwell's pentagram of companions to raise high their banners bustling through the galleries of the University out onto the large campus quadrangle, where a crew erected scaffolding. Johnny Esquire's Harley circled the quadrangle, his effigy scissored from some Elvis movie, circa *Girl Happy*, acoustic guitar strapped to his back, pulling up alongside the scaffolding whereupon he climbed up on the platform. Slinging the guitar across his torso with Rockabilly versions of Dylan's *Motorpsycho Nitemare* and *All Along The Watchtower*, he proved a crowd-gatherer, drawing students to a convergence on the aural web of his voice. Saturnian faculty staffs were powerless inside their Administration building as the student proselytes dislocated themselves from the ritual of the commencement of a new semester and vocally responded to Eddie Phoenix mounting the scaffolding, banners unfolding around him. "Graduation Day will be your Conscription Day! Do you want a Tour of Duty? Now Cambodia's airspace has been violated!" Wedging through the periphery of students a phalanx of young women led by an Amazonian thigh-and-groin masterpiece of a woman rammed forward for the scaffolding. Half-climbing and hanging off the grid while her companions began vigorously rocking the structure to bring it down, the red-singleted woman raised her arm and exposed her potent hair, inciting the females in the crowd to: "Tear down this fatuous idol, Man!"

Lift Up Your Feet, Here Comes The Revolution. Jason Palmer pulled Miranda Westwood to safety from the turbulence inside one of the University's galleries as the student sculptures streamed free of the metaphorical mosaic pursued by baton-wielding Police. Mimicking mannerisms of Archangelic greatness, Eddie Phoenix brazenly wrestled with the Amazonian *revoltée* beneath the half-collapsed scaffolding, his last cry of: "500,000 GIs deserve to be immolated!" engraved in the consciousness of the trampling students eager to avoid the blows from the Police batons. Hearing the explosive throttle of the Harley, Miranda ripped her arm free of Palmer's grip and sprinted for the motorcycle circling the quadrangle, only slowing as Johnny Esquire accelerated down an arcade, across a lawn towards a car park and exit to the main roadway. From the Physics laboratory Palmer thought he glimpsed the faltering gaucherie of Laura Devonshire pressed against a stele of Spanish sandstone, unwilling to enter the raging flood of students dispersing everywhere. A Molotov cocktail shattered the window of the Physics laboratory.

How Can We Step Free Of Three-Dimensional Space? Billboards inset amid the geology of the sand dunes addressed Laura Devonshire's minimalist music as she passed through their metaphoric tapestry with Jason Palmer. Debris from the explosion in the Physics laboratory earlier marked his flesh with the stigmata of revolution, combat stripes in his skirmishes with the fallen Archangel, to which she listened indulgently, then indicated the film crew trailing them across the beach: "Our suspension in this *Inferno*, as you call it, how long will it be, and why do you say we must climb free of the film of three-dimensional space, yet you would imprison our images on two-dimensional film in that camera?" Her struck tuning fork's humming expansion of resonance vibrated free of the subatomic particles of Lichtenstein dots coalescing on a billboard in an image of machine guns blasting skyward. Spinning Tao, a black helicopter rose above the horizon of billboards, blades scything the air, banking low to avoid the machine guns erupting from the Lichtenstein.

Promethean Lyricist. Stale smells, fried eggs and mushrooms streaking unwashed plates, characterized the recording session organized by **EOS** Records, with *The Pléiade's* underground ethos now interrogating new lyrics by Christopher Featherstone. Sharpening the scythe of the melody more rhythm tracks were laid, then the vocalist approached the drop-microphone fingering back the locks of his hair, while Featherstone stood at the engineer's shoulder.

> Wear a mask like Lucifer, or Mephistopheles if you prefer,
> Clothed with Revelations, the Gospel's dedication.
> Bring on the masquerade where generations played
> Horsemen of the Apocalypse, and Anarchy has the sting of whips.
> Freedom and slavery are one and the same tyranny
> With National Guardsmen dressed in fascist emblazonry.
> The President is asleep folded in his dream
> But dying youth is not his theme.

Listening to a tape of the recording in her glass-walled office, Bridget Lovegrove glimpsed a middle-aged Troubadour packing ice around a wound in his psyche, but remained puzzled with this Promethean aspiration to fire up youth to rebel against the fallen Archangel. Outside, expressionist figures of summer lightning strode across the storm-ridden clouds above the city, and the pavements were awash with rain sizzling from the heated asphalt. Then the temperature plummeted, perhaps re-freezing the ice holding Featherstone's heart, and stepping away from the louvered window she said: "Christopher – your new friend, Jason Palmer, what did he mean when he said, *Whom have we to imitate on this movie set of a world here but our superiors?* Did he mean, spiritually, or ...?"

Chance Meetings. "Look, Alexander is naked to me, even with his clothes on." Laura Devonshire's *crème fraîche* unleashing of her violin's Aeolian breeze, allusive with the wit of a gourmet, sweetened the moment. "As he must be for you, Aquilina." From the dormitory window Simon Freeman observed the summer cruiser of a Chevrolet negotiate the milling students gathered about a Gang of Five holding up traffic with banners strung across the roadway. Followed by a film crew, Jason Palmer brushed aside a cordon of protestors and hurried towards the dormitory. Hand-in-hand, running the gauntlet, Freeman and Aquilina avoided the revolutionary disputation, made the midnight-blue street-rod and escaped. "Will Laura relinquish her virginity to this Don Quixote tilting at Lucifer, or Eros?" Amused by Aquilina's half-serious question, until he recognized the *Ann-Margret* chrome leg-extensions of a Harley slipstreaming behind him, he powered up the volume of the car radio, energized by *Proud Mary*, and opened fire with the street rod for the next quarter-mile. Movingly illuminated by in-slanting sunbeams, Jason Palmer turned away from the window listening to Laura's ethereal accuracy placing violin phrases from Sibelius' Concerto, her torso's impearlèd ice beginning to melt before his cosmic surfer's ethos *brooding on the charmèd wave.* Superb copyist, her strawberry lips emboldened by a creamèd smile, kissed by a mouth telegraphic with a Seraphim's ardor, challenged by its eroticism, Laura breathed: "Isn't it strange how one man's kissing becomes like another's where love is missing?" Answering the door she coyly ushered Alexander Chamberlain inside, his thought's bonfire lighting up his expression, consuming the atmosphere's oxygen, suffocating the moment, each actor delivering a consummate performance.

Letter V. Fabian Roxburgh to Christopher Featherstone. *Biblical, the Ashau Valley is a crevasse into which the world has fallen, from which even napalm fireballs can't suck the will-to-fight from Charlie, who counter-attacks with rockets-over-Saigon. Lonesome and solitary I exist in the dark junctions of makeshift bars and haul out my typewriter to prepare 'Nam's eulogy. In your letter you conjure remembrance of God's Image and chastise me for not caring for my own but the monolith of Communism is too powerful a deflation of simple faith in Him. Why is the North so magnetic, why do these metal filings align themselves politically to its pattern for waging war, why do we continue to day dream of co-habitation with alien ideologies? On the roadway yesterday we passed a scorching envelope of a tank consumed by a fireball and the screaming souls of occupants hung in the fetid air unable to peel away their flesh seared to metal. Well, I raise my glass to an eternity of martial engagements ahead of humanity, because when Communism installs its divinity on Earth the dictatorship of the proletariat will want to storm Heaven!*

Letter VI. Fabian Roxburgh to Bridget Lovegrove. *Beautiful Sphinx always on the loom of my thoughts, how I need your celestial lambency, how I need right now to be imaged in your mind a hero, but I know I passed before your inscrutability with the equipage of a simian into this twilight zone of an existence. Even in the boondocks you continue to ambush my contemplation endangering my life. The fighting GIs here have to endure the nursery rhyme sing-song of the political figures Stateside who speak of the war as a sideshow, so we listen to Radio 'Nam for inspiration before descending into the Valley of Death ... Indian Giver and Games People Play! I have written separately to Christopher ...*

Portrait Of The Archangel (III). Silver arms arrayed after the lovely curvature of a jade vase, with effortless elegance the violinist brushed against a table on which lay half-a-pomegranate, juicy and red, the leather armor of its penetrated case aflame, certainly emblematic of their intimacy. Christopher Featherstone caught something of Jason Palmer's provocative, slow-burning flammability silhouetted in purple shadows against the glowing sun descending below the balcony of his Oceanside apartment. He overheard her say: "Yes, green fruit, Jason ... I lack ripeness." The hyperbole of her incandescence momentarily obscured the form of schooner nearing the shore, and he knew he and *she* were abandoned to each other until Judgment Day, which had him brooding over the Portrait of the Archangel. (i) **PHYSICS** – Banking left-and-low the bubble-eyed helicopter swooped across the bow of the schooner just as Paradise was dying in the complexion of the fallen Archangel. Was a hole truly empty? (ii) **CHEMISTRY** – The Supreme Rebel canonized himself in the DNA code of Eve's innocence for transmission through futurity. Rigidly bound in this DNA pattern the inflexibility of every generation continued to besmirch the light of the soul. (iii) **BIOLOGY** – God solved the placement of the Scorpion in space-time's continuum given Eve was absolute for promiscuity. (iv) **PSYCHOLOGY** – Embedded in rhetorical brain-waves, who in his passion acts out his creations, the fallen Archangel displayed the Milky Way against the evening's purple brilliance, a cosmic spillage of semen exampled for every Adam to aspire to. (v) **ECOLOGY** – *Gnomes*, toys for the Archangelic Croesus, embellished existence with reefs of gold on which were shipwrecked the hopes of humanity aspiring to set sail for the Promised Land. Palmer watched Featherstone walk away aureoled with his Portrait of the Archangel and later he and Laura strolled along the foreshore, swam naked in the darkened ocean before unlocking the star of her heart, unpacking its fusion, its radiance magnetizing the fallen Archangel. Did she sense she was chained to the cliff-face of existence, Archangelic waves rising to dash against her soul, wash her away into eternal darkness? Palmer determined to preserve for her the peace of a white swan, gliding across the Milky Way, her original wings perfectly folded, spiritually unassailable.

Press Conference. Paulette Taylor's frontispiece as publicist for **WHAAM!** emphasized Pop Art's poetry, for clever staging visually encrusted her marblesque postures against projections of various of the genre's masterworks upon a backdrop's screen. Questions probed word-of-mouth suggestions acts-of-defilement would be perpetrated on-stage, to which she suavely responded: "We have been expulsed from Paradise ever since a serpent punctuated Eve's vein and humanity continues to suckle at her breast. Naked, man is but mind, and quite simple with it, naked, woman is but body, alluringly beautiful. The waters of Aquarius begin to flow through our Age, our play is but one bubble surfacing to cast a rainbow across the stage, then **WHAAM!**" Before the laughter subsided, Paulette a visualization of Danaë awash with its golden wave, Cornell Bedford-Brown leaned close to Celeste Hawthorne's ear and whispered: "If I were a Pop Artist and you were my Muse, I would have you gild the shore of the world's galleries like foam-born Aphrodite!" Looking like a soul threshed from its husk, Eddie Phoenix stepped forward beside Paulette, his anthology of gestures worthy of the fallen Archangel's, for he observed Jason Palmer striding down the aisle of The Playhouse, wresting a microphone from a sound-recordist. "Souls drift from their fourth-dimensional spheres into these emulsions of flesh for an Eternity of deformation under the aegis of the fallen Archangel ..." Phoenix leapt horizontally from the stage as a spear aimed for Palmer's heart. In the ensuing *mêlée* **WHAAM!**'s free publicity quotient soared.

The Eliad. "You say you can crack the ice, but can you melt it?" Free of the chaos inside The Playhouse, Celeste Hawthorne responded to Johnny Esquire's importunity, his pubescent manliness, his GI stubble regenerated so he resembled the metaphysical singer extraordinaire, Elvis. "Perhaps you will decay handsomely." Johnny Esquire indicated the parked Harley chopper and they manoeuvred through the fragmentary conversations of the pedestrians. Both paused at the curbside where Celeste looked at his reflection in the wing mirror, where she commented on his photogenic resemblance to the famous pop star. Seemingly legendary, forgotten in Time, Elvis' figural transformation of late revived memories of *The Eliad*, to which Johnny Esquire referred. "I'm thinking in Elvii again now." Appearing in the frame of the stage door, Miranda Westwood resembled Iphigenia's heroic dream of metamorphosing into an Arcadian breeze, for she stood watching Johnny Esquire with the symmetry of a sculpted statue themed for sacrifice.

There's A Brand New Day On The Horizon. (i) **LONG LEGGED GIRL (WITH THE SHORT DRESS ON)** – Elvis' fallibility proved an astute moral lesson for Johnny Esquire standing in Celeste Hawthorne's upper studio running the teeth of a comb through his hair's black corona while she leaned forward from the waist over a modern chaise-longue. Evaporative body-splash coloured the curvatures of calf-and-thigh revealed by her stretching free of the short dress. "So, how does Johnny Esquire visualize himself in '69? Your conquests are circulating in manuscript, did you know?" Trued to an imaginary chalk-line she measured him physically for the space of her bed. (ii) **ANYWAY YOU WANT ME (THAT'S HOW I WILL BE)** – Pressed deep against the sirène's lips, his self-realised DNA image resurrecting inwards-and-outwards in breathless kissing, he was sexually crushed to the pulp of a pomegranate, juice flooding his palate. Thoughtless of mortality, free to choose who he was every moment, he was ready to lay his being in a soil of nothingness, become an existential disputant with the world. Celeste asked: "Which of us then is hallucinating from too little sex? The kernel of the almond is ripe, just gently peel back the shell ..." (iii) **DIRTY, DIRTY FEELING** – Silkily flowing Beaujolais, surgically naked for sex's anaesthesia, coupled in the cartouche of the bed, their *ballet mécanique* more credible than Nureyev-and-Fonteyn, Celeste performed an erotically believable dying swan smothered by Johnny Esquire's expiring Hyacinthus. Her orgasm's butterfly impatient for flight in its chrysalis inhaled the aroma of the hyacinth. (iv) **FOR THE MILLIONTH AND THE LAST TIME** – Held within the yin-and-yang of the bed frame, encompassing sexual sin in completeness, its full sphere, not just a quadrant, the languid peacock fan of her pubis, its vineyard of leaf-forms curling, they watched the sulphur-coloured hues of another dawn splash the window. "You are a handsome enough warbler, sexually." Richer sap gathered in the bole of his eucalypt, oozing, eddying, channeling for the incision through which to spill free, and Nature's symmetry climaxed in sexual symbiosis. (v) **PLEASE DON'T DRAG THAT STRING AROUND** – Her pencil's draughtsmanship captured the romantic ignobility of Johnny Esquire's post-coital sprawl *à la The Death of Chatterton*, her ice-cool introspection precisely graduating the tones as moonlight filled the window frame. Later she positioned his guitar as a continuation of his physique's arabesque, and touched chalk to paper while he ate breakfast, a strangely esoteric moodiness ebbing and flowing from his portrait bust at the table.

The Star In Her Blue Heaven. Gunning his Chevrolet, Jason Palmer signaled the film crew to follow and accelerated after Johnny Esquire's Harley, the sunburned moon spotlighting the helicopter banking from the east. Amid the sand dunes there lay an astrolabe's esoteric mirror, an augury as naïve as Miranda Westwood's face searching the traffic for the Harley and Johnny Esquire, the Star in her Blue Heaven. Kneeling in the sand awash with moonbeams she might have been a forlorn Antigone, then she asked him: "Why do you varnish yourself in that expensive aftershave?" Standing on the ash-coated crest of a dune as a searchlight from the helicopter swept the maze of billboards, he replied: "To disguise the overpowering stench of my incarnation." Soluble light bled around and through the tall stele of his torso's architecture as the helicopter hovered like a spider on its web waiting to strike. "Did you know Fabian Roxburgh?"

Chekhovian Drollery. Descending the geometrically sculpted *steps of Justice* from the courtroom the cast and crew of **WHAAM!** under Paulette Taylor's guidance approached the news teams. Metaphorically clothed in *haute couture* soaked in the colour of a dozen bleeding roses, Helena Steele conceptually defined a new martyrdom, the neo-Platonic feminism of a twentieth-century Hypatia, an allegory silk screened against the dramatic stage platform of the Law Courts. Dissolving through the heat-haze Christopher Featherstone observed Calvin Westwood and Cornell Bedford-Brown avoid the Press and disappear inside a Rolls Royce. Inside the timbered court room

Helena Steele's Chekhovian counsel, black-robed in mourning, had dissociated the riotous behaviour from its political subtext and fabricated a script biased against the obscenity of the production, soliloquized on moral outrage. But how had Eddie Phoenix insinuated himself as a clerk-of-the-courts? Words were laughingly exchanged: "Now there goes a woman drunken with the blood of saints!" Standing on the foundations of Justice, immoveable, Featherstone answered: "Then she is the Las Vegas of the world's cities."

The Geometric Hour. A beached skeleton of a boat lay before the geodesic dome of a dune flowing with tresses of sand in the sea breeze. Clouds reminiscent of liquefying time-pieces billowed upward on rising currents of warmth inland from the beach. Alexander Chamberlain's Eros adrift in this moonscape, a Pop Art version of *Revelations* drained of its metaphoric imagery, walking beside Laura Devonshire while Jason Palmer set up the cinematographer to capture their diurnal portraits, experienced the sensation of falling through a sea of liquid glass and being swallowed. Amid the fluidity of ocean waves, dunes and clouds Laura lifted her violin and moved off playing phrases from the famous Sibelius Concerto.

Hour Of The Angelus. Jason Palmer's ghost of Sardanapalus lying propped between the feminine thighs of sand dunes surveyed the surrounding *jade calm* while inland sails of white cloud filled with shadings from grey-to-black smoking the horizon. Crouching like a remnant of shattered amphora, Lt. John Kirby gathered fossilizations of sea shell, brittle symbols of the late-sixties echoing the drone of war. Morphological apparitions abounded here as the Hour of the Angelus passed and Venus de Milo's profound torso, *la femme invisible*, emerged and approached the throne of sand dunes suspended in a massive cloud-form.

Led Into Captivity. Las Vegas burned in a lake of fire, neon encrustations elevated from the surrounding desert's pool of darkness, jewel in the palm of the fallen Archangel dominated by the *wingèd scroll* of the International Hotel unfolding against the cloth of sky. Glamorous butterflies pinned in a wall-mounting the chorus girls resembled castaway Angels with the strings of their harps fraying from the frame of Heaven. Scorpions infested the desert sands and bleached skulls surfaced under the fierce winds sweeping the terrain. Checking-in, myriad tourists converged on the strip of casinos divided from their spiritual selves, tickets for the floor-shows selling fast, the Wheels of Fortune spinning twenty-four hours a day, the Sands of Time running through the hour-glass seemingly endless.

The Greatest Profile In The World. Rehearsals for **WHAAM!** intensified following the indecisive court appearance, although edged by tensions sustained through the Director's nervous breakdown, and Johnny Esquire's solo although narcissistically molded around Miranda Westwood's flute-singing persona, polished the silver of Paulette Taylor's urn of **ME**. Sheltering in the curtains at the wing of the stage, Eddie

Phoenix's gargoyle presence cast a metaphoric shadow across the production, the fossilized shell of his skull existential with Lucifer's resurgent echo of revolt. Charmed with himself, Johnny Esquire, *Mr. Acrylic* exhibiting *The Greatest Profile in the World*, riffed the *Peace Symbols* number from a plastic Eldorado Cadillac while the backdrop painted by Celeste Hawthorne featured Eros and Psyche in coitus modeling the now-famous sign: Miranda roller-skated dream-like figures across the stage.

> Ain't it a crying shame
> To have lived before I died?
> Certainty is for fools you cried
> But who am I to blame?
> Peace Symbols jangle from your neck
> Peace Signs painted all over my ties
> And butterflies sewn on your Levis.
>
> I think therefore I am
> Embroidered across your shirt
> Can't erase the pain of my hurt.
> Now you've proved existence a scam.
> Peace Symbols jangle from your neck
> Peace Signs painted all over my ties
> And butterflies sewn on your Levis.
>
> You wear your Levis so tight
> And the butterflies seem to move.
> But what does it all prove
> You're drifting outa my sight.
> Peace Symbols jangle from your neck
> Peace Signs painted all over my ties
> And butterflies sewn on your Levis.

Skate-dancing along the sidewalk Miranda tracked the Harley Davidson parallel as far as the intersection before Johnny Esquire felt the squeeze from *Priscilla* high on the pillion and abruptly accelerated away. A midnight-blue street-rod crawled alongside the curb and Simon Freeman gestured for her to swing into the rear seat. "Someday I will succeed in saddling up that Proteus!"

Cracking The Eggshell. Helena Steele's materialization in the frame of the doorway as ebbing afternoon whispered through the smoke-clouded haze of the communal room telegraphed a new feminine style unshadowed by the insular misogyny of Man. Preparing lentils-with-vegetables, the flower child opaquely woven into the weave of incense-laden space, came to recognize the broad-shouldered stele gazing down at a stripped-down engine-block as if assembling it in her thoughts for placement in the chassis of her soul. All scarlet bougainvillea with crushed tomato lipstick, an apotheosis of sexual feminist dynamism, Helena extravagantly sketched her Amazonian intent when moving to an ancient Remington typewriter and reading the mosaic of words on a page, said: "Tell Fabian Roxburgh and Christopher Featherstone they have broken the eggshell and step forth into a New World, that others have strapped on the wings of the Milky Way before them but succumbed to the hubris of the masculine Gods."

Symmetrical With The Lineage Of Seraphim. Singing, Orpheus strolled the sky's resplendent rim afire with sunset, and lifting off the ocean the sea breeze assumed Aeolus' radiant face sweeping around the ethereal cartography of Laura Devonshire's presence on the foreshore playing her violin. Visible was her swimming soul within the statue of her torso as the fire of Eros became vulcanized on the anvil of the horizon. The sand at her naked feet was burnt to powdery ash. "I listen to your obscure conversations and take away with me whatever I fancy might lead me deeper inside myself." Jason Palmer circled the immortal idea manifest in her marble block spiritualizing the beachscape. His visceral tenderness kissing her preserved the purified white sheet of the Infinite in which she stood enshrouded. She visibly witnessed in his face an invisible diamond through which flowed transphysical light, refracting, unresisting, dazzling, radiating from a mystical centre symmetrical with the lineage of Seraphim. His Promethean kiss unbound her heart's chakra from the wheel of mortality and when he raised his hand the seven stars of the Pléiades settled on his palm. Casting her Horoscope later in his Oceanside apartment while she phrased her violin through the Brahms Concerto, he said: "The Great Fire of London in 1666 – note the significance of the numerical, 666 – ignited from the wingèd touch of the fallen Archangel's flare, forty-years after Francis Bacon's metaphoric death."

Poignant Moments In Suburbia. Lazing by the Kingsley family swimming pool with Aquilina who was bronzing up her Greek patina as Psyche scorched by Eros, Simon Freeman spoke of how quickly the flowery promise of the Summer of Love wilted, became a sordid milieu, how the sunflowers outspread like sacrifices before their idol quickly shriveled. Aquilina caressed the bejeweled sparkle of water with fingertips: "Yes, the beauty of your ugliness as one of the flower children, here in my mind's eye, overpowers me. You can hold the prize of a different kind of happiness if you wish." Ascending perpendicular, the drive in movie screen's flat two-dimensional slice of space soaked through with the late-sixties domestic felicity of *Bob & Carol & Ted & Alice*, sophisticated model for youth of the coming generation. When he unrolled a poster from **WHAAM!** showing a full-length photographic representation of Alexander and Aquilina simulating coitus posed in the trend-setting Peace Symbol, Freeman asked her: "How can fidelity endure in our generation? Lying under Alexander for this portrait, and I know your faces are not recognizable, were you livelier than you are in the flesh with me?"

Ulysses And Nausicaa. Luscious, creamily amber oil flowed into the motor of the midnight-blue street-rod, Simon Freeman wielded a grease-gun and the chrome extension forks of a Harley Davidson gleamed in the spatial frame of the workshop's open door. Johnny Esquire dismounted tinctured in dazzling sunlight and entered the workshop where immediately his illumination lessened. An impeccably decked and accoutered dragster, its craftsmanship worthy of Vulcan, symbolized a quest for redemptive speed to escape the subterranean realm of three-dimensional space. "Just tell John Milton when he comes to Drag City the Phoenix will burn him up!" *Ann-Margret's* stunning legs seemed liquid in the glass of space as the Harley throttled and accelerated away. Paddling into small-breaking surf at the beach later in the day, Freeman clothed himself in the cleansing subtleties of silken water, silently rode waves parallel with Jason Palmer, rejuvenated by the session's tranquility. Against a silver-sanded dune, imbued with winsome celestial grace, waving as Palmer's Malibu beached itself on the foreshore, he recognized Laura Devonshire, her soft-curled hair reddening with the passion ebbing towards her head.

Re-incarnations Of DNA Imagery. Albert Moore nudes and Victorian Christs, the commune assembled for the *bed-in* commemorating the marriage of John Lennon and Yoko Ono, the apartment's décor littered with paraphernalia, *detritus moraine*, from the Summer of Love. Christopher Featherstone enquired after Helena Steele's visitation but the fatigued *créateurs de mode* swathed in bed linen had well-and-truly severed themselves from the Christian faith embodied in *Revelations*. Any symbolic resemblance to the Elvii had been erased, the original Rock musicals of the demi-god had discolored to tribal wall-paintings, the men again resembled the misogynist Victorian figures from daguerreotypes, and the women descended Burne-Jones staircases. Featherstone noticed a sheaf of wheat nestled in the arm of the reclining flower child. Bending low he could just make up the inscription on the attached card: *To desire prosperity is to dance with the cornucopia of delight* – (signed) *Eddie Phoenix*. (i) **The Garden of Adonis – Amoretta and time** (J. D. Batten) – Embellished with brilliantly fresh blossoms the youth of the flower child was doomed to wither, lose the invigorating pallor of orange sunsets, just as she had lost the wings of an Angel. (ii) **Ajax and Cassandra** (Solomon J. Solomon) – Gratification is inevitable in three-dimensional space where sexual force spirals the length of torsos; Featherstone visualized Samantha Westwood languorously sheeted on the bed and himself Ajax sweeping her up in his arm, striding from the apartment. (iii) **Helena and Hermia** (Edward Poynter) – The tesserae of hippies glued in mosaic since the Summer of Love had begun to crack, Fleur and the flower child looser threads already in the weave of the time despite their sewing themselves together for this *bed-in*. Featherstone settled back on the sofa in his office as bronze-curled sunlight darkened in the space of the window, listening to Beethoven late-String Quartets.

Christ And Apollo Mirrored In The World. Television images of the populist *bed-in* lingered on in the news bulletins. Rocks smashed the screen, Lennon's pretentious pacifism carried no credibility with the Gang of Five, the pentagram of revolutionaries competing with the Peace Symbol as representative of the Age's youth. Rebellion against the war in 'Nam was a glass shard thrust between the generations of America. Painted toys from the Summer of Love, The Beatles stifled under their over-dressed personae, perhaps inspiring Lennon's robing himself Christ-like in beard-and-winding-sheet, while Elvis' wave of Apollonian physique adorned the glass of space again with Olympian grandeur. Cymbals-and-symbols clashed on the University campus when the Police and National Guardsmen charged the anti-war demonstrators. Pained by Miranda Westwood's desertion of the *cause* Stephen Maxwell fought with reckless ferocity, his passion to *kill off Vietnamization* untamable by the smooth-talking politicians protected behind the façade of Authority. His threshed soul pastorally burned, scorched by Miranda's indifference, so he offered himself to the Revolution as a quixotic sacrifice. Lennon's glass spectacles fractured, his myopia ironic considering his detestation of Christ as the Supreme Singer between Orpheus and Elvis!

How To Mold A Peace Symbol. Johnny Esquire amused himself on stage of The Playhouse, misbehaving like a Stanley Kowalski hairstyled *à la Elvis*, wielding the axe of a black Stratocaster, the nymphs in the production coming together patterned after metal filings around a magnet, Miranda Westwood jamming with her flute, but whose sonorous torso was she musically ravishing? Organized by Paulette Taylor, the principals of the cast dined together, very *bon viveur*, and Miranda monologued on the clash of combustible planets in the show's Horoscope, preparing them for the explosive publicity when **WHAAM!** opened. Paulette's romantic enjambment with Cornell Bedford-Brown, twentieth-century poesy in the modern style, psychologically invulnerable to Victorian *mores*, her sexual self-publicity, upped the voltage of the cast's enthusiasm. Negotiating the algebra of coming maturity, Miranda erotically curved the slices of space-time by perfuming Alexander Chamberlain's face with kisses as copious alcohol smoothed angular morality from the evening, she determined to extract golden ore and mould a Peace Symbol from this excursion on the stage!

The Torsion In A Rosette Window. Weeping candle wax metaphored the slippage of Time, the flame's half-light embroidering the voices of the String Quartet, when a knock at the office door awakened Christopher Featherstone. Shadows filled the inside-and-outside pane of glass on which his name was boldly lettered until rosettes of bullet holes spread fractured petals all the way to the frame. To whom then belonged the image of the human persona reflected in the glass of space-time? How many forgotten books, paintings, songs and movies melted from the ever-burning candle of Time? Death's torsion ultimately challenged the eminence of the DNA spiral beginning to delude humanity, effortlessly slicing through the latter's presumptuous silhouette dancing across the world's stage. A cream-coloured *coupé* torched by moonlight, its metallic DNA horizontal and four-square on the roadway, sped from the office block, Amazonian tresses freed to the summer breeze, a released scarf saluting the low-flying helicopter which swooped across the freeway.

A Vibrating Field Of Ionized Plasma. The metaphysical abstraction of a torso fragmented from existence, its linear finality, yet touchingly relaxed, conveyed to Jason Palmer Life was nothing but an assumed comedic identity and death the human persona's goodbye quip as it tap-danced from the stage. Reeling in a vibrating field of ionized plasma as detectives and forensic people searched for *prima facie* evidence with intricate thoroughness he cast his spirit amid the nomadic galaxies spinning through Eternity. Bridget Lovegrove, a purling brush having ignited her hair's blushing coppery-red silk following the phone call, stumbled through episodic memories on entering the office, unable though to cross the space and reach the reflective curves of Palmer's Michelangelesque marble half-collapsed against the window-sill. Cracks in the façade of his classical incarnation heavily shadowed his communion with the infinitude of black where he wandered a horizon of *nothing*. All the corners of the office slept now with an anguished repose. On the spinning turntable a late Beethoven String Quartet silently revolved, even the existential overload of its drama subordinate to Death's sonata-for-two-instruments performed earlier.

Religion Of Lost Souls. Faith's Pop Art *Chartres* opened in a blaze of publicity, nymphs-and-satyrs were conceded their nudity, the audience aroused enough to absorb the radiance of the mosaic of scenes tinted with the chemistry of a stained glass window as if viewing another Sistine Chapel, or the Papal walls adorned with Raphael's frescoes. After all, actors were simply beings from a world of illusion, stars fallen from the realm of Heaven onto a performing stage, robed in costume or naked flesh, lost souls all. Unveiled eroticism would become an acquired taste as consumable as *fast food*, and the sight of Sin copulating with Death a sure-fire ticket-seller to the masses ... **WHAAM!**

Theater Of The Absurd. *"Author of evil, unknown till thy revolt, unnamed in heav'n, now plenteous as thou seest these acts of hateful strife, hateful to all, though heaviest by just measure on thyself and thy adherents: how hast thou disturbed Heav'n's blessèd peace, and into Nature brought misery, uncreated till the crime of thy rebellion!"* ... (John Milton)

HOMMAGE à CHRYSLER CORP

How The Spanish Make Love. Magisterial, arabesque Celeste Hawthorne stepped from the stairhead onto the studio platform, bearing her painter's smock on which a smothered palette and brushes lay crossed. *Décolleté*, her unbuttoned blouse, hanging free, fluttered gently caught by the mild autumnal breeze wending through the open window of the studio. She held the bowl of her palette aloft and breathed over Cornell Bedford-Brown's reclining torso:

> Las ascuas de un crepúsculo morado
> Detrás del negro cipresal humean ...
> En la glorieta en sombra está la fuente
> con su alado y desnudo Amor de piedra,
> que sueña mudo. En la marmórea taza
> reposa el agua muerta.

The sky was plated in an effusion of tangerine against the glass-paneled studio holding her unfinished *toilette* in a delectable chiaroscuro speaking of their post-coital time-shift. Uncomfortable, uncleansed in his unpressed suit and rumpled business shirt, Bedford-Brown turned the ignition key in his brand-new Chrysler, remembering Celeste's autonomous sexuality, her rather militant misogyny-in-reverse, her Delilah-solution in emasculating men by imprinting them in chalk naked on reams of paper. Mesmerizing, sweeping him up in her pirouetting Toreador's cape at last night's party, and he was hornèd with the potency of a Spanish bull, she had subdued him whispering Spanish as they danced and plying him with Tequilas set up on the bar like in a Western movie. Money molded in the styling of the Chrysler effortlessly power-steered away from the curbside and he thought he glimpsed Celeste's silhouette darkening the glass panes of her studio.

Encounter On A Showroom Floor. "*Devotion*, Simon, is as a falling star, brilliant against a night-sky, but fast-fading, ephemeral." Aquilina Kingsley dragged her illustrative fingertips along the sleek torso of a Chrysler revolving on the showroom floor, modeling the actress, verbally fencing with him, adding: "*Devotion* to your dragster exceeds what is natural in a modern man, I cannot dress in steel, my voice is as a religious castrato compared with a turbo-charged motor, weak and limp. Laura too complains about the amount of time you are spending with that idle seraphim-in-a-cartoon, Jason Palmer, both of you chasing your Prince Mephistopheles." Simon Freeman half-laughed, quizzical, remembering the one-sided conversation as he slumped behind his desk in the office rifling through paperwork and new-model Chrysler specifications, smelling the odor of sanctimoniousness oozing from his pores. Men's hairdressers were being bankrupted across the city and suburbs as masculine culture stylized itself ready for the coiffured promise of the seventies-to-come. How could simulated fornication have become licensed for the stage, with naked torsos assuming primacy over dialogue, and how sharp-toothed and predatory advertising had become with its bolder imagery and minimalist verbal captions; tossing aside the paperwork he realized the hippie communes out in the suburban prairies were doomed, the counter-culture revolution had failed. A shell of mortality poisoned with imperfections, Prince Mephistopheles in the guise of Eddie Phoenix, moved among the gleaming Chryslers his arrhythmic footsteps echoing in the quietude.

The Beau Monde Of The Age Of Aquarius. Flecked jewels, the lively young girls half-skipped, always conversational, towards the drive in theater's refreshment kiosk while Alexander Chamberlain and Simon Freeman lounged in the midnight-blue street-rod leafing through the script of the evening ahead. Miranda Westwood loomed up at the car window, her mouth's raspberry sorbet fizzing with impertinence: "What a setting for the *beau monde*, Butch Cassidy and the Sundance Kid! Alexander, I almost didn't recognize you with your clothes on. Very monkish looking, quite the Puritan." Beyond the precincts of the drive-in theater the deep rumble of a Harley Davidson given full throttle reverberated along the adjoining street frontage. Both leaned forward and turned up the volume of the car radio as The Fifth Dimension's *Aquarius* resonated the air-waves.

The Getaway. "Who was Miss Miranda Westwood looking for?" Aquilina Kingsley allowed Simon Freeman to lick her ice-cream cone. "Her angelhood, I should think." Scuffles erupted in the projection room above the refreshment kiosk, a film-frame froze on the screen then its melting, consumed image dissolved away and the tocsins of car horns crescendoed. Slamming shut the door of the street-rod, Alexander Chamberlain sprinted for the refreshment kiosk, quickly recognizing the familiar Amazons causing the disruption. Free-swinging, iconic in watermelon-red, a broad-shouldered Amazon flung the discus of a can of film skyward, the frames unraveling like the tail of an exotic kite. Climbing back inside the street-rod as Freeman turned the ignition, he watched her leap into a cream-coloured *coupé* and speed for the exit, running her tyres against the curbing before swerving into the adjoining street. Bottle-necked at the jammed-up exit, Aquilina tongued a smooth dune of ice-cream sitting atop its cone: "Someone should cast that woman's Horoscope!"

Reading A Lesson In The Old Morality. Sheltered from the cool onshore breeze by the screen of a billboard titled *Hommage à Chrysler Corp* Simon Freeman spread the woolen blankets side-by-side on the slope of beach sand and the couples lowered themselves onto the magic carpet. The moon's Persian slipper was buckled with a dazzling star. Knees up, enclosed tight by her arms, Laura Devonshire listened to the breathy kissing, very aware of Alexander Chamberlain's sexual *plastique* stretched out alongside her, the dynamic of their asymmetry contrasting the intertwined ribbons of their friends on the adjacent blanket. "The sexual peace I make on stage with Aquilina is symbolic, Laura, I'm thinking only of you. Listening to the gasps on opening night, I knew you would be the envy of all the women in the audience; you are irresistible, but why this tension over my nakedness?" Standing, peering down at her friends' straining horizontality, Aquilina half-moaning with pleasure through her mouth pressed to Freeman's, Laura smiled: "Alexander, Virtue is no longer coy about undressing herself since she goes about without a chaperone, and you spoke like a Poet when you said to me: *Love has the brevity of a syllable sighed in Eternity*. Nature is an antiquated courtesan, overflowing with copulating beasts and insects … listen to them!" Taking his hand, moving them from visible-to-invisible, Laura walked him away from the billboards and their Pop Art imagery of automobile mouldings along the foreshore deeper into an opaque midnight, the ebb-and-flow of the audible surf an enervating presence.

Entombed. A leaf effortlessly brushed from a branch and drifted light-as-a-feather before settling on a stone. Shaken, screaming through her renownèd tranquility, the flower child became disoriented shopping in the supermarket and cast aside the limp torso of her cheesecloth blouse, lining up at the checkout with a trolley full of yogurt. Fabian Roxburgh's tattered and fading obituary lay half-curled pinned the corner of an album cover on the wall, Ten Years After's **UNDEAD**, and the flower child stood listening to the valedictory *I'm Going Home*. Finished in the bathroom, Fleur-as-singer-actress struggled to find a rhetorical equilibrium through which to balance her sister's surprising grief for Christopher Featherstone against the tenets of the Summer of Love instilled in her psyche. Test-driving a brand-new Chrysler, Simon Freeman sounded the car horn's tocsin and Fleur spooned some yoghurt between her lips, kissed the flower child and bounded down the steps of the apartment block, swinging herself in the back seat. Aquilina Kingsley's libidinal luminescence sprayed its Teen Magazine stylings across the stage of The Playhouse, her naked Eros-and-Psyche episodes holding the audience's deep-seated lust caught on the sticky web of her voice. Following the matinée performance they unwound from the rigors of the Show at a nearby bowling alley where Fleur was paired with Alexander Chamberlain. Existentially tuned-out, existentially turned-off, the flower child still stood washed in the immediacy of *I'm Going Home*, her life-force's taper guttering, only reviving with Fleur's returning kiss.

Empty Pedestals. "Simon, pull alongside!" With parallel simultaneity, the Chrysler sedan traveled side-by-side with Bridget Lovegrove's vehicle so Aquilina Kingsley could speak through the passenger side window. Hair rippled by the breeze, Bridget roused herself to verbalize a thought: "In the ruined Parthenon of his life he wanted to install me as Pallas Athena. Moving through the days I'm simply flexing the suture, so it won't heal. And there have been so many marketing strategists come to promote the lifestyle of Heaven ..." Only the rushing wind sounded as the curving roadway propelled the vehicles on arcing routes away from each other. "Simon, how long has it been since we've seen that Chevrolet?"

A Metaphysical Boutique. Probing the boutique mirror, swinging her reflection through costume-changes, Miranda Westwood imagined the mysterious ghosted-figure melting amid the racks, increasingly visible through last year, friend of Fabian Roxburgh, himself exiled in Vietnam, and shuddered to think of a bullet tearing through her flesh, staining the costly fabrics adorning her.

Dreaming The Tao. Eddie Phoenix ascended the elevator to the thirteenth floor of **KRISHNA inc.** and stepped through into a sanctum freighted with allusions to the Tao of Lucifer's miniaturization. "Eternity has awoken, and the nightmare of the Archangelic fall was a dream after all. Here in the architectural structure of our faith, embedded in the vertebrae of the city weighted with his thought, we will no longer be the mere whim of a dream, but transform existence's light operetta into a revolutionary act!" Lifting off the landing pad atop **KRISHNA inc.** the helicopter arced across the city and followed the arterial freeway system's spectacular Tao, ribbons of space choked with traffic, serpent jeweled with the scales of infinite car hoods beneath an early autumnal sun.

Letter VII. Fabian Roxburgh to Bridget Lovegrove. *Has the King of Hearts fallen from the deck of cards, pierced by a bullet hole? Has he fallen through the perforation in space? He questioned self-existence with rare omniscience, challenging our supposed knowledge of ourselves, but I do profoundly suffer his loss to us as a friend. Perhaps the alchemy of our Age has worked him into unalloyed gold, too pure now for this world, just as your hair's glorious aureole is if I remember dipped in the colours of Heaven setting in the sky. 'Nam's real estate value is now worthless, death is her agent, VC microbes invade and paralyze all industry except the export of body-bags stamped for the USA. Perhaps I might forge a breastplate of immortality here in 'Nam, or my playing card too might wear a bullet-hole. Please shelter the King of Diamonds in your hand!*

Letter VIII. Fabian Roxburgh to Fleur. *Our hair will fade to grey, Fleur, yours perhaps to a blue rinse, and we will have to re-invent ourselves. The thinness of this war's libretto, especially the operatic stiffness of the North Vietnamese delegation singing their Nationalist monologue in Paris, debilitates the GIs, they feel like cardboard cut-outs placed in the boondocks for target practice, engagements here are so sporadic and indecisive. A visionary frontispiece, an antique* *architrave has collapsed, the leaves in the Book of Fate were not transparent, that realization is a specter I'm wrestling with here so far away from you; the bubble has burst and I'm gasping for air.* **WHAAM!** *might just be your redemption, re-ignite your experience of a world marketed as a shooting gallery, resuscitate your commercial heritage. Why be an anti-heroic couplet with some drop-out hippie? Am I still* **then** *to you or have I evolved to* **now***?*

Portrait Of The Archangel (IV). (i) **PHYSICS** - "What is the foam scattering from the lip of electro-magnetic waves breasting space since time-zero?" Dissolving a sugar cube's scalar quantum values in the parabola of his coffee cup, Eddie Phoenix pondered Jason Palmer's verbal sketch tilting at a likeness of the fallen Archangel, his attempted dot-portrait linking electronic masses as miniscule as 9×10^{-28} grams. Hovering offshore before the Oceanside apartment, identifying Palmer's burnished shadow on the balcony, the helicopter's spinning rotorblades made incisions in the sun; a stele fell flat from the horizon across the ocean coloured like a spillage of blood from a wound. Cookie-cutter star-forms blazed through the elastic fabric of the fallen Archangel's immense magnitude, burning up the energy he had cooled to absolute zero in his quest to wrest three-dimensional space from God. (ii) **CHEMISTRY** – Three-dimensional DNA hourglasses carbonized the crystalline spheres of fourth-dimensional space, tightening the coil of Man's consciousness about the sweet glucose molecules of the fallen Archangel, twisted the strands into an unbreakable chain. (iii) **BIOLOGY** – Scorpions scurried across the northern sweep of sand dunes, models for the fallen Archangel's plated fingernails clinging to the infinite particles layering the Earth, a behavioral pattern of devolutionary drift, not evolutionary progress. (iv) **PSYCHOLOGY** – Thought's stratosphere iced-over to absolute zero, Man's brain-waves barely oscillate, and concepts sit in his consciousness like the seeming icebergs of the stars adrift in the Milky Way. (v) **ECOLOGY** - Sub-atomic particles imbued with the brain-waves of the Archangel are as distanced to walking man as the stars are, so sketching a true portrait of the arch-fiend, capturing his likeness in three-dimensional systems is an illusory dream.

We Rose Up Slowly Like Swimmers In A Shadowy Dream. A plaited sculpture-in-motion on the wave, Simon Freeman surfed the autumnal swell inlaid on the entablature, a raised hand dragging along the crest's architrave, while on the foreshore Aquilina Kingsley and Laura Devonshire conversed. "How can I be horizontally relaxed with Alexander on stage, nude, yet aroused to the point of insensibility with Simon, fully clothed?" Overlooking the beach, astride the Harley Davidson, Priscilla posed *à la Pharaoh* on the pillion clasping the ribs of Johnny Esquire, the couple seemed enclosed inside an invisible Pyramid. "So, you haven't surrendered to him the necklace of your virtue?" Aquilina's enquiry chastely hymned her own inclination toward Freeman. Rapidly decelerating, a Chevrolet braked alongside the Harley and a kinetic exhilaration visibly stirred Laura, but she moved too slowly for just as Johnny Esquire propelled the motorcycle away it dragged the car in its slipstream. A breeze agitated her symphony of curls into a flow of semiquavers of delight as she gazed after the Chevrolet. Sequenced in tear-away mode on a wave, Freeman reveled in Arcadia's imagery of still-warm light, water, motion and chastity, and when Aquilina waded out they sank back into the surging whitewater kissing.

Analytic Tendencies. Pine trees raised their spires against the horizon. The eastern skyline was unusually on fire with purple tapestries inset with the moon's succubus sucking light from a sun dipping below the horizon's curve. A helicopter negotiated the brightening shoals of the Milky Way. Sharp pine needles carpeted the earth, millions of fallen arrows wasted in the Archangel's assault on fourth-dimensional space, realm of the human soul and always the true setting for the conflict between Good and Evil. Meditatively immersed in the physiognomy of the grove of pine trees, crunching the needles underfoot, Jason Palmer climbed back inside the Chevrolet and turned over the motor, remembering Christopher Featherstone's words scrawled in blood ... *circuitus spiritualis*. Rolling a blow-up beach ball among the sand dunes tinctured by moonbeams he mused for hours over the two-dimensional warpage-effect, and when daylight came returned to the Oceanside apartment, looking up the business phone directory for architects; he would design three-dimensional models and enmesh the fallen Archangel!

Brother Love's Traveling Salvation Show. Atypical of the non-engagements in 'Nam between the NLF and the US forces, the anti-war demonstrations Stateside starred hundreds-of-thousands of open combatants, posters advertising this irony flooding the campuses, and a louder voice gathered momentum: **THIS IS A WHITE MAN'S WAR!** Stephen Maxwell's Gang of Four feverishly harangued the student body from make-shift trestles, moved phalanx-style everywhere, adopted tactics the NLF rigorously shied away from, large-scale physical confrontations. Basic tenets and assumptions inherent in the Western Democracies were questioned for their validity in the modern world and the sticky web of Communism woven across South-East Asia strengthened its anchorage to Russian and China. While death numbers of US personnel in 'Nam steadily increased to 33,641, a figure brandished by the Gang of Five across banners and placards, threads hoping to enmesh thousands more protestors, physical fatalities from the demonstrations were insignificant, the psycho-political damage was designed to cripple the West for generations-to-come. Albums spinning on turntables in the West promised youth they were **ON THE THRESHOLD OF A DREAM!**

Christopher Featherstone's Memorial. The nerve of his libido still electrified despite his sexual emptying-out with Celeste Hawthorne, his emotions in free-fall, Cornell Bedford-Brown signed into the Health Club for a session of lifting weights and *Crimson-and-Clover* reflections on the reviews **WHAAM!** was drawing from the critics. Cycling an imaginary *Tour de France*, measuring his heart rate, fuelled by lust for Celeste's sexual palette, pursuing the dream of a supernatural masculinity, rebuilding himself against Judgment Day, he caught a glimpse of Eddie Phoenix observing him inside a wall-mirror. Radio air-play of selected tracks from the cast's album, memorial to Christopher Featherstone as lyricist, eluded the listeners, so Johnny Esquire ramped up the voltage of his solo number in **WHAAM!** for release as a single, and television appearances were booked. Introduced by the turtle-neck sweatered *sidewinder* MC on a popular variety program, entering the camera's eye astride his sleek-limbed *Ann-Margret* Harley Davidson, very photogenic in his ersatz Elvis-style *à la Viva Las Vegas*, Johnny Esquire brilliantly illuminated the screen with his version of *Burn The Candle*.

Oooo, that fabulous rock'n'roll
Stealin' like a phantom over my soul.
It's the life I dream,
All the drama of my scene.
They tell me Burn The Candle at both ends,
But I'm hopelessly tangled up in emotion.
Always ready to catch on fire
Just like Chekhov ridin' A Streetcar Named Desire.

Oooo, they say rock'n'roll's immoral,
Leads to acts unnatural.
But let's have some amusement
And then tell the President
Go Burn The Candle at both ends.
Get yourself tangled up in emotion.
Be ready to catch on fire
Just like Chekhov ridin' A Streetcar Named Desire.

Oooo, rock'n'roll will never die,
Though time is on the fly.
And when my girl's dancin' it seems
Her dress is fallin' apart at the seams.
Cos she Burns The Candle at both ends,
Got herself tangled up in emotion.
Always ready to catch on fire
Just like Chekhov ridin' A Streetcar Named Desire.

Oooo, rock'n'roll is the Great Pretender,
And talkin' up romance is slander.
While time's playin' at bravado,
With Fate catchin' at shadows.
So Burn The Candle at both ends,
Get yourself tangled up in emotion.
Be ready to catch fire
Just like Chekhov ridin' A Streetcar Named Desire.

Buried in the psycho-sexual core of Celeste's bed with the obeisance of a leopard, her carved Eros astrally reconstituted as chalk on the sheets of her sketching folios, Bedford-Brown turned up the transistor radio on the table, listening to the DJ spinning *Burn The Candle's* 45.

Metaphysical *Frottage* Beached In Existence. Sliding incandescently from the Chevrolet, visually irradiated by the moon, blue moon of loneliness, Laura Devonshire floated like a bell-tone across the crests of sand dunes, discovering a cream-coloured *coupé* half-buried in a finely-sifted drift. Adrift like so much metaphysical *frottage* himself, Jason Palmer nuanced the memory of a long-lost Jazz riff glimpsing the torso of the *coupé*, its baroque paradigm of a tomb full of impudence, but Laura's orchestrally-trained ear heard the low-throbbing cello of the helicopter first. A Police forensic team cordoned off the surrounding dunes and arc-lighting bleached the billboard images crowding the scene. Laura kneeled in the sand and brushed grains from a black disc, a 45, with a fiery pink label **LESBOS** label: the artist's name, **HELENA STEELE**. Piece-of-jigsaw missing, the blue moon lay blackened with the helicopter's imperfection, the scene seemingly a mystery to everyone but Jason Palmer who interpreted bizarre meanings from the cloth of all the imagery in which they were enmeshed.

"I'm An Actress!" "Simon, treat me gently, carefully, I'm just a bubble of a working girl in which my feelings display themselves. Prick me and I'll burst, I'm an *actress*!" Sexily smoldering through her mischievous ironies, Aquilina Kingsley smoothed down her lacquer-tressed hair, having convincingly kissed Simon Freeman inside the brand-new Chrysler parked in her driveway. Pushing the Chrysler up to eighty, Freeman reflected how her monologues were preferable to cut-away conversations, and being inside her silky bubble of emotions refreshed his sense of identity, but cruising the Oceanside boulevards he searched for the Chevrolet. Steadily burning arc-lights illuminated billboards set among the sand dunes like cinema screens, carrying fragments of a portrait he had glimpsed in Jason Palmer's wallet, a Private Investigator he spoke of elliptically, and whose photograph featured in the newspaper. Appearing to physically cling to an immense mouth emerging across the space of the billboard (but whose?), Laura Devonshire shimmered in the efflorescence of the Chrysler's headlamps.

Television Is The Medium! KRISHNA inc. bought advertising space on television, offering the counter-culture devotees the Maharishi Phoenix's rose garden of petals to meditate upon, and Miranda Westwood's appearance in the commercials playing the flute, offered further aesthetic pleasures to contemplate at the downtown ashram, thirteenth-floor. Troubled on behalf of Calvin Westwood, one of the new sixties multi-millionaires, financial investor in **WHAAM!**, Cornell Bedford-Brown undertook an investigation into **KRISHNA inc.**, taking the elevator and already breathing the smoking incense as he ascended the floors of the skyscraper. Of Amazonian build, with Ursula Andress shoulders, setting her dress on fire, a half-glimpsed tall woman brushed by him into the elevator as he emerged, and stepped across a harvest of rose petals into the sanctum of the ashram. Playing the flute, cross-legged on the floor, Miranda Westwood and a Summer of Love flower child with cymbals on her fingers, improvised a melody while other nymphs unbound a swirling turban of lotus petals about their heads. Rising, cobra-hooded, Maharishi Phoenix ghost-touched Bedford-Brown's forehead in *blue* with a fingertip and signaled they watch a television screen pulsing to clarity with a current affairs segment focusing on **KRISHNA inc**. Swami Phoenix struck the interviewer like an unerring serpent: "Christian Adam was sublimely cuckolded by Lucifer and Eve, a very tired bedroom farce, a mischievous masquerade, and humanity is to forever drinking poison from the burning lake. Come to Krishna, who swan-dived into the flaming poison and cleansed the river of existence: Come to Krishna, unfurl your clothes and swim naked in him, he will fulfill your desires." Letters requesting initiation into **KRISHNA inc**. out-numbered the lotus and rose petals covering the floor.

Apollo Slays Python (Delacroix). Irreversible falling sensations infused Jason Palmer's astral dreaming in the Oceanside apartment, and just prior to dawn Apollo's effortless descent, an expository *deus ex machina*, and slaying of the presumptuous Archangel's gliding Moray eel revivified him for the Eternal Quest set down in his Zodiacal stars. Apollo's ethereal flame crystallized from a billion fourth-dimensional suns surged through the microcosmic space between the sub-atomic particles composing his torso and darkness slithered away. Palmer experienced an explosive onrush of air as the Chevrolet accelerated down the boulevard, and he was coasting on four celestial wheels of a chariot whose bearings were scintillating jewels not metal, rising not on air, but *aether*!

Olympus On Ida (GF Watts). Who walked more beautifully than Laura Devonshire scrutinizing his chameleon thoughts radiant with his Fate's martyr complex? Crossing the sand dunes with the choreography of a falling star illuminating the cream-coloured *coupé* entombed before the headstone of a billboard portraited with Christopher Featherstone she was so many twisted curls of motion sprung with rainbowing perfume. Redeemer of mortality, her triadic beauty was centripetal with the Solar Bride contemplative on the horizon, walking together on the tapestry of dunes coloured by the sunset her heartbeats were synchronized to Immortality's.

The Penitent Magdalene (Antonio Canova). Kneeling on the sun-swept floor of the Oceanside apartment as the crystalline spheres of his heliocentric universe shattered with the impact of a falling stone through glass, sifting through gathered memorabilia unfamiliar to her, Laura Devonshire *was* the sculpture, her face echoed Magdalene's gazing over the crucifix of photographs arranged there. Space's languor eventually stiffened with a sudden sea breeze ruffling the stilled Galilee of the ocean visible through the window. University's worldly turmoil, anti-war riots and demonstrations, contrasted the serenity externalized in the hypercubic space of the apartment. Laura began to visualize the still-forming face masked across the three-dimensional sculpture of billboards among the sand dunes. Pale moonlight bled blushes from Magdalene's exquisitely composed face, and meditation became virginal, a rising lotus whose roots might be sunk in pollution but whose glowing awakening was rapt with understanding.

Interior With A Violin Case (Matisse). Elegiac, Brahms' Violin Concerto burnished the apartment's post-romantic painterly motifs, the aura of space beyond the window crackled with autumnal colours, while Laura Devonshire maintained her guardedly aristocratic air. Chromaticism surged from the violin, phrases floated as if on a stream of cosmic breath exhaled by an Archangel walking the golden galleries of the sun, so rapt was Laura's penetration of the weave of music, her *color* soaking its fabric. Jason Palmer's Arcadian solitude, a millennial displacement from Greece's Golden Age, his endless contemplation of the slices of Time, individualized moments screened by consciousness, assumed the airiness of Eternity as bow-and-string separated and a vibrant silence descended. Laura reverently laid the violin in its case, a torso infatuated with its life-giving soul!

Coffee, Sex And WHAAM! Aromatic coffee flowed from the silver spout into a white cup and milk swirled from a jug held by Celeste Hawthorne. Her movements about the studio possessed today the intimate musicality of Vermeer's brushstrokes, and though he had attempted to scrape her portrait from the canvas of his thoughts, like lines once spoken, vanishing, the actor within kept revisiting them and her erotic beatitude. She articulated sex as a sequence of meditations, her smooth nakedness lithe amid the wave of sheets as suave as an Ode, each session of coitus a stanza awaiting transference to her sketchbook in coloured chalks. Cornell Bedford-Brown inhaled the aura of coffee, caught in the lightning-flash of her creative intelligence sketching his transience, his microcosmic refraction through the prism of her existence, raying sensation he could observe be not be *inside*.

> Tal vez la mano, en sueños,
> del sembrador de estrellas,
> hizo sonar la música olvidada
> como una nota de la lira inmensa,
> y la ola humilde a nuestros labios vino
> de unas pocas palabras verdaderas.

Seated in the half-empty Playhouse, feeling his cosmopolitan varnish encrusted with chalk-dust courtesy of Celeste's libidinous temperament, Bedford-Brown was by now super-saturated with **WHAAM!**'s Pop Art impressionism, the artistically modelled nudity as prosaic as the drinking of coffee. Paulette Taylor stalked the front office, all zest and exuberance, setting up schemes for the transmission of **ME**, ever the mistress of innuendo for the Press whom she cultivated with a blithe eroticism borrowed from the Pop Art imagery of **WHAAM!**

The Geography Of Dante's Inferno In 3D. Working the steering wheel of the half-submerged, cream-coloured *coupé*, its physique's plasticity prostrate before its forensic futurity under Police supervision, Jason Palmer visualized in the surrounding sand dunes the symmetry of Eden collapsed into three-dimensional space. Australia's desert-coloured antique geography, a red-hued and bloodied elemental spirit, a bizarre continental shape imprisoned in the Ocean of Time, and its shipwrecked humanity embodied the condemned of Dante's *Inferno*. Tragically, this post-Eden time was non-linear, the stop-watch hadn't started, ruby blood from the fallen angels seeped and crystallized everywhere, the muscle of the human heart carried the infection through the body's DNA staircase, energized the mind to formulate acts of madness. "Simon calls you a kind of cosmic frontiersman blazing a trail through the wasteland of three-dimensional space, signposting the way for others in your Chevy, but whatever does that mean?" Footprints in the soft-crusted sand resembled the outline of hooves from Man's featherless biped, fossilizations of the journey from Eden, perhaps projections of an image for the planned Moon landing scheduled for mid-year. Aquilina Kingsley skipped off across the moonscape after Simon Freeman carrying Palmer's response in her thoughts: "I have stepped through the mirror of three-dimensional space in which the Sun God, Helios, reflects a starry version of Himself, *upon* Himself, that I might draw the world up to that mirror and say: *Look here, upon this picture, and on this; the counterfeit presentment of two brothers, Michael and Lucifer. See, what a grace was seated on this brow; Hyperion's curls, the front of Jove himself, an eye like Mars, to threaten and command, a station like the herald Mercury new-lighted on a heaven-kissing hill, a combination and form indeed, where every god did seem to set his seal, etc.*"

♪ **The Melody Haunts My Reverie** ♫. A cartoon blueprinted from a modern dress Delacroix lithograph on the theme of *Faust*, Eddie Phoenix circulated among the lunchtime audience of University students gathered in the auditorium for a recital, tall in his Cuban-heeled boots, the fallen Archangel's mirage in the mirror of three-dimensional space. Trailing star-dust from the cream-coloured *coupé*, crashed chariot in the wasteland of the Earth's *Inferno*, Jason Palmer found Phoenix's slipstream as Laura Devonshire led the musicians on stage to perform Cesar Franck's Piano Quintet: at his suggestion she had formed a String Quartet of post-graduate friends and named the ensemble, **HELIOS**. A sympathetic Archaii, feminine Archangel, kissed Laura's sisterly face and Franck's spiritually sensuous music filled the auditorium like sunlight shimmering in stained glass, and Phoenix's ebony Delacroixan lithograph fled through the shadowy interstice of an exit pursued by Palmer. A menacing frontispiece likeness of Mephistopheles, Phoenix swung behind Johnny Esquire on the Harley and Palmer's Chevrolet did not catch another glimpse until the motorcycle crossed a hunched bridge shaped after a dragon's vertebra. Backstage following the recital, Laura entertained Alexander Chamberlain, bringing his shadow to a rare luminosity, so Palmer hung back with Aquilina Kingsley who joked that **WHAAM!** was now playing to the emptiest Playhouse in the world. Fluid with the poetry of the Franck Quintet winding the Chevrolet towards the ocean, the music's wave-of-aether magnetically drawing him surfside, Palmer paddled the Malibu into his translucently sheer beachbreak for a free-spirited session until the helicopter disturbed the perfect symmetry of the sinking sun. Surfing a wave's entablature was more thrilling than carving the Parthenon.

I Can See The Whole Room And There's Nobody In It. "Christopher told me you were the accountant alluded to in *Revelations*, double-entry bookkeeping is the gift you bring into the world." Glazed, unfocused, Bridget Lovegrove listened to the young man who had stepped into her glass-panelled office, his obscure sketch reminiscent of Christopher Featherstone's descriptors, his exaggerated style filling the emptiness metaphorically surrounding her. "I recognized you from his description of your head's alchemical rose: perhaps our thoughts can waltz a melody together around his remembrance. The birth and death of extraordinary men are fixed points of arrival and departure drawn by set-square and compass in three-dimensional space, that we all might trace out patterns for ourselves, be re-engraved on fresh tablets to their specific spiritual geometry." Bridget's desk-bound journals, themselves a geometry of accounting modelled on the leaves turned by the Angel of Records come Judgment Day, lay closed as he guided her along the aisle away from her office space and opened the door of his Chevrolet, driving her down to the beach where the cream-coloured *coupé* sat in the open-air theatre of sand dunes. Becalmed offshore, anchored in stillness, floated a schooner, ghost ship lost on the Sea of Eternity, although an elegiac sounding, autumnal flute roused a gentle breeze like a sweep of thought through the mind.

An Opera Staged In Eternity. With the heart of Carmen in her operatic breast Helena Steele crossed the roadway causing the gleaming Chrysler to brake suddenly, luminous with a killing style of walking catching Cornell Bedford-Brown's attention, for he recognized her now as the Amazon Queen leading the assault on **WHAAM!**. Perhaps she should be written into the Arcadian Pop Art world-picture of the Show to energize the spatial flatness of Celeste's backdrops. Later he caught up with Jason Palmer and they contrasted their existential differentiations on what their metaphysical choices were, especially when he mentioned the towering Amazon, and her Toreador flirting with his Chrysler. An ochre sunset swirled colour through the late-afternoon sky. The figure of a young woman dived from the schooner dusted in the saffron aureoling the sinking sun. Gripped in the paradox of Eternity's unchanging sameness, Palmer crossed a sand dune dressed in the sun's after-glow, silhouette of an earthbound soul wrapped in funereal purple, knowing the Spirit of Infinity had dreamed him, that is all!

V
THE GREAT AMERICAN NUDE

Whose Ventriloquist Echo Are We? Ventriloquist's echo, hollow with the new rhetoric for a freer moral code on the threshold of 1970, Paulette Taylor summoned up the lineage of Eden and naked Eve in the celebrated Garden, jostling with the staid-suited newspapermen who crowded her descent of the steps from the Court House. Rolls of posters for **WHAAM!** under her arm, exhibits of immorality but selling steadily among the youth, she wielded them like Siva in his stylized dance to descend towards Cornell Bedford-Brown's idling Chrysler. Layered beneath her smart business suit, her torso's luminous cream of sensuality wore the fabric's stain like sin's embedded stigmata, and climbing into the Chrysler as phallic microphones brushed her person she left the dour newspapermen with a smile's *dishabille*. Her crimson mouth's ventriloquism, over-rouged to provoke a spectacle in Court, deliberately compromised The Playhouse's management who would read the column inches in the morning papers and announce the Show's closure. Later, Bedford-Brown leaned against the bathroom door frame watching her in the shower-stall drag the towel from side-to-side across her shoulder-blades, the gelatin translucence of her naked breasts inviting his touch: "Time to free the prisoner, Eve, bored in her Eden, and I'm relying on you being an available Adam whenever I make the right move on you!" Pop Art's ideal sexual shallowness, canvases isolated from a chain-of-being, the plateau of the bed-as-installation perfectly scaffolded Paulette's vision of coitus.

Who Could Solve This Cryptic Crossword Clue? Intersecting cryptic crossword answers, vectors describing the two-dimensional length-and-breadth of Paradise Lost, Eddie Phoenix and Helena Steele moved off at right angles to each other, leaving Johnny Esquire holding the common square of sidewalk pavement they had occupied before the entrance to **KRISHNA inc.** "Harden those biceps, Atlas, if you have any, you'll need them to raise *Paradise Lost's* Twelve Books!" Laughing, Phoenix pushed away from the Chevrolet idling by the curb, snapping his fingers to The Beatles' *Get Back* audible from a transistor radio at a passing teenager's ear. Creeping forward the Chevrolet trailed the haughty stride of the Amazon, filming her with its fender-mounted camera; how was Jason Palmer to staunch the leakage of these effusions into three-dimensional space from the fractured labyrinth into which they had been cast? Who was the angler beaching them on the shores of the world? Breathing as if naked, swinging hips and legs in *that* motion unique to feminine thighs, Helena Steele presumptuously stepped from the sidewalk onto the roadway and cars braked to a screeching halt.

Zen For The Pop Generation. Eros' **I** stood modeling a crucifixion in Time, Psyche half-collapsed *à la Ingres*, lights brought up the slashing witticism of Roy Lichtenstein's oil and magna masterpiece, *Yellow and Green Brushstrokes*, expressive emblem of Zen for the Pop Generation. Campaigning against the censorship of the *moral majority*, University students frequented The Playhouse, canvassed widely to ensure **WHAAM!** survived its negative press, **THE GREAT AMERCIAN NUDE** parties were the rage on campus, 'Nam seemed yesterday's news. The erotic optics of sexual intimacies assumed the *frottage* of liquid brushstrokes, splashes and drips of ecstasy became emblems of *satori*, epitomized by Eros and Psyche self-enlightening on stage every evening in **WHAAM!**.

> *(Eros)*
> I stand alone in your gallery of faces
> Dying memories, flaming roses
> Thoughts leave silent traces
> As the tomb slowly closes
> Falling In Love Again
> Falling In Love Again
> We're the young and the beautiful
> Just two shadows of one fool
> *(Psyche)*
> I'm my shadow's shadow
> Chained to passion's solitude
> Temptation's deep as a cello
> And guilt's a universal mood
> Falling In Love Again
> Falling In Love Again
> We're the young and the beautiful
> Just two shadows of one fool

I Just Want To Go To My Room. "O, Alexander, Laura, what a lovely montage of echoes, dinner together, perhaps we can scramble the egg!" Aquilina Kingsley, loosened by alcohol yet self-possessed, very different to her expressive nudity written into **WHAAM!**, scanned the plates and cutlery in equilibrium on the tablecloth, adding: "We should take advantage of these spaces while my parents are away, my brother's old room has not been slept in for two years. Simon, come to the silken crimson pillows of my mouth." Velvet-gloved together on the sofa, their dinner-table collage fractured like a Cubist painting, kissing fully clothed, Alexander Chamberlain widened the fissure between their withdrawing mouthes, sensing the cause of Laura's alienation. Self-mirrored in the space of her eyes she was surreally arabesqued in a secretive embrace with Jason Palmer, the metaphysical poseur who had visited The Playhouse and remarked: "Why did Pop Art miss surfing in its iconography?" Aquilina introduced Simon Freeman into the Hollywood museum of her bedroom, her gestures loosened now from the pages of a D. H. Lawrence novel, holding him in a tranquil seizure, kissing, her fingers exploratory, refusing though to undress. A crumpled pillow and bunched bedcovers camouflaged the unwritten scene in **WHAAM!** where Eros and Psyche mutually *scrambled the egg!*

Department Store Fresco. Miranda Westwood extended her leg parallel to the lengthened fork of the Harley Davidson, compared arabesques with *Ann-Margret's* chrome frigidity, but Johnny Esquire failed to appear at the stage door so she climbed the steps and entered The Playhouse. Somewhere a light burned illuminating the scene settings and stage props for Eros and Psyche's *Great American Nude* sequence. A dressing room door stood ajar and muffled gasps could be heard. Her face modeling a bitter-sweet swoon over Johnny Esquire's shoulder, Paulette Taylor hugged his torso's lascivious armor, she took her baroque ecstasy in full view of Miranda as the motion of his flesh became more sluggish too. Walking the city streets awash with neon, fending off the come-ons from cruising cars, Miranda gazed into a department store window, at the sylph-like mannequins and her half-reflection off the glass, suddenly realizing they were facsimiles of Paulette Taylor!

How Does Music Name The Flute? "If God had a name, was nameable, couldn't we then address Him with our problems?" Teasing, Miranda Westwood leaned her arms along the roof of the Chevrolet and laid her cheek against her hand, curious for Jason Palmer's reaction, but he just swung open the door and they patrolled the city streets. *Hair* by The Cowsills filled the cabin, but she was more marketable as *pavlova-with-peaches* with her girl-next-door beauty and heiress status, despite her flute-playing persona in **WHAAM!** and infatuation with Johnny Esquire. "My father, Calvin Westwood, one of the new millionaires, believes he is God to me, his rebellious daughter, Eve. Hey, do you already have an Eve for this movie you're making?" Lit up with arc-lamps, the marina's quay spotlighted the approaching Chevrolet and Miranda's disembarkation, the camera set-up following her along the jetty towards the Westwoods' moored schooner. Microphones picked up the interplay between the onshore breeze and the flute music drifting from the schooner, both competing in longing to name Deity, metaphors for His expressiveness. With her face profiled inside a round porthole window, leaves from the pages of last year's **JACKIE** journal blowing in the space of her thoughts, Miranda began to appreciate her mother's loss measured against her own.

The Two-Dimensional Floor Of Paradise Lost. A very metallic Eddie Phoenix, colder than fiery ice, giving Jason Palmer the stare of Voltaire diluted to its marble fixity, said: "Miranda Westwood, the millionaire's daughter, is a child of her time, and a candidate being considered for the next *Great American Nude*, and if she succeeds she can ride pillion with Johnny on the broad highway of the floor of Paradise Lost." Overnight showers had saturated the lush lawn of the park where a kookaburra swooped and gathered up a rubbery lizard in its beak, the bird stony-eyed and unblinking with its prize capture, briskly taking to wing again. "You cruise this world's highway in that rustic Chevrolet as if it had wings and you had the blue thoughts of the azure sky there, but dark clouds are already rolling in." Phoenix, exemplar of philosophic hooliganism, smiled with the indestructibility of marble as they crossed the park into the city where skyscrapers formed up in mountainous ravines through which plunged the swift-moving river of humanity, tight within Lucifer's gravitational orbit.

Sexual Physics. Feeling the boundary of his mortality mirrored in the stinging salted tear in Laura Devonshire's eye, his cerebral libido on stage nude in **WHAAM!** just a burst bubble to her, Alexander Chamberlain's wound oozed with the poison, *jealousy*. "Coitus is inevitable," Aquilina Kingsley whispered, close to her friend's ear as the crack of snooker balls resounded on the billiard table. "Simon fumbled, very incompetent, because my strategy is to remain clothed, requiring him to think about how he was going to pleasure *me*, instead of just himself. I told him he had better not hug me as if I were a mannequin." Laura rested her cue on the bridge and watched the ball cushion off a *red*, but her thoughts were role-playing to another impresario's script, Jason Palmer's, who kissed her with the intensity of Brahms' Violin Concerto. Aquilina read the lesson and recited it: "Are you mortal to this Jason Palmer then? He brings a moonless night to your reverie, but your human eyes can't quite make out his elusive black cat ... you know ... but I see the electricity bristle your hair when he purrs and rubs up against you." How effortlessly Aquilina masked herself in monologues and preserved her purity with Alexander, a prodigy with her voice even while the hue of her naked complexion compromised the loins of the audience, while the tincture of Laura's flesh was frosted to his arousal.

The Swami Reads A Horoscope. KRISHNA inc. mirrored a late-autumn sky chilled with cloud-forms resembling the auras of Angels. Having scaled the peak of the skyscraper and re-designed the interior offices of **KRISHNA inc.** and dressed as Swami Eddie Phoenix, the Voltaire of exiles arranged a convocation of flower children around a sand-box centered on the floor, the Australian flag beautifully rendered within its boundary. Rhythmic finger-bells sounded by the flower children accompanied Miranda Westwood's flute sucking oxygen from the space of the office and converting it to sound, dulling the sensorial world, creating a Stygian flow for the soul to glide from this three-dimensional world, but to where? Paulette Taylor presented a parchment inscribed with a Natal Horoscope to Swami Phoenix for his interpretation: Jason Palmer's! Helena Steele's formidable presence dominated the glass-walled space of the window, bleeding all the red from the Australian flag into a broad-shouldered jacket, statuesque amid the supple reeds of the flower children, her psyche deaf to any call-to-repentance as she scanned the Horoscope over Phoenix's shoulder. "Five planets in air signs! Have we considered the symbology of *air* in our strategy against this troublesome Palmer, this middle-earth pilgrim? Air is invisible, unlike earth, fire and water, it is breathed and sustains existence, three-dimensionally. How then do we suffocate his spiritual aspirations? How do we stop inhaling him ourselves, infecting our consciousness, for his mystic oxygen leaves the stain of Faith? Look where these fourth-dimensional Planets overflow into the two-dimensional map, from which he arises three-dimensionally, an Archangelic social climber suppliant for Lucifer's abandoned crown in Heaven!" Flame ignited in oxygen, Helena Steele walked across to the fiery altar of a Zodiacal egg's representation on Phoenix's desk, pondering the Horoscope in her hands: "I'll burn this sphere of space he inhabits and he will vanish!"

Skyline From Planet Of The Apes. Bob Dylan's *Nashville Skyline*, as languorous as the undulations of smoke rising in the apartment, rolled back the political turbulence structured around Lt. John Kirby as he moved by a stripped-down engine-block centered in the room and crossed to the Pop Art flower children seated on a sofa. He picked up the fragments of a torn letter on the floor at the younger flower child's naked feet. A bearded hippie, self-enlarged with counter-culture wisdom, dislodging a soup-can sculpture as he moved said: "Lieutenant, I see you've strapped on your wristwatch for the countdown to Eternity. White-man-with-black-soul is going to need Eternity to cleanse himself of his sins." Air-brushed for silk-screening to a Pop Art canvas Lt. Kirby idly tapped an ancient Remington typewriter ... *From 'Nam With Love* ... the very model for a Lichtenstein! Bearded hippies huddled on the floor by the sculpture of the engine-block summoned up images from *Planet of the Apes*!

Letter IX. Fabian Roxburgh to Bridget Lovegrove. *"Seize the tableaux!" is the military cry, and I'm referring to specific Hills in the highlands of 'Nam, terrain even the poetry of Dante and Milton could not describe for all their gift with words. Your news leaves me denuded of purpose and meaning. Watching the surgical strikes on the boil of the Hill, I seem to be the only imagist able to pierce the skin surface of earth and feel the poison coursing deep through the veins, spreading the length-and-breadth of 'Nam, with the carbuncle of Saigon waiting to burst with the inflammation. The ceiling fan spins, my image in the mirror can't be mine, a transistor radio somewhere is playing Wedding Bell Blues, and my character is brushed in the space of a war zone with the shadowy forms of Grunts ascending a Hill without hope of salvation. Lying beneath the ceiling fan in my room in this fetid city I drift off in a dream of St. Julian the Hospitaller, myself, exchanging skins with the leper, 'Nam.*

Letter X. Fabian Roxburgh to Bridget Lovegrove. *I speak your name aloud ... Bridget ... and the echo pries open my thoughts to remember your warmth and calm tranquility. The tenderness with which you write to me is a grace more soothing than prayer. You said you had* *found your head leaning against the painting,* **HOPE,** *on the wall of Christopher's office and experienced a strange transference reviving your spirits. So do I lean my thoughts against your memory in the ominous shadow of the Hill, an inverse funeral urn littered with skeletal remains, and find strength to thread the labyrinth, find my way home. 'Nam is a vast cage in which the animal, Man, is loosened from conscience and restraint, to sink or rise, to shelter beneath the wing of the fallen Archangel or step into the light of Paradise in death. I feel impaled on the quill of an Archangelic feather, the ink I spill across the page is sulphurous with his negativity. After these letters will my seeing you again unsettle you too much?*

Letter XI. Fabian Roxburgh to Bridget Lovegrove. *A disheveled chorus line, Grunts descend the Hill, upturned urn inscribed with the aftermath of tumultuous fighting, more despondent than the fallen from Paradise Lost; so Communism will triumph, humanity's colonization of the Earth will be repelled, the Archangelic Dictator can celebrate a victory. The other evening I dreamed of you again, surrounded by clusters of men, a moment of metaphysical flamboyance, I know, but the ache of separation intensifies my feelings for you, I draw such comfort from the sensation, being bereaved here in life.*

Letter XII. Fabian Roxburgh to Fleur. *My existence is still rough-grained, still in formal mourning, I'm still a castaway beyond redemption, but the brightness of your caricature described to me, in* **WHAAM!,** *balances my darkness. Here all is painted in a canvas of blood so knowing your life is backdropped by harmless Pop Art scenes against which you are modeling your existence is instructive in a metaphysical sense. I have Lt. Kirby's piece,* **From 'Nam With Love,** *before me now; has that Pop Art brushstroke in red, Helena Steele, been arrested yet, no one will write of her to me? So your bearded room-mates took umbrage at my description of them as unholy, obese reincarnations of Caribbean pirates, guitars having replaced their cutlasses, and say I deserve this exile! Well, I shall maintain a respectful distance and close our Book of Fate, leave those pages to posterity.*

Portrait Of The Archangel (V). (i) **PHYSICS** – What did the grains of sand on a beach cognize of wave-foam bubbling over and soaking through the space between them? Jason Palmer's late-autumn surfing sessions elliptically alluded to the glory of free-spirited seraphim before the Fall with the trail of his surfboard chalking the wave-faces in pure lines. Now he remembered cruising the waters of the desert to the island of Las Vegas, neon domes and minarets aglow summoning the faithful, and the golden sphere of the sun descending behind the wingèd enfoldment of the International Hotel. Laura Devonshire, chilled by the offshore breeze, stripped down to a bikini, shivered as he explored the metaphysics of sand grains adhered to her abdomen like Benday dots, and stood by him on the balcony of the Oceanside apartment as he gazed up into the clear night sky at the stars and the black foam soaking through the space between them. (ii) **CHEMISTRY** – Napalm soup spilled from the bowl of the sky across the jungles of 'Nam on the news bulletins. Balls of string lay on the floor of the Oceanside apartment, diagrams of molecular rings and chains, *polymer spinal columns of the fallen Archangel,*

Jason Palmer called them, as Laura Devonshire's beautiful hourglass form practiced her violin. "What is C-O-O-H?" He spoke of two-dimensional binary alphabets, of the freemasonry of the double helix, of the hundred-thousand-billion miniature suns compacted in the darkness of the human form, and the scissors of rays of light cutting her shapely arabesque from the cloth of space. (iii) **BIOLOGY** – During Intermission at the drive in theatre, while they ate hamburgers and studied the screen through the Chevrolet's windshield, Jason Palmer asked: "What height may a man achieve in two-dimensional space?" Brando's *The Appaloosa* screened after Intermission, the scene with scorpions concentrating Laura Devonshire's fears, the Caliban revelation of the famous actor's performance haunting her Miranda for days afterward. Palmer kissed the soft glucose of her mouth and filmed her in the rib of an abandoned skeleton of a boat half-buried in the foreshore of the beach. Clouds dappling the flanks of the sand dunes created an effect of motion. (iv) **PSYCHOLOGY** – Through clustered clouds stars faintly beamed, linking up a gravitational web across which the fallen Archangel extended his consciousness, but would Laura Devonshire standing on the balcony of the Oceanside apartment repulse him? Her violin playing shuddered with a kind of emotional seismology and her posture evoked the loins of a rift valley; Eve's evolutionary adaptation to the twentieth-century, especially strolling across the tapestry of sand dunes beneath evening's sunset-of-colors, held back the chill of star-lit space, the psychology of a Fall. (v) **ECOLOGY** – Gathering fossil intelligences along the foreshore but unaware of geological space-time Laura Devonshire merged with the membrane of sky as the late-autumnal sunrise emblazoned the crest of sand dunes. Kissing her, a crystallography of salt layering his mouth, inbreathing the 47% by weight of oxygen composing her, Jason Palmer imagined her orgasm as a microcosmic model for the death throes of a star.

Comic Book Images. "Who is *The Great American Nude* ... Garbo ... Ann-Margret?" Cornell Bedford-Brown posed the question to Celeste Hawthorne as she supervised the arrangement of a mixed media Pop Art tableau on stage of Psyche and Eros, nude, comic book style, replicating Rossetti's *Paolo and Francesca da Rimini*. "Garbo and Ann-Margret, they're Swedish." On the news bulletins the Apollo 10 lunar module descended to within 10 miles of the Moon's surface, its brilliance reminiscent of a radioactive isotope, and later on the bed her naked breast glistened as if in affinity with the curved illumination of the globe. All eroticism was no more than a synthetic Pop Art display, Eros and Psyche stenciled on the canvas of bed sheets, limbs-and-torsos slightly varying but held fast to a web of lust. Bedford-Brown pondered his latest orgasmic peroration strangely troubled by Celeste's unknowable experience of the momentary oblivion and was struck with the image of the lunar module's nipple touching the curvature of the Moon's breast. Poster designs for **KRISHNA inc.** filled her sketchbooks. Half-asleep in the semi-darkness he observed her tip-toe rising up the staircase to the studio with wings of neon aglow suggesting a soul freeing itself from a subterranean vault.

A Taste For The Satyricon. Flower children lifted straight from poster designs for **KRISHNA inc.** attended a matinee performance of **WHAAM!**. Faces drawn with dead-pan *sang-froid* milling around backstage after the show, they suggested to Cornell Bedford-Brown stray thoughts from God's *blue period* abandoned to Earth, having lost all memory of who they are. Psyche's voice carried to him, and laughter, with the phrase ... *a sixties boulevardier*. Youth's stretched skin, nude on stage, visually smooth as classical sculpture, innocence yet to model repentance, was touched by light and held in the soft folds of the brain as a vision. Charged with this contemplative thought he pondered the origin of humanity's solitary and super-subtle God, His Triad-of-Oneness, impressed in the soft brain tissue of the Cosmos. Arm-in-arm two sister flower children, perhaps bizarre wave-formations in God's brain, or Krishna's, silhouettes of the late-sixties, linked up with Miranda Westwood and disappeared beneath an **EXIT** sign. With all the loyalty of a flirtation Paulette Taylor emerged from a dressing-room, always an erotic enjambment of Victorian *mores* with a taste for the *Satyricon*, the sunset of her raspberry lips camouflaging a persona possessed of the decaying softness of an over-ripe apple.

I'd Rather Sink ... Aquilina Kingsley smoothly swung her torso and released the bowling ball, holding her sculptural pose until the remaining two pins rocked back to stillness. "O, Simon, lead me into temptation! How does this laughter become my face then?" Foot-tapping the wooden floor in her bowling shoes, Aquilina marked her scorecard, mischievously side-glancing at her friend: "So, no more dateless evenings living in the dormitory then. I can hear you sighing for Babylon, and your violin playing is bringing Jason Palmer closer to you than your own shadow." Half-leaning from the midnight-blue street-rod, Simon Freeman whistled and Aquilina skipped across the roadway, followed by Laura Devonshire, the car radio playing at full volume, *Lay Lady Lay*. With the street rod's legato acceleration, smooching Simon's ear, Aquilina addressed the Pop Art coolness of Laura and Alexander together on the rear seat, addressing him first with amusement: *"I Know How You Must Feel, Brad."* He understood her reference, but Laura didn't when she pleaded on her behalf: *"I'd Rather Sink ... Than Ask Brad For Help!"*

Surrealist Exhibition 1969. Sublimated sexual ecstasy transformed the beachscape late-in-autumn when a sequence of billboards was erected among the sand dunes based around fragments of Salvador Dali's obscure painting, *Masochistic Instrument*, with Laura Devonshire's nude torso holding a melting violin, and further erotic intensities engendered by her representation in *Three Young Surrealist Women Holding in their Arms the Skins of an Orchestra*. Jason Palmer organized a solo violin recital among the dunes as crowds visited the surrealist exhibition, Laura half-freezing for her Art, model for **THE GREAT AMERICAN NUDE**, delicious lure for the fallen Archangel! "Laura, how could this Archangel not see his image in God? Out there I can feel cosmic breezes filling the spinnaker of the fallen Archangel's wings." A silver seam of stars glittered in the night sky. Puzzled, Laura succumbed to his stylized lovemaking, her arousal muted yet intensifying too as he placed cotton wool between her toes, run his fingertips along the alabaster arabesque of her leg and began painting her nails a vibrant red. Lying on the bed with the tranquility of a frosted autumnal leaf slowly melting fissures in the cosmic mind opened as she beautifully warped space.

Troubling As An Erotic Dream. "Who is this metaphysical beachcomber? Look in the mirror, at the languorous pleasure seeping from your glances when your eyes cut him out from a crowd." Alexander Chamberlain's words substituted in her thoughts what he was singing on stage, Eros-to-Psyche, costumed nude, as troubling as an erotic dream, only as engaging as a trans-physical sensation. Laura Devonshire sat in the darkness of the half-empty theatre more embarrassed by her best friend's nudity, its hollow rhetoric, duetting a false promiscuous exaltation, Eros-and-Psyche mummified in the Pop Art brushstrokes of the scenarist's designs. Alexander fully clothed, walking her across the lawn to the University dormitory following the evening performance, remarked how he always felt he was skating across thin ice until she glanced into his eyes, whereupon he felt himself fall in and freeze. Trying to lighten the mood in the midnight-blue street-rod, Aquilina had whispered in her ear: "Laura, let him see your *champagne*, you'll find his bicep very risqué." Rain began falling.

Opera Among The Clouds. Walking like a ribbon of film through a projector, Helena Steele's *noir femme fatale* paced Johnny Esquire's Harley along the curbside, the motorcycle's baritone rumble obscuring their verbal exchange, her jacket dissolved in poppies contrasting the grayness of the afternoon. Free-swinging away she passed through the revolving door of the skyscraper and could be seen taking an elevator to **KRISHNA inc.** just as a chopper descended out of sight onto the helipad on the roof. Pacing about the lobby of the skyscraper with Jason Palmer, a feather held in the palm of her hand, a beautifully polished stone in the other, Bridget Lovegrove's chromatic redhead with the pure soul of a blonde was irritated by his answer to the commissionaire: "*I Am Supposed To Report To Mr. Bellamy.*" Taking the elevator to the rooftop they circled the chopper limp on the helipad. Palmer sat in the bubble cockpit hooded like the helmet of an insect. Eddie Phoenix and Helena Steele emerged onto the rooftop as showers of rain swept in from the west. Helena's bloodstained jacket burned through the gathering downpour while a *Liebestod* sang in Bridget's mind, the elevated stage of the helipad atop the skyscraper terraced by clouds peopled with an audience of Angels drawn in fourth-dimensional space.

Liebesduett Among The Dunes. A mechanic suspiciously overhauled the helicopter while clouds compassionately burst with rain and Jason Palmer's saturated voice, clean-washed by the shower, said elliptically: "Here is a lobster held fast in the *fisherman's* hand. The world is being cut into the magnificent jewel of a Maltese Cross from which the fallen Archangel's shadow will be banished forever." Wiping his dripping overalls initialed with **SF** the youthful mechanic, fetchingly handsome beneath a White Sox baseball cap gave Eddie Phoenix the thumbs-up sign. Hawk-on-the-wing, the helicopter banked away from the skyscraper, while Bridget's face awash with raindrops mingled with tears despaired of Palmer's courteous mannerisms, but she accompanied him out among the sand dunes where the excavated cream-coloured *coupé* lay semi-revealed. Angling in low over the billboards as the sunset faintly burned up cloud on the horizon a helicopter suddenly stalled and plunged into a sand dune with a shudder and rising pall of black smoke, dark souls wriggling free of the constrictions of three-dimensional space!

Habitation. The curved scimitar of the International Hotel lay on the earth reflecting Las Vegas sunlight. Untangling the skeins of his own mythmaking Elvis rehearsed his voice's ignition of his soul-in-the-world. Las Vegas' erotic burning on the tableau of the surrounding desert evoked Biblical reminiscences in the thoughts of the famous singer. Crossing the lobby of the hotel, adrift in glistening silk, caressed by her white underwear, Paulette Taylor moved to the elevator, even among so many glamorous women a seductive Eve, standing in the minds of observant men as **THE GREAT AMERCIAN NUDE.** What would be the longevity of the stele of the International Hotel on the floor of Paradise Lost?

THE UPANISHADS, WHAAM! And 'Nam. Masked by a paperback titled, **THE UPANISHADS,** her motif of concealment, the flower child strolled among the serene waves of sand dunes, while offshore the storm-churned ocean, feeling the pure milk of her desires rise in the gourd of her breasts. Ambrosial sunlight burst through the fabric of cloud and enveloped Jason Palmer aglow on the crest of an adjacent dune, a seraphim emerging from the cracked eggshell-effect, fully winged, and the lotus of her face peered from behind the book. Wreathed in incense while vigorously whisking up a dressing of mustard, vinegar, garlic, olive oil and cream, Fleur observed her sister cooking the pancetta, singing excerpts from **WHAAM!** as she peered at the golden bread on a baking tray in the oven.

> Rallying 'round the flag
> Is getting to be such a drag
> Like failing life and joining the marines
> Can't substitute for the rock'n'roll dream
> They say money is the root of all evil
> And in $500 suits you'll find Dante's devil

Lt. John Kirby hunched over a battered Remington typewriter testing the boundaries of language in describing his experiences in 'Nam while the flower child settled cross-legged on the sofa engrossed in **THE UPANISHADS** and eating the pancetta salad. A newspaper column caught his eye, brief notification of a helicopter crash among some sand dunes.

Discovering The Décor Of An Ode. "Consider the Planck-moment: who fired the cosmic gun shattering the crystalline sphere of three-dimensional space into proliferating galaxies?" Listening, Bridget Lovegrove sensed the Universe throb, synchronize with Jason Palmer's heartbeat as they gazed upon the smooth syntax of the dune's calligraphy. The blackened shell of a helicopter contrasted the cream-colored *coupé*, both models of spiritual petrifaction amid the elegiac dunescape beneath wintery skies, with the ghosts of Eddie Phoenix and Helena Steele journeying onward now with the existentialism of those first shock-waves generated when the silver bullet fired from the cosmic gun touched the planes of three-dimensional space. Foam flew from the churning waves. Entering the Oceanside apartment, Bridget adjusted to the submarine lights, discovering the décor of an Ode, space sliced into planes resembling movie film, and confronted her own Pop Art reflection impressed inside a mirror. "Bridget, we are archetypes, you and I, already dreaming ourselves entering the stadium at the end of Time's marathon. Like film reversing through a projector, the fragments of the galaxies are re-forming, becoming a mirror again, and our reflections here will withdraw from its space." Amazed at her emotional dissolution in the idiom of his speaking voice, she asked: "And where is Christopher's reflection, where has it withdrawn to?"

What The Reviews Of WHAAM! Said. Tastefully shadowed the gallery of nudes choreographed a succession of Wesselman multi-media paintings. Psyche's sexual yeast inflated the presentations, moonbeams flooding the stage, Zephyr's breeze revealing her nakedness inside the folds of a Greek chiton, her rapturous marble torso-and-limbs classical enough to exhaust the aesthete reviewers among the audience. Eros and Psyche wound-and-unwound DNA helices in their rendering of **THE GREAT AMERICAN NUDE,** their sexual acts being *à la dérobe*, their Pop Art transitions through everyday suburban poses against the scenarist's designs so many extrinsic embellishments to coitus, what the audience paid to witness. A wild-eyed charioteer, inwardly troubled, strangely unreachable, Simon Freeman drove as if pursued by Furies, Aquilina Kingsley unnerved by his percussive behavior. Leaving her standing in the rain in her driveway he reversed the muscular street-rod back onto the roadway and punched the car forward like a blow from the heavy-weight champion of the world. Aquilina had noticed a frayed newspaper photograph on the back seat of the car, the drooping burnt wings of a crashed helicopter and in print a eulogy to the inglorious deaths of its occupants. Questioned, he said: "Aquilina, for me there was no choice, choosing you, anymore than there is a choice for Palmer to engage in combat with the fallen Archangel." On stage her Wesselman nudes became more painterly, less sculptural, more remote, and even the sugarcane juice squeezed from Miranda Westwood's flute-playing could not sweeten the scenes, Psyche and Eros conveyed a very limpid classicism!

The Great Drama Of Salvation. Simon Freeman's figural transformation, his moodiness and drift back toward hippiedom, his sudden abandonment of the midnight-blue street-rod, of the Chrysler showroom, his half-fearful repertory of musings in hearing the whirr of chopper wings everywhere came to the notice of Jason Palmer. A gigantic billboard of the downed helicopter rose above the sand dunes varnishing the exterior of the sky's canvas of clouds. "Simon, all humanity is eternally drifting towards the precipice, only the sweet breaths of the Archangels holding them back as they sway on the edge. There is no safety net across the plunge to the floor of Paradise Lost. The down-draft of the fallen Archangel's wings is irresistible to all but a few. I see a burning glare in your eyes. Isn't Phoenix indestructible?" Together, locked in the Oceanside apartment, visited by Bridget Lovegrove, they compiled accountancy journals balancing Good-and-Evil and composed charts of the two-dimensional skin of sand remembered from the dunes where they planned to imprison the fallen Archangel. Sleeping soundly at midnight they felt the breaths of Archangels soothe them of the frictions of three-dimensional existence. Rising at dawn they were actors in the great Drama of Salvation!

Every Man Has A Flaming Star Over His Shoulder. Virginal-with-irony, a *cliché* of polished pearls necklaced Paulette Taylor's naked throat, and a gloved fingertip teasingly brushed them when she caught Cornell Bedford-Brown's eyes from across the room. How she moved among the guests with the treacherous rhythm of a rattlesnake! Bedford-Brown stepped away from a backdrop of Warhol's *Flaming Star* Elvis as Johnny "Guitar" Esquire, always sexually ill-mannered, constelled a sequence of pop star gestures in Paulette's space before gripping her *rattle*. Miranda Westwood attempted metaphysical incantation assuming her mere thinking about Johnny Esquire as her companion would interpenetrate his emotions and embed her portrait there beside his ever-mirrored *self*. Moving among the exhibits following the party, so many shadowy mosaics, Bedford-Brown cautiously approached the *Flaming Star* Elvis, hearing Paulette's sexual *rattle*, and could make her out pressed up against the famous pop star, her naked legs locked around Johnny Esquire, a *ménage à trois* on **THE GREAT AMERICAN NUDE**. Faintly, drifting above the rhythmic *rattle*, a melodically floated flute seeped through the scene, a sound-form fossilized in a heart of stone.

Elvis Speaks! Space's bronze-colored glass through which the human shadow passed warped with the figurative magnificence of the celebrated pop singer performing on-stage in Las Vegas. At the press conference, his summer-bronzed marble rendered pliable, he chiseled a transmission from the Eros of his own Psyche: *"I will take full responsibility for the acts of my generation. While I am ELVIS, I will surfeit on the full spectrum of life's experiences. Remember, I was born to unimaginable poverty, neglect and anonymity. I've been making an ascent of the levels of Dante's INFERNO one-by-one, and if I be lifted up will lift my generation with me. I'll suffer, sure, and absorb the suffering of my generation through myself, to lessen it for others. I will henceforth ask for suffering every day of my life, and ask for the strength to transmute it with grace."*

VI
HAMBURGERS & PASTRIES

The Soft Hamburger. Investigators excavated the fossilized structure of the downed helicopter from the soft geometry of drifting sand dune. Drizzling rain emerged from banks of lowering cloud half-obscuring the surf breaking offshore. Images of the helicopter and of Elvis *à la Flaming Star*, Ann-Margret *à la* **THE GREAT AMERICAN NUDE**, and a once-flashy red Chrysler peeled from billboards weathering among the dunes as winter storms ravaged the coastline. The verdict handed down read: Pilot error. A tattered etching of hippiedom's ur-reality, Simon Freeman understood now he stood for everything fictional in a world nothing more than a montage of random viewpoints, realized he was simply peeled on to the fabric of space-time as were the images on the film-strip in Jason Palmer's camera. Ragged, unkempt, without a shell to spiral into as rain wept from the ebony sky, he ordered a hamburger at an all-night stand and sat watching the city's neon signs flash with damp color, vacuous ciphers making up the existential code-word: **NOTHINGNESS**. Hunched inside his jacket's face-framing collar he bought a ticket and entered the half-empty theater already darkened for the opening scene of **WHAAM!**

The *Cantabile* Violin. Darkness' inertia becalmed Laura Devonshire's violin, very Sibelian in mood, when Jason Palmer's statue squeezed from the tomb of three-dimensional space, the crease between two walls in his Oceanside apartment, and said: "Every human persona is a knot in the tightrope of *Being* stretching from here to Eternity, and must be unraveled as we ascend out of Paradise Lost. Lucifer, the fallen Archangel, is a cosmic spider designing new webs in which to catch us, and only speed, the velocity of your violin, can snap the threads binding us to space-time." Later, between rain-showers, they strolled down to the beach where the skyline was laced with frozen cloud, conscious she was merely a beautifully feathered parrot talking to him: "Jason, see this Delta symbol I've drawn in the sand. I feel I am pressed into this corner, and the angle is becoming more acute. When we return to the apartment I am going to play you a Paganini *cantabile*!" Palmer experienced Laura as an emanation from his heart lost in the golden rose of the Sun God Helios, wandering three-dimensional space playing the violin.

A Softening Political Will. Winter softened the lapidary centre of Revolution so the Gang of Five gathered in the University library and scribbled anti-war marginalia in selected books and magazines for the edification of student readers. A World Conference of Communist Parties galvanized some street theater but more earth-shaking was the creation of a Provisional Revolutionary Government for South Vietnam by the NLF, its tremor of implications picked up by the seismograph of radical students, who took to the streets in celebration. All over the radio was the phenomenal *Bad Moon Rising*, and never off the flower child's turntable, although the live-in hippies smoked their time away with *Crosby, Stills & Nash*, especially on *Marrakesh Express*. "Look, man, Eternity creates these elisions of tension, and we're finding those spaces to live in, you understand?" Jason Palmer's film crew caught on the wing a voice's improvised dialogue. Fleur balanced coffee and pastries on a tray moving around a sculpture of Campbell soup cans positioned in the centre of the room. Vocal harmonies more abrasive than *Crosby, Stills & Nash* serrated the pages of politicized conversation between Stephen Maxwell and the corduroy-clad hippies, both pursuing undiscoverable dreams amid the terrain of Paradise Lost. Television footage beamed in from 'Nam further brutalized America's tender psyche and the casualty figures felt like a scythe thrust in the wound; especially indignant was news the NVA had reoccupied Hamburger Hill!

The Soft Helicopter. Silk stockings sheer the length of her extended leg's arabesque, Paulette Taylor accepted she was simply an inserted quotation in the blank verse drama of Eddie Phoenix's attempted seduction of the world, the ideal of these sexual self-immolations harmonizing with the revolutionary tenor of the times. Striding the stage of **WHAAM!** she noticed Cornell Bedford-Brown pondering a fresh *objet d'art* the production's scenarist, herself a veritable Carmen, had introduced a *soft sculpture* of a downed helicopter, similar to the shell she remembered on the news bulletins. An unkempt figure with a turned-up collar emerged among the front stalls as **WHAAM!'s** chorus drifted on-stage to begin rehearsals, oblivious to the kapok-and-vinyl helicopter and its possible symbolic import, although the wandering hippie appeared to stalk its presence from the shadows. Suddenly, Aquilina Kingsley's Psyche leapt free of the stage apron and flung herself into the arms of the hippie stranger, her Aeschylan cry filling the auditorium, a stark visual reminder of the continuing power of the Odysseus/Penelope story!

Simon, Where Have You Been Living? Simon Freeman's re-emergent legibility, his torso worthy again to be a sepulcher for his youthful soul, freshly showered and shaved in Laura Devonshire's dormitory apartment, encouraged the question about his disappearance. Aquilina Kingsley hunched forward as a delicious selection of pastries tempted him to speak: "Virgil rescued me amid the terraces of the freeway cloverleaves, guided me through the maze of moral discoveries I needed to experience for myself. Aquilina, what nightmares! Always the scorpion tail of a helicopter, the barb of poison paralyzing me, and I fell like an extinguishing star from Heaven into such darkness ... Jason though has the key to the bottomless pit! ..." The miniature pastries sweetly melted in his mouth and the burning sunsets experienced by his psyche were no longer populated with helicopters falling in a blaze of brimstone from the sky like battalions of rebel Archangels surrendering their spiritual light. An equine fear widened Aquilina's eyes, grasping how far now he had centrifuged from the center, until Jason Palmer's seer found the pathway back through the maze. Laura's violin unwound a thread through the labyrinth which Aquilina felt after to caress Freeman into a deeply peaceful sleep amid the groves of Elysium.

The Soft Delacroixs. Celeste Hawthorne bit fulsomely into a vibrant red apple, tossed it in a gentle parabola and Cornell Bedford-Brown juggled it, before sinking his own teeth through the stretched skin and into the crisp body. Soft Delacroixs, her oil studies, swimming forms in liquid color, had become her companions, the croissant breasts of Greece Expiring, the melting Women of Algiers, a whipped cream effect Portrait of Chopin, a banquet of rich dishes making him aware of his own displacement. Although Hamlet and Horatio in the graveyard scene with the soft skull raised from the earth, a premature rehearsal for Judgment Day and the Resurrection, contrasted Celeste's promiscuous flower, Ophelia, poetess of madness, grief swirling in a bouquet raised to the chapped lips of Death. Jolted by the allusions energizing his mood, Bedford-Brown pondered the ledger of her accounts, her financial draughtsmanship, as she ascended the stairs to the studio and ushered in a rag-tag Gang of Four student activists, soft-flesh representatives who had modelled for her oil study of Delacroix's *Liberty*!

A Commission For Soft Portraits. Thin rain fell against the exposed winter sun like a watery glaze of subdued oil paint. Her voice as spicy as minestrone soup, Paulette Taylor formed a heroic couplet with Johnny Esquire surveying the photographic evocations of famous celebrities lining the walls of the obscure gallery: "My flawless short-haired version of **ME** defines my opposition to those medieval hippies there, sandal-footed, knotted, unwashed tresses, everything screaming *desolation*." Fleur and the flower child, approached by Jason Palmer, listened to him enunciate descriptors, invocations to call the iconic celebrities to life from the tombs of their frames. (i) **ELVIS** – Apollo embodied in the continuum of America, impossibly handsome, simultaneous with the Voice of the Sun God. (ii) **SHELLEY** – Adonais flighted in stellar dreams, immortal singer of the sylphs. (iii) **ASTAIRE** – A melodious spiritual etiquette of romance figured in perfect motion; Newton's Laws flowing through the microcosmic world; the inspirational physicist's apple caught in elegant movement. (iv) **REMBRANDT** – Illumination gilding the spiritual victories of the Saints. (v) **MALLARMÉ** – The watercolors of a flute arabesquing erotic impressions in a mirror. Ô miroir! Eau froide par l'ennui dans ton cadre gelée, que de fois et pendant des heures, désolée des songes et cherchant mes souvenirs qui sont comme des feuilles sous ta glace au trou profond, je m'apparus en toi comme une ombre lointaine ... (vi) **KEROUAC** – Post-war Amercia's most poignant image, Lonesome Traveler, the plimsoll line of a lost generation. Escorted by Johnny Esquire, his equipage as cavalier as Elvis in his ascendancy, Paulette Taylor spoke as usual of **ME**: "Johnny, how the absorption of one's self in the macrocosmic sweep of this galaxy of stars, and the assemblage is lucid, enhances **ME**, *le style, c'est l'femme*!"

How Softened Silica Hardened Into Thought. Grids of glass walling circumscribed **KRISHNA inc.** as Miranda Westwood's flute-playing quietened with the tension of light ebbing from a precious jewel. "How sustainable is thought?" Eddie Phoenix posed to the languid devotees arranged with the canon of a vow before a sand box placed in the center of the floor of the suite. "Thought has been the links in the chain of our descent as we heroically chose to create our own space and our own time in which to fulfill dreams as numerous as the grains of sand here." Gentle tones from the finger-cymbals wielded by the flower child were picked up by the microphones for relaying across the air-waves in the evening news bulletin. "Yes, the sandman cometh!" But how long could the imperious vertebra of human thought hold? Beyond the broad thirteenth floor window the architectural giants of skyscrapers defied the horizonless infinitude of space, embedding themselves in earth for Eternity. Adoring the lens of the television camera, the crown of his head a torso of turban, symbol of self-thought weighty, sculptural with the triumph of creation, Phoenix dipped his fingers into the loose sand and raised the chalice as an offering.

Mise-en-Scène For A Rock'n'Roll Movie. Half-tearful, half-playful, a work of art deep in winter's stippled pool, Aquilina Kingsley slid across the lane's approach and released the bowling ball towards the pins, holding her Age of Aquarius pose before snapping back to attention. "O, Simon, look how you've skittled my affections! Laura, step up to the mark and deliver yourself, you have the ball in your hand. Alexander, is there any fun in Calvinism, compared to swinging down the lane of a bowling alley with Laura?" Still stooping her practice shots as they exited the bowling alley, Aquilina was impastoed in splashes of illuminated neon, and didn't glimpse the low-slung red Chrysler crawling the curbside, Eddie Phoenix half-leaning from the window, Gospel-rider of Lucifer's chariot. Audible on the car radio was *The Pléiade's* new single:

> Here she comes walking down the street
> And the mannequins in the windows all tremble.
> Who would believe anyone could dissemble
> Emotions that seemed so sweet?
>
> Hey I'm walking up to her along a street of glass
> Yeah, I'm walking up to her along a street of glass
> And all she does is blow me a kiss as I pass.

"Simon!" Bodily flinging herself, Aquilina wrapped Simon Freeman in her arms as he grabbed Phoenix by the lapels through the Chrysler's window, wrestling him back as a foot stepped on the accelerator and the car propelled forward. Inked over by a cloud-burst, the eye of the moon released tears of raindrops as the red tail-lights of the Chrysler teasingly blinked through the shower. Alexander Chamberlain guided his friend back from the curbside wondering if he would ever recover tranquility's plateau again now he had been tempted by the frontispiece of *Paradise Lost* as ink-blocked to the pages of their lives by Jason Palmer.

Frothy Spearmint Thick Shakes. Deep inside the soft, spacey echo chamber of a winter wave, chilled through in his pose, Simon Freeman allowed the screening façade of water close over him; hippies did not surf or cruise the boulevards in red Chryslers. Strolling through the illusionistic space of Jason Palmer's Oceanside apartment, startled to discover Laura Devonshire equipoised on his wingèd arms, he glimpsed a series of bizarre collages, described as architectural designs to trap and imprison the fallen Archangel in two-dimensional space. Described as his genealogy's heirlooms, folios of sketches signed by Celeste Hawthorne captured the impression of a cavalcade of incarnations, historical dressings shaped around the same allegory, the pursuit of the fallen Archangel. Smoothed to the surf's wave-rhythms, Freeman felt himself attaining again something of his purest translucency, and later he indulged in a frothy spearmint thick shake, one of his generation's true Pop Art creations. Emotional alliances and allegiances were rooted in the earth of a genealogy of incarnations, he grasped after that truth, for how was he to know whether he was aligned to Ascendant Archangels or the fallen Archangel? Moving along the sidewalk, surfing the pavement with his skateboard, crouching low, hanging five, his head haloed in a face-framing collar, he pondered why Alexander Chamberlain had abandoned his Christian map to salvation.

Letter XIII. Fabian Roxburgh to Bridget Lovegrove. *How soft space can seem, how plastique, especially the silhouette of Hamburger Hill's primitive three-dimensional perspective, Paradise-on-Earth for a surgeon. 'Nam is a mobile field hospital, kind of like Paradise Lost for the fallen – I received a communication from Jason Palmer and the refrain of his words echoes on in my thoughts. As your portrait does with the closing of my eyes. Our souls walk through a tempest onto the turbulent sea of three-dimensional incarnation. Christopher has drowned. Salt stings my still-raw emotional wound. I was an imaginary pallbearer. I close my eyes and see you stand, correctly poised beside the coffin, in cleansing showers of rain. Have you a special memory, like the monastery and his footprints in the sand leading off to the horizon? Jason wrote of Death's special intimacy with us, being the womb from which we are born into a celestial world, so I wrote to him and asked which stellar keyhole there in the night sky will open Paradise for Christopher. Yesterday I witnessed the harassed flight of a Madonna and child along Route 66, as the highway is christened, as if the journey were somehow magical, leading to the Promised Land. Babylon is fallen! will be the cry in Saigon when the NLF finally squeeze the juice of Democracy from the winepress of 'Nam. Saluté!*

Letter XIV. Fabian Roxburgh to Bridget Lovegrove. *I am scheduled to uplift Stateside soon — New York, I believe. What does 'Nam's multi-dimensional map look like? I'm thinking of Flanders in 1916. Of what inner experience is 'Nam an objective projection in three-dimensional space? Charlie is very frightening, capricious with treachery, some mythological earth-sprite, very dangerous, from the decayed world of a Tennyson poem on the Arthuriad. Standing against the skyline, every Grunt is a stele encrusted with the memory of a gunslinger in the Badlands — Send in the Cav! What is 'Nam an imitation of? Up in Da Nang there is brutal hand-to-hand while on Radio 'Nam Elvis' spectral voice is singing In The Ghetto as if he means it. Perhaps the urban Grunts are remembering their 'hood and thinking may be 'Nam is safer after all. Bridget, who can prove the bombing of North Vietnam is unethical? Nimble-toed Grunts under brimstone fire come down off the mountain where they have been contemplating the Ten Commandments, and trudge that darkened lonely street back to Saigon's Heartbreak Hotel ... In The Ghetto!*

Portrait Of The Archangel (VI). (i) **PHYSICS** – Odalísque, on the divan in Jason Palmer's Oceanside apartment, the ghost of Madame Recamier reclined as Laura Devonshire, beautiful meniscus as lovely as a wave's or soft sand dune's, with melting Time liquid in her eyes. Traversing the city's psychic *nothingville* with him in the chariot of his Bel Air Chevrolet, wandering out among the cool afternoon sand dunes, where she indulged him with the aural folds of her violin's embroidery, she listened to his description of a repoussé bronze Archangel mysteriously shaping from a massive billow of cloud. With the mortise of fingers joined to hers, he said: "Laura, the physics of causality in our Euclidean space is a ballet no more substantial than the foam feathering from the crests of those waves. Look at the granulation of the Milky Way, an infinitely supple wave, breaking up, the sky's mirror there an illusory ceiling." Later, on the balcony of the apartment he partially undressed her, exposing a breast, and with a soft felt pen drew the hyperbolic geometry of a triangle. Molding his hand to the stretched curvature of skin he further quantified the beauty of an equation there: flesh festooned in Greek. "Upon the soft hyperbolic curvature of your breast Pythagoras' famous theorem will find no resolution, for the angles of this triangle, as you can see will always be less than **Phi**. Lucifer out there in the night sky fills the zero curvature of Euclidean perspective, his blackness silvered by the stars exploding into being from beyond his uncharted two-dimensional plane." Together they timed *The Maximum Speed of Raphael's Madonna* with Dali's *Soft Watch at the Moment of First Explosion* and meditated the oily waves languidly rising with the dawn when there was a momentary suspension of winter breezes. (ii) **CHEMISTRY** – The chemistry of Dali's *Portrait of St. Jerome*, the ferocity of his double helix's disintegration before the full force of the fallen Archangel's hunger to feast on the human soul, precipitated an on-air dialogue between Jason Palmer and Eddie Phoenix, the venue a Christian broadcasting station. A flute touched Miranda Westwood's jellied mouth, her music so much spiritual meringue, her posture in the sound-studio holding the torsion of a sirène, while Phoenix's commentary possessed the inchoate appetite of the fallen Archangel. "These illustrations of yours, polymer strings modeling the rebellious Archangel's double-helix unwinding through Eternity, and your assertion his cosmic dust besmirches the mirror of Heaven to our sight, is pure fallacy. Palmer, this dust has no mirror of Heaven to cling to!" Sweet glucose issued from the flute, the music's visceral body-curve like viscous caramel sauce, its reverie upon the radiant darkness of the sub-atomic world, a deep-sea space, unwinding a complexity of molecules inspiring Palmer. "The *rose* is our last remembrance of the heart of Heaven, precipitate on Earth, just as the *lotus* is remembrance of Heaven's mind." Clasping Miranda by the hand, Palmer placed their wet footprints on a pathway deeper among the dunes where the raked sand evoked interference patterns. "Miranda, consider, in the labyrinth of the brain's electrical circuitry, what is the actual content? Chemistry's nirvana is for energy to become inert, and we are rigidly bound to the fallen Archangel's genetic code!" (iii) **BIOLOGY** – *Démodé* in medieval hippie embroidery, the flower child, svelte silhouette from a Waterhouse canvas, observed from a distance the outstretched hand of Eddie Phoenix, the punctuation of his finger gestures, poised like a scorpion's tail to strike Jason Palmer. Why did his words cling to the submerged biology of a feminine torso like raw barnacles? Palmer approached, smiling as if he had just slipped a banana peel under Phoenix's feet: "Man is Lucifer's universal prey, although his deception and revenge upon Heaven seems misplaced in us, for if you remember Jaques' lamentations over the deer in *As You Like It*, how can we undertake war on God?" (iv) **PSYCHOLOGY** – Seated upright in the flawless Chevrolet, Bridget Lovegrove, illuminated by the psycho-sexual catharsis of her Freudian remembrances of Christopher Featherstone, dowsed the fire of Eros in the cool waters of Jason Palmer's voice. "Fabian writes of the turbulence in America as a psychological transference of energies from the death-obsessed tensions in the minds of the Grunts in 'Nam. Macrocosmically, the maelstrom of galaxies there flowing with slow-motion Tai Chi towards each other, are two cosmic warriors engaged in combat. See the spinning slash of sabers, sleeve-draped arms reaching forward – I think the style is called Wing Chun." (v) **ECOLOGY** – Across the rippled two-dimensional plane of beach sand spread before Celeste Hawthorne lay imaged the electronic shell of the fallen Archangel; Jason Palmer spoke of God snapping Lucifer's heel in battle and his subsequent fall through seven-dimensional space ... **WHAAM!** She gazed upon the incandescence of his white cockatoo, and later in his Oceanside apartment felt him tickle the soles of her feet with a feather. Why was he fascinated with her naked heel illumined by light slanting into the room?

Conversation Piece I (Aquilina Kingsley speaks). "Simon, lend me your lips again, where you breathe my name! I have so much unabsorbed emotion for you, and I cherish your wisdom to romantically knit your life to mine. Just think of me on stage as playfully stylized and silhouette me in your thoughts against the looser morals of the time. For you are the statue of a man, *the man*, I would ransom from this Archangel for any price he named. Now, hand-in-hand, let me ask you Alexander, a Christian, and circumcised?"

Conversation Piece (II) (Alexander Chamberlain speaks). "Bared to the world on stage, yes, Eros is circumcised, against the looser morals of the time. Flesh is a burr that sticks, but eventually falls away. Consider, what if our Grandmother Eve had been circumcised? ..."

Conversation Piece (III) (Laura Devonshire speaks). "That would be to feel like a petal-less flower. But the sweet kernel of the almond in its soft shell hardens as it ripens in season. Alexander, Jason and yourself are equivalents in handsomeness, if you have contrapuntal opinions of each other and of me."

Conversation Piece (IV) (Alexander Chamberlain speaks). "Yes, you feel after his cosmic loneliness, listen to him burnish his fiction with theological allusions, and enjoy being showcased in glass. Cast off the works of darkness and climb into an armor of light with me. Salute me with a kiss."

Conversation Piece (V) (Simon Freeman speaks). "Why is Jason in the frame here? The shattering of my statue leaves me abstracted in inertia. Aquilina, surely I am too dull to be at the center of your existence. The beast rose up from the sea and submerged Phoenix. How can I sink further into the abyss and reverse his rescue in time?"

Conversation Piece (VI) (Alexander Chamberlain speaks). "Laura, in the election of grace is this man a prophet? He tickles you with a barbed feather. A satyr's hoof is imprinted on your torso. Last time I saw him he was wearing a medallion suspended from his neck carrying your portrait."

Conversation Piece (VII) (Laura Devonshire speaks). "How bizarre that you should map a Christian's progress playing Eros on stage, your faith exposed, but I can see you are bound up in a chain of jealousy. Jason Palmer levels me off to a serene tranquility, and I enjoy accompanying him on his excursions of metaphysical thought."

Gift Of The Gods. Lounging full-length along the *chaise longue*, bringing a Jupiterian elegance to an age fracturing with public promiscuity, Paulette Taylor imagined hearing a psychic scream vibrate the aether ...*Johnny! Johnny!* ... and thought she glimpsed an astral Miranda Westwood in the dressing room's chiaroscuro. Her *alchemical engagements*, particularly with Johnny Esquire, their modeling in black-and-white, freshened up the publicity for **WHAAM!**, and the illustration in **OZ** magazine of her caricature holding his *chemistry flask* while it sexually bubbled was pure genius. Shifting shadows of the Absolute, penumbras of romantic longing never to be surfeited, solidified in Miranda's world, and the vanilla extract of her flute-playing, flavoring her essence of adoration for Johnny Esquire, turned mourning black. Helian sunshine on an overcast winter's day, Johnny Esquire's Harley Davidson chased down a familiar Chevrolet on the freeway, rocking the motorcycle's gleaming *Ann-Margret* legs to seduce Jason Palmer's attention. "Palmer, are you still traveling your Road-to-Damascus then? Still waiting for the spiritual **WHAAM!** to open your eyes to blindness? Lucifer welcomes us all into the mighty crematorium!" Swinging open the car door at the curb before the towering House of **KRISHNA inc.** Palmer surprised Bridget Lovegrove, who pivoted on her Tao's temptation and slid her svelte derriere inside the Chevrolet. "They tell me you're a bloodied Archangelic hero dying lifetime-after-lifetime in combat with Lucifer. How can you never weary of dying into Eternity like this?"

Venus Rising Against The Scalèd Serpent. Clouds effervescent with winter rain hovering above the undulant sand dunes filled the translucent envelope of the sky. Scarves of onshore breeze fresh with the aromatic chemistry of sodium chloride softly wrapped up Laura Devonshire in sheaths of airy texture before slipping away from her presence on the crest of a dune. Later, burning arrows of sunlight pierced recumbent clouds languorous with Original Sin, as Laura stepped back inside the Oceanside apartment in her soft, heel-less slippers, light a brilliant yellow in the distant rain-showers. Bach's enameled Partita for violin elasticized space, summoning up the turbulence of muslin fabric about the *frottage* of her loins, where Jason Palmer laid a healing hand upon the suture of Creation, source of Man's seepage into three-dimensional incarnation. Together they studied a sheaf of drawings of hands Gabriel Rossetti had prepared for his *Dante's Dream* composition, and for which Palmer had commissioned a sonata for violin-and-piano. Fingers of sunlight beamed through chiton-folds of Venusian clouds rising like foam from the visible ocean framed in French doors of the apartment. Luminously *à la antique*, Laura musicalised all the feminine myths impressed in the fabric of space-time, inspired his quest to wrest the sacred Hesperidean fruit from the crimson-tinted jaws of the scalèd serpent whose underbelly slithered among the cloud-forms in the sky.

The Psychology Of Peripheral Vision. "Please, invent me a gesture so I may lacquer in gold the chiaroscuro of my nudity!" Psyche dramatically implored Eros, representing a vinyl and stuffed kapok tableau of Rembrandt's *Danaë*, while visible in backdrop as through a window was Roy Lichtenstein's oil-and-magna *Temple of Apollo* soaked in Helian sunbeams. Nudity-dressed-as-Art captivated the audience, humanity's sexual surfaces-in-quotation traceable in the coitus they created, imaginatively or otherwise, in the privacy of their suburban homes. **WHAAM!**'s *raison d'être* in Paulette Taylor's publicity blurbs engendered sex as a motif essential in every household décor, beautifully air-brushed on the canvas of suburban life, an alchemical tableau around which all existence should be assembled.

I'll Hold You In My Heart (Till I Can Hold You In My Arms). Fragments of billboard images peeled, fluttered and blew away, stripped by wind-and-rain, as Bridget Lovegrove visualized a feathered hieroglyph ascend from the coffin traveling in the long black limousine. Troubled by cross-over faiths she listened to excerpts of the transmission *From Elvis In Memphis* hurting that Existence's vertigo had spun Christopher Featherstone so cruelly from Earth-to-aether. Lyrically sentimental, Elvis attained a metaphysical plateau with his singing even as his famous Warhol edition *à la Flaming Star* disintegrated, metaphoring Featherstone's loss for her, for he would always be *Gentle On My Mind.* Suddenly an unfamiliar hippie half-buried in a turned-up collar brushed by as the sky deepened to ebony. Moving on, viscous with sadness, she attended a matinée performance of **WHAAM!** in a half-empty theater, the florid nudity and raw musical stagings unable to assuage her as did Elvis' singing of cosmic breadth. Posed like a juvenile Lucifer on his throbbing Harley Davidson, Johnny Esquire attained a monosyllabic version of the famous singer, his heart simply a plastic rose whose petals would never blow, like the billboard images.

Ice Cream Kissing. Eddie Phoenix amiably masked himself as Roy Lichtenstein's young officer in *The Kiss*, Paulette Taylor the shamelessly beautiful, golden-wigged Aphrodite, abstracting their fleshiness for the Press conference, infusing their promotion of Paradise Lost as a desirable destination with ethereal colors, and a light romantic mood. "Truly, we are indeed mortal to changes in fashion, and sex is a melting ice cream under a summer sun we pant to lick, even as it vanishes. I say, invent your own flavors! Cut the fashion of sex to your own palate and taste its mortality." In her creamiest voice Paulette Taylor addressed the would-be virgins among the Press-corps to bring the brightest blushes to their thoughts. As flashbulbs popped they energetically kissed, sanitized like a comic strip couple, simple advertisement for the kaleidoscopic fall into Paradise Lost.

What The Vinyl Hamburger Symbolized. Sensitive to the threnody of 'Nam, hungrily lawless with self-righteous alienation, the Gang of Five punctuated the comic strip innocence of **WHAAM!** being advertised in the media with anti-war demonstrations. Pledges from academics and intellectuals safe in their stuffed kapok ivory towers, venturing out onto the streets but softly cushioned inside cadres of students, signatories to endless petitions, conspired to lend credibility to the anti-war movement. Medieval flower children fallen from Bayeux tapestries now embroidered the youthful conquerors assaulting the barricades of the Establishment. Kapok and vinyl hamburgers symbolic of American commercialism now appeared borne aloft by the demonstrators, referencing the mincing of the Grunts on the infamous Hill in 'Nam's highlands. Bitter, I-told-you-so speeches accumulated, senatorial censure sounded from Capitol Hill itself. Loss in war now became celebratory as victory!

The Horizon Of Space-Time Tilted. Eros and Psyche sexually consummated their Myth inside a *papier-mâché* helicopter, fallen Archangel, reprising their familiar duet:

> *(Eros)*
> Oh let me be ... your Corinthian column
> *(Psyche)*
> Oh let me be ... your Cave of Darkness
> *(Eros)*
> Oh let me be ... your Temple of Solomon
> *(Psyche)*

Oh let me be ... your Ark of Eternal Sadness

Cornell Bedford-Brown pondered time's instability on the fulcrum of space, eternally unbalancing humanity, embodied in the ragged anti-Pop youth concentrated on the flighty Psyche onstage, adoration and aspiration dramatized in his desolation. Later, very tired, leaning his head against Celeste Hawthorne's *soft Delacroixs*, while she prepared high tea as was her fashion, he contemplated Jason Palmer's doctrinal challenge mounted against the fallen Archangel. Backstage after **WHAAM!**'s evening performance, drugged with the mournful flute expressive of a virgin's mouth impastoed with lipstick, watching Psyche's quick-change from nudity to fully dressed to keep her date with her anti-Pop silhouette waiting in the corridor, he experienced a declension of faith in the efficacy of existence to achieve anything. The flute's invisible embouchure floated music through the silence then trailed after Johnny Esquire's departure with Priscilla. Plato had emerged from his Cave of Darkness into blinding light, the Temple of Solomon tilted History and the Ark of fabulous memory surrendered its Mystery before humanity understood its significance.

More Soft Portraits. "Is the face indistinguishable from the soul's?" Jason Palmer posed the question to Fleur and the flower child. "How impertinently this mask intrudes itself between our third-and-fourth dimensional selves." A libertine couplet, imagistic in tone, Paulette Taylor and Johnny Esquire scented the present with the past, Archangelic lavender the aroma, her torso floating around the gallery as if in a silk handkerchief, her chiffon breasts equipoised like serene marble. Eyes on the face of the walls, the frames beckoned: (i) **BOB DYLAN** – Harlequin with fabulous stories to tell, in a voice like acid-etched glass. (ii) **J.G. BALLARD** – A Master of imagistic prose flashing with the deliquescence of a jewel still covered in Jurassic mud. (iii) **BAUDELAIRE** – Aristocrat of Requiems to Beauty, his poetry sublime tattoos on a body of forbidden vices. (iv) **MOREAU** – Miracles of champagne-gold guilt bleeding through innocence. (v) **STEVE McQUEEN** – A clean-cut ice carving with a face of nothingness. (vi) **VERONESE** – High Renaissance musician-of-the-brush, divine celebrant of the Feast's temptations. Miranda Westwood's flute-softened lips in Veronese-red were moistened with champagne as Johnny Esquire's hand touched Paulette's sizzling couture. The Tao of framed portraits presided over a space-time in which they were guaranteed an after-existence!

Pinball Wizard. The sky's blotting paper effect soaked up the inky washes of sunset. Like a visored helmet Johnny Esquire's plumèd quiff collapsed across his Grecian forehead. Swarming locusts of the shadowy fallen, pedestrians visible from the thirteenth floor of **KRISHNA inc.** moved along the city sidewalks, while inside Eddie Phoenix festooned a sandbox with lotus petals cupped in the flower child's palms. A paradigm of the new virgins the flower child visualized from the lines drawn in the sandbox the fallen Archangel's re-emergence as a scrawled signature in the Book of Life. Phoenix had promised to psychically re-organize the interference patterns generated by her association with Jason Palmer. Running, dragging the hem of her floral embroidered wrap-around skirt along the pavement, caught in the headlights of the Chevrolet, she slipped out-of-sight into a pinball arcade, the brilliance of illuminated flashes electrifying the scene, and from the speakers poured The Who's rock-opera, *Tommy*.

Only The Strong Survive. "Am I still here, in the sixties?" An ever-moving baroque torso, the red Chrysler cruised the freeway interchanges, circling a cloverleaf exit, while Simon Freeman's question caught a wave of light's birth centrifuging from center-to-circumference through his existence in space-time. These torsions of the human persona in the *plastique* of three-dimensional space bled as painfully as Christ crucified in stained glass and lit up by lances of sunlight. Aquilina Kingsley, bewildered herself inside the melting silica of *being-and-existence*, stripped to the cliché of soft feminine sculpture, breathed: "Tell me, Simon, have you the sensitivity to measure how deeply I've fallen for you?"

BACKSEAT DODGE – 38

What Milton Saw. A rain-drenched moonscape striated with rivulets of patterned sand lay screened behind façades of billboards. Reversing the crimson-coated Chrysler through the loosened sand, framed by the motion picture camera traveling side-by-side with the vehicle on tracks, Simon Freeman succumbed to Psyche's allegorical innocence, her nudity's seductive white chocolate in **WHAAM!** just the patina for a Myth. The camera panned from the Chrysler's grille-work to the billboards arranged like so many fabrications of origami in the soil, markings for the fallen Archangel's LZ, his representative flower-myths. Alexander Chamberlain suffered under the toxicity of these Euclidean concepts devised by Jason Palmer, presentations of his revolutionary act of defiance towards Lucifer, fantastical fictions in which he had psychologically cast Laura Devonshire as his female lead. With a fender-mounted camera the dazzling Chevrolet and its charioteer filmed the illusory vistas of the city's cloverleaf interchanges and the baroque automobiles negotiating the curved structures. Gifted with this Miltonian inheritance as a fallen Messiah, Jason Palmer strode across the translucent silica of sand dune, soaked with the tears of Angels, measuring the decibels of echo reverberant across the aeons from the Archangel's *crash*. Wind, sea and undulant wing-of-dune generated inexhaustible transitions of energy, presided over by the celebrity faces peeling from the billboards, eyes of the blind gazing across the terrain of Paradise Lost.

Where Have All The Archangel's Feathers Gone? *Haute couture* ostrich feathers adorning the swaggering super-models parading the length of the cat-walk, regenerations of the wings of the fallen Archangel, gilding these sub-celestial embodiments of Eve, first among humanity's *fashionistas*, floated by the lens of Jason Palmer's movie camera. Soaking his gaze in winter's brief sunset, barely visible as a jeweled incrustation as clouded thought brooded on the horizon, Palmer listened to Laura Devonshire's pellucid violin, aerial with the full wingspread of an Angel, summoning a fiery brilliance to light up the space of the Oceanside apartment.

"Esoterically, the Moon is a mummified corpse there in the museum of the sky, holding some profound Mystery, the hieroglyphs indecipherable. Earlier I saw a flock of birds shaped in the wing of an Archangel." With a fingertip he reached up to peel the crescent moon from the sky and place it on Laura's forehead.

Raking The Sand Of The Mind's Zen Garden. Like a covering of mold on fruit the glittery flesh of the sand dunes crystallized a reminiscence of the archaeology of Lucifer's thought. Jason Palmer meditated in his own mind's cultured Zen garden raking the sand into some enchanting symmetry, forms soothing to a bruised psyche. "Laura, I am in the forge, what will my Creator image?" Lit with the fanaticism of a Zen monk, Palmer's complex mapping of an excursion she could not accompany him on, had Laura desperately unraveling the skeins of melody her violin playing had bound him in, Merlin-and-Nimue revisited. Asymmetrically balanced now inside the cabin of the Chevrolet, extraneous to the rhythms of Palmer's space-time fusions, his transcendental engravings taken of the Archangel's *crash* with his bizarre Zen rakings, Laura fled from the car at a red traffic light, severing the glowing filaments of the web woven by her violin.

Doctrinal Transposition. The splash of a mood's shadow saturated the hippie commune building; *Crystal Blue Persuasion* flowed reverberantly across the space of the apartment as Eddie Phoenix stood framed in the doorway. Catalyst for a chemistry of forbidden shadows, moving with the mechanization of the faithless, his physical precipitation there in the cube of the room, the sisters tender with the naiveté of Mary-and-Martha, Phoenix dragged his shadowy wingspread deeper into space. Wrapped in their many-colored robes inwoven with allegorical moments from the hippie-sixties, their Stations-of-the-Cross, Fleur and the flower child did not initially register the presence of Paulette Taylor in her long-sleeved white gloves until she emerged from behind Phoenix's shadow moving up the wall. Awkwardly phrased questions, verging on the obtuse, were posed by Phoenix enquiring whether communications had been received from Fabian Roxburgh or Lt. John Kirby, speculation about their deaths being circulated by numerous sources. Shadowed in the semi-darkness, Phoenix resembled an agitated gargoyle leaning from a façade, while Paulette Taylor gazed at the tableau of a mounted engine block, perhaps puzzling over its significance. Thunder-and-lightning swiftly crackled, a window was brilliantly illuminated, lamp-light in the living room flickered, faltered, before reviving, and Phoenix was gone with the speed of a shadow vanishing through a wall.

How Eros And Psyche Make Out. Just classical teenage weekenders, Psyche and Eros musicalised coitus onstage in a replica of the famous **BACKSEAT DODGE – 38**, space inside the theater lit with Apollonian sunshine while outside the scene was of dripping ink saturating the parchment of the night sky. **WHAAM!**'s diminishing audience, mostly out-of-towners now seeking refuge from the storm, needed an injection of controversy, hence the insertion of a further scene, with coitus tastefully evoked in a new song ... *It's a teenage world, of parties and falling in love etc* ... and new verses to a familiar one:

(*Eros*)
I saw the best minds of my generation
(*Psyche*)
Crash and burn from too much veneration
(*Eros*)
So we're taking the Road to Perdition
(*Psyche*)
Letting go this bourgeois attrition
Driving coast-to-coast in Maybelline
Just hanging out from scene-to-scene
They say money is the root of all evil
That in $500 suits you'll find Dante's devil
Cruising these terraces of Hell
Sure feels like living in a wishing well

Hurrying through the rain into an all-night diner, Fleur shook off the clusters of droplets, remembering Jason Palmer calling them Angelic tears shed for humanity, falling through space to cool the floor of Paradise Lost. "Every evening we close our physical eyes and our three-dimensional incarnation sleeps, but fourth-dimensionally we remain eternally awake. Argus, the fallen Archangel, and his cracked mirror in our physical world, Eddie Phoenix, understand this, and their mission is to close the Third Eye forever, bring eternal night to the fourth-dimensional realm." Fleur listened to Jason Palmer's rapier whisper pierce her multi-dimensional persona, felt multiple hearts open up tempering the steel of his words passing into her consciousness. "And this is why your guardianship of my belovèd sister is so important? If her eye closes, so does her generation's? Our generation's?" Suddenly, the glass of the diner's mirror erupted with the feather-in-a-fashionable-hat, and Paulette Taylor stood by their cubicle like a taper-lit candle-flame.

Sexual Materiel For Building A Golden Calf. Cracked and chipped marble, veined to over-ripeness, spillages from pomegranates and figs, overlaid the sexual palimpsests modeled among the sheets of the Las Vegas hotel suites. Soothed by these Byzantine erotic extravagances, Eddie Phoenix escorted Paulette Taylor through the spectacular mirrored lobby, reflections of themselves multiplying with thoughtful benevolence, for both had just risen from among the bed sheets in their suite satiated with orgasms. Fresh-cut in the *Vegas* of his hard-won individualism, the supreme gambler Lucifer charted those unparalleled, as-yet-unattempted extremes of idiocy at the Wheel of Fortune, and having lost the spin, resignedly assumed Kingship in the asylum of three-dimensional space specially created for his Fall. Stepping free of the lobby onto the famous Strip, Paulette beside him like a vertical mass of rouge comparable in motion to her horizontal sexual postures, looking up from the dazzling splashes of neon lighting up the desert city, he realized the Helian medallion in the sky could be melted down and shaped into a Golden Calf!

How Do We Recognize The Fallen Archangel? "What a dispersion of feathers!" Vegas chorus girls, so many galactic clusters of fallen Angels, filled the entertainment stages of the casinos, orchestrated an Islamic dream-time for martyrs to the Archangel's cause. Miranda Westwood caught *Priscilla's* refrain as she trailed Johnny Esquire among the roulette tables, his Horoscope mix'n'matched with hers folded in her purse, both natal and transiting planets aligned as she visualized their lovemaking would be on the circular hotel beds upstairs. Colors from the poker machines bled across her as she leaned into them, watching the grouped conviviality of the meeting with Eddie Phoenix and Paulette Taylor, all star-crossed lovers. Fanning feathers opened and closed around the chorus girls like Archangelic wing-beats Lucifer manifested lessening his crash to Earth.

Example Of Zen Laughter. Languidly exaggerated while moving down the supermarket aisles, as Fleur updated her with Jason Palmer's wild description of Eddie Phoenix's threat, the flower child dipped among the frozen items for a tub of yogurt, conscious of the tracking movie camera and settling herself into his obsession with the fallen Archangel. "Fleur, did you ask him to explain your theme in this movie?" Outside in the parking lot a red Chrysler reversed into a vacant bay. Aquilina Kingsley helped load the shopping bags and they accelerated away leaving the movie crew stranded. "Empty film-frames, but Palmer will imagine some dramatic twist, I'm sure," Aquilina laughed. "Have you ever seen him laugh?" The flower girl nonchalantly shrugged, but Simon Freeman obliged her: "Yes, laughter's breeze has wrinkled and lined his otherwise smooth face. Don't let his Miltonian seriousness, the blank verse of his thinking fool you, metaphysical laughter does burst from the lotus of his thoughts." Laura Devonshire attested to his luminous laughter, its safety-valve effect, its reflexive weapon used against the fallen Archangel. The flower child insisted on being dropped-off outside **KRISHNA inc.** and approached the revolving doors with a walk like oil spreading across water.

Viva Las Vegas. Postcards from Las Vegas began arriving, postmarked the same day as if they represented metaphoric film-frames of an evening-in-the-life-of-Eddie Phoenix, purgatorial cartoons of the Desert City. (i) **Paulette Taylor at Sunset** – Scarlet berries crushed against her lips, evening gown loosely flowing from her sonneteer shoulders, yielded a visceral impression this Wesselman nude had embraced the fallen Archangel himself and embarrassed his sexual affectations. (ii) **Eddie Phoenix holding a 45, The Ballad of John and Yoko** – Site of Elvis' proposed Resurrection, Vegas' Cave of Darkness mimicked the rebellious leer of Phoenix's mouth, with Lennon's singing voice like white cocaine powder in the throat. (iii) **Johnny Esquire emoting Elvis-style** – Many are called but few are chosen, and while this ribboned cavalier flirted with the image of greatness he could only ever be an echo in the Tomb. (iv) **Miranda Westwood sweetened up like a candy-apple, disguised under a towering, black-velvet hairdo** – Yin, but to whose yang, certainly not Johnny Esquire's, although Jason Palmer experienced a pain in his rib-cage! Side-by-side the collection established the *dramatis personae* and their expectations in the City of the Fallen Archangel.

In The Year 2525. Scripted by Jason Palmer, the flower child rode the elevator to the thirteenth floor of **KRISHNA inc.** and entered the inner sanctum, lazily observed by the would-be feminine deities in their Eddie Phoenix designed saris, gently tapping finger-cymbals to some faintly perceived music. Arranged in a sandbox, designed from colored crystals, lay a representation of the Australian flag, mandala for the resurgent Archangel, and as instructed, the flower child placed the imprint of the sole of her naked foot among the stars of the Southern Cross. Aghast, the deities ceased tapping their finger-cymbals, swept the hems of their saris across the floor and peered into the sand-box; a spell was broken!

Requiem For Brian Jones. Images of the Hyde Park concert, abbreviated though they were, held the commune brothers-and-sisters spellbound, as if this event presaged the truly apocalyptic ending of the sixties. What did the leaves of days in the remainder of the calendar for 1969 hold now? Holding Simon Freeman's hand, Aquilina Kingsley guided him by her statuesque parents, still traumatized by his earlier regression to hippiedom, and into her bedroom. Rain stippled the family swimming pool visible from her window. Sealed up in a tomb of sentiment he breathed the sachet of her dress as she encircled her arms around his neck and they kissed. During that evening's **WHAAM!** performance, a *Requiem For Brian Jones* insertion in the show included a montage of Rolling Stones songs.

Too Young To Die-Into-Eternity. "Laura, you could say my identity has been vanquished in this maze you have woven; you have proved no Ariadne, letting go the thread, and the Minotaur has ambushed me." Alexander Chamberlain's rehearsed speech, searching to balance the horizontal Tao of his affections for Laura Devonshire, against Jason Palmer's elliptical pretensions to have her die-into-Eternity with him in his quest to imprison the resurgent Archangel, misunderstood the *frisson* such an adventure engendered. Clashing pins-and-bowling balls, the metaphor of the lanes, the aggressive posturing of delivery, the scoring of points, the teasing of Aquilina Kingsley, shook free some of the star-dust from Laura's dreaming, coaxed a flicker of conformity from her recent other-worldliness. "Reconciled after our frightening experience, this Psyche and her Eros have died together, although my parents are traumatized. Your Eros there has already been naked in your dormitory, remember?"

Letter XV. Fabian Roxburgh to Bridget Lovegrove. *Uplift, Bridget, and I will soon be Back In The USA, but I'm feeling the aorta of '69 has taken too much shrapnel and is beginning to lose too much blood. God, what a waste if the end of incarnation equals the end of* *the world. The smokescreen of the first troop withdrawals has descended across 'Nam and you probably read of the visit to North Vietnam, well-publicized, to negotiate the release of three POW's, one of the infamous Chicago 8 grand-standing himself for the World Press. Such a stone sinking into the abyss drags others into its vortex, and we wonder why we have eddied to this place at this time. Right now I feel my cosmic loneliness, especially as Jason Palmer has written of you, calling to my mind your beauty, how you radiate like a Strauss tone poem ... Jason had in mind, Death and Transfiguration, but then his mind is orchestrated that way. As for the Roxburgh world-picture, trying to forge an identity for myself in your life out of this cycle of loss and reunion, morally, I have the persona my feelings and actions deserve for me. Do you remember the famous photograph of the burning Buddhist, his ceramic vase of a person glazed in flame, an image forever besmirched in the smoke of this conflict's brimstone? I think of your self-immolation to attain Nirvana, your fabulous Ode To A Grecian Urn, how I would like to lead the procession to the sacrifice, but like Keats and the Buddhist I am simply a tourist, a sixties tourist, looking for Nirvana. So I have climbed for the moment from 'Nam's stagnant pool and adorned myself with a Peace symbol medallion on a chain to wear on the streets of New York.*

Letter XVI. Fabian Roxburgh to Jason Palmer. *New York's fresco pleasantly aerates the imagination, the vast amphitheater of Central Park like Eden-in-summer, no grasses here are weighted down with droplets of spilled blood, no faeces-smeared nails or arrows are driven through flesh by a trip-wire. But I have picked up my pen because Kennedy's fatuous comments on the operation for Hamburger Hill (as if he could ever comprehend what the moral high ground means) have been thrown into relief against Chappaquiddick Island. The Grunts dug in against soul-destroying mayhem on Hamburger Hill, Kennedy takes to his feet for a marathon, fleeing from Mary Jo Kopechne abandoned in a car wreck, and his excuse? Will he be court-martialed and executed for this heartless desertion? I am Back In The USA trying the scissor the imagery of last year's memories from my existence, because America is finally the only Hope for a Lost World, and another Kennedy intrudes upon our consciousness. O! Brave New World!*

Portrait Of The Archangel (VII). Jason Palmer's metaphysical explorations into the psyche of the fallen Archangel matured amid the immense quietude of the semi-desert wave-motion of sand dunes where the immediacy of the night-sky allowed him to formulate the following: (i) **PHYSICS** – Fuzz-box black-radiation soaked the filthy rag of three-dimensional space, through which rotated burning stars as cleansing unguents, sweeping up the gaseous effluvia, bringing a sparkle again to every surface. If three-dimensional Physics were a fashion-house for the fallen Archangel what gravitational freedom did he in fact have designing quantum models? The wide-brimmed millinery of the galaxies were insertions of curvature impressed in the slides of cosmic space-time, models whose invisible hands gloved in star-dust raised toasts to God with hyperbolic Minkowski grails. Dior, Cardin, Yves Saint Laurent or Courrèges, who emerged from the Archangelic planes of mentation and emotion reflecting a truer symmetry and more accurate cross-sectional slices in their precipitated designs? (ii) **CHEMISTRY** – Mystical carnation, gentle flower whose blossoming ballet in space evoked the divergences of the DNA spiral, issued from the barrel of a National Guardsman's rifle like a bullet's freeze-frame emergence. Eddie Phoenix's mockery was like burning acid to the tapestry of the Christian faithful making up the audience in the television studio. "Following the trajectory of your thinking is comparable to a mirrored reflection trying to escape the two-dimensional frame of its existence. Where can it go? Inertia holds the DNA spiral in a quantum world where human thought lies shadowed in perpetual isolation." Annoyingly, Miranda Westwood's flute-playing shifted through space with a throb of religiosity, a carnation of sound turning itself inside-out, rivulets of waved-petals exulting in three-dimensional space. (iii) **BIOLOGY** – Appetites feasted at a *Satyricon* for the legacy of immortality but the dissolution of *Luxe, calme, et volupté* into a residue of bone soon disentangled the soul from the Tao of incarnation. The flower child's deer-like fragility, her clouded flesh an olfactory manifesto for **KRISHNA inc.** labeled incense sticks and body-oils, was no armor against Eros' arrows, soft-tipped though they were. (iv) **PSYCHOLOGY** – Traumas impressed in the museum of the fallen Archangel's mind reverberated their cause-and-effect across the screen of human thought and experience, precipitated the dysfunctions between the metaphysical soul fused with a three-dimensional physique. Rescued by Jason Palmer from entrapment in a precipitate rain-storm with lightning, sinking back into the upholstery of the Chevrolet, Bridget Lovegrove discussed her strange correspondence with Fabian Roxburgh. "He fears becoming now poisoned foreign substance introduced into the living organism of my life, as if the silica of his person, his carbon and oxygen will diminish my spirituality. Where can he have received such ideas from?" Bridget's psyche ruffled with the resonance of a windswept harp, soothed by the rainbow aura of her soul, wingèd Angel always musical-in-motion and able to vibrate free through the *strings* of quantum worlds. (v) **ECOLOGY** – Sound sculpted invisible forms in space, their precipitations onto the two-dimensional plane of a sand dune mutating and evanescing like the expansion and contraction of the fallen Archangel's wing-span. Now the impearlèd moon resembled a jewel inset in the shimmering raven's wing of the night-sky. Jason Palmer's unstainable white cockatoo glowed against the velvet curtains in the Oceanside apartment when caressed by Celeste Hawthorne's fingertip.

What The Moon Landing Symbolized. Seeking to quell the rococo disturbances generated by Fabian Roxburgh's correspondence, relieved he had abandoned the badlands where mist-and-hills dangerously intermingled in 'Nam's highlands, Bridget Lovegrove gazed upon the jade brazier of the moon, anticipating the climax of the space capsule descending to its surface. "Symbolically, Bridget, the space capsule is a metaphor of the soul remembering back deep into aeonic history, and its three-dimensional landing in incarnation. In 1492, Christopher Columbus chanced the frame of two-dimensional space in which humanity's consciousness lay imprisoned, and his discovery freed us to think again, three-dimensionally. Soon, architecture underwent a Renaissance, the flat-earth thinkers had to challenge space again, and the legacy today is cities of skyscrapers, mass communications, and above all flight. Now, in 1969, this moon landing will usher in four-dimensional thinking, but how that will externalize ..." She listened to the abstract cordiality of his voice, the cubism of his speech rendering multiple-planes of meaning simultaneously, but what electrified her feelings was the sensitive Third Eye enclosed in his bronze forehead waiting to melt through.

Scheherazade Unveiled. Storm warnings kept the Westwoods' schooner safely anchored in the marina. **WHAAM!**'s balance sheets occupied Cornell Bedford-Brown's thoughts, the skyline half-visible through a porthole was no Pop Art silk screen, and Samantha Westwood's half-ruined Beauty lounged like an erased frame from *True Romance*, a comic strip waiting to be filled again with promise. Above the elliptical rim of her martini glass her gaze traced lines of perspective to some far-off horizon of remembrance he could not fathom. All existence was theatrical and the ever-tightening mainspring of the drama for a woman was: How can my beauty survive? Running as slanting rain lashed the quay, Bedford-Brown reached the Chrysler determined his experience's palette would be meaningfully applied to the squared-up canvas of his existence, and as he drove through roads awash with the downpour caught at the impressions offered by Celeste Hawthorne's *vie de Bohème*. Wandering about her studio-loft's Freudian dream, starring a cast of personae from Delacroix's *œuvre*, he flashed her a thought: "Why do *1001 Arabian Nights* emerge, crowd me on this stage?"

Headpiece-And-Tailpiece. Orgasm's existential moan, the physique's staccato moments, lovers' effigies from Antiquity, a sky beyond the studio-loft irradiated with electro-magnetism, these were the sensations of *Eros* entombed and resurrected in coitus with Celeste Hawthorne. A headpiece-and-tailpiece to a romantic tale, *Eros* and *Psyche* bookishly poeticized coitus and then turned the page, Celeste charmingly mirrored in her voice.

> El amor pasajero tiene el encanto breve,
> y ofrece un igual término para el gozo y la pena.
> Hace una hora que un nombre grabé sobre la nieve;
> hace un minuto dije mi amor sobre la arena.

What was Delacroix's classical memorial in his Hamlet lithographs copied by Celeste: Lust cradled in the begging bowl of the skull reduced to wind-blown dust?

Riding To Damascus On BACKSEAT DODGE – 38. Alexander Chamberlain's ecclesiastical boyhood, a sunburned St. Paul tanned by biblical sea breezes, undertaking imaginative visitations of the Seven Churches, contrasted this transformation into a Sabbath-breaker, his manhood's dilation into pagan eroticism, yet Jason Palmer seemed focused on Laura Devonshire. The **BACKSEAT DODGE – 38** was no Prophet's chariot, coitus (if simulated) with Psyche was no scripture reading on the Wages of Sin, rather a nexus where spiritual and sexual pleasures intersected and from whose web he could not free himself. "Yes, the actor, Eros, is my extension, my ennui! I am now the surface face of a clock, not its internal workings, and I'm winding down. Do you really understand how an actor runs-down time from the man he was born-to-be?"

Could Vegas Be Transposed To The Desert Of The Moon? "Poets will offer you the golden apple of the Moon – there's a hard core to swallow." Eddie Phoenix's witticism mirrored an allusion to the original Civil War in Heaven in the floating corpse of the Moon. Banks of television screens carried images of the lunar capsule and the tension of its impact on the powdery surface, the descent of the ladder, but the moment was a slow-down, a decrescendo, compared with the sumptuous surreality of Vegas, the dance of the Astronauts stilted against the carnival of show-girls. Paulette Taylor omnisciently transcribed the lineal chain of Byzantine imagery moving through Vegas like a serpent-in-a-vacuum. Here the fallen Archangel effortlessly unloaded his psyche of memories of the *crash* as the crowds gathered around the roulette and blackjack tables. Who could resist such a reef-of-gold exposed and blazing in the desert of the world?

Metaphysical Dimensions Of The Dream. Cornell Bedford-Brown glimpsed his dye shadowing the lithograph of his presence in the studio-loft, where the bed's tossing boat, floating, now becalmed as a wave-of-sheet, while his soul sailed with Celeste Hawthorne on *The Raft of the Medusa*. Astronauts now gazed upon a pearl shelled in the oyster of space a quarter-of-a-million miles away, so devalued by the fallen Archangel and then redeemed by the Buddha and Jesus, but what would be its final epitaph sculpted by Time? Had the shadow of the Absolute lifted with this visitation of the Moon? Filled with liquid the brush soaked paper as Celeste began a watercolor of herself watching him sleep. But the brush could only compose abbreviated gestures, biases of torso-and-limbs, iconographic motifs, losing the metaphysical dimensions of the dream powering them. Leaving the watercolor sketches of himself in motionless suspension on the spatial slides of paper, Bedford-Brown re-entered the tableau of the city, perhaps unconsciously searching for the *Bel Air* Chevrolet he knew would be cruising the streets. Virtuoso at emptying the sky, Lucifer wove the Chrysler and Chevrolet together along the curving camber of the freeway, a calming conjunction of metaphysical geometries, like a pearl maturing inside an oyster shell.

After-Shocks. "Are we to seriously believe, the microcosmic DNA chromosomes evolved *reason* and *laughter* under their own sub-atomic volition?" Jason Palmer's question evaporated before the spacious languor of sand dunes, ecological spirals of the Earth's DNA, but his tone was good-humored and peaceable, sensitive to Aquilina Kingsley's misunderstanding these pearl-grey models. "Then these billboards, slices of two-dimensional space as you say, pasted up with images, are your interference in the fallen Archangel's DNA design for the Earth?" Simon Freeman externalized the smoke of thinking from the fire inside Palmer's mind, and her laughter held up in space with the transparence of crystal. "Well, your voice is duller on subsequent hearings. Fortunately the tsunami of this mythical *fall* which seems to obsess you has ebbed, and we're all stranded on the same beach, making our own way back to Paradise." Aquilina fashioned a thoughtful enough response, adding: "Words are just toys to you, you set them in motion like spinning tops, and we follow them like children. Hasn't the Apocalypse passed?" Emerging from the inner curves of a receptacle of dunes with the slices of billboards receding into the distance they allowed the shards of existence lacerate their forgotten memories like the abrasions of Time on a once-precious statue. While the wing of a hand passed along the symmetry of the crimson-fleshed Chrysler and the sea breeze decayed in the wave of Aquilina's plasma of hair, Palmer posed a question: "Tell me, would you travel on stilts, extensions for a featherless biped, or by wheels in a sculpted chariot?"

Xenophobia. Illumined by bizarre linkages, Fleur regarded Jason Palmer's theological intimacy with the Archangel's *crash* as baroque artifice, although his xenophobia exerted a fascination on her sister, the flower child, who stood beside him with the clarity of a reflection in water. As if emboldened by Palmer's ever-watchful eyes the flower child suspended eating from the tub of yoghurt and contemplated the synthesis of images in the photographs spread for their viewing. (i) **Vegas-from-the-air.** Laid on the inside of the desert's shell was the cornea of Vegas, imperfect pearl, aureoled by a dim circlet of illumination, the reddened fire of the fallen Archangel opening to the plain of Paradise Lost. (ii) **Hueys-from-the-1st-Cav.** Armed-and-dangerous, emergent from serpentine smoke-trails uncoiling over 'Nam, the war-horses symbolized the technological reunification of the fallen Archangel's war-machine. (iii) **Footprints.** A montage brought Armstrong's plimsoll impression on the lunar surface together with the flower child's footprint decorously laid in the mandala of Eddie Phoenix's sandbox, an etude of mystical poignancy, designs of eternal placements, and reminders of the sacrament of incarnation. Modulating the moment through emotional key-changes they sped across the two-dimensional plane of the city in Palmer's Chevrolet with the photographs curling in the curve of the flower child's lap. Eyes later roamed the night sky for the glow of the space capsule's fire-fly in space.

A Deep-Red Rose. Brushed in the feathery plumage of twilight, wind caressing the terrestrial plasma of her hair, the flower child let ripple the thermal conductivity of her torso wrapped in cheesecloth-and-sari, indulged Jason Palmer's colloquial asides referencing uncountable incarnations trying to still the turbulence of Paradise Lost. One *Tempest* per lifetime, one exile in lamentation and forgetfulness, but thousands of embodiments! Had she been grafted to Lucifer's stalk as he implied, too somber to flower, pungent with sulphurous odors, but now this anointment would transfigure her, the bracelet of her heart's petals would perfume space like a deep-red rose? Palmer illustrated for her the Earth's pot-of-gold at the end of the Cosmos' immense ebony rainbow spangled with glittering stars and showed her his sulphur-crested cockatoo, the flaming leafage of his spread wings, letting her visualize in the bird his own soul caged in darkness. Stunning thighs of white-fleshed eucalypts stained by sunset strode across the landscape.

Man And His Image. Together they mounted the spiral staircase to Celeste Hawthorne's studio-loft where a tea-and-coffee silver service was laid on a table. Thought's plateau touched on the opacity which had fallen between Man and his Image, metaphored in oil paint gracing canvas, in three-dimensional architecture clothing consciousness in structured symbols, and of love wrestling its aerial and earthy dominions. A consonance of torsos clustered in chalk on paper contrasted the news bulletins where US Forces and Viet Cong ebbed-and-flowed in their battle for The Citadel, a mere 25 miles north of Saigon. Against these grainy black-and-white images the lithographs were rhythmically inert and Bridget Lovegrove remarked on Fabian Roxburgh's romantic exile: "He writes of surfeiting on his absence from the world, that Saigon's crumbling Byzantine Christianity is doomed, but I know his actions and his feelings sift different states of his experience." Bridget's chalked emergence from Celeste's sketching emulated the metaphysical sickness-at-heart in Delacroix's *Cleopatra*, her head's sovereign crown visceral with interior thoughts on what-is-to-come. Visited later in her office by Cornell Bedford-Brown he sensed in her speaking voice a water-colorist's medium, fast-flowing but porous as the paper in her accounting journals, as they discussed **WHAAM!**, and their dining-table talk that evening reminisced their impressions of the Westwoods.

Prince Charming Searches For Cinderella. Untouched, the sandbox carefully colored-in with the map of Australia, still carried the impression of a lovely footprint in its Sea of Tranquility, and one-by-one Eddie Phoenix placed the foot of each of the flower children in his entourage there, a sublime Cinderella-moment for **KRISHNA inc.**!

Footprint As The Medium. Reading, masked by the book's cover, *Up The Down Staircase*, listening to the latest hit record on the radio, *Spinning Wheel*, the flower child ignored Jason Palmer's movie camera filming the *mise-en-scène*, and his bizarre monologues on the meaning of the sole of her foot, what its placement on the Earth's surface might mean. How many of her footprints had he photographed out among the sand dunes? A deep-red rose leaned on a gently curving stem from a uterine vase. On the balcony of the Oceanside apartment he studied astronomical charts and she observed him reaching out as if to touch stars, sky-writing some Physics equations through soft-slices of space's twisting curvatures: intuitive symmetries of thought. Only comfortable with right-angular, linear, straight-ahead roadways she enjoyed cruising in his mythical chariot, but became characteristically unsettled when he parked among the intrinsic-and-extrinsic curvatures of dunes where he placed her footprints in the soft viscous sand. Workmen repairing concrete paving outside **KRISHNA inc.** were recalled to the site by Eddie Phoenix complaining of a feminine footprint setting in the wet cement!

Transfiguration. Houris-in-**KRISHNA inc.**, navigating their way to Paradise with the code-music of finger-cymbals and Miranda Westwood's flute, the flower children ambulated through the city streets under monochrome skies, practitioners of disengagement from Western Civilization. Luminously black winter skies through which pencils of sunlight beamed evoked the prophetic closure of fourth-dimensional space over the bottomless pit. The tapers of skepticism burning in the penciled sunbeams barely illumined the scene. Gunning the Chevrolet, chariot forged from the Mind of God, Jason Palmer accelerated from the freeway flyover, the dying thunder of Elvis singing *How Great Thou Art* lost in the deluge of rain. Soaking up the texture of this crisis, the flower child hummed her hit parade of songs, disconcerted why Palmer had restrained her from dipping a virgin foot in the pool of his bed, as if he were first waiting for a transfiguration of their clouded flesh. She loosened her freshly shampooed, luxuriant tresses, listened to his monologues, glanced over his tulip-bulb style drawings of multi-dimensional space, but still he declined to touch the sheath of her orchid. Now the storm's full-force cracked the branches of eucalypts, tearing wood cried in pain, and everywhere gentle petals were weighed with raindrops, while Palmer conjured up for her the image of root-systems groping deeper into *terra firma*, tangling up in darkness, shunning the light.

Self-Realization. After the storm had passed and the sun again rifled the milky cloud-drifts the following morning, Jason Palmer stepped to the French doors leading onto the apartment's balcony, and said: "These are not the *windows* I want to open, do you understand? During the night as you dreamed I caught glimpses of your hair swarming across the pillow in the lightning-flashes." The flower child's lips touched an apple's heel before biting deep into the flesh. These glissandos and tinglings of sex embodied in the minutiae of Woman's simplest gestures contrasting the sensations of slashing hail of last evening, a masculine orgasm, lashed his sensibility as he peered through the cool panes of glass, realizing his loins could never become chastened in the wave's whitewater washing up the soft beach sand!

VIII
ACRYLIC KISSES

Letter XVII. Fabian Roxburgh to Bridget Lovegrove. *Ariel's art is never causative, and neither is mine, for flying into Belfast I entered a kind of captivity only able to react to events there. How do those words go: For a man hath no greater love than to lay down his life for his brother. Perhaps the Protestant Orange Order visualize themselves as a resurrected Templar Order with Ian "no surrender" Paisley their Grand Master, for the Catholic paramilitary priesthood here, a new Inquisition parading in their hoods, have unleashed a tempest of violence even Prospero could not quell. How will this all end, in public burnings, mass hangings, midnight executions? Everything here is economically ransacked, vandalized, and anyone would think Belfast were another Jerusalem as a monument to spiritual pilgrimage. If I eventually shipwreck myself on your shores again, will you be my Miranda, will you look at me and say: O! Brave New World, that has such a man in it? Fire from armored cars keeps this Apocalypse fresh with images of evil.*

Letter XVIII. Fabian Roxburgh to Bridget Lovegrove. *Being a late-sixties bachelor I parade myself around Saigon (which is beginning to feel like Paris, 1940) in bell bottoms, tune into Radio 'Nam and catch Johnny Rivers' tribute to the Mekong, (I Washed My Hands In) Muddy Water, and I do have some fashionable facial hair. Charlie however has his own iconic clothing, especially as summer is deepening, the heat is building (torrid is the in-word for it), and this provides an opportunity to catch the US Forces sunbathing. Picture sleepy coves of white sandy beaches, Malibus gently riding the easy swells, snorkeling weather, a few games of social tennis, drinks at leisurely Saturday night dances, and I will conjure for you the holiday resort of Cam Ranh Bay, where I'm flying in for some R&R. Lying back in the warm sand I think often of Charlie out there shoveling through labyrinths of tunnels, fixated on the political goal, reunification under Communism, and become so sick at heart I start to vomit. Or is it sun-stroke? Charlie raided the US hospital here, inflicting enormous psychological damage, the happy vibe has passed, the critical mass has been reached, 'Nam is well-and-truly blown wide open. The Grunts here want to go back to the farm ... Now!*

Portrait Of The Archangel (VIII). Jason Palmer, accompanied by the flower child, her physique enervated with the effortless beauty of a lotus, and contrasting the tight DNA braids in her long tresses, strolled among the slices of billboards fraying under the southern winter storms, glimpsing in the Archangelic façades the subatomic particles of Benday dots. (i) **PHYSICS** – Bundled in Galilean space-time, geometer of parallel planes, the fallen Archangel's photons entered the billboards as Benday dots, alerting Palmer to possibility his portrait lay impacted on the screen behind them. Stereographically the Archangelic portrait twisted space in four-dimensional vectors, their strings peeling off slices like billboard images which floated through space-time. (ii) **CHEMISTRY** – What is Chemistry's anti-Nirvana? Of what manifestation of bonding does annihilation take? Palmer gazed at the electron-clouds of Benday dots, his fingertips handled the braids of the flower child's tresses, the Archangelic spine precipitated from the Planck-moment to Infinity. Could he persuade her, as a religious gesture, to take scissors to her braids, sever the fabulous strings holding space-time in bondage to the fallen Archangel? (iii) **BIOLOGY** – Flesh's anomalous viscosity, erotically pro-creative, intensified the drowning of the human persona in space-time, the ever-unraveling strings of the DNA spiral insufficiently attached to the roof of Heaven for Man to climb free of the bottomless pit. (iv) **PSYCHOLOGY** – The leaking hollow tooth of the fallen Archangel's psyche, his metaphysical venom, paralyzed humanity's brain-waves, froze living chromosomes of thoughts of divinity into a complex of Benday dots arrayed on the slices of space-time. (v) **ECOLOGY** – Kneeling, a fingertip touching the flank of a dune, Jason Palmer raised the grains of sand adhering to his flesh, surmising the incalculable number of these silica Benday dots painting the canvas of the beach scene. Sliding through the space between the billboards, sensing the thin layers of shadow, how they were palpable with the fallen Archangel's presence, he visualized the fountain of quantum-foam bubbling at sub-atomic levels, remembering how heavy winter rain splattering on surfaces everywhere evoked its turmoil.

A Quartet Of Strolling Players. Strolling into The Playhouse for the afternoon matinee performance of **WHAAM!**, Alexander Chamberlain was arrested by Laura Devonshire's presence, emerging from an alcove, no longer shaded with those thoughts of Eternity the tempter, Jason Palmer, had obscured her in. "Alexander, while you might have been as urbane as carved stone towards me of late, I have been too placid, like a tamed sea-horse, afloat in a current I couldn't control." Suddenly, the gargoyle of a face, tarnished in Las Vegas' neon-brightness, intruded and Eddie Phoenix said: "Yes, Eros, she is as pure as free-flowing grain in a smooth plank of pinewood, but we all have a gnarlèd knot of imperfections, so be careful! Look, she's vivid scarlet, and you're Robin Hood green!" Combing high his quiff, Johnny Esquire sauntered into the foyer, announcing as he took Laura's bowing hand: "Palmer told me making love to this romantic song transported him to a plane where he could see the Universe as a crystalline raindrop sliding from a cosmic lotus petal. Splash!" Reflective counterweights, the lovers maintained a tense equilibrium while Phoenix and Esquire exited inside the theater proper, then etched a kiss overflowing with rumination on the meaning of romance in the late-sixties. **WHAAM!** and its Pop Art pastel washes of nudity for the *Now* generation only twisted the threads of sexuality into an insoluble algebra whose equation was too deep to fathom.

Christian Physics. "Do ripples form in water like parallelograms? What does this tell us about anything?" Jason Palmer's doctrinal crusade addressing the audience of born-again Christians hopelessly tarnished his credibility with their feverish self-righteousness. "Look at your neighbor, Sin is always cleverly disguised as an actor performing among us. Listen, Sin's soliloquies are fantastical with the *either-or-question*: Am I pre-destined for carnal pleasure, or purity? Lucifer's acrylic kissing of Eve, your own wife or girlfriend, soon has her dreaming her soul's molecular make-up is compounded with the chemistry of his, and the gentle flame of the Angels becomes the harsh fire of lust."

Elvis As Captain America. Zen geometry in the fine-grained beach sand, scratchings on a mirror to Bridget Lovegrove's understanding, rendered him a translucent semblance to a Beat poet from her college years, but more troubling was the matrix of his questionable performance before the born-again Christians. Speeding in the Chevrolet they had trailed behind Johnny Esquire's *Easy Rider* Harley, his Captain America incarnation as a roustabout Elvis, another meaningless immersion in the mythology of the late-sixties, everything being to her now a thoughtless refrain on the death of Christopher Featherstone. Together they pondered the longevity of the stele of **KRISHNA inc**. and Goethe's alignment of architecture with a hymn-in-stone. Elvis' moralistic 45, *Clean Up Your Own Backyard*, certainly a strange choice for a single following *In The Ghetto*, unless a continuity of social consciousness was being invoked. Herself ravishing acrylic, *Priscilla's* Egyptian avatar, two-dimensional as a fresco, peeled her palimpsest from the papyrus of Johnny Esquire's torso and swung free of the Harley Davidson's pillion. Such Zen-like moments had been story-boarded by Jason Palmer; she recalled the folios of collages spread across the floor of his Oceanside apartment.

Scenes From WHAAM! (i) Opening in a neon-lit diner with Oldenburg's famous soft sculptures on the menu, waitresses in a chorus-line serenaded Eros and Psyche in their quest for sexual gratification. (ii) Eros and Psyche traveled the length of a gallery where mixed media versions of Wesselman's *Great American Nudes* came alive, tastefully shadowed, chorus to the mythological couple's romantic ballet. (iii) Smooth-as-acrylic, Eros and Psyche frolicked in Red Grooms' *Hollywood (Jean Harlow)*, abandoned to the rapture of promised fame, hurrying toward the threshold of consummation before the lights came down. (iv) The tableau of *Backseat Dodge – 38*, Psyche's leg extension visible, her loins dancing with Eros as erotically as those of Cyd Charisse setting the movie screen ablaze with her sexual presence. A bulging file of press cuttings and feature articles reviewing and analyzing **WHAAM!** lay beside Cornell Bedford-Brown on the front seat of the Chrysler, as did autographed copies of the show's album and 45s. Idling at a traffic light he glimpsed Bridget Lovegrove crossing the intersection; she suddenly stumbled as if his thinking had caught her up by the ankle. Now he understood Jason Palmer's reference to her as a lamb dressed in a Golden Fleece!

Vesuvius! Paulette Taylor's sharp-edged woodcut sexuality, plotted like a geometric ballet, created around the arrangement of his existence the glowing filaments of web lit up like Las Vegas in its desert setting. Cornell Bedford-Brown felt his inhibitions melt like a crust of Arctic ice as her orgasm flowed with the heat of smelted copper and her teeth bit into the honeycomb of his shoulder. Perhaps her orgasm was as allegorical as the hoof-like sweep of her pubic hair, the Faun's imprint so tempting to measure one's own dimensions, brimming over with earthy flavors; her acrylic lips relaxed with exhausted kisses, languid with flushes of luxury. Bedford-Brown raised his torso's skin-area from hers as if lifting a film of mosaic decoration from a Pompeian fresco.

Johnny Esquire And The Aeneid. "Yes, I am exhausted with my own nakedness, and dream now of casting it off when **WHAAM!** folds." Aquilina Kingsley stepped from out of the tomb of classical allusion, emerging from behind the shadow of the thought as Laura Devonshire tuned her violin and Miranda Westwood drowned her thinking inside arpeggios of flute-music. "If I am no more than an illustrated stanza of erotic poetry, may my next role be Isabella in *Measure For Measure*!" Whenever Miranda caught a glimpse of the Trojan survivor, Johnny Esquire, Aquilina shivered now seeing her illumination fixed on the page of space, Dido-the-salamander eager to burn, self-consume in poetry. **WHAAM!** proved to be no dialectic victory for Woman and the precocious fireworks of Psyche's nudity lessened with each salvo of a performance, the charade of simulated sex on-stage an unintelligible tableau from the back-stalls, and besides, what moral self-discovery had the cast made? Johnny Esquire's profanation of their dramatic chiaroscuro with his behind-the-scenes sexual liaisons with Paulette Taylor, another Dido to his Aeneas, this time silhouettes on the wall of the Cave of Darkness, fulfilled the existentialism sung by his hero in *Heartbreak Hotel*. Among the cast-and-crew the infamous couple was referred to as the Roustabout-and-the-Fornicatrix!

Zen Moments Among Hippies. Handing her a Zen stone and a mallet-and-chisel, Jason Palmer said to the flower child: "Here, carve your true name there." Amiably *plastique*, her face all cloud-free tranquility, the flower child held the rock's Zen skull in the palms of her hands, her smile a sudden burst of flame upon the cup of a taper. "There is no I-ness in the inner presence of such a stone, man," a hippie nodded sagaciously, dressed in the buckskin-with-tassels of a Wild West figure. Fleur walked from behind the engine-block mounted as sculpture in the communal living room increasingly intolerant of these Quixote Messiahs trying to unravel her beloved sister's virginal intricacies, their thoughts certainly not on Immaculate Conceptions. She had seen some of the rococo footage's *découpage* for Jason Palmer's movie, troubled by the pendulum swinging between repentance-and-sin, feelings torn by rose-thorns and healed by the petals, but sensed her sister was no companion for him in the long cosmic nights of his loneliness. Miranda Westwood's flute sank away into emotional quicksand as she suffocated by the sofa, straining, sieving her feelings through the darkness of Johnny Esquire's indifference.

Following A Sign. "Distortions in Jason Palmer's portraiture, this Expressionist Christ, belie his cool self-righteousness, for he is the very Robespierre of romantic minds." With these words to the Christian journalist, Eddie Phoenix climbed aboard the helicopter and ascended from the roof of **KRISHNA inc.** leaving his entourage of flower children like survivors from a shipwreck. Folding the Christian newspaper in which his photograph appeared, Jason Palmer turned the ignition and the Chevrolet followed the helicopter's flight-path, a journey towards the emerald sea bordered with the warped cartography of sand dunes and a skyline deeply ingrained with undulations of cloud. Coiling pythons of smoke curled up from the moonscape of sand dunes as *Put A Little Love In Your Heart* came on the car radio.

Who Cast The First Stone? Rain delicately lustered with sunlight fell across the drooping wings of the Archangelic helicopter. Like a crushed Zen stone the cockpit of the helicopter kissed the lip of a dune. Papers drifted in the heated eddies rising from the helicopter, floating off across the sloping dunes, while sunlight gently fizzed on the emerald sea. A soaring eagle appeared, talons extended, coiled in the twisting python of smoke as Simon Freeman stumbled through the sand inside a face-framing collar. Like the tearing tissue of a tapestry the waves of sand dunes embraced the image of the fallen helicopter. Memories of the cream-colored *coupé* abandoned by Helena Steele's ubiquitous presence, so electric she could jump-start a car just by touching the ignition with a fingertip, rose from the magic mantle of sand dunes in its tragic after-existence, companion-in-arms to the downed helicopter. "How will I erase the image of this skull from my thoughts?" Simon Freeman's mortal blood cooled while Jason Palmer's Byronic impasto glowed, statuesque now, in-the-round, his face designed for spiritual coinage, an avenging Archangel!

Good Morning Little Schoolgirl. News bulletins ran with the phenomenon of a 3-day Festival at a location called Woodstock, helicopters buzzed the log-jam of traffic down *groovy highway*, the impossible-to-manage crowd and the commune-dwellers began to hyperventilate the vibe of their feelings, as if they had missed the Crucifixion. Aromatic with fresh-baked bread, serving her latest casserole, Miranda Westwood caught elisions of conversation above the Ten Years After album, *SSSSH*, spinning on the turntable, a mood-setter for the talk about Woodstock's epochal event in the history of Hippiedom. *Crêpes-with-maple-syrup-and-oranges* accompanied analysis of the Establishment's vendetta against the Chicago 8, and Ten Years After worked their way through *Good Morning Little Schoolgirl*.

Zen Surfers. Fluid and restless, waves-of-cloud flowed across the sky, the Chevrolet's wheels like Achilles' chariot, dragged the red Chrysler in its slipstream, both vehicles chasing down Johnny Esquire's Harley Davidson speeding for the underpass. More handsome than a Teen Romance cartoon hero, Johnny Esquire had gathered a distressed Paulette Taylor from the mortuary room at the hospital, perhaps hoping the speed would centrifuge the blackened aura of despair from her consciousness. Eddie Phoenix's irreligious exertions, his anti-Christian *exposés*, his blow-torch approach as the fallen Archangel's messenger, climaxed with a prodigious wipe-out as he surfed the wave-of-sky on a stormy afternoon. All exultation, the flower child wandered the sand dunes with the Zen stone in her palms, making sure it was cleansed by washes of sand, rain, breeze and music, for she recognized somehow this spiritual talisman held the serene beatitude she longed for. Emerging from the underpass Jason Palmer slowed observing the Harley Davidson's after-thought inter-penetrating the distance, and remarked to the flower child: "Inertia! Remember, the fall of a stone is harder than a feather's, but both obey the same Law."

What Is A Kiss? Shoulder-blades naked, her vertebra reminiscent of a Mosaic staff, in a body-clinging black evening gown whose *décolleté* burst a thousand light-bulbs in the cameras, Paulette Taylor attended the gala Awards Night with Johnny Esquire in gold lamé on her arm, his statuesque idol threatening to break the Ten Commandments. Celeste Hawthorne's posters lining the grand entrance to the venue were astonishingly vibrant Pop Art representations of the **WHAAM!** stage settings, her *homage* as she was a nominee that evening. Acrylic kisses ornamented a thousand cheeks, although Johnny Esquire flirted with the cameras, publicly mouth-kissing the actresses, chorines, set decorators and costume designers, merciless with his attentions, but when he tongued a surprised the red-hot favorite for Best Actress Award, she turned to the bank of up-thrust microphones and tossed them: "What is a kiss? As an actress I tear up the page of a script on which it is written!" Cornell Bedford-Brown surveyed the silhouetted *derrieres* beautifully upholstered for the evening, enthralled with the stylized candor of their showmanship under the brilliance of the lighting, but during the lavish buffet the failure of **WHAAM!** to influence the critics began to sting, for this evening was always the apotheosis for the Theater. Johnny Esquire's rapier was out and flashing, his handsome equipage, his emblazoned singularity, contrasted Jason Palmer's Zen style, ceremonial, face-down, and who was he escorting, Fleur, the flower child, or Bridget Lovegrove?

A Psychedelia Of Floral Metaphors. Touching up lips smudged by Johnny Esquire, smoothing fabric over hips and *derriere*, the mirrors glistening, perfume breathing from inside of wrists, the convocation of women talked. "Johnny will dance **ME** into the breaking dawn," Paulette Taylor delivered with the tone of an absolute monarch. "Physically, we are a double-echo, if you understand my meaning." Stung as if by a bee pleasuring a blossom, holding the pollen but nothing else, Miranda Westwood still felt his lips inlaid on her mouth, but Fleur had already re-capped her tube, saying: "Too many have already sketched the eunuch for me to prize his dancing. Now his kissing of me has further poisoned the illustration. What about you Aquilina?" Checking for any shadow in her armpit, Aquilina Kingsley laughed: "As an actress I meditate on the great lovers of women on a writer's page, but I will only cruise for kisses on-stage, from part-to-part, and if Johnny Esquire follows me on a pilgrimage from role-to-role, well ..." Laura Devonshire listened to her friend's teasing of Paulette, before adding: "Who told me Esquire's quiff stands up like a uraeus, an s-for-sex? Jason Palmer?" Over-rouged lips re-appeared among the guests, perfectly traced arabesques until the collision of laughter's interference patterns hallucinated their psychedelia, and there were too many red roses for Johnny Esquire to deflower with kisses.

Zen-Koans. Soft cloth evocatively embroidered with moonlight plunged Alexander Chamberlain's thought into a reflective pool as he escorted Laura Devonshire toward the red Chrysler. Ligaments of light torn apart, the Milky Way flowed with the trajectory of Lucifer's Fall, the wounded Archangel's *howl* pitched to wavelengths no longer audible to human ears, although the amplification of these latter-day guitar-heroes aspired to capture it. Jason Palmer's elliptical will-o'-the-wisp, his peripheral super-realism all evening appearing as fragmented slices of quotations from Zen-koans, circled into Chamberlain's pathway, Bridget Lovegrove's taut magnificence at his side, she too as abbreviated as a classical aphorism. Laura's rose-petal frosted over by the sudden fall in temperature now threatened to melt. "Alexander, return to your study of the spiritual archaeology of the supreme Actor, your first inspiration, His script will bring you your greatest performance." The flower child drifted from the venue toward the car park with the Zen stone in her palms, the sounds of Eternity pressed within its heart, even the cry of the fallen Archangel!

Tantra Is the Mantra. The Moon squeezed between enfolding cloud-forms as if to reaffirm Bridget Lovegrove's brilliance. Wreathed in the smoke of her fragrances she closed her door and leaned against it hearing Jason Palmer's footsteps recede toward the driveway. Sexual designs etched in the ceiling of Laura Devonshire's thoughts were a Chinese dragon twisting and turning in spiritual ecstasy. Eros metamorphosed into Alexander Chamberlain, more a Tantric Taoist than a tempted St. Anthony, and amid her bedroom's stage décor he brought to her pubis the pulsation of a bulbèd rose. Oxygenated by kisses, Psyche allowed her sexual stream of sensation turn the wheel of her thoughts, her speech in Simon Freeman's ear always an anthology of allusions, until the moment of tremulous blurring, the accelerated cruise into orgasm experienced in his dragsters. Johnny Esquire's alchemical imitation of the famous pop star, rhyming their sculptural models, dreamed of Ann-Margret's hair rising like the sun above his sexual horizon, burning them both in tendrils of flame, a sweet immolation beyond Paulette Taylor's comprehension if not her experience. A raven's ebony wingspread of darkness limned the shadows in the climb to Celeste Hawthorne's studio-loft where Cornell Bedford-Brown's after-presence of a Faun already lingered.

A Curtain Call. Half-hidden in shadow, undressing, Celeste Hawthorne exhibited the flimsiest slice of enameled torso, allowing the gold-filigree of her voice illuminate parallels between desire and its fulfillment.

> Cierro los ojos y el negror me advierte
> Que no es negror, y alumbra unos destellos
> Para darme a entender que sí son ellos
> El fondo en algazara en la suerte,
>
> Incógnita nocturna ya tan fuerte
> Que consigue ante mí romper sus sellos
> Y sacar del abismo los más bellos
> Resplandores hostiles a la muerte.

Dressing before a mirror as space became grey with dawn, Celeste's eyes just above the shoulder of his tuxedo, she remarked how he would gaze into the reflection of himself but not look at her, to whom he found himself saying: "But I can see your reflection behind me. And haven't I kissed you more warmly than this cool glass can?" Quicksilver sketching strokes musicalized a sketching pad as he puzzled why their sexual embracement never seemed to level her off to a state of tranquility and placidity. Disheveled in the crumpled tuxedo he descended the studio-loft and climbed inside his Chrysler the previous evening's ephemeral hallucination an end-moment like the final curtain fall on **WHAAM!**.

Johnny Esquire's Kiss. Miranda Westwood's tears splashed the torso of her flute lying across the palms of her hands: the walls of the communal apartment rocked with *Honky Tonk Women* at full volume, shattering the sweet delicacy of her crème caramel moment. One of the sleepless hippies, re-heating her casserole, came over and sat cross-legged on the floor, sweeping a sarong around his knees against the cold. "Better the flute than trigonometry. Flowers *blossom*, the music *knows* itself, but where are the daffodils in mathematical formulae? I've heard you give music intelligence, and that is important for our time, you understand?" How could she capture Johnny Esquire's lips in the flute's embouchure?

Christ In The House Of Mary And Martha. "The poisoned well supplying the Marriage at Cana, the water basin used for the washing of the Disciples' feet, Joseph cast in his wishing well, what are these homespun morality tales but children's stories for the credulous?" Eddie Phoenix's natural smolder within the domesticity of the communal hippie apartment block, his carapace of affectation with Fleur and the flower child, sounded an echo in the tomb of the living room, he betrayed his ignorance of the *groovy vibe* essential to communication with them. Fragments of a letter from Fabian Roxburgh caught his eye: *A visionary frontispiece, an antique architrave has collapsed, the leaves in the Book of Fate were not transparent, that realization is a specter I'm wrestling* *with here so far away from you; the bubble has burst and I'm gasping for air.* "But, man, **KRISHNA inc.** is too heavy for us, too *straight*, you know what we mean? Too *straight* a vibe from the ungroovy past, yes?" Arrogance, intoxication and artifice alloyed the evening and the salve of Miranda Westwood's flute was absent, its metaphysical purity, its emanation as if from a dream, and the dialectic remained gravitationally bound with Eddie Phoenix's voice.

Miss Lovegrove's Day At The Office. A fog of methane ice, Bridget Lovegrove's torso, nebulous and milky, stepped from the shower stall, her hair's plasma of electromagnetic waves a cloud of cool gas red-shifted in emission. Later, entertaining Cornell Bedford-Brown in her office space, her flesh now cool as a crescent of sand lapped by the winter surf, she marveled at his cavalier accounting practices with **WHAAM!** and assumed Calvin Westwood's wound had re-opened and was leaking. "Miss Lovegrove, **WHAAM!'s** bubble has burst and Miranda Westwood has vanished, so have you heard from anyone who might know her whereabouts?" Visiting the Oceanside apartment, where the door was answered by a flower child spooning yoghurt from a tub with her finger, her languor soft-laden with Eastern perfumes, Bridget entered the room's cube following the wingèd arc transcribed by the schoolgirl's hand. Was she Jason Palmer's sibyl unstitched in space from a lovely Eastern tapestry? Palmer himself, immortalizing some long-forgotten art, emerged from his sojourn of loneliness walking the moonscape of sand dunes as the bleak winter edifice of sunset crumbled on the horizon.

Intrigues. "Armored in her bronzed inhibitions, Miss Westwood protects her virginity from those strolling pedestrians called actors, besides, I understand she is not the prize Johnny Esquire is aiming for." Jason Palmer spoke but his eyes followed the soft chalk outline of the flower child, her curvaceous vocabulary obviously an embedded sketch in his existence, unfinished, her eroticism strangely oblique, perhaps like Miranda Westwood's. "I am aware of ... *intrigues* ... Have you received a letter from Fabian recently?" Bridget Lovegrove's voice left a tingling touch vibrating space which chiseled away at his bravado with her. A sunburst across Eden, her hair suggested sugared candy-floss on the lips, and as she regarded the incandescence of his white cockatoo, whose tongue was visible inside the shell of armored beak, Palmer realized something of her own art in releasing bound souls frozen in immobility. "Miss Westwood vanishes upon inward journeys, Bridget, where she can be independent of wealth and birth, where she is free of predestinate romances dreamed by her family."

Lost And Found. What did waitresses masquerade? Columbines to the Michelin-cuisine of their creators, fanciful starched up in a star-like purity, the waitresses moved among the exclusive clientele like actresses whose movements were precisely blocked on-stage. Jason Palmer soon recognized the prim iconography of Miranda Westwood's face, her posture disciplined as if for atonement, her voice explaining the menu's culinary heritage, her hairstyle severe in a no-nonsense bun, everything about her person molded to a classical etiquette. A little erotically entangled in the murmur of her voice audible at an adjacent table, Palmer mentally printed off copies of herself from his original remembrance of her and marveled at her transformation, this fresh image emerging from the palimpsest of space she occupied. Afternoon shadows enveloping the schooner moored at the marina cast deep-toned reflective patterns across the water. Walking along the quay, Miranda acknowledged the Chevrolet with a glance, her torso a sudden conductor of electricity bringing sunlight through a cleavage in the clouds, then Palmer heard and saw a helicopter swooping in low from the ocean through the mouth of the marina entrance.

Existence As A Roll Of Dice. The dazzling white cockatoo playfully pecked at Bridget Lovegrove's fingertips. Here was a woman capable of reversing the shattered mirror of the Milky Way so Lucifer could visualize himself again in that brightness he was graced with before the Fall. "The bell has rung, I see, and school is over." Referencing the flower child, Bridget teased him affably enough, adding: "She's hardly a spotless lotus anchored in mud, or is your mission to cleanse her petals?" Arriving well before curtain-time, mingling but not socializing with the pre-crowd audience, they glimpsed Paulette Taylor fluent as usual on her pendulous spider's web, and Eddie Phoenix slightly behind her like a stagnant wing feather, their sexual torsion flattened to a Euclidean frame. "Can we eat a poem?" Cornell Bedford-Brown asked, referring to the **MALLARMÉ** insertion in **WHAAM!**, an immense stuffed kapok dice with images of the actors on its faces, rolled across the stage. Under street lights the flaming crest of Bridget's red-gold tresses feathered in the breeze.

Aquilina Kingsley's Zen-Koan. Seated on the bonnet of the red Chrysler, Aquilina Kingsley observed him struggling in the opaque *frottage* of whitewater, a romantic castaway with his talk of quantum-fields, the milk-shakes of sub-atomic matter, while further offshore Simon Freeman flawlessly performed manoeuvres on a towering wave. Skipping down to the foreshore with a large towel she gently rubbed Freeman's dripping hair, his ears, nose and lips iced over with cold, and while warming him up in the Chrysler with kisses, said: "On the beach in summer you must be a candidate for a flirtation with every pretty girl. And from your surfing style I can see you would have the resilience of air to a wing!" Listening to him later swapping stories of their evangelical boyhood with Alexander Chamberlain, she told Laura Devonshire: "Sometimes the blade of a plane runs over wood and hits a knot. I'm so thankful Simon and I have left it in our lives as a thing of beauty in its own way, something for our memories to pass across knowing the rest of the beam is lovely and smooth."

Mythological Moments. A helicopter stained the sun's sinking sphere and light bled around the curved surface of a stone's Zen inertia held in the palm of Jason Palmer's hand. Wrapped in a negligée of dreams, an allure of tranquil flight, centrifuging to another firmament, the flower child left him isolated in the loneliness of the Universal. From somewhere drifted a faint sound, the pop song, *Sweet Caroline*, someone's romantic longing freed of metaphysical complexity. Dawn's roseate terrestrial glow captured Palmer paddling his Malibu into the surf, the ocean's transferences of incalculable energy epitomized in the zenith of a wave's curve, the virginal flow of water as cold as ice caressing his torso. Checking out the airport he too awaited the arrival of Lt. John Kirby, surfed to exhaustion, the flower child excitable beside him, trying to evade the stalking presence of Eddie Phoenix and Paulette Taylor, Prometheus and another Pandora, the tension in their mobility contrasting the soldier's lowest ebb of endurance.

Hippie-Speak. "A man engaged in coitus is a little like a crawling caterpillar, you pray will metamorphose into a butterfly." Overheard decorating her conversation with the hippies, Paulette Taylor easily drowned their voices, while collapsed on the sofa, Lt. John Kirby scanned the column-inches of a newspaper, switched-off having heard the flower child had abandoned **KRISHNA inc.** and was beachcombing with Jason Palmer. Disrespectful of the uniformed Lieutenant, the hippies were his architectural antithesis in their loose-fitting kaftans and *Sgt. Pepper* paraphernalia and the sound of Paulette's high heels symbolized for them the parade ground, long abandoned by them. Conversation moved through mellifluous windings and when the trio left Fleur to search elsewhere for the flower child, the hippies were unanimous in their aversion to Paulette: "Man, she sucks her aura after her like a metaphysical balloon filled with corporate-speak!"

On The Threshold Of A Dream. Slanting fragments of imagery were grafted onto the parallelogram of Jason Palmer's shooting-script but could the camera-frame compose them with intelligible meaning for a movie audience? (i) Above the ballroom of the ocean, the shimmering and shaking chandelier of the night sky flashed as a memorial to the fallen Archangel's crash through three-dimensional space. (ii) The Moon, imprinted with Man's pleated foot, burgeoned like the pearl of Lucifer in the oyster shell of Paradise Lost. (iii) Miranda Westwood's Poussin transformation in her classical masquerade as a Michelin-waitress, sweetly composed as a vanilla *soufflé*, her lips liquid with pomegranate dressing, a culinary wound seeping through her psyche. (iv) Eddie Phoenix *en flagrante* with Paulette Taylor, his torso's coital rotation a flask intermingling Lucifer's chemistry, the lash of her fingernails biting his flesh *Opus Dei* style, their sexual arrhythmia overflowing with late-antiquity's end-of-the-world desperation. (v) The edible vegetable cheesecloth garments favored by the flower child hanging from a shower rail to drip-dry, and their layering across her pubis' grove of sandalwood and myrrh. (vi) Hands rolling dice, the meaningless probability of numbers revivifying the tension between inertia and aspiration. (vii) The frieze of an incandescent white cockatoo, sulphur-crested, in the domestic Masque of the Oceanside apartment, a stilled moment with Bridget Lovegrove evocative of a Pompeian cartoon.

A Model For Everyman's Pietà. Immense acrylic lips composed of Benday dots and spread across billboards kissed the sky. Horizontal space-time slices layered as the

HOUSE OF KRISHNA inc. modeled a stairway erected from the floor of Paradise Lost looking for the empyrean realm. Mandalas arrayed in sand blasted by the winter storm evoked humanity's *second death*, the dissolution of form to sub-atomic milkshakes of matter consigned to the flask of the bottomless pit, where the Nobel laureate, Lucifer, is the master chemist. Footprints in the sandbox on the thirteenth floor of **KRISHNA inc.**, the pavement outside the skyscraper's revolving doors, Armstrong's pleated impression on the Moon, the walking sequence visible across the dunes, would be all that remained of the human experience on the palimpsest of three-dimensional space-time if there was no spiritual levitation from the blank verse of *Paradise Lost*! Acrylic kisses liquefied by Angels as air and water impressed the faces of humanity collapsed in their etheric arms in a *pietà*!

IX
GOOD MORNING ... DARLING!

Shipwrecked With Delacroix's Orientalism. What quintessence of romantic grace could be drawn out of the satiety of red chalk trespassing the cream sheets of Celeste Hawthorne's sketch-pads? Erotic tendernesses caressed the page, Celeste's imagination aerated by imitation of Delacroix in his *Odalisque* mood, although Cornell Bedford-Brown *à la Sultan* disrobed was an illusionism rendering him uncomfortable. Like smoke from a furnace the *noir-and-rouge* chalks arabesqued across the page with a sensuous flow reminiscent of her love-making, and she would add the intertwining radiances of her water-colors later, melting the lines into contours of flame. Further symbiosis of their eroticism flowed through her voice speaking favorite Spanish poetry, how she would style her, *Good Morning ... Darling!* while physically studying him with her eyes over coffee-and-croissant.

> Cada beso que doy, como un zarpazo
> en el vacío, es carne olfateada
> de Dios, hambre de Dios, sed abrasada
> en la trenzada hoguera de un abrazo,
>
> Me pego a ti, me tiendo en tu regazo
> como un náufrago atroz que gime y nada,
> trago trozos de mar y agua rosada:
> senos las olas son, suave el bandazo.

Her voice hovered amid the aromatic fumes of coffee, her torch-singer glances sexually curved like a croissant, they exchanged wound-for-wound there in the studio-loft while his burning nakedness enflamed the pages of her sketch-pad in red chalk.

How To Salute The Australian Flag. A collage's inserts, skeletal tracings with the two-dimensional inertia of paper cut-outs, the very cosmetic artificiality of erotic art,

Eddie Phoenix and Paulette Taylor were sexually glued to the bed sheet. Paulette's drum-skin tautness of flesh stretched across her abdomen crawled like a caterpillar under Phoenix's perspiring solar plexus, the baroque gasps of this, her *Good Morning ... Darling!* orgasm a convulsive Desdemona-effect. How quickly though, brushing her hair, Paulette's mirrored eyes froze to ice as if trapped within the cool glass. She was Margarete's potently realized after-image actually seduced by Faust! Reeling in drunkenness with his victory, Phoenix ascended to the thirteenth floor of **KRISHNA inc.** King of the sixties' idiot Messiahs and stepping across to the sand-box containing the mandala-flag, placed the sole of his bare foot beside the flower child's imprint there. The fingerprint of Paulette's pubis lay burned in his consciousness.

Love's Religious Conversion. "How can on-stage sex, simulated as is it must be, arouse anyone when every evening Eros and Psyche are queued to a schedule by the writer's Acts in the drama?" Whispering where on-stage she projected her passion, Aquilina Kingsley's iridescently placed humor, well before her anticipation of ecstasy's singularity, relaxed the sexual tension between Simon Freeman and herself. "Good Morning ... Darling!" The *élan* of Aquilina's romantic cadences, her pancake breasts aroused in feeling his own heartbeat, her air of acquiescence to his own brand of provocative and free-wheeling counter-culture exhibitionism, revived his sense of there being a metaphysical salvation after all in falling in love. Her creation of verbal tableaux, perhaps stage practices garnered from **WHAAM!**, embedded him deeply but richly in an orgy of feeling, and the authenticity she exuded before, during and after coitus caught his imagination in an inflated idolatry. "Simon, Jason Palmer has sensed this spiritual force, for that is what he would call it, with which you have penetrated the flame in my heart, and where you stand martyred, burning for righteousness!"

Taoism Brushed On Space's Parchment. Serenity characterized the flower child's sexual lapses, the squaring of hearts together in three-dimensional spacetime, for she sat on the bed cross-legged, Eastern-style but modeling a pyramid, whereas Jason Palmer inwardly glimpsed himself as a stiffly upholstered Archangel. Spring's freshening on-shore breeze loosened her rainbowing sari into undulant wings of fabric as she half-leaned forward into the balcony railing and Palmer's loins brushed her *derriere*. Serenely flighted in acrylic white feathers, sea gulls hovered, buoyed on the air currents above the spacious amplitude of the emerald ocean, the translucent shell-of-pearl foreshore, the milky lips of the waves evocative of her *derriere* as the irresistibly merged. Rarely painting space with her voice, the flower child conveyed her *Good Morning ... Darling!* by tilting herself toward his sexual geometries, his monologues overlaid with symbolism. "Among those poetic embroiderers of the sea who have not surfed, not sculpted statues from the fabric of the wave, not stood before *The Sunne Rising*, transformed themselves into swooping angelic imagery in the ocean's gymnasium, who would you follow on such a spiritual pilgrimage as this we are embarked upon?" He taught her to probe an orgasm's Taoist void, be a seer of its calligraphy soaking learning through mind and heart, gently curve herself like a blossom-laden bough over the stream of running life while his hand sensually cupped her breast through the fabric of cheesecloth.

Adam's *Roustabout* Cruising Into The Sunset. *Primo tenore*, Johnny Esquire, forever wandering about in the singing of early-sixties Elvis, songs like *I Feel That I've Known You Forever*, imagined Paulette Taylor disguised in the melodies as Eurydice to his Orpheus. Untroubled by the emotional dilemma of alienation posed within the pop song, Paulette sexually isolated him from his Elvis apparition long enough to smooth his misogyny in coitus, transfer his vocal mannerisms to his loins and chain himself to memories shared together through the aeons. In Vegas' Eden of russet West, where Adam and Eve abandoned lucidity, where their souls' palimpsest of incarnations began, where Eternity stood statuesque with God, two desert roses were grafted in sin tingeing the skyline a potent tangerine. Surprised by such feminine mobility, Johnny Esquire's *Good Morning ... Darling!*, just caught the erosive flow of Paulette's hip-swinging derriere setting the hotel foyer ablaze with erotic vibrations. Following in her slipstream, Elvis' *Roustabout* incarnation, pulled after her like a puppet on a string, he intuited now the debate between Faith versus Revelation, and then climbed after her into the chariot of his soul parked for him by a car hop.

Was Petrarch's *Laura* A Violinist? Consummate kisses irradiated with dramatic suddenness as Laura Devonshire's reticence vaporized and the space of her University dormitory inbreathed to embrace her and Alexander Chamberlain. How he had dreamed, Eros winning Psyche on-stage every matinee and evening performance, of inventing some romantic narrative, unfolding it line-by-line, kiss-by-kiss, starring Laura and himself, always diminishing the vividness of consummation in deference to the nuances of embrace-and-caress. Searching for theological synonyms, illustrations of affinities for the opening of her eyes to him, he practiced fulfillment nightly with Aquilina Kingsley where they martyred themselves in nakedness. Now, like a rose burning up space, Laura disoriented him with an explosive onrush of kisses, and the width of her finger-spread spanning her violin's fret-board transferred its sensuous vibrato to his torso. The evangelical blaze of his boyhood revived with falling-in-love, and the erotic compression of Virgin-and-Bridegroom oozed with a delicious spiritual nectar, and in a fleeting moment he was thankful for Jason Palmer weaving their strands together. Paradigm of a virgin, Laura's supple velvet arabesque as her liquefied clothes flowed away from her contours so transcended Aquilina's easy nudity, he understood **WHAAM!**'s marketing strategy was doomed to failure. Ivory-throated with her violin nestling there, her bowing arm swooning under the weight of music, Laura welcomed him the following sunrise with, *Good Morning ... Darling!*, as if delirious with immortality. Petrarch's *Laura*, effusive in her incarnations in *Sonnets*, immersed him in the kissing of a hundred-petalled rose, as they intermingled and swayed like flower and breeze embracing.

Castaways. Raising the lid of her treasure-chest of Spring dreams, Bridget Lovegrove gazed skyward at the infinite shattered pieces of their china flying forth as the Milky Way, her sexual jewel squandered on Calvin Westwood, inexhaustibly luminous, yes, but a moment unreachable now. And she had been drinking the poisoned ink of Fabian Roxburgh's letters, only to be revived every Spring morning by the blowing of almond blossom, with the promise of almond-green to come, but for her? Chivalry aureoled Jason Palmer's attentions, his obvious affection anchored in a serenity of faith that Fabian's black-beamed rays of writing were exaltations of love for her, but then his own vocabulary of divinity evoked such a spectrum of variations on the theme could she believe him? Like Christopher Featherstone, he too was shipwrecked on a reef of neo-Platonic symbolism, a castaway wandering the shores of the world's lagoon, another Robinson Crusoe, perhaps doomed to perish in the quest for the archetypal spiritual moment floating across the pages of the screenplay she had been able to glimpse. Who would ever say to her, *Good Morning ... Darling!*, revive the heavenly fire of love barely smoldering in her heart?

How A Woman Self-Pleasures Herself. Casting herself in the mold of the perfect Michelin-waitress, Miranda Westwood precisely ironed her uniform, turning the pages of a cookery book, abandoned now to privacy where she shielded her romantic precocity from Johnny Esquire's indifference. Thankful for Jason Palmer's decorum, sensing his own Muse too was Solitude, she abbreviated her sexual grammar to the caress of I, although the glove of a masculine voice worn to caress her in-the-mood, and to awaken her with, *Good Morning ... Darling!*, did bring her faltering along the groove to fulfillment. Dylan's *Lay Lady Lay* on the radio atmospherically harmonized with her desires, voluptuously soulful in intensity, then the moment passed and the man who could sing her portrait from the frame, Johnny Esquire, cool as Apollo on a pedestal, sculpted marble, luxuriated in her thoughts.

Commotion. Bursting free of the barricades, charging the US Consulate with banners modeled on the classical Roman armies, harangued by the Gang of Four, the mourners exhibited a wave of grief for the now-celebrated and revered revolutionary felled by Time, Ho Chi Minh. Violence, cold in its immaculate self-righteousness, legitimized by the excursion by US Forces in 'Nam, turned the hearts of youth to stone, except they now wept for the deceased Ho, idol of revolutionaries, expeller of Imperialist running-dogs, face on all the placards, name on all the banners. Stephen Maxwell initiated the rhythmic incantation of the name, Ho-Chi-Minh!, while effigies of Lt. William Calley were burned in the street, outrage building with the formal charges laid against him over the My Lai massacre. Wailing choruses of Lennon's *Give Peace A Chance* eased the conscience of youth, the song was taken up as Ho's epitaph, and Stephen Maxwell forged monologues for the gathering students, a veritable Coriolanus in his speeches on the cringing embarrassment of the *Silent Majority* over the My Lai revelations. Ho's death changed nothing on the revolutionary agenda, he was succeeded in transition by a committee pledged to continue the liberation of South Vietnam with ruthless efficiency, while the youth of the Western Democracies linked arms, swayed and sang, *Give Peace A Chance.*

Swing Down, Sweet Chariot. Days of Spring surf, sweetened by the song all over the radio, *Sugar Sugar*, leavened resonances of serene pleasure as Simon Freeman's face emerged from the marble block of a wave's frothy crest and shook free the crystalline water droplets. Working beside Jason Palmer on the theocentric dragster, its motor's Jovian thunder, chariot of the God of Speed, he experienced again the pulsations of drama which had plunged him into Purgatory, but now the choreography of days was focused on the dance along a quarter-mile ballroom. In the workshop Palmer's classic Chevrolet was raised on blocks with its chariot wheels removed. Together they measured the *narrow way* of the race-track, straight, designed for speed's penetration of the space-time continuum, while above the infinite circumference of the sky's immense bubble burst with sparkling star-light. "Think of this flowing strip as the Jordan sluiced across Paradise Lost, centrifuging again on the Centre. Our centripetal pilgrimage, full of bravado, rooted in temptations to rebel across a spectrum of ideologies, has actually numbed our spiritual dexterity, but we will become our Age's Ezekiels!" Devotionally white, chastely dramatized on wave-entablatures, radioactive isotopes ignited by the sun, they surfed through the early days of Spring.

Fall And Redemption. Half-running, high heels catching in cracks in the pavement, Bridget Lovegrove imagined she glimpsed Fabian Roxburgh vanishing among a crowd of student protesters causing a disturbance on the city sidewalk. Long-haired, mustachioed, wielding a banner-on-a-pole like a broadsword, the leader carved a pathway through the elephant grass of pedestrians and Bridget was flung against a storefront window. She recognized Miranda Westwood bending low, squatting, hands raising her stately arabesque from the grid of the pavement, and guiding her inside the department store. "Did you see Fabian?" Miranda's ear caught the rhythm of her breathing his name, then the store window glass shattered and splinters became embedded in their hair and clothes. Disinterestedly spinning the accounting journals on Bridget's oak wood desk, Miranda surveyed the office space through the open door, exhausted from the overflowing restaurant at lunch time and argumentative exchange of words with Stephen Maxwell. Bridget's ragged woodcut illustration came back from the washroom, unfamiliar without her attitudinal elegance, and brooded like a wine-stained rose seated at her desk, although her fabulously designed face soon relaxed its thoughtfulness. "Miranda, Fabian doesn't speak like the rest of the world, have you noticed?" Voices mysteriously dissolved in the air, words vanished, imperfectly recalled by memory, and for some reason Bridget thought of the words of Jesus from the Cross as recorded by history, whether what He actually spoke would ever be redeemed.

What Do The Billboards Say? Like a comet proceeding tail first, the sleek *Ann-Margret* fork extensions of the Harley Davidson accelerated out of the cavernous underpass, wheeled onto a cloverleaf and merged with the flowing traffic. Themes codified in the billboards lining the freeway were: (i) **MUSICAL** – *I'll Never Fall In Love Again*. Heroes-and-Heroines of advertising campaigns visualized in imagery comparable with expensive Pop Art works, cosmetic products, clothes, shoes, hairstyles whose consumption would transfigure the most mundane man-or-woman into a demi-god or demi-goddess. (ii) **LITERARY** – *Romeo and Juliet*. Twiggy-as-Juliet, underage nymphet speaking poetry, purifying the romance of fashion of middle-class, middle-aged *mores*, the Ideal pleasure being the wearing of clothes. (iii) **CINEMA** – *The Party*. Half-twist and squeeze the lemon of two cultures into the martini of Western Civilization and meditation evolved into riotous comedy, the black-and-white world of *La Dolce Vita* is colored in rainbows of lightness-of-being. Swinging free of the motorbike outside The Playhouse, Johnny Esquire varnished in leather *à la Elvis* from *Roustabout*, re-combing his quiff of slicked-back hair, saw **WHAAM!**'s lights dimming on the marquee.

Theme For A Dream. Jolted by the explosive, sustained revving of the dragster shuddering through the workshop, Aquilina Kingsley gasped for breath. "Isn't this machine dangerous? Who are you going to attack with such force under your fingertips?" Dressed in his *Viva Las Vegas* overalls, Jason Palmer answered her with bold, level-voiced insouciance: "On the labyrinth of the drag-strip I intend to melt-down the fallen Archangel, bring him back to the periphery of two-dimensional space, the Euclidean grid from which he has escaped." Kissing the fresh almonds of her eyes, Simon Freeman invited her to climb into the dragster's sculpture, anti-art she called it, and grasp the wheel. "Aquilina, as Jason says, our voyage through the sixties attains its terminus this summer out on the dragstrip where we combat Eddie Phoenix." Side-by-side in the hairdressing salon with Laura Devonshire reading magazines and gossiping, tresses tousled with length, asymmetric minimalism now *démodé*, Aquilina gave her friend the teleological stare. "Did Jason Palmer walk you into his Zen garden?" Laura studied the glossy Rubensian lipsticks lifting from the mouthes of the models, out of the pool of the page, while the hairdresser's fingertips played with her tresses, pondering how to re-sculpt them. "He spoke of the fallen Archangel as freeing himself from the heart of a stone, as if I could grasp the meaning in such obscurity. Then he covered my hands and wrapped them around the glowing mane of a crimson rose, burgeoning with softness and fragrance, and I began to understand degrees of liberation. The density of the stone wielded carelessly could crush to delicacy of the rose." Lit nitro flaming from the dragster burned before Aquilina's eyes.

Letter XIX. Fabian Roxburgh to Bridget Lovegrove. *Playing Green River continuously, the Grunts are dreaming only of the bayou, the journey home as Cross-Tie Walkers, hungry for the feeling of Grace. A new dynasty begins to encompass the battleground of 'Nam, and the NVA has penetrated the Mekong delta in numbers for the first time, experts in the art of tunneling, so what if the US controls air-space. Out in the boondocks I was sliced up by elephant grass, zig-zagging through the shoulder-high stuff, but the scabs are falling off as the skin heals.*

Are you still holding one end of the golden cord for me, as I'm lost in this labyrinth, everything I file is spiked, but I keep a copy for my memoirs. The Grunts aren't listening to THE BAND, although I think Across The Great Divide is a perfect leaving-on-patrol sing-along number to buoy the spirits, overflowing with poignant ironies, and should baffle Charlie if he's listening. Suddenly though your name isolates a rare brilliance in my life here, and I remember your head surfacing through a wave at the beach, aureoled with smiling sunlight.

Letter XX. Fabian Roxburgh to Jason Palmer. *I'll Be Home For Christmas. You write to me again of Eddie Phoenix and the Gang of Four and their collusion in a piece of Street Theater representing the G.I. as a Chocolate Cream Soldier, and I understand there is publicity of rebellious Grunts refusing to go on patrol. Perhaps the suburbs of Vietnamese Saigon reflect the pessimism in black Harlem, and the media draws parallels between oppressed peoples, but one glimpse of Manhattan, a stroll down Fifth Avenue, tells me neither Communist Saigon nor black Harlem can be the future of the world. Now the first consignment of troops has returned Stateside (30,000) VC and NVA infiltration will escalate, for they already carry the momentum sweeping down from Hanoi, a trail of ants, unstoppable until they nest in Saigon. Where will I be on that day? Thank you for your words and photographs of Miranda, Fleur and her sister, and rescuing Christopher's collection of Beethoven String Quartets for me. Of all decades to be young in ... the sixties!*

Portrait Of The Archangel (IX). Standing before a large rectangular mirror with the flower child, studying their artificially created reflections, Jason Palmer spoke to her of the fallen Archangel and how he had genetically polished up Darwinian man to his current Western incarnation. Mirrored in clear glass with the precision of a photographic image, radiantly polished, pondering the strangeness of their duplication, its esoteric meaning and purpose, Palmer asked: "What is space-time's true three-dimensional geometry?" Dipping a finger in her tub of yoghurt, the flower child wrote on the glass: J^3. Were her eyes especially permeable to the mysteries of space-time? (i) **PHYSICS** – Pursuing relativistic visions, lured deep into microcosmic realms by the photons of Benday dots splashing across the screens of his billboards, Palmer considered motion, his movements from the Oceanside apartment (here), to the sand dunes (here), to The Playhouse (here), all accomplished in *time*, yet the miracle seemed to be he still retained his identity within each of those spaces. Parked in his Chevrolet at the drive in watching the massive screen framed by the windshield he recognized here was an inertial space of two-dimensions. Projected images flowed across the screen and he was haunted by the revelation of the fallen Archangel imprisoned as that space while Man's incarnations came-and-went in scenes, but did Lucifer actually change, wasn't his inertia eternal? (ii) **CHEMISTRY** – Electron-clouds of Benday dots metamorphosed in L^2 (Luciferan two-dimensional space), it was always zero-time for the fallen Archangel, while Man was psychologically immersed in the illusion of unfolding happenings, simultaneous with each other, occurring on various spatial segments of the screen, as identified by the sweeping eye. Within the J^3 space of the Chevrolet the flower child passively allowed Palmer to remodel in his thoughts the anti-Nirvana of her chemistry, where the cosmic joke of Existentialism assumed a more telling focus, for they were simply colored images sliding across the movie screen of the fallen Archangel's blank consciousness, vanishings! (iii) **BIOLOGY** – What did the movie screen tell Palmer of the drowning of the human persona in space-time? What was the relationship between his spatial displacements from incarnation-to-incarnation and *time* differences? Wasn't there an individually special J^3 (Jasonian three-dimensional space) screen for each of his moments in being-and-existence in *time*? Now the mystery inherent in the evolution of cinema became apparent to the revelation of Man's relationship to the fallen Archangel! (iv) **PSYCHOLOGY** – Decoupling, not in a Freudian sense, which was but immersion in imagery fluidly projected by consciousness onto the inertial L^2 screen, a mere entertaining Broadway show, a ballet by Dali, brought into sharper focus how space actually lost its Benday dots with the flicker of the projector of time, then re-formed, giving the appearance of continuity! (v) **ECOLOGY** – Of what fibers then are these Benday dots composed, how are their particular curvatures and torsions shaped into compositions of quantum-foam, who holds the projector? Lucifer's spectacular inertia, free-falling with angels according to the curvature of acceleration: $a = f/m$, illuminating the mind to gravitational force as they collectively hit three-dimensional space (L^3) and establishing for Eternity the paradigm of the *crash*!

Decoupling In Jasonian Space-Time. Puzzled, still drowsy, the flower child awoke and thought she heard Jason Palmer say: "Good Morning ... Darling!" Grids of intersecting screens were arranged across the floor of the apartment as she swept a sari around her waist and dragged the hem after her, the geometric alchemy of the structures perhaps related the lipstick markings he had drawn across her torso while she slept: Infinity-and-Eternity symbols in four dimensions. For hours he contemplated waves stroking the sand on the foreshore. Meeting up with Simon Freeman and Aquilina Kingsley in the red Chrysler he spoke of himself now as a charioteer of Einsteinian space, as another Phaëton imprinting plastic space, burning-up L^2 with the blaze of his passage through time!

Raking A Zen Garden. Jason Palmer held the Benday dot of his Zen stone in the palm of his hand as if it were the key in this quest to ID his singularity. Sunbeams projected onto the horizontal screen of the ocean, light sparkled, waves rippled, but what did the sea image to the Sun God, Helios, what did Phaëton's momentous plunge signify, his burying himself in two-dimensional space? He quietly raked a Zen garden from the beach sand, created a dialogue of wave-fronts, asking the question: "What is the center of *no-thing*? What, how does it *hold*?" Sidling up to Paulette Taylor at a cocktail party, her decadence adorning the mirrored slices of space displaced by the *time* differences in her movements within the room cubed, he drew from her the flexure of a question: "What is the end then of the scientific, Darwinian, **ME**?" Émigré from the Court of the fallen Archangel, Eddie Phoenix, already in early Spring scarlet with sunburn, introduced himself into the frame of the conversation, bas relief sculptures against the screen of a blank wall, so many Benday dots raked into human symmetries. A literal but shallow emblem, broadening the panorama of Palmer's incarnation among them, Phoenix explained: "This Phaëton would lasso the Earth and drag the planet across the rubbery fabric of space closer to the solar brightness of Helios."

March Against Death. Gatherings of anti-war protesters assembled across the grid of the city oblivious to the geodesic history of a sub-atomic particle within the galaxy. An irreversible fusion of forces coalesced to resurrect those famous scenes evoked by John Milton in *Book One* of *Paradise Lost*. Banners ironically splashed the slogan, **MARCH AGAINST DEATH**, across the intersecting planes of the cityscape. Shoulder-to-shoulder a phalanx of marching protesters led by the Gang of Four formed-dissolved-formed rebellious characterizations on the screen in 3D for the filming television cameras. Only the thump-thump heartbeat of a helicopter flying low could swallow the soundtrack of the chanting protesters.

All Youth Are On Fire. Bonfires of burning draft cards celebrated the President's announcement of the cancellation of November and December's call-up, then was over-shadowed by the commencement of the trial of the Chicago 8, more elastic stresses distorting the imagery on space's L^3 screen. Santana's album assaulted Jason Palmer as he mingled with the hippies iced-over in kaftans, rendering the earlier Baroque period of the sixties more Rococo, vividly ensouled in the dancing of the flower children, no longer Bernini-twisting the night away. The album covers of **ELVIS IS BACK** and **THE BAND** were framed on the wall side-by-side as metaphors signifying the unparalleled transformation of youth through the sixties, and especially for Lt. John Kirby disillusioned with his *GI Blues* tour of 'Nam, Palmer ensured *Whispering Pines* was played for him to slow-dance with the flower child. When the talk nuanced the *policy* of the Progress of Vietnamization following demonstrations-in-sympathy with the injustice of the Chicago 8 trial, and newsreel footage of the National Guard's interactions with the protesters screened on television, the hippies rejected Palmer's latest peace-offering, Grand Funk Railroad's *On Time* album, sensing in the choice some mordant comment on their lifestyle.

The Night They Drove Old Dixie Down. Boxes of candles and black armbands, cards printed with prayers, rolls of toilet paper bearing the surly portrait of President Nixon, formed a pyramid in Fleur's apartment, while couriers spread across the city delivering the emblems to tens of thousands of youth being galvanized for Moratorium Day. Jason Palmer's suffocation of the mood with **THE BAND's** anthem, *The Night They Drove Old Dixie Down*, had him banished from the apartment, and when he interviewed noteworthy Christian groups for appearances in his movie, teasing them by playing *Rag Mama Rag*, he despaired the human orgy of Benday dots populating the successive screens of space would never achieve satiation. Immolated in inertia (L^3 screens), the fallen Archangel allowed the myriad Benday dots assemble on the battleground, fluidly interact, interchange, create the *frottage* of quantum-foam and expend unimaginable energies through slices of time, for his patience now was Infinite!

Scene In Scarlet And Black. "Well, beauty is fashionable in black trimmed with scarlet!" Paulette Taylor's mannequin with penciled-in eyebrows swiveled on high heels, dramatizing herself in fabrics with vivid immediacy for the photographers on the arm of an equally dashing Johnny Esquire. Movie theater audiences spilled onto the sidewalk as Paulette's salamander passion, her clothes fabric bleeding with dozens of crimson roses, swung across the pillion of the Harley Davidson, carrying herself with the pietistic sweep of a Cardinaless from *La Dolce Vita*. Patrons drifted away from restaurants, entertained by the spectacle, wondering who the celebrities might be, then a red Chrysler cruised alongside the curb, rolling up to Miranda Westwood. Behind her thinking's ellipsis lay the shape of a puzzle yielded up for Aquilina Kingsley to solve, then the wistful young heiress walked on, her motion's malleable softness returning as the tail-light of the Harley Davidson disappeared.

Chimera In Red Chalk. All fluid tenderness, the tip of red chalk moved in a radiantly clean arabesque across the pale sheet of paper, Celeste Hawthorne's fingers bringing the mask of his face to life, her calligraphic form of romancing imbued with trans-sexual sensations difficult to understand. He had seen a dewdrop poised on a rose petal, both fragile with mortality, and then she had shown him her incredible Technicolor web of a copy of Delacroix's *Abduction of Rebecca*, vibrating the stillness of Nature's contemplative Art. But what would be the existential residua of these sublime moments now the embrace of their time together was loosening?

> Dormir, vivir, morir. Lenta la seda cruje diminuta,
> finísima, soñada: real. Quien es ses signo:
> una imagen de quien pensó, y ahí queda.
> Trama donde el vivir se urdió despacio, y hebra a hebra
> quedó, para el aliento en que aún se agita.
> Ignorar es vivir. Saber, morirlo.

Threads of red chalk, shadows of texture rose from the weft of the page, cast of a face in a two-dimensional sliver of marble, but it would be forever silenced, unkissable!

Memorable Moments As The Sixties Fade. Brushing her freshly shampooed Godiva-tresses, and binding them hippie-style, the flower child ambled across the floor of the apartment, her gaze transiently remote, perhaps longing to slip down the mud slides seen on the newsreel footage from the Woodstock festival. Did her vision filling the mirror possess aroma, self-illumination, sensation? Bi-lateral, divided in half, straight-line Zen asymmetry, no more aware of her true identity than the magnificent white cockatoo, she vacated the space of the mirror with her at times unbearable quietness. Embalmed, decorative of the time, freighted in her whimsy of cheesecloth fabric, she communicated in a language redolent with Miltonian amnesia, her blank verse silences stretching into the length of a book. Lying naked amid the cool waves of the bed sheets she possessed the transparency of the ocean caressing a lovely coral reef. Visiting the Christian broadcast station with him, lovely as Mary Magdalene in her epiphany, she breezed by Eddie Phoenix, the burnt-out coals of his eyes dropping to measure her sandaled foot. Breaking away from the Christian commentator briefing him on the program's structure, Jason Palmer sauntered over to her: "And here we were, with an expectation of Lucifer himself, instead we get this Phoenix!"

The Quest. "A Journey to the Center of the Earth is unimaginable, let alone A Journey to the Center of Paradise Lost!" Alexander Chamberlain erased the classic Ptolemaic motif of crystalline spheres red-raw with fire-and-brimstone and sought solace in the dynamism of Spring cloud-in-motion freshening up the azure sky. "You say it can be filmed, but is that reality?" Tough-mindedness lay tactilely exposed in these out-of-focus enthusiasms. His affectation as an Ovidian Eros now fast-fading, Chamberlain rendered visible his tendernesses toward Laura Devonshire now the oscillations between peace-and-disorder had smoothed out, although Jason Palmer's abstract vocabulary threatened to flood, its high-tide had already swept her away once before. Suddenly he materialized, as if with psychic spontaneity, bearing alchemical symbols in his aura, the evanescent flower child, his fanciful Zen-muse, impressionistically illumined beside him, talking of this Quest of A Journey to the Center of Paradise Lost!

Voyage Of Discovery. Running with a dog-on-a-leash, a pacing red setter, Bridget Lovegrove seemed to Jason Palmer strung-and-tuned for harmony, her rhythm classical, all lyrical shapeliness, perhaps a Proustian memoir in her flowing Auroran tresses, a new incarnation of Albertine! Later, Jason Palmer drove down to the marina where moored yachts slumbered under Spring skies, while others slipped free of the breakwater for the open sea, drawing from him reminiscences of the voyage of Vasco de Gama, from whose journeys the sails of three-dimensional space unfurled and filled for future generations. Now the journey through the sixties was climaxing, what would be his remembrance of this time, what observances would he memorialize? Strolling beside Bridget and her red setter, he paused and drew calligraphic Zen-lines in the sand, walked her amid the architectonic vault of billboards where realism-and-surrealism were counterpoised, whereupon she said: "Our navigation of life needs a fixèd star in unclouded skies to guide us. Am I looking for an Archangel, or a man?"

Romantic Sonatas. Cello-and-violin in the String Quartet briefly tuned for a performance of the Franck Piano Quintet, Laura Devonshire strongly-etched in an evening gown, her exaltation in the music celestial. Silhouetted against her fiancé backstage, all romantic discord between them resolved, Laura's acrylic lips melted Alexander Chamberlain's mouth with kisses, while Jason Palmer exited quietly with the flower child, her cheesecloth fabric under moonlight evoking her as a sizzling moth.

Walking her out onto the existential isthmus of sand dunes where his Zen garden had been mobilized to waves of raked earth he impressed her with his evocation of time-zero. Tremulous in her gauze of cheesecloth, her emblematic shroud juxtaposed with the foam lit by moonbeams lifting off the surf, she welcomed his unsullied romantic gentility if puzzled by his absorption in her space-painting as some Angel rescued from Paradise Lost.

X

WE ROSE UP SLOWLY

Cryptic Imagery From 1969. (i) Who were Angels of Ice, and who Angels of Fire dramatized in three-dimensional incarnation, threaded through the metaphysical tapestry of the year? (ii) A dragster's comet, all breathless velocity, trailing a flashing plume like Bridget Lovegrove's hair as she sprinted along the foreshore, fixed an image in Jason Palmer's mind; entranced him with possibilities on how to unwind the fallen Archangel's cosmic DNA. (iii) All over the radio-waves, *Something In The Air*, emotionally engaged Stephen Maxwell and the Gang of Four who saturated their thinking with Revolution, took the song as an anthem, an Oracle shaping what their future held. (iv) Eddie Phoenix pinned to **KRISHNA inc's.** gold mine, the compass of his spread arms inscribing a sphere widening to embrace Paradise Lost, the skyscraper's throne re-instituted the etiquette of Lucifer's hierarchy. (v) Nixon's television appearances climaxed with his fatuous pleading for National solidarity, confirmed by his overwhelming Gallup Poll victory, even as the World's political machinery began swinging more solidly behind the Communist insurgents.

The Mansion Of Three-Dimensional Space. Of what was the helicopter a symbolic distortion? Pulsating, rotor blades cleanly scything space, the helicopter leaned forward like an armored aerial spirit and sped across the sun-swept prairie of sand dunes. Jason Palmer's impassioned ideological debates on Lucifer's monumental artifice, his vision of the falling Archangel's trailing fabric, burning wings rushing into the Absolute Zero of three-dimensional space, was accompanied by footage of space capsule re-entries into the Earth's atmosphere. His authorship of the calligraphy inscribed across the sand dunes, and explanation of Lucifer's rippling wingspread embedded in the patterns, did not impress the Christian journalists and their Pauline strictures as evidence of the Archangel's re-awakening, they would not read the *signs*. Parked in a bay outside **KRISHNA inc.** where the doors of the Mansion were revolving free, Palmer leaned across the steering wheel, nauseous, sickened with love for the promise of *Paradise Regained*, the hand of the flower child touching him unable to assuage his disquiet. Lying in the Oceanside apartment as afternoon's shadows gathered from the two-dimensional squeeze of planar walls he spoke in a delirium of his metaphysic suffering across the millennia and his dream of crucifying Lucifer's physique with compass and T-square within such a space. How could the human persona so arrest the soul in a torso's DNA chemistry and sentence that fourth-dimensional presence to three-dimensional imprisonment?

University Wits. "Is this arabesque here Jason Palmer? Whose voice is this echo?" Unshaven, his delirium easing, Palmer addressed his mirror-image while the flower child lounged against the door-frame offering him her tub of fruit-flavored yoghurt. Wheels spinning off the kilometers the Chevrolet searched the freeways lined with billboards as tonal as Pop Art installations for co-ordinates to identify where Lucifer's shadowed soul might be imprisoned while the car radio pulsated with *Come Together/ Something* back-to-back. Then strolling through the University grounds, raising a military arm to Stephen Maxwell hurrying by, Palmer led the flower child over to the water-feature stretching along the façade of the library. "See how painterly the lotus frees itself to bloom." Smoky wave-foam embedded with tracings of dusk reminded him of Bridget Lovegrove's silhouetted coiffure as she agreed to sit behind the wheel of the excavated cream-colored *coupé* among the sand dunes. Earlier at the lotus pool in the grounds of the University he had tossed a pebble in its stilled water setting up agitated ripples centrifuging against the stone walls. They were all embarked upon such a pilgrimage of wave-motion through the mind of Lucifer!

Eve Transcendent. Picturesque in her red-haired chromaticism, Bridget Lovegrove modeled an apogee of beauty poised tip-toe in her dazzling short-skirted tunic, preparing to volley the tennis ball back across the net. Sipping iced lemonade by the sun-shade, an immobile vase, if nobly sculpted, Jason Palmer talked with Aquilina Kingsley, remembering her on-stage violations by Eros, her nudity ghosted in the minds of the audience, her famed publicity now simply a handbill pasted in someone's scrapbook. Bridget's muscular dexterity, an exuberant palette of torsions modeled on the pedestal of the two-dimensional tennis court, scripted pivotal moments synonymous with his thinking of what calligraphy to rake from his Zen garden. Evenings in *Drag City* unchained Bridget's being from the pedagogic fictions of her commercial world and she spoke of the nitro-buzz's poetry of pure speed as a linear sequence of thrilling orgasms. Soaked through with perspiration her tennis tunic erotically clung to her loins as she accepted a glass of iced lemonade from Palmer.

Tonight I'll Be Staying Here With You. Iconography for an erotic nocturne themed after Delacroix's *Odalisque Reclining on a Divan*, Cornell Bedford-Brown felt the electricity of Celeste Hawthorne's chalk crackling the paper, his naked torso forming there in a cloud of chalk-dust. Celeste's fingers re-sculpted contours of his pose as if he were a block of malleable marble, her voice's androgynous softness and ever-mobile lips swooning with Spanish poetry, as if *The Bullfighter Was A Lady*! Hers was an

Art lustered by lithographically expressed feeling bodied in her speaking voice as she sketched. Kissed, her pancaked breasts became aroused, she said he had Matisse's hand in the act of drawing out her orgasm as their pleasures intersected on the stretched canvas of her bed sheet, but they were only ever symmetrical with each other in coitus. How had he become so blindly absorbed in her realm of desire?

Led Zeppelin II. *Cosmic Blues* exploded the apartment walls, Police squad cars pulled up outside the apartment block, music's solar breeze rushed from the open windows onto the street, and the hippies welcomed the officers with three peace-loving words ... *Whole Lotta Love.* From the heroic chronology of the *G.I. Blues* Elvis '60 evolved a heavier flagship, Led Zeppelin '69, and the chimera of the Summer of Love, its daisy-chain of petals blown away by the cosmic force of *What Is And What Should Never Be*, the pieties of the Maharishi deluged in under the thunderous supernova of *Heartbreaker.* The rainbowing bubble of hippiedom burst asunder and all the leaves from the calendar of the sixties blew, swept into oblivion by *Led Zeppelin II*, where was Hendrix now, where was Clapton, for the canvas had been scraped and an explosive image surfaced through the palimpsest? For hours the flower child sat gazing at the album cover, spinning the record from dawn-to-dusk, dreaming of coitus with the *sound*, the thrillingly voiced lyrics, no longer paying any attention to Jason Palmer.

Facets Of The Fallen Archangel's Jewel. Johnny Esquire journeyed *From Memphis to Vegas: From Vegas to Memphis*, cruising by white-columned Graceland and the waved wingspread of the International Hotel, singing Roustabout *à la Elvis* working the clubs for the tourists hoping for a glimpse of the ascendant Star. Hair raked with Zen-thoughts he swung *Priscilla* on the pillion behind him as autograph hunters descended on the Harley Davidson and steered out onto the famous Strip as sunset fired up all the neon. Belting out Rockabilly memories as if his lungs held the entire world's air, spreading vanity's peacock tail like an ever-young Apollo himself, he engorged his throat with the militarism of G.I. Blues and crooned his way through a songbook of movie favorites. Las Vegas' neon jewel inset in an ocean of desert webbed with roadways, *Priscilla's* smudged mascara, her celebrated ziggurat of ebony hair Delacroixan-black, complemented the scenic setting, her Egyptian Cleopatra gilding Johnny Esquire's Caesar prophetic of some momentous happening on the threshold of the seventies.

A Meditation On Forgetfulness. Meditating on his battered skateboard, curving across an embankment of concrete, Simon Freeman rolled by the dazzling Chevrolet where Jason Palmer half-slumped against the radiator grill, *Suspicious Minds'* mythological coruscation issuing from the car radio. "Is forgetfulness a gift?" Running the skateboard away from the Chevrolet, Freeman swooped around the embankment practicing some surfing moves, his question welcomed by Palmer for it echoed a thought in his own Gospel, promised a world soon to be saturated in forgiveness for falling into space-time with Lucifer. Side-by-side at the drive in, the Chevrolet and red Chrysler modeled tandem sculptures on a tableau, romantic etiquette abandoned in pleasure's buoyancy, agony seized and transfigured in a kiss, and original joy bonded to memory. Laura Devonshire's gaze in the semi-darkness slipped by Alexander Chamberlain's halo of hair and she imagined she saw shadowed within the Chevrolet side-window frame, the flower girl's silhouette astride Jason Palmer. Suddenly, the question she had heard Freeman asking all week, deepened in resonance: "Is forgetfulness a gift?"

Elvis In The Gambler's Capitol. The desert surrounding Las Vegas presented an immense two-dimensional plane. Like baroque royalty, the famous pop star and his entourage swept through the entrance foyer into the International Hotel, full incarnation of the Platonic Idea of Beauty and Simplicity, and all space seemed to spiral around his Archangelic presence, Vegas' terrestrial plasma felt the disturbance of force to its core; Elvis would challenge Lucifer in his gambler's capitol! An evening November sky guttered disquietingly as the fallen Archangel's poisoned luminescence washed up the façades of the casinos and high rise hotels but the pop star had already experienced the geography of Eternity in this psychic war.

Extracts From A Broadcast Christian Dialogue. (i) Eddie Phoenix – "I am the lion's jaws holding the Lamb, my teeth sparkle and drip with the wisdom of Lucifer. (ii) Christian commentator – "This famous pop star is a lustful goat, a satanic fornicator." (iii) Johnny Esquire – "*Priscilla* naked is the most perfect of God's sculptures, she is Eve's eulogy, an Angel's spiritual narcissism." (iv) Jason Palmer – "Lucifer's wings are a collapsing peacock-tail, a spread of the colors of Pride, fanning only to brood on the pageant of the fall from Grace into spacetime."

Fleur's Peace Symbol. "Is a symbol intelligible to itself? That's your question, right, man?" Jangling the Peace symbol suspended on a chain, seated cross-legged beside the mounted engine-block sculpture, Joe Cocker's *Delta Lady* saturating air-space, the hippie drew breath to clarify, his comprehension tangential to Jason Palmer's. Eyes followed the crowned ornament of the flower child in her excited but unheard monologue with Fleur, while the hippie murmured, barely audible to Palmer: "*She Came In Through The Bathroom Window.*" Joe Cocker's raspy voice seemed a profound illustration of the hippie physique. Displayed on the wall of the apartment was a large colored poster of a nude couple in coitus circled by a bouquet of flowers, their sexual postures laid out in the Peace symbol.

The Buddha's Electronic Pattern. After visiting the University library to meditate on the goldfish pool, where the sight of a lotus, religiously disrobing, a shiver of nudity as the dress-petals unfolded, Jason Palmer returned to the Oceanside apartment where stood his Pop Art soft sculpture discarded for **WHAAM!**. The sculpture represented a stuffed kapok version of an equation: $4\pi GM$. To Simon Freeman he described the geometry of his ratiocinations on the strands of their incarnations webbed together in the three-dimensional space-time continuum. Later, surfing the sumptuous wave-fabrics together, creating lyrical sculptural impressions, dipping heads in the white-foam trimmings, raking the ocean with their Zen calligraphy they struck the young women on the foreshore as emanations, a flash of gamma rays. Aquilina Kingsley emerged from the chilly Spring snow-drift of whitewater to taste Freeman's salt-fleshed kisses while the flower child unfurled her Matador's cape of a sari and stood in her bikinis. Cleansed of her suffocating Indian oils by the ocean's chlorophyll pigments, the flower child sank into the blowing petals of whitewater, sublime deva of a liquid lotus, a botanical meditation freed by the thinking of the Buddha!

Bring On The Court Martial. Jefferson Airplane's *Volunteers* scorched paint from the walls of the hippie commune, a provocative commentary on the news bulletin footage where a montage of screen-time assembled the following: (i) Vice-President Agnew, piously abstract, initiated a controversial debate on the media's anti-American bias on the conduct of the war in 'Nam, not knowing how to starve the revolutionaries across the globe of their oxygen. (ii) Heavy US casualties in the volatile Archangelic space-time continuum of the DMZ, 22 dead on the occasion, building the tsunami of sorrow Stateside, all flowing from a poorly written film-script over-seen by the President. (iii) Gunpowder in the wind created a riot in Washington, tear gas canisters instead of the napalm exploding across the jungles of 'Nam: perhaps if a further 250,000 troops were shipped in ... (iv) My Lai survivors get their infamous fifteen-minutes of fame.

Bringing The Boys Home. *Laocoön* unlaced of his serpents, Fabian Roxburgh crossed the tarmac into the airport building, his identity's lineaments lost on the pages of reportage from 'Nam, his letters to his friends, although Jason Palmer's embrace lent the war some *trompe-l'œil* depth, established fresh linear connections with space's Western panorama again. "Still walking the broad Tao to Paradise Lost? Coming home from 'Nam I've booked out of *Heartbreak Hotel.* Are my fault-lines too visible, will Bridget's eyes freeze to ice when she sees me?" Showered and shaved, dining on Italian cuisine as a golden sunset lacquered the aquamarine ocean beyond the balcony, Roxburgh tested his mannerisms on Palmer, washed his psyche free of the spillage of blood he had witnessed, allowed shadows to embrace his understanding of the war, invoked his romantic self to come forward. A sunflower followed the golden sun, its geometry, its sphere of raying petals tilted like a true devotee, and Roxburgh absorbed the image into his consciousness.

Surfing As Romantic Meditation. Seeking the perfect choreographic romantic placement, Fabian Roxburgh gazed across the sparkling ocean, his mind's sky clear blue again, his torso revivifying with the flow of stanzas gracing a Byronic poem, and asked the question: "Is there one equation then measuring the distance between Heaven and Hell?" Honey-blonde young women in stylized semi-nakedness, mouthes torrid from a night of kissing, relaxed on Technicolor beach towels, and Roxburgh steadied himself with the thought Eternity could not be encompassed in a single lifetime. On a transistor radio could be heard the song of the moment, *Na Na Hey Hey (Kiss Him Goodbye),* but Jason Palmer's Malibu was already slapping the whitewater and with wingspread arms was paddling for the off-shore peak. Surfing brought a further restoration of symmetry, every parabola of descent across the wave-walls with the fluency of a sunbeam, releasing the effervescence of happiness, Zen-laughter Palmer called it. "Jason, before this epiphany subsides, and while you think about my question on the distance between Heaven and Hell, let me call on Bridget Lovegrove!"

O! For A Helmet Of Invisibility! A golden compass of sunlight mysteriously traced a *glissando* along the pathway leading to the front door of Bridget Lovegrove's home. Parked in the Chevrolet, Jason Palmer listened to the car radio, Joe Cocker's version of *Darling Be Home Soon*, while the flower child climbed into the front seat, steadying her tub of fruit-flavored yoghurt against spillage, and marveled how she personally raked space with Indian oils as loose-fitting as her cheesecloth-and-sari. Fabian Roxburgh's centrifugal emanation paused at the opaque screen of the front door and rang the bell, imagination's anthem for every Ulysses returning from an Odyssey, and then Bridget stood inside the frame as the Chevrolet eased away from the curb.

Redemption Inwoven With Visionary Images. The dove of Bridget Lovegrove's emotions was stained by a bleeding heart. Fabian Roxburgh felt he had burst free of the membrane of a curling wave. Penitence intoxicated him as affection crystallized in her emotions portraited before him, a web of crises inter-threaded the sight of each other after so many months, especially the death of Christopher Featherstone, pain still to be transformed into faith. A sunburst gradually impregnated every pore of the dark cloud between them. Still, the labyrinth of the passing year was impressed with silhouettes yet to step forward and speak, vibrations in the heart's emptiness needed to gain momentum, voices began to interblend, layering words together in a stanza of romantic poetry. Fabian reveled in the abstractions of thought and emotion, their ethereal elixir, for they alone could resurrect the lost time between Bridget and himself, and he remembered Jason Palmer's white cockatoo, its penchant for humor, even as Bridget's lovely dove bled with droplets from her heart for him!

An Evening Of Impressions. Visible from the restaurant was the upper lip-curve of a spanning bridge, Whistler-lights shimmering in the oily river, and Miranda Westwood's transfiguration at the table illuminating the menu. After a brisk walk by a massive billboard peeling with a *Final Show* banner across a Celeste Hawthorne **WHAAM!** backdrop, Jason Palmer escorted the flower child into the fast-rising restaurant, popular with Showbiz *Beau Monde*, the kitchen an applause-winning stage in itself. "Is it possible for an actress to walk the stage six-or-seven times a week and still bring fresh insights to the role?" Miranda's chopped mint eyes scintillated at the question, but her voice was a teaspoon of honey, Michelin-sweet as she guided them through the menu; had the yoghurt been washed from the flower child's fingertip? Palmer ordered the rotisseried duck, wittily comparing his own lacquered tan with the bird's, while Miranda's professional silhouette, immaculately beautiful amid an aura of aromatic cuisine, moved away. Later, slipping free of the sari, the flower child stood on the balcony of the Oceanside apartment, bewildered by Palmer's whims, feeling his teeth's imprint softly bite her shoulder.

Moi, Je Ne Saurais Vivre Que Nue. Bridget Lovegrove's thoughts coalesced to an imaginative oil painting of the Pietà. Emotional splinters from the Cross still lodged in her bleeding heart as midnight struck on her wall-clock. Fabian Roxburgh acquiesced to the visitation's symbolism for her, he felt the lance wound his abdomen, accepted the idea of her kiss brushing his cheek and stepped away from her home where the mold of the night-sky's black breast was perforated with trillions of stars. Naked, headily perfumed in Indian oils, the flower child answered the door and ushered him inside, where Jason Palmer knelt among pages of film-script and matching story-board representations of scenes, a moment enkindling a quizzical glance: "Pleasure is an Angel's wing raising flesh from the scourge of pain." Palmer's belated aphorism flawlessly performed, contrasted Roxburgh's traumatized psyche lashing his flesh. The flower child's statue, suave as late-nineteenth century French verse, idol-in-ivory, brushed the lyre of his thoughts with his singing remembrances of Bridget.

Visiting The Tomb Of The Nameless. Kneeling in the oasis of dune, Fabian Roxburgh touched the entombed, cream-colored *coupé*, his leveled arm symbolic of a Davidian gesture, or Poussin, until he heard the stronger thump of a helicopter approach. Sunset's paroxysm of energy veiled the helicopter, then its silhouette emerged from the splitting pomegranate of Hell, the atmosphere surrounding the sand dunes sweetened though with the perfumed oils lifting off the flower child's cheesecloth garments. Invited by Simon Freeman to the tourney of dragsters, Roxburgh asked after the midnight-blue street-rod, but all his thoughts were filled with the image of the cream-coloured *coupé's* arrogant quotation half-buried in a dune. Driving over her cousin, Bridget Lovegrove stepped away from her car and approached the assembly area, her beauty redolent of that golden haze surrounding the verse of Pierre Louÿs, although the metaphysical reverberations of twentieth-century drag racing did echo a projection propelled forward in time, from the chariot racing of the Ancient World. Dreaming in sleep, Helena Steele swung her limbs free of the cream-colored *coupé's* tomb, *Les Chansons de Bilitis* on her lips:

> "Ce n'est pas la mort qui m'a enlevée,
> mais les Nymphes des fontaines.
> Je repose ici sous une terre légère
> Avec la chevelure coupée de Xanthô.
> Qu'elle seule me pleure.
> Je ne dis pas mon nom."

A Question For The President? Could a circling compass disfigure the sphere it inscribed or would the circumference always run true? Einsteinian motion bending the plasma of space occupied Jason Palmer's thoughts even as the flower child joyfully twisted her Krishna-sway over the crests of sand dunes. "Bridget was terrified I planned to climb into the dragster's harness. We talked, of her feminine powerlessness to free Christopher's face from her mirrored space, and I of my every thought being a dream where marriage reigned." Palmer's calligraphic Zen-profile lifted in bas-relief from the raked sand, as he turned to Roxburgh and said: "The Ocean there invented the wave; who invented us?" President Nixon assumed center-stage on the news bulletins, his lines tired now as he briefly soliloquized on the policy of Vietnamization, unaware of an acidic irony sizzling his words, for just as he spoke of the policy's momentum carrying the war to an honorable conclusion, the Communist insurgents launched dozens of affirmative strikes across the country. Could a circling compass disfigure the sphere it inscribed or would the circumference always run true?

Abandoning The Caravanserai. Distorted cosmic sunflowers adorned the free-flowing color-energies, the psychedelic vision of the hippie van as inner-space vehicle parked in the street below Jason Palmer's Oceanside apartment. Pausing, hesitating for a fleeting moment on the sidewalk, looking up at the balcony, waving goodbye to Fabian Roxburgh, as Frank Zappa's *Hot Rats*, the *Willie The Pimp* track drifted across the street. A caravan of Hippie vehicles tail-to-tail slowed behind the parked van, then the procession moved off, and Roxburgh waited for Jason Palmer's Chevrolet to appear. Frank Zappa's guitar solo stretched the length of the Milky Way across the night sky.

A Flight Into Inner Space. Johnny Esquire danced *Ann-Margret's* chrome-legs ahead of the caravan of hippie vehicles speeding away from the city into the countryside, carrying with his person astride the Harley Davidson all the luster of the sixties, headed for the horizon of the seventies and the destiny unborn in a new decade. A helicopter rose from the landing pad atop **KRISHNA inc.**, its ornamental design embellishing the cult of Maharishi Phoenix as Paradise Lost's spiritual savior, for the hippie generation was launched on a flight into inner space. Sweeping through the summer countryside Johnny Esquire glimpsed in passing the *Tree of Life* blackened by fire, the hippies hit the tocsin of the car horn in recognition of the sign, while being previewed on the car radio was *Midnight Rambler* from the *Let It Bleed* album, reflective of the suture the sixties had opened up in the psyche of youth. *Ann-Margret's* tireless dancing limbs were rested at a roadhouse where the flower child secretively phoned Jason Palmer.

The Future Of Christianity. "Let us bind up the sheaves of our harvested lives and walk from this three-dimensional field of conflict forever!" Addressing the Christian Convention from the podium, Jason Palmer suspiciously glimpsed Paulette Taylor like a symphonic discord of Chaos handing round her Publicist's card: was she promoting a new Broadway musical based around the drama of Golgotha? Like a coronet, painful memories were guiltily worn around the heads of these over-zealous Christians, esoterically bleeding from the thorns they had arraigned themselves in against the hippies who had stolen their thunder in the press and media across the globe. Confronting Paulette, Palmer said: "Tell Phoenix his propositions carved in fire may have scorched the psyche of the flower child, but the sub-atomic **YOU** is doomed to endless recycling through three-dimensional space-time. Does he know you're another Judith to his Holofernes?" Unable to balance his metaphysical estrangement from Laura Devonshire he sank himself into the Lethe of flowing dunes gazing up at the transitory fragments of the Milky Way, fractured splinters of a Cosmic Cross where the Christ stood in four-dimensional space breaking our Fall into three-dimensional space-time, preparing to melt all back into a sublime Unity.

Leaves From The Great Folio. His early-summer face already a bronze-cast, Jason Palmer half-hung from his soul's dazzling chariot, a respectful distance from the erotic symbiosis of Paulette Taylor and Cornell Bedford-Brown in animated conversation on the sidewalk outside the edifice of **KRISHNA inc.** Eddie Phoenix strode through the revolving door his footsteps striking flint on the pavement, a Promethean spark igniting the Way to Paradise Lost as he advanced on the couple. Laura Devonshire would have received his packaged gift by now, delivered to her University dormitory, his Zen rock in which could be discovered the elemental dawn which broke across Paradise Lost aeons ago; he knew she would understand his preference would have been a diamond! Her Corinthian chastity, a purified Temple pillar standing tall, violin in hand, would saturate Alexander Chamberlain's relapsed Christian with a redemptive purity transforming Eros into Charity. She had been his gift to the young actor! His ringing declaration to the Christian Convention echoed on: "How was it possible Donne's ears, his intellect, were deaf and numb to Shake-speare's Great Folio? Was it because he knew the True Author and would never endanger him with a loose word? Lucifer strides through three-dimensional space generating Chaos, laying Paradise Lost to waste, are our ears hearing his discords, are our intellects numb to the puppets speaking his lines? They betray him to us with every word they speak upon the world's stage!"

How To Illuminate A Romance In Arcadia. Bridget Lovegrove dipped her head backwards under a wave's foaming brilliance, the vector of her tresses like a propagation of electro-magnetic pulsations in cosmic plasma, a red-gold *Aurora Borealis*. A romantic, thermodynamic equilibrium was being re-established here in the ocean's plasmic resistivity, while sunbathing on a rainbow-filled beach towel her torso-and-limbs glowed over the whole electro-magnetic spectrum of emotion. "You've sewn me up in your fabric of moral behavior, and I believe a spiritual body can be sexually free." The media reported forty-thousand G.I.'s had now perished in the killing Fields of 'Nam! Calling by Jason Palmer's apartment, briefly, he walked about the cubed space with his white cockatoo gripping his finger, and passing a mirror joked: "O, miroir! Sing to me of myself as I look at you, show me my soul's four-dimensional sculpture, tempt with his handsomeness!" Roxburgh left him aureoled in a glow of Hellenic obedience, his eyes scanning the ocean for the turquoise Greece where his soul dwelled in fourth-dimensional space. With a fingertip, Bridget delicately caressed the white cockatoo's sulphur crest, while a gentle breeze of golden light crept onshore and ruffled the Platonic bird's feathers, and Roxburgh intuited she was thinking of Christopher Featherstone. Walking back to her car, he said: "Bridget, is love fire, or water? I have been swimming and surfing with Danaë, yet, the ocean best evokes the enclosure of love, for how do you sever water, how might it be wounded and emotionally bleed, how is it controllable except by channeling? Light refracts into a spectrum, but what depth water has!"

Love Is Like A Red, Red Rose. Gold dust drifting from Bridget Lovegrove's hair filled the palms of his hands. An epicurean rose fluttered as the petals of her clothes fell away from her loins. Pleasure lay silhouetted in the wall-mirror as he kissed the rose's martyred lips; the turbaned red rose was jeweled with a dewdrop. Evening's red rose beyond the window curtained the moon. A lovely vase's torso on the sideboard could not move to the rhythm of a rose's perfume, although its curvature echoed the aroma, visualized its undulation, and then Bridget's voice crystallized sensation in space: "Fabian, all Diana's pleasure is overflowing in my loins!" Layers of Venetian glaze coruscated as his lips touched the Golden Fleece.

Sleeping After Sex. Sleep's keen awakedness brought pagan reflections to Fabian Roxburgh's thoughts. Languid now, pleasure sleeping in acquiescence, perfumes slowly undulated from Bridget Lovegrove's flesh, the portrait of his mouth sculpted on hers as she dreamed. Can content self-comprehend itself? Cleaved together after orgasm, Roxburgh felt their loins were together in the perfect place, and dismissed the intrusive thought the moment might be the epilogue to their tragic-comedy. Rapture satiated eased to thoughts of sensuous illumination. Bridget lay molded in the endless sleep of a marble-fleshed St. Teresa fingerprinting her heart with unendurable ecstasy. She described his caresses as sweet mercury. Sex was indeed religious in its Baroque extremism, perhaps humanity's only reminder of that ecstasy looked forward to in our spiritual reunion with the soul!

Remembrance Of Our Scripted Lines. Topaz, emerald, lapis lazuli, sun, sea and sky shimmered with the dawn of a summer's day. Visible offshore from the apartment's balcony, sails from a flotilla of yachts imprinted space, a sequence of screens filling with the land-breeze. For Jason Palmer, his finely-wrought sensibility conscious of light's flexible intelligence, its refraction into the seemingly infinite imagery forming in space, the yachts had the feeling of a skater's blade dancing on ice as they passed across his line of vision. With evangelical Pauline energy he had stormed the storeys of **KRISHNA inc.** after Eddie Phoenix but he and the multitude of flower children had vanished, leaving him feeling like the famous face-hider, Peter, who momentarily lost his sight on another stage two millennia ago, although the Supreme Prompter could have assisted with the remembrance. He stepped away from the classical penumbra to meditate across the unfurling scroll of sand dunes. Inertia gripped these December days, incandescent as they were with topaz, emerald and lapis lazuli brilliance.

What Candles Symbolized. Appearing on an obscure late-night television program featuring speculative religious viewpoints, Jason Palmer offered the following challenges to the panel and studio audience of born-again Christians eager for martyrdom. (i) "Imaged from the L^3 screen of space-time, Lucifer is well-recorded as aspiring to storm Heaven, but he can only light human candles, and how far do their flames stretch? Physical wax eternally melts, and while he seems to have an endless supply, even his Archangelic wings of infamy cannot fan the flame universal rebellion." (ii) "Lucifer has molded the cosmos open to our eyes after his own martyrdom, encompassing a three-dimensional plane I refer to as L^3, a hieroglyphic abbreviation. Our eyes only see reflected shadows smoothed in the glass of L^3, but we know of way showers who have glimpsed the Olympian beauty of heaven, and for us to catch a glimpse of this Paradise our sight must first be sealed up in the tomb of death." (iii) "Voices on the newsreel footage from 'Nam, our moment in time's L^3 space where the shadow of Communism is lighting candles to hopefully smother our glimpses of Paradise, are saying they *fight because that's the only way to stay alive*, and, *to let up is to die*. Therefore, let us carry a splinter of the True Cross in our sides, ignite our candles with Helios' illumination." Palmer turned the ignition of the Chevrolet pondering how many among the viewing Christian audience carried incarnational memories as participants in the infamous martyrdom of Hypatia.

An Aesthetic Of Sadness. Evening lyricized sunset in the reflective mirror of the moon. All the degrees of the compass were inscribed in the glowing lunar circle rising in the east. Relinquished into the arms of Alexander Chamberlain, modeling the levitation of fashion through all styles, rejuvenated in a chiton, Laura Devonshire met his eyes in the Chevrolet's side-mirror, then leaned in at the window, fingertips resting there. "Jason, someone said you were planning another moon-shot, it must have been Aquilina. A new year, a new decade, will you feel quite at home there? Please remember me with affection, as I do you. Your friends will never abandon you, your Quest, may be!" Laughing, Laura sealed the moment with a kiss, lip-to-lip but without the stimulus of Eros there, so Palmer wheeled the Chevrolet away from Drag City. The moon coalesced all starlight into its transcendent sphere just as a window inset in a wall absorbed illumination into its screen. Did a crystal design the architecture of its geometry and the equations to explain it? The moon's buoyancy held the cool lushness of a flower blossom floating on space's black water.

Elvis: 1970–1979. Screens freezing in space a spectacle of moments, celebrated the personification of a demi-god whose Apollonian gifts spanned the years, 1960-1969, the collage arranged in a three-dimensional grid within the cubed apartment Jason Palmer's *Hommage à Elvis*. Hair's impulse to bloom through the sixties' generation surrendered its Hellenic perfection modeled by Elvis, descending into a disheveled imitation of Christ's tendrils, without understanding the metaphor of the vine. Exhibiting the collage at a Gallery, Palmer questioned Paulette Taylor, her dyed hair like blackened glass, touching on Eddie Phoenix's disappearance, but her sexual veneer remained impeccable as she proudly raised her scorpion's barb when he alluded to the lion's jaw being powerful, the tooth being penetrative. A hand moved across the collage as if brushing away cobwebs and he understood the gesture. Vengeance would smolder on in the crucible of L^3 space-time, the labyrinth of screens upon which they would all enact their scripted roles would remain perilous, erasure would be swift, but Elvis, 1970–1979, what was his destiny in this momentous battle to regain Paradise?

Hell's Angels. Descending over Altamont Raceway, a spectral helicopter whipped at the seething New Year's Eve crowd thinking of *The Dawning of the Age of Aquarius*, but this was no Angel bringing Elvis home in 1960, his vision emerging from the door an unimaginable triumph, the scythe of the chopper's spinning wings announced the Coming of Death!

1970
(DESERTED CITIES OF THE HEART)

CONTENTS

I
JOURNEY TO THE CENTER OF PARADISE LOST

Love Story à la Mode. Ethereal, semi-liquescent, the burning flow of sand dunes resembled undulantly polished white-gold glass blown by Aeolus, established in space a field-of-dreams. A whiff of Indian musk ballooned on a breath of offshore summer breeze. Sandalled footprints patterned the softening translucence of a sloping sand dune. How had he become abandoned on the Loom of Time with this captive flower child who dressed to breathe only in cheesecloth? Eternally humming *Raindrops Keep Falling On My Head* her spirit lingered in the halcyon twilight fast-fading from momentous sixties Rock Festivals. Through the dust-powdered windshield of the classic Chevrolet she was watching him measure the dazzling crested pearl of a sand dune. Time lay scrambled in her mind like a configuration of computer code ... **IOIO**. A dazed, convent-raised minimalist who had shed her baroque Catholicism, she now only tuned into the esoteric sitar solos within Monterey's space of her mind, using the resonance to ask him: "What is the theme of your movie?" Barefooted, she later swirled across the loose sheets of shooting script arranged on the floor of the rented apartment, spooning fruit-flavored yogurt between her comatose lips. The fiber of cheesecloth pooled at her feet evoked a pedestal her naked torso stepped away from with the insouciance of a karmic gesture. Enmeshed in lustrous thoughts, the symbolic canopies of Krishna and Buddha igniting his consciousness concentrated on the spectacular sunset soluble to sky-and-ocean, Jason Palmer visualized himself bound on a Journey To The Center Of Paradise Lost!

Critique Of Pure Reason. Showing his endorsed visitor's pass, Dr. Philip Byrne followed directions toward the spacious studio soundstage where over the years filmed versions of *The History of the World* had been reminisced, noticing as he did so the massive Chevrolet which dominated the parking bays. A Chariot of the Gods had been squeezed into three-dimensional space: Jason Palmer's seraphic wraith clung to the vast vehicle, but where was his *physical* presence? Stepping from the pulsing summer sunlight through a doorway onto the soundstage, Dr. Byrne rather clumsily kissed his brother's ex-wife, ever sensitive to her sexual aphrodisiac, bewildered by her infatuation with Palmer's Miltonian seraphim and his obsession with the tireless fallen Archangel. Above head-height there ranged a cool bank of television sets screening soundless images from the interminable war in 'Nam, or as Palmer preferred, that *exploratory skirmish testing whether Paradise could be regained*. With his fabulous chariot four-square in spacetime he seemed to be visualizing himself as the right wing of a resurrected Angel in Michael's Legions. "Philip, this is a Love Story?" Diane Blake's flesh under the studio lights had the resonant hues of fine stone. "Mmm, *à la Mode*, Diane." Torched huts silhouetted patrolling American GIs, chopper sorties carved up the sky, tanks bruised the decimated earth as canopies of undergrowth collapsed in fireballs of napalm. Was Palmer planning to slap the *Critique of Pure Reason* on the table at the Paris peace talks?

Speculative Questions. Inside a wood-panelled office adjacent to the studio proper, Diane Blake kneeled and manoeuvred on the floor in a covertly sexual posture while unveiling Jason Palmer's gift, compromising her supposed erotic withdrawal following the divorce. "Diane – you have chosen to revert to your maiden name." Dr. Byrne had often seen her empirical submergence in Vermeer's domestic décors, but Dali's? "Who is she, Philip?" The painting was raised from the floor and placed upright atop a low cabinet for viewing. Light bleeding through louvers brought colours to seemingly float upon the surface of the painting. "Mmm, the now-celebrated feminist, Germaine Greer, or her theoretical contours at least." Dr. Byrne frowned, for the portrait was painted *à la mode* Dali's exquisite Madonnas, quantum physics style, and now he would have to read the feminist's book. Logical space, did it exist anymore, considering the dissolution of boundaries? "Eve's spiritual disintegration, her amoral responsibilities abandoned in crossing the boundary from Paradise, clashes with the feminist's assessment of our sexual history as it stands on the printed page." The juxtaposition of the chair Diane was braced against and the television screen flowing with live-action footage from 'Nam signaled a new interdependence, sharpened for all of them the cinematic design of the imperfect world Palmer conspired to redeem. "*If I Were A Carpenter*," he murmured, thinking of her collapsed world following the divorce, then added: "From the fragments Philosophy has bequeathed us, can we construct again Paradise Lost for redemption, is it enough to be armed with the *Critique of Pure Reason?*" Illicit resonances swirled about them with the accelerating rhythm of Germaine Greer's disintegrating portrait.

Portrait In Pythagorean Geometry. Still photographs laid out in the form of a Pythagorean five-pointed star made up some mythical portrait of a persona capable of traversing space extraneous to the cubic volume of the Oceanside apartment: (i) the city's thick-textured treacle river in the dead of night, the word, **STYX**, penciled on the back. (ii) a studied close-up of a man's Achilles heel. (iii) a slab of lit marble doubling as an altar. (iv) an unsheathed samurai sword crossed with a shining javelin. (v) an Ingres cartoon of a woman erotically bound for sexual bondage, her face superimposed with Diane Blake's. Jason Palmer had to be taken seriously! Did Diane realize she was to be another Andromeda sacrifice, chained to the cliff-face of the steep descent into Paradise Lost, a seductive lure for the fallen Archangel?

The Death Of Ophelia. A symbology of vertical and horizontal shadows geometrically lengthened across the flat, two-dimensional planes inside the compact jewel of the Oceanside apartment. The photographic portrait arrayed in a pentagram had vanished from the floor now these intravenous purple shadows displaced light in the volume of the room. Obsequious shadows bowed before Diane Blake waiting in attendance upon Jason Palmer, unnoticed by her, for she eyed the captive flower child who drifted by pulling the petals from a rose with all of Ophelia's deadpan innocence. More startling was her glimpsed presence in the open-doored bathroom leaning over the filling porcelain tub, a naked volume of derriere, tipping salts and rose petals into the water and trailing her fingertips across the surface. Palmer occupied himself feverishly studying the architectural designs she had procured and remodeled at his request, and with which he hoped to imprison the fallen Archangel forever on a two-dimensional perspective grid, freeing humanity to ascend fourth-dimensionally. How could any of this make sense to a modern woman? Seated *à la mode* in an armchair was the mysterious figure of Lt. John Kirby, the famous President in his Washington Memorial his model, whom Palmer introduced to her as *the soul of 'Nam in Purgatory.* Who were these characters? Were they perceptive annotations to the finished shooting script? Diane found herself having to resist a powerful subliminal pull: the Germaine Greer portrait had all the momentum of a threatening, accelerating sexual causality. Why this fervor to place duple spatial dimensions between the fallen Archangel and humanity? "Diane, all these very precisely ruled lines of blueprint you've drawn here – is drafting a sexual experience for you, an erotic release?" The wayward flower child seemed to aurally suck Palmer's question from space with her visual submergence into the viscous volume of the full bathtub. "Let the ink flow, smudge the thin line, soak the blotting paper." How keening was the draughtsmanship of shadows pressing against the precise cut and line of her severe business suit as she rolled up the blueprints: Lt. Kirby seemingly had vanished through their interstices!

Negotiating The Terrain Of Paradise Lost. Lengthy speed-sequences shot with fender-mounted cameras challenged the *ennui* of yet another slow summer afternoon's filming on the beachside boulevards. These masculine exhibitions of bravado and motivity galvanized the film crew after the claustrophobic stasis of the studio soundstage and the laborious setting up of arranged in-door shots. "We've been given back the speed of Angels!" Jason Palmer's lane-hopping chariot endlessly cruised the fabled circuit of Oceanside boulevards. Wearing a white T-shirt boldly imprinted with a portrait of a youthful John Milton, he half-leaned from the grandiose Chevrolet engaging the occupants of passing vehicles with his vision they undertake a modern adaptation of the famous chariot race of Ezekiel with the fallen Archangel. Little did they know he was objectively leading them into the labyrinth of a transcendental dialectic in blank verse, twentieth-century style. Framed in the rear vision mirror, the ghosted eyes of Lt. John Kirby searched other perspectives, other meanings from the geometry of the boulevard grid. The terrain of 'Nam exploded in his mind with the physics of Dali's disintegrating Madonnas, for he had failed to solve the equational probability of Vietcong land-mine placements, become a victim of logical rather than factual space. "Apple-and-serpent! We need more than their knowledge today to negotiate the terrain of Paradise Lost." With bravura, a leather-jacketed motorcycle courier Palmer had been employing dramatically braked up to the camera placement where Dr. Philip Byrne loitered, swung her leg over the saddle and shook free her tresses to the hot summer breeze. Who was this Artemis of the freeway interchanges, and who the unfortunate Actaeon she was hunting?

Rare Orchids. "Can you blueprint off a copy of Time for me?" Dr. Philip Byrne sought a flash of enlightenment as he surveyed the manufactured faces come to the surrealist canvas of Las Vegas to play against the munificent gambler, Lucifer. The look-a-like blondes statuesque in their fur wraps, enclosures like washes of milky whitewater which shouldered the waves at the beach Jason Palmer studied for hours, each torsoed *Jayne Mansfield*, *Diana Dors* and *Marilyn Monroe* loaded with spicèd orchids primed to burn for the handsome singers taking the supper club stage. Diane Blake's starry-eyed following of the languorous-limbed singer manipulating the microphone cable's serpent as if it were alive and threatening to coil about his limbs and torso, conjured up memories of her own pre-marital years as a cherubic fifties teen angel. Dr. Byrne obliged: "Johnny Esquire, Diane. Hardly your Perseus, I would have thought." Jason Palmer's intense gazing across the table at her sculpted bust as Johnny Esquire reprised Dean Martin's uniquely stylized singing, Rockabilly rhythms filtered through lush orchestral arrangements, evoked how Time was still hunting down all fugitives from the fifties who had so far escaped the scythe of death: *You've Still Got A Place In My Heart ... The Door Is Still Open (To My Heart).* So many *outsiders*, so many loaded guns in the wrong hands! At another table Dr. Byrne recognized Lt. John Kirby, rendered a wraith by the meaninglessness of a land-mine planted in the fertile tropical earth of 'Nam, its sudden spurt of explosive growth into a spectacular flower visually fragmented in the orchids worn near the hearts of the women listening to Johnny Esquire croon. "Diane, Paradise Lost is not a *fact*." Seated with Lt. Kirby were Eddie Phoenix and Paulette Taylor, her publicist's mouth as mobile as Jupiter's *red spot*. Diane's fabulous fifties coquette of recent memory was so different to the rationally suited woman of 1970, especially when she had asked him: "Tell me, who is this flower child Palmer's sleeping with? She moves around his apartment without any clothes on, as naked as the roses she deflowers all day with her fingers, when they are not smeared in yogurt. Where does her one-dimensional cipher from the late-sixties squeeze into the grid of Paradise Lost he's mapping?" Jealousy voiced these questions, and prompted his answer: "Diane, you're the chosen draughtswoman mapping this delusional Paradise Lost for him, leave this sexual distortion to straighten itself out." When Johnny Esquire swung into

(You're The) Devil In Disguise he suddenly realized Palmer and the unholy trinity at the other table were striding down the aisle toward an exit.

Eyes Of The Sixties. Confidently steering one-handed, Jason Palmer wheeled the imposing Chevrolet into yet another circuit of the city streets paved with an image of the sky, pedestrians modeling postures from a frieze around the altar of a tall building plaqued – **KRISHNA inc.** Cars were dueling post-biblical chariots circling the structures precipitated in Paradise Lost. They effortlessly cruised, measuring the length and breadth of the broad avenues, computing the weight of the ascending skyscrapers, tamed classical moldings of precipitated thought, but could the building masses hold the fallen Archangel pinioned to the two-dimensional plane long enough for humanity to make its escape? Crushed together on the rear seat behind Palmer, Paulette Taylor and Eddie Phoenix were computing other desires, her lovemaking a good-humored set of Paganini variations, his stentorian blank verse, the Paul Newman-as-hustler school of romantic poesy. Static interfered with Palmer's favorite radio station bringing a jagged edge to the songs he hoped would piece the night together.

Whole Lotta Love	- Led Zeppelin
Don't Cry Daddy	- Elvis
When You Awake	- The Band

Each circuitous passage criss-crossing the city tightened invisible astral bonds to bind the elusive Archangel. The banks of red traffic light rendered every intersection a speed trap for mobile Angels on a mercy mission. Surely this undeniably beautiful woman with the large classical face handsome as carved ice, perhaps capable of melting, streaming everywhere, grasped the significance of the nocturnal hour? His faithful courier relentlessly trailed the Chevrolet. Over-his-shoulder, Palmer said: "Paradise Lost fulfills Archimedes' Law of Displacement on a cosmic scale. What is not generally realized is the seemingly infinite three-dimensional space of the Cosmos is actually the fallen Archangel's quiescent, monolithic form camouflaged in the depths of absolute zero, waiting to rouse itself again to the intensity of the Planck-moment." Parking on a yet-to-be-completed section of flyover that peeled away from the cloverleaf interchange, Palmer swung open the car door and stood admiring Diane Blake's unerring placement of an architectural sequence of billboards he had commissioned, Eyes of the Sixties: **ELIZABETH TAYLOR's, JFK's, AUDREY HEPBURN's, J.G. BALLARD's.** Oblivious to the cosmic import of these signs, the couple on the back seat were still socializing the causality of sixties sex, and Palmer marveled for a moment at the shallowness of space, the very breathlessness between two pressing mouthes. The motorcycle courier's headlight zeroed in on his prophetic presence surveying the scene. The time, 3am, brought a dead calm to the city, opportunity to invent a moment of redemption.

The Seventh Seal. Standing off to one side with tightly folded arms, Diane Blake observed the progress of this interview for a controversial theology program in the city's public broadcasting studio. Pontificating like Bertrand Russell sitting-in on a CND rally, model for a conscientious objector as the legions squared up to face off in a revival of the war between Heaven-and-Hell, the interviewer began innocuously enough: "Dr. Philip Byrne, respected authority on the literature of alienation, Jason Palmer, described here as Theologian of the Apocalypse, welcome to today's broadcast. Jason, if I might test the waters of Theology with a statement you had published in a recent film journal, quote: *God has let loose the camera into the world so we might remember everything.* Isn't the All-Seeing Eye of God sufficient, a lens capable of distinguishing Good from Evil?" Diane focused on Palmer's broad expanse of shoulders as he leaned forward and took a sip from a glass of theological water standing on the low table. The interviewer irritatingly lit and sucked a pipe. "God is indeed the Director, I am His cinematographer. The movie camera loaded with film is sharpening for humanity the monumental imagery of Paradise Lost as it develops in our spacetime continuum. Film itself is a two-dimensional medium where we can imprison the fallen Archangel for Eternity. A can of movie footage is the ultimate seal mentioned in *Revelations, chapter five.*" These simply expressed propositions struck fissionable resonances in Diane's psyche, blurring Faith and Doubt in an unsettling cocktail. "Dr. Byrne, would you care to comment on these extravagances?" Her ex brother-in-law had initiated sexual manoeuvres with her but she was still drawing very precise lines of blueprint in her strategy with him. "Certainly, Wittgenstein's world-as-totality-of-facts, not of *things*, shifts our perspective in a dramatic way. As we can't actually *show* thought, it is timely for us to consider the possibility the Archangel will always prove as elusive as the chemicals mixing together imagery on a reel of film. Indeed, our question should be: *What will be his next image make-over, his next Oscar winning performance?* I think Jason has caught a good likeness of this Archangel's solipsism." Diane's gaze measured the masculine spirit-level of Palmer's squared shoulders, and the telling handsomeness of his transphysical expression as he spoke again: "*Facts* do not equal *things* in the new theological algebra." She felt the perspectives of her own loins converge feelingly with the lines of his manly torso: startled, she realized the leather-jacketed courier he sponsored had brushed against her elbow trailing an inflammable odor of oil and gasoline on the studio air.

Sounds Of Silence. Lovely sand dunes swelled-and-receded about Paulette Taylor's stilled presence with the power-filled delicacy of Rachmaninov's Rhapsodic 18th Variation on a Theme of Paganini's. Softening gold *Camembert* watches and melting silver keys meditated in the silky sand at her naked feet, her pillbox-red toenails bold discords in the sonata of colours on the beachscape's palette. The easy flow of crests evoked brushstrokes of oil paint against the canvas of the azure skyline. "What really matters to Palmer, paraphrasing Wittgenstein, is what he can only ever be *silent* about, and there is some ruined Parthenon fragmented on the Acropolis of his imagination."

Dr. Byrne's blithe commentary was a jangling of out-of-tune bells: Paulette was listening for the glowing harmonies of the sun's cymbal resonating space.

An Evangelical Moment With The Fallen Archangel. Piqued by her abandonment, Diane Blake hobbled up to a sidewalk café table after snapping the high heel of her stiletto in a cracked paving slab, and wasn't conscious of Eddie Phoenix stepping from the pillion seat of the courier's motorcycle until he leaned over introducing himself. There was an odor of the evangelist about this shadowy figure, tattooed with the authority of the Scriptures, but whose, God's or the fallen Archangel's? They ordered coffees, the planes of his face as thin as strips of celluloid being matched, and when he smiled his face's skin folded like film failing to run through a projector. Sulphur's smelling salts abruptly focused her awareness and when she asked after Palmer for something to say, he built a pyramid of sugar cubes on the surface of the table, scanned what was visible of the sky and mumbled something about him being a mere feather fallen from the Archangel's wing, temporarily blown aloft. The dismissive undercurrent in his voice didn't fool her though. Crescendos were beginning to hammer with Wagnerian insistence in her heart, Brunnhilde's heart, for this *lost feather*, and her loins were feeling sexually tickled when she was in his presence. She gasped aloud when Phoenix precipitately reached across with his fingers and explored her shoulder-blade. "Just measuring you for a pair of wings, a black swan's!" he grinned fiercely, his psyche now visible in the long, jagged shadows cast by the nearby skyscraper.

Song Of India. Offshore, a flotilla of yachts lay becalmed on a summer ocean set to blue ice. Curiously stirred by the undulant sand dunes which resembled an enormous wing gilded with sunlight and beginning to stretch for flight, Diane Blake's fingers caressed the gold necklace stinging her flesh, while the architecture of her steelèd clothes became increasingly malleable with perspiration. Patterned tire tracks converged on Jason Palmer's sculptural Chevrolet, fabulous chariot of the sun molded by Vulcan, waiting as patiently as the stilled yachts, like her sexual yearning, amid the flanks of sand dunes veined with windswept striations. Metallic sitar sub-tones birthed on the air from multi-dimensional sources, aimless motifs, so many temptations hoping to catch the ear of the brooding Archangel.

Basilica. The Chevrolet's chariot wheels smoked on the melting asphalt. Piloted by Eddie Phoenix, the chopper's rotorblades whipped updrafts of loose sand into a blinding storm which swirled about Diane Blake poised on the impearlèd crest of a dune. Seated beside Jason Palmer in the Chevrolet was the flower child, her rampant nipples pressing through the damp fabric of cheesecloth she favored: had anyone told Achilles this Iphigenia was plighted to be *his* bride? Diane imaginatively caught his design here on heavy-wingèd thought, how to catch the dark Archangel and pin him to the two-dimensional perspective grid laid down among pillowing clouds of dunes with javelins of jeweled sunlight, perhaps with the sweetness of Bernini's *Ecstasy of*

St. Teresa, for Lucifer too was a *feather* come loose from God's plume. Now she understood him sending the mysterious leather-clad courier all over the city with her silver cans of film, delivering ultimatums to the Archangel. Perhaps he even expected Satan to draw the mighty sword of light offered by the Sun God and commit seppuku! Shadowy ideograms raced across the beachscape, ciphers announcing the fallen Archangel had awakened.

The Gulf Of Tonkin Incident. Crouching low-in-motion under the spinning rotorblades, Dr. Byrne hurried away from the bubble-glass cockpit of the helicopter with the openness of his irritation visible, his movements counterpointed by the cantilevered floors of a car park adjacent to the roof of the skyscraper's landing pad. Jason Palmer's Chevrolet had powered from the vortex of energy created by the circling chopper, leaving Diane Blake abandoned among the sand dunes. Dr. Byrne then had glimpsed the motorcycle courier offer Diane the pillion seat, watched as Artemis' waist was clasped with both hands and *the two-wheeled gypsy queen* accelerate after the Chevrolet. Seeing Diane pressed forward against the leather-bound Artemis he now despaired of ever exploring the theology of her loins, the chapters of *Revelations* within the papyrus leaves of her pubis. Hadn't he brought her out to the sand dunes so she might sense the contours of his feelings for her in their lineaments? Lt. John Kirby stepped through the doorway leading inside the roof of the skyscraper. Americans were the Olympian Gods now withdrawing-with-honor from the exhausted battlefield of 'Nam: they had suffered enough casualties in a forlorn war, and were going to bathe their conscience in ambrosia Stateside on Parnassus to forget the mined rice paddies of the Mekong delta. In a flash of inspiration he grasped an outline of the revelation Palmer was ever pointing him toward, and swung a glance up into the sky. "Yes! The Gulf of Tonkin Incident! Of course, there's the trigger setting off his adolescent psyche. *And the wrath which becalmed the Greek fleet was appeased.*" Dr. Byrne laughed at the futility of this quest as the elevator plunged to street level.

Acceleration, Deceleration, Acceleration. The saturnine opaque bubble of the flighted helicopter with Eddie Phoenix at the controls sparred with the pursuing Chevrolet. Was Dr. Byrne sun-struck with midsummer madness? Jason Palmer eased off the accelerator, glanced across at the flower child indifferently licking fresh yogurt from her fingertips, then braked, before reversing back towards the chopper's take-off zone, a space where the sand had miraculously re-assembled into the Peace Symbol. No doubt Dr. Byrne would be lecturing Phoenix in the cockpit of the helicopter on *what we cannot speak about we must pass over in silence* – the Iago solution. From the sun's positioning in the afternoon sky there was still plenty of time to shower and formally dress for the book launch. He paced about the disturbed juncture of sand, an explosive wound in the earth, sucking suture where the chopper had ripped free of gravity, sign of a fourth-dimensional zone of entrance-and-exit for the Archangel, ironically youth's popular Peace Symbol. Sand dunes striated with bursting veins were evidence of a struggle to flex free, for the very flesh of the Earth now held the fallen Archangel's muscles, a physical union long consummated. On a whim he had signaled Diane Blake to climb astride the pillion seat of the courier's motorcycle and join the Chevrolet's artifice of pursuit. She too had witnessed the wingèd Archangel rip free of the sand dunes and escape towards *Pandemonium* where their blueprinted, two-dimensional perspective grid lay spread to capture and sluice him in its mineralized lake.

Persuasion Through Pride And Prejudice. Grains of finely powdered sand drifted to outline her bare footprints on the polished timber floor when she stepped across its surface. "My stiletto's heel snapped earlier: perhaps my tripping up was a metaphor?" Jason Palmer paused awestruck by the image of her footprint photographed in wood-grain, virginal as Eve's pressing into the earth following her expulsion from fourth dimensional space into three-dimensional incarnation: was he Adam cleaved to her side? Then her flexible bare feet of exquisite sensibility, her toes stretching in motion, crossed the floor of the apartment to the bathroom. Fresh trails were opening up to his spiritualized scent. A fleshy vision of Pallas Athena had fallen into the space of his Quest, messenger from Olympus: if only she were visible to himself alone! What false dream could he telegraph Eddie Phoenix, endlessly circling three-dimensional space's lost Paradise armored in his helicopter? He had cursorily dropped off the flower child at his own apartment knowing she would bathe herself in musk all evening. "Are you and that flower child from the sixties, sexually involved?" She talked of her own marriage as a *Madame Bovary* existence, so confusing and puzzling to her sensibilities following the freedom of her Brigitte Bardot adolescence and its evenings of cinematic kisses. "Sexually involved?" he stalled, equivocating: "Like trailing a *ménage à trois* with her cobra-hooded guru." Her silences were loquacious with interiorized thought. Palmer himself was thoughtful studying the metaphoric layout of her kitchen as he fingered an oval benchtop-with-mounted-basin, sterile ceramic womb imaging her pre-coital intensities. While her fingers leisurely released the buttons from the holes of her blouse she ambled about the apartment describing the origins of its Ingresque décor. A soundless television screen exploded with artillery mis-hits on last year's Hamburger Hill fiasco. A documentary analysis of the war in 'Nam convened there within the thrall of silence in her living room contrasted the flawless stone hues of her own flesh as she slipped free her shoulders from the blouse and strolled back to the bathroom. "I rather expected the ambience of an airport departure lounge ... an installation if you like, for your lovers." She hummed *Suspicious Minds* in the shower as he poured himself a drink and wandered about. Absence cooled everything, including the vast emptiness of three-dimensional space beyond the sphere of the Earth. The Archangel though was sure to manoueuvre for her. But how, where? Touching a selection from her bookshelves he could intuit with what perseverance she had peeled back the leaves of Jane Austen's novels for the romantic Holy Grail in this, an anti-romantic existential Age. "Jason, while you shower, I'll press your clothes, if you wish." As an architect, how readily would she accept the make-over forming in his thoughts? They could call in Dali's interior decorating flair, and bring off a Mae West effect! He watched the studied spontaneity of her aristocratic wrists as she reached for the ringing phone. Her

Hello overflowed with solitude. He knew reading her body language, listening to her hushed voice, the caller could only be the self-styled *Archangelic Messenger*, Dr. Philip Byrne!

Portrait Of The Fallen Archangel (I). The high-circulation tabloid of humanity's psyche fed on this scandalizing portrait of the dark Archangel, composed from the following collage: (i) **LITERARY** – Camus' *Le Mythe de Sisyphe* ... (ii) **MUSICAL** – The Beatles' *Yellow Submarine* ... (iii) **VISUAL** – the eleven politically damaging, if not militarily damaging, infantry assaults on Hamburger Hill ... (iv) **ART** – Dali's *The Persistence of Memory* ... (v) **POLITICAL** – the collective Sivan-like arms of the North Vietnamese Peace delegation in Paris.

House Of Atreus. New-Wave feminism's prophetically striding Joan of Arc manoeuvred on-stage beneath silkscreen posters of her book cover suspended on cords from the ceiling, a provocative visual tapestry for the assembled media chorus. Hostess for the book launch, Paulette Taylor orchestrated applause with the energy of a Berlioz overture, herself beautiful as aristocratic ice, leading the tall authoress to her place of honor among the assembled guests. Germaine Greer, fresher for her sojourn through the sixties, physically structured after the quasi-magisterial ruin of an Amazon, allowed herself to be guided to a table piled high with her celebrated feminist masterpiece, **THE FEMALE EUNUCH.** But here was no face to launch a thousand ships! "Our gathering at Aulis for the sacrifice of Iphigenia! By the way, where is the flower child?" Dr. Philip Byrne's brusque attempt at humor failed to ally Diane Blake to his cause. "Diane, am I to understand Jason Palmer intends talking theology to this woman?" The authoress boldly unsheathed a fountain pen inscribed with the script of her name, and dedicated the first copy to Paulette Taylor, whose longish face glowed as fresh as an iceberg under an Arctic summer sun. "This Clytemnestra of sexual *mores* is the moral embedded in the fairytale tragedy Palmer has scripted for his cameras. Beware becoming enmeshed in her tapestry." Diane Blake, herself quintessentially Greek, was particularly vulnerable to frosts, the smoke of dry ice swathed her indifference to him, at least sexually. "Palmer is resentful his own proposed image for the book cover, you've seen the painting, *à la mode* the Dali *Madonnas*, remember?, was rejected outright, and he read to me a selection of her serpentine sentences slithering across the rejection notice she sent him." Who was tempting whom? Now muscling his way to the head of the queue, Jason Palmer thrust a copy of *Gulliver's Travels* against the authoress' breast, once famously bared for **OZ MAGAZINE.**

Salome Dancing In The Weave Of Gustav Moreau's Canvas. Crowning the evening's schedule of entertainments was a special presentation for the guests: placed on a low pedestal stood a massive eggshell. The sculptor stepped forward and cracked the egg open. Castor-and-Pollux reclined within the curvatures of the halved egg. Applause was halting and sporadic, bringing a vitriolic speech about philistinism from the mouth of the continental sculptor, who stormed off in a tantrum, Toscanini with a mallet-and-chisel. Paulette Taylor quickly signaled for the music to begin, which brought forth the appearance of a water-color Salome dancing in the weave of Gustav Moreau's canvas, encrusted with jewels, all erotic suggestion even for the jaded Modern Art palates of the society guests. Salome's companion was a living fifties Lichtenstein cartoon, modern of course, elegantly romantic in the American way, if rather a little bland and colorless. The moral followed. Both women artistically undressed, the exposure, the stripping back a telling analogy, for what was the difference now between their respective nakedness, how indeed had Woman's development progressed over a century's evolution, let alone a millennium's? Germaine Greer's impassive vacuity of expression stared out from a billion film-frames, from museums overflowing with canvases, stood on the pedestals of statues gracing the galleries of History: unexpectedly she suddenly attempted Salome's celebrated pose!

Eve's Head In Einsteinian Space. "Palmer surprises me with the rigor of his intention: he still plans to explode this dour Eve's head in Einsteinian space, the spillage of milk analogy popular in Quantum Physics." Dr. Philip Byrne's expository remark leveled over the rim of his champagne flute was overheard by the prowling courier, still in her aromatic leathers, skin of a sexual panther. "Who killed *her* heart?" Malice's corrosive geometry sand-blasted the façade of ritual and the authoress abruptly abandoned the book-signing. Even copious champagne couldn't lessen her mouth's special truculence, while the toughened glass of her eyes was ever measuring the distance between Jason Palmer and herself. *Gulliver's Travels* masqueraded as a pact with a *Mystery School*! Foggy London was more her milieu, not this bright southern Hellas. "She's had words with Palmer. He began by asking her of whose flesh she was formed. Her riposte amused him: *Not of a father's!* He then spoke of her precious vocabulary, its sorcery of austere vices and wondered whether she might be persuaded to take the cups of her bra in hand and release her feminine breasts to the guests. She obviously knows something of his quest, for she countered with: *This caricature of an Archangel from the leaves of the Scriptures, where is he then among this crowd? I've searched for him, but can't find him, even in my dreams. Therefore, surely he's not factual. Or is this movie you're making only metaphorical?* Palmer then presented her with a lavishly wrapped box containing a costume exactly designed after the one which graces her book cover, asking her to slip into it for him."

The Finding Of Iphigenia! Slowly-revolving ambulance lights bled across the enameled layer of sheet whose temperature had fallen to that of the sand dunes wrapped in darkness beyond the apartment complex. Diane Blake's hue-of-stone emerged from inner labyrinths of thought into the night air with the magnificence of a caryatid: *The Finding of Iphigenia!* Wheeled on a stretched trolley toward the open doors of the ambulance, the flower child's recumbent nude *bas-relief* beneath the draped sheet evoked the winsome flow of sand dunes, a graceful epiphany of a soul's abstracted motion. Eddie Phoenix's trolley appeared outlining his stark evangelical mask beneath the powdered dune of a white sheet suffocating him. Now reduced to a black Delacroixan lithograph, this Mephistopheles' dionysiac exuberance had been stilled by a single overdose of Eternity. Jason Palmer lay a copy of **THE FEMALE EUNUCH** on the virginal catafalque of sheet, an abyss of text for the evangelist to descend into during this journey. Running parallel, the Chevrolet and ambulance cruised the lustrous black highway, Palmer's gaze focused on the bonnet statuette modelled after a likeness of Germaine Greer's naked torso remembered from **OZ** Magazine.

The Fragility Of Cheesecloth. Anticipating his caresses, the flower child had assumed the pliability of Indian temple sculpture visualized from magazine cuttings littering the floor. Two recumbent effigies adorned the relief slab of the bed. Tremulous sitar music jangled Diane Blake's senses as she beheld the modesty of the flower child, now a fragile blade of grass, sheared from the lawn of three-dimensional space. "Is she? ..." Asleep on the altar of the bed? On the silent television screen tanks sheltered GIs repelled by gunfire pouring from the stones of a Citadel. "Awake in a transphysical world? Yes. She'll fall asleep if she regains consciousness *here*." Diane Blake bent at her knees and picked up the fragility of the flower child's favored cheesecloth garment, redolent as always with the heavy scent of musk. A perfume-burner smoked near the mortuary shape of the bed. Approaching the bed she brushed against Jason Palmer while still fingering the cheesecloth fabric through whose weave all her hopes had expired. Cresting the outlined curve of her leg was the tufted dune-grass of her pubis, chilled to winter stillness. She lay there a serene piece of sculpture ready to be sand-papered completely smooth and delivered to the temple for installation. Her rootlessness was now fixed to the earth while her face was already assuming the pallor of a lotus blossom. Inch-by-inch the GIs advanced across rubble toward the crumbling Citadel. Palmer recalled how he would play with the grains of sand clinging to her dark navel like so many stars to a *Black Hole* in space. The evangelist, Eddie Phoenix, burdened with the imagery of Paradise Lost cooled beside her, ready for his torso's composition of electrons to disperse into the infamous lake of liquid black fire. He still lay unsigned though, pale as a sack of grains of rice poured into the beggar's bowl of the bed. Here was comparable poetry for Homer's triumphant evangelism of Troy's celebrated siege millennia ago!

Corpus Hypercubus. Jason Palmer now made preparations for full combat with the fallen Archangel. While summer's heat-wave threatened to perspire in a thunderstorm he supervised the erection of an imposing edifice among the cream-crested sand dunes. Dawn's metallic brass sunburst found him wandering the sand dunes' infinite particles of inlaid eggshell while the construction crew erected his portrait of Germaine Greer in swirling strips of wire, through which currents of wind and light flowed. Dr. Philip Byrne visited the site with Diane Blake as evening's copper patina emboldened the beachscape's forms. "I perceive his thought's logical picture here. He wants to make love to this Greer woman across all the millennia. But his adversary, the Archangel bestrides all Time like the convex of sand dune there, unsettling his hopes. And she of course visualizes some kind of mystical ascension for her career with the launch of this book ..." Diane Blake had heard Palmer was making endless *papier-mâché* models of Dali's *Corpus Hypercubus* in his apartment. She thrilled to contemplate his stretched nakedness covered only by a sliver of white silk loincloth! Then she trumped Dr. Byrne with a wry smile: "He understands, Philip, the only way he can defeat the Archangel is to fill *all* space with his *own* mind. Do you see now, Archimedes' *Principle of Displacement*? Can I displace *her* though?"

The Thing Seen! Life's mortuary awaited the disappearance of the sun from the heaven's skylight. The modest torsos of reclining sand dunes blushed with sunset and the spiritually-clothed purple moments approaching from the east, out of cloud-breaks as the thunderstorm stalled, presaged a climactic moment of engagement. Germaine Greer's constructional portrait formed a Black Hole's immense magnetic field drawing forth the stars from the cloth of evening. For Jason Palmer, famed charioteer of Chevrolets, ebony space was a marble quarry to be chiseled with so many billions of Sun Gods, even if only their inextinguishable light remain visible to three-dimensional eyes. The glorious portrait exploded with swirling electricity! Bursts of iridescence carpeted the sand dunes and brought a *flambé* glaze to the sky. For an omnipresent moment all three-dimensional space collapsed into the head of the fallen Archangel, his crownèd omnipotence seared with pain, then the solidity of the statuesque portrait shattered to billions of electronic stars whirling in space. All the visible galaxies arrayed above were his three-dimensional brain-waves! Tomorrow the flotilla of yachts would be free to cross uncharted horizons. Paradise Lost still resembled burning phosphorus in the chemistry of Palmer's psyche. Then, the charred right wing of the fallen Archangel was glimpsed lifting free of the crest of a sand dune, spangled with billions of stars!

II
THE LAST DAYS OF ELVIS

The Eliad I. *The globe of Elvis' head holds the World's song, and his divine ancestry is emblazoned in the wonder of his face, and in the splendor of his voice. Behold, here before you is the Tomb of the World, where Elvis is God's commemorative statue arising triumphant from the chaos of History. Elvis is white, but comely O ye Daughters of America, white as the Pentelic marble from which classical Greece was sculpted.*

A Model For The Death Of Elvis. His white linen summer-cool suit fluidly aglow in the shimmering heat-haze, Dr. Philip Byrne visually traced the flower child's evanescence across the deserted sand dunes, wandering shepherdess in search of lost time. What symbology had Jason Palmer alluded to, defining incarnation: "*Being's enfeebled fragmentation in a hostile continuum.*" This captive flower child, one of Palmer's whims, with her eternally becalmed expression devoid of any twentieth-century *angst*, idly traversed an earth laid waste by Poseidon. Around her the peaceful dunes mediated between thought-and-desire, their thinness-and-emptiness as expressed in the line between the planes of sand-and-sky. When pressed, Palmer became theatrical, verbally sketched her as his *Perdita of the Sand Dunes*. As his shoes annoyingly filled with sand, Dr. Byrne imagined hearing her sexual confessions, already no doubt a lifetime's listening. Unhurried now he paused in the curve between two dunes, intrigued by the convergent perspectives, finally grasping Palmer's painting of the scene as a Gauginesque paradise from which spacetime had been extracted. The horizon was simply an etiolated arabesque of fine-grained sand. Turning, he glanced back ... *nothing!* How did Palmer propose to build a new race from this decomposition? Light foamed about the crest of a waved dune as the flower child rematerialized, her tender nipples stiffening through the damp cheesecloth, loading the future with her untrammeled sexuality. About her presence the drained spaces of earth and sky imaged three-dimensional time sucked into a fourth-dimension: she slipped over the crest and vanished leaving the confluence of still dunes, a cipher of her twentieth-century pantheism. By the foreshore a *Wooden Horse* of billboards composed from idolatrous images of Elvis dominated the screen of the beachscape. Dr. Byrne strolled among them visualizing in the composition a sphinx-like riddle: Elvis perhaps as Oedipus Rex, blind king! Then he suddenly realized, here was a model for The Death of Elvis!

A Strategic Analysis. Dr. Philip Byrne perused some questionable documents located in Jason Palmer's Oceanside apartment, observed by the nonchalant flower child who dipped a forefinger into a container of yogurt and sucked the viscous flavour, her unstifled *naïveté* a subliminal irritant. (i) An aerial night-time photo of the land-grid of Las Vegas, laid bare on the web of the desert, with the glittery jeweled spider of the fallen Archangel visible. (ii) The musculature of a department store mannequin outfitted in one of Elvis' Vegas costumes, an armor cleverly arrayed in the seven spiritual charkas sculpted after jeweled lotuses: another religious icon had arisen and breastplated himself for battle with the Archangel. (iii) A *G.I. Blues* movie poster plastered with a diagonal caption: **ELVIS MUSICALIZES THE COLD WAR!** (iv) The palmistry of Elvis' handprint. (v) A montage of the famous pink Cadillac, gleaming hubcaps and all, as Ezekiel's chariot. (vi) Various soft *Camembert* watches from Dali's canvases, for *Time* is Lucifer's principal impersonation, God's being *Eternity*. Here was an identikit of the Archangel conceived by Palmer, but the question remained, what could be the inner significance of Elvis' incarnation?

Death-By-Vegas. Slow afternoons finally succumbed to the exhaustion of the desert's timelessness when Vegas-time metamorphosed into an imperial porphyry evening beneath the shimmering chandelier of the night sky. *Incognito*, Jason Palmer cruised the strip's heavy traffic with a fender-mounted camera, endlessly filming the spinning chariot wheels of the saloon cars and convertibles. Brilliant neon-washes relief-mapped Johnny Esquire's upper torso sculpted behind the wheel of his *coupé* idling at a red traffic light. Beside him sat his glamorous consort, modelled after the famous pop star's wife, heavily penciled, her hair's gouache ziggurat poised behind the glass windshield like the death mask of Nefertiti. Haunted by the receding horizon of natural light, Palmer's camera trailed the *coupé* all the way to the waved wing of the International Hotel's standing monolith. Eddie Phoenix sprang forward dressed in a car hop's uniform, *à la mode 77 Sunset Strip*, and opened the *coupé's* door, a sentinel in this Pompeii of modernism, guardian of the mausoleum where the pop star would be ceremonially interred ... Death-by-Vegas!

The Theme Of Resurrection. "Elvis' exhibition of himself on stage in Vegas is a series of sculptures on the Theme of Resurrection," Dr. Philip Byrne elaborated for Diane Blake, his glance straying among the crowd, for he thought he glimpsed Eddie Phoenix masquerading as a waiter at the function. "Johnny Esquire is Phoenix's clever decoy of course ..." Diane froze the drypoint clarity of her line within the spaciously mirrored foyer. "A decoy, for what? Assassination?" Her increasing attentiveness toward Jason Palmer irritated him. So splendid dressed in saturating waterfalls of glass, she nevertheless shadowed some inhibition he couldn't quite fathom, still, architecture's oblique sexual geometries of plane-and-angle enhanced the mysteries of her beauty. Perhaps he should devise geometric responses to her indifference, become more sexually Euclidean, conjure Magian symbols on her flesh with his fingertips. Striding on stage to thunderous applause, the famous pop icon's resurrected persona possessed a symbolist air with his fusion of Aeschylus, Freud and Caruso, publicly, while his private life might inspire an updated version of Huysman's *à Rebours*. Diane manoeuvred herself close against the apron of the stage, model for a Mary Magdalene stroking the New Christ's white shoes, readying herself for a *Love Me Tender* kiss. Las Vegas energized the desert as an embodiment of the fallen Archangel in his most glamorous if frivolous mood, for he was Time's supreme gangster and archetypal gambler: of course the roulette wheel would someday stop spinning and the party be declared over. Was this Elvis' spiritual message?

The Eliad II. *"I am contemplating how God's pencil is shading us on the canvas of Life. We can be so easily erased. How can I summon up a feeling of timelessness in my own life? God bequeaths to me His breadth here in the world. Who has not heard of Elvis? Whenever youth convene in the future to sing and celebrate their freedom from the tyranny of the past, it will be because of me. My spirit will be moving among them. For my generation, I am its meditation on Time, Memory and Immortality!"*

Desert Song. Beneath the stone-sharpened Abrahamic blade of the moon, the early morning skyline, Las Vegas' spiritual boundary, stretched away as bloodied as dyed embroidery. Dusted in early sunbeams a caravan of speeding chariots followed the pop Ezekiel's trailer across the Mosaic sea of sand. The desert city's radiant jewel strangely dimmed with every approaching sunrise. Why had the pop star abandoned the insular wingspread of the International Hotel? And why did this dead-sea of congealed sand preoccupy him as a source of pilgrimage at this time on the threshold of the seventies? In the near-distance beside the parked trailer, the famous weaver-of-song still in his show-stopping Bedouin white jump-suit, stood clearly visible to the entourage accompanying Jason Palmer, his head anointed now with oil-of-sunlight, his voice audible echoing across space. "Who turned this world into a forlorn desert?" Diane Blake's rhetorical question floated from her lips like the fading Vegas bursts of neon absorbed against the brightening horizon. "Yes, it has been observed, Nature possesses an appalling sameness ..." The motorcycle courier approached at a speed catching them all by surprise. Attractively outfitted in leather, the courier leaned close to Palmer's ear. Unable to finish his conjectural statement about Nature, Dr. Philip Byrne watched Palmer swing astride the pillion seat and the motorcycle accelerate away, pamphlets fluttering free, so many galaxies issuing from a Planck-moment. Dr. Byrne snatched at one: the advertisement, simple enough, pictured a glossy International Hotel, scene of Elvis' triumphant resurrection, or, as Palmer preferred: *His Josephian casting into the well!* All insolence, their chauffeur, Eddie Phoenix, kicked at the settling sheaf of pamphlets, and was heard to mutter: "Behold, the Mount of his inheritance!" Clocks ticked, but when would the time come to abandon Las Vegas' modern Babylon?

Bringing It On Home. While Jason Palmer's flower child love-interest browsed the local supermarket aisles, Paulette Taylor indulged her own sexual shorthand, its jotting pad brevity, with Eddie Phoenix in the Oceanside apartment, his Valentino incarnation. As her torso ululated swiftly and his silent movie touches slid across her hairless inner thighs, perhaps measuring the emergence of his as-yet-unborn child, another banished Archangel readying to corrupt the world, he focused on the transmission coming in from a Las Vegas television studio, a religious program featuring Palmer and Dr. Philip Byrne as guests. Still pre-orgasmic, Paulette studied the plumbline of his smoldering silence, its chemistry in the quiet apartment something of a resurgent aphrodisiac, the molecular model of an orgasm she had experimented with, tried to decode without success. Finally, the fingers of one hand slipping a breast back into its bra-cup, she strolled over to the television and turned up the volume. An interviewer was addressing a keening Palmer, very Hamletian in mood, as always remolding the script: "So, what then is your theological argument here, how is this pop star a vindication of Darwinism?" Eddie Phoenix's expression honed its imagery of malevolence, and with her palms cupping her breasts in the bra, Paulette suddenly felt the fallen Archangel in three-dimensional depth-and-outline limned in her coitus with him. Palmer's voice overlaid the sensation: "In this world's desolation, a rose blooms, a chalice burgeons, waves of perfume flood space. Time waxes with the white light of Elvis' brilliance, but of course its magnificence is destined to wane, the Law of Friction has been set in motion just for such a purpose." Paulette became conscious of the flower child's sheaf of spices loading the air, a shedding of autumnal leaves, as she entered the apartment. Her shopping list might prove enlightening. A question was put to Palmer: "How will Elvis attain the true *Art of Dying*, like his illustrious forbears?" The flower child's wandering eyes were interminably lost in her own post-coital forgetfulness, as if she and Palmer had been lovers for millennia and every erotic sensation exhausted aeons ago. "Like Jesus with Lazarus, Elvis calls the antique world back to life." Seated alongside Palmer in art deco chairs, Dr. Byrne was observed to wince at this expression of spiritual patriotism, although his white-on-white summer-suit conspired to idealize his cynicism. The flower child idly scooped yogurt with a finger as the androgynous motorcycle courier knocked at the open door.

US Male (2:42). Montaged cinematic imagery materialized from the projector beams flooding the movie theater's *Cave of Darkness*, unraveling short-cuts of Elvis' birth-through-death timeline, all synchronized to the 2:42 of *US Male*. Jason Palmer's *decoupage* of the frames evoked the polished facets of a skillful lapidary's cutting some precious jewel. Tonally pure, Elvis sang *The Way to God* without existentially describing it, although his Sirian presence, brightest star in the world's constellation, fixed a pattern of divinity. The vitality and elasticity of his cosmic hair crowning the monolith of *The Man* nodded, and earth and sky shook. How will he die? Buried in his pink Cadillac, itself a priceless armor of metals, a wondrous shield, his Cleopatra beside him in his Mark Antony mood? His hero's spirit, experiencing unquiet in life would sleep in peace when death came. Dr. Philip Byrne observed Johnny Esquire and Paulette Taylor slip away quietly with the screening still-in-progress. "She's becoming quite the socialite with her sexual favors," he whispered to Diane Blake. "I sense you're more cerebral about whom you're willing to touch loins with." Palmer's shadow caressed the screen presence of the pop star's black-haired bride: but was she Elvis' Salome, or Mariamne?

The Eliad III. *"There is a Freemasonry embodied in my name: **ELVIS**. I created and brought to America a ceremonial whose gestures, postures, rituals and initiations have with the passage of the sixties begun to lose their original Mystery, for everyone now mimics them, dilutes their significance. To be the ONE, then to see these transient reflections focus the gaze of America once reserved for myself is devastating, emotionally. This must be how God feels when the pathetic human mind is allured by the myriad illusions which flash by it. As darkness descended this evening I sat watching the glass of my bedroom window crystallizing to onyx. The emptying of light from the frame metaphored the emptying of light from the pane of my mind."*

Have You Fallen For This Equestrienne? Whistling *In The Ghetto*, the sepulchral theme song of the fallen Archangel, archetype of the *Angry Young Man* in three-dimensional space, the projectionist handed cans of cine-film to the leather-jacketed motorcycle courier. Unfazed by Jason Palmer's attentive question, its mystery to her, Diane Blake answered: "In what sense do you mean, *fallen?*" His senses responded to the delicacy of her slender ankle, and gentle trapezoid of foot naked as it touched the floor of her apartment. "Light is the voice of Time's dramatic poetry enunciated in space's theater." Templated together against the tissue of the movie screen, dimmed in a negative near-darkness, he kneeled and began tracing the geometry of her leg-stance with a fingertip, confessing how as a filmmaker he was haunted by the coming **LAST DAYS OF ELVIS**. "Observe the spatial capacity of my film-frames, Diane. How can I squeeze three-dimensional depth-of-field into two-dimensional space? Hold the analogy, and consider how can I then impress fourth-dimensional experiences within three-dimensional space? How can my soul pick up my human persona and *be* itself in this screenplay? Let us imagine we are fourth-dimensional souls rehearsing these human personae in the drama of the world. Souls incarnate in three-dimensional space, create a human persona, and it all goes wrong ..." Diane peered back through the radiant darkness toward the projection room and physically started. Film mysteriously rolled, catching them in an intersection of projector beams, throwing their silhouettes against the movie screen.

Sex & Saigon. Fingers separating two Venetian louvers, Jason Palmer scanned the street where Johnny Esquire and Eddie Phoenix loitered by the chrome front-end moldings of his parked Chevrolet, twin fifties time-travellers adrift on the threshold of the seventies, as mystified as everyone with Elvis' startling resurrection, passive witnesses to the event's burying of the sixties. Talcum drifted to the wood-grain floor of the apartment outlining Diane Blake's footfalls. On the television, a soundless orgasm of artillery hits rocked a town under siege. When she answered the phone Palmer x-rayed her: how could this etching of bones be instinct with intelligence? Could he invent with her a new sexual *moment* ready for the movie cameras? He glanced across her bookshelves for inspiration. There was always the auto-eroticism of the novel, perhaps Molly's soliloquy from *Ulysses*. She raised her fingers to her hair and exposed the sexual hollow of an armpit. The flash of a hand-gun was frozen in the television's 'Nam retrospective to enhance the *frisson* of the street execution captured in the streets of Saigon during Tet. Below, Esquire and Phoenix, Paulette Taylor's sexual Castor-and-Pollux, cockily sparred with each other as they laughed and sauntered off down the street. Who mediated between life-and-death? What was the *and*?

Towards An Orgasm. (i) **CUBISM** – Diane Blake disrobed from a dress-suit tailored to her conservatism's underlying sexual mannerisms. A champagne magnum fizzed when shaken: Jason Palmer visualized her in a garment composed of newspaper print across which sexual paint spilled. Later, her presence in the cubic space of the shower stall, awash with soap suds, undercut a million reproductions of Renoiresque nymphs bathing *al fresco* by pools and streams. The geometry of modernism eroticized Pythagoras. Kissing, they lay at right angles to each other, only their mouthes physically touching, while the seductive aroma of percolated coffee hung in the air. (ii) **RONDEL** – The sphere of the eye imaged existence's primary circle, the horizon of vision itself the secondary circle, both models for fallen space's claustrophobic enclosure. Palmer's tongue caressed the softness of a peeled ruby-red grape. The sinking sun framed by the window cast the aura of a pomegranate into the space of the apartment. How sweet the seeds tasted! (iii) **BAROQUE** – Palmer remembered cruising the city's baroque cloverleaves in his Chevrolet. What monumental sculptural arteries energized the fallen Archangel's heart! *Diana* emerged from the shower stall wearing the marble of a swimmer's nudity. Millions of suburban swimming pools were modelled on her torso's curves. His orgasm resembled Actaeon's death throes. (iv) **ARABESQUE** – What was this supine *thing* laid with teasing equilibrium on the moonscape of the bed? Palmer's fingertips followed her body's sinuous, slow-flexing line, only pausing at her tightly linear pubis, entrance to a metaphysical absolute. Here was a cast contoured in the very flesh of his sexual desire. (v) **ROCOCO** – She made a gorgeous cartoon for transference to the fresco of her bed. Already a crown of stars was visible in a flash of sky domed in his imagination. More arousing though was the vine leaf, the incurling frond of her pubis. (vi) **SURREALISM** – Sex's metaphysical *mal de mer*, a flooded coastline, a spillage of spume, disturbed the Pythagorean geometry of classical *Being*, became a textural dream of subconscious *Existences*. Even their dinner conversation was a calculus of insoluble dream-states precipitated into edible forms.

Diane Nude, Seen From Behind. The motion of undressing was for Diane Blake an exercise in ritual invisibility, a first-time moment of chilled-through marble, of inhibition shadowed by metaphysical expectations. Jason Palmer's Aeschylan intensity may very well be carved with modern insights but her own compass of temptation was fluctuating wildly enough. His Pythagorean notion of stripping sex to line-and-circle, his seeing her sculpted on a pedestal on the mosaic-tiled floor of her bathroom, generated about him an emotional turbulence comparable with Greek drama. He kneeled with fingertips searching the sculpted space the line-and-curve of her body occupied, the plasticity of her womb, and murmured of acts related to the conceptual deaths of Elvis. How quickly he curved sex from sentimentality to melodrama, propping her naked against the scented pillow, encouraging her to blow soap bubbles, bringing her wrist lower so the swelling *plastique* burst upon contact with her nipple. A seismic shudder went deep, deep, oars swept a placid river in unison and suddenly existence possessed the texture of an ancient tapestry. Diane filled the bedroom with herself in her ecstasy. A *feather* remained buoyed aloft!

The Eliad IV. *"My body is a copy, a mere tracery, a shadowed contour sunk in the pure water of this mirror. How the chilling ice hugs my physique. O soul, let me see your Beauty within, let me be the radiance of your Intelligence diffusing itself! O soul, be the sculptor of this statue! Find within this block of marble the perfect lineaments of your Form, and disengage them from the world to gaze upon."*

Elvisacidalacidesoxyribonucleidacid. A comparably lovely resonance of percussive yellows flowed with the eurhythmic repetition of sweeping sand dunes. All day sunbeams had stung the hemline of the flower child's bikini bottoms. Her naked upper torso was soaked in marine smells, wave aromas, from breasting the ocean swells as she stepped across the miniature camera tracks like some captive Chryseis, or amoral Cressida on the foreshore of Troy. Dr. Philip Byrne stood in his white linen suit scrutinizing the tracking camera as Palmer conjugated the perspectives of the sand dunes among which stood a *Wooden Horse* of billboards. The billboards collectively made up a portrait, molecules in the chemistry of a pop star, the composite fragments forming links in the chain of Elvis' being. Palmer had conjured the arrangement from Diane's architectural consciousness, her portfolio the inspiration, so Elvis modelled the *Illusius* of Phidias, his most recognizable feature though, his glorious head, missing, except perhaps fourth-dimensionally. Dr. Byrne massaged his neck as the flower child levitated from a cushion of dune warmed by her derriere. In passing, Palmer's fingertips caressed the curve. When he then turned to face the sun a flood of yellow sunbeams washed the youthful portrait of a seraphic-faced John Milton, silk-screened onto the cuirass of his white T-shirt.

Beautiful As A Wreck Of Paradise. Space inclined and swayed with the twist of the DNA spiral. The azure Magritte sky was ablaze with unseen angels. As for the polished enamel sand dunes, they possessed the purity of the dreaded abyss' silence after the ringing chorales of Heaven. The waves of dunes were kinetic impulses aroused by the fallen Archangel as he prepared for his lonely voyage through three-dimensional space, point of disembarkation, Planet Earth. Stretching the length of the beach far off into the heat-haze lay a parade of sunbathers. Already at work among the sand dunes, a construction team was assembling an immense model of a reclining pop star from sets of blueprints delivered by the motorcycle courier. Doomed Protesilaus, Lt. John Kirby's ghosted photographic presence, a mannequin in aviator-style sunglasses reminiscing all the fallen GIs in 'Nam, appeared on the spiritual crest of a dune dazzling with the sheen of a polished pearl. Startled by the low pulsating throb of a helicopter rising and banking behind Lt. Kirby, perhaps the vibration of his thought, the crowd of sunbathers resembled G.I.s on R&R from the war torn beaches of 'Nam. The beachscape evoked a vision of what 'Nam would resemble after God had scourged it. Jason Palmer, stripping off his Miltonian T-shirt, strode forth across the beach like some Byronic swimmer of space, evocative of that first great modern poet of a man to perish on the shores of Hellas. And, presiding over the whole landscape, the *Illusius* of Elvis made the universal, *existential*!

Ecumenical Council 1970. "Cliff! Cliff! Cliff!" rose the audience chant, but a Wurlitzer jukebox on stage unexpectedly lit up with *Suspicious Minds*, prophetic lyric on the certainty of the Fall of Man. Christian evangelists had circulated posters and flyers across the city all week advertising this event, a Eucharistic revelation to be delivered by the *British Elvis*. Jason Palmer ambled across the boards from the wings of the stage, microphone in hand, ignoring the lectern prepared for the guest speakers ... *We're caught in a trap* ... accompanied by three virgins all aglow in white, puzzling the expectant audience, more so when he physically dramatized his spoken word. *"Come up hither, and I will shew thee things which must be hereafter.* The fallen Archangel is the Supreme Artist of the Absurd, yes, and we are his materials, his uncut marble, his canvas-and-paints, his unmolded clay. How he taunts the Creator with these, our sacrificial forms of mortality. Lucifer, the playwright, would steal Eternity, but space grows weary of Time and he knows it. Behold! ..." Rolling spheres of fiery napalm ballooned over tropical foliage, and barren-pitted earth screened as a backdrop, a seared landscape of fire-and-brimstone, an apocalypse readily identifiable by the audience. Jeers from deep within the auditorium gathered momentum. Like spilling mercury flowing through Time, brawls spread and the mass of people heaved. Dr. Philip Byrne thought he glimpsed Eddie Phoenix masquerading as an anti-war demonstrator, vigorously assaulting the born-again Christians. Nursing an unsighted blow delivered to his cheekbone, Dr. Byrne shepherded the flower child through the surging exit out onto the sidewalk. *"And whosoever was not found written in the book of life was cast into the lake of fire,"* resounded in Dr. Byrne's ear.

The Eliad V. *"Observe how these Army dress blues harden my torso into an ironically detached pose. My feet will journey no further in this incarnation. Why should I travel from land-to-land, I am no longer a pilgrim. Graceland shall be my soul's Temple. Yet, I am still a forgery of Apollo, some fatality aureoles my physique's classical perfection. Who will inspire me to acquire beautiful habits but my soul? Can this idealized canon, this hallowed Parthenon of a body-column nourish me spiritually in the years to come?"*

Milton à la Mode. In Dr. Philip Byrne's eyes, this metaphysically floated obsession of Jason Palmer's to be the filmmaker of the liberation from Paradise Lost, began to climax with his choreography of Johnny Esquire, staging him in a compendium of Elvis movies re-shot in a succession of décors ... Vermeer, Ingres, Dali and Pop Art among them. Moreover, on rented soundstages across the city, *Elvis* was filmed in Daniel's lion's den, on Fellini's rotating Laurentian grill lifted from his *Satyricon*, as Job and Oedipus Rex, for the famous singer was already otherwise consigned to a footnote on the pages of Hollywood, a formulaic *extra*. Up-to-the-minute in relevance, *Elvis* was cleverly montaged with scenes of the North Vietnamese delegation in Paris. Viewing the *rushes*, Dr. Byrne watched the totemic Greek Elvis suffer for humanity. The fabulous icon was now healthy again after years in the wilderness, if still a man of Byzantine moodiness, sculptural and untouchable themed in *white*. The roustabout, crop duster, deep-sea fisherman, southern simpleton and itinerant nightclub singer had successfully eluded the allegorical understanding of all the media, Palmer excepted.

Curriculum Vitae. (i) **THE BEGUILING OF MERLIN** (Edward Burne-Jones) – Alchemist of his generation, Elvis submits to incarnational bondage within the fallen Archangel's hallucinatory space, his well-illustrated look and gaze a facet cut from the jewel of his soul-in-travail. (ii) **THE LAMENT OF ICARUS** (Herbert Draper) – A freewheeling aerialist, Elvis magically falls into incarnation, *Blue Hawaii* style! (iii) **HYLAS AND THE NYMPHS** (John Waterhouse) – Elvis' soft-chalk physique heralds the depth Time graces the Antique World with, as mythology segues into cosmology. Always haunting this singing philosopher is the circular existence of identity's pool. (iv) **THE DEATH OF CHATTERTON** (Henry Wallis) – Adulterer with a sublime face carved of fragrant soap, Elvis ravishes even that nocturne which is the Dark Night of the Soul, his dying being a dazzling completion even as his singing throat cools. (v) **THE DEATH OF MARAT** (David) – Elvis' nemesis models a revolutionary Archimedes, the Che Guevara of his time, a *papier-mâché* roustabout of a politician-made-good, a counterfeit imprisoned forever within a frame of canvas. (vi) **ISABELLA AND THE POT OF BASIL** (William Holman Hunt) – Orpheus' head, scion of every flower myth, the very herb of adolescence flavoring successive generations, watched-over and guarded by a luscious Priscilla.

Caprices. Tableaued on the bonnet of his gleaming Chevrolet, Mendelssohn piano *Caprices* racing through the corridors of thought, spotlighted under the evening sky by the single headlamp of the stationary motorcycle, Jason Palmer considered: Am I *subject*, or *object*? The epaulettes of the Milky Way shimmered along the wingspread of the fallen Archangel. Inside the Chevrolet, Diane molded her breast with the palm of a hand, and turning her head aside saw again the letters of condemnation from various Christian sects spilling across the rear seat. "Tell me, is your own rebellion born of the Arch-Rebel's?" What was he doing now on the bonnet of the car gazing up into the sky, hoping to spiritually scramble the fallen Archangel's brain-waves? Earlier they had visited stonemasons contracting ever more elaborate cenotaphs for Elvis' tomb. Only the inscribed epitaph remained constant: *He fell in the battle to regain Paradise!* The nearby ocean condensed to sparkling crystals under starlight.

Rock'n'Roll. As the exquisite glow of metaphysical sensation faded from her loins Diane Blake lay back on the cool sand following with her eyes the night sky's flow of pearls. Already Jason Palmer's sexual image drawn across the topography of her body was laid in fast-fading colors. Her fingertips brushed the surface of beach sand. No doubt he would illuminate the significance of their lovemaking's symbolism for her. "Diane, the possible forms derived from thought are as numerous as the grains of polished sand lining this beach." What was he thinking during coitus? Probably unstitching the Milky Way's embroidery, unraveling the Archangelic thread, but what image would he weave from so many solar masses, the head of Elvis? In his presence it was impossible not to think.

Is Elvis A Thought? Parting the compass arms of her legs from the fulcrum of her pubis at a Masonic angle, Diane Blake climbed astride the motorcycle's pillion and folded herself against the leather-jacketed courier, illegitimate emotions for Jason Palmer blurring her thoughts. He followed them in the Chevrolet for some distance. The planetarium inside the fallen Archangel's head was aglow with cold stars. The ebb-and-flow of the war in 'Nam troubled his spirit as a preliminary skirmish by the Arch-Rebel's forces testing America's Forces of Light. Stars evoked the U.S. flag lackeying in the tidal delta of the Mekong. On a whim Palmer pulled over and plunged into the viscous ocean for a Byronic swim toward the beacon of an anchored schooner. What could he distil from the breaking wave of galaxies apart from a sense of Time's overpowering tedium? Elvis' glorious hair was a supernova of anti-matter shaped after the *frisson* of the night sky. Diane's erotic contortions on the sand earlier demonstrated her architect's feeling for layout and composition on space's three-dimensional grid. Already his memory of her had the feeling of an ancient tapestry from which Luciferan figures emerged and disappeared. But this was the destiny of fourth-dimensional *being* crushed into three-dimensional space!

The Eliad VI. *"Bring on the Dark Night of My Soul for all rebellion in my heart is quenched. This hand, once snapping its fingers at convention, now describes a limp adagio. My very stature forces this severance from light, plunges me in darkness, but my saturnine innocence, my gentleness, my diaphaneity shall remain a sacramental visualization before the world. And pleasure? I'll float upon an endless stream of wealth and opulence and ride in monarchial triumph through Memphis!"*

(There Will Be) Peace In The Valley (For Me Someday). Infinity cast a semi-tragic aura in temporal three-dimensional space over the Canaan of another incarnation. Las Vegas, chosen scriptural site for Elvis' retrospective of sculptures of himself, sacrificially resplendent in the logical picture of God's Thought, lay in the valley of the Shadow of Death. Embedded on the floor of Hell, crucible for the alchemy of the fallen Archangel, Vegas emerged as a low-lying neon-mist, geometric city for his manifestation in space-time, a chemistry of perversion. Idling by the roadway in his Chevrolet, Jason Palmer ignored the taunting helicopter skimming the asphalt, watching dawn animate the sky's stained glass with pure gold, his feelings for the transformation heightened to a crisp excitation. "The furnace begins to spark and roar. Elvis is our radiant Star of the Morning reigning over this desert Thebaid." An alien Ruth embodied out-of-her-time, the flower child's incarnation beside him was simply pigmentation on canvas, she appeared oblivious to the significance of Vegas' apparition burning up in the distance, or the low-flying helicopter. "Elvis and myself have stalked this Archangel from incarnation-to-incarnation, been interred in life's mortuary beneath the sun's low-slung skylight there thousands of times." Accelerating down the highway across a landscape modeling that for a future lunar colony, a gambler's Canaan, he thought of Elvis and the previous year's Moon landings. Elvis was a vibrant vein of light pulsing within Vegas' compact jewel, his name was everywhere. The International Hotel's persona beckoned, a subliminal architectural torso wingèd against the otherwise precision of horizontals denuding the landscape.

Madonna Without Child. Workmen continued remodeling space within the gallery even as the exhibits were being positioned on the dust-covered floor. "I understand you're financing the refurbishment ..." Dr. Philip Byrne guided Diane Blake by the elbow between to sheet-draped exhibits. "Was it a planned childless marriage?" His surface all dense blank verse, Eddie Phoenix silently introduced himself into their *tableau à deux* by stripping the sheet from an exhibit. Diane gasped, recognizing a fragment of her apartment recast as an airport transit lounge scene. "Childless marriage? That I would be a Raphael *Madonna-without-child*, you mean?" Her verbal recovery was swift. She circled the plaster-of-Paris representation of herself, bare-footed, in bikinis, dancing *The Twist* in her apartment's airport lounge. "Quite the *cause célèbre*, mmm? Were Palmer and yourself, *sexual*?" Phoenix's metaphoric showmanship, dressed in workman's overalls, further extended to swirling the sheet from another tableau. Euclidean diners sat at a table seeking a workable solution to the theorem on their plates, a yellowing, curling flower of *The Female Eunuch*, artistic *nouvelle cuisine* indeed! "*Sexually*? In what sense? Surely you agree, he's rather sexual for the Greer woman, not me. He visualizes my womb as an L.Z. for generations of incarnations-to-come, a laboratory no less ..."

Gallery '70. Glossy magazine coverage reported audience consternation at the public showing of the tableaux later that evening: (i) Herms of Elvis '56. (ii) Oath of the Elvii – "So long as I draw breath I shall never cease singing." (iii) The Male Eunuch – figural representations of the fallen Archangel. (iv) The wall-mounted front-end of a Ford Skyliner convertible with bonnet statuette modelled after the flower child, while mannequins of Jason Palmer and Diane Blake engage in coitus on the front seat.

(v) Germaine Greer – *The Great Australian Nude*, setting Elvis dreaming of Vegas' Thebaid.

A Fading Festival Poster. Iphigenia was borne away, stretchered toward the ambulance on the gleaming aluminum altar of a trolley. With the breeze rising, tomorrow the ocean would be ablaze with colorful sails. Jason Palmer knelt beside the motorcycle's spinning wheel, fascinated with the geometry of *circumstance*, its circular motion, a mathematical formula with meanings far beyond the crude articulation of language. The pink Cadillac stood outlined against the curvilinear sweep of the flyover. Off to one side with his Priscilla look-a-like, Johnny Esquire was heard to remark in a southern drawl: "They've gone to Jesus." From his vantage point crouched over the headlamp's shattered glass embedded as mosaic in the asphalt, Palmer contrasted the cool objectivity of the priest-like ambulance attendees. His fingertips cupped the bowl of the headlamp's chalice from which the golden thread of light guiding the flower child through the world's darkness was now extinguished. Although some distance away, Diane Blake sensed his pain as a bow's slide across strings of an out-of-tune violin, and contracted inward, struggling for breath. Only a memory now was the flower child's perennially fatigued manner, a helpless Briseis, a fading festival poster. No more would Palmer explore the sexual delta of this time-stalled Mississippi Queen. Diane was witnessing him engaged in a theological argument between life-and-death: "I absorb the overflowing richness of the setting sun's colors into the dream of living so I might die textured with Eternity." Dr. Philip Byrne's clever offhandedness when confronted by the flower child's chalk outline drawn on the asphalt appalled her sensibility: "She was too wristy with the throttle. By the way, where's Phoenix?" The lyricism of surgery couldn't save her this time from the severity of injuries even if the ambulance priests could have transferred her immediately to an operating table's altar. In a surrealistic context the canon-and-fugue of the operating table and her prone torso would compare with a composition by Bach performed by a chamber orchestra of medical staff. Diane shuffled, felt as responsive as a mere shadow-puppet in a theater, but who was her puppeteer?

How Would Elvis Philosophize His Death? Tawny orange, the setting sun burnished the late-afternoon sand dunes. Twilight's gradual dispersion brooded over the still-hissing ocean. Diane Blake's poised shoulders were still aglow with the glorious sunset. Jason Palmer emerged from the *Wooden Horse* of billboards placed among the ashen dunes. From the crest of a dune where Dr. Philip Byrne joined her, she could make out the finished constructional portrait of **ELVIS** a team of volunteers had been working on all week. Since the death of the flower child, Palmer had been avoiding the presence of Elvis' *torso*, his *physique*, rather focusing the touch of his gaze on his philosophizing *soul*. The incarnational model to be sacrificed would create a Tao transcending the spacetime continuum. "I've heard his intention here is to detonate a nuclear device, two-dimensional of course," Dr. Byrne began. "Elvis is to become, literally, the *atomic-powered singer* under which title he was publicized during his first

Vegas engagement in '56." Elvis's portrait exploded multi-dimensionally in swirling spirals of electricity. A glaze of flesh-peeling napalm smeared all spatial surfaces. The dunes rocked in the suicide throes of the fallen Archangel trapped in two-dimensional space. Harmonic disturbances subsided in a subtle, smoky haze and only a lightning sketch of Elvis remained visible. His head hymned the music of the spheres above the onyx seascape.

The Eliad VII. *"For me, singing's obsession has been a struggle comparable with the spiritual torsions of Michelangelo's sculpture: the Voice of God would burst free! Singing has brought me a Palace in the Land of Grace, where I knew freedom for the first time in my life."*

III
EINSTEIN & WORLD WAR III

Physics & Revolution. Diane Blake's fingertip bent a Venetian blind's louver. Beneath the University clock tower framed in Spanish sandstone, Jason Palmer's audacious leather-clad courier waited astride her motorcycle, a tableau attracting the curiosity of milling students, themselves a montage of political activists bringing the concept of a Pop Art *happening* to revolution. Palmer, the academician, now there was an incongruous image! She winced with sunburn, feeling branded with a red-iron across her shoulders. Behind her, Dr. Philip Byrne had separated himself from the convocation of physicists and crossed the laboratory. "Well, Diane, the battleground has shifted!" She glimpsed Palmer now swing *a tergo* across the pillion seat. "World War III will be fought *here* against the fallen Archangel." An erotic *frisson* engendered by Palmer *a tergo* with the courier proved irresistible. "Palmer has formulated a plan: he's on a subatomic mission to capture and imprison Lucifer in this laboratory." Illicit responses inwardly massaged her as she conjured again electrified sensations re-experienced when he palmed her *Mount of Venus*. "Diane ..." She day-dreamed them both lying coupled on the foreshore, sand draining away the wave's kiss. Was he haranguing the political activists from the pillion? The courier's leather-clad fingers gripped and twisted the motorcycle's throttle. Lt. John Kirby's ghosted presence slouched by a particle accelerator, the eye of their generation's conscience severely shaded behind aviator-style sunglasses.

A Revolution In Painting. Rich lodes of cultural ore coalesced to materialize in the University architecture's miraculous vibration of Spanish sandstone. Strolling with a fifties stiletto roll to her carriage Diane Blake was a sensual garnish to the scholarly ambience of this hallowed seat of learning incarnate from some Spanish Golden Age. "In essence, Time is trigonometry ..." Crossing a quadrangle they were jostled by students dressed in a pastiche of army fatigues, shaking anti-war placards and chanting: *"Kent State ... Kent State ... We won't debate!"* Swept along by the raging human tide they were streamed toward a hastily erected platform where Eddie Phoenix wielded his weapon of a megaphone. Shadowed by Lt. John Kirby and Johnny Esquire on the makeshift political stage, Phoenix strutted about in torn and patched jeans, a headband badged with anti-war slogans. Wearing a Che Guevara T-shirt, expostulating *Look Back In Anger* style for the hippie *Hell, no, I won't go!* generation, he verbally enflamed the students to storm the Physics laboratories and level the University stone by stone. Then Johnny Esquire hustled forward strumming an acoustic guitar and singing Dylan's *Talkin' World War III Blues*, even though he rather resembled a *roustabout* Elvis lost in a time-warp on the Paramount movie lot. But Diane was less enthralled with these political gestures than her companion, Dr. Philip Byrne, and her attention scanned a group of arts students moving large canvases across the lawn. She recognized immediately the director of these students, Raphael Summers, someone she had dated years ago before her marriage. The bizarre backdrop of canvases floated by peacefully, an icon to a period when painting was once an incendiary act. The abstracts seemed somehow familiar in their imagery. Then she remembered the papers scattered about the laboratory with their subatomic particle tracks, magnetic fields and sheets-of-lightning effect. The canvases evocatively emotionalized Physics with color-ores, the residue of angels fallen into two-dimensions, the mineralized space of Paradise Lost, if Jason Palmer's assertions were to be believed. Later, on the evening news bulletins, she caught footage of a spectacular bonfire of paintings in the University grounds, shuddering with Palmer's intuition this was a metaphor describing how the angels fell into the Lake of Burning Marl. Also visible in the glow cast by the erupting flames were the forms of Eddie Phoenix and Lt. John Kirby.

At Every Instant Of Flight I Am At Rest. Esoteric transmissions from three-dimensional space's continuum visited Jason Palmer as these dreamscapes following his explorations of Elvis' movie *oeuvre*. (i) **WAVES** – Stationary with a softly melting Dalinian watch shaped after Elvis' face, he measured the time required for a single sand dune's wave to flow, perhaps the duration between the famous singer's incarnations. (ii) **MIRRORS** – Brain-waves, galaxies of physicists, including the thought-patterns of Newton and Einstein, voyaged on a sea of marble stars pursuing the albatross of the fallen Archangel: Elvis-as-gunslinger mirrored on aluminum by Warhol approached his showdown with Lucifer. (iii) **GRAVITATION** – The moon-flight's manned capsule returning into the Earth's atmosphere and splash-down re-enacted Lucifer's Phaetonesque fall into the Ocean of Time, a mirror shattered and a wave was created for humanity to surf through Eternity. (iv) **MAGNETISM** – In the dance of electromagnetism his hand grasped and pulled the sash of the Milky Way, spinning the torso of his silver-footed Thetis, Diane Blake, across the bakelite ballroom of the Universal Studio.

Raking The Sand. The Archangelic *Outsider's* shadow had carved its two-dimensional headstone over the flower child's prostrate torso, the flowery Zodiac of her sari skirt evocative of her sexual stylizations on the cusp of the seventies, as young women contemplated a freer existential self-definition. Eddie Phoenix too had raised her naked foot with his hand and kissed the ring with which she adorned her big toe, had sucked yogurt from her index finger, breathed the pungent nasturtium of her flesh, sexually adhered to her like bark to a smooth-fleshed eucalypti. Jason Palmer levitated from the tatami mat and left the apartment to meditate the dunes of his thoughts on the deserted beach. She had effortlessly adjusted herself to the Zen austerity of his re-fashioned apartment space, absorbed as she was in the artifice of the late-sixties purveyed through the *Alice-in-Wonderland* sideshow of Lennon-and-Ono, those dream-shaped playing cards, cartoon-figures distorted in the world's mirror. Leaving her asleep in the solitude of her dreaming's pre-Planck moments Palmer settled himself among the flute of waved dunes meditating between sun-and-surf within the space of his Zen sand garden. Dr. Philip Byrne visited him later that morning, while he was drawing a rake across the washed-out grey sand, creating marvelous waved patterns, a transcribed image of the sound of a breeze flowing through sharp pine needles.

Paradise Lost's Archaeological Site. "What on earth are you doing?" The flower child suddenly appeared out of the sun, the fallen Archangel's *agent provocateur*, shadowing Dr. Philip Byrne with her customary blank incomprehension, seemingly unaware of the bankruptcy of their sexual nocturne. "*Doing?* My brushstrokes are exposing layers of Paradise Lost's archaeological site, mimicking the fallen Archangel's brain waves so I can better understand the magnitude of his Fall." When the couple receded along the beach, Palmer stood on the crest of a dune studying the sand patterns, suddenly realizing they modelled an arrangement of Diane Blake's pubic hair lying against her flesh! In the interstice flowing between two dunes could be visualized the tail of Lucifer's bruised divinity, a slither of shadow impossible to grasp. The flower child would sit cross-legged on the tatami mat spread across the floor of the Oceanside apartment listening to Deep Purple's *Black Night* guitar riff over and over. Was the sand garden actually meditating *him*? Was *he* drawing the rake, or the sand drawing *him*? "What is this Zen garden of yours imagining about us?" she had asked. How could he rake for her Dali's famous painting, *The Persistence of Memory*? Still, the dandelion-petals of her throwaway consciousness intrigued him. One morning he dropped an open book in her cross-legged lap. "Plunge into the frame of three-dimensional space, dissolve into the text. Life is fraught with the instability of walking across a rubber tatami stretched thinly in space, with the moral code of $E = mc^2$ defining how we should act."

The Space Of ME. Silver platters of *hors d'oeuvres* and glittering champagne flutes accompanied the energetic bursts of conversation echoing off the gallery walls. "Lucifer is only as free as the length of the chain of his thought, and there is an immense amount of inert black coal spaced between the Galactic Gods sweeping their sabers of white fire into its depth." The silent paintings on the walls were themselves *homage*, an abstract mosaic of radiance, scales on the dragon-space of the fallen Archangel. Caviar flavored Paulette Taylor's welcoming smiles, cut to the deeper crimson of her gown, while her fingers sewed a dance in the air as she manufactured her wonderful repartee. "Forgive the *Disharmony in Red*. I call it, The Space of **ME**! Now, what's this I hear, you've applied to become a patent's clerk, or something ..." Jason Palmer motioned himself by her with the mannered jadedness of a sculptural presence from *Last Year at Marienbad*. "All the better to get the world thinking on *time*!"

Sweet Bird Of Youth. Dr. Philip Byrne tossed him a well-thumbed copy of *The Female Eunuch*, eyeing the factual presence of the freshly hung canvases, the *raison d'etre* for being there, itself a conundrum of course. "Paulette, she's caviar among fallen Archangels." Dr. Byrne sensed irony in Jason Palmer's description, conscious of the aroma of his own fingers. "And these paintings, are they *existential*, and in what sense?" Did he mean the magisterial displacement of Diane Blake's breast profiled in space? Certainly, her abrasive glances in his direction alluded to a classically muted eroticism paginated somewhere in her psyche. Palmer gestured with *The Female Eunuch* like a Southern hot-gospeller might, but his words were for Dr. Byrne. "I feel myself no more than a framed portrait, hastily executed, hung here in space. These gestural paintings paint *us*!" The nuances of Dr. Byrne's surfacing nausea became visible as Diane conversed with the gallery's director, Raphael Summers, and Palmer played ornithologist, the observer *par excellence*. "In a moment of pique, before she met you, Diane told me about this *Sweet Bird of Youth*, Raphael Summers, how they were once, many years ago, the two wings of a bird. An albatross I should think. I wonder who will prove their *Ancient Mariner*, yourself? I haven't been able to bring myself to tell her he's become quintessentially *Greek*." Born three millennia too late, a triptych of marginalized Muses made their glorious entrance to polite applause ... Lorna, Jasmin and Donna Lee. "*Greek*, you say? In *that* sense?"

Equations, Muses & Paradise Lost. Searching for ever more profounder secrets to the fallen Archangel's *mystery* by a process of fourth-dimensional osmosis, Jason Palmer hostaged himself to the University physicists, sinking his sub-atomic consciousness through the febrile web of their abstruse equations chalked across the blackboards. Bunkered inside their on-campus laboratory, armed with photographic equipment and a mythology of *The Equation*, he awaited the arrival of The Muses, Lorna, Jasmin and Donna Lee, who had been lured by his promise of a paper on the physics of Paradise Lost for a prestigious scientific journal. The rather stiff-backed physicists, myopic geniuses in tobacco-soaked tweed jackets and flared bowties, pondered his elucidation of their equational dialogues in metaphysical phraseology, and his questioning of them on the possibility of coitus in a cyclotron. **JASMIN** was stenciled in black ink across the flank of an intersecting storage accelerator. Beyond the windows of the laboratory turmoil reigned. Student activists had set up barricades to resist imperialist authority. The Muses in borrowed white laboratory coats flirted with the physicists, unself-conscious of aromatic arabesques of breast-and-thigh naked under the fabric, ready for the revelation of Science to advance their careers. The Milky Way galaxy itself was focused through the lens of The Muses' physics!

The Muse – Clio. Lorna, whose delectable pale loins thawed as she obligingly stretched prone, horizontal along the laboratory table, welcomed the surveying eye of

Jason Palmer's camera, content to indulge his viewing of her as a galaxy being swept by a telescope. A montage of ripple-tank interference patterns, radial propagations exploring orgasm's wave-speed and distance-time relationship, with the transverse pulse of her breasts traveling along the elastic medium of her flesh, overlaid Palmer's perception of the human body's relationship to the sub-atomic spatial dimensions of the cosmos. Scripted beforehand on his theme, she obliged him without coloring her embarrassment until he came to diagram the wave-front of her orgasm, studying the soft galaxy of her abdomen vibrate up-and-down, contract-and-release, whereupon she saturated film-stock. In a time-lapse sequence he would share with her later in the physics theater he illustrated her orgasm as periodic circular waves, and draw for her a microcosmic correspondence with the macrocosm's expansion-contraction through three-dimensional space.

The Muse – Urania. Jasmin, alluring sex goddess of quantum mechanics, whom Jason Palmer pleaded to engage in coitus with him inside a particle accelerator, gave him an emphatic No!, dooming their nuclei to existential loneliness, denying their sub-atomic matter an emblematic embrace beyond the constraints of space-time. She did allow him, as pre-scripted when he danced a stick of chalk across the blackboard in an ejaculation of equations, to photograph her solo orgasm's vaporization curves, and pen the famous energy-of-an-electron equation across her abdomen with a tube of lipstick. His montage of her womb wherein was suspended a solarized star, and carefully-timed microcosmic bubble trails, evoked how decorative our coverage of space was ... *as above, so below*!

The Muse – Terpsichore. Donna Lee, whose terrestrial magnetism generated an electronic dance, sweet whirling dervish, about the nucleus of her microcosmic presence conjured up the center of a spiraling galaxy, space's promiscuous flower afloat on the waters of *nothingness*. Jason Palmer photographed and celebrated her navel as a microcosmic equivalent of the famous Puerto Rican radio telescope dish confirming the existence of her orgasm's gravity waves. Her torso lay as a single bar magnet with the iron filings of her orgasm evidence of a powerful field-of-force. Again, he lipsticked her torso with subtextual equations completing his Archangelic make-over of The Muses, delving to measure the plateau of pleasure beyond pleasure.

A Joust With The Fallen Archangel's Evangelist. "The bend-sinister on the Shield of Space, is *Time*. Nothing can go faster through three-dimensional space than light. Imagine a vast rubber sheet stretched through the cosmos: have you even tried running across a trampoline, how its space bends when impacted. *Light* itself is space. We cannot escape. Our persona's image is doomed through inertia to eternal visibility within the spacetime continuum." Dr. Philip Byrne sat upright, rigid in his pin stripe suit listening to Jason Palmer provoke the religious fraternity tuning in to the Christian television program. Opposite them, the freshly scrubbed interviewer shifted uneasily in his chair, his inertia a troubling inertia against Resurrection Day. "Time is *relative*.

And what was the Savior's *transfiguration* but the switching on an electro-magnetic current lighting our existential claustrophobia. Exciting, yes, worthy of Renaissance masterpieces, *because there was no tangible power source*! However, what we must grasp is the truth the whole pseudo-mystical edifice of Heaven is actually built on the Laws of Physics, as the fallen Archangel groveling on the sulphurous floor of the Burning Lake well understood. And as for this cipher of an Archangel, only calculus can measure his immeasurability." Diane Blake's deliciously delicate floral sun-dress fluttered gently just off-screen, contrasting the courier's chrysalis of leather, a viscous skin of desires, but for whom? Why were the cameras still rolling when the floor manager was signaling *Cut!*? "Lucifer is The Great Male Eunuch, permanently locked in one position, onanism ..." What was Palmer doing with these incendiary comments? Dr. Byrne half-rose from his comfortable chair at arms-length then sank back. "Our soul is our fourth-dimensional bodyguard." Palmer was inciting the Archangel as if he were real and personally tuned into this obscure program's transmission. Surfeited, aggressive as if stumbling in drunk from the Marriage at Cana, Eddie Phoenix suddenly appeared, muscling his way on-screen, shouting: "Beware his virginal loins, his lustful mind! You only want to become existentially entangled in *her* pubis!" Furniture was knocked over in the melee, a stand-up fight ensured, fists were thrown and parried, then the horizontal spear of the courier was hurled at the Archangel's evangelist. Swinging at Phoenix, Palmer grinned into the tracking camera: "Thus we bring the Archangel's anger to completion, and, *voilà*, emptiness ...!"

Object At The Center Of Curvature. Stepping through the studio door into the radiant heat of the parking lot, Diane Blake paused, adjusting her eyes to the glare, before approaching Jason Palmer, knowing he was considering her person reflected both in the convex mirror of the Old Testament and the concave mirror of the New Testament. Was she to be his Mary Magdalene at a Crucifixion, or Resurrection? As she neared him she imagined his psyche a fogged photographic plate, only his glistening porcelain teeth visible as he smiled, although the kaleidoscope his presence threw out into space promised a fascinating Tao. With him she sensed the stillness of that abyss between a two-dimensional image of the I and its three-dimensional realization, I AM. *Agony*, as he repeatedly said, was synonymous with *distance*. His fingertips were idly caressing the statuette of herself gracing the bonnet of his Chevrolet. She grasped his dilemma: the eye of God sought **ME**, to know **ME**, to image **ME**, but the human persona stood on the page of three-dimensional space in frivolous *Italic lightface*! Climbing inside behind the wheel his only words were: "Come visit me at the beach."

The Spontaneity Of Emptiness. A smearing *gouache* of wave-foam overlapped the smooth beach sand and soaked away in a billion bursting bubbles. Diane Blake's eyes followed the Tao of a dune's wave, coming to focus on a hut of palm fronds erected on the beach, and Jason Palmer's esoteric beachcomber absorbing the ebb-and-flow of the ocean as a tranquilizer as he patiently raked the sand in to a Zen garden.

Dr. Philip Byrne had warned her: "Beware his *laissez-faire* morality, Diane. He sits by the ocean all day with that nymph of his, the flower child, imagining himself some crazy would-be Zenophyte, moving through a labyrinth of incarnations to confront the Minotaur himself." She spread her colorful rectangle of beach towel beside a Tibetan sand-mandala and stretched herself along it absorbing the warming bath of sand. "May I enter your mind's Zen monastery?" Jason Palmer squinted in the direction of the sunny, relaxed ambience of the dunes where he caught the flash of the sun off the lenses of Dr. Byrne's binoculars. "Why are you raking this sterile sand? Isn't that a pointless expenditure of energy? I thought of you earlier during the bikini contest, how your ecstasy has turned analytical, how your presence here has become imprisoned like a face-in-a-mirror." Very tenuous linkages existed here, tenderness was overshadowed by the Stygian flow of dunes, as if his feelings for her glided with their elision slopes-and-crests. Her flawless maillot sweeping through the curve of her arched back, down over her *derriere*, possessed for him the modesty of the sand dunes now Dr. Byrne's presence had vanished. "What amazing forces are deployed in the space between two people!" The ocean's aquamarine iridescence sharpened the thermal convection between them, sun-anointed pilgrims concisely embedded together in the curved slices of three-dimensional spacetime. "Is thinking too arduous for you?" She considered the wave-of-thought propagated by his responsive question amid the beach's monotonous motifs. Her mind rustled with the breeze moving through palm fronds. "Well then, tell me how I can make of my heart this moving sand-pattern, how it may emotionally shift under the breeze of my thinking." Hadn't Dr. Byrne said he was fighting simultaneous battles in different dimensions? "Diane, as an architect, is algebra one of your strengths? Water there equates to a fair representation of two-dimensional space, wouldn't you agree? The air rushing by, feeling us, shapes forms in three-dimensional space. And fourth-dimensional space is ... x. Messages in bottles drift ashore from the ocean of Time. At every instant of flight I am at rest! This sand-pattern represents an infamous baptism, the Planck-moment when the fallen Archangel dipped into the pool of three-dimensional space, an Achilles-effect, one hopes. His gravitation *is* the structure of the spacetime continuum." Her shoulders were beginning to blister with sunburn. "What's the time?" Palmer moved from under the palm fronds. "I'll consult my shadow."

The Physics Of Interference. The helicopter's pulsating sound-waves rose above the dissolving crests of the dunes. As a spatial entity describing a mood's stagnation the helicopter climbed a spiral ramp over the palm frond hut with Eddie Phoenix visible behind the glass bubble of the cockpit. Drifts of loose sand were soon in chaotic motion, whipping towards where Diane Blake was scrambling away, the tilting horizontal plane of the spinning rotor-blades catching the sunlight and splintering the beams against its shield. Her beach towel's mandala swirled upward and was gone. Phoenix's grinning expression beside Lt. John Kirby at the controls precipitated the sediment of hate loading his psyche. The helicopter hovered above the flimsy hut stripping away the palm fronds and obliterating Jason Palmer's Zen garden to an arrhythmy of re-constituted patterns. To avoid the stinging sand Diane plunged into the ocean.

While the helicopter was fleeing, Palmer studied the Physics of Interference which now patterned his Zen garden, wondering what metaphysical exploitation he could extract from the model.

Proof Of The Archangel's Perishable Nature. Emptying sand from his shoe, Dr. Philip Byrne stood by the car watching the motorcycle courier approach, her veneer of black marble modelled on Elvis in his '68 Special, sculpted for imaginary pleasures he shrank from. How had he ever imagined too the flower child would be a carnal pomegranate? So much for Jason Palmer's aspiration to reverse the Planck-moment! The courier delivered a satchel of documents she had intercepted for him, but her sly glances were for the flower child sprawled across the car seat, perhaps jealous of the ease of her self-effacement, her languor as Palmer's metaphoric Angel. Dr. Byrne flipped open the satchel and fanned the documents across the bonnet of the car. Laughing suddenly, he paced about, a ridiculous figure, then stopped himself seeing contempt blaze up in the courier's face. "Your faith in Palmer is justified. He has proof of the Archangel's perishable nature."

Edge Of Relativity. The sculpted spaces of Diane Blake's apartment flowed seamlessly, brought him the sexual tension of a Vermeer interior as he cruised her rooms, wandered by a mirror's very straight reflection, while her wardrobe rainbowed a chromatic dispersion of clothes. Time though would empty her treasury of Virtues. His eye and nose isolated a pair of sixties white leather dancing boots: Diane Blake *A Go-Go*! Lighting emitted an atmospheric glow, leaving him with the whimsy of an impression: what did these aromas describe to him of her beauty? Diane stepped free of the bathroom her flesh coloring to apricot. Underfoot, the carpet's supple feeling of her in motion sent up a sweeping wave-of-emotion. Poised for a moment centered in the bedroom she mimetized the voluptuous figure upholding an Olympian lamp. Jason Palmer ambled back into the living room and placed Johnny Esquire's bizarre parody of the Elvis 45 on the turntable ... *Edge of Relativity*! "Your secretive after-thoughts of us?" He referred to her tablecloth design of solarized photographs. "Yes, you gave me the idea, and the way your flower child eludes the grid work of spacetime." Her phonetic kisses swelled in resonance from the depths of an emotional space he couldn't fathom. "Drink her fast, Jason, she's a yogurt-shake of a girl," she teased, alluding to the flower child, her melting voice untwisting his psyche. She magically released the shadow of his thinking from the compressed junction of two walls and her fantasias of architecture freely discussed with him led him to probe the fallen Archangel's blue-printed presence on the grid of space-time. The face of a Bodhidharma lingered in the mirror as she brushed her hair's aureole. She collapsed across the bedspread with the languor of dissolving sugar, a naked Columbine lounging on porcelain. When would she discover he had carved Isaac Newton's name on her window-sill?

Sexual Relativity. "What is this?" A bemused Diane Blake frowned, as Jason Palmer leaned into a blade of sunlight beaming through the louvered window. "Our sex manual?" Palmer, touched by the lucid intermixture of media, her linear supplication contrasting the straight-edged sunbeams, observed: "Perhaps, after all, only in temptation is there hope of salvation." (i) **MECHANICAL WAVES** – Sex's mechanical wave is a disturbance in the equilibrium positions of matter, the magnitude of which is dependent on *location* and on *time*: a source of energy that produces a disturbance and an elastic medium to transmit the disturbance. (ii) **TRANSVERSE WAVES** – Sexually, are those in which the displacements of particles of the medium are *perpendicular* to the direction of the propagation of the wave. (iii) **LONGITUDINAL WAVES** – Sexually, are those in which the displacement of particles of the medium is *parallel* to the direction of propagation of the wave. (iv) **STANDING WAVES** – Sex is produced by the interference of two periodic waves of the same amplitude and wavelength traveling in opposite directions: the intensity of her orgasm's dimensionless *sound* reaching new acoustical thresholds.

Regard Time With Suspicion. Sexually mobilized by the Physics manual, their coitus modeled on an intricate dance of equational gyrations, Jason Palmer deftly maneuvered Diane Blake across the University campus from Lecture Theater to a movie retrospective on Marilyn Monroe, to a photographic exhibition featuring his triptych of Muses embracing the pornography of Science. University mathematicians sexually teased thought with their mappings of *Riemann surfaces*, every equation like erotic glue, temptation itself, unfathomable like the Bay of Portugal! "Diane, the trick is to regard *time* with suspicion, and acknowledge equations have an actual existence in *space*. Remember, Paradise Lost as an event in the spacetime continuum was first witnessed by our souls aeons ago, in incarnation, but can now only be remembered in equational Physics." Sex's change of wave-speed at the interface of two media blurred with the chalk-white panoramas of scribbled equations against the ebony night-sky of the Lecture Theater blackboard. The irony embodied in the equation was its unintelligible lucidity. Soul-time elapsed between events was not necessarily the same for all observers. "We'll discover split images of the Archangel in these equations. I'm talking the relativity of simultaneity. I can hear the Archangel's laughter bellow through these equations. He *understands*, Diane, and that gives him his eternal edge."

The Geometry Of A Chance Meeting. Shocking Blue's *Venus* red-shifted from a passing car, and armpits heady with breathing hair, the Greer woman paraded her dreary socio-sexual realism along the city street, her walk as menacing but sexually predatory as a samurai sword stripped from its sheath. Jason Palmer had glimpsed her left-right asymmetry in the crowd and slip-streamed behind her, oddly attracted by the attitude in the residue of her motion. Indeed, the parable of her equation became sexually entwined with the distances of his imagination, but would he want her to *Walk A Mile In My Shoes*? Would he surf the Styx for her redemption, this mother all Achilles'? She was no aesthete's dream of a Botticellian woman! In the geometry of this chance meeting speculative possibilities began to accrue in his mind with every whisper of her thighs in motion. (i) **GEOMETRIC** – the area under the curve of her breasts, imperfect parabolae capable of haunting even Euclid, the texture exuded the quality of sterile sand dunes. (ii) **SONIC** – the sexual peroration of her membranes, resonances sweet as the hum of tuning forks, splintered gasps of ecstasy into a kaleidoscope of cadences. (iii) **ORGASMIC** – the sympathetic vibrations of reeds, strings and columns of air involved coitus in Physics, more, a mouth's poise froze with a smile. She communicated a potent sexual fairytale, but which one, had it been written? Then there was the girth of her hips, space, volume and the *frisson* of particle acceleration in coitus, her orgasm's probability wave, of high-and-low intensity, a thought as emotionally overwhelming as a slow summer sunset. Did she spend her lonely Saturday evenings grooming her toenails?

Glimpsing The Archangel's Shadow. Gliding by a department store window in the city, Jason Palmer glimpsed in reflection the torso of the familiar Cadillac creeping up behind him at six-o'clock, an attenuated silhouette dwelling within the subliminal eye of a day-dreaming Bernini should he be walking the pavement. The Archangel's contrapuntal *provocateurs*, Eddie Phoenix and Johnny Esquire, were shadowed inside, but were they trailing him or the Greer woman? A strong gravity pulled him nearer with every sexual compression of her walking style. Windows rhymed the images of the Cadillac and this female eunuch creating *doppelgänger* effects and the ticking clock of his consciousness reacted to the gravitational fields of both warping torsos. Suddenly she swiveled on her prophetic feminine curvature, launching in his mind a thousand hips down the catwalks of the fashion houses, and advanced on him with eyes of toughened glass, her mouth a steel girder. A bend-sinister tail of shadow was cast across the sidewalk when Eddie Phoenix stepped away from the idling Cadillac adjacent to the curb. *Kentucky Rain* dramatically deliquesced in space, theme-song for Germaine Greer! What monumentally condensed monoliths the skyscrapers modeled. Moving clocks ran slower than stationary clocks, and the timing of her just-published book stood in the publishing house like tightly-folded Angels' wings. As Palmer considered the ignoble Archangelic strength of a meditating skyscraper, Greer's rectilinear face confronted his: perhaps if he smeared her with cold cream ... but Phoenix guided her by the elbow toward the open door of the Cadillac before he could finalize the image. Now he grasped something of the Archangel's somber virility, his theological desolation etched with the loneliness of a long-distance eunuch, marathon runner *extraordinaire*. Architectural stability, as Diane Blake assured him, was the very cornerstone of Paradise Lost!

Maybe In A Billion Years! Pages of abstruse equations fluttered to the floor of the apartment in the eternal struggle with gravity, one of such breathtaking conceptual elegance its haughty mien challenged the flower child's warpage of space. Wrapped in the flowing cone of a sari skirt, her upper torso naked, the flower child knelt to shuffle them together, all warp-and-curve in the spatial fabric of the apartment. "Who then is the Lawgiver of the Laws of Physics?" Dr. Philip Byrne dutifully considered Jason Palmer's impassioned question. He recalled the debacle of their break-out from the

University campus an hour ago, Palmer clasping the papers covered with these infernal equations as if they were more precious than the Dead Sea Scrolls, how they had run the gauntlet of the student activists. Palmer of course became confrontational, taunted the students as the *bête noire* of all political activists. Thankful to have escaped uninjured Dr. Byrne abstractly caressed the flower child's posture with his glance, sexually stirred by the physical presence of her squatting like that over his keening loins. "So, you've stolen these equations from the consciousness of the Archangel, to use against him? How?" The flower child's transitioning Waterhouse cartoon intrigued Dr. Byrne, but how dangerous was her sub-romantic hippie philosophy? Falling asleep, she *existed*, waking up, she *existed*. "Think about it, Philip, when the Archangel has surfeited on every conceivable experience and chooses to remodel the ratio of the circumference of three-dimensional space to its diameter, what then? The residual *unformed* will still be his field-equation." Maybe in a billion years! Palmer hunched over the television screen, as usual mesmerized by the latest newsreel from 'Nam, where paths of ionizing particles streaked the tropical cloud-chamber, high-speed tracers searching the emulsions of human flesh. Blurred in the flashes was a ghosted clash of shields with a droning voice-over commentary. Come daylight and the armor of the fallen Angels rolled on battling for supremacy in 'Nam. Momentarily distracted by the screen from his own sexual tension, Dr. Byrne didn't register the flower child begin running the zip of his trousers up-and-down with her fingers.

I Dreamed I Saw St. Augustine. The helicopter's low-frequency wave-pulsations as Jason Palmer approached across the tarmac were pitched higher according to the Doppler effect. Lifting off the floor of Paradise Lost the helicopter banked away towards the Radioscience Laboratory with the vast pointillist lake of the city in the distance. His faithful courier's feminized Martian demeanor was focused on the massive dishes aligned like parabolic mirrors to concentrate the trillions of rays of the solar Angels descending from Heaven to rescue the fallen ones. Palmer heard her voice-print cut through the wave-pulsations: "Aren't you in effect, a classical *Outsider* here?"

Energy = Power x Time. All afternoon Jason Palmer and the energized Martian courier had erected a perpendicular transparent screen in his apartment and pin-pointed the grid of inner city streets there. On the equatorial and longitudinal planes spatial displacement was occluded. Now they followed the photons of car headlights below the helicopter's flight path guided toward the city by some invisible wave-field. Coming to the beautiful symmetry of a cloverleaf interchange the helicopter banked to follow the immense curve of concrete wings spread before the altar of the city. Palmer stood beneath a flyover while the courier waited in the torso of the helicopter. The traffic simulated an earthquake's wavelength measured in kilometers. When he looked up at the sky what struck him was the resonance how the Archangel's cosmic quake unleashed waves across three-dimensional space whose wavelengths were measured in light-years. Suddenly he heard screeching tyres, the Cadillac skidded beside the stationary helicopter, the dark-grained figure of Eddie Phoenix leapt out and muscled in beside his wrestling courier. With Herculean strength of mind he ascended the physics of the Archangel's limp wings and turned his gaze toward the Divine City. The delicate curved screens he intuitively sensed, their transparence soluble to human movement and therefore only metaphysically detectable, arraigned the miracle of the continuum of spacetime as a cut-up of instants of time!

The Only Change Is Constancy. Resistivity was wholly dependent on the identity of the material and its temperature. With the city geometry at play, Jason Palmer motioned his Chevrolet through the schematic diagram of streets memorized from the translucent screen in his apartment's converted war-room, *He Ain't Heavy, He's My Brother* on the car radio, working the brilliance of Einstein's insight, gravitational force = acceleration force, the famous Principle of Equivalence. He measured each circuit's internal resistance. Archimedes' Principle of Displacement held true of course. This incarnation of the Archangel in the inertial medium of the city, its streets forming networked resistances in series-parallel, meant he would always occupy a space equal to himself, he would not in fact be in motion. While idling at a red traffic light he inscribed a couple of equations on a corner of the dust-covered windshield. There was a consequential finality about an equation. Cruising on as if in a closed loop he waited for the helicopter to emerge from the vertical passage between the spacetime screens of two skyscrapers.

A Tabula Rasa For All To Scribble Across. Legs iced in black leather the motorcycle courier swung free of the pillion and her footsteps incised curls of sand on the otherwise smooth flank of a dune as she descended to the foreshore. Dr. Philip Byrne and others were studying the oscillatory force of Jason Palmer's raking of the sand. "This Zen garden camouflages the trauma of World War III, its spiritual confrontation first initiated when Paradise was lost to humanity, and taking place in his psyche. You might say he's been raking the patterns of the fallen Archangel's brain waves. Doubt though refuses to arabesque into Faith." Germaine Greer, her expression suffused with solemnity, struggled to focus on the visceral waves of thought, follow their refraction, she was rather irritated by the dialectic between cheesecloth-and-torso as a breath of breeze stirred the musk-soaked fabric about the flower child. "Am I in some kind of danger?" She might be Juno to his sun-drenched beach Prospero! Dr. Byrne peered along the shoreline where the mint-green ocean curved away. "We all are, that's the point. Here we have if you like a model of the fallen Archangel's mind stripped nude. Further along the beach there a bikini contest of semi-nude Angels is in progress, a microcosm of his feminized physique, full of temptation." The courier scooped up handfuls of grains of sand smoothed to perfect crystals. Now he understood. The beach was a blackboard, but who was reading the invisible equations inscribed there? These mandalas waved in the sand, washed by the flow of dunes, were a trap laid for the Archangel!

Bismarck On 'Nam And World War III. *The great questions of the day will not be settled by resolutions and majority votes but by blood and iron.*

The Mass Of A Body Is A Measure Of Its Energy Content. Flashing Police lights reflected off the surface of Diane Blake's hand-held mirror. Her breasts swelled deliciously with each gasp. White-coated physicists were being interviewed beyond the Police cordon for the evening news bulletins. Dr. Philip Byrne puzzled why this coquette of Physics should be infatuated with Jason Palmer, who, like his illustrious predecessor Aeneas, had made good his escape from burning Troy. Fire fighters covered the shell of a linear accelerator with cascades of foam, quantum-soup was over-heard from one of the physicists amid serious laughter, but it was too late for Eddie Phoenix and the flower child. The perfume of humanity's narcissism floated from her face-mirror, a delicious probability-haze, the thought of her lineaments being anywhere and everywhere a profound enticement, but how could he explain that to her? Reconstructing what had happened, it seemed Phoenix and the flower child had entered the three kilometer long linear accelerator and imploded the tunnel as they were propelled the length of the structure. Of course, only their sub-atomic essence completed the journey, attained a velocity greater than 99.999% of the velocity of light. "Talk about experiencing the nausea of life's vertigo." The ambulances wouldn't be needed. Buttoned up in their alcohol-soaked white coats the physicists were talking thermodynamics to the television cameras and explaining the acceleration of an electron ... $\mathbf{a} = \mathbf{F/M}$, moving on to Einstein's revelatory equations. They studied the arabesques, the gestures of their equations as he would a woman he dreamed of having coitus with. Like Diane Blake! "Dreams are familiarization flights of the psyche. He was attempting to reverse the Planck-moment and assault Paradise. Palmer is obsessed with the Quantum Archangel's *particulate unpredictability* as he calls it, questioning the *locality* with the Christian broadcasters. Watching you confront the fiction of the mirror's face there reminded me of something he said as we parted: God has allowed Lucifer the mirror of three-dimensional space to act out his petulant moods. I asked him then at what *moment* he fell in love with you. His response, the perfect minimalism, the Zen calligraphy of your eyeliner pencil wielded to define the wave of your lovely face." What did anything matter now? "The vertiginous loss of Paradise has warped us all in this spacetime continuum." Phoenix wouldn't rise from this trans-metaphysical arabesque for aeons. Fusion and vaporization, the physicists talked on searching for the infinite in their kaleidoscope of equations. Tragically, it appeared, the electrons in the torsos of Phoenix and the flower child hardly had time to get pushed at all, let alone get near the velocity of light!

Untying The Knot Of Destiny. Everlasting oil-of-sunlight coated the ocean's existential space stretching with the flexure of gravity. Feathered arrows of time pinned his soul's incarnations to the screens of space arrayed moment-by-moment since the fall from Paradise. A glowing blade of angled sunbeams cleaved the space between the waves of two sand dunes. Jason Palmer waited for the afternoon's coda and its cadences of richer color to flow through time's screens. The shoreline tilted as shadows began to fall from the dunes across the Zen garden. In the freeze-frame of *now* the quantum-façade lay at peace. Light was refracted into any realm only by apertures containing very small dimensions. As the fabric of sky smoldered and twilight brooded over the ashen dunes he remembered the Planck-moment's aperture as the fallen Archangel's immense cosmic drag of energy into three-dimensional space. Conversely, a black hole's aperture was ascent back into fourth-dimensional space, even the Archangel's gravity could not hold back light! The Big Bang was a rush of fallen Angels into this three-dimensional cave, a diluvian lake of ebony fire cooled to absolute zero, a zone of Einsteinan field-equations awash in quantum-foam, the laughing Archangel throwing every frame of past-present-future into three-dimensional space to see what order would evolve. From a reddish-hue to salmon pink, evening began to blur all contours into an indistinguishable symmetry. Soon *distance* became an inferno of stars and Palmer stood up to read the sky's blackboard. The Archangel's dusky *frisson* of nudity loomed and pressed through the fabric of space. Palmer's soul, metaphysician wingèd for disengagement from its human personae, steadied his vertigo with the swirling radii of unreachable constellations in deep space where there was no up-down. Above the onyx seascape the solar winds dispersed leaves of stars ... one leaf fell!

IV
LINEAGES OF TRANSMISSION

The Poetry Of Vorticism. The humming glissandos of Miranda Westwood's traveling perfume, a bouquet of temptations arranged for modern tastes, perhaps sub-titled **THE WOODSTOCK GENERATION** as sociological fallout began to vibrate the youth of the world following the Festival, overlaid the traffic flowing through the Euclidean cloverleaves which regulated the diastole/systole of the city. Woodstock's vehicle-of-consciousness as a latter-day Dionysia frayed Dr. Philip Byrne's nerves as he had been tracking Jason Palmer for some days through the terrain of automotive manufacturing plants, touched by the abrasive poetry in the fermentation of metal-and-plastic, the ever-fresh stanzas rolling off the production line with the new spirituality of loaves of bread for a consumer market. However, he conceded jealousy was kneading the dough of carnal bread here, and he was plummeting toward a center of existential nausea with the swiftness of the fallen Archangel himself. Escorting Miranda to the promotional dinner in honor of Germaine Greer, *femme eunuch*, he was surprised his nausea with the world might be easing under the influence of her company, although her seemingly aloof naiveté had so far forestalled all her spiritual fortune-seekers. The car plunged through an underpass and his psyche heaved with emotion-sickness. "Chanel No. 5?" Dialogue was cryptic but over-burdened with association. Who had cast the mold of this beautiful young woman whose torso resembled cream squeezed into a gown of chocolate éclair? A sharp thorn of pornographic thought caught at the allusive fabric of his psyche. Co-joined with the Archangel he could park the car on the verge and engage in coitus with her against a concrete pylon where silvered moonbeams might spray the tissued flounce of her evening gown: a Faustian dream!

Lineage Of Transmission. What lineage of transmission inspired the Vorticist poetry of *a racing car is more beautiful than the Wingèd Victory of Samothrace?*

Mixed Media. Guided by astrological charts discovered among Jason Palmer's possessions, mingling with guests in the vaulting mirrored foyer prior to dinner,

Dr. Philip Byrne sensed the presence of some monumental *Ego* structured within the torso of the hotel's subliminal architecture. A bank of television screens replayed footage direct from Khe Sanh deluged in a rocket-firing blitzkrieg, cutting to choppers laying down a carpet of withering fire into NVA troops exposed in Hell's no-man's land. Applause announced the magisterial entrance of the Amazonian eunuch, Germaine Greer, and Dr. Byrne replaced his champagne glass on a passing tray, eager to study this charismatic teaser whose journalism had robed men in the darkest grain, if deservedly so. Miranda Westwood swiveled away from the black-and-white television images, captured by Eddie Phoenix's glowering eyes under a promotional boater crêped in American red, white and blue, a touch of flimsy calculated to infuriate the Greer woman. "Now, *that* man is uncultured, no pearl!" In a sweep of motion the loquacious flower child pressed two packets of letter into Dr. Byrne's hands before slipping away between the interstices of the guests beginning to move into the dining room. Momentarily confused before placing the packets inside his tuxedo, Dr. Byrne isolated Phoenix who had observed the transmission, his psyche as naked as *Laocoon and the serpents*, Paulette Taylor swinging off his embrace like a sexually bowed viola wielded like a phantom Paganini. While maneuvering among the islanded tables toward Miranda he felt Phoenix grip his shoulder. "Tell your philosopher friend we're thrusting the sickle in deep and scything, *Doktor*!" Locusts and scorpions were the pets leashed to this Zapata's psyche. God might be unnamable in the modern world, but how was this reconcilable to Elvis' singing *Don't Cry Daddy*?

The Law Of Entropy. Attempting theological evasions over dinner Dr. Philip Byrne palmed the packets of letters from his tuxedo and briefly examined them. Miranda Westwood suddenly broke off her sidelong conversation, remembering: "I overheard *that* man earlier negotiating for those *billets-doux* with a leather-clad courier in the foyer. He was cradling a crucifix as if ready to perpetrate some *sexual* violation with it." She motioned herself like banana crêpes inside the oozing rum butterscotch sauce of her evening gown. What a contrast to the colloquial mime of the Greer woman's statue, a persuasion to seek the Narrow Way of Virtue, whereas the *femme eunuch's* marble eyes hardened in the face of some Roman matron: Mark Antony's wife on hearing of his dalliance with *the serpent of the Nile*! Jason Palmer desired to cloister himself with this feminist Amazon? Electrified with righteousness, a hooded monk, a wild Caravaggio from *The Decameron*, burst through the dining room doors like an annunciation on The Law of Entropy for the fallen Archangel, and space fractured as the audience rose to its feet from the sumptuous feast and applauded.

Journey To An Infinite Interior. Stellar Benday dots layered time on the canvas of space. The vast ceiling soaked in ebony light, unclimbable and unassailable, canopied the moonlit coastline of the southern beaches of Hellas where Jason Palmer welcomed Dr. Philip Byrne within the cyclopean eye of the motorcycle's headlamp. Lucifer's crash through the window of three-dimensional space had splintered into trillions of fragmented stars composing the image of a cosmos in Benday dots. Was Creation then a Pop Art joke? "See, Philip, the fallen Archangel's dark energy pervading space, compositionally, seventy-percent!" Waves washed his monk's borrowed plumage, a non-luminous façade, fluid without the traction of mathematics, perhaps a metaphor for the fourth-dimensional soul imprisoned in spacetime. Barefoot, her gown's meringue coffee frothy with whitewater, Miranda Westwood waded by the foreshore, peerless in her feminine ambivalence to Palmer's cache of mythologies about Lucifer. "Buried deep out there, and in the quantum foam of our beings is remembrance of the Archangel's original awakening in this space-time continuum. We too rose from the same solitude of his Fall. Did it happen, Philip?" Against the horizon flowed the contour of a sand dune pearled by moonlight, a void either side of an arabesque, nothingness reflected in the sky's distorting mirror. "Cast the millstone of the human ego into the ocean and feel it plunge like the Earth's stone in plastic space." Palmer handed Dr. Byrne the spiral shell of a mollusk.

I. Palmer to Diane Blake ... *How do we smooth the jagged microscopic surfaces of being-and-existence, those inflationary bursts of human thought-and-feeling? About me this evening a warm mantle of sunbeams has fallen across the shoulders of the horizon, a robe of pure divinity. I raise my hand high waiting for it to be clasped by an Angel's. But what a fiction the construction of space is, and as for our flawed dramatis personæ sleepwalking through time, the Masque ran out of original ideas aeons ago. How quickly spraying waves of quantum-foam are swallowed again by the sheer momentum of the plastic ocean surging through cycles of ebb-and-flow. Similarly our surface tension here in three-dimensional space experiences a gravitational squeeze, our affections warp-and-ripple, we acquiesce to the turbulence of being-and-existence, past-and-future unobserved by us. Whose Empire is these Deserted Cities of the Heart? Come with me then to the monastery of Eden, hear the rhythmic euphony of the voices, walk with me into the heart of my Zen garden and lose forgetfulness of existence. Lose all to gain all. I am Journeying to an Infinite Interior breathless with such spacelessness as renders our world claustrophobic! Cassandra is a monochrome messenger who can be trusted ...*

II. Lieutenant John Kirby to Eddie Phoenix ... *In my crisply laundered fatigues listening to transistor radios, idly playing cards, trading stash, supervising the tractors securing the LZ's perimeter, I'm commanding this war like a John Wayne movie, standing tall because the incoming is only for show in cinemascope. How's my hippie baby doll, the flower child, is she still dreaming of me walking through the meadow of death, ignoring the nightly newsreels, leaving time alone? Everyone's stripped and dusted down digging in, the camouflage webbing doesn't keep the sun out, but the wet's coming day by day – they know where we are, they know where we want to be, and like the rice paddies will keep comingseason after season. Tonight we're expecting a shadowy swarm of locusts ...*

Armor For A Monastery. Laid with the precision of pieces placed for an immense jigsaw puzzle, circular stained glass windows Jason Palmer had inspired the University students to design and cast in secret, were arranged on the campus lawn like two-dimensional bowls of spectacular color listening to the euphony of the sun. A large pantechnicon reversed closer to the lawn's perimeter. Dean Martin's bi-lingual singing of *An Evening In Roma* could be heard on a transistor radio. Students carefully gathered up the resolutely flat breastplates of colored fire solidified in glass, armor for a monastery, and carried them across the grassed quadrangle under the imposing Spanish sandstone arches of the clock tower. A heavily penciled Priscilla look-a-like sat framed in the window of a monumental black saloon watching an on-campus war unfold between rival political factions over participation in the Vietnam War. Soon she vanished behind smoky windows and the chariot's spinning wheels rolled away across the asphalt. Palmer's stained glass breastplates tasted the light rays in a blaze of vibrations as they emerged from beneath the arches. Eddie Phoenix tossed aside his anti-war placard and sprinted toward the cavalcade of brilliant windows. With a hand, Palmer restrained Diane, sensing Phoenix's intention and willing to allow the desecration unfold, for the energy eddying around the political fracas needed some climactic act to siphon it off. Diane gasped as Phoenix leapt feet first at the altar of a disc held upright by two students and plunged through its space: the image was a Technicolor fifties deification of herself in molded glass, dynamically penetrated in a way beyond-sex. "Did you feel the psychic tremor? Diane, he replicated the Archangel's crash into three-dimensional space, the dissipation of spiritual reflections the visible schism between Heaven and Hell occasioned. How extraordinarily clear everything seems. He knows I've planned your escape from the *Ego's* imprisonment and intends to hunt you down, chain you forever to the spacetime continuum. Don't look puzzled, I'll explain later."

In A Monastery Garden. Musical Latin chants in full-throated Gregorian ease echoed as far afield as a spreading olive grove where flocks of pink-and-grey cockatoos settled on the boughs to listen. Leaving an orchard of sun-ripened pomegranates, Jason Palmer surveyed the ultra-smooth arcs of sand dunes undulating between the abandoned monastery and the nearby ocean. Accompanied by his courier, slithery as a Zen brushstroke and as visionary in her defiance, and some volunteer students from the University, he approached the crest of a carefully chosen sand dune, textured like softly colored chalk against the sky's brilliance. From a transistor radio crackled a song in ephemeral collision with the Latin chants: *Instant Karma*. Renovations of the crumbling monastery were being prepared, the blueprint hypothesized from Pythagoras' famous theorem and Quantum Mechanics, a conjunction whose translucence would provide an explanation of what was seen on the surface, but would prove mirror-black in seeing the explanation itself. Borne by the magic carpet of the shifting dunes a caravan of splash-painted hippie vehicles emerged from distant dust clouds, prompting in Palmer a sense of urgency as the students scrambled to the crest of the dune and set the first jewel of a stained glass window there. A *hole* in three-dimensional space had been created at last aligned with the geometry of the rising-and-setting sun. The Daliesque beachscape unlocked Palmer's intuitive sense of reality-in-time, turned the key opening up a new monastery of the mind where even the anxiety of happiness was unknown, where the elusive *there* was eternally *here*. Coated in psychedelic color-patterns, the hippie vehicles were lined up caravan-style and doors opening, the passengers disembarked in breathing, flowing kaftans. Palmer x-rayed the disguises and recognized Johnny Esquire, Donna Lee, Eddie Phoenix and Paulette Taylor among the party, a sexual *pas de quatre* whose symmetry he would have to unbalance.

Eve And The Law Of Universal Gravitation. Sleep and silence descended over the monastery with the coming apogee of the autumnal equinox, although the space inside Eddie Phoenix's head reverberated with the recessional velocity of a splittable atom. Bandaged and limping slightly from his earlier plummet through a stained glass window at the University, he brooded away the afternoon siesta gazing across the parchment of sand, Earth's developed negative of Paradise Lost, smirking to the sounds of muffled coitus being attempted in an adjoining cell. *She* was deferentially insatiable of course, and Johnny Esquire was hardly monkish for the loneliness of a cloister, unless to meditate on an orgasm. More pressing amid this negative-image Garden of Eden was how to devise a suitable *Temptation for St. Palmer*, lead him into captivity as a prize for the Fallen Archangel to diminish further the heliocentric Paradise of the Solar Deity. How to prepare Palmer's entombment without the possibility of resurrection. A solitary monk with a scythe slung around the neck of his cassock resolutely walked by, mind fixed on God's work, toiling away in three-dimensional space with the steadiness of a spiritual compass misreading true north. Paulette Taylor, poised in her tremulous but familiar *dishabille*, finally sidled into his cell biting into a highly polished red apple. "Palmer has been out among the dunes with his windows, coordinating those holes in space you mentioned, arguing classical Physics is simply a game of *Charades* devised by God. The whisper about the corridors here is he plans designing another Luxor-Thebes complex with the architect he is sleeping with, Diane Blake. What dreams they share! Presumably, for an Exodus of some kind. If you can be bothered in this heat, he's scheduled a transmission for the monks this evening."

Vermeer, Archimedes And Time. "The Art of Dying is academic, surely." Dr. Philip Byrne was laconic but with a twist of insolence, for ahead of them Diane Blake entered a pharmacy to collect her prescriptive oral contraceptive pills. Motifs were tangled up in a skein of fragments impossible to weave together. Raphael Summers was an unwelcome presence, like some of the masculine figures haunting Vermeer's paintings, and etiquette veered askew on closer observation, for how had his intoxication with *her* quietened to sexual indifference? Obviously the *body* didn't convey the truest perception of Woman. They followed her the length of a canyon of skyscrapers, Dr. Byrne mesmerized by her sleight-of-hand sexuality, and the swirl of her hemline set in motion by a casual sweep of fingers. Summers' voice deliquesced through the depth-of-field: "Sexually, I'd classify her as a Vermeer, erotic in her mental repose, but not my era at all. A radiant apparition must eventually fade." Noteworthy was their Duchamp-like reflection in a façade of office windows. "With what then does this friend of yours, Jason Palmer, propose to displace time?" Paradise Lost's Manhattan-dream vanished in the memorable fabric of her top's off-the-shoulder diagonal sweep as she turned in profile tipping a Coca-Cola bottle to her lips. Dr. Byrne no longer desired to be etherically locked on the canvas of space with this questionable phantom held in the mind of Vermeer: "He sees himself as a reincarnation of Archimedes, ever fascinated with the city's displacement, its overflowing of space." Diane quickly swung astride the pillion of the courier's motorcycle and disappeared into the traffic flow. More Vermeeresque dialogue flowed from Summers: "I understand the controversial Greer woman is flying out to some monastery to interview this latest Messiah for OZ magazine." Was this some coded message? Dr. Byrne immediately thought of the aberration of Jacques Villon's Cubist portrait of *R. Duchamp*, realizing that its image was mysteriously pressed as a water-mark into the pages of Lt. John Kirby's letters!

III. Palmer to Diane Blake ... *Who am I? A fabricated metaphysic, a mirage, Diane, a fragment of phenomena in eternal exile in the world's playhouse. Am I instinct with wisdom? A model for a civilized world? O for the consummation of just one moment, one glorious moment glimpsing the* **NOW**, *of being nowness! Antiquity overawes us, but who can truly conceive the imagery of the Future? What immortal days, years, eternities unknown to us, Futurity has. Only the other day I was browsing names already inscribed on the Scroll of Death, comparing them to those in today's Book of Life. Little wonder my mind is in training for a Monastery in Eden, that I'm giving all my strength to yield, taking casts of my thoughts and hammering them on an anvil, firing and folding them to create a weapon capable of slaying* **HIM** *plunged deep in the hidden places of Self ... my* **SELF**! *Nothing is more arduous of attainment. That is why we delay this confrontation until the end of time and condemn the soul to the martyrdom of endless human personae. So my theme is to moralize on our Commonwealth of famous Anglo-Saxon alchemists!*

IV. Lieutenant Kirby to Eddie Phoenix ... *Illion is ours! Yes, Philosophy and Patriotism stiffen the US of A's imperial ensign flying over our LZ. Our 'Nam captivity is in a phase of transformation, artillery shakes the earth, shockwaves radiate, craters fill with relentless downpours, but the feet of the conqueror shall not be moved. Still no letter though from Baby Doll. They came out of the putrid jungle's green mist smelling of vomit and breached the barbed wire perimeter for some of the hand-to-hand grunt, like devils possessed. Revenge and atonement was relentless but we fed them our best unwrapped bronze candy with hard centers until they were gorged to bursting. F111's tore apart the concave of the ethereal sky and later we strolled among corpses masked in perdition. Incessant rain began to hose down the charred carcasses. I'm scheduled for tomorrow's airlift ...*

Diamond Vehicle Of The Fallen Archangel. Slow motion astral transmissions sequenced Jason Palmer's meditation on time's volumetric relation to space, especially now the monadic eyes of his stained glass windows inset on the crests of dunes caught the peripheries between the third-and-fourth dimensions on the wing. (i) Las Vegas' hallucinatory model of Paradise Lost loomed in fast-fading light across the desert floor, posed in a defiant posture of existential indifference. Anti-Parthenon, crowning jewel of a negative-image Acropolis, center of the Archangel's non-spiritual city precipitated forward in time upon a vast plain, all horizons were dazzled by the visualization. (ii) What revolutions exploded across the skylines of time bringing cries of anguish from world-rolling-on-worlds, and generations who were cast into neon lakes burning with eternal fires. (iii) Desert Queen, scarlet odalisque, chakras of glowing red hot coals of neon, lying seductively on the couch of earth ringed by compassionate stellar gods radiant in the empyrean, her sirenesque glamor irresistible to the teeming millions of her subjects. (iv) His feeling of *mal de mer* with the Ocean of Time has climaxed with comparison of the patterns of oratory of Las Vegas and the monastery, respective voices of the Fallen Archangel and of God – Las Vegas' streets so many corridors in the Archangel's monastery.

Oath Of The Elvii. *The Wonder of You* coalesced pilgrims to Las Vegas like encrustations of sequins on brocade. Time commanded this City on the Plain, a glittering monument frozen in inertia by day but melting through the night, draining off and absorbing the blazing red sunsets from the sky's pit of darkness. Regattas of thousands of cars maneuvered through the strangely becalmed streets. These circling chariots assaulted the flashy battlements of the besieged city. A clean-limned Elvis and ravishing Priscilla were glimpsed, both accoutered Vegas-style, descending an elevator, rumors abounding that *married chastity* had disordered this Cleopatra's imagination and that her Caesar himself was gilding the Scarlet Whore's wasteland with his sexual prowess. Nevertheless, the landscape of Elvis' face and his slender, still youthful-seeming energy was a model summoning a legion of classical icons to the modern consciousness in remembrance of a Golden Time. Blackjack and roulette apprenticed the Colonel to the Archangel, fabled high roller himself, mathematician ever calculating the odds, and Elvis was another Isaac brought by Abraham to sacrifice. Dr. Philip Byrne and Miranda Westwood strode free of the hotel lobby into the over-lit architectural space of the Strip. A mosaic of murals erupted, so many jeweled hues, geometric figures scattering in ashes of neon fire, yellow roses bursting from a crystal vase. Miranda spun along the sidewalk, her torso fitted inside her dress like a port-soaked fig, her mouth meltingly glutinous, a deft crayon sketch rendered mobile by the dispersion of neon. What an altar for unripened Iphigenias Las Vegas proved! An ebony limousine cruised up to the curb and a door swung open. **ELVIS** presided in visual flashes over the sexual currents of neon electricity igniting the already overflowing golden cup of the tarnished city.

V. Palmer to Diane Blake ... *Evening's solitary hours for me are a rich tapestry of temptations. Your memory descends with them over my Isle of Patmos. There, your thought captures me gazing across the breaking surf at Paradise's unattainable horizon. Silence the invocation, I AM, in my throat, my heart, my mind and what am I? Spiritually mute! Fragments of a dream from a Golden Time fuse to my imagination as I stand here, toes poised on the rim of fourth-dimensional space, peering into the Void. Flowing away to the horizon is a sea of molten glass shot through with fiery beams. The monastery's island is awash with waves of dunes flowing to and from an eternal silence of infinite spaces my heart falls toward in hope. But I have placed* *my key in the door of time and turned it. Truly, Diane, there is no trap quite as gripping as the trap I have set myself ... Le Premier Homme. How have I grown into this double-identity? And this insoluble feud between the Archangel and myself prolongs the resolution of the fifth act of the Drama we are starring in. For how long was the Myth of Sisyphus prepared in Lucifer's heart while he commanded the cornucopia of artistry which is Paradise? Your winged thoughts come to me with the transparency of a migratory bird-of-paradise, for truly there is only flight ...*

VI. Lieutenant John Kirby to Eddie Phoenix ... *Fighting is a kind of inspiration, but where does it come from? Violence is our existential revolution-in-progress. Principles of Law and Morality guide our resurgent patrols through the limp, rain-sodden geography of 'Nam as we turn the empty pockets of Communism inside out. My foxhole is the tomb I enter every night thinking of my Baby Doll, guardian angel, and where I wreathe myself in the smell of her remembered incense, how it smokes my hair and flesh. You say she's left the Ashram for some monastery? Killing is as addictive as sex. How do firefights occur? Well, out there across the mud plain, wading through the water-logged grasses Charlie is listening for the twang of someone's aftershave, tasting radio waves on the air from a transistor, and caught in the lure of our stupidity can't resist the opportunity to test our resilience. Morning comes, will I or won't I step on a mine? Guilt has been apportioned here on the battleground, Charlie is to be punished for political deviance. Charlie reads guilt into everything too, but disputes who the guilty party is. Funny that. Moving off, the drenched grasses swallow us whole. Does the mine magnetize the individual footfall, or does the foot seek the trigger? Either way the rag doll ascension is sickening to behold, a crucifixion in space, arms outflung begging forgiveness, a raising, a lifting backwards of the upper torso, then the slap back to a watery earth. Sampans drift on a spectral River Styx ferrying the souls to Hades. Heavy-fire, cross-netted for effect, choppers are sweeping in at tree-top level. Casualties mount. Reprieve. For incoming is a vaulting, combustible deluge of napalm, brimstone filling every cavity of undergrowth, a fiery couch laid for human sacrifices. Liquidized torsos. Solar flares visit the earth and taste us. Retrieve our dead and wounded. Grasses splashed with blood: bloodied trails leaking everywhere ...*

Découpage. FRAME 1. Dipping slightly tail-first the helicopter landed and Germaine Greer crouched forward under the rotorblades. Eddie Phoenix welcomed her clearance of the helicopter with a libation of the local vintage. Monks in cassocks formed a chorus in attendance against the Pythagorean façade of the monastery. **FRAME 2.** Arms linked, a crescent sweep of dancers kicked high, their feminine softness plated with brilliant birds-of-paradise plumage over minimalist tunics. Las Vegas showgirls undulated their arms at full stretch like wings. **FRAME 3.** Germaine Greer showered her *femme eunuch's* torso under the supple tongue of the Milky Way, soaping the dune of her abdomen, her eyes lingering on the sword of diamonds presented to her by Jason Palmer. **FRAME 4.** A lemon crust of neon thickened the cake of Las Vegas standing on the platter of the desert. Streams of asphalt flowed from all compass points like cables, culminating in the town's explosive short circuitry, a desert opal veined with shimmering electricity.

Matins. "This oasis welcomes the coming of the midnight-hour for it cools the Archangel's wings." Jason Palmer's opening words for the convocation accompanied the distant Gregorian chants of the monks. "The Archangel is a faultless fencing master, his timing of passes is impeccable, and he has proved invincible in three-dimensional space, but this is his Achilles heel for he must wield his artistry through Lieutenants armored in flesh-and-blood." Germaine Greer fingered some individual diamonds pressed into the handle of the mysterious sword he had presented her with. "Physics is the crystallization of God's poetry in Laws. Our eternal problem is the fallen Archangel is himself a thought in God's own mind. The Supreme One's own energy and mass, His inertial component." Mesmeric chanting of **THE WORD** by the monks symmetrized Palmer's chording of his thoughts. "Hands are on the vine, the grapes have ripened and the wine-press waits. At the end of the road stands the monastery. Spectators who simply line the route take aeons to arrive ..." Sediment gathered in the bowl of the crucible of Christianity. Later, brushing up against Germaine Greer and Eddie Phoenix in a darkened alcove, the latter was heard to rasp: "This Clytemnestra of anti-war demonstrators is handling the sword which will separate you from your concept of yourself."

Beginner's Luck. Reeling in his ceremonial symbolism *à la Elvis*, from casino-to-nightclub where bevies of perfectly shaped women loaded every horizon, Johnny Esquire teamed up with Miranda Westwood after she had come adrift from Dr. Philip Byrne's protective chaperoning. Las Vegas was a frontline city in a cosmic war, an entertainment for the battle-weary where erotic rejuvenation was the keynote, where beginner's luck was a certainty. Esquire woke first toward midday in the hotel room and ordered breakfast. The razor keen fluting of their torsos in coitus had him feeling like a shelled oyster this morning. His impression of sex with Miranda was a swimming in pomegranate marinade. With so many fluttering feathers in the Archangel's wing it was effortless to pluck one and tickle desire. After showering he planned to walk-in-white through Vegas with the gypsy, Elvis.

Clytemnestra's Slaying Of Agamemnon. Miranda Westwood crouched *à la Ingres* while dragging Johnny Esquire's razor along her lathered calves. Mirrored with lush creaminess in the cool space of glass she was enfolded *a tergo*, the curves of her derriere clenched by his fingers while Bobby Darin's *18 Yellow Roses* spun on the turntable in the lounge room. Himself an early-sixties reminiscence of Elvis-as-roustabout, Esquire had caught her attention just as she was making a self-luminous movement toward sex, summoning up an orgasm's surging rose within the space of her hieress' life. In a flash she intuited something of the famous pop icon's thoughtful lasciviousness in Esquire. Dr. Philip Byrne questioned her intimately about her dreams, as her Freudian patron, speaking of their experiential path, their koans of conceptual transcendence, whereas Esquire devoured her silky tortellino lips and devised erotic alternatives to the missionary exploration of her sexuality. Should she confide last night's dream to Dr. Byrne? Hands gripped her pelvic musculature. She had been jolted awake by

Clytemnestra's slaying of Agamemnon! With a bemused Esquire she had surveyed the equations lipsticked over her thighs and torso, bizarre stigmata empathizing with some climactic happening: sex's passionfruit pulp flowed. Esquire obsessed over his early-sixties 45s, playing them incessantly ... *Come See About Me* ... *Chains* ... *Runaway* ...

The Minimalism Of Physics. Night descending aureoled in a mysterious emanation of magnolia fragrance, unsourced, Jason Palmer strode westward from the stone façade of the monastery to the periphery of the dunes, visualizing the sky as an immense Zen garden carefully patterned with glittering fragments of stardust, the leap from finite-to-infinite seemingly effortless. "I am *myself* the Fallen Archangel, imbued with his abandoned tenderness, his precipitous vulnerability, just as he is *myself*." Laughing, lost amid the minimalist interior of atoms in his own quantum torso, echoing the Milky Way's spinning charka of inter-threading stars, he salaamed to time's endless Nomad passing him in the desert of existence, and resumed his journey.

Frankie & Johnny Rock Vegas. Agitated, stained in a wash of neon's caramelized pineapple, Dr. Philip Byrne paced about the sidewalk while Johnny Esquire slipped inside the unstoppable limousine and gave Miranda Westwood the brush-off through the window as the vehicle gathered speed again to roll away. She had entered an arena of metaphysical existence every bit as dramatic as the Coliseum. Here, defined by the chimerical scripture of Paradise Lost, existence's residuum was carefully calculated to induce nausea at every throw of the dice. Lucifer's Las Vegas journey negated any concept of absolute rest one might foolishly have. The primeval Gambler threatened to characterize the star-uncrossed lovers as a modern *Frankie & Johnny*. Jason Palmer's apocalyptic disappearance, except in an epistolary sense, brought home to Dr. Byrne the conflation of emptiness which was Las Vegas' pastiche of Paradise Lost, and the rich nirvanas embodied in singular men pausing briefly on their journey in the Earth's incarnational caravanserai. So much astonishing phenomena bound one's self-centeredness to possession of illusions. Miranda pounded the palm of one cupped hand with the pestle of another. Her torso's flute of champagne fizzed before ambling off. Dr. Byrne followed: why weren't their gestures symmetrical? Gilded in flooding topazes, tinted in falsifying splendor, the illusory Midas-touch of the Gambler himself, Heaven and Hell vanished in a glimpse of her Venetian glass evening gown. Who *was* Jason Palmer? Who cared?

The Palace Of Futurity. Eos' appearance in the horizon's royal door flooded the Palace with illumination. Darkly, weightily embodied, the velvet bedspread of sand dunes traversed by Jason Palmer vibrated horizontally, the Archangel's wings rhymed during the night to the stasis of the Milky Way now began to awaken with movement: Las Vegas' caravanserai descended into inertial sleep. Why had he been condemned to spectate for aeons on the travelers passing through the Earth's caravanserai, co-ordinates fixed to spacetime field equations they could never solve. Time's sponge was well and truly squeezed dry. Glorious peacock eyes the Archangel shook to dislodge from his wings, the stained glass windows stored the Ptolemaic spheres as a memory against the heraldic immolation of space by time. Wandering the interstice between two dunes, raised bra cups of the reclining Earth Goddess, Palmer listened to a distant vibrating undertone, a low frequency throb rising in pitch as it neared. Life's journey was plummeting from zenith-to-nadir as Cassandra maneuvered Providence toward the golden path leading up to the Palace of Futurity.

Germaine Greer's Materialization In Space. Two custom-built versions of the moon buggy dueled along a tranquil stretch of shoreline. A medieval brightness suffused the horizontal arabesque of sand dunes. Faithful as ever, the courier abruptly altered traction and wheeled her Ezekiel chariot in an arcing semi-circle causing her pursuer to adjust his thinking geometrically and almost flip his vehicle. Observing the spiritual tussle of these machines, Jason Palmer did not immediately perceive Germaine Greer's materialization in space, framed within a stained glass window cresting a dune, her bared Amazon breasts freed to the caress of a softly palmed breeze lilting in off the ocean. Semi-naked, heiress of Tantalus, the lioness of feminism approached him, obviously looking-back-in-anger across the somnolence of Woman's time in incarnation, her feelings' blood ebbing back to form a heart as hard as stone. No child would make the consecrated passage from her loins into mortality. She had shattered the mirrored likeness of herself so she might never be reflected in posterity. For a moment she stilled the delirious confusion of the polyphony of existence with her Amazonian pillar. How *young* was time? Woman's time? The moon buggies moved to the famous tick of Newton's biological clock!

The Rape Of Germaine Greer. Jason Palmer tirelessly meditated his displacement in space. The arrow of temporal time, horizontally straight in curving space, cruised amid the quantum frenzy of existence like an endlessly stretching one-dimensional string plucked by God. Castaways beached together on a stage surrounded by the sonically perfect amphitheater of dunes, he observed the climax of the rape of Germaine Greer, potentially one of the twentieth-century's exemplary tragediennes. The blazing furnace of the sun poured a stream of light along the interstice between the negatively saddle-curved flanks of two smooth dunes. Eddie Phoenix's airborne chariot, *deus ex machina*, made a shattering transit through the lustral wash of an emblematic stained glass window: finally then, the perspectives of his physical presence succeeded in shifting toward an astral plane commensurate with the Archangel's mortuary space. Darkness pierced Germaine Greer's eyes as this thermal faun embraced her in an orgasm spreading a crimson tapestry across the satin sheet of sand. A chariot had crashed to the floor of Paradise Lost. How perfectly these pieces matched up in the jigsaw puzzle of spacetime. Lucifer's exothermic liberation intensified as the flower child expired face-up, garlanded with crystalline sand: she would sleep until he aroused himself and summoned again his legions to the phalanx of rebellion. Phoenix languished too, but in the loins of a prophetess, both soon to be colder than Greek marble worn by time.

VII. Palmer to Diane Blake ... *The twist in the DNA helix, is it an elaborate joke? Or the favored dance of the fallen Archangel spiraling from Heaven to Hell? What is the mystery in movement? My mind drifts with these sand dunes in a kind of pas de deux across the screen of space. Elvis & Priscilla. Their conceptual deaths are already pre-ordained, I'm sure. Call it the intuition of the Elvii. Elvis' masculine martyrdom is spiritually aligned to Orpheus', Bruno's and Francis Bacon's, whereas Hypatia, Joan of Arc and Blavatsky are feminine exemplars of Priscilla's transfiguration. You told me once Elvis has manufactured Priscilla's persona, shaped her very torso, face and hair for the remembrance of all Time. Unquestionably. Contentment, happiness, what are they but emotionally charged images crayoned on the canvas of existence to contrast the shadows which would otherwise soak us up. Aeons ago you and I set out on a journey thinking we understood the physics of Time, but the friction, the mechanics has burred our transitions between three-and-four-dimensional space. Time's language is inscribed in silence, its harmonies have faded and memory is as the Moon, glowing only in reflective brilliance against a backcloth of forbidding darkness. Too long have I stood outside my soul in ignoble solitude walking the corridors of the Earth's monastery. Like Socrates I should have been Death's bridegroom ...*

VIII. Lieutenant Kirby to Eddie Phoenix ... *Imagine a tawny orange sunset capable of engulfing all space. If only I could cast my memory into the urn of death and sleep for Eternity. I'm standing outside of myself as the corpses are coming in: how physically heavy they are among the slender grasses of 'Nam. Elongated silhouettes winged with shadow are moving across the ruinous landscape brooding revenge. What are the incidental features of Death's portrait? Playing cards lie scattered ... the bloodied Jack of Hearts ... nearby is the crematorium of a tank, and the souls of its occupants spiral up in smoking balloons like so many cartoon captions. The Way of 'Nam is an aimless circularity. Patrols leave the LZ from the embrace of choppers and return to them wrapped tight in the coil of destiny. Death's portrait resembles the face of irrationality. We plunge on into fire as if into refreshing water. Stars come out at night, wind-soaked in rain, such a lyrical ejaculation inviting us to drink of oblivion ...*

V

BRING ME MY BURNING BOW

Waves & Circles. Festooned carousels and Ferris wheels symbolically revolved against the dusk-smeared sky with the brilliance of Archangelic chakras. Through peak-and-trough a rollercoaster's wave-train undulated, allegorical vehicle of Einsteinian physics, the supporting grid work arranged and illuminated after the H_2O hexagonal lattice, all clinging to space's curvature. Immaculately dressed and polished equestriennes leapt through near-faultless rounds at the gymkhana being staged on the floodlit arena as twilight descended over the fairground. Launched on the rollercoaster with the flower child's Krishna cartoon braced beside him, Jason Palmer reveled in the amplitude of waved track measuring the relativity of distance traveled and time elapsed, for his unification with Physics repositioned his power ratio with the fallen Archangel and he experienced satori: an illuminated moment would remain eternally illuminated! Since rescuing the flower child from the Ashram a week earlier they had moved from a succession of sitar recitals on the University campus to Sanskrit readings of *The Upanishads* in the original to the visceral rebirthing of sex in his Oceanside apartment, charting these moments of spacetime history on a graph, experiencing the *frisson* of their non-changeability, knowing them to be immutable. Now she swayed alongside him among the fairground arcades tonguing her candy floss on a stick and listening to the voices of the Fortune Tellers rising above the noise of the crowd. From the conceptual energy inherent in the fairground fun rides he sensed something of the implosion of the wave of the cosmos collapsing back. Later, in his apartment, she fell back with the inertia of a tidal starfish onto the watered silk of the bed, her spangled sari slipping free of her tanned waist. While her fingers had wreathed the sculpted statuette on the bonnet of his Chevrolet earlier with their aura of aromatic incense, the distant Ferris wheel circled her face with a spinning mosaic of encrusted light, a lovely Byzantine decoration.

Unrealizable Erotic Fantasies. From his stationary frame of reference at an upper pavilion window overlooking the gymkhana in progress, Dr. Philip Byrne scanned the length of the rollercoaster through binoculars, remembering Jason Palmer extolling to him the Principle of Equivalence, but missing its inherent eroticism for him. Propelled forward, Palmer's moving frame of reference began its journey, then twin beams of light flashed simultaneously, one opening the door of futurity, the other opening the door of the past: which imaginary doorway opened first?

Equestrienne. More visually compelling though was Diane Blake's extraordinary equestrienne, floating over a high wall with her pubis rubbing the pommel of her saddle, a sexual warpage accelerating her toward orgasm. Eddie Phoenix brusquely shouldered his way inside the pavilion across the threshold, the classical mechanics of his persona, their metaphysical absolutes, as tired now as a reading of Milton's *Paradise Lost*, his physique's frame dragging the poem's spatial grid in his slipstream. His piqued expression telegraphed his *angst*, his temporary depletion of a power-to-weight ratio now Jason Palmer had maneuvered the flower child from *his* frame of reference, the Ashram! Diane in space's negatively curved saddle astride her immaculate stallion eroticized Einsteinian Physics!

The Drum Roll Of Eternity. How was it possible to be sexually aroused by Doubt? Pleasurably fatigued yet standing in radiant clarity following the evening's gymkhana, Diane Blake unsaddled her magnificent horse in the stable adjacent to the jumping ring, while Eddie Phoenix clung to Dr. Philip Byrne's elbow, ever the oracle of Paradise Lost and wearing his persona like the shell of a crustacean. Did she find the aromas seeping from these centaurs an aphrodisiac? *"Doktor*, I can soften this *rock* for you."* Too bad about Sir Isaac Newton's perfect constructs of absolute space *and* time! Dr. Byrne thought he heard the drum roll of Eternity ... Phoenix had suddenly vanished, ever seeking to ransom them all to spiritual dishonor. Diane's jodhpurs and severely cut jacket would have him signing away his soul! Dr. Byrne dreamed of the strophic symmetry of her coitus, trained with the precision of a gymkhana, but later, parked below her lighted window as the hours passed, he thought he glimpsed Phoenix's presence saddled up in the dark-bodied limousine slowly cruising the length of her street.

The Age Of Names. Coiled with the irregularity of the 'Nam generation's free verse attitude to Issues, walking the photographic exhibition catalogue-in-hand, Dr. Philip Byrne stopped and gripped Diane Blake's elbow, steering her towards a group of titled amphorae portraits stenciled with captions: (i) **Sartre** – the moving clock of a Black Hole, his facial contortion expressive of nausea. (ii) **Elvis** – the marble disc of the Theater of Dionysus silk-screened with Apollo's fourth-dimensional presence. (iii) **Mao** – a hide-and-seek moon. (iv) **Che Guevara/Yves St. Laurent** – dissimilar mirrors of two minds. (v) **Warhol** – painting's sanitized toilette. (vi) **Fonteyn/Nureyev** – the sexual density of two I's. (vii) **Germaine Greer** – *A dear happiness to women: they would else be troubled with a pernicious suitor.* Diane asked, puzzled: "Where exactly am I located here?" Lately, *non sequitirs* had characterized their conversation, and her sexual lucidity proved inaccessible. Too sunburned to squeeze into a one-piece maillot, she was clothed only in perfume beneath the bright but loose sun-dress over a string bikini, its Benday dot pattern a maddening locus of unassuaged desire. Faces watched them from the surfaces of the amphorae.

Dreamscapes. Sheathed in a molded, clinging T-shirt, Jason Palmer posed himself *à la Brando*, with his muscled arms crossed, studying the geometry of shadows forming within the cubed room, knowing he would have to engage them in a metaphysical dialogue. The soluble slap of sandals advanced then receded proving space to be a sticky medium of transmission. Tight-wrapped in a sari, the flower child propped a hip against the frame of the open door, wearing a bodhisattva's crescented smile on her calm face, her soul's lithe rotation on the axis of her physique a natural temptation for a rebel. Many axes flowed from these conjunctions: soul-and-body, desire-and-discipline, their eventual termini reached where Paradise Lost was reduced to the simple integers of light-and-shadow. She moved, her curving hips caressed by the fabric of the sari breathing myrrh and frankincense. The angle between two walls balanced good and evil on its fulcrum. Walking into the ocean of sky up to her loins she was splashed with foaming stellar semen from a galactic wave. Palmer abruptly awoke. Reclining Buddha-fashion beside him on the bed, the flower child was sensually brushing the length of his naked torso with a long-stalked lotus. Now he grasped Eddie Phoenix's mission ... *brahminicide*!

The Surrealism Of Dalinian Physics. "This deluxe dove of peace has him, and his mind, caged in the Ashram of her body. Already he's fragmenting with the surrealism of Dalinian physics. She brings a very visceral religious ecstasy, if you know what I mean." Modeling a fragment of feminine Greek sculpture, an Amazon equestrienne perhaps, having dismounted, Diane Blake curved to remove her sandals before hurrying after Dr. Philip Byrne along the cream-laced foreshore, her physique's carriage of an indefinable radiance, something imperishable. The throbbing mantrum of a helicopter vibrated the still azure of the summer sky, the pressure of pulsations like armor plating around a phalanx of fallen Archangels. Ambrosial wave-foam churned the shoreline and swept up the beach clasping their legs while the helicopter circled overhead. Distilled myrrh mingled with coconut oil lotion on the crisp air. Then rotorblades beat elision semaphores across the exquisite slopes of sand dunes, sketching the decomposition of Infinity, the geometric ciphers conveying the calligraphy of a new challenge to Heaven being mounted by the fallen Archangel. In the near-distance, *Krishna*, buoyed on a carpet of jasmine petals listened to a sitar, circled by cross-legged devotees, his postural complements, so many astral travelers shipwrecked on Earth. Diane approached and studied them more closely, becoming confused when she thought she recognized Jason Palmer impersonating the contemplative *Krishna*. More worrying were the silhouettes of Eddie Phoenix and

Lt. John Kirby moving along the crest of a vanishing sand dune, scene of an existential loneliness more threatening than the promised Paradise of these devotees as fragile as lotus blossoms. The stylized technology of the helicopter hovered low and whipped up a storm of sand.

Media For A New Mythology. Against the linear attenuation of the sand dunes, the disintegrating fragments of Eddie Phoenix flashed across their flanks embodied in the shadowy ciphers cast by the helicopter's rotorblades. Conscious of her peeling sunburn, metaphor for the skin of their Age flaking from the Body of Time, Diane Blake fanned herself with a publication borrowed from a Krishna devotee, before noticing the glossy cover photograph: a burning Buddhist on a Saigon street. *Krishna's* chakric wheels of fire beautifully painted on his torso brought to her sensibility with some force how the paradigm of the Age was shifting, and she pondered time's distortion of accepted reality, and her own ambiguous identity in the world's theater. These overheated images melted the soft frame of space: (i) The Phoenix helicopter embossed on the sun's golden escutcheon: the fallen Archangel as a master technocrat. (ii) The flower child's watercolor hair awash with *Krishna's* azure body-paste: love-potion ground from the substance of the stars. (iii) Jason Palmer's elliptical remark: "I'm miming my own reflection here in three-dimensional space, they can fight that!" (iv) The lacquer of his all-over Krishna body-paint washing off in the surf; a reflective skin created for dissolution. What was the message here? There must be some psychic causality perpetuated from one incarnation to another? Glistening, Palmer re-emerged from the membrane of the ocean just as the helicopter peeled away from the sun's golden altar, a wisp of darkening smoke, charcoal foam lifting off a wave of Pride. "Diane, can you forgive this condensation from the sublime melt of our spiritual unity, for, incarnating, the soul sacrifices its androgynous self. I am dismembered. Will you piece me together again?"

KRISHNA inc. Spaced extrinsically across the cityscape, fresh billboards advertised **KRISHNA inc.**, a laundering operation for the fallen Archangel's age-old currency of self-glorification. Itself an imposing sculpture parked out front of a skyscraper's waterfall of glass, a Rolls Royce decorated in fading psychedelia *à la the Summer of Love* had a seated Buddha mounted on its bonnet, the vehicle a gilded personage, abstractly figurative to be sure, but suitably uxorious for a Swami. Dr. Philip Byrne guided Diane Blake up the steps toward the skyscraper's revolving doors, feeling her centrifuge further to the periphery of his existence despite these transits of nearness. "Have you heard, they've taken to addressing Jason Palmer as *Citizen Krishna*, an amusing sobriquet, wouldn't you say?" She had briefly worked for the consortium of architects responsible for the building. Smoothly levitating the floors in an elevator, conscious of a run in her stocking which flawed the pure sculpture of her leg, she remembered with delight Palmer's appraisal of her with a Blakeism: *The nakedness of woman is the Work of God!* So why was he shaping himself to the elastic stresses of this Krishna imagery? She mused on the mirroring effect provided by the elevator's dark-glassed interior. No vestal Venus, she imagined the surrealism of their nudity when the elevator opened on the twentieth-floor of the corporate building.

Unholy Trinity – Phoenix, Esquire & Taylor. Germaine Greer scribbled statistical truths for **OZ** magazine in a notepad, readying a collage of thoughts, ruminations on the runes of the controversial publication, how to widen its circulation. A vibrantly colored sand mandala lay composed in the center of the twentieth-floor suite: model of the Australian national flag as a sexual tantric sutra. "We're putting down roots, man." Entrepreneurial gurus and Correggio virgins cross-legged on the floor tapping finger cymbals circled the mandala. "Are we communicating?" Eddie Phoenix was the ideological center here, capstone in the Ashram's corporate pyramid, Paulette Taylor flashing her porcelain-capped teeth, his ministering angel always creating the impression she was in sexual motion. Beyond the windows ranged the steep glade of skyscrapers, so much high-rise water glass awash with the sky's infinitude. What was the marketing ploy here, and the geo-political significance of Germaine Greer's journalism for **OZ** magazine? Diane Blake was acutely conscious of her physique's observable surface before the gazes of Johnny Esquire and Eddie Phoenix, wreathed as she was in the hypnotic musical energy of the finger-tapping cymbals. Were these Templars planning to abduct another Rebecca?

The Margin Of An Ocean Of Release. Jason Palmer's chivalric untying of her sari exposed the flower child's gold-dusted pubic hair to a sky glowing with a declining sun. He undressed his Creator's bride beneath foliage of decaying sunlight for an *al fresco* consummation. Bronze undulations softened her flesh so she evoked a sculpture covered in a pale tangerine negligee. Fraying gold tassels hemmed the fluorescence of waves undulating the margin of an ocean of release, the modulation of a moment comparable to the folding-back of the flower child's sari. Where the iliac contours of infolding sand dunes merged, Palmer's courier leaned forward across the handle-bars of her motorcycle, her gaze unusually evasive of reality, her jet-black leather jacket badged with the sinking image of the sun on the horizon. One-dimensional, mineral, she then repulsed the sun's silk-of-gold swathing every surface on the beach, flattened against the occident skyline, a remotely inaccessible I in *bas-relief*. Palmer ignored her immense inertia and began molding colored sand into a mineralized elixir of Physics equations about the flower child's red chalk cartoon.

Saga Of Neither/Nor. Eden's achingly beautiful radiances cascaded across the horizon. Passively astride Jason Palmer's horizontal pelvis, curvaceous with the grace of a summer thunderstorm's willowy rainbow, the flower child held all the expectation of a night-blooming lotus as she stretched and contracted for *the* caress. Visualizing a kaleidoscope of sexual variations from her dexterous silhouette astride his hips, Palmer quickened like a blank canvas under the brush of a *plein air* painter, a Monet feverish to capture the burst of snow-crested ocean waves. Incense wafted free of her musk-tainted flesh on a softly contoured curve of breeze lifting around and off her flower child torso. The ripple of sand dunes flowed beneath his prone torso, the crystalline grains forming on his flesh into a polypeptide chain, model of their coital symmetry, lineal descent from Adam and Eve, hippie drop-outs from Paradise. Trillions of sand grains were compacted to Brahma's celestial torso perfumed in pleasure. The flower child's undulations wove together so many strands of rope chaining them there on the abdominal plexus of the God. Bracelets slipped down arms to wrists, and anklets tinkled. Palmer's palms caressed a supple-hipped fig while around them the dunes were smeared with luminous moonlight. Cradled like a lotus in a balmy sheath of breeze she languorously arched until the undercurve of a breast was lit to evoke a sliver of moon. Afterwards, the metaphysics of her beach dancing, unleashing the fullness of her ecstasy's boundless infinitude emulated the flowing semen of stars, so many diamonds dazzling against a velvet sky.

A Night At The Opera. Summer's sequence of days seemed structured after the *découpage* of a movie, whether Godard's *A Bout De Souffle*, or the longueurs of *Cleopatra*, Jason Palmer couldn't decide which. Like Paradise's infamous fugitives, the flower child and he abandoned the Oceanside apartment and the prying surveillance of Eddie Phoenix, leaving him to guess patterns of behavior from the transparencies of their liaison. Moving randomly from motel to motel he gathered her magazines and began to measure radii of desire for the Eve in all the women pictured on the pages. Any meditative tinsel had been well and truly airbrushed from the glamorous faces. During this time he began a series of cut-ups *à la Burroughs*, using *The Koran*, the *Old and New Testaments*, *The Secret Doctrine*, *Tao Te Ching* and *The Upanishads*, spooling the famous teachings through the time-loop of his own consciousness. Then, in the evening, after she had allowed him to shave her golden-haired pubis, they cruised the inner city streets where the neon brilliance conjured up the vast set of an opera ... *Aida*.

Dante, Blake & Hamlet. "The stratification of each embodiment is terraced in Time for the archaeology of consciousness to rediscover and interpret. There is no more stunning revelation than the soul is trapped in bars of shadow cast by incarnations locked into the matrix of Time. Theologically, it is essential to consider this, the spacetime continuum is not scientifically abstract, but susceptible to all vibrations of mass-energy, feeling the lightest touch of God's fingertips." Leaving behind a furor of physical disturbance he had aroused among the guests in the television studio, Jason Palmer collected the flower child from the motel and drove over to the University where he delivered a seminar titled: *Dreams – ideological quests in search of the soul.* Hurrying away from the bored audience they visited a succession of courtrooms, terrestrial image of the spiritual trials to come on Judgment Day, reflective Dantean moments, the flower child a non-communicative Virgil. Then they sauntered among consumers in supermarket aisles, Blake and his Angel, surveying the housewives on their understanding of the Tantra of sex, while the flower child hummed *Jerusalem*. Existential consumerism ruled on these suburban terraces of the *Inferno*. From there they wandered through hospitals and post-operative recovery rooms, he the famed ghost of Hamlet, where he delivered another favorite Blakeism to the prostrate patients otherworldly with the after-effects of anesthetic: *Expect poison from the standing water.* Together they existentially explored the grid of three-dimensional spacetime turning upon the edifice of *Heartbreak Hotel* in Paradise Lost. Dr. Philip Byrne finally tracked them down to a motel where they had booked in under the names of Dante and Beatrice. Palmer discussed with him his latest musings on the scalpel of Krishna's sitar making spiritual incisions in the infected body-of-consciousness of humanity. Should he opt for spiritual surgery, or should he rehearse Hamlet for his final battle with the fallen Archangel? "You could prepare the parable of the Prodigal Son," Dr. Byrne suggested off-handedly.

Analysis Of A Cocktail Party. Immaculately gloved to her elbows, Paulette Taylor circulated among the guests with her walk's cobra motion, remarking to Diane Blake: "She's as well-preserved as a slice of wedding cake." Germaine Greer, theologian of the new *ism*, feminism, peeling away layers of the fallen Archangel's celebrated gender bias ("Quick, name the feminine hierarchy of Satan's counselors in Pandemonium."), arrayed her textural themes like warring Amazons against the scriptures of Mythology. "She is a swooping falcon no man will draw a hood over." Paulette's white gloved arms undulated like twin cobras poised to strike.

To Create A Little Flower Is The Labor Of Ages. "Where is he, has anyone seen the deluxe hustler? Johnny Esquire? He told me he'd like to press me between the pages of your book, *The Female Eunuch*, sexually." Paulette Taylor's libidinous fingers were incongruously gloved for the trays of *hors d'oeuvres* being passed around as companions to the book. "The last time Eddie Phoenix and I exchanged eyes, I said to him: Since there is nothing other than **ME**, of what can I be afraid, myself?" Germaine Greer's impenetrable face, prow of a trireme, deep-space sci-fi vessel, followed Phoenix's passage around the room, her own ungloved fingers skimming caviar from a tray. The red carnation dapper in Phoenix's lapel imaged a metaphoric wound. By his side, the flower child held her palms together in the spiritual handful-of-petals gesture, a nice touch. "Who among us can peer into the future? *My* future?" Germaine Greer winced, a rictus she would make famous, like her book, the geodesic deviation of her skull design modeling an uncut diamond smudged in carbon dust. Johnny Esquire's parody of the famous singer's mannerisms elicited amused applause from the guests.

Frieze. Hunched over the radio, Paulette Taylor concentrated on the pop song, *American Woman*, while from the upper floor hotel window Jason Palmer observed three lissome lotuses floating in the swimming pool. The tiled mosaic resembled a grid on a canvas where the sunbathing lines of the tanning beauties intersected, crossed and touched with the grace of a Renaissance cartoon. "Eddie Phoenix's ploy with **KRISHNA inc.** has all the transparence of a Warhol silkscreen." Paulette kicked off her stilettos and began rolling the gloves from her elbows, always the flirtatious stylist, determined the future would not become more virtuous, extolling in the gesture her aversion to the virginal alignment of her sexuality with the Greer woman's. Lorna, Jasmin and Donna Lee lifted their derrieres up onto the concrete frame of the pool's canvas as the water took on a shimmery sheen from the brilliant sunlight, their laughter echoing around the concourse of the motel. Paulette obliged his placement of her against the wall of the motel room in a sequence of sexually piquant postures: (i) **MARILYN MONROE** – the erotic wings of her nose were echoed in the curves of Paulette's derriere. The full white one-piece bathing suit and Pythagorean triangle of pubic fabric engendered desires more intense than anything Eve striding naked from Eden could evoke. Her hair's polished platinum mollusk curled off her forehead would survive her dead torso's driftwood washed up on the shores of California. (ii) **BRIGITTE BARDOT** – Columbine in a modern Parisian setting of the *Commedia dell'arte*. Pop Art beauty of the sixties, who was her worthy Harlequin? Pouting, her oil paint mouth possessed an appetite for giving illusion for illusion, erasing even the Lolita-like nakedness of her teenage years in the eyes of all beholders. (iii) **CATHERINE DENEUVE** – Diana's burning bow strung with arrows of ice as they plunge through the masculine heart. She symbolized the infinite space between *homme* and *femme*. Could he soften her hieratic sensibility, kick-start the voltage of the cinema goddess now the sixties were over? (iv) **KIM NOVAK** – Here was a face capable of breaking Everyman's spiritual will! Her hieroglyphics, her formulae, had assumed a presence in his reverie, her romantic style's sexual implosion opposing the infinity of space beyond the walls of his Oceanside apartment.

On The Road With Blake. A Rolls Royce car door ornately stenciled with **KRISHNA inc.** swung open as Eddie Phoenix and Paulette Taylor emerged from the skyscraper's revolving doors and strode across the pavement. Inside the Rolls, Johnny Esquire and Germaine Greer, busy scribbling in a notebook with a fountain pen, shuffled across the seat making room, their conversation's dialectic conceits around *The Female Eunuch* a biting straight through the rind of a fresh lemon, or the taste of her epicurean loins. What had she written? *The road to excess leads to the Palace of Wisdom.* The Rolls took a scenic route through the construction of new suburbias, this filling of the vacuum of Paradise Lost, an otherwise purposeless excursion, metaphor of Life's original journey from God and the waywardness of a return. Driving through the traffic with the controlled flamboyance of a Spanish bullfighter, the uniformed chauffeur resembled a two-dimensional cut-out of Lt. John Kirby, the soul of 'Nam adrift on the circles of Hell, unfolding his darkness as sunset ignited the ocean to resemble a lake of cool fire. Publicist for **KRISHNA inc.**, Paulette Taylor pressed back into the upholstery, identified the song on the car radio, *Everything Is Beautiful*, flipped open her compact mirror and began applying a fresh tube of lipstick to her mouth, the martinis of her glancing eyes visible with Phoenix's existentially taut sexual presence in the rear vision mirror. Already the invisible Archangel had incarnated his DNA spiral within her womb, his globules of matter clung to the texture of her uterus, ready to ascend the helix's free-swinging stairway. Jolted with this realization, she paused with the lipstick against her mouth and wondered about her sexual encounter with Jason Palmer, when she asked him: "Tell me, are you a rock, or a reed, then?"

The Female Eunuch, or Medusa? Official records of *Births, Death & Marriages* occupied Jason Palmer's days as he constructed elaborate familial bloodlines, laying expansive collages of data and photographs from a variety of sources across the floor of his Oceanside apartment. A modern Medusa, Germaine Greer, drawing upon metaphysical parallels, conjured some alchemy of golden publicity for *The Female Eunuch*, even while sexually floating herself with the security of an iceberg in Arctic waters: the stylessness of her prose confounded criticism. While the flower child ambled barefoot across the mutating collage, spooning yogurt between her comatose lips, Palmer searched on for Truth's *bona fide* watermark on the pages of Knowledge, visiting public libraries and bookstores. A crest blossomed from so many pages, an image requiring divination: *Suffering Is Infinite* (bannered underneath a watermark resembling a segment through half a lusciously ripe pomegranate). When evening descended he would glimpse the co-ordinates of Lt. John Kirby's self-contemplating shadow opposite the balcony of his Oceanside apartment. Disturbing intuitive flashes evolved from the collage tentatively titled, **DEATH CHALLENGES LIFE**, for a theme emerged from the familial bloodlines of Thanatos-and-Eros: the fallen Archangel planned marriage-and-pregnancy with Paulette Taylor!

Poem Of Ecstasy. Fulsome, dense with sylphic thought, a curtain billowed inward lit with spores of sunlight. Dazzling with inwoven breaths the curtain undulated. From a pyramid of Cezanne fruit bowled on the table the flower child chose Sir Isaac Newton's apple, her gesture's stretching of space contrasting the typeset headline forever fixed on the two-dimensional page of a newspaper: *13 US Personnel Killed in Da Nang Ambush.* "So, what is the meaning of these collages?" Glancing from wall-to-wall inside the apartment he realized the three-dimensional planes (E^3) were frozen in a forever-moment, unlike the apple's sphere, already altered by the flower child's bite, and being chemically transformed inside her stomach. Why wasn't his Hamletian figure in the graveyard of 'Nam in soliloquy over Yorick's skull? His nostalgia for the anonymity of Time deepened in intensity. Scriabin's translucent mysticism channeled through his *Poem of Ecstasy* rendered the space of the room a cube of aural topaz as the trumpet blazed. "These collages? My design for a winnable war!" The swinging trapeze of their acrobatic conversations, very linear, invariably stilled to question-and-answer. Her waif's voice was worn like an Ashram's sheath. "Jason, who is Diane Blake?"

Equation Defining Doubt. The loom of chalk-white sand dunes threaded their Tao. Jason Palmer reclined on the crest of a dune, sand scooped by a palm trickling through his fingers, visualizing the palette of a billion sunrises, the patina of a trillion sunsets which had lit the sky since the Archangel had made of Earth's Eden his Thebaid of dissent and alienation. Trekking among the empty sand basins as bleached and washed-out as a Turner watercolor they came across the abandoned monastery. As she swung the incense of her arms, the flower child's finger-bells found a hypnotic rhythm, scintillations counterpoised against the crumbling architecture of the monastery. Further off were the stained glass windows of his imaginary inner cathedral and the skeletal frame of a half-buried moon buggy. Hunched over by Doubt he stooped and finger-wrote the energy-of-an-electron equation in the sand. Light's dispersion through the virgin torsos of the stained glass windows and her single word answers to his questions, the Zen of adolescence responding to adult koans, cleaved his understanding of the relationship between the microcosm and the macrocosm. What was the amplitude, the circumference of the floor of Paradise Lost? He too had shrunk himself inside the nucleus of an atom! Atoms were sensorial glowworms negotiating the darkness compacted in three-dimensional space. His soul maneuvered within the subterranean space of his body by their light! Night brought forth an ideological configuration of stars, precious jewels in the treasure house of Brahma's mind, the glowworms of every comet electric with His thought.

Love In Las Vegas. "Who is Diane Blake?" Cooling off waist deep in the foaming shallows of whitewater with the flower child, Jason Palmer watched the loosening girdle of the Milky Way and remembered a journey he had made with Diane, arriving in Las Vegas just as the mellowing varnish of evening sunlight was drying on the sky's canvas. Initially, from a distance, Las Vegas represented an enormous oil painting in the style of John Martin's wrath-filled revelations: Vegas as a biblical incarnation! Sunrise in the desert city was actually the midnight hour. Lines of taxis and limousines stretched from hotel to hotel as if the guests believed Las Vegas was sanctuary against some impending cataclysmic disaster. Bursts of neon-cloud shot through with perpetual lightning bolts of garish color, a darker spectrum though to Paradise's, symbolized by the waves of galaxies ebbing from the Earth's plunge into deeper darkness, displayed the awesome psyche of the fallen Archangel, the Supreme Gambler. Neon smelt here of fire-and-brimstone! From the rodeo of touring the casinos, to playing centaur-and-centauress in their hotel suite, they attended the gymkhana in which Diane was competing, moments radiantly counterpointing each other, a conjunction of classical idealizations. By day, after sexually brushing the lyre together they sunbathed, motionless, beside the liquefied jewel of the swimming pool, before retiring again to the suite where they slept out time. Later that evening, by chance, he discovered a Christian radio station broadcasting readings of *Revelations* from Las Vegas, architectural model perhaps for a New Jerusalem!

Show Girls! Elvis glimpsed pausing to climb inside his Cadillac, and turning to glance and wave at his fans, evoked blown golden pollen lifting off the filament of a wilting lotus. Before the Cadillac pulled away from the marquee, Jason Palmer handed him a copy of *The Female Eunuch*, with one of Diane Blake's ornate hairpins placed between the pages, a whimsical gesture noted by the new Apollo with a frowning smile. Finding the architectural analogy, she described the famous singer as *power pinioned in the classic Herm of a man*. God walked the Earth under many aliases!

Library For The Damned. "If I asked for my bath to be filled with milk, the staff would oblige. So you plan to steal away Germaine Greer's image? Is there a sale price?" The fallen Archangel spread his plumage in feathery neon colors across the floor of the desert. Las Vegas' quantum-theory presented as a three-dimensional model of his atomic structure, architecture of alienation and isolation, every neon globe a pulsating particle in the fabric of his gambler's consciousness unreconciled to failure. They drove beyond the city precincts following Diane Blake's elimination from the gymkhana to where the easel of Las Vegas against the zero of the sky stood precipitated like a library for the damned, a painting swept into being by splashes of neon. Highways receded into radii of shadow across the vast desert where Nature was in a condition of obsolescence. While Diane dozed curled up on the car seat, Jason Palmer felt the sand's granular abrasiveness under his feet, and marveled that the Eternal Gambler would outpost his consciousness here on the throw of a dice: a Mallarméan moment! Marooned on the atoll of Las Vegas, Infinity dreamed on, shipwrecked tourists beaching themselves in the high-rise hotel/casino complexes, scalping tickets for the famous singer's evening resurrection at the International. Driving back, he remarked to Diane that the Archangel had swallowed the whole world, to which she sleepily smiled a riposte: "And Las Vegas is his dyspepsia?"

Good News! Standing against a film of embroidered tapestries extolling the virtues of **KRISHNA inc.**, Jason Palmer elaborated on his spiritual theme, how, like a counterpoised leitmotif, *Revelations* existed in all Scriptures. Good news for God, not so good news for the fallen Archangel! Dr. Philip Byrne found himself laughing as Palmer discoursed on Jesus-and-the-quark, conjuring, wreathing descriptive *colors*, *flavors*, *charms* from these extra-physical forces, which actually *increased* their power of attraction with distance instead of decreasing. Using the fabric of the tapestries he musicalised harps of galaxies strung with stars, swept by electromagnetic breezes, the audience seated on soft cushions surrendering to the symphony of imagery, the calligraphy of his speaking voice's unfamiliar syntax. "Space has heard, is hearing, and will hear, simultaneously, the sounds of all Time." Although chaperoning the flower child, who sat on a cushion at Palmer's feet, undulating with the elasticity of Indian dancing, Dr. Byrne could only sense the equine aroma of Diane Blake's jodhpurs stretched between her thighs, and hunger for the mold of this sexual equestrienne of a woman to envelop him. "Can humanity be persuaded to re-evaluate their relationship to Lucifer?" Stepping with Palmer onto the roof of the skyscraper where the helicopter waited, Dr. Byrne weighed an appropriate answer: "You wielded God's spiritual baton in there with all the credibility of a twentieth-century Harlequin!"

The Ultimate Model Of Matter Is Proving Eternally Elusive. Placard carrying Christian groups assembled and stormed the headquarters of **KRISHNA inc.**, the enamel of salvation polished in their expression of righteousness, the stones they carried emblems of Lucifer's unrepentant heart. Jason Palmer quickly identified Germaine Greer in the vanguard, a surprising positioning of herself, the tall taper of her womanhood crowned by a wick he determined now to light and melt her persona's waxed enamel, rendering her a lamp within the world's tomb, or womb. Under a shower of rocks and shattering glass the atom of another spiritual revival disintegrated!

Quanta. Students erected a frieze of Jason Palmer's collages around the walls of the Physics laboratory. They understood the message of his *Revelation*, how they were all simply subatomic particles roaming among the stars, ionizing each other, producing visible pathways, and demonstrating the exclusion principle that no two electrons in the atom of the cosmos possessed the same set of quantum numbers, not even in Infinity. He showed them the phosphorescence of the Universe was a wave-characteristic and diffraction-pattern emitted by the electrons in Brahma's torso. "*Voilà!* My reflection, ladies and gentlemen, is simply a painting-on-glass!"

Preparation Of A Mausoleum. Perspiration super-saturated with salt slowly eddied toward the dark jewel of the flower child's navel. Late-afternoon's raga drifted across the dunelike fragments of her prone torso, a pure lithograph on the crumpled page of the bed sheet where he brought closure to their sexual tableau, that artificial metamorphosis into spiritual ecstasy and the famed *little death.* Her orgasmic flash transmitted through tightly closed eyes rippled with a succession of chords struck on the sitar, resonating beyond terrestrial space, as if in anticipation of her ultimate journey to come. Under his fingertips her smooth skin felt as silky as a calm ocean shot through with blushes of sunset. One of Life's most compelling transactions was now completed. Leaving her, Jason Palmer walked away from the apartment complex's façade armored in bronze from the glowing sunset, and strolled down to the beach. Captured by a fragment of thought the sun's jewel became sealed again in the casket of Time: the delirium of space's prison cell starved his aspiration until he climbed the crest of a pearl-grey dune and planted the cross of his torso-and-outstretched arms there. He marveled at the swiftness of his shadow moving on the axis of his torso, the pantomime of existence supremely imaged in the scene. Earlier in the apartment he had smeared her in equational Physics, seduced her thoughts from the Iphigenia-sacrifice she was destined to make by modeling her as famous sculpture, all for a mausoleum of feminine marble: *Ecstasy of St. Teresa, Apollo and Daphne, Diana,* and *Niobe.* Completing her version of a late-sixties spiritual child for him she braided garlands of jasmine petals through her free-flowing tresses.

Crisis? What Crisis? The sun's globe trembled on the curving blade of the ocean's horizon with the resonance of an annunciatory trumpet bell. Shadows lengthened across the Zen garden of scrolled beach sand. Sheaves of sparks glazed the hooded mask of the helicopter rising over the ashen dunes. The armor of an eggshell cracked! Lucifer half-bent backward under Archangel Michael's thrusting luminous sword disguised as a sunbeam. Jason Palmer drew a lesson from this struggle, welcoming the discipline of his own asceticism, in becoming as infinitely small as the stars readying to sparkle forth. He awaited the pinholes of light to break through the eggshell of Paradise. Suddenly though a stasis of darkness closed around the burning wreckage of the helicopter and garish flames licked at the indigo skyline.

Transliteration. Brahma slumbered, submerged in the cosmic ocean beyond three-dimensional spacetime. The stars' effluvium exterior leaked through God's interior reverie. Discovered some time later in Jason Palmer's Oceanside apartment was a long-scrolled collage, a referential map of the Universe hemorrhaging with the flower child, the amphora of her body contoured in galactic arabesques, Brahma's dream. She was finally a lily-of-the-valley raised among a field of stars!

VI
WRECKS OF A DISSOLVING DREAM

Les Muets. "The poetry of Physics, spacetime field equations, Philip, paradigms. What else constitutes the essential metaphor describing Paradise Lost and the City of God?" Leaving the plebeian suburbs and journeying along the teleological freeway toward the city precincts Dr. Philip Byrne pondered Jason Palmer's question. Thought segments of concrete and asphalt laid a logical *way* along which he was committed to travel. A lone motorcyclist accelerated out of the darkness alongside the car. Had Palmer provided an escort for his negotiation of the *way's* conceptual maze? Her shoulders were hunched inside a bomber jacket, a lovely effect conjuring the fallen Archangel's descent across the periphery of three-dimensional spacetime, his flesh prickling with the event's imagined recollection. Headlamps lit up the phrase, **LES MUETS**, emblazoned across the bomber jacket. Wheeling from the cloverleaf toward an underpass he glimpsed the escutcheon of the Chevrolet's grill on the cobra crest of a rising flyover. The flyover's soaring wave had yet to complete itself and flow back into the ocean current of roadways washing against the city foreshore. Palmer's eventual completion of his own question seemed definitive enough: *"The cistern contains: the fountain overflows."*

Changelessness. Untrammeled by her lost innocence, Cassandra symbolically leaned across the bonnet of the Chevrolet *à la the pose* from Dali's *Young Virgin Autosodomised By Her Own Chastity*, gazing at the charcoal spires of the city skyscrapers. These half-obscured images, monumental fossilizations, symbolized a universal trauma, sullied reflections from a City of God on which the sun never sets. For Jason Palmer the windshield frame presented a panorama evocative of the scene of spiritual dereliction conjured from the blank verse of Milton's epic poem: (i) *out of the earth a fabric huge rose like an exhalation* – The freeway's eviscerated torso resembled a vast fossil of the would-be Archangelic Superman, status black, heroically proud in less than sovereign banishment. (ii) *stretched out huge in length the Arch-fiend lay chained on the burning lake* – A *Laocoon* tableau, the geometric city stood scaled in strings of neon wrestling with spools of cloverleaves, bound in gravity waves of chaos generated by the Archangel's existential presence. (iii) *then with expanded wings he steers his flight aloft* – With the mauvish-pink coming of dawn blending through tangerine-orange, the wings of the cloverleaves spread, opened, gathered all inbound traffic, held the armored vehicles gridlocked, the dissipating shadows so many terrestrial ashes scattered before the streaks of light. (iv) *the sudden blaze far round illumined hell* – Sunrise's fountain overflowed the horizon's cistern and the sky resembled the veined grail of the metaphysical flower of the City of God. (v) *sonorous metal blowing martial sounds* – Organ chords drummed across the embankment slopes as the phalanxes of cars generated their magnetic lines of force about the core of the city. Cassandra glared back through the windshield and pouted at the disinterested head posture of the flower child who was idly flicking through some glossy periodical to pass the time.

Rebel Without A Cause. A long black Lincoln Continental, model favored by the pop star, exited an underpass into a torrential volley of arrowed sunlight, a power display demonstrating the ease with which the fallen Archangel must have been restrained in darkness after his challenge on the City of God. Eddie Phoenix, Archangelic hoodlum, half-leaned from the passenger side window as the Lincoln Continental drew level with Dr. Philip Byrne. "*Doktor*, Jason Palmer has gone all sentimental, he wants to bring the Archangel and his Deity to a Socratic dialogue. What could they possibly have to say to each other?" Sarcastic laughter hung for a surreal moment in the sun-warmed cinematic space they occupied. Dr. Byrne watched the surgical apparatus of cranes-in-combination operating on the freeway's prone torso, surely a moment worthy of the maddening verse of Lautreamont!

East Of Eden. Pages of a magazine titled **LUCIFER'S JOURNAL** fluttered with the rustle of wings on the seat beside Jason Palmer as he caressed the Chevrolet free of the loins of the cloverleaf interchange. Filling up at a gas station he pondered how to unlock the ambiguity of his relationship with the flower child. His metaphysical séances with her, endeavoring to open her eyes into his eyes so she might synthesize with his nostalgia for *Revelations*, had rather loaded down his lashes with heavy black kohl, brought a spiritual dip in his line-of-vision. She had stared blankly at the hymnal nakedness of the phallic pylons and failed to comprehend the freeway billboard signage illustrated with thick arrows, her connectivity with the world being too discordant. Her favorite occupation was wandering supermarket aisles sampling exotic foods from the shelves. Sex with her too was like exploring a universal solitude, becalmed as she was in the disequilibrium of modern life, the declension of the sixties attained, the ascension through the seventies beginning. Cruising the coastline at dusk he marveled at the convex arabesque of the horizon spilling eternal waves toward the beach. Colored in ochre coral the smooth surface of a sand dune momentarily shone with the brilliance of an egg, and he thought of the marble thighs of St. Teresa, undulant with spiritual ecstasy arrowing the length of her torso into her heart. The solar monocle fell from the aristocratic face of the sky.

Lucifer's Journal. Conceptual permutations intrigued Jason Palmer as he smoothed the heat-curled pages of the magazine and scanned the paragraph headings: (i) **NOW is Sufferable!** (ii) **Disobedience is Freedom TO BE, or NOT TO BE!** (iii) **I Rebel, therefore I AM!** (iv) **God IS Dead!** Editorial question: How then is the Archangel to be condemned? Clever photographic montages with Diane Blake and himself dressed like resistance fighters for the Archangel's lost cause spilled across the pages, suitable transfers to imprint on T-shirts for the world's rebellious youth, very marketable on the threshold of the seventies. Looking closer he recognized himself among anti-war demonstrators at the police barricades, Diane holding a banner which read: **FUTURE = NOTHING!** How purposefully she strode across the sidewalk from the office building and tossed her own copy of the Journal onto the passenger seat of the Chevrolet.

Lao Tzu's Free-Way. "How can we escape being shipwrecked on atoll Earth then? Is there life after death?" Diane Blake gazed up at the passing windows with a subliminal ache for the imagined sexual dramas unfolding behind curtains drawn across each bedroom's mini-theater. The messianism of Jason Palmer's in answering defied the zenith of negation the world had attained, his confidence energizing but surely unsustainable: "Don't we prove it? Diane, this Chevrolet is a divine chariot, our uniformly moving frame-of-reference, unsinkable." The pair of Journals lying half-across one another on the rear seat underscored caesuras of silence, the free way in which he evoked and described *limitlessness*. Flooded with perspiration she felt herself sexually soaked in phosphorus remembering the luxurious brushwork of his caresses, how he brought her to inhabit multi-dimensional space simultaneously with himself, naming the fusion *teleological coitus*. Fingers pulling at her professionally tailored *décolleté* blouse, she blushed for her fleshy pearl dissolved in the clasp of moistening lips, and hurriedly turned on the car radio where *Up Around The Bend* was playing. Why this endless fascination though with the motion of traffic sweeping along freeways? What did the obsession portend? Over and over he had taken to repeating: "Free ... *way*. How can there ever be a *free* ... way? And to where?" His still-youthful skin's stretched Florentine bronze profiled a half-rotation which caught the reflection of her desire's solitude. "The relativity of distance traveled and elapsed time lies foundering on this atoll of three-dimensional spacetime like the wreck of a dissolving dream." He had become for her a collage of such tactile moments, always mellifluous in his provocative assumptions. If only her flesh caressed by luscious underclothes were as cerebral!

Is She A Vermeer, Sargent, Or Lichtenstein? Scintillas of ideological intelligence excited his glances, rhythms of interior mental architecture transposed from the City of God suffused his DNA structure and defined his personification on the canvas of three-dimensional existence. Conversation centered on the yoga of the automobile-as-chariot and the astral travel of their personae through spacetime. Some of his favored evocations were images of armored personnel carriers, Hueys and tanks negotiating the forbidding tropical terrain of 'Nam, the percussive armor-plating a metaphor for the engagement of forces on the burning lake of Paradise Lost. The weight of Diane

Blake's plumage propped by her hands became so much erotic ectoplasm. Frozen mirror-images they posed a question: How could a three-dimensional image reduce to two-dimensions like this? Three-dimensional, they touched, whiffs of perfume embroidered the pressing of flesh, so why weren't their two-dimensional mirror-images sensing ecstasy, or were they? Precisely matched inside the two-dimensional space of the mirror they were sexually indivisible, Diane trembling with the absorption of her breast between his lips, and this instantaneous duplication of arabesques struck Jason Palmer, for was there a simultaneous line-of-transmission right now from fourth-dimensional through three-dimensional spacetime? "All possibilities exist simultaneously." Evening's presence as they cruised the Oceanside boulevards conjured dreams of a pastel Hellas filtered through the skies of the City of God last glimpsed by the legions of Angels falling over the precipice into darkness. Driving through the evocative washes of these watercolor moments he was conscious of her vibration's sexual blur and his mouth still tasting her breasts outlined in her gown's plunging *décolletage*. "Diane, on the curve of space you beautifully illustrate a goddess in *bas relief*. Your conceptual elegance is breathtaking." During their sexually evocative afternoon together she felt herself shifting from a symmetrical Vermeer, through incandescent Sargent, ending up a Benday dot Lichtenstein, her orgasm quantum-sized, an ignition of the star-stuff, her pubis an exploding pomegranate. "A goddess in *bas relief*?" she joked. "On A Grecian Urn?"

Bringing On His Existential Crisis. Symbolic days stalled in city traffic inspired Jason Palmer's appreciation of the skyscrapers' tableaux as signifiers of the Archangel's identity, his existential crisis floored on the grid of three-dimensional space. Down the dark aeons the immobility of his existentialism, a superhuman resignation to pessimism at the very extremity of non-believability, the Archangel's *rock of ages* contemplated time amid an absence of sweet sunshine. Surrounding the cityscape, the cloverleaves' musculature writhed in slow-motion with the agony of rebellion, of incarnation condemned to immobility, emblematic of the Archangel's crusted extremism. The *wheel's* sudden proliferation proved the proposition: *Idea precedes manifestation.* As the Chevrolet's fuselage taxied the runways beneath the facets of Archangelic eyes encrusted in contemplative skyscraper windows, Palmer realized how the city modeled a seven-dimensional presence in *real* space. Held in the city grid, the Archangel's anatomy was ultimately inextricable from God's! Slow-motion waterfalls of glass, frozen fjords, towered over the pedestrians hurrying *nowhere* along the sidewalks. In Palmer's diaphanous vision Cavaliers and Roundheads formed imaginative icons for God's faithful Angels and the proletarian Archangel. Images from the ongoing battle for Paradise Lost in the tawdry terrain of 'Nam, like a soiled and drooping US flag, its stars discolored, movingly filled the evening news bulletins.

OZ Records. Publicizing Germaine Greer in a glorious Marilyn Monroe wig, a wry parody of *Some Like It Hot* feminism, Jason Palmer launched a 45 rpm recording by her on an obscure label, promoting her on billboards across the city. When the single's

A-side, *I Want To Be Loved By You*, flawed by the rasping edge of Germaine Greer's voice failed to be picked up by the radio stations, he transformed her into an incarnation of the Jane Russell of feminists, belting out *Diamonds Are A Girl's Best Friend*. Dr. Philip Byrne caught the platter on the air-waves and his porcelain vase shattered.

Camus In Drag City. Diane Blake clutched her throat and paled at the lucidity of Jason Palmer's sanitized indifference, the classical beauty of his *machismo* as the mechanics strapped him into the slim line silhouette of the dragster. Woman's beauty was extrinsic to the masculine pattern, and Diane's sympathetic fragility as the engines revved to deafening decibels awakened her to the suffering which is Eternity. The *tabula rasa* of the quarter-mile, for some reason a legendary distance of unknown origin, but spiritually significant to Palmer, awaited this waltz of mortality with death. "Is this existential choice the right freedom for you?" Beneath the almost swooning fall of sunset and the molded embellishment of the rising moon, an antique aura cast across the sixties pervaded the disused track as clandestine crowds gathered, sensing some intrinsically metaphysical manifestation about to unfold. In answer to her existential quotation, he replied: "Gravitation is irresistible, it pulls me into embodiment. What will loosen me again?" The hood closed and the visible path of the linear accelerator was readied for slippage into acceleration. High-octane rocket fuel created explosive thrust-and-acceleration. "Who is in the other dragster ..." Heart pumping as the shimmering exhausts, pools of liquid fire, propelled the competitive dragsters forward with a sonic acceleration tearing space asunder, she repeated the question. Burning up like a subatomic particle the other dragster began disintegrating. "O, some guy called Eddie Phoenix, they tell me ..." Diane's hand gripped her throat tighter as the dragster disintegrated into tracings of obsolescence and flaring rocket fuel torched the indigo skyline. That Palmer would renounce Eternity for the brevity of existential speed was relativistic behavior which tested her belief in his patience to wait for her in the *Now*. Drenched in the aroma of rocket fuel fumes she wondered whether she would ever find a *way* into his narrative. Dissonances clustered in the distance as the image of masculine vulnerability dissolved in the allusion the fallen Archangel's crashing chariot on the floor of Paradise Lost.

Sculpture In Foam. Fire trucks hosed the skeletal fabric of the dragster, coating its blackened torso in a preservative of foam. Siren wailing, an ambulance sped along the trajectory of the linear accelerator. Attendants in starched whites rolled a trolley up to the sculpted dragster while the particle tracks from its disintegrating torso still clung to the retinas of the crowd's eyes. Death's space was a theorem full of vacancy and airiness mocking the crushing indifference, the closure of incarnation with its compendium of abstract gestures. Jason Palmer's dragster decelerated, dragging an inflated parachute, his double-handed grasp of the steering wheel controlling the hilt-and-pommel of the long sword-thrust of the sleek machine. The dragster's silver flash underlined the black clouds billowing from Eddie Phoenix's dying machine, then the latter's torso became sculpture in foam. Like Hamlet, Palmer had succumbed to the vertigo of existential choice knowing *arrival* and *departure* were simultaneous. His parallel joust with Phoenix decided forever the respective probabilities of their faiths. He gradually came to focus Diane Blake's anxious face close-by, overwhelming his sense of otherness, her soul's equipage poised with the conundrum of a Sphinx, as flakes of foam floated across the tarmac. Fumbling between his knees he retrieved a copy of Germaine Greer's 45rpm record and offered it to her hovering, benedictional hand.

Confronting The Minotaur In The Labyrinth. Atonal silences themed the absurdity of this latest venture to penetrate the depthless psyche of the fallen Archangel. Stars bright as diamonds brought human aspiration to the precipice of absurdity so vast were the distances between them, yet a pervading nostalgia they could be reached defied their immeasurable depth of silence. The Chevrolet slowed and idled before cyclone fencing beyond which lay crumpled and rusting car bodies stacked in neat tenements on the soft sand. "Where are we?" More pertinent might have been her question: "Who are we?" The inner labyrinth of car frames visible through the windshield and illuminated by the Chevrolet's headlamps signposted some kind of abstruse bearing on the floor of Paradise Lost. "Diane, welcome to my hermitage. Speed's poetry finds its residual cadence here in this existential wreckage." She exhibited the miracle of Zen patience awaiting his enlargement of the meaning in his *non-sequitirs*, but the kernel rarely ripened for her. How had she hooked up with this offbeat anti-hero searching the shoals of three-dimensional space for a restorable Hellas? Did he mind her sleep-walking beside him? Galactic tidal distortions drifted above the automobile graveyard. He seemed to be made up of words from Paradise Lost. Seated side-by-side in the capsuled tomb of a black Lincoln Continental impacted both front-and-rear in a two-dimensional collision they sensed in the upholstery the after-presence of other passengers-in-darkness, wraiths lost in the interstice between life-and-death.

Germaine Greer & Les Muets. Dr. Philip Byrne's fingers loosened the knot of his tie as he stepped into the claustrophobic space of the ramshackle recording studio. Conjunct with the angle of two walls the flower child listlessly turned the pages of a glossy periodical. Her exotic caged-bird separation from the devotees at the Ashram gave her a synthetic ambience in the space of the studio. Jason Palmer crouched over a mixing desk in the cramped control booth speaking via a microphone to the performers in the studio proper. Session musicians patiently rehearsed the musical arrangements. Germaine Greer's ephebic lips mouthed some lyrics: she was braless under her T-shirt, the perspiration-soaked fabric clinging to her nipples, the very body of **OZ RECORDS**. But would she have the lyric feeling for pop music's Tao? Fame's contract had even titillated this resolute woman. Hearing from Diane Blake about this latest caprice, this musical collage, Dr. Byrne was intrigued and wondered what anthemic portraits the celebrated feminist might conjure from the silk screen thinness of her voice. Palmer was obviously establishing the rhythms of his desire for her through the fictitious moments of pop songs and casting them in the semi-permanent roundel of a disc. Now the tape was turning and emotion cascading off-the-wall. Lorna, Jasmin and Donna Lee joined Johnny Esquire as back-up singers, their voices purer moonlight polishing the flinty granite of Germaine Greer's. Fragmented by frailty, her voice attempted to modulate through the romantic styles of the early-sixties, but only the quintessential harmonies of the back-up singers were reminiscent of the era, Germaine Greer linked the musical notes in a splash of colorless Benday dots. Palmer's hastily handwritten notes accompanied the song list for one side of an album, whose working title was: **THE GREAT PRETENDER.**

THE GREAT PRETENDER. (i) **BOYS CRY.** Frosted with the acid of Irony these teardrops overflow from the transparence of betrayal discovered. Germaine Greer would not wipe away this boy's tears, her voice freezes them to ice in his eyes. (ii) **SHOUT!** Insulated in *nothingness* since time immemorial, feminism's howl of defiance shatters the sculptures of male deceit in romance, strips petals from the cosmic rose, echoes the fallen Archangel's cry falling out of love with God. (iii) **HE'S A REBEL.** The desert blooms again with Germaine Greer & Les Muets evoking an aviary of asexually colored birds ... God is dead! Germaine Greer wittily sings **SHE'S A REBEL,** her pride fleetingly transforming her voice into exaltation. (iv) **YOU DON'T OWN ME.** Lyrical self-exploration powered with centrifugal force and I dream of coitus with Sleeping Beauty. (v) **THE GREAT PRETENDER.** Here is the Female Eunuch nasally singing through a marijuana haze, creating her future self in the future ... but tomorrow never comes.

Eternity's Heraldic Presence. Lozenges of beautifully framed stained glass windowed the ashen flanks of the sand dunes. Igniting the horizon, the sun began to blaze more fiercely while the moon bathed on in the cooler azure, and every three-dimensional boundary ruptured. A psychedelic finger-painting drawn across the canvas of space, the flower child stood upright in the speeding moon buggy holding the rollover bar, the lustral rhythms of her tresses surrendered to the onrushing breeze, her sari fluttering open at her pelvis, so many possibilities diaphanous within her resistless innocence. Heart-filled, exhilarated with his soul's emanation, Jason Palmer swept by the jeweled fires of Byzantium igniting the crests of the dunes. Motion appeared to cease as they entered the realm of a Dalinian canvas, the landscape's assemblage transcendent with time. Isolation's transparency was perfectly visualized in the *nothingness* of the sky's azure pane.

Visitation. Under the monaural disc of the sun the flower child stepped towards the high-water mark of the shoreline, the hem of her sari sweeping patterns in the loose sand reminiscent of his Zen garden. Her untrimmed tresses floated with the grace of an Angel's in a Renaissance painting, very Correggioesque. As for the Zen garden, Diane Blake had wittily remarked: "Is this Jason's Gethsemane?"

Shipwrecked. Skeletal ribs of a beached fishing vessel lay like a fossil in the bleached sand. Contemporary juxtapositions faded through the quietening patterns and only the speech of the wave-and-the-voice-of-the-breeze was audible here. The curved framework of the shipwrecked vessel resembled the ribcage of a skeletal angel crashed to earth. The hue of levitated consciousness assumed a turquoise glaze from the weightless radiances aureoling the curvatures of dune and shipwreck. A generation had been shipwrecked on Bikini atoll where the detonations sounded like the fallen Archangel crashing through three-dimensional space.

Beyond Time. The moon buggy lazily trailed behind the flower child's elastic Indian dancing, stylized on a radiant web of cascading sunbeams, her hand motions molding light into narrative thought. Jason Palmer had set his mind's iceberg adrift in this vast ocean of burning sand. Paradigms were perfect in the sense of there being no shadows, no inferior copies, just a sun-baked luminosity with crystalline thoughts like salt crystals dissolved in the ocean of time. A glowing bracelet on the flower child's wrist and her sari trimmed with woven threads provided liquescent undulations about the clustered symbols of her dancing arabesques.

Camus & The Resistance. Holding the pictured sleeve cover of *The Wonder of You*, Dr. Philip Byrne sensed from Diane Blake's quietude the pulsations of a yearning rose. "Diane, are you having an affair?" Ostensibly, they were exploring together Jason Palmer's textbook of the city freeway interchanges and the skyline architecture, for a glimpse of the fallen Archangel in their geometric cubism, but alienated by the concept he could be located and imprisoned within the tracings of their three-dimensional labyrinth. Dr. Byrne wanted more than Polaroids of his ex sister-in-law, he wanted to experience her eroticism's molten magma himself, penetrate her surface beyond these photographs of her coalescing on the screen of space. "In a Freudian sense, Philip? We both know his true affair is with the Greer woman. Romantically, I am sized to zero in the scheme of things. But I think of him ... continuously." The freeway's modulus divided, as she added: "If only he knew, my atom is splittable." A web was being woven in Dr. Byrne's consciousness from which he would never successfully extricate himself. "Would he catch your falling star? Milton's blank verse is set in his mind like these concrete cloverleaves are in the mind of the city. Ultimately though, thought's speed is trapped by this geometry. We're hopelessly lost in a continuum." He waited for answering thoughts to fall from the lips of the beautiful prophetess: her torso's sticky space of microcosmic particles held. "Well, Diane, Adam and Eve eventually had to leave the bridal suite of Paradise." He felt too keenly the dislocation of time she engendered. How could he keep leashed the abstract expressionism of his passion for her? "Is he behind this new recording group, Camus & The Resistance? He spoke at a tangent, philosophizing on World War Two's resonances in three-dimensional space, and how his war on the Archangel primarily occupies fourth-dimensional space, where our world's circle is but a mere cipher in the sand of Infinity. Perhaps he was alluding to the microcosmic battle on the sands of Iwo Jima." What possibilities Diane might crystallize! "According to Palmer, World War Two was a mere ideogram cast in spacetime, a representation of a vaster conflict glimpsed on the pages of *Paradise*

Lost. In a sense, although he wouldn't confirm it, he views the response of the US space program as the forerunner of another Exodus." Diane purposely lay naked on the vibrating web beneath the dome of his consciousness as she asked: "Does Jason see himself in the lineage of a Mosaic prophet then?"

Combat. Liberally applying coconut flavored suntan oil to her arms the flower child would never grasp the truth that no lotion could purify the marbleized colors of the human psyche. Jason Palmer turned the ignition key and the moon buggy moved off across the curvaceously serene sweep of sand dunes. Time-zero haunted his memories of these inflationary parameters so reminiscent of a vibrating string. The breeze had finely penciled ripples on the enamel surface of sand while whitewater girdled the curved foreshore, and as his fingertips lightly brushed these evocations he remembered the invisible wrinkles of the flower child's orgasm, very sixties in its reticence, still overwhelmed by the resistive drag of the frigid fifties. A distant but regular low-frequency *whump* of rotor blades announced the shimmering mirage of a helicopter above the watercolor flow of sand dunes. And still the onshore breeze sang through the tresses of the flower child's hair.

Escutcheon. High on the lip of the unfinished flyover's breaking wave, Jason Palmer's magnificent chariot surveyed the immense tableau arrayed below, the cavalcade of an end-to-end car crash staged for a photo-journal spread in a new Technicolor periodical being readied for the newsstands. Drag force within the illusory vacuum of space culminated in a stunning symphonic image, choreographic configurations more descriptive of a generation exhausting itself on the plains of Paradise Lost, as attempted in the very tiresome *ennui* of The Beatles' valedictory *Long and Winding Road* being extolled on the radio. Cameras flashed, focused on Lorna, Jasmin and Donna Lee modeling *femme eunuchs*, off-the-rack soft cover versions lifted from the celebrated feminist's book. Lorna strikingly evoked Waterhouse's *Lady of Shalott* seated in a coffee-colored Cadillac convertible. While the publicity shoot proceeded, Palmer scanned the urbanized terrain of this Paradise Lost where the flexible ambulation of the freeway cables slithered like a muscular anaconda gripping the torso of the city. Across the globe millions of gridlocked cars linked up as chain mail to armor the Archangel for one last combat with God. Well, let the existentialist sword of the Archangel cleave past, present and future, his Chevrolet's escutcheon was impregnable!

Milton & Modern Warfare. " ... *move in perfect phalanx to the Dorian mood of flutes and soft recorders ...*"

Conversational Signatures. "His contention is that the automobile's High Renaissance period is beginning to turn on the cusp of Mannerism." Dr. Philip Byrne's observation eluded Paulette Taylor. "The glory of his Michelangelesque Chevrolet has passed, and he won't be consoled that truth is existential." Her forthrightness, *whom here is not transgressor?* mode, amused him, especially the way she telegraphed the Morse Code agnosticism of the Age. "You're saying he has the sensibility of an impending catastrophe? Not a very original observation, surely. And for how long has he been practicing this asceticism, hundreds of incarnations?" Here was a modern woman written from the pages of *The Female Eunuch* ready to slip into and fill the form of her future. "By his reckoning, Paulette, some four million years." Warhol's stationary cameras filmed continuously. Paulette attempted sly humor: "Only four? Whenever we occupy the same space I sense he's just another Adam living in dread of his freedom. Sexually, he's a tuning fork sounding the perfect pitch between *Being-and-Nothingness*, the hollow *and*." Here was the woman attempting the social coup of the millennia, to bring the two warring Deities to a Symposium! Dr. Byrne perceived a Roman legion of shadowy lovers massed for coitus with her, but he only dropped one name: "And Eddie Phoenix?" Presumably Miranda Westwood would manage the catering. "Sexually? He talks endlessly about exhumation, about annihilation being undreamable, unrealizable, of *nothingness* being fullness, of *absence* overflowing with presence. My passion is for the status quo, scales evenly balanced, the fulcrum being **ME**." Listening to her wield the technology of existentialism, Dr. Byrne took out and slipped on sunglasses, the visceral routes in-and-out of the city swarming with *thronging helms and serried shields in thick array of depth immeasurable*. A helicopter rose, the insect-fabric wings of its rotor blades whirring.

Sleeping In Brahma's Dream. Evenings, *a bout de soufflé*, while the image of the sun blossomed into a pearl within the crust of the moon against black-velvet skies, had them surrendering time to the certainty of the screen-world at a succession of suburban drive-in theaters. Existence solidified about this indulgence of nightly reverie, the establishment of a routine of continuity, exploring a repertory of moods created on the two-dimensional movie screen. Jason Palmer coolly noticed the fabulous pink Eldorado Cadillac and Johnny Esquire's Priscilla look-a-like, thickly made-up like Cleopatra in her royal barge. *Cleopatra's* dreamy adolescence must have melted with the juvenilia of *The Female Eunuch*! Encouraged by Palmer the flower child kissed him with her psychedelic mouth and during the movies took to spray painting slogans across the parked car bodies, what he called *Woodstock-moments* later. Day-following-day descended into the consequential *découpage* of these evening movies at the drive-in theaters, a visual encyclopedia setting his imagination browsing the residua of the sixties. Crimson petals squeezed tight, her psychedelic kissing, initially timorous before his sexual impudence, soon became creamed ice whipped to foam, and folios of Indian oils opened with the leaves of her sari. Priscilla proved angelic but ultimately marriageable. Having abandoned the flower child, Palmer collected Diane Blake and they trailed after the Eldorado Cadillac. Diane's languid sinking astride his pelvis, doing what couldn't be shown on-screen, his sucking the sweet fig of her lower lip, became their physiques' mandala, their ideological coitus, like her erotic holding of the pommel, foot in the stirrup, swinging into the saddle at the gymkhana. Later, sleeping in Brahma's dream, he came to the realization how all humanity practiced the asceticism of becoming infinitely small in every individualized spermatozoon and ovum pearled within their torsos. Was observation of the genetic DNA models as enthralling as the broader film of their lives screened before a four-dimensional convocation of souls abstracted from any outline of flesh? Or even a movie audience abstracted from these two-dimensional recreations in celluloid?

Double-Features. (i) **THE APARTMENT/IRMA LA DOUCE** – Here was a cryptic crossword of sixties employer/employee relations, a malarial existentialism infecting the psychology of flesh. Desolation beat the heart of fiction in our lives, architectured in Shirley McLaine's streamlined gamin features, and Jack Lemmon's willingness to debate *everything*. (ii) **THE FUGITIVE KIND/THE CHASE** – Brando among the leaves of Plutarch's *Lives*, with the Crusaders before Jerusalem, at Agincourt even, he would always be an image-carver bringing a visual finality to any mythological scene. Now adrift on the cusp of the seventies, having refused through the sixties to be cut to cinematic lithographs of social realism, could he champion a Renaissance? Or would his brooding enmity of a Titan be forever overshadowed by the new breed of actor? (iii) **L'AVVENTURA/CONTEMPT** – Truth melted to nougat on the Mediterranean. On the ebb-tide of desire ... *mal de mer*! Bardot's peeling away the skin of the movie screen to reveal the *Nothing* there had the Technicolor freshness of a pulp cartoon. Both films lay classical traps for Truth. *Thou who didst waken from his summer dreams the blue Mediterranean, where he lay, lulled by the coil of his crystalline streams, beside a pumice isle in Baiae's bay, and saw in sleep old palaces and towers quivering within the wave's intenser day ...*

Milton & Modern Warfare II. " *... Then with expanded wings he steers his flight aloft, incumbent on the dusky air that felt unusual weight, till on dry land he lights, if it were land that ever burned with solid, as the lake of liquid fire ...*"

You Love ME, I Love ME. "Doktor, are you *The Spy Who Came In From The Cold?*" Eddie Phoenix's voice bled the perfume from a blossoming black rose, the fallen Archangel's official imprimatur in the cosmic War of the Roses. Visible in the rear vision mirror with an arm draped across Paulette Taylor's shoulder, her flesh cooled with jewelry, he adequately suggested the Archangel's contemporary fabulist, his glance capable of unraveling the spool of cloverleaves they had been cruising for an hour or more. Dr. Philip Byrne's eyes fell away from the mirror thinking of Jason Palmer's reminiscence of Paulette: "Handling her is like fingering a peeled, hard-boiled egg." 'Nam's nomadic refugee, Lt. John Kirby, sat beside him at the wheel staring straight ahead through the windshield into a future generous in its promised *nothingness*. The tumult of Hamburger Hill was inaudible in this city traffic. As for Paulette, she was no Shavian virgin either in the *Commedia dell'arte* performance the Archangel was staging in metropolises across the globe. Traffic slowed in the approaches to the inner city as the anti-war demonstration was in full clarion swing. Phoenix murmured close to Dr. Byrne's shoulder: "Our victory is assured. America's chocolate cream soldiers in

'Nam are melting away in the searing heat. Behold this demonstration, Doktor, *For this infernal pit shall never hold Celestial Spirits in bondage.* Next time you see Jason Palmer, ask him from me, does the *Way* know its destination?"

Four Sides Of A Square. The horizon delicately underlined the Void. They scoured the automobile graveyard for traces of Jason Palmer's visitation, knowing his penchant for the crumpled beauty still detectable in the crashed chariots' shells of despair. Only incandescent dust stirred as they rolled along the aisles. The geometry of Lt. John Kirby's vacancy from the front seat beside him held the blank verse of a life brutalized by Time's indifference. Why was Paulette Taylor treading water in Eddie Phoenix's psyche? From where did she derive her mimetic skill and negotiator's smile? "Is she still following us?" The motorcycle courier's apparition focused his eyes on the screen of reality. Dressed in black leather she might have been ebony lightning bursting from the mind of the fallen Archangel!

Transmission. Tuning the car radio into an unscheduled transmission from a Christian radio station as they sped along the unwinding ribbon of highway back toward the city precincts, they listened to Jason Palmer's voice against an obbligato of the gospel song, *Just A Closer Walk With Thee*: "*Who would lose, though full of pain, this intellectual being, those thoughts that wander through Eternity, to perish rather, swallowed up and lost in the wide womb of uncreated Night, devoid of sense and motion?*" Renaissance perspectives cluttered everything of course, but for the first time Dr. Philip Byrne imagined the Archangel's sharpened definition limned on the city grid. Compared to the city's western Renaissance altarpiece, he thought Palmer rather resembled an unfurling Chinese scroll painting. Paulette Taylor shifted the bulbed vase of her hips in the plush upholstery. Eddie Phoenix's consciousness would shape her halo to the lineaments of the *Absurd*. Tall skyscrapers modulated immense magnetic fields into suburban patterns from their energized hubs. "Palmer aspires to be a mountaineer, ascend from floor-to-peak, but what's beyond Everest?"

Milton & Modern Warfare III. "*For who can yet believe, though after loss, that all these puissant legions, whose exile hath emptied heav'n, shall fail to reascend self-raised, and repossess their native seat?*"

Embedded Brushwork Of Shadow. What underpainting was showing through the palimpsest of these events? Easing back the accelerator, Dr. Philip Byrne pummeled the steering wheel in frustration, his own aspirations to rescue Diane Blake long-dead in Eurydice. As afternoon declined toward evening the city blocks assumed the series of voltage and impedance diagrams, with their equational solutions to problems, scribbled across **LUCIFER'S JOURNAL**, a magazine they had collected from Jason Palmer's abandoned apartment. Somehow the Lincoln Continental had made a voltage jump and power-curved off a cloverleaf, giving them the slip. An Archangelic brushwork of shadow coating the city brought a stronger definition to currents of color beginning to glow along the geometric circuits. "How deeply are you embedded in Palmer's narrative?" He phrased the question to Diane as the resplendent sun streamed up an avenue and impacted the windshield. A sense of figurative displacement intensified.

Crash Of An Archangel. Minus the drag of friction the moon buggy sped across the glowing sand. He experienced the exhilaration of a Horseman aboard a Huey riding across 'Nam. The crash of an Archangel was a retrospective revelation in the sense of Time taken by light, of distance traveled, since the Planck-moment: events being witnessed in the night sky were simultaneous with their historical occurrence. Supernovas of white-foamed waves breaking across the beach of the cosmos were therefore reverberant across the whole sweep of Time. A floor of crystallized chaos lay spread about the moon buggy. Jason Palmer wondered how gravity had been disciplined by the Archangel to keep humanity earthbound. Equations imploded toward the convex sun dying on the horizon. Each sand dune resembled the physical space of a bleached skull. A flock of high-flying birds created a lovely V-effect. All imagery floated immersed in a sea of gravitational fields.

ΑΒΓΔΕΖΗΘΙΚΛΜΝΞΟΠΡΣΤΥΦΧΨΩ. The ocean's garment lay sewn with the cloth of the Presence. Sand dunes dissolved and reformed, evoking the shell of the world-egg. An existential fluidism congealed in the insatiable eye of a helicopter ascending from the interstice between two dunes. A vermilion sunbeam gently touched the glass of the cockpit. The helicopter motioned through an ungainly Stravinskian ballet against the eastern tapestry of the late-afternoon sky. The engraven geometric whorls of the Zen garden spread along the beach mesmerized the falling helicopter. Consumed in a ball of frigid phosphorus the helicopter began its luminous decay. Blackened pages from a burning journal dispersed to ash on rising thermal currents. The textures of electricity and magnetism blended in the bloodshot tidal foreshore. Jason Palmer's asceticism released him to the macrocosm. Every crystalline grain of sand became a star in the evening sky. His spermatozoon became a galactic comet. On the Atlantean width of his shoulders he bore the cosmos!

VII
DNA: SPACE'S CURVATURE IN TIME

Danseuses de Delphes. Applause ornamented the tutelary goddess of feminism as she descended the gallery's spiral stairway. Announced by Paulette Taylor to the thronging society guests, the celebrated feminist indulged her persona before the flashing cameras while standing her book's statuary on a pedestal. A pianist played Debussy while *hors d'oeuvres* circulated on trays. "What do you think of this Female Eunuch's investiture? I heard your own eunuch, Jason Palmer, speak of her as sexual exercise for a Zen monk." Eddie Phoenix unconsciously twisted the gallery program in his febrile fingers into a DNA spiral but Diane Blake's eyes gave him the *Mona Lisa* burn. Silhouettes in *bas relief* on a Grecian urn, three Graces in Ionic robes rhymed themselves to the Debussy music with a kind of frictionless motion, gifts Paulette yielded up to the society columnists, embellishments for the muscular tome balanced on the pedestal. "Come, circumambulate the Kaaba with us, we have Eternity to rise again if we wish." Her own metrical feet sandaled *à la Grecian* she spooled the guests tighter about the pedestal. Circuitously cruising the gallery, Dr. Philip Byrne replenished his glass and peeled Diane away from Eddie Phoenix, guiding her toward a canvas-lined wall. Unintelligible juxtapositions characterized the exhibits, many themed on 'Nam's psychic upheaval, generational loss terraced in the prose of oil paint and focused in the somnolent presence of Lt. John Kirby brushing up against the guests in battle fatigues. "Diane, these visualizations, the gallery itself, evoke what? Are we inside the mind of Lt. Kirby? You and I clearly missed *The Magic Bus*. For all we know ghosts may be standing here finishing the canvases. All creation is illegitimate ..." Holding his signed copy of *The Female Eunuch's* still-life, with its controversial jacket-design of melting Semelean gold, Dr. Byrne stepped away from the gallery entrance onto the sidewalk. The Three Graces had preceded him and were performing *West Side Story* on the pavement in the direction of Johnny Esquire's idling Cadillac convertible.

Voiles. Fateful cloth-of-angels, the gently billowing spinnakers slackened as the breeze ebbed and motion slowed. While the sun slumbered compliantly on the ocean surface, so much smooth enameled flesh calmed by summer's intense warmth, only a continuum of foaming wave-crests carpeting the far-off reefs suggested movement. Jason Palmer stood at the prow of the schooner's supple draughtsmanship gazing shoreward at the beachscape of Paradise Lost. How was it possible to lay down a *Way* on the directionless ocean? Since the breaking of darkness with the transition of dawn they had been cruising the coastline. A sudden spiraling ellipse of birds rose from the glittering armor of the sea. Brushed in aromatic coconut cream oil, Miranda Westwood emerged from the galley balancing plates of papaya salad, a serene matchless statue with the smoothness of rondure, her late-adolescence a libretto for a pop album. The mesmeric undulations of the ocean were paralleled onshore in the dunes visible through the schooner's telescope. Using the telescope herself she had confessed to spying on him, watching him rake his Zen garden, maneuver a surfboard all over the supple waves breaking across the nearby reef, before offering herself as Nausicaa to his journeying Ulysses. Fruit suffused with viscous sweetness melted into her mouth. She understood his dissolution in the solubility of spacetime. Cruising on the schooner was reposeful during this time when he was infatuated with so many false images. Then there was the way she combed her hair entwined in sunbeams slanting across a sky moving with the *pas de deux* of wind-and-cloud. Offering him her fork of succulent salad she alluded to her sexual intrigue with Johnny Esquire. The suitability of the *sphere* in Creation fascinated Palmer as he listened, especially the designated equidistance of every surface from the center inherent in the model. The implications of this were profound. As the picturesque center of her voice centrifuged he realized he might have been debating her immanence within his own future sexual life. Floating with the ocean's elastic potential energy he conjured in his thoughts the mass of the Earth ... 6×10^{24} kgs.

Le vent dans la plaine. "Lt. Kirby delegated Eddie Phoenix to be your spiritual chaperone?" Illustrative grains of sand adhered to his fingertips. Lulled by the rhythmic pulse of the quiescent dunes they wandered the labyrinth of sand waves, all the angles of Nature's freemasonry as smooth as the breeze. Their dialogue of conversational silences endured the passage of time, were exalted in her illumination amid the symmetrical modules of dunes. The flower child's single-minded contemplation of *nothingness*, her childlike façade as bland as a now-fading poster image advertising some late-sixties Rock Festival, her resolute naivete and numbness might have been signs, stigmata of a psychological wound sympathetic with Lt. John Kirby's sacrifice. With the breeze freshening, Jason Palmer scanned the arched vastness of the dunescape's wavelength, hearing the faintest echo of thought like geometric crystals in her mind, a Zen monologue intelligible only to the breeze. Waiting patiently offshore, the schooner might be insurance against the shipwreck of existence, their abandonment on the floor of Paradise Lost forever. Each grain of sand on his fingertip held the molecular repository of the fallen Archangel. Maybe she visualized these dunes as ice-cream molds in the mirage of summer's fierce heatwave, that after-burning conflagration from the Battle for Heaven. Now Shiva's matted cloud of ebony hair transformed the inner shell of the sky east of the dunes. Agitated mountain ranges of shifting cloud lifted high over the plain of sand waves. Crossing the crests where his Technicolor *nocturnes* in stained glass lay half-buried, they sought sanctuary in the abandoned monastery, where she sheltered with the sensitivity of a rococo virgin from the chorus of a Rock Opera. Over the sand dunes the summer thunderstorm animated the seemingly inanimate, cleansing the stained glass windows so they vibrated again with liquid imagery, and the flower child drifted from cloister to cloister, his own thoughts preoccupied with the orbital radius of the human persona about the fixed point of its soul: specifically, Being's elasticity in the spacetime continuum. Under a cloud-burst he felt the full weight of the Archangelic wave crashing on the shore of Paradise Lost and generating the tsunami of History across quiescent space, initiating the concept of Time, that mysterious emblem yet to be adequately deciphered of meaning. When the sun re-emerged a massive billow of white cloud bled with a shadowy Maltese Cross, deep purple, set sail across the ocean of the sky: the cloud-galleon concealed the treasure chest of the golden sun. Later they ventured back to the beach where his patterned Zen garden had been despoiled but was echoed in the wrinkled age lines which now blemished the once-smooth skin of dunes.

Les sons et les parfums tournent dans l'air du soir. Miranda Westwood organized a dinner party by special invitation only: Johnny Esquire declined pleading rehearsals for his next supper club engagement. His fragmentation of the collage tarnished Miranda's mood. Illuminated like a talking photograph, her torso's *sponge-dressed-in-strawberry* appetizer ushered Jason Palmer and Cassandra into the dining room where Dr. Philip Byrne entertained Paulette Taylor and the celebrated feminist over pre-dinner drinks. Coffee flowed from a silver spout and a game was improvised from the conversation. (i) **CHAQUE FLEUR S'EVAPORE AINSI QU'UN ENCENSOIR** – Paulette Taylor: "Yes, I collaborate with Eddie Phoenix's hologram. He is the very melodist of nihilism. I am the lyricist. Your God can only offer me a mortal husband. What I am offering is my *finest hour*. You talk of Creator and Creation. Is it your likeness on which the world is modeled?" Her beautiful Jupiteran face of refrigerated ice sexually melted Dr. Byrne's libido. Her whole persona was sculpted in bondage to **ME**. (ii) **LE VIOLON FREMIT COMME UN COEUR QU'ON AFFLIGE** – Jason Palmer: "Holy Parcae! Fate sugars its poison to my taste. I come to restore sociable uniformity in the world. Yes, women read *The Female Eunuch*, accept you as their ideological mentor, but will they ever come to an understanding of the tragedy of Paradise Lost? Now is the time for a geological analysis of the **SPHINX**. The aridity of the desert in which the **SPHINX** reclines landscapes our abandonment of Eden." (iii) **UN COEUR TENDRE, QUI HAIT LE NEANT VASTE ET NOIR!** – Dr. Philip Byrne: "Which of there angels in stained glass do you choose to guide you back to Eden? Look out! Actaeon, here is your Diana! Her criticism's teeth-marks are all over you. Miranda, I assure you, Jason has seen a woman's infatuated smile die as quickly and darkly as paper burns. Doubt is all. Women are skilled inquisitors and torturers, very religious in romance. They say Man learns through suffering ... what does he learn?" (iv) **LE SOLEIL S'EST NOYE DANS SON SANG QUI SE FIGE ...** - Germaine Greer: "I will be your Iphigenia. I have posed nude before the world's camera. The jacket design on my book cover looks soft, but it will prove to be the spine of summer, just as my silhouette echoes a tall building's. Under my pumice caress all men will be smoothed to my will." (v) **TON SOUVENIR EN MOI LUIT COMME UN OSTENSOIR!** – Cassandra: "What is it we are waiting to happen? I am his Peri corseted in leather, Jackson Pollock's chaos falling from his fingertips, the movie everyone misses, a sculpture's abandoned Ideal. Read my sexual mime, erotically embrace me with more than your voice, break my emotional celibacy ..." (vi) **VALSE MELANCOLIQUE ET LANGOUREAUX VERTIGE!** – Miranda Westwood: "Orpheus wanders Paradise Lost forgetful of his Eurydice. Pleasure's whirlpool is the black fig of my virginal pubis!" Smears of star-foam freshened the luminosity of the night-sky, expressing the secretive after-thoughts of Miranda Westwood and Germaine Greer.

Les collines d'Anacapri. Waist-deep in the oval canvas of a mirror, Miranda Westwood may not have been conscious of her perfume's glissando, its erotic timing as they squeezed into the schooner's cabin, Jason Palmer holding aloft a bottle of her father's classic wine. "Johnny warned me about you, said you're a very classy Byronic swimmer, no Leander. I've never been consanguineous with a Faun before ..." He palmed the bottle's curve to steady himself against the sensual implosion of her presence within the confined space of the aromatic cabin. "When will these centuries of revivals end, when will there be Peace on Earth? Are you wondering why I have shifted my affections to you? The breadth of your shoulders excites me, they could support the whole world." She measured their width with her hands. Over her shoulder he contemplated the silvered mirror, its reverse side blackened to allow reflection but not a seeing through, becoming a receptacle for fleeting impressions to flow across. The murmurous waves below dreamed of the schooner's cleaving hull, anticipating a regenerative journey, liltingly seduced the vessel buoyant with Jason Palmer and Miranda Westwood. "All evening your eyes banqueted on the Greer woman: she's just a rough oil sketch by ... Moreau?" Was she being confrontational during their undressing to probe the strength of the flaw of infidelity in his psyche and ease her own virginal paralysis? "I was comparing Germaine's master version of the *New Woman* with her previous incarnations." Miranda smeared space with sex as she stood, feet pooled by burgundy lingerie, one hand lightly brushing the isle of a bared breast, waiting for the inflammable moment, coitus' florid idyll to commence. Nude too, Palmer felt an accelerating microcosmic whirl of quantum-galaxies in his scrotum as she poured two glasses of wine to moisten their lips. Under his kiss she ecstatically folded to a sculpted position in the bunk, more like a flow of pomegranate syrup his tongue swirled to savor, for her evocative autoeroticism of eating at dinner earlier was unquestionably a prelude to sex later. His mouth yielded to her fabulous fig, then the pomegranate burst, sweetening the tongue's palate more than wine or cuisine. Buried together in the longitudinal casket of the moored schooner they crescendoed with a tarantella rhythm, even as a deep-buried name heaved from her lips ... *"Johnny"* ...

Des pas sur la neige. Zen's center of gravity resolved chaos following the rain-shower's dissolution of Jason Palmer's sand garden. The purity of raking the dove-grey sand against a nearby dune's long-breathed exhalation brought him moments of supreme harmony. Patterns fell into the mold of silica under the now rain-free sky which resolved the tensions in his Physics field-equations being washed away by wave-surges flowing up the foreshore. Later he became aware that Lt. John Kirby was shadowing him from the legato sand dunes undulating the length of the horizon. Cassandra too passed through the vividly ornate spaces of the stained glass windows cresting the dunes. Lt. Kirby had been reduced to a black chalk drawing against the cartoon of the sky as he walked the petrified wave-mass of dunes. Sunset's napalm spray liquefied the sky. Lt. Kirby moved among the tidal pools arrayed like so many bloodied footprints, his mind in chaos, wrestling with the plasma waves of napalm flooding the quantum-fields of 'Nam, computing the inflationary expansion of billows sucking up human flesh. That evening Palmer dreamt of Miranda Westwood, her face carved from a Grecian column on a pedestal-with-Corinthian-headpiece, her torso and limbs lipsticked over with Physics equations.

Ce qu'a vu le vent d'Ouest. Cones and cylinders burning high octane rocket fuel brought a *fauve* blaze to the purple evening. *Drag City* shattered the classical, pastoral Poussin world as surreally as Cubism did nineteenth-century painting: another Athens had arisen, passionate with youth and speed. Space was now reoriented to speed, whether the vigorous tremolandos of the accelerating dragsters, or the waltzing space capsules journeying the vacuum of space to the moon, and time too suffered compression under some inexplicable force driving the world. What had suddenly stirred the Archangel's inertial psyche in this direction of motivity? "Miranda, tell me, what do you hope to salvage from this beached Ulysses?" Leaving *Drag City* with her, turning the ignition key in his car, Dr. Philip Byrne was conscious of the cherry finish to her lips, ready for the salutation of a kiss. "O, Jason? ... Waking this morning, I discovered equations lipsticked all over my flesh. Only upon waking can you tell you've been dreaming."

La fille aux cheveux de lin. Centerpiece in Paulette Taylor's publicity campaign supporting the release of *The Female Eunuch* was a masked ball. Under the sparkling brilliance of chandeliers, a Panathenaic procession of guests advanced the length of the ballroom to be received by the celebrated feminist, made up in the remembered glory of a theatrical Amazon. A whimsical moment arrested attention from Germaine Greer's statuesque column, teasing her psychology, for a number of women approached holding a mask of her likeness on a stem up to their faces, all indistinguishable from one another, then peeled away to stand against a wall. Dr. Philip Byrne's *Ascelpius* studied the dramatic unfoldment of procession and the confusion modeled in Germaine Greer's statuesque presence receiving the guests. "Diane, could this be a love-token offered by Jason Palmer?" Masks replicated the Germaine Greer *look*, an extravaganza of narcissism surprising even Paulette Taylor. "Yes, I trace the romanticism of *Mercury* here. Jason is quite comfortable with his life role as God's messenger." A ravaged Andy Warhol was ushered forward, glimpsed in a *Jackie O.* mask, Laurence Olivier presented as *Othello*, symbol of his own unrepentant misogyny, then Jason Palmer's wingèd *Mercury* danced *Hygeia* from *Ascelpius'* side as the music began. "What is this latest dance craze called?" The Stroll-like movement of parallel dancers allowed conversation. "I believe it is called *The Double-Helix*." Diane Blake's *Hygeia* made the dance's anti-romantic swerve at the head of the queue, and when they had circled back to join up again, she asked: "Whose lipstick is on the mouth of your mask? Smells like cherry red to me. Does she kiss you as fervently as she brings her lips to the embouchure of a flute?" Passion's heliotrope coiled among the guests all evening, except an icy *Hygeia*, blonde physician of souls awash in milk, all spiritual monochrome in her display of affection. Germaine Greer's proud Amazon presided over the festivities armored in the breastplate of her feminist formulae, her tanned upper torso molded from shoulder-and-breast with the rigidity of bronze, her refusal of *Mercury's* invitation to dance prompting his fingers to flirtatiously touch and trace the sexual inlay work. "Our torso is the soul's decorative surface garnishing three-dimensional spacetime. Sculpted here beside you, I am cup-and-cupbearer awaiting the kiss of your lips."

La serenade interrompue. Fingers resonated the Spanish guitar strings. Castilian steel, the rhythm flashed with the flourish of a Toledo blade. Visible beyond the windows of the auditorium, under the Moorish architecture of the University, the leather-clad motorcyclist disputed revolutionary dogma with placard carrying students dressed *à la Che* and *à la Mao*, a mute habanera. The guitariste evoked famous cities of the Iberian peninsular, quested after the melodies and rhythms of their architecture, materialized their idea in sound. Eddie Phoenix positioned himself prominently beneath a Spanish arch with a megaphone, fracturing the serenity as vividly as the Cubism of Braque and Picasso translated guitars on their canvases. Crashing through the doors a revolutionary cadre began assaulting the bourgeois audience while chanting slogans from Mao's *Little Red Book*. Cubism's pictorial representations violated three-dimensional space in a final triumph of revolutionary fervor.

La Cathedrale engloutie. The cathedral city floated in space on a sand-reef. A stream of asphalt crossed the moonscape. Baroque Cadillacs dueled along the empty stretch of highway. "On this isthmus of sand I can savor the intoxication of being free." Jason Palmer's eyes roamed the cleft perspectives of spacetime and came to focus on the origami of Las Vegas blossoming in the desert, smoldering conflagration, grandiose self-assertion, tremulous aberration of a Holy City glowing with Lucifer's brightness. "*Free*? In a Sartrean sense, surely?" Dr. Philip Byrne's shoe scuffed the earth. The fallen Archangel had seriously tilted the geometry of fourth-dimensional space releasing his narcissism and fogging the mirror of three-dimensional space with his image. "Philip, is this the treasure laid up for us by the Archangel?" Shrugging off an immediate answer, Dr. Byrne attempted to engage the soporific eyes of the flower child lounging in the Chevrolet. "Three-dimensional space exists as thought, therefore the Archangel will think and create." What a chasm lay between the double-helixes of Diane Blake and the flower child! "Elvis was at the wheel of one of those Cadillacs, another Ezekiel plunging toward the center of Paradise Lost shielded by his aerial guardians. He's the spiritual worm embedded in the poisonous rose of Las Vegas." The extension of the horizon possessed a boundless depth. "Here we have the final fossilization of the Archangel. Time's excavation has dug up for us his breastplate from the floor of Paradise Lost. Behold!" Dr. Byrne sensed an epiphanal moment had struck. "And you intend to claim this cuirass for yourself as a prize?" When an ochre-washed evening descended and a bloodied tide of dissolving sunlight flooded the plain, the Chevrolet made an approach to the sub-Byzantine world of Las Vegas. "How many times has it been imaged, the soul as a traveler in the caravanserai of the body, exposed to the desert of the world?"

L'Danse du Puck. Desert *fauves* in a dust-filmed Chevrolet, they cruised the dream-world of Las Vegas, following the jeweled clasp reflecting off Priscilla's blue-black Cleopatran hairstyle. A wax museum of archetypal Eves dressed at the very frontier of sixties-colors seemed tranquilized under debauched caresses of neon. Cruising the fabulous Strip, car-hopping with superlative timing, Pyramus and Thisbe whispered idealisms, while all around them the color-soaked faceting of the hotels and casinos pulsed with the hyper-active heartbeat of the Archangel. The slim white tapers of pretty teenage girls in bell-bottoms leaned against idling cars, smoothly demure hustlers unable to consciously endure the brevity of existence. A prophet in search of theological proof, Jason Palmer cruised the streets for hours as if lost in the Minotaur's labyrinth, finally numbed by Las Vegas' idyll, so, for how much longer would the thematic fibers hold?

Ministrels. "Pure raindrops fall to earth, gather into a spring, rush into a river and finally meander ... where? ... why?" Jason Palmer's masquerade as a Physics professor scribbling equations across the blackboard of the University lecture theater had a minstrelesque ambience. A paper airplane sailed across the auditorium. "This Term's assignment is to set down the field-equations describing the following: *Him the Almighty Power hurled headlong flaming through th' ethereal sky with hideous ruin and combustion down to bottomless perdition, there to dwell in adamantine chains and penal fire.*" After-shocks from Mao's Cultural Revolution were reverberating through Academia. Restless students outside the windows could be heard chanting ... *There is no reason for anything to exist at all!* ... while Palmer used the closure of the blackboard's frame to elucidate the phrase, *Theos agnostos*, with a mosaic of equations. "Human thought is a Minstrel in black greasepaint, and what has thought's creation unfolded in Time? The seers of Physics have always talked the language of the Gods." Unexpectedly, Johnny Esquire drifted into the lecture theater strumming an acoustic guitar and singing Elvis' arrangement of *Tomorrow Is A Long Time*, accompanied by the Three Graces in starched white coats. The students, daydreaming heads absorbed in the revolution of mathematics and the field-equations of Paradise Lost, found voice as the tantalizing Graces flashed their naked torsos inside the white coats. A Molotov cocktail crashed through the glass window scattering the students. Flame and smoke erupted, besmirching faces. Slivers of glass encrusted Palmer's jacket. Visible beyond the shattered window was a wave of placards ebbing and flowing with the battle between students and mobilized Police. The Three Graces stood in shock, their white coats swabbed in blood, abandoned by the students crushed in the exits. Palmer's minstrelesque smile defined the moment: "Is there sex beyond the after-life of our three-dimensional spacetime continuum? Welcome to the University of *Pandemonium*!"

Reflets dans l'eau. The schooner's mathematical angularity cleaved the tilting plane of the porphyry ocean. Dawn brightened in limpid pinks and golds, the exegesis of a spiritual peroration reminding humanity of the distance of their *fall*. Miranda Westwood volunteered her family's schooner to the three Maenads so they might convalesce, and talk to her of Johnny Esquire. Jason Palmer too soaked up time aboard the schooner. He visualized a fleet of yachts as triremes stroking an ocean lit with Eos' golden tresses. Here one could experience the melt into *nothingness*. Fins of cloud surfaced to cleave the thin plane of the sky. Miranda's handsome Orpheus modeled after the famous pop star would no longer thrill guitar strings with restorative healing, being a casualty in the war between God and the Archangel. Lorna, Jasmin and Donna Lee sunbathed in half-silence while Miranda swabbed and dressed their battle wounds, unimpressed that the Physics students were industriously computing equations around the ghost masses of high-energy particles from the explosion shredding their white coats. Helios steadily looked into the mirror of the ocean from space. Drifting in a space of one-pointed perspective, Palmer sensed something of the ecstatic calmness inherent in time before the beginning of Time.

Hommage à Rameau. Dr. Philip Byrne initiated Diane Blake into the existential psyche of French New Wave filmmakers, their viewing of the retrospective providing a striking contrast, for the current generation had evolved with flowers for voices. (i) **AND GOD CREATED WOMAN** – Bardot's ambrosial hair spilled from the arabesque of her naked torso, a masculine thought made flesh for the delectation of the audience. The Mediterranean sun warmed her sexual being against Dufy's breezy and colorful brushwork. (ii) **LAST YEAR IN MARIENBAD** – Imaginary conversations in whispering pianissimos, reflections caught in splintered psyches where mirrors aroused the tautest emotional responses, froze them. Here, alcoves were abandoned, oracles silenced. Verbal residue settled into monologue. (iii) **HIROSHIMA MON AMOUR** – Is the world really perishable? Violence as simplicity itself, quiet as the shrouded umbrella of a mushroom, a descent into darkness. The origami of a love affair curled with radiation burn. Love remained an enigma, even while the mind bled memories of a nuclear idyll. (iv) **JULES ET JIM** – The metaphysic of a *ménage à trois* dominated by ambiguous identities, sexual mime, unknown dimensions of the feminine psyche, and Jeanne Moreau's ripe-curving mouth.

Mouvement. The flower child's naked torso and limbs caressed the texture of space within the afternoon light of the apartment while he contemplated the figural dynamism of leaves radiating from rose and lotus buds. When the sea breeze lifted off the ocean later and cooled the curve of her torso, she occupied herself squeezing the golden mass of radiance pouring through her fingers, and from his angle of vision, Jason Palmer perceived the relationship between the mass of light particles and the energy of its vibrating string flowing through the hand of the flower child. Enjoying coitus later in the afternoon quietude, her orgasm like the ignition of a star, he wondered if she understood the significance of the billions of sharp-scented white stars birthing in his own scrotum. White signified the shadow of divinity cast across the world.

Cloches à travers les feuilles. Cecil B. de Mille's cast of thousands assembled in the city streets, the anti-Vietnam Moratorium bringing traffic to a standstill. From the steps of an inner city cathedral, religious leaders harangued the surging crowd with platitudes extolling the brotherhood-of-man, that all-men-are-brothers, even Communists, while bells tolled a *Requiem*. The fallen Archangel's immersion seeped through the stone blocks of the edifice, erected as a piece of sanctified Paradise on Earth: it too was *lost*. Baroque surges of blood congealed Jason Palmer's sculpted physique as he watched the television coverage on the evening bulletins, recognizing Eddie Phoenix masquerading in the cloth-of-righteousness on the steps of the cathedral. "Now he's extolling everyone to take Mass-and-Communism twice a week!" The killing fields of 'Nam seeped with a tracery of particles, a glowing fog, as images were intercut with coverage of the Moratorium. Accompanied by the legato lyricism of the flower child, always amiable listening to him discourse on the war in 'Nam, he drove over to the city cemetery and walked among the aisles of graves. In their tranquil loneliness, deaf to the religious Mass sang in their honor, these fallen youth had been summoned in the dream of incarnation to sacrifice themselves on behalf of the Freemasonic-brotherhood-of-the-Archangel!

Et la lune descend sur le temple qui fut. Parked high on the breaking wave of a flyover, Jason Palmer surveyed the white-hot quietude of galaxies slumbering in the violet pool of a midnight sky softened only by a glowing moon. Templed on a geometric grid of streets, the city buildings resembled parallel chords of precipitated music, but not so much Pythagoras' *Music of the Spheres*, rather Milton's more martial blank verse. The cold space between hot galaxies intrigued him, this spread cloth of irradiating blossoms in the garden of the sky. Whose caress spun and undulated the galaxies? Out of the brilliance of a pointed star, Cassandra approached him on the brooding lip of the flyover's poised wave. Rapt with stillness as lacquer flakes from the jade moon peeled and drifted earthward, they watched and waited. "Revelation has always decoded the secrets of the Universe to us in our ancient incarnations. Now we need the chimes of Physics equations to awaken our recognition, annotate the memories we carry with us in our DNA: Space's Curvature In Time! Look how the braided galaxies there weave a quilt of stars. There are formulae in the lacework we will understand only through Revelation." Together they faced the voyaging sea of marblesque stars until dawn streaked the horizon.

Poissons d'or. "Shall we do the *Baudelaire Waltz?*" Paulette Taylor's unexpected question hung in the voluminous space of the cathedral before dissolving into the imagery of the stained glass windows which glowed like weightless bubbles. Her sexuality's narcissism threatened even Eddie Phoenix's revolutionary ardor, made his overtures seem like blissful endearments. She peeped into a confessional space contemplating its erotic morphology, already bored with their sexual plateau, hungering for more dangerous Alps, a Matterhorn, or Mont Blanc perhaps, to take her breath away. More immediate was Germaine Greer's sexual identity, the *Amazon Queen of Feminism*, and Jason Palmer's elusive motivation to synthesize coitus with her on the palette of a redemptive spiritual life, paint her character in Zen calligraphy. Now her vase's still-life, too cool a reflection, lacquered with the inscriptions of Feminism, waited by the nave where light falling through the stained glass windows suggested impressionist goldfish in an aquarium. "Isn't it a truth that all the angels who fell were masculine?" Phoenix listened to her question, pleased she enjoyed polishing such nuggets in the vein of her mind: let Jason Palmer sift in the stream of her thought, wade there with his *pan*! As for Paulette's insatiable sexuality he would prepare for her a palette, not Rembrandt's though, but Andy Warhol's!

Brouillards. Amorphous fogs thickened over the ocean and burgeoned along the foreshore of the beach, dissolving the verges of every boundary, the seascape aromatic with pungent odors. Conscious of the season's equinoctial progress, Diane Blake crossed the Rubicon of a petrified wave-mass of dune in the shadow of Cassandra's leather-clad monk, her emergence gilded in pearls of condensation. Harmonic disturbances in the psyche of quiescent vapor soaking through her clothing jolted her with the realization the young woman was dying even as she was becoming more vivid in their lives. Jason Palmer's rigorous meditation on the koan of the fallen Archangel was enthralling her own imagination. Now he sat within a sand mandala on the beach absorbed by the fog's pollution, circled by devotees unfolding a language sacrosanct with isolation from the realm of three-dimensional space. This hunger for invisibility puzzled her as she waited for his recognition of her presence. She toyed with impromptu thoughts, that Cassandra was his *zero*, his *non-being*, his shadow's *non-shadow*, then irritably emptied her mind, until a question burst forth: "Who on Earth are you?" The koan of Einstein's famous equation elucidated a hypothesis: *Form is emptiness and emptiness is form – mass and energy being directly proportional to each other.* But so what, when hearts were engaged in transmissions to each other? Palmer raised a palm of sand crystals, the very composition of the Cosmos itself, and allowed them to stream through his fingers. Was she smiling?

Feuilles mortes. Freshly bronzed by fourth-dimensional suns, the Ashramic devotees drifted away with the thinness of silence. The ocean's non-figurative fluidity enhanced the theological idyll of their arrangement in the circular Yin-and-Yang symbol on the foreshore. Could she disentangle him from this emptiness? One thing was certain, they somehow proved passivity was intense activity! The signage of his Zen garden had her visualizing an interior waved thought, his immeasurable aloneness, but she sensed their portrait in Physics was of binary stars, and perhaps together they could overpower this Archangel. "You say this mandala is a *vehicle*, to carry what, where?" While the vanishing devotees rolled back the onshore mist so the chemistry of crystals glistened again, he realized there was neither fog nor sky, neither was movable, and the balance of space was simply *equidistance*. Diane Blake's imperial amalgam of bodhisattva and burnished woman had been brought to the beachscape to exhibit compassion within light-filling space. "Leaves falling to the ground, equal orbiting planets, equal orbiting galaxies, equal souls gravitating to Earth. Gravitation is neither here, nor there. Our original face before our parents were born is neither here, nor there." Infinite meanings trickled with the sand flowing through his fingers, the thoughts sieved through his mind.

La puerta del Vino. Intermingled ribbons of musical curves flowing from the auditorium tautened the image of Heloise-and-Abelard's heads tongue-kissing against the prose of Spanish architecture spiritually identifying the University. While the program of Indian ragas established a mood of spiritual aspiration for the respectful audience, two figurative torsos, sculptural in shadow against porous Spanish sandstone, were engaged in their own sonorous sexual carving, a sonata whose crescendo attuned its dynamic to the *bolero* of Time. Paulette Taylor smoothed her dress in the smoldering glow of the bombed-out Physics laboratory. Time scintillated on every note cascading from the sitar. Eddie Phoenix belted and zipped his trousers but his attention was focused on the revolutionary smoke from the student fires still bleeding across the quadrangle. Suddenly, the celebrated feminist loomed beneath a Spanish arch with a piercing gaze, her mouth a tight-lipped hyphen, her presence a momentary distraction for Paulette. "Elopement is romantic non-conformism, and unpacks the promise of frenzied, illicit sex. You know I feign comprehension of everything, except **ME**." Phoenix held a transistor radio and was maneuvering through the compass dial for the clearest reception. "I know I do have too much of a *type* of beauty, but then existence is so fulsome of **ME**." Prolonged and respectful applause spilled from the auditorium and layered the scene in a shroud of peace.

"Les fees sont d'exquises danseuses". Three Graces celebrated *Land of 1000 Dances* about the mock-up of a downed Huey painted with anti-American slogans in Vietnamese, the chopper seemingly *crashed* in one of the University quadrangles. Students idolatrized this totem in a sing-song monotone which periodically erupted into chanted slogans. Eddie Phoenix paced about with his transistor radio, clearly anxious about a scheduled broadcast. When he glimpsed the flower child's late-sixties lithograph among the crowd he brusquely separated her and they vanished into some shadows. Her passivity struck a chord of virtuous idealization with the youth demonstrating, but perhaps not with the celebrated feminist. Germaine Greer's Amazonian presence awed the female students who were now confronting the consequential perception of their *otherness*, that they were not masculine Archangels. When the radio transmission came through Phoenix gathered them together to listen. *"Yes, I have been tracking through our three-dimensional spacetime continuum the psyche of Communism's would-be assassin."* Phoenix sniggered at Jason Palmer's presumption. *"Science fails to grasp that the chaos of quantum-space is the psyche of the fallen Archangel. Science would have us believe Lucifer has been erased from the space we occupy, then he colors in a cartoon of his ongoing rebellion in 'Nam for us. Some of us disappear from frame-to-frame in this increasingly syndicated cartoon. But what is this death? The soul conceives of the body as a tool to carve itself a place in the world. Of what significance are the affections of a sculptor's chisel, or completed sculpture? Let the creative breath of the soul breathe across the coal of the mind and fan the 1000-petaled lotus there into blossom. How it blooms, opens up in a seven-dimensional Buddhic sky ... "* Phoenix dashed the transistor radio to the pavement. "Now I think is the time to erase the palimpsest of Jason Palmer's embodiment, smash the sculpture, turn the Archangel's chisel upon his soul!"

Bruyeres. Dreams, trembling the leafage of his thoughts like rays of light spilling from the sun's cornucopia, visited Jason Palmer during this period of aloneness wherein he strived to resolve the crisis of metamorphosis, the eternal problem of delayed-choice now he had incarnated in the fog of three-dimensional spacetime. The Physics of birthing feminism had him reconstructing Germaine Greer's persona from the monochrome prose of her celebrated book. Thoughts of her were layered in the strata of her mind alongside the ethereal sculptures of Physics equations. Surely Einstein's field equations weren't simply vibrations his sensitive mind had received from the fallen Archangel's cosmic thought-patterns? In the gravitational field, the tidal ebb-and-flow of his dreams, they explored together **FRICTION**, exchanging atomic particles of themselves in experimental coitus, the Amazon a model of the co-efficient of sliding friction. Basking in the nostalgic idyll of these dreams he caressed too the famous Nefertiti bust whose features were transformed into the feminist's, and he could later rationalize away the intimacy by acknowledging that the paintings, sculptures and equations created by his mind were standalones, just as he was his soul's creation. More troubling though was his dream of the Planck-moment's bursting pomegranate, and the scattering of the Archangel's seeds through endless time. Here was an equation, perhaps derivative after all from the devious Archangel's psyche, whose gravitational constant would haunt all space for all time.

General Lavine – eccentric. Sex's stimulant sharpened the sting of the Archangel's accusative cry against Heaven's inertia – Einstein's inspirational unraveling of the mystery of mass and inertia coalesced with Milton's blank verse: Lucifer storming

Heaven will exponentially increase his inertia and never increase his speed to attain the velocity of light, and is therefore condemned to eternal darkness! Images of this comic General and his Legions amused Jason Palmer as he observed Eddie Phoenix and Paulette Taylor from his Chevrolet parked opposite his Oceanside apartment. Phoenix had obviously coerced the key to the apartment from the flower child. Inside, Paulette stood sensing the texture of the four walls, and especially the space of the mirror which was shadowed with fading sexual puppetry, Palmer and the flower child in coitus. Sex framed a syndicated cartoon sequence, *ménage à quatre*. Phoenix had hoped to surprise their wandering Orpheus planning to reunite him with his Eurydice! Orpheus-and-Eurydice eternally entwined in death in a sexual DNA curvature: she experienced a *frisson*. The whole floor of the apartment was papered with the covers of an obscure magazine titled: **FEMINISM**. More remarkable was the observation that each cover of the successive subscriptions (yet-to-be-published) exhibited but a fragment of Germaine Greer's air-brushed face, and only the complete set made up her composite image in fullness. Phoenix waited, the fallen Archangel's eccentric General, occasionally glancing at Palmer's two-dimensional domestication of the feminist rebel and the series of provocative sexual sketches she featured in. Coupled with Paulette he devised jugglings, impersonations, provocations, lobster-moves of his own in three-dimensional space with which they would confront and torture Palmer upon his return to the apartment.

La terrasse des audiences du clair de lune. KRISHNA inc. successfully negotiated a financial takeover of the cash-strapped Ashram with a view to transforming it into a commercial enterprise. Contracts were signed by the signatories under a moon-drenched sky adding luster and an aëry influence to the commercial proceedings. Eddie Phoenix, allowing an aesthetic fissure in the mask of his pessimism, coolly presented the presiding Swami with a sand-sculpture of the Australian flag, the emblematic allusion mystifying the spiritual guru. The flower child was isolated from among sari-clad dancers until she stood free beneath the moon's soaring buoyancy, the conceit appreciated by the Swami, an answer to his ceaseless prayers to be accepted in Krishna's erotic cortege. Silver tonings enriched the luminous sky, the moon's crystal ball clouded with light, the stars on the Australian flag glistened, and the dancers sculpted lotus plants around Eddie Phoenix's jewel-crested cobra. Couldn't she feel his ice burn, melt to an intenser coldness? Radiances intermingled as the saris swirled in celebratory dance beneath the pearl-light of the moon.

Ondine. Legs spread open beneath the smooth sheet of the ocean, Miranda Westwood immersed her hair so it streamed, melted away, reposed as in a bath of liquid light, while Jason Palmer sunbathed on the schooner feeling the evocative motion of Debussy's *Préludes*. Last evening moonlight gracefully scrolled the indigo skin of the ocean, loosened tresses overflowed Miranda's swimming torso, so many transitions of sensitivity manifest through the spectacle of observable reality. Bliss was an enticement engendered by her stained glass effect now on the ocean surface, a Miranda-moment brushing with fingertips the seven-dimensional lyre of his consciousness into tapestries of melody. Magazine print had tattooed her derriere once the misted fog of her clothes had dissolved from the geography of her torso, ebony streaks contrasting the silver moonbeams of her swimming Undine. He had squeezed in the door-frame of the onboard bathroom while she showered, and fragments of Germaine Greer's magazine lips had swirled away from her thighs, soft as a kiss. Drying herself after the swim she presented the curved flank of her arabesque's syrupy pear for his delectation but misjudged his appetite. Oblivion's enervating balm was already thickening about her psyche as the ocean became carpeted in vibrant yellows.

Hommage à S. Pickwick Esq. P.P.M.P.C. An Oresteian trinity of vengeful players commanded the Gnostic spatial power of the Gallery. The famously alliterated Germaine Greer brandished the shield of her book cover, *The Female Eunuch*, as a veritable feminine Rameses, but without Athena's intelligence, Aphrodite's beauty, or Hera's *lese-majeste*, and stepped forward to the podium. Immediately, the masculine members in the audience were emotionally de-magnetized, more charismatic was Paulette Taylor peeling a long-glove from her hand. Although skillfully managed by Paulette, the presence of the feminist possessed the allure of an idolatrous totem, the aroma of passion decayed, she maneuvered with the autonomy of a buffoon, and then she opened the hyphen of her lips to deliver a challenge, usher in the Germaine Greer Epoch: "Gentlemen, does the physique of *Superwoman* embarrass you? I use the word, *gentle-men*, advisedly." Open disobedience among such a distinguished array of guests would be regarded as unseemly so conversation over *hors d'oeuvres* defused the Amazonian assault from the podium. It was whispered beneath the Rose a mysterious guest was expected, more handsome than Apollo, more beautifully voiced than Orpheus, another Archangel disguised in the identity of the most famous singer of the Age. When *God Save The King* began, expectation took a sharp inbreath, then Johnny Esquire made an entrance, royalty failed to materialize, God had abandoned the world. Jason Palmer made his assault on Germaine Greer later, unannounced, magnetized by her beauty's strange asymmetry: a *Clytemnestra-effect* was his witticism to Paulette. The feminist's imperious response was felt with the shuddering impact of Clytemnestra's axe: "Him? I am no tree to be bound by tendrils! Will someone smudge this comic book drawing from the frame?" Stung, overhearing this, Palmer ventured a riposte: "Lucifer's profile, a feminine thinker, would bestride the world. But what if this statue here was for a measured moment to actually *become* Hermione, in her soul's posture, and grace us with her thoughts and feelings? Do the printed words on the pages here image *soul*?" Germaine Greer's fabric of sculpture awaited her sculptor, and Eddie Phoenix's observation anchored each at their respective distance, referring to Palmer. "He's simply the rotation of a fixed line about a point. He slaps one's face with the glove of Physics." The eyes of the Idol suddenly delved for Palmer's center of gravity, but he was already joking with Johnny Esquire's matinee idol about succumbing to the glamour of an existential anti-hero playing the supper clubs of Paradise Lost.

Canope. Strolling the Tao of the military cemetery with Lt. John Kirby, where the sands of Time gathering in the sunken caskets were for scattering across the floor of Paradise Lost, Jason Palmer contemplated the following: (i) Sleeping in *matter* the soul dreamed, yet nevertheless felt the persona's imprint engraved upon it, to perform as sexual decoy so humanity continued to propagate in three-dimensional space. (ii) Time erased the curve of itself as it progressed, screen-by-screen, bringing a seeming dissolution of all experiences and images – where were the reels of Time eternally stored though? (iii) To take a core sample of human thought and feeling and do a geological analysis would reveal substance as old as the Earth itself. (iv) The Great Beast, *Existence*, hungrily fed off the vast shoals of human thought and feeling, engorged itself until the Leviathan awaited slaying by Apollo. Lt. Kirby's chaste remoteness resembled a vanishing inside the Archangel's cosmic ice-floe. Palmer clouded his vision with remembrance of erotically sinking back with the flower child like cushioning autumn leaves falling to earth. But she had already assumed her Ophelia mask with Lt. Kirby her absent Hamlet. The fall of the DNA spiral into spacetime sculpted patterns filled with everything but Truth! When evening came and the sands of Time could be seen falling through the hour-glass of the sky they stood gazing at the dazzling white crosses, thinking of the urns buried in the earth.

Les tierces alternees. Reversing off the flyover's stationary wave, the Chevrolet re-entered the weaving flow of traffic, while visible in the rear vision mirror Eddie Phoenix and Paulette Taylor lounged *à deux* with a unique kind of sexual familiarity. Now the spokes were exactly inserted in Ixion's wheel and Jason Palmer felt himself secure within the frame. "They tell me you want to lift the hem of the Greer woman's peplos." Was a Black Hole the spindle in the Cosmic Wheel? "How pointed, that someone with your Christian Virtues should be seeking sexual satori with feminism's very pagan goddess!" Motion spooled along the ribboned freeway as the tape of Phoenix's voice unwound. "A reliable source informs me her torso has the texture of a rind of fruit, the casket of a pomegranate." Passing the University clock tower constructed from blocks of Spanish sandstone, Palmer formulated that Time commenced ticking with the energizing of Paradise Lost. "Rumor has it you've been seen with Miranda Westwood." Paulette's dulcet narcissism bent like a reed before the reflection of his eyes in the mirror. Indeed, they had dined *à deux*, and after swimming together all day her prune-like flesh became soaked in sexual Port ... but with Johnny Esquire! Palmer cruised through the ensuing silence. "Phoenix, you of all people should agree with me, we need to become more aerodynamic. But you should also know, the rims of my chariot wheels, once bent cannot recover their original circularity, no matter how much hammering we give them."

Feux d'artifice. Bastille Day! The horizon's arcing blade bloodied with the radiance of the Sun King's head had celebrated aeons of debauchery. With the winged rays of sunset mirrored on the *frottage* of ocean, the schooner had set sail for Eternity. Only a veil of white surf fringed the reefs. Eddie Phoenix burned in the glass-paned window space of the low-flying helicopter. Suddenly, the pomegranate exploded, the galvanic upthrust of force somersaulting Jason Palmer into the fast-darkening ocean. He surfaced to a crimson patina, but visibility springs from fire, its nature was to illuminate. A wingspan of watery fire struggled to lift free of the ocean. Had the Archangel collapsed back? Still dazed before the burning casket of the schooner all he could focus on was the gravitational constant's final triumph. The radiance of the Sun God's monarchy suddenly dimmed. He swam towards the schooner but was repelled by the oblation in fire. *Where was Miranda Westwood?* Even the jet of appearing galaxies couldn't quench this concentration of fire. The schooner's raw salmon belly liberated aromas of pomegranate molasses. Night was swallowing her raspberry mouth. Mortality banqueted on her. Now the listless water dragged the charred keel of the smoking schooner under. The curling volute of a wave beached Palmer on the shore. An elastic emptiness filled his consciousness until Nausicaa's voice echoed there.

VIII
NOTES TOWARD A SUPREME FICTION

Who Possesses Space? Black-and-white newsreel footage of the University's Physics laboratory ablaze, bizarrely intercut with Jason Palmer's controversial Christian broadcast screened that evening on a current affairs program. Cross-legged on the sofa, ignoring the surreal montage on the television screen, the flower child idly rotated the ring on her big toe, coolly negligent of the students' insurrection or her lover's metaphysical campaign against the fallen Archangel. Dr. Philip Byrne hunched forward beside her and raised the volume when the commentator's voice-over finished, and he realized Palmer was talking: "Our issue here is, who possesses space? What we are witnessing in this afternoon's footage is a modern version of the burning of the Reichstag. These angels of ice are interwoven with the fallen Archangel's fire, their confluence in three-dimensional space generates his own Third Reich, successfully ruled over by him now for *thousands* of millennia ..." Seen in grainy imagery, slowly swinging from side-to-side in a swivel chair, his air one of a distracting, hypnotic rhythm, Palmer ignored the civilized interjections of the other guests, the Archangel's fellow-travelers. The flower child unconsciously hummed The Carpenters' *Close To You*, and Dr. Byrne recalled her idly attempting to create forms of origami from pages of screenplay Palmer had strategically positioned across the floor of the Oceanside apartment. Dr. Byrne said to her: "Why don't you give your tongue some exercise, and walk it with me in conversation once in a while?" Spatially, her flower child's eyes possessed a Matisse glaze. Covering a babble of cross-over voices from the sandal-wearing studio guests, fresh images of exultant student demonstrators fuelling the University blaze were flashed up on-screen, generational allegiances crystallizing from the chaos. Retreating then reappearing, the flower child lazily spooned yogurt between her unimaginative lips, a mouth of silences. "World War III, like all historical wars, will be fought over possession of *space*. However, let me pose to you an enigmatic question: Should we ever empty three-dimensional space of the Archangel, *where can he go?*"

Flowing In The Archangel's Time-stream. Unrolled architectural blueprints spilled to the floor of the Chevrolet. Diane Blake had helped him extrapolate the Archangel's architectonic image, measure the lineaments of the Titanic combatant as he centered in on rendering Pandemonium's metamorphosis. **KRISHNA inc.** formed an audience chamber of Pandemonium, and the blueprints of the building, two-dimensional in themselves, nevertheless allowed a translucent *seeing through* to its core structure unimpeded by actual steel and pre-stressed concrete. Crossing a city bridge with Diane, Jason Palmer paused to glimpse the materialization of rare black swans sailing on the river, negative images of Lohengrin's manifestations: *Ride A Black Swan*! Together they flowed in the Archangel's time-stream, beneath glass waterfalls illumined by the sun, and he contemplated Truth's deepest darkness compacted in mineralized space, the loss of Paradise. "Diane, why is God unnamable?" What a nexus for self-exploration the city presented! He observed the dance-like graffiti-motion of the pedestrians moving along the conveyor belt of the sidewalk, presences eternally brushed by the torsos of skyscrapers, muscles in the being of the embodied Archangel. With day dying into late-afternoon he returned with Diane to her office, another inner space being measured up for eternal inhabitation. While space thickened with descending evening and the bejeweled dreams of light-filled skyscraper windows glowed against an amethyst skyline, they cruised yet again through the city's thoroughfares, conscious of a millions eyes observing their every move. What a seemingly vast illusion of emptiness lay behind the ink brushstrokes of these skyscrapers!

Hermione And Desdemona. "Crystal cities?" Diane Blake's question challenged Dr. Philip Byrne's Othello-on-Cyprus persona: how would she ever understand the bitter lashes of Leontes' jealousy across the tender romantic image of himself? How plastic was her sensibility? "Crystal cities, architectural portraits, precipitations of the auras of the Archangel Michael's Legions ... Jason Palmer's words, Diane." Together in her office they examined the unintelligible draughtsmanship, blueprints for a city designed after the structure of a jewel, powered at its heart with ... *love*? Dr. Byrne half-lunged for the window, reeling from Diane's evocative fondling of Palmer's monogrammed handkerchief, some soft olfactory manifesto perhaps, the origami of their coitus. A dryness touched his voice: "Has he told you he regards himself as a diamond destined to cut the glass of the sky and free us from the Archangel?" Where could he take this conversation? "We will pass with the ease of light through a pane of glass. Windows have always stood before us as meditational devices. The idea is lucidity itself, a classical thought. Church windows were invocations for the congregation to rise and pass through into light, but the Archangel held them well and truly buttressed ... " Could she conceivably fill the mold of Hermione? Did she know Eddie Phoenix visualized her as Desdemona to the Archangel's Othello? Dr. Byrne ached for her to play Procula to his Pilate! "Philip, thank you for these insights. Architects are symphonists. For me these skyscrapers *sing*!"

Triptych. Diane Blake's triptych of bedroom mirrors symmetrically angled to freight space with her curvaceous presence stood festooned with a collage of lipsticked equations. Could she believe her eyes were windows in the Chartres architecturally designed by her soul? She brushed the lyre of this thought while gazing upon his reflection. He imaged sex too as intertwining parallel helixes! Naked, luminous in his portrayal of a chivalrous Angel bringing his diamond-body to slice through the discolored glass pane of three-dimensional space, chromed in the reflective triptych of mirrors, Jason Palmer lay sculpted on the pedestal of the bed, his legs chiseled under the dune of sheet, a stylized drift of sand, as always contemplating the spiritual tensions within Physics equations. Emboldened, she delicately peeled back the bedsheet as if it were a two-dimensional skin, unveiling his exquisitely finished musculature, the classical signature of a demi-god imprinted on the casket of the bed. So why did he murmur: *Shelley, à priori Bruckner*? Such cryptic fragments of dialogue characterized their relationship, perhaps the way jewellery accessorized a woman. Her eyes sinkingly closed as the length of his fingers sexually measured her. Her orgasm came as a long-breathed glissando, the length, breadth and depth of a poem by Shelley or a symphony by Bruckner!

Anatomical Lesson. Weekends, trying to make of their time together a Pythagorean symmetry, they traveled vacant beachscapes in the moon buggy talking of crystal cities, crossed the boneless sweep of sand dunes visualizing architectural jewels materializing free in space. Testing the resonance of a hypothesis, they also made helicopter passes over the theoretical tracks incised in the anatomy of dunes by the moon buggy. Patterns subconsciously emerged, as if to resemble those a surgeon made on a patient's torso prior to its presentation on the operating table. Jason Palmer began to form the distillation of a perfect stereotype, a moral guide, and he even had her thinking astrally, with her attuned to the immense reclining torso sweeping below the helicopter, and in the near-distance the flattened intersecting axes of the Archangel's mental space, there stood the earthbound city! She gripped his arm as the conceptual grid of the city quickened her heartbeat. God knew she of all people was ill-equipped to incarnate moral absolutes! Troubled with the recognitions he triggered, she said: "You told me the continuum of every city is contiguous with the unseen sacred cities raised in fourth-dimensional space, built beyond the horizon of the Archangel's mind, and ours. How can I accomplish the architectural alchemy you're asking of me?" Together they followed the radii of freeways extending from the thoughtform of the city. Were these the lesions he imagined he would surgically remove?

Sing Your Way Out Of This! Watching Johnny Esquire rehearse the band and back-up singers in the cramped recording studio while the engineer finessed over the deck, Dr. Philip Byrne cast an eye over a song list saturated in nostalgia, a primer of the Absurd: (i) **DEVIL IN DISGUISE** – The singing of one's way into the heart of every Eve, to illuminate romance and searchingly probe the meaning of Woman.

(ii) **DEVIL OR ANGEL** – Paradise Lost pared down to a two-minute pop song, Lucifer's megalomania sung for a teenage audience. (iii) **LITTLE DEVIL** – Hope springing Eternal in sprightly caricature. (iv) **SYMPATHY FOR THE DEVIL** – Sorry, but that Evangelist's salvationary days enter the sunset of Time, even though the lyricist's palette of words would paint a canvas for the millennium. (v) **DEVIL WITH THE BLUE DRESS ON** – Germaine Greer's favorite, for she regained in the listening her lost *otherness*. Have mercy! How well the singer caught his experience of Woman on his lips! (vi) **SHE'S GOT THE DEVIL IN HER HEART** – And God Created Woman! The jingoistic voice of the singer belted out a cryptic warning: she could just as easily have God in her heart. Johnny Esquire paraded the sensibility of the supreme dandy, his stylistic resemblance modeled on the Age's glorious Apollo currently musicalizing his fate in the supper clubs of Las Vegas. Miranda Westwood squeezed her luscious cream torso from the singer's embrace as they huddled together listening to causality riding the grooves of the acetates spinning on the turntable.

Threading The Maze. Day after day a classic Chevrolet was observed cruising the horizontal crossroads of the Way, the car radio tuned to the most requested song of the moment, Freda Payne's *Band of Gold*, chaste hymn for *The Female Eunuch*. The time-bound Cubist cityscape, faceted with windows incestuously reflecting elusive self-thoughts, lured Jason Palmer into its labyrinth of existential experience and axes of surreality to test the Archangel's palpable strength. The world's coliseum was circled for a spectacle. Celebrant of the automobile's triumph as spiritual chariot he joined a caravan of roaming hippies free of societal convention and journeyed with them for a week in quest of unfixed boundaries. Although fastened to a car seat they understood this was his inward journey away from physically participative three-dimensional space. They believed his vision of the City of God and that he was the architect for its materialization out of *Revelation*. *She* materialized one halcyon red-rose evening tapestried with the illusions of her generation. A lovely, if naïve flower child traveling with the caravan fondled his silences with revivifying caresses, rather than embalming rituals and mannerisms so in favor from Woodstock, so he abducted her from the phantom of a lover absent in the rice paddies of 'Nam, and returned with her to the city's refuge of sweeping cloverleaves. With the delicacy of arcing rainbows she sliced her silhouette through his Zen space, bringing with her a fragmented collage of *non sequitirs* and a quiescence breathing the flavors of yogurt. Sexually, she possessed the geometry of a flower's architecture, her petals *blew*, a little too passively though.

The Subterraneans. Dressed in curving, stretching black leather, Jason Palmer's courier browsed the vault of the gallery for a list of prints featuring Burne-Jones and the Victorian era's Angels-in-the-House, women who never conveyed to the viewer they were pleasured in consummation. From the shadows she imagined she heard sexual ululations. Movingly solicited by voyeurism, companioned by the painted women institutionalized in myth on canvas, stepping with the militancy of a virgin toward a violation, the courier carefully concealed herself in shadow. Icons from a

Pompeian fresco, Eddie Phoenix's satyriasis of Paulette Taylor before an unrolled print of Burne-Jones women descending a staircase was being covertly observed by Raphael Summers in a conjunction fraught with erotic tensions. Rigidly outlined, Raphael Summers mimicked Phoenix's intensity, bold as a satire by Juvenal, his spillage a visceral jolt. Why did Jason Palmer only ever greet *her* sexual overtures with Zen's hand slap?

Portrait Of A Lady. Fresh from her orgasm's still narcissism, reminiscent to the observant eye steeped in nineteenth-century eroticism, of an image fractured in a lake of water as a breeze brushed its surface, with sexual palimpsests glowing about her aura, deepened by the rouge of oil paint framed against the wall, Paulette Taylor advanced to the podium like a mannequin wandering in from Paradise Lost. What dynastic beginning was she planning with the fallen Archangel through this incarnation? For a telling moment she paused, as pictorially still as an Egon Schiele portrait dressed in Gustav Klimt's raiment, the true **ME** of her narcissism's metaphysic, then the aesthetic pendulum swung to Germaine Greer's entrance. If the Fall was masculine, and the temptation of Eve a seduction of feminine Angels-in-the-House-of-the-Lord, then the keening theatricality of Germaine Greer, her script, was a more valid document than Milton's tome, Paradise Lost. Paulette's twist to introduce the celebrated feminist was always a gesture heavily smeared with: *What of ME do you apprehend?*

Revolutionary Party. "Are we of the regicide party then?" Germaine Greer's sly witticism defined her ideological power-curve. The Three Graces, once-chaste icicles melted by Jason Palmer in the linear accelerator of his aura, created fluid magnetic lines of force about the core of the feminist as she circulated among the guests with champagne and a selection of *hors d'oeuvres*. "Now, there's a woman pierced by a shaft of fears." Eddie Phoenix delivered this aside from his Archangelic pose before a famous Cubist portrait showing what the reflection of its human personae resembled when the soul looked into the three-dimensional world's mirror. Dr. Philip Byrne drained his champagne flute and turned away from Raphael Summers' parallel illustration beside Eddie Phoenix, evocative of an ill-balanced world hanging off its hinges. Seeing them together, Paulette Taylor was observed fretting, her posture striking, reflective of a mirror's asymmetry of **ME** petulant with jealousy. Diane Blake was obviously dreaming a dream-within-a-dream as Dr. Byrne approached her. "Diane, were you attentive to the scene played out just now? Germaine Greer's Queen Gertrude face stiffened to a tragic mask as Phoenix stage-whispered his desire to be moss sexually clinging to her stone." Jason Palmer's Ashramic *toy* floated up to Germaine Greer with a bouquet of **KRISHNA inc.** publications, unquestionably a teasing gesture by this twentieth-century Nietzsche who philosophized with Physics equations. Diane's sigh resembled a whistle of steam. "What is it about Beauty that makes of men idolaters?"

Pagodes. Diane Blake's chili-red lips curved in a half-smile reflected off the mirrored inner wall of the elevator they were ascending to the inner sanctum of **KRISHNA**

inc. Martyrdom assumed an idealized corolla in the mind of an adventurer seeking its experience, a compelling fascination for erasure from the canvas of existence Dr. Philip Byrne could not understand. Diane conceded religious devotees were magnetic needles to martyrdom's lodestone. Stepping through into the plush pagoda of office space they faced a platform shaped after the moon's crescent, where Eddie Phoenix's impersonation of some unfamiliar deity lounged with bold impudence. The sonority of Miranda Westwood's flute quivered with spice-coated melody as semi-clothed nymphs performed an Indian dance. The nymphs elegantly and effortlessly rotated clockwise on a right-handed-thread of motion as if securing themselves to three-dimensional spacetime. Diane leaned and whispered in Dr. Byrne's ear: "Just don't expect me to supplicate before this capital **I**." As the collective dancing imagery mutated the flower child was recognized shimmying back into an entranced sutra of motion. Boxed in on the floor was a magnificent colored-sand mandala of the Australian flag. Tiring of the conceited monologue, Diane realized the nymphs were so many genii rising in obeisance with Eddie Phoenix, torsos in puppetry with his thought, so many sweet communion wafers melting on the tongue absolving him of the sin of carnal delights. Atop the skyscraper's cloud-free sundial they boarded a helicopter and followed the river's snaking arabesque in the direction of the University.

La soiree dans Grenade. A *String Quartet* of physicists made musicalized gestures in free air before lowering hands to the blackboard and evoking a raga of mathematical equations. Chalk-white *strings* attached to the thoughts of the physicists unraveled across the space of the blackboard, so many entangled characters creating a reality by objectifying their locality: *heard melodies are sweet, but those unheard are sweeter*! The eloquent grace of these equational portraits struck Jason Palmer as the physicists' pinups of God and His Archangels. As his eyes followed the sinuous curves unfolding from the chalk's silken skein he heard the approaching *habanera* rhythm of a low-flying helicopter. The physicists paused to listen too, disrupting the electronic velocity of their chalk and Palmer gazed into the non-locality of the blackboard. Again, the light from the pieces of chalk flowed, creating an inexhaustible fountain of equations across the blackboard's canvas. Only a shower of rocks and Molotov cocktails shattering the windows disturbed the séance of physicists as they spontaneously computed equations describing how space was dragged with the moving of objects. Youth's on-campus battlefield encompassed the Physics laboratory, which even the elasticity of equations and their revelation of the quantum-world of sub-atomic particles could not shield from destruction. Einstein's masterly choreography of field equations somehow transcended the chaos engendered by the quantum-world on the façade of Law and Order. Palmer's eyes lingered on the chalk's attenuated ray of light unraveling a model for universal mourning, even as the fire crews strong-armed him to safety from the burning building. Overhead, the swish of the helicopter's samurai blades cleaved through billowing smoke trails: could humanity truly see what it was immersed in?

Jardins sous la pluie. Jason Palmer's raking of his Zen garden unearthed a skull, perhaps washed from sand dunes flowing across the beachscape like a petrified river of the Underworld. The Baptist's head rose upward to meet the rising sun, Sir Isaac Newton's head might be said to have lifted to meet the apple, and this skull being tenderly palmed, had it ascended into the light it once enjoyed? He turned to Cassandra who waited by the smoked-glass windows of tidal pools on the beach, gourds filling with the memories of millions of late-afternoon skies: "Ulysses? ..." All day Lt. John Kirby could be observed wandering the curvilinear perspectives of the dunes as if searching for his own skull, and a consciousness of who he was, some kind of certainty that he possessed *existence*. Mimicking the famous statue of the discus thrower of antiquity, Palmer hurled the skull from within the brushstrokes of raked sand towards Lt. Kirby's waiting presence. "There's a soul separated from its reflection of itself on the mirror of three-dimensional space!"

Postcards For A Feminist. Germaine Greer's compendium of inflationary moments as an Amazonian persona coalesced into a pose steeped in an irony of *male*volence as she flipped the postcards onto Paulette Taylor's desk. "What does this unintelligible juxtaposition plead for, what does the clairvoyant want from me?" (i) **PROSERPINE** (Dante Gabriel Rossetti) – "Fornication is biological, twisted into the spiral of DNA code. Sexually suffused, my brain cells are engorged with the blood of the pomegranate. Be the green leaf I can spiral with." (ii) **THE MEETING OF DANTE AND BEATRICE** (Henry Holiday) – "O Plotinian moment! You bring my soul's eye into my mind and draw back the lid. Of what is coitus a delirious symptom? Accept my very plastic sensibility and enamel me in salvation." (iii) **DANAIDES** (John William Waterhouse) – "Let us discover Hellas' placement in the Underworld together, and be master-mistress of sex's electricity lighting up this realm, be the tragic convergence of two destinies, challenge this most dangerous of utilities. Together we will write the book of our Divine Author, the perfect Androgyne!" (iv) **UNCONSCIOUS RIVALS** (Lawrence Alma-Tadema) – "Indelibly inscribed over the marbleized arch of our lives is the phrase ... **PARADISE LOST**! What is it then that we are waiting to happen?" (v) **OPHELIA** (John Millais) – "Shall we swim in sex together, you and I?" Eddie Phoenix smirked from the shadows of a corner of the room, working a switchblade like a samurai sword. Germaine Greer's emotional celibacy had all the veracity of one of the postcards Jason Palmer presumed would beguile her.

Ouranos & Gaia. Who raked the city into its Zen garden? Roman palimpsests intrigued Dr. Philip Byrne's survey of London as the helicopter leaned forward in its flight path toward the existential scaffolding of the current city precincts. How was he to convey to Diane Blake in meaningful words Jason Palmer's intention of burying the fallen Archangel in the city grid's sarcophagus? Burning marl flowed along the untangled skein of motorways, the picturesque avenues converging on the Shepperton film studios. Now the helicopter banked and the archipelago of skyscrapers evoked a mighty leviathan. Palmer had mysteriously talked of shuffling the screens of time and laying out varying arrangements as if they were a pack of playing cards and the hand we currently held could change in an instant ... *an instant of cosmic time*. He spoke too of three-dimensional space's networked sewer unrolled beneath a levitating Paradise. Clearly visible was the Archangel's resistance hardening to armor in the densely cubed volume of the city. *Deus ex machina*, the disk of the helipad atop the European headquarters of **KRISHNA inc.** beckoned.

Biblical Times. Pages from an underground Christian journal swirled up and were flung against Dr. Philip Byrne as he crouched low and moved away from the whirring blades of the helicopter. Turning to Diane Blake, he allowed himself a wry witticism: "Paradise Lost: no exit!" Then he glimpsed the shadowy presence of Eddie Phoenix, armed and dangerous, a figure of Everyman's existential ancestor, clasping her by the elbow and pulling her towards the helicopter. A moving flash emerged from the elevator shaft, *Jacob's Ladder*, and a torso resembling Jason Palmer's wrestled Phoenix away from Diane, faint light glinting off a switchblade's tempered steel. Fists flew imbuing the evening stillness with frenetic motion. While Phoenix sprawled with the figurative solidity of concrete, a dying Othello, Palmer scrambled Diane aboard the helicopter. Dr. Byrne puzzled over the strength of one man ranged against the epic thickness of the city's torso: could he actually bring off his biblical feat? For something better to do he captured a flying spread of journal on the wing and read the text in the dying light.

Unsafe At Any Speed. Jason Palmer lay wrapped tight in a corset of bed sheet, so much cold-painted masculine marble, foreshortened in the wall mirror, hands clasped behind his head like wings. His penis' line of erotic verse defined the bedscape's sexual *Sturm und Drang*, had her *looking* not thinking, stammering with amatory eloquence. "Jason, is my form of Beauty truly beautiful?" This charismatic warrior-philosopher whose caresses raked her desires into sublime waves reminiscent of his Zen garden, could ultimately position her to spiritual advantage in the scheme of existence and for the cosmic battle looming. The *adagio* from Mahler's Fourth Symphony dissolved the glacial rigidity of the bedroom walls as she sprawled on her stomach, conscious of the curve of her derriere reflected in the mirror's impenetrable iceblock, feeling the openness of every feminine physique to *penetration*. High above the city in the helicopter, when glancing across at his handsomeness she had a flash of his *imitatio Christi* entombed by the Archangel, then noticed a vehicle streaming down the motorway below draping a silken banner stenciled with: *Friends of Jesus*. Her fingers tenderly gripped his pubic hair's emblem of masculinity then relaxed. Earlier, he had been sexually formed under her in the shape of a Zen koan. Now he probed her own meditative sex, touching her toes and curved instep with his lips, then coitus brought a full romanticism to the bedspread's palette. Later they went cruising in his fabulous Chevrolet. Perfumed in pleasure, Mahler evanescing in her aura, she spoke of her ex-husband: "Sexually, you mean? The façade of a building with a revolving door. What did I know then? ..."

Ambassador. The dilution of antiquity brought too much translucence to the imagery filling the screens of Time. Dr. Philip Byrne struggled to unearth his characterization tapestried within the folds of memory from his own University days. **KRISHNA inc.** partitioned off reality from its interior stage, and stalked its *dramatis personae* as relentlessly as a playwright did their text. "Jason Palmer is fixed upon the rediscovery of a trans-geographical home for his visionary self. He speaks endlessly about *non-locality* and the mystery of abstracting death from ourselves. He talks of becoming *ourselves* beneath the veil. Perhaps you can use this quasi-divine interpreter, being particularly sensitive to sexual entanglements, to legitimize these incantations. Test his Archangelic strength, send him gifts of Hesperian fruit." Listening with an oblique expression, all his thoughts impersonations of Lucifer, Eddie Phoenix proceeded to kneel before the colored-sand mandala of the Australian flag, and began sifting the sand with his fingers, despoiling its sugared perfection, but was he listening, and to whom? "Well, *Doktor*, what invisible transitions are you making here? I understand you want to *gorge* on your brother's ex-wife, but you're not the negatively curved saddle she's riding. She's actually helping Palmer untwist the chains binding Ixion. Diane Blake is the cactus of his lust, the sting of the scorpion ..." Standing up, Phoenix walked over to the office window, his patience eroding like the disfigured mandala. "This Eve has discovered *choice*, without experiencing the sexual nausea the Greer woman writes up so fervently."

A Fabulous Fifties Teenage Coquette. Diane Blake diarized the evening's tactile richness of caresses, hand-and-pen achieving a sexual *pas de deux* across the pages, describing with guiltless exuberance the discovery of her true erotic reflex. A rosebud had eased into a full *soufflé* of petals under touches of sunbeams. *What am I symbolically fulfilling here?* Jason Palmer initiated her in the orgasmic language of warps-and-ripples, the slowing of time in ecstasy, fulfilled her expectation's electricity with the revelation of his own gratification's linear contour, and a sword of pleasure passed through her as effortlessly as light through glass. He described the evening's encounter as prose, *novelistic* sex, but the Mahler *adagio* levitating emotion strengthened their sexual connection as Art for Art's sake! Remembering herself as a fabulous fifties teenage coquette she had flirted endlessly with mirages of Elvis, thought she had married one, Dr. Philip Byrne's brother, but Jason Palmer's transfiguration vanquished so many naïve illusions. Elvis' warp-and-curve crossing the horizon of the seventies seemed light-years from his crossing over from the fifties to the sixties: *I Just Can't Help Believin'* was on her radio.

Germaine Greer's Debut Album. Paulette Taylor marshaled representatives from the press gallery and supervised the distribution of copies of Germaine Greer's debut album on **EOS** Records, although she richly caricatured **ME** in her presentation. Holding aloft the album cover as cameras flashed and microphones hustled for position close to the feminist's mouth, Paulette read off the dedication: **TO ALL THE GIRLS WHOSE BOYS ARE IN 'NAM**. Reviews began to appear over the following weeks in Underground journals and magazines, crafted from an unknown pen suspiciously reminiscent of Jason Palmer's style. (i) **JOHNNY ANGEL** – Feminism melts in gentleness, steeled with the sheen of a Toledo blade, as the fountain of Greerism overflows with an old Shelley Fabares #1. Spectral with a Velvet Underground rawness (like the whole side), our feminist chanteuse attempts to unpack her heart from its ribs of ice, but the platter doesn't quite melt as the original did, eight years ago. (ii) **EARTH ANGEL** – But wait! Is this feminist humor cut in wax? Alas, her voice flows with the paralysis of a glacier, sung straight, in parody, like a reading from the columns of **OZ** magazine. Forgive the pun of her voice's *eunuch* (unique) telegram singing style: the message is everything. (iii) **TEEN ANGEL** – Does the Amazonian feminist possess a sense of humor? Here she vocally wanders Paradise Lost in search of just one feminine being, a woman-Orpheus looking for a man-Eurydice, her voice like dead leaves swirled by an autumnal breeze and scraping along the floor of Hell. (iv) **BLUE ANGEL** – The big O? This gilt-wood frame of a voice is peeling, its posture's very erectness a chromed accessory to the vehicle of the melody, charioted Velvet Underground style. (v) **ANGEL** – How will posterity assess her tinting the rich Renaissance fresco of the Elvis song? She brings the inelegance of graffiti, simpler brushwork than Hans Hartung could express, convinces us she lacks celestial parentage. Sales were minimal, restricted to collectors with an eye to the future, despite Paulette's cultivation of influential music journalists and her sexual willingness to entertain them.

Gymkhana. Horsebound, armored in jodhpurs, beautiful centauress, Diane Blake animated the tapestry of flowing dunes beyond the Zen garden as she descended to the foreshore with the grace of a mounted Aphrodite. Rain-dampened sand flicked from the hooves as she galloped along the foreshore. The horse pranced away from whitewater washing up the beach. Erotic energy tugged at Diane's supple arabesque commanding from the negatively curved saddle. The horse's lyrical exuberance contrasted the stilled transience of the wind-swept sand dunes, the volatility of the ocean and the sculptural passivity of the Westwood's schooner anchored offshore. Addressing himself to the inevitability of the wave, Jason Palmer plunged into foaming bubbles of whitewater and swam out to the schooner anchored amidst the canvas of split horizons of sky and ocean.

Nudes à la Physics. Ignoring Eddie Phoenix's flick knife blade flashing from the shadowed niche in the gallery's basement, Dr. Philip Byrne examined with several University physicists a bizarre frieze of symbols pasted up on one of the walls, or were they precipitated ectoplasm from fourth-dimensional space? Paulette Taylor, manacled to uncharacteristic etiquette by the presence of the physicists who were emotionless and straightforward, barely controlled her keening sexuality, her coital matrix of personal allusions. Dr. Byrne began to suspect Phoenix and she had sexual rendezvous here, that they discovered the mysterious frieze and hastily phoned him with the news, anxious for his interpretation, suspecting Jason Palmer of an act of sabotage. "If we disentangle these strands, and I'll illustrate with this chalk, we might describe a marriage, a union of computer code." A physicist tapped the **Phi** symbol with the tip of his chalk, but Dr. Byrne believed the sequences were interpretative scenes documenting Paulette's pornographic proclivities, watched over by the voyeuristic faces peering out of the two-dimensional prints and canvases. What was Jason Palmer's moral here? That being visible to two-dimensional embodiments, like those on famous canvases, we three-dimensional travelers were like Gods? The physicists conferred together and passionately probed the math embedded in the simplest of equations. Terraced in the sand dunes beyond the Zen garden were horseshoes ... **Omega** ... and the imprints of cleats ... **Theta** ... elusive ciphers in the cryptology of Palmer's warfare with the fallen Archangel. What a sexual sadness mediated from the faces and impoverished erotic arabesques of the two-dimensional Burne-Jones women!

Sarcophagi. Dissociating the illusory boundary of three-dimensional *Self*, Dr. Philip Byrne crossed the crust of sand dune and discovered Jason Palmer contemplative over a serene fragment of late-afternoon Eternity enskied in a tidal pool. A golden stream flowed into the bowl cupped on the foreshore, brilliant epiphany escutcheoned on a shield, cosmic chalk inscribing space with form. Offshore, a schooner drifted beyond surf shot through with the sinking sun, these timelessly variable sunsets deepening spatial effects, a veritable Zen dream for the new Arcadia of Australia. Dr. Byrne peered over Palmer's shoulder into the miniature underworld, horizontal vision suddenly becoming vertical, his thoughts neither entangled nor empty, and when he glanced up again into the eye of the sun watching over his mortality, he experienced for a moment freedom from attachment to the world's illusory imagery. Solitary in his dream, tasting the sun's bursting pomegranate, awash with the flowing juice, Palmer sat with the omniscience of a sand dune within the meditation room of his Zen garden's mosaic, surrendering to the symbiosis of oil paint and the weave of canvas, three-dimensionally expressed. Together they walked back across Eternity to the courier and her motorcycle, where the flower child breathed upon and wiped dust from the rear vision mirror with a section of her sari decked with golden embroidery. Silence enfolded their journey in the Chevrolet through the city's dense Archangelic mandala, the treacherous reefs of freeways closing off the sarcophagi of skyscrapers. The flower child's fingers fondled the hem of her sari while she gazed out the window at the city's vibrational design positioned in spacetime. Reading Palmer's thoughts, Dr. Byrne considered the Archangelic mind, its profound motionlessness, no one going anywhere, his psyche's pattern structured after the sarcophagus of the city. With a forearm the flower child rubbed the streaky car window. Recognition's fading coal darkened with the coming of evening and Dr. Byrne reflected over the discords engendered by his attentions toward Diane Blake, how the silhouette of his purpose lost out to the light of Jason Palmer. He had to accept the mirror of Diane's mind had been demagnetized, his sexual spores could not cling, they could only ever be balanced at two points of an extremity, like life-and-death.

Mobilization. Dragsters' explosive speed propelled Jason Palmer and Eddie Phoenix along the quarter-mile in a symphony of Berliozian exuberance, a crescendo of acceleration and deceleration analogous with the momentous crash of the Archangel through the Planck-moment into three-dimensional spacetime. Did Diane Blake grasp the context here? When the Archangel brought space into being through his mind he set it racing with *time*, the rhythm of a poetic fatalism sculpted in John Milton's blank verse, a multiplicity of turnings in the Way that Palmer intended to telescope into a straight quarter-mile. Phoenix's incineration in his exploding vehicle sublimely captured the actional grace of fire repelling darkness. "Diane, he was bound to the Wheel of Time, to his Way, to his journey, but I take the point, there is something of crass incivility in death. There, in the sky, his chariot wheels keep spinning, but even the brilliance of all that wave-spume dims into dark matter. Jason Palmer understands this is only a Pyrrhic victory at best."

A City Composed After Miltonian Verse. Jason Palmer's Chevrolet slipstreamed behind the Lincoln Continental crossing the city bridge at speed. A sulphur-colored coating dusted the cityscape's geometric meditation. Drawing level with the Lincoln Continental's smoked windows before the camber swept the vehicles in parabloae away from each other, Palmer pondered their respective journeys and considered the analogy of two cans of paint, one red and the other yellow, mixed in their one-way-only union, for the process could not be reversed. A jaunty piece of jug-music came on the car radio ... *In The Summertime.* Life's incandescence ebbed from the Renaissance synthesis and serenity of the Imperial Palace with this descent into three-dimensional spacetime. Of course, Paradisal cities were imaged as squares, analogous with memories of fourth-dimensional space! Thinking of the Ashram and the decrystallized figurine of the flower child in her flowing sari, he remembered her first words to him: "Where do you live?" Spontaneously, he answered: "On the quantum-horizon ... *The Pleiades.*" As the city's neon illumination strengthened he cruised the avenues between the blocks of skyscrapers, the day's legion of pedestrians no longer strolling the Archangelic catwalk, yet the silence possessed their after-resonance, the collective memory of the millions who now slumbered. Who possessed whose space? While idling curbside before the monolithic building of **KRISHNA inc.** he glimpsed the Amazonian carriage of Germaine Greer hurrying towards the familiar Lincoln Continental. Eddie Phoenix's would-be Monarchy would now starve in pre-stressed concrete with his banishment to the three-dimensional space of the Archangel's dream: he should have familiarized himself with Milton's blank verse.

Calling Dr. Byrne. While comforting a distraught Paulette Taylor in the hospital's emergency room, Dr. Philip Byrne brought the fast-fading light of his own mind to the penumbra of meanings cast by the evening's events. They were all immersed in temporality, their personae so many parallel darknesses, subtle with inexplicable enigmas, like the tears falling from this woman's eyes. All-cried-out she straightened her shoulders, but her face conveyed the fractured imagery of a mind unable to decode the theological frameworks of *Fall*, *Incarnation* and *Redemption*: even her grieving, the funereal purple of her swollen eyes, conveyed a latent coital charge and eased their benumbed paralysis. Approaching, Jason Palmer's leather-clad courier brushed her lips against Paulette's cheek and whispered something in her ear, the intimate *frisson* of their contact physically unbalanced by the ambulances rolling away from the hospital into the cityscape's hierarchy of darkness. Error cleared from Paulette's eyes: "Now I understand the **ME**, and the **NOT-ME**!"

Espionage. In the division of light from darkness, rays passed through the window and projected onto the wall a silk screen silhouette of shadowed leaves moving in the wind, a bird on a branch, but what was truly *moving* here, the wind, the branch, the leaves ... his mind?

Zenophobia. Time's unfolding length of screens frozen like a waterfall tumbling from a Chinese cloudscape modeled Eternity's Zen koan. Diane Blake's materialization of a perfect city composed of crystal occupied Jason Palmer's hours of contemplation within the symmetry of his raked Zen garden. How to bridge again the abyss and synthesize the division between three-dimensional and four-dimensional space? A femininely youthful Li Po, swirling with the intoxication of music, the flower child was discovered wandering the sand dunes' meditation rooms, Ophelia-without-flowers, a sculpture of loss and abandonment, searching everywhere for the Golden Age of her mind. Dr. Philip Byrne figured Palmer had laid her mind to rest in the sand patterns of his Zen garden. Ultimately, were Jason Palmer, Diane Blake, the flower child and the sand dunes inside or outside his own mind?

Visual Paradigms And Linear Connexions. Amphibians stretching on the beach of Time, the sunbathing beauties assembled into an equational mosaic on the sand, would eventually be washed-over by the incoming tide: the bull-horned moon in the sky resembled the clean fingernail of a God caressing the fabric. Evening's immersion of the Zen garden in light of stained glass delicacy had Jason Palmer philosophizing on the illusory volume of space *per se*. His thought's equational haiku pitched a pendulum from Heaven-to-Earth. The fingernail of God brightened as Earth's pendant jewel was clasped and smothered in a blackened hand. Evolutionary bursts of diamond from the carbon darkness traced breaches in the fallen Archangel's psyche!

MARSHAL OF THE MASQUE

A Mid-Summer-Night's Dream. Lithe *Lamia* in black leather, Cassandra, dark energy swept up from the floodtide of the Milky Way, gunned the throttle of her motorcycle and wheeled across the parking area until the Chevrolet fell into the cone of her headlamp. *She's Got The Devil In Her Heart* being sung by Germaine Greer could be faintly heard from a car radio. Above the city the moon's silver profile lay incised in the watery glass of the sky. "Cassandra, the screenplay calls for more Puckish behavior, a rousing of jealousies." She recalled Dr. Philip Byrne's injunction as she observed Jason Palmer lounge against the bonnet of his Chevrolet as if searching all the solitudes of existence for *Him*. "Who is the inhabitant of this song?" She determined she would kiss his masculine lips with the tenderness of a dewdrop precipitating on a peach. Together they focused on the towering skyscraper lit up with **KRISHNA inc.** in neon, presumptuous Monarch of the City, and measured the city precinct's radiating strength, muscled by freeway interchanges, a torso of steel and pre-stressed concrete fibers. As a fashion stylist he carried a new icon silk screened on his tee shirt, an image of Francis Bacon. Cars were lined up alongside the Chevrolet, the occupants engaged in sexual gymnastics, youth nurturing the paradoxical seed of romance in a fallen world. Finally he half-turned to capture her eyes: "Let's strap on our parachutes and sky-dive into Paradise Lost!"

Cul-de-sac. Gifted with parallel moralities, a woman ripened by her attentive mother's generation, Germaine Greer advanced across the gallery accompanied by Raphael Summers, a pairing of the Virgin and the Priest at the birth of a New Religion. They were two of the Age's smart-people, the very installation of a *Concept*, radiating the luster of a Destiny. Dr. Philip Byrne, magical in his materializations, overheard some words Summers half-whispered in the tall feminist's ear: "If only this sketching hand, with its pencil or colored chalk, could capture everything on the wing day-by-day as the writing of words can." Expectancy subdued the buzz of the assembled guests to a kind of background radiation, no doubt left-over from the *frisson* of Jason Palmer's

Planck-moment earlier, when he installed a Pop Art assemblage of the couple as a *Pieta* in reverse, Germaine Greer oddly persuasive as a crucified Virgin. This feminist deity was for the creation of a new Universe, and her voice possessed the cadential curve of the falling Archangel's theology in its proposition: "Now that I am free, I can do whatever I choose!" Dr. Byrne deftly lifted a champagne flute off a passing tray. Paulette Taylor's, *come on and place me in your foreground*, posture diminished the feminist's credibility and sociability, or perhaps the basement tapes Summers was circulating of her coitus with Eddie Phoenix had tested her own amoral archetype: virginity never looked better!

Parallel Spaces That Will Never Touch. Dabbing the corners of her mouth with a starched handkerchief, Paulette Taylor soliloquized: "Lunching today at a café, I chose the *Bruschetta*, and observing the shape of the crowd striding along the sidewalk, I knew my determination to always choose **ME** was a piece of sublimity." Dr. Philip Byrne studied the existence of the canvases, conscious they were parallel spaces that will never touch, being evocative of that mysterious horizon between three-and-four-dimensional space which eternally haunted Jason Palmer. *The Female Eunuch's* Bible in her hand at a press conference, Germaine Greer spoke of a woman's metamorphosis by choice until Palmer's witticism brought her lips to a hyphenated close: "Accept the Gospel of Eve's heroism, having plagiarized her chromosomes and walked away from Man to lie between the pages of a book." Unfashionably dressed, unlike her electrifying Grandmother, Eve, the feminist's derriere modeled the curve of an empty barren vase, but miracles were looked for every day, *à la Cana*. When she was alone did she simply fall asleep? Eddie Phoenix extended the Archangel's portrait deep within the boundary of the world's canvas. Still, Germaine Greer was of a marriageable age, although her facial physiognomy suggested she had tasted enough heartache for one lifetime. Leaving the Gallery, Dr. Byrne read off allusions from the opaque night sky, marveling how the galaxies were twisted into the weave of space's plasma, reminiscences perhaps of the DNA spirals magnetizing matter into intelligent human form. Suddenly the flower child was at his elbow, biting into a crisp apple, an anomaly causing him to laugh aloud.

Revolutionary Physics. Art Nouveau creations suggesting space's lineaments to be less *sticky*, Lorna, Jasmin and Donna Lee toyed with the equations flowing across the blackboard, the white chalk matching their laboratory coats, enjoying this quasi-sexual interlude with the Physics staff. As they frolicked with the galactic skywriting of chalk equations the campus outside the laboratory erupted, anti-war demonstrators unleashing showers of fiery particles in a microwave hiss that metaphored all the probabilities of quantum physics. So many baroque chalk-strokes, the theoretical nexus of equations, a robust musical liaison between the String Quartet of physicists, could only antagonize and inflame students now politicized to the dream of monolithic order promised by Communism. While time dilated and space curved, the physicists unbuttoned the laboratory coats and intermingled the milky emissions of their chalk equations with the snowflake symmetries of the Art Nouveau girls, invoking serendipitous discoveries: sex mimetized space's three-way curvature into the positivity of the sphere, the negativity of the saddle and the zero of an infinite plane. These gravitational entanglements freshened the adventurous mind for the challenges of a *Theory of Everything*, in coitus electro-magnetism and the quantum soup interfused.

Pageants. *Mise-en-scène* from Jason Palmer's film-in-progress, tentatively titled, **MYTHES**, coalesced these images: (i) **JASON AND THE GOLDEN FLEECE** – Wingèd hood ornament, Cassandra breasted the evening air-waves with the nuanced grandeur of a demi-Amazon as the procession of classic Chevrolets cruised the Oceanside boulevards, modern triremes of a latter-day *Argonautica* wresting the Golden Fleece of Time from three-dimensional space. Youthful allegorist, Jason Palmer evolved from the palimpsest of spacetime's continuum models composed of etheric textures which he wove into his film-fabric. (ii) **CASSANDRA** – Pinball machines illuminated the panther skin of Cassandra's leather jeans as they strolled the amusement arcades and tested the physics of the game. Her face criss-crossed with Mondrian's boogie-woogie neon-colors, she rebirthed something of the Trojan Age, became his perfect companion on this quest to retrieve the Golden Fleece from The Center of Paradise Lost. (iii) **THE FALL OF TROY** – Curving away from the blackened cityscape pressed to the mirror of space, Jason Palmer's Chevrolet journeyed to the automobile graveyard by the sea, silver-sanded under moonlight, Cassandra's aloof modeling beside him carnally asexual and therefore intensely arousing. Above, the Milky Way's trellis loaded with stars possessed a diamantine brilliance underscored by the hiss of waves breaking on the nearby shoreline. Cassandra unbuttoned her shirt and exposed a pure white brassiere cupping her breasts, while the anguished torsos of the stacked automobiles lay crumpled under the weight of Paradise Lost's gravity. Essences dilated, an aroma of sweet lavender circumferenced the moment, moonlight reflected off splashing jasper foam: was this how beauty yielded itself up to sin? (iv) **ATLANTIDE** – Lying outstretched on the cooling sand of a finely-grained dune, propped on both elbows, molded for a tableau in marble, or Egyptian ebony, Cassandra waited for his luminously handsome *Atlantide* to release the tension in space and move. Moonbeams stole across his physique and the iced-over stream of time flowed. The *Golden Fleece* lay impaled and the Argonautica set sail under a spreading spinnaker of stars.

"Angels Fell, But Where?". A violinesque breeze swirled about the navel-effect on the anatomy of sand dunes and the slender dune-grass curved before its soft pressure. Strikingly lithe, anything but boyish-looking though, Cassandra strolled with him by the abandoned torsos of automobiles, the moon-drenched moment sexually inlaid with exhaustion, listening to him expound on the 100 billion galaxies as being quantum mechanics expanded to a cosmological locality. Jason Palmer paused before a fractured windshield and drooping wings of car doors, smelling in the salted dune-grass aromas of Eve's pubis, spreading across Cassandra's flesh through the palimpsest of the feminine DNA spiral, a dance of perfume with which he twisted. Bare-chested, having stripped off his Francis Bacon tee shirt, he half-lay with Cassandra on the crest of a dune watching waves effervesce to whitewater ... *Ill met by moonlight*. Suddenly Diane Blake appeared from the moonlight in her perfection's profundity, as if an astral presence, her voice's poetry the mold for an irremovable stain: "Coitus by moonlight!" Lying there, the iridescent bulbs of Cassandra's brassiere evoked slivers of moon peeled from the sky. "Jason, you molded my eyes to *see*, so why should I be surprised at the distortion of this image refracting through my tears? You have cast me adrift, left me desolate amid the ruins of spacetime, when I was sleeping so peacefully ..."

Icon On A Tapestry. The Einsteinian bending of space still posed lingering questions. Jason Palmer contemplated the increasingly emaciated devotee reclining across the sky, the inflationary shiver of the Milky Way's meditative torso exemplifying non-locality. Evolutionary bursts of diamond effloresced from the carbon darkness in a beautiful origami of galaxies making up the lotus flower of the Cosmic God. In these galactic conversions of mass/energy the fallen angels skated the ice of a profound solitude. The Milky Way herself leaned from space with the flickering impression of a blossom-laden bough of cherry blossom on a night-darkened stream.

Welcome To My (Quantum) World. Entering the sunken stream of moonbeams drained between two dunes, Dr. Philip Byrne and the flower child heard voices pitched to filter through the ocean's wave-hiss, the quantum-scene strangely stilled. Still eating the Hesperian fruit of a pomegranate, the flower child confounded his sensibility with her incessant allusions to a mythological presence, her gestures annotating the ethos of the Woodstock generation, her tenuous cravings for some sphere of peace in which to incubate eluding him. Searching the quantum-world of the beachscape they glimpsed the physicists illuminating the altar of a sand dune, subsumed to etchings by the gleaming but very cool silver of the moon, these Abelards of Physics, and the Three Graces, being placed against the sky's plenitude of darkness in amoral arabesques. They had obviously abandoned the laboratory fire-bombed by anti-war demonstrators and were seeking Jason Palmer's palliative refuge-on-the-beach in which to consummate their equational proof of gravity-waves. Dr. Byrne described their moon-dreaming to the flower child: "You would think sex-and-mathematics were exclusive of each other in the mind of a physicist. Does the morality of mathematics support coitus? The purity of mathematics is devalued, unless of course Lorna, Jasmin and Donna Lee are pure symbol, or a fog of equations to be defined and understood." Erotic turmoil was a skein of sensation the flower child might understand and make sense of, but her emotional celibacy was as rounded and dense as a perfect pomegranate prior to splitting and bursting open. A throbbing helicopter prowled the coastline, its searchlight probing the foreshore from the dark insect-like eye of the cockpit, creation from the thought of Physics but unimagined by Sir Isaac Newton as he waited for the apple to fall into the palm of his outstretched hand.

Scene Cast In Pearl-Grey. Falling together into the interstice between two sand dunes as the helicopter's searchlight swept across the flanks of pearl-grey sand,

Dr. Philip Byrne and the flower child came to inertial rest in each other's arms, a moment's epiphany loaded with myrrh and sandalwood aromas. If gravity contracts what makes the Universe expand? Jason Palmer's perceptive elucidation that in Eternity time was invisible, indivisible like a glacial sweep of ice, struck him with the force of the circling searchlight's cone holding them in its field, a slice of illumination separated from the darkness. Half-blinded by the glare they staggered across the powdery sand down to the foreshore and focused Palmer's monastic cell fiercely ablaze, perhaps a metaphor of the burning villages in 'Nam, models of spontaneous combustion. Later, the physicists and Three Graces joined them on the foreshore, dressed in milky laboratory coats, and they stood together at the perimeter of Palmer's smoking Zen garden. Offshore, a schooner lay at anchor, visible in the dying flares cast by the burning cell, a silhouetted figure outlined on the deck. But where was Jason Palmer?

Gnostic Propositions. Standing together amid the Zen garden whose rakings were filling with ash, the group resembled stylized motifs on acid-etched glass, overarched by diamantine fragments splintering the jade sky. The Gnostic trinity of physicists discussed Jason Palmer's propositions: (i) The cosmos was simply **ONE** equation scribbled on the blackboard of three-dimensional spacetime human thinking delved and unraveled, theorizing on everything. (ii) The Planck-moment was the fallen Archangel's chalk touching the blackboard of three-dimensional spacetime's continuum, becoming humanity's equational Physics. (iii) Setting time's fuse alight, melting its glacier, so it consumed itself as it progressed, was evidenced in the sky by the ash of stars falling away into oblivion. Loosening hair twisted by the thermal currents of breeze, the feminine aesthetes enticed the physicists toward the deeper shadows between the sand dunes for a session of coalescence. Dr. Philip Byrne imagined the mathematics of sex scrawled across the rippling parchment of sand would be visible to Palmer in the morning when he returned to the Zen garden: may be he would visualize parallels in both patterns.

Earth, Sky & Ocean. Could he break the code of the sand dunes' horizontal DNA helixes? Ringlets of fine-grained sand danced in the whispering breeze under Jason Palmer's footprints skimming the crests of the dunes. Amid the ashes of his hermitage lay the koan of his Zen garden. Life's empirical submergence in the biological *frisson* of the twisting dance of the DNA spiral lay patterned in waved silica before his eyes. Auroran tresses of sunlight shook free of the Sun Goddess, Vesta, fiery with exultation on the horizon, one glance able to transform the most somber colors lost from Paradise and pressed into the darker brain-waves of humanity. The succulent lip of the solar mouth breathed across the cool horizon, aerial image of a kiss to be felt from dawn-to-dusk by the Goddess' devotee. In casting his imagination's net across the ocean of space-in-time, Palmer's infatuated consciousness had beached a kaleidoscope of ecstatic visions, his mind burst with brilliance, the seams of his emotions interfused with his thoughts coruscated. Thought's zen-waves coalesced a chemistry as intrinsic as this potent evocation: time's relationship to the continuum of the Cosmos was as salt's to the ocean, where fluidity became crystallization. Vesta's uncontaminated beauty, grace crowned with unstainable Hellenic light, eased the agony of captivity in Paradise Lost while Palmer pondered the ocean from which appeared the origami of a flotilla of yacht sails. Now he had discovered the true axes of reality how was he to balance his ascent back into the heart of the Sun Goddess?

"Have You A Billet-Doux For Our Sister?" Inspired and emboldened by the horizon of divinity emblazoned with the Sun Goddess, Jason Palmer crested the shore-break and swam toward the schooner anchored offshore, the lovely origami of yacht sails beginning to disperse westward. Swimming, traceless on an ocean of consciousness, galaxies of bubbles laced in white rising to the surface from his stroking arms, he felt the sun's expansive radiance flowing ahead of him, beyond the torso of the looming schooner, itself a silver bow new-bent under Heaven. Miranda Westwood, her limbs brushed in melted coconut cream, unfurled the ladder for him to climb aboard, her eyes regarding his dripping torso the way a Hellene contemplated the classical statues of Greece. She held up a pair of high-powered binoculars. "Watching you, I thought you dived out of the sun into the ocean: what a powerful swimmer you are, for a piece of classical sculpture." All around the schooner the ocean's litmus paper soaked up the burgeoning sun. A curved placenta of dune lay burnished with a luscious glow, the embryo of his Zen-garden a signifier of their births-to-come in the spacetime continuum of past-present-future. Sunburn like streaked rhubarb followed the contours of Miranda's classically feminine bikini-line during the moment's long-breathed glissando. The wave-particles of the distant dune's arabesque were simultaneously energy-and-mass! "Have you a *billet-doux* for our sister?" The question surprised him? "Germaine Greer? Miranda, we're unrhymable. Is she below deck?" Her laughter possessed the vibrance of a Michelin-chef's sauce. "There are *two* below, yes. They've been fornicating all night like two beached fish flapping about on soft moist sand. They tell me her orgasm is comparable in energy to salmon swimming upstream. She *dies*, only to survive and talk about the after-death experience, at length." He watched her thumbs gently peel back the mysterious flesh of a purple-black fig for the delectation of his salty lips. A white-feathered bird, chalked from azure space, gently settled on the overhead mast.

Discoveries. Rifling through Jason Palmer's papers, watched over by the flower child sucking an icicle from the open frame of the door, Dr. Philip Byrne was intrigued by a portfolio of architectural cities, so many photographic portraits of the Archangel. Listening too as a transistor radio played *Ain't No Mountain (High Enough)*, he realized the flower child had brushed against him in her disdainfully chaste manner, disturbing his ability to focus and make sense of the material. (i) **ATHENS** – Palmer wrote: *Here is where all modern history, geography, philosophy, science and artistry became synchronized to Time. Athens, classically Mediterranean, womb of all intellectual riches of our subsequent incarnations, vestal spring limpid with the palimpsest for future geological cities. Pattern of the unchangeable, beginningless, Athens was Civilization's Planck-moment!* (ii) **CAIRO** — Palmer wrote: *The Archangel's Pyramid of Time cubed in the desert of Paradise Lost, now* *flashing minarets globed with his physical weight. Muezzins, the Archangel's monologists, intone the agony of the Fall across his vast wasteland.* (iii) **DELHI** – Palmer wrote: *City hostage to Chaos, dust-layered in rotting immutability, a colonization of the Archangel's imagination, Delhi-on-the-Ganges has forgotten the Buddha in His 1000-petalled lotus fragranced with Paradise.* (iv) **PARIS** – *Geometry squeezed into a trapezoid, an existential physiology shaped after the Eiffel Tower raised to the empyrean in multiple dimensions, Paris-on-the-Seine (sane) patterns the nausea of the twentieth-century, humanity's unwillingness to confront the Archangel.* (v) **NEW YORK** – *City-of-Time-Square untying the tangles of European everything in a quintessence of Pythagorean space: behold the sky blocked in dreams!* Licking creamy apricot yoghurt from her index finger, the flower child strolled barefoot around the apartment like a chimera from the best-selling pop song, *Mama Told Me (Not To Come).*

Circumambulations Of The Ka'aba. Gridlocked on the frozen fjord of the freeway in his Chevrolet, Jason Palmer contemplated the warpage of space thickened with skyscrapers and the heavier curvature modeled from the cloverleaf interchanges. There was no reining back the wave of the city now! Elvis' spiritual heroism through the sixties, his haunting of the air-waves with the beauty of his voice's poetry, certainly aroused the Archangel, for anti-war demonstrators were gathering for a succession of marches through the world's premier cities. Trailing the familiar Cadillac along city blocks, knowing Johnny Esquire had his Chevrolet framed in the rear vision mirror, Palmer pondered how he could unbalance the za-zen of the Archangel's mind, to bring the ecstasy of his own emptiness of *form* to the consciousness of the populace. No more than God was Elvis intelligible to the current generation! Circling-the-square of the pedestaled skyscrapers aroused a fresh dynamism to mount the escalator of Jacob's ladder and ascend. The car radio station reprised soul music: *Don't Play That Song.* The Cadillac abruptly swung away onto a descending undercover parking ramp.

Age Of The City. Peering into the iridescent coruscation of the tropical aquarium in Diane Blake's office, Jason Palmer suggested: "If this sculpted city beneath the sky's azure ice is a materialized thought, perhaps Ocean is the Archangel's stomach." Laughing at the extravagance of the words, Diane gazed through the expanse of window frontage into the sky's nothing of *beyondness*, as always unbalanced by his reflective oratory, his words always allusive of many meanings. How could she design crystal cities as a counter-solution to the image before her? Arrayed like brooding monks, the muscular torsos of skyscrapers and arterial limbs of Archangelic power writhing in space as freeway interchanges, disturbed her equanimity, while her emotions were stirred into a muddied pool of jealousy over Palmer's flagrant unfaithfulness. His face was visible through the liquid jewel of the aquarium set in the office. The livingness of hope became inert, she felt herself weightily inlaid, encased in an architectural mind, an imageless Image, but of what? "Will you come to the Gymkhana with me?" Were these skyscrapers inside-or-outside her mind? "Diane, there is no *inside*, or *outside*." Palmer wrested his eyes from the aquarium, puzzled why his remark sparked this circuit of electrical faultage between them: what was too complex about the fabulous architectural fabrications he had laid across her desk? "Look, there is an all-weekend Rock Festival coming up, after the Gymkhana. We can dress up as hippies, lose ourselves in a space where every moment will be as real as any other." Gridlocked traffic below moved like a slippage of ice periodically melting.

Would The Equestrienne Deliquesce? Sublimity *à la mode*, arms linked in rhythm to the unfolding raga of evening, exquisitely finished teenagers swung along the sidewalk, minds undisturbed by the multi-grained textures of Paradise Lost. Jukeboxes powered up inside pinball arcades with the hits of the day. Riding pillion behind Cassandra, Diane Blake cruised the Oceanside boulevards scanning the unknown faces which streamed in and out of the amusement arcades, conscious of the feel of unfashionable leather which armored Jason Palmer's courier, perhaps a metaphoric skin she dreamed of shedding at the moment of enlightenment. Unable to surrender to the leather skin, Diane witnessed everywhere, conversation and laughter as the teenagers sucked and tasted lips, so many anonymous identities flashing by the motorcycle: she remembered the tension of her own virginal teenage years when she dreamed of a romantic fabulist who would write up her future life. Cassandra's soft plasma torso loosened inside the stiffened leather skin, so she focused on the pose-and-exhibition of the teenagers, arms draped over shoulders in garlands of generosity, a definition of the Age's *Baroque'n'Roll* self-awareness: hopefully these opaque causal linkages would become clearer as the Seventies progressed. The boulevard's tarmac seemed to sense the spinning wheels of the motorcycle. When Cassandra did speak her words formed a firm crust around the softened flesh of her voice, but could she be believed? Breaking at a red light, Cassandra glimpsed and recognized Johnny Esquire first, leisurely combing his Elvis quiff, his pose trying to model the summation of the artist-in-history, but among the current of teenage girls he was flirting with the fate of Scylla and Charybdis. Diane's fingers spontaneously tightened their grip on her waist and the leather skin crumpled. Had she left her fingerprints all over Cassandra? Seen emerging from a cinema whose marquee was ablaze with **FELLINI SATYRICON** were Lt. John Kirby and the flower child. She had glimpsed a dog-eared copy of Petronius' surviving fragments lying on the coffee table in Palmer's apartment. Cassandra's head swung left but Diane still caught sight of Palmer and Miranda Westwood shuffling on the sidewalk as if it were a chessboard's horizontal plane; two scorpions in a circle of neon fire!

Scene à la Fauve. Diane Blake swung free of the pillion seat and hurried across the intersection. Hip-swinging beside Miranda Westwood, Johnny Esquire eventually sauntered off, his metrical footsteps as rhythmic as the geometry of his pristine Elvis bell-bottoms would allow. Confused, her modesty ablaze, Diane was well aware she displayed there on the sidewalk an outline of emptiness, an existential transparency Jason Palmer's eyes were photographing for his coffee table book on the refugees from Paradise Lost. At least an appearance in his book would keep her available to him for decoration! From her vaguely expressed hope they would be two Titan colors warming the canvas of existence together, she now felt a shift in intensification, as if they had become two bold Fauve colors juxtaposed but not harmonizing. Palmer was purveying here Paradise Lost's fun-house mass of distorting mirrors in which she could glimpse herself. Was this how the Archangelic eye visualized the world?

Theoretical Romancing. Twisting free of the aromatic weave of fashion-conscious teenagers beginning to raise the decibels of the amusement arcades, Jason Palmer descended the broad stairway to the beach and sighted the schooner's furled sails, the visible verticality of its masts dripping white against the ebony sky. He washed off the boulevard's neon watercolors by stripping down and plunging into the shorebreak and swimming out to the hull of the schooner. Miranda Westwood tipped over a rope ladder and welcomed him aboard. In the quiescence of his dreams she nuanced a fizzy lightness of *rococo-cola* sex, the buzz of a baroque-style flute filtered through the tapestry of **FELLINI SATYRICON**. When they reclined on cushions under moonlight as if off the Isle of Capri, and she invited him to measure the compass of her tanned legs on the deck of the schooner, he could only say: "In the relativity of this *moment*, can its mass curve the space which holds you?"

The Fictitious Playground Of Existence. Radiant heat-waves rippled and slow-danced amid the small valleys of sand dunes. An onshore sea breeze sculpted the dunes as they backdropped the Zen sand-garden. Rising from the robe of sand molded after energy's suppleness, Jason Palmer felt the angular crystalline grains pressed into his flesh as he strolled down to the foreshore. The sun's aromatic swelling buoyed the wings of a schooner afloat offshore. He dived into the ocean to prove elastic space would bend, and to search for holes in the Archangel's sea of energy. A visionary moment communicated how the swirling Universe was but the solar plexus chakra in the torso of a Cosmic Brahma! Feeling the plasma's turbulence he began to understand the wilting lotus of his own solar plexus, a spiral galaxy of energy whose mastery was essential to still the turmoil ripping space asunder with the fallen Archangel's presence there.

Stalking The Tao. "Philip, consider the proposition, only the hollow space held by the curve of a chalice makes it valuable." Dr. Philip Byrne surfeited on the touches of fissionable sunbeams weaving the Zen garden's raked patterns into an harmonious interplay of light-and-shadow. Jason Palmer, breezy and self-assured, unscrolled more of his theme as they surveyed the Zen-lines raked in the sand: "Why would the soul, our fourth-dimensional presence, vacation here in three-dimensional space, like a tourist, unpack its trunk in my mind?" Talking Tao like this would inevitably precipitate a crisis. Moving off across the crystalline sand, Dr. Byrne offered him a stalking proposition: "Fanatics are universally sheets of clear glass, and all things must pass through them first for validation: fanatics are the pane by which something can be known."

A Fount Of Greerisms. Shadows attempting to squeeze into the space of light simply vanished! Yet Germaine Greer's full-bodied Hippolyta sustained her presence and approached the metaphorical ruins of Jason Palmer's existence, shadowed by Eddie Phoenix's amorphous contour. Already the nerve-ending of all their prejudices were becoming excitable with the presence of so many literary exhibits. From which Zeus though did this Pallas Athena spring fully armed? "Aboard the Westwood's schooner I dreamed of swirling your hair's torso while we read passages from Physics journals together." Phoenix's arc of surveillance encompassed Palmer's psyche, and emerging from Germaine Greer's contour he surveyed the emotional destruction effected by his verbal lightning-bolt, removed his sunglasses and even attempted a smile. "No armor of Cardinal's robes, no Krishna war-paint, no Zen koan will erase the rebellion sown in three-dimensional space by the fallen angels. We will be in Paradise Lost the *impossible*, rather than be in Heaven, the unimaginative *possible*." Later, bound to the wheel of his solitary existence, seated on the cooling beach sand as sunset colored the tidal pools glowing along the foreshore, Palmer was again visited by Dr. Philip Byrne, curious to know what had transpired earlier. "What did the tall prophetess say to you?" The sun's opaque mirror dissolved into the ocean. "Something personal, from Baudelaire ... *J'ai plus de souvenirs que si j'avais mille ans.* Surfing the pastel reef-break adjacent the sweep of sand dunes where his Zen garden lay, his feet calming the sea, Palmer imaged triumphant seraphim incapable of sinking into spacetime riding the waves of futurity.

Elvis' Gravitational Field Curves Spacetime. Stretching a sculpted arm across the plush upholstery of the Cadillac, Paulette Taylor extenuated her half-revealed breasts and inner thighs to the pop star's heavy-lidded gaze, the glimpse of whiteness as intense as an imploding galaxy. The Cadillac's transcendent conception glided through shimmers of neon-fire toward the curving façade of the massive International Hotel. The skyline was electric with Las Vegas' *nothingness*. The *frisson* of sound-waves permeating from the supper club where Elvis emoted *Love Me Tender* maintained the flexible curvature of the sculpted hotel against the flat-planed landscape.

Las Vegas Casts A Spectrum. A fabulous chorus line of casinos dreamed from the poetry of Baudelaire danced in brash neon, acolytes illuminating the altar of Las Vegas standing under a cathedralesque sky. Letting fall the curtain's sumptuous textile, the famous singer moved about the rococo interior of the hotel suite, gun-and-holster strapped under his arm, wondering whether he would reach the horizon of the next song. Would there be an assassination attempt on stage tonight? Floors below his sealed-off hotel suite Miranda Westwood posed nude on a wave of marblesque sheet. Evening's spectacular approach had unleashed across the sky all the colors of Paradise's spectrum, and from a distance the city possessed the delicacy of Venetian glass, sweet illusion. Parked on the highway at the city precincts, Jason Palmer beheld in awe Las Vegas' iconography, the Archangel's sunflower blooming in a coat-of-many-colors for the sun of darkness. A magnificent Monte Cristo treasure was caved in Las Vegas, unapproachable except by the Chosen One, but would Elvis symbolize the tomb of a generation's mortality? Every evening the curved, protective wing of the International Hotel seemed ready to take flight from Las Vegas. Dawn's cresting brilliance soon diminished the artificial brilliance of Las Vegas. A Cadillac running the marathon of Time sped by Palmer's Chevrolet, Elvis' Apollonian leitmotif being the driving scherzo of the twentieth-century's symphony. Braking hard, Palmer glimpsed the Cadillac and the figure striding across the desert ripping open the ice of his white jump suit, as if releasing his soul in ecstatic flight, flawless miniature of a mighty Seraph. Elvis' fluorescence flared in its gathering of Las Vegas' spectrum into one beam of white light!

Art Nouveau & The Theory Of Relativity. "Mathematics formalized in equations visualizes for us the unseeable." Solidified strokes of chalk raked the Zen garden of the blackboard in the Physics laboratory. The chalk-white cluster of equations formed the *dramatis personae* in a cosmic tragedy. Unquestionably, imagery reaching the eyes via the medium of light happened in the *past*. But the slender Art Nouveau arabesques in chalk proved spacetime was a continuum, the solar flare in the sky was a frozen image eight-minutes old! Outside the laboratory the anti-war demonstrators had breached the police barricades and were streaming across the University quadrangles, a placard-waving Eddie Phoenix in the vanguard, his own slogans though on the blackboard were inflammatory with the espionage of quantum physics. The Three Art Nouveau Graces naked inside crisply starched laboratory coats puzzled over the blackboard's equations where the chalk had the looseness of the Milky Way's liquid flow against a night sky. Seemingly unaware of the maelstrom descending on the laboratory the physicists unbuttoned the white coats and the Three Graces stepped free in a linear swathe of Art Nouveau movement. A window shattered and a Molotov cocktail arced through into the laboratory's spacetime continuum.

How Small Is Small Then? Brushing flecks of foam from a curve of exposed breast, Jasmin asked: "How small is small then?" Whenever flame flared across the adjacent quadrangle, Lorna and one of the physicists could be glimpsed playing Pyramus-and-Thisbe *extempore* by a thick-boled tree. Allowing fingertips brushed with chalk to adjust the laboratory coat, Jasmin listened: "Our flesh cushions a cosmos of sub-atomic particles with the properties of waves. Imagined ourselves shipwrecked survivors on a galactic atoll of quantum physics, immersed in a sea of quantum-foam." A parade of *shipwreck* cartoons projected across Jasmin's mind. Fossilized in the silence of time the University burned. Eddie Phoenix's silhouette searched the embers of the Physics laboratory for the DNA of Paulette Taylor's unborn child.

Paphos Is An Anagram Of? Tanned, her Amazon's upper torso armored in breastplate sexually inlaid with Theseus' romancing of Hippolyta, Germaine Greer imperiously welcomed the Panathenaic procession of guests celebrating the launch of *The Female Eunuch*. Society photographers moved the length of the ballroom capturing on film the pyrotechnic costumes, eager for the deadpan Germaine Greer masks to fall away once obeisance had been made to the imperious Queen of the Masque. Dr. Philip Byrne promenaded the patio with three familiar feminine *faunesses*, their aromatic swish of aromatic autumnal leaves a more somber dance compared with the orgy of colored fabrics mingling inside the ballroom beneath sparkling chandeliers. "Paphos is an anagram of ..." A visually stunning tableau on the lawn gathered streams of admirers. *Daphne* began her metamorphosis in an abrupt sexual swerve from *Apollo's* fingertips. Leaves were already transforming her waved hair, then a revivified Miranda Westwood lightly danced away with resplendent Johnny Esquire in pursuit.

Heartbreak Hotel. *Mercury* vaulted from a low-slung balcony onto the patio and tried to unravel the *faunesses* with a pirouette of dance movements toward the ballroom entrance. Long toughened by Nature's masculine law they fended off his challenge and arm-in-arm strode through into the emanation of brilliance beaming from the chandeliers. "Ugly Ducklings paddling life's stagnant pool, determined not to metamorphose into swans, as good as dead in the water." Dr. Philip Byrne recognized the Byronic *Mercury* surfing the wave of evening, his combative mannerisms evaporating behind mask-and-costume, his wrestling the Archangel for the Earthscape of Paradise Lost temporarily on hold. *Hygeia* approached, tearing asunder the Veil of Antiquity. Would she recognize Jason Palmer? "I've danced, strolled the ballroom with every figure of a man, but all they can offer me is a fabric of archaic remembrances to dance with. So I've come downstairs from wandering the upstairs bedrooms ..." As she swept her masked eyes skyward there were secretive, indefinable infinities ablaze in a longing sigh she breathed, so much emotion seeping from *Heartbreak Hotel*. *Mercury* lounged in shadow as a *haute monde Columbine* sauntered by, all iridescence, her costume bubbled with eroticism, the tufted damask velour of her pubis crackling in reflected light. "I am existentially self-evident ... **ME**!" A black helicopter briefly circled the grounds before descending to the lawn.

Phoenix Aflame. The empty bowl of the moon tipped to scoop the burning torso of the crashed helicopter bleeding elastic colored oils across the canvas of beach sand. Was it simply *A Midsummer-Night's Dream*? Bravely plunging through the shorebreak and swimming out to the anchored schooner, Jason Palmer luxuriated in the pomegranate molasses of the ocean now oozing with the reflective flames cast by Paradise Lost, dreaming of Miranda Westwood's feminine shape awaiting him, succulent but sweetly firm, *à la* the inner cavity of half-a-pear!

X
TIME-ZERO

The Elegance Of Nothingness. Chaos lay sequenced in the architecture of the sky and Jason Palmer realized the Cosmos was simply the interior of an immense particle accelerator, itself a blueprint how to shrink the universal panorama, render the fallen Archangel in a grain of sand atop his fingertip. Light reflected off the paper-thin mask of the moon, but balsamic vinegar stains clung to all forms within the automobile graveyard. With graceful torsion, freeing her untrimmed tresses, Cassandra slipped free of her shirt and shadows peeled back so the surrealism of her presence faintly glowed in the thin wash of moonbeams: she possessed the quintessential elegance of a gauche model for a resurrected angel. Palmer saw analogies in the constellated enlargement of the Cosmos and the time-zero of the inert automobile graveyard as he meditated on the relationship between a curved chromium fender and the sweep of the Milky Way. Mimicking a playful sexual sophisticate, emerging from a smokily languorous mood the birthright of all women, Cassandra had recently self-enlarged her idealization and layered her mouth in vermilion rainbows for him to smudge, draw off the poison of her erotic passions. *Drag City* had beckoned earlier, where an *Argonautica* of speed-empowered chariots moved beneath the spreading spinnaker of stars: Lucifer had dragged the mirror-image of Paradise with him through the *Planck-moment*, and it shattered into trillions of fragments on the floor of Hell. Favoring chariot wheels, the Archangel fired up his armor, metallic volumes faceted with a blaze of high-octane fuel, but Palmer's flashing comet conquered Eddie Phoenix's land-cruiser which crashed to Earth like a burning meteor. Whose *eye* was monitoring the Cosmos' sculpted *plastique* unwinding with the slowness of time?

Shall We Sing A Te Deum For Paradise Lost? Dr. Philip Byrne listened off-camera to Jason Palmer setting forth his arguments in the metaphysics of Pythagorean solids, geometric insights baffling the pedagogues in the audience. He concluded: "Time is motionless at light-speed. Why? Our error is to build existence on the premise Time flows. Time is now ... now ... now ... flow is illusory. You see me schematically illustrated here before you, but this physical persona is my soul's aura, a gravitational force warping spacetime. I am simply a warpage of space." Howls of outrage from the Christian-based audience erupted into physical confrontation when Eddie Phoenix muscled himself on-set and assaulted Palmer. A cry was heard: "Feed the lamb to the jaws of the lion!" Studio furniture was up-ended in the melee's flexing of the scene's spatial canvas. The staccato abruptness of each moment-with-an-ending tested Palmer's hypothesis, with the Christian's reacting to what they perceived was the tarnishing of their theology. Parked near the television studio's transmitter, Dr. Byrne waited for Palmer's appearance, waving him across the baking asphalt. "A mass, as exampled by my torso, or pure energy such as music, warps the fabric of space, proving the indivisibility of the **ONE**. This was scientifically demonstrated just now when Phoenix commanded his flying torso to curve space, and in attacking *me*, struck at *himself*!"

Scenography. (i) **ROCK FESTIVAL** – Electronic musical smears transmitted at high volume from the group on-stage, resonating across the vast outdoor arena, seemed to precipitate in psychedelic washes over the buses and VW vans parked on the periphery of the property. From fulsome hippie beards there issued psychedelic butterflies floating in rainbowing strobe lights. Dressed in homespun fashion awash with decalcomania, Jason Palmer guided Diane along *Groovy Way*, through the suspended haze of marijuana smoke, among a younger generation undergoing sociological metamorphosis. Traffic was backed up for miles along the freeway approaches, all headed for this expanse of earth layered with pitched tents, portable toilets and tens-of-thousands of devotees right into the *love groove* going down on the stage in the near-distance. Afternoon thunderstorms soon turned the whole arena into a lake of mud for frolicking in ... so much *brown acid*. Palmer amused himself among the devotees, introducing thoughtful comments: "Does this *rock* know who I am?" (ii) **RECORDING STUDIO** – Dr. Philip Byrne pressed himself against the wall of the studio reading the *New Musical Express* while Eddie Phoenix vigorously caressed the mixing console. Attempting a self-referential version of an early-sixties composition, *(She's Got The) Devil In Her Heart*, her voice as charred as fire among autumnal leaves, Germaine Greer breathed like a whispering temptress into a microphone while Phoenix stirred together rhythm tracks overlaid with Aeolian strings into the mix. In the *timbre* of her voice he was still searching for those Archangelic sub-tones for capturing on tape and carrying into Eternity. Dr. Byrne cast a glance over the paper's chart placings as the gaunt-voiced songstress brought her special malformation of feeling to the lyric. Still, he had heard a festival bootleg being circulated by Jason Palmer, and knew Phoenix was chasing down a copy of the record's horizontal perspective, suspecting the grooves were loaded with an Archangelic message caught and pressed there. Bob Dylan's *New Morning* was communication at the speed of sound, mere wisps of energy when compared to the symphonic walls-of-sound unleashed by solar flares. Dr. Byrne's eye caught a paragraph deep in the paper speculating on the possibility of Dylan and Greer recording a duet together ... *When I Paint My Masterpiece*? (iii) **LAS VEGAS** – Exiled on the latter-day Isle of Patmos, surrounded by a sea of sand, Elvis fingered the Hebrew **CHAI** suspended from his neck and stepped from the elevator, a walking revelation of the New Jerusalem. Another macrocosmic presence simultaneously advanced across the lobby of the International Hotel as the chakric roulette wheels of the fallen Archangel burned up space. In a moment of pure Elvisness, he spoke: "Well ... well ... well." Dylan, bleeding with neon, feeling the translucence of revelation in this meeting, nodded to God's gypsy: "*Tomorrow Is A Long Time.*" They stood framed by the elevator's Jacob's ladder. Miranda Westwood drifted by as the two mighty Atlantides, sculpted male pillars, Joachin &Boaz, clasped hands and talked. "Apollo has been searching for His Prodigal Son through the ruins of the late-sixties, but a *New Morning* has dawned with the seventies. Until now all he has found in the world have been imperfect copies of the perfect form of Elvis." The Apollonian singer smiled and answered: "Why is the Tao's bowl always empty? Well ... well ... well, God looks even through the fallen Archangel's eyes. Have you followed the moon shots? Distance evokes a luscious curve to the geometry of the Earth, yet, here, at the surface, what turbulence!" The imagery of two voices increased their distance, reflecting on the metaphysics of their respective singing as Revelation!

The Geometry Of Flattened Spacetime. Cruising the Painted Desert scene in the Cadillac's *Golden Calf*, Johnny Esquire, Miranda Westwood, Eddie Phoenix and Paulette Taylor tuned into one of Las Vegas' Christian radio stations listening to a broadcast. Las Vegas' baroque nothingness exampled kinds of bleak beauty for the thoughtless gamblers adrift in its existential spacetime geometry, the flattened desert an apt metaphor. Jason Palmer was lampooning the fallen Archangel, provoking Phoenix across the air-waves with imagery of rebels-in-agony: "What was the Archangel's expulsion through the *Planck-moment* but Paradise's sewerage system flushing away!" Suddenly, astride his Harley, the famous singer's blur of spiritual animation cruised by the Cadillac, light glinting of the neck-chain and its Hebrew **CHAI**, Joshua before the walls of another Jericho! The desert expanse evoked a sheet being rolled upon itself, and away in the distance space resembled a thin one-dimensional line. Humanity's metaphysical salvation lay limned in the juxtaposition of Palmer's transmission and Elvis' Joshua before the walls of Jericho!

Cubism. Cubic phalanxes arrayed in space, the city presided over squadrons of gridlocked cars, and there stood the existential finger of **KRISHNA inc.**, a gravestone stele for the *Now* generation. Beside Dr. Philip Byrne, oblivious to the lashing and writhing serpent of the interlocking freeway interchanges, the flower child buried her lips in some rubied nectar of pomegranate juice. Her virgin's spices savaged space with a maelstrom of unassuaged desires. Interfacing spatial dimensions, fragments not tapestries, the skyscrapers fossilized the simultaneity of spacetime even as the traffic advanced. The flower child modeled the moment of *temptation* so enchanting to humanity their unquestioning obeisance to God slipped from consciousness. Jason Palmer was hardly your quintessential revivalist armed with the sword of repentance, rather a jitterbugging quantum dancer within the spacetime continuum, the questioning Hamlet of the Principle of Equivalence.

The Brassiere And The Moon. Broodingly shadowed by Cassandra on his forays into the city during this period when *Cracklin' Rosie ... Lookin' Out My Back Door ... Lola* were all over the air-waves, moving along the Lethe of freeway flowing into an Infinity of life-ever-after, Jason Palmer comprehended light rays were a corridor in time he must enter and walk. Motioned by the freeway's rhythm into the vortex of the city, the in-curving spiral of cloverleaves a reverberant event-horizon, he contemplated Diane Blake's architectural creation, **KRISHNA inc.** until the sun began sinking low. Misplaced in the acute fundamentalism of spacetime etched with the illusion of death he searched for his inheritance of a pair of Archangelic wings. Everywhere he looked he saw the God-created mirror of three-dimensional space wherein was imaged a flash of Himself. Before evening's drag racing extravaganza began parachutists slipped down a depression in the sky's spatial fabric in a spectacular display of quantum physics. Kinesthetic flight stood sculpted in the electrifying poses of the colorful dragsters. Palmer's dragster imaged a searing meteor, Vulcan's masterpiece, sizzling with speed as it burned up the quarter-mile. The furnace of the deep purple skyline at sunset intoned: Utopia is this way! Later, even the hornèd moon paled against Cassandra's more luminous brassiere as she stretched across the gentle slope of a sand dune. She evoked Lord Leighton's *Flaming June* drained of its orange aura when Diane Blake stepped across the sand and discovered them in an arbor of rising moonlight.

Drip Drop. "Have you seen Raphael Summers' candid camera footage of the illustrious couple amid the basement's mute artworks?" Atonal ice clinked in their glasses over the question. Dr. Philip Byrne provided a quicksilver expansion of the topic, his motif though transitional: "Diane was acutely embarrassed, the irony eluding her. Dali's *Autumn Cannibalism*, an *eating* of each other, I believe. Very unrehearsed expressions, unlike your commercial pornography. They were as close-weaved as oil to the canvases which witnessed the act, but is it modern art in an existential sense? Summers himself was no doubt a *Metamorphosis of Narcissus*, tight-fisted. But tell me, your radio excursion to annunciate the recapture of Paradise Lost, surely a little premature?" Miro's biological surrealism, myriad spermatozoon of the fallen Archangel congealed in the drip school, ironically framed Germaine Greer's entrance into the gallery accompanied by her entourage of feminists. Pushing by Dr. Byrne, raising the Bible of *The Female Eunuch* with an evangelical gesture, Jason Palmer approached the hewn stone of monolithic Woman, herself standing as if entranced by her new self-definition. Feminist minders leaned forward to shield her, a gold-embossed invitation falling from the book's mask to the floor where it lay as inert as her face. Palmer's elliptical masculine geometry, so generous of Antiquity's legacy left her unmoved, their textural styles were too dissimilar. Following the official portion of the book launch a special screening of Raphael Summers' notorious film amused the hangers-on over cocktails, drawing observations that the *dramatis personae* standing, lying and crouching in the lonesome paintings stacked against the walls, modeled figurative parallels with the lamentations of Paulette Taylor and Eddie Phoenix in coitus. Outside the gallery, Palmer caught up with the feminist, elbowing his way to her side, whispering across her Amazonian guard: "The physics of your persona obviously believes each moment is frozen in time's block of ice, but even ice yields to its melting point."

Equine Mathematics. Gripping both reins-and-pommel, Diane Blake effortlessly levitated a svelte leg across the saddle, became the Sagittarian woman *par excellence*, symmetrical to spacetime, dreamed herself unseatable, a centauress. When the horse's head nobly caressed space both modeled in unison the simplicity of carved Pentelic marble prepared for the Parthenon frieze. Diane's formal competition equestrienne fabrics solidified to her musculature as flesh did to her horse's torso: Pegasus printed its proud hooves in the receiving earth. Both were companions engaged for some mystic mountain-ascent, a poetic chimera, an imaginary dance across the sky, and Jason Palmer felt something of their royal embracement. Diane's featherless biped, perfect in her immutability astride Pegasus at the Gymkhana, defied gravity, possessed the freedom of a singing voice: their musicalised dressage unfolded across the square of soft-textured earth and space molded torsos to uniform motion. Sir Isaac Newton marbled in the monument of his thoughts, Palmer derived from dressage's serene restlessness, its arabesques of buoyancy, the infinite weakness of gravity, for a pomegranate electromagnetically bonded to its branch feebly fell away. Pegasus waltzed across the palm of earth. Vault-and-curvet, moving through a sonata of refined emotion, purveying the elegance of energy *vis-à-vis* the inelegance of mass, the centauress sculpted spatial patterns imbued with universal truths. Entropy's equation lay imprinted in the soft sand! Dismounted, separated from the visceral magnetism of her horse and its relaxed sternness of will, Diane removed her helmet and stood in her dust-covered riding boots: was she essaying the possibility of romantically riding him in the saddle!

Masked Ball I. Leer or surveillance, was the celebrated feminist's gaze for the passing parade of women holding *her* deadpan mask to their faces, mirror-perfect after Hippolyta's imagined reviewing her Amazonian warriors? Her torso maintained a monumental dignity as the masked women curtsied. The narcissism of the female eunuch betrayed she was untroubled by creative intelligence. Wall-to-wall the feminist's mask radiated ... emptiness.

Masked Ball II. *Columbine* vividly emphasized the artifice of **ME!** as space was shaped into origami with the transformation of her fan's verticality upon opening. One-dimensional, two-dimensional, three-dimensional, four-dimensional, the fan's space, a kaleidoscopic hemisphere of angles and surfaces, was woven into multifarious rhythms by her hand gestures. In this masked ball of statuesque symmetries *Columbine's* flaming Medusa caught plummeting Icaruses in mid-flight beneath the rotunda of spinning chandeliers.

Masked Ball III. Tresses of plaited silk adorned a reputation finessed like priceless Venetian glass as *Hygeia* felt the shape of *Mercury's* hand dance her beneath the brilliant chandeliers across the ballroom. *Pierrot's* moon-face slowly rose among a cluster of masked beauties, clothed in silvery satins, glittering with the scintillations of the ocean's fabric, his lunar reflections palely illuminating the guests. How did this Masque evolve from the opening pages of John Milton's *Paradise Lost*?

Masked Ball IV. *Asclepius* unraveled a trio of pirouetting *faunesses* on the patio as they observed a sexual nocturne motioned across the lawn by a fleeing *Daphne* and pursuing *Apollo*; the geometry of corkscrew hair dusted by chandelier light evoked silver fractals of beauteous energy. A fauness withdrew the shell of a mirror wherein the dazzling pearl of her face floated in its pool. These silken moments veiled in the slender torso of time illustrated temptations subtle with symmetrical consequences for future incarnations.

Masked Ball V. Time's statuesque personae dressed up the thoughts of the guests as they circumambulated the bronze-plated Amazon Queen pedestaled before a framed gilt mirror in all her classical insouciance: *The Female Eunuch* commanded the Masque of Time, half-diamond, half-rhinestone, a tough lyre for any would-be master musician to aspire to conquer. Wandering by the gilt mirror with flighty impudence, Mercury asked her: "So, what music does the harp of this mirror make?"

Masked Ball VI. "Here come *The Subterraneans*! These personae are our souls' DNA sub-sets. Dancing there, *Hygeia* mimes Diane's healing inflexions, and her truth in my life burnishes the armor-plated persona which cuirasses my incarnate soul. She's a romantic dream ripening from the mold of Physics!" Saturnian circles ringed Hygeia, her dancing possessed the efficacy of a spiritual ritual designed to bring healing to the world.

Masked Ball VII. Marvelously and inventively scripted by *Mercury*, the stilted Queen of the Amazons undertook the dramatization of Einstein's *Relativity of Simultaneity* for the guests, moving them through into a large study landscaped with a model electric railway. Posing, a lovely fauness held against herself a cardboard placard on which was printed in boldface ink: **Simultaneous events in one frame of reference are not necessarily simultaneous if viewed from a different frame!** A slouching, would-be Archangelic figure, all pumice sarcasm in attitude, *agent provocateur*, moved ineffectually among the crowding onlookers. Germaine Greer played station-master, with whistle-and-flag, setting the steam engine and passenger car in motion. *Mercury* provided the commentary as the *faunesses* rotated more revelatory cardboard placards: "**There are no instantaneous interactions in nature** – Press closer and visualize this miniature train as a moving frame of reference. We, as observers from the embankment here, are a stationary frame of reference. **There is a maximum possible speed of interaction.** You will say simultaneous events are occurring before our eyes, but

Einstein says *simultaneous* can be proven to be *relative* to viewers in different frames of reference. Here comes the steam engine now. Within the passenger car is a source of light sending a beam both forward and backward, simultaneously. **The maximum possible speed of interaction is the speed of the electromagnetic interaction.** Let's wait for the locomotive to return to our embankment, and this time be prepared for the beam of light designed to open and close both the front and rear doors of the passenger car. From our stationary frame of reference, does the front or rear door open first? **The speed of the electromagnetic interaction is the speed of light.** To us stationary viewers the rear door opens first! To a person standing inside the passenger car operating the light, the doors will open simultaneously. Profound? **The speed of light is the maximum possible speed.** Observe my torso, how it has moved a little distance, from room-to-room along co-ordinates of length-and-breadth, then up a flight of stairs, a vertical axis. This is three-dimensional motion. Yet, my torso has matured, and moved a considerable distance through time, adding an extra dimension. Tomorrow I am scheduled to fulfill an appointment arranged at **KRISHNA inc.** where the building stands in the city. At an appointed time! Only light does not age. Therefore time is inconceivable at light-speed."

Measuring Wavelengths On Space's Grid. Footprints lay as if hammered in the metallic surface of early morning sand dunes, awaiting the glazes of sunlight which would soon coat them. Like a Zen-mind still within the drifting wind of time, the salted sea breeze lay heavy over the sand dunes laden with diaphanous crystals of sunlight, Benday dots of the Helios' portrait. Latin Gregorian chants haunted Lt. John Kirby's *retroussé* phantom, existential drifter from the rice paddies of 'Nam, measuring the geometry of the dunescape like a Hamletian soliloquy, as bewildered as the Elizabethan hero. His displacement from the perspiring killing fields of 'Nam brought that war's lens into sharper focus. Eos' flash touched the scrupulously polished fold of the conch shell balanced on Jason Palmer's hand as he too followed the symbolic melodies of flowing sand. The semi-abandoned monastery gathered to itself a powdery glow of talcum mist as waved sand-drifts gathered about the foundations of the structure deepening its spiritual solitude. Stained glass frosting jeweled the wavelength of sand dunes. Incense was silhouetted as the flower child's musk-scented penumbra crystallized from the veil of surreality solidifying out from the solar presence cresting the horizon. Intelligence beamed from Eternity into temporality along wavelengths of light, slowing to the visibility of a sand dune's crest-and-trough. On her fingertip the flower child presented to Palmer a crystalline atom of sand not understanding the miniature jewel was ultimately the true physical repository of light's intelligence. The horizontal monastery floor was overlaid with billions of grains of sand impressed with her naked footprints.

The Musculature Of Food. Presented with a printed menu, Jason Palmer allowed the fingers of one hand to tenderly caress her upswept hairdo, this heroine smoothly contoured in the red light of designer couture, clinging like water flowing over her when she showered prior to dinner. **PINEAPPLE CRUSH**: Miranda Westwood's rhythm with the silver cocktail shaker evoked a mid-sixties Go-Go dancer aloft in a cage above the discotheque floor. Tasting her creation, flavors and strong textures were languorous on Palmer's tongue: white rum, orange liqueur, lemon slices and pineapple. **RARE ROAST BEEF SERVED WITH CAPSICUM RELISH, POPPY-SEED SKORDALIA AND STEAMED LEEK WITH CARAWAY**: Seamless stitching characterized Miranda's transitions across the screens of time erected for his existence to receive her impression. Thinly sliced beef with the rawness of a full-summer sunset, enriched with red and yellow capsicum relish adorned his plate, the food curiously shading toward the tanned sunburn of Miranda's flesh: he conjured too memories of her Brazilian inner thighs, the close-cut stubble of hair like a sprinkling of poppy-seed. He thought of Physicists as inspirational and intuitive trackers, having discovered for the intrepid Plainsmen-to-come, *Black Holes*, the fallen Archangel's footprints. **PASTA WITH CRAB MEAT, GREEN PEAS, CHIVES, CORIANDER, PURPLE AND GREEN SALAD**: A menu designed around the Uncertainty Principle! The smear of crab meat on Palmer's palate proved an agitation of flavor comparable with the turbulence of quantum-foam at sub-atomic levels. Pasta's DNA spirals were as rubbery as Einsteinian space. Coming off the ocean, odors drifted aboard with a faint wisp of breeze, leaving Palmer to ponder the proposition that existence must embrace the totality of past, present and future simultaneously and equally. The sea remained as smooth as pasta and as *al dente* as the slight slippage of Miranda's breasts inside her traffic-light red dress when she changed position. In coitus she might exude to his taste red cabbage, asparagus, white wine vinegar and Dijon mustard, a heady cocktail of enigmatic sexuality. **POACHED PEACHES IN LEMON SYRUP SERVED WITH ALMOND CAKE**: Dessert pantomimed a sexual drunkenness where conversation flowed like an uncoiling stream of water, rivulets peeling off before soaking deep into the texture of early evening and vanishing, no longer remembered. Bowled with cream, the confection of dessert sweetened the anticipation of coitus later, a bath in honey, the lyrics of kisses like the pop songs on the radio, caressing tongue and lips.

Existence Lived At Its Extremity. The schooner lounged on the water-bed of the stilled ocean. Upswept like a tight-fitting helmet, Miranda Westwood's coiffure gleamed against the cushion, her head cushioned in a state of dream-induced quiescence, while her fingertips abstractly skirted his loins. Jason Palmer's thoughts were strung together as finely as the linkage of stars distanced in the sky, reflected on the flat mirror of the glassed ocean. Here was a fusion of emptinesses! Miranda's physique curled up as relaxed as a pool of strawberry jelly whereas his tauter structure reclined on the deck of the schooner after Dali's *Rhinocerotic Figure of Phidias' Illises Suspended in the Middle of the Bay of Cadaques*, tableaued on the plinth of the oceanic subconscious, only the furled sails crossed on the upthrust masts piercing the gaping hole of the sky's nothingness. Then, flesh aglow with a classical bronze evening, sunburn's citrus brightness defining the perimeter of her bikini lines, she positioned herself astride his sculpture with the smoothness of olive oil oozing over a summer salad. They suggested an exalted configuration as the Sun God's brilliance delicately varnished the Moon Goddess, a beautiful symmetry of sensations, perfect uniformity, a sculptor and sculptress with transforming touches. A chaste dew of perspiration crowned her nipples and pomegranate molasses sweetly flowed. With the schooner becalmed, sails limply set in the sky's burning ice, Palmer's torso slipped over the side of the vessel into the water's cooling caress.

Sketches From Paradise Lost. Leveling off above the indissoluble mass of freeway traffic, the helicopter moved through the air without leaving trails, a contrast with the rigidly patterned cloverleaves below: were they inside an immense mirror of illusion, a magician's sleight-of-hand stage-show? Physically crushed into the space of the cabin with Diane Blake, he began to reel with a realization they were all dwelling in the blank verse of *Paradise Lost* being recited by the fallen Archangel, just as the color of sulphur powdered the horizon. Tomorrow's exile at the Fall became Eternity! Or was existence simply dramatized thought? Diane revivified and squeezed a gesture of recognition, for visible below, curving around a cloverleaf was the stylized mold of Jason Palmer's '57 Chevrolet, chariot of a demi-god, or cartoon ideogram? Dr. Philip Byrne's sidelong glance confirmed, she belonged in the squareless realm of a spatial paradise of someone else's making, here in three-dimensional space she was simply a sketch of the Divine Feminine lost, adrift in a dark world. Space's three-dimensional eruption with daybreak cast a film of illusion, the sense of an anonymous creation, over the fallen Archangel's construction of Paradise Lost, the psyche of humanity forever fragmented by the crash. How sentimentality brooded over their lives with irresistible Archangelic force. "Diane, is space *something*? Up here, the greatest fullness of space is Infinite as you can see, yet so empty!"

Goethe And Architecture. The helicopter effortlessly blew away from the landing-pad atop **KRISHNA inc.** and disappeared between the towering skyscrapers whose burnished windows reflected golden sunbeams. Descending the elevator, Dr. Philip Byrne marveled at Diane Blake's insular romanticism, her voice extolling how skyscrapers were actually raised by mantra, were solemn crescendos, chordal symphonies embodied as architecture. An emission of poetic fragrance issued from the kernel of her voice, assumed the perspectives of a romantic space whose resonance he had caught from observing Jason Palmer converse with her. Then there was Palmer's obtuse analogy that the freeway system of cloverleaves styled the thinking Tao of the fallen Archangel, was his engraven mobility and method of marshalling the energy of humanity in his combat with God. When the elevator door opened the hollowness of the cave of the offices of **KRISHNA inc.** beckoned, where a massive Led Zeppelin poster created a new mandala, signaling the Age of Festivals had passed; Woodstock's evocation of flower children had attained its apotheosis and was in decline. Dr. Byrne had been mesmerized by the sketches in blueprint of crystal cities drawn by Diane at Palmer's request!

Time-Zero. "There is no **ME**, only the **non-ME**! I can only exist in time, have meaning in time." Paulette Taylor's self-reverential posturing by the aquarium of colorful tropical fish irritated a more-than-usually pensive Eddie Phoenix, his Paracelsian-look as Jason Palmer ironically phrased it, quintessentially the anti-Christ. What had Germaine Greer testily whispered at the Masked Ball: "Her orgasm's a brisk one-liner!" Dr. Philip Byrne shuffled and gazed down at the new sand-mandala embedded in the floor, a replica of the first Led Zeppelin album cover, ominous model for the launch of the next generation of spiritual Icaruses. "This redemptive bird-on-the-wing needs to be brought to earth." Phoenix pushed away from the window and with a magician's flourish swirled a velvet cloth from a largish portrait freshly varnished standing in its exhibition frame against the wall. Germaine Greer expressed herself succinctly: "I ask for marriage as I ask for an early death." Dali's *Raphaelesque Head Exploding* had been repainted with Germaine Greer's head ironically substituting for the original, obviously commissioned by Palmer for presentation as a taunt to Phoenix: what was the subliminal message here, the dynamic regeneration of the celebrated feminist out of the disintegration of her image by time? In a flash, Dr. Byrne apprehended now that time was the Archangel's interlinked chain mail resisting and deflecting the transfiguration of Michael's blazing Sword of Light! Gathered at the window they observed Germaine Greer exit the building and walk across the forecourt to the curbside Cadillac's Golden Calf and climb inside, choreography of a modern ballet.

Light Unfreezing Form To Motion. Salt crystals on his tongue, rocked in the cradle of a breaking wave, Jason Palmer exulted in the softness of his chosen Tao, where he could carve up existence without disfiguration, and wear the ocean's close-fitting brocade translucent to his flesh, lending him the macrocosmic sensation of being amid the swirling quantum-foam of the galaxies. He was a quotable image for Paradise Regained! The ocean possessed an imageless Image as it swept toward the machismo coastline. Waves sizzled and fizzed and formed a white saccharine film coating the perimeter of Paradise Lost. The vault of the sky's cupola smoked with light, sediment floating earthward from the last battle for Heaven. Again and again during this time he unsheathed the blade of his surfboard to carve, dance to the ocean's sirenesque lure, be swallowed in the meaningless movement, and then later when the sky's furnace fired up in the late-afternoon he stopped by to collect Diane Blake to cruise the boulevards with her. Blown by the on-shores, roughed-up to a Monetian canvas, the white-capped ocean bleeding with sunset evoked a feathered wing of the fallen Archangel.

Unwinding The Slowness Of Time. Sunbathers rose from the silver-sanded beach at dusk like so many casualties precipitated to Earth during the war between Heaven and Hell, their exodus emotively portrayed in Granados' *El amor y la muerte*. Passing like light through smoked glass, shadows cast by time, the sunbathers abandoned the beach as the last waves tingled with sunset's fading glory. Exuberant crowds were exhilarated by the performance of the fast-moving chariots at *Drag City*, speed raging amid the inertia of three-dimensional space: gasps accompanied the prophetic disintegration of

Eddie Phoenix's dragster in a fireball, a microcosmic image of the falling Archangel's Planck-moment. Later, having de-constructed the meaning of the dragster's event-horizon while at the drive-in, watching *Love Story*, Jason Palmer understood the burning silhouette's sign: the photographic magnification on-screen of the two fated lovers only highlighted the two-dimensionality of space unrelieved by time. Leaving the drive-in he wheeled the Chevrolet toward the automobile graveyard. The skeletons of stoical chariots were heavy black pencil studies beneath the *plastique* of galaxies stationary at the speed of light in a Benday dot arrangement across the night sky. "Diane, these subliminal cadences intoxicate me with reminiscence of the Archangel's chariot falling out of Heaven to crash on the floor of Hell. Following the indescribable tempest of the Planck-moment, we now find ourselves consciously shipwrecked in these seemingly calm waters for Eternity. If only we could cleave ourselves again to the illumination lining the innermost sky of our thought. Instead, look how we are being filtered through the banded tesserae of shadow-designs cast by these fallen vehicles!"

Abandonment. Evanescent moonbeams held sustained the resonance of bowed cello strings playing through the orchestra of stacked car bodies. Time's ambiguity as a conceptual fourth-dimension troubled Jason Palmer: who got time moving? How slowly the undulant wave of the galaxy was breaking up. Embers of memory scattered by time faded like red-shifting stars, the depth of the fall from the Planck-moment sounded no bottom. Could the moon be set in rectilinear space? Inlaid ivory, Diane Blake proved the indivisibility of differentiation, and the pre-Universe knowledge illuminating her eyes spectacularly lit up his imagination. The Archangel tragically gifted humanity with images of the Image, and as he lifted himself to embrace to Milky Way flowing across the night sky he longed to draw a comb through those tresses!

Time BEGINS, Space IS. Moonbeams filtering through the mesh curtain shadowed her sleeping torso with a suggestiveness of wings of feathered mail. How was he to explain to her that their time between incarnations was simultaneous, and only embodiment dramatized, individualized to flow of *moments* experienced in three-dimensional spacetime? So many imperfect copies proliferated, sketched in three-dimensions, emulating one another, all stiffening toward the bias of caricature, but they were all simply Lucifer entering into his own synthesis of shadows. Yet, with perceptive prescience through their confluent mouthes kissing, she had breathed: "Here in the coldness of space I hold myself close to the sun." Sleep immobilized apprehension, but still her glissandos of fragrance hummed with the Brucknerian *adagio* softly playing in the other room, music forming a radial asymmetry with the arabesques of coitus. She awoke confessing to him how she felt in her loins the temperature of a crimson rose, glimpsed in the mirror the paler dune of his derriere contrasting the bronze patina of his arabesqued torso and limbs. What unseizable thoughts he expressed! In coitus she experienced a sword passing through her with the sensation of light through glass, frosted, translucent, transparent. Tissues were deliciously squeezed and curved, no doubt as space was by gravity: earlier he had rolled off her black fish-net stockings and contoured the bedsheet across her pubis after the drapery of the Milky Way. Sexually, she knew he was attempting the supreme breathlessness of death.

Theory Of Everything. Bending to attain wholeness, Jason Palmer raked anew his Zen garden, impressing his signature, transcribing the arabesque of his brain-waves, waiting for the crystal pane of the late-afternoon sky to shatter. Composed of silica, the Earth was potentially molten with glass-holding light, a conceptual alchemy where his dreams of crystal cities originated. Quantum Physics celebrated the complexity of each grain of sand, with each droplet of concentrated silica imprisoning the glow of liquid glass waiting to illuminate itself and the world. Visitors wandering the psychological layers of dunes glimpsed a modern Zen monk raking away the ashes shed by the sunset's lustral fire. The flanks of the sand dunes wore a sheen of precious oriental silk sensitized to fingertips of light fading a caress. Symmetrical forces folded over the chaos of the quantum world, the quantum-foam of a blood-orange late-afternoon sky, aftermath of the battle between Heaven and Hell. Cassandra saw the glow of his passion for her subsumed in the decaying sunset and descent into darkness. What did she understand? Squeezed among the Planck-lengths of the Zen garden each grain of sand circumscribed the seed of a future Universe. Peering into his eyes, hearing the new words he invented just for her, she glimpsed the *end* eternally visualized in the *beginning*.

Deep-Breathing Yoga. Thrusts of decaying sunlight pierced the flesh of shadows staining the copper beachscape. Arrowed in martyrdom, standing on the golden sands as if preparing to take flight into fourth-dimensional space, wearing for armor the lacquered opulence of sunset's bronze glow, Jason Palmer used these fading minutes to farewell his beach sculptures and the Elvis hoardings constructed within an amphitheater of dunes. The ocean's lovely Zen zig-zag of wave-fronts breasting the shoreline seemed to flow earthward out of the sun's radiantly spacious heart opening on the horizon, its metaphysical immanence preparing to absorb him on the in-breath. Time was now beautifully empurpled in the orient sky where stellar fingerprints twinkled behind the veil, signaling an ignition of *deaths*, of abandonment of the constraints of the three-dimensional spacetime continuum. From this crystalline astronomy of a quantum world could be heard the faint pulsations of an approaching helicopter. Palmer's deification in his own mind as a broad-shouldered demi-god, his Apollonian teeth stars of the first-magnitude as he released Cassandra with a smile, stood against the monumental decomposition of the sky as the sun slipped lower into the horizon and the helicopter elevated itself above the slimline crest of a sand dune. Accelerating his footsteps along the interstice between two dunes he suddenly intuited the fallen Archangel's Achilles heel imaged in the Elvis hoardings: a moment could never change, being eternally defined upon its own screen, and the light which illuminated each moment could never leave the three-dimensional spacetime continuum, except by absorption through a black hole! Light's moment of victory over darkness eternally *is*! The hooded airborne chariot cruised to a pause directly above the Zen garden, whipping the waved sand into a frenzy of quantum chaos, symbol of the *second death*, model of the soul's occult time machine, then headed offshore toward the schooner. Open strings exploded with electricity, the wiring of Palmer's constructional sculptures sparked and erupted briefly, the portrait of the celebrated feminist was rendered a mere lightning-sketch, the spiritual iciness of her mouth's burning marl throwing the world a smile. The charred, smoking shell of the schooner soon drifted shoreward, a bier for the fallen Archangel, limp wings drooping in the Ocean of Time.

A Blackboard As Microcosm Of The Night Sky. "With World War III's insurgency so deep-layered in our three-dimensional spacetime continuum, how do we receive the Supreme Commander's dispatches, what is our line of communication?" How could the Pythagorean geometry of the fallen Archangel's battle plans be made intelligible to this new generation of students? Beyond the Physics laboratory student activists were breaching the barricades and fires began to erupt in adjacent buildings even as Jason Palmer hurriedly chalked a sketch reminiscent of Delacroix's famous *Death of Sardanapalus* on the blackboard, layering the image across some equations. "Equations! Equations wrest the strategic design of His battle plans from the mind of God! They are our tactical tools to bring us victory at last. You physicists are humanity's spiritual codebreakers." With the sensibility of Goths the truculent students ransacked the buildings. The University's *soirée* had obviously been unable to harmonize the dissonance of the advancing anarchists, the sitar recital was abandoned and the metallic discords of instruments of destruction wielded by the students drummed through the Spanish sandstone corridors. Pyrotechnic equations, formulae of conversations with Deity, exploded from the blackboard's night sky with the radiance of supernovae, formless, soundless, and incorporeal, yet a glimpse of His magnificence in microcosmic space. Equations crystallized the catharsis of illumination intrinsic to understanding the fall of the Archangel. A door flung open: "Hey, there's a riot going on!"

Tactical Maneuvers. (i) **ELVIS** – Entrusted with the Voice of God to save the world, the now-famous singer initiated a genesis of regeneration, and for a moment all youth believed the *Now* was Eternal. (ii) **EINSTEIN** – Did Relativity and Quantum Mechanics parallel Heaven and Hell, the macrocosm and microcosm? What is the probability of the fallen Archangel storming Heaven and wresting the Crown from God? The Angels of Quantum Theory are excited by this probability, that there is enough Time for this to occur. (iii) **JASON PALMER** – The discovery of a sequence of cross-sectional photographs and complex blueprints of model crystal cities were circulated among physicists rather than engineers, being components in a strategy to launch a publication titled: **THE ARGONAUTICA OF PHYSICS IN QUEST OF THE GOLDEN FLEECE OF A UNIFIED THEORY OF EVERYTHING.** (iv) **LUCIFER** – The twentieth-century's impact on the gravitational fabric of the spacetime continuum necessitated healing the millennial tapestry: the fallen Archangel could only perish in *annihilation*, yet the quantum connections of his sub-atomic particles permeate the Universe, exist side-by-side with humanity's!

Journey To The Center Of Paradise Lost. Investigators puzzled over documents discovered in Jason Palmer's beachside apartment. They signposted a significance in *Drag City* and the mystery of Linear Accelerators as freeways in the high-energy world of quantum physics. Clever collages pasted up on the inner walls of the apartment decoded analogies between a sub-atomic electron compacted in his physique and his soul, how both *waves* registered on the screen of space-time as **ME**: should I choose to *look* at the quantum particle or my soul's photon? Asymmetrical baroque duelists steeped in differing Principles across the millennia, Eddie Phoenix and Jason Palmer would climax their marathon in the copper-lined concrete tunnel of the sub-terra Linear Accelerator, time machine photographing the *second death*. The Geiger counter clicks of Paulette Taylor's stilettos echoed off the gleaming metallic surfaces of the tunnel stretching away like an immense one-dimensional powerline. The tableau was slammed shut for a ringing of the anvil and the fallen Archangel's irretrievable banishment for another cosmic cycle. Eddie Phoenix had never mastered the combat weaponry of mathematics! "The true practice of Tao is diminution!" Rebellion was chaos, resolved only by fast-breathing, every sub-atomic photon dreamed of becoming jewel-encrusted light-substance, a wave of luminosity with the brilliance of the Milky Way. Accompanied by the physicists and the Muses wearing starched, immaculate white-coats, Jason Palmer prepared Eddie Phoenix and Paulette Taylor for the thrilling Dionysia of quantum physics, the apotheosis of their ongoing sexual *pas de deux*. Let them string their happiness along into the bliss of oblivion, into abandonment to *nothingness*. "Welcome to *Drag City*! Let's tie up these strings without using a knot!"

Coda. Now only a voluptuous cluster of subatomic particles accelerating the freeway of the Linear Accelerator, the androgynous Archangel no doubt enjoyed the panoramic view of the microcosm afforded him: special detectors analyzed his spray of electronic architecture. The quantum jitterbug twisted into a fusion in this sub-atomic Land of a 1000 Dances! "They've become again simply a cloud of probabilities ..."

www.ingramcontent.com/pod-product-compliance
Lightning Source LLC
Chambersburg PA
CBHW060812030726
47503CB00002B/458